The Meridian Anthology of Early American Women Writers

From Anne Bradstreet to Louisa May Alcott, 1650–1865

EDITED BY

Katharine M. Rogers

A MERIDIAN BOOK

MERIDIAN
Published by the Penguin Group
Penguin Books USA Inc., 375 Hudson Street,
New York, New York 10014, U.S.A.
Penguin Books Ltd, 27 Wrights Lane,
London W8 5TZ, England
Penguin Books Australia Ltd, Ringwood,
Victoria, Australia
Penguin Books Canada Ltd, 10 Alcorn Avenue,
Toronto, Ontario, Canada M4V 3B2
Penguin Books (N.Z.) Ltd, 182–190 Wairau Road,
Auckland 10, New Zealand

Penguin Books Ltd, Registered Offices:
Harmondsworth, Middlesex, England

First published by Meridian,
an imprint of New American Library,
a division of Penguin Books USA Inc.

First Printing, August, 1991
10 9 8 7 6 5 4 3 2 1

REGISTERED TRADEMARK—MARCA REGISTRADA

LIBRARY OF CONGRESS CATALOGING-IN-PUBLICATION DATA
The Meridian anthology of early American women writers : from Anne Bradstreet
to Louisa May Alcott, 1650–1865 / edited by Katharine M. Rogers.
    p. cm.
  ISBN 0-452-01075-6 : $12.95
  1. American literature—Women authors. 2. American literature—Colonial period,
ca. 1600–1775. 3. Women and literature—United States. 4. American
literature—19th century. I. Rogers, Katharine M.
PS508.W7M47 1991
810.8'09287—dc20   91–6769
                                                              CIP

Printed in the United States of America

THE MERIDIAN ANTHOLOGY OF EARLY AMERICAN WOMEN WRITERS

Here is writing as diverse as it is rich in scope and emotional power—works of fiction and nonfiction by those who conformed to conventional expectations of women's writing and those who defied them. There are actual letters, many of them personal, like Abigail Adams' passionate outpourings to her husband, John, and the first autobiographical narrative of Indian captivity: Mary Rowlandson's sensational account of her capture by Algonquian Indians. There is the moving poetical oratory of Frances Harper, as well as Sojourner Truth's compelling oratory on the rights of women and the abolition of slavery. And there is an excerpt from the first American bestseller, Susanna Haswell Rowson's 1791 sentimental classic, *Charlotte Temple*, and a lively, humorous character study from Harriet Beecher Stowe. Encompassing a wide spectrum of experience and expression, this outstanding collection celebrates the rich heritage of literary creativity among early American women.

KATHARINE M. ROGERS is a research professor of literature at American University. She has edited the *Selected Works of Samuel Johnson* (a Signet Classic) and coedited with William McCarthy *The Meridian Classic Book of 18th and 19th Century British Drama, The Meridian Anthology of Early American Writers: British Literary Women from Aphra Behn to Maria Edgeworth, 1660–1800;* and is the author of *Frances Burneg: The World of "Female Difficulties."* She lives in Bethesda, Maryland.

To Maggie, Chris, and Tom

Contents

Introduction

THE FIRST COLLECTION of original poems produced in America was written by a woman, Anne Bradstreet. The circumstances of its appearance tell much about the situation of a woman author in the seventeenth century. In her "Prologue," Bradstreet acknowledged that many of her contemporaries thought a needle fitted her hand better than a pen, and she asked for a parsley wreath instead of laurel; nevertheless, she insisted on her right to express herself in poetry. She could not have done so had her father not given her an education superior to that of most women, or had he and her husband not supported her intellectual pursuits. Her poems were published because her brother-in-law took them, without her knowledge, to a publisher in England.

Although Puritan society as a whole assumed that women should be subordinate and tended to distrust intellectual activity on their part—John Winthrop, governor of Massachusetts Bay in Bradstreet's time, attributed a young woman's insanity to her overindulgence in reading and writing—Puritan religion did promote literacy and self-examination in both sexes. Women, as well as men, were expected to present a history of their spiritual experience in order to become full members of the church. Bradstreet's "To My Children" is an example of this form, and some of her finest poems examine her difficulties in subjecting her love for earthly things to her resolution to submit to God's will.

Despite the patriarchal structure of all the established churches (apart from the Society of Friends), religious feeling played an important part in liberating American women's creativity and enterprise. It was religion that inspired Mary Rowlandson, Elizabeth Ashbridge, and Jarena Lee to record their conversion experiences, religion that inspired Ashbridge, Lee, Sojourner Truth, and Sarah Grimké to preach and lecture. Grimké used Biblical arguments to rebut the Congregationalist ministers who rebuked her for speaking in public; the first consequence of the Fall, she claimed, was Adam's impulse to seize dominion over Eve.

It seems likely that the relatively unorganized conditions of frontier life made it easier for women to expand conventional limits. Gender restrictions on who might write may well have been obscured in a community where women and men struggled side by side for survival and there was no literary establishment. In England, no woman of education and refinement comparable to Mary Rowlandson's would have been exposed to the harrowing adventures that she recounted so vividly; in this case, uniquely American subject matter created a new form. The two best-selling novels written by women in the 1790s, Susanna Rowson's *Charlotte Temple* and Hannah Foster's *The Coquette,* show perhaps a little more sympathy for their erring heroines than do the English sentimental novels on which they are modeled: Charlotte is an almost innocent victim of seduction, and Foster enlists our empathy for Eliza's reluctance to marry the boring though estimable Reverend Boyer.

The feature that most clearly differentiates late eighteenth-century American women from their English contemporaries was their concern with politics, developing from their experience of the Revolutionary War and the foundation of the new republic. While Englishwomen typically avoided politics as an unfeminine subject, Americans such as Mercy Otis Warren and Abigail Adams were as caught up in republican enthusiasm, as zealous for liberty and equality, as their male relatives. It was considered entirely appropriate for Warren to publish plays lampooning the Tories and a partisan history of the American Revolution. The political ferment stimulated her friend Adams to the radical thought that women should be included in the new government.

These seventeenth- and eighteenth-century women were exceptional, however, and none made her living by writing. In the nineteenth century, many women became professional authors, though at the price of accepting certain conventions about the proper way for women to write. Significantly increased literacy and leisure, together with technological improvements in printing and communications, greatly enlarged the market for books and periodicals. And this market was strongly influenced by upper- and middle-class women, since it was they who made up the bulk of the leisure class and to whom cultural matters were often relegated while their men pursued business and politics. This created a specific demand for women writers to meet the tastes of women readers. Nina Baym estimates that women produced "close to half of the literature published by Americans between the War of 1812 and the Civil War."[1] Editors in the popular press actively encouraged their women readers to write. The number of female authors was increased by the fact that writing, which required no credentials and could be done in the privacy of home, was the best career opportunity open to women. Unfortunately, the same factors caused the field to be overcrowded. Sara Parton's ("Fanny Fern's") autobiographical novel *Ruth Hall* makes clear that even talented writers had to struggle to get published, even successful ones were liable to be financially exploited. The essayist Mary Abigail Dodge ("Gail Hamilton") discovered in 1867 that her publisher regularly gave her a smaller royalty than he did men.

Moreover, most women had to write in intervals snatched from domestic responsibilities. Elizabeth Cady Stanton lamented the difficulties of composing closely reasoned speeches "while I am about the house, surrounded by my [five] children, washing dishes, baking, sewing, etc.," with "seldom . . . one hour undisturbed in which to sit down and write."[2] Harriet Beecher Stowe wrote to help support her family while raising seven children and struggling to run a household without enough money. Sarah Orne Jewett explained why Stowe's work is marred by imperfections: "You must throw everything and everybody aside at times, but a woman made like Mrs. Stowe cannot bring herself to that cold selfishness of the moment for one's work's sake."[3] Elizabeth Stuart Phelps's story "The Angel over the Right Shoulder" poignantly dramatizes a woman's realization that

[1]Nina Baym, "The Rise of the Woman Author," in *Columbia Literary History of the United States,* ed. Emory Elliott et al. (New York: Columbia University Press, 1988), p. 305. Baym's essay is an excellent discussion of the situation of women writers from 1810 to 1865.

[2]Stanton, Theodore, and Harriet Stanton Blatch, eds., *Elizabeth Cady Stanton, As Revealed in Her Letters, Diary, and Reminiscences.* 2 vols. New York: Harper and Brothers, 1922. Reprint. New York: Arno and The New York Times, 1969. See below, p. 475.

[3]Qtd. in Judith Fetterley, ed., *Provisions: A Reader from 19th-Century American Women* (Bloomington: Indiana University Press, 1985), p. 378. This book is recommended for its selection and commentary.

she cannot fulfill her intellectual needs because of her family obligations.

Nevertheless, some women managed to attain enormous success. Lydia Sigourney was probably the first American poet to support herself and her family entirely by publishing poetry. Her verse, along with the similar productions of other women, so dominated the market that it came to define poetry for the average American reader. The greatest best-sellers of the midcentury were Susan Warner's *The Wide, Wide World* and Stowe's *Uncle Tom's Cabin*. Fanny Fern was the highest-paid newspaper writer of her day. Women edited as well as wrote for periodicals: Sarah Josepha Hale wielded great influence for many years as the editor and editorialist of *Godey's Lady's Book*, which was overwhelmingly the highest-circulation magazine of its time.

But women's newly validated right to wield the pen and to work as professional authors was predicated on the assumption that they functioned in a separate feminine sphere. This was a private sphere, in which women were to use their gentle influence to promote the domestic values of love, sympathy, pure idealism, and family ties; it was sharply differentiated from the public sphere, where men used power to pursue worldly success, to compete aggressively, to determine political issues. Women's sentimental novels and poetry, regional sketches, and commentaries on domestic life were approved and appreciated, but they were not expected to range into the public realm. Lydia Maria Child was a successful and respected author, so much so that she was awarded library privileges at the all-male Boston Athenaeum, but when she published *An Appeal in Favor of That Class of Americans Called Africans* in 1833, her book sales fell off, the children's magazine she edited failed, and the Athenaeum revoked her library privileges. *Uncle Tom's Cabin* was acceptable, despite its political content, because Stowe appealed to right feeling and condemned slavery as an attack on the sacred values of home and family.

Women wrote with a heightened consciousness of gender, of what subject matter and style were appropriate to their sex. They were encouraged to adopt a "feminine" tone, indicating that they were emotional rather than rational beings, who neither aspired to nor were capable of claiming power. Bradstreet's metaphysical wit would have seemed as unsuitable to nineteenth-century sensibility as Warren's vigorous political argument. Even when Bradstreet grieved over the deaths of her grandchildren or Judith Sargent Murray advocated tenderness in child-rearing, they did not adopt a consciously feminine tone. Nineteenth-century women, on the other hand, disarmed potential opposition by self-deprecation, matter-of-fact unpretentiousness, effusive feeling, or scatterbrained inconsequentiality. Caroline Kirkland presented her insightful reports on frontier life as "desultory sketches, . . . a meandering recital of common-place occurrences"; Fanny Fern's columns have the appearance of spontaneous chat; Alcott played down her harrowing service in an army hospital by a humorous matter-of-fact tone, as if she were relating the trials of managing a house and family. Dodge both used and mocked gender stereotypes in her essay "My Garden" (1862); first, she pretends that it is necessary "to know whether the story-teller is a man or a woman" in order to call up the right set of feelings, and that she is obligated to admit her sex, lest she mislead her readers by showing them "a vigor of thought, a comprehensiveness of view, a closeness of logic, and a terseness of diction, commonly supposed to pertain only to the stronger sex."[4] Then she proceeds, in the body of her essay, to flaunt the inaccuracy, digressiveness, and fanciful sprightliness that supposedly characterized women's writing.

Although many of these women were critically acclaimed in their own day (in contrast to more modern times), they were judged in terms of their own sphere, which was not equivalent to the unrestricted world of men. A contemporary reviewer of Fanny Fern's *Fern Leaves* understandably deplored the fact that such a slight work was "*the* book of the day," but he went on to link its limitations with the author's sex: "Where are the original, the brilliant, the noble works, in whose publication we might take a lasting and national pride, from whose perusal we might derive delight, instruction, and elevation? Where are the men to write them?" He exhorted men to publish books "for the hope of the future and the honor of America. Do not leave its literature in the hands of a few industrious females."[5]

This reviewer blamed women for restrictions that, Mary E. Bryan recognized, men had imposed upon them. In an essay of 1860 she complained: "Men, after much demur and hesitation, have given

[4]Fetterley, *Provisions*, p. 427.
[5]Qtd. Joyce W. Warren, intro. to Fanny Fern, *Ruth Hall and Other Writings* (New Brunswick: Rutgers University Press, 1986), p. xxxvi.

women liberty to write; but they cannot yet consent to allow them full freedom. They may flutter out of the cage . . . they may hop about the smooth-shaven lawn, but must, on no account, fly." They must not grapple with metaphysics nor "with those great social and moral problems with which every strong soul is now wrestling," nor must they "go beyond the surface of life, lest they should stir the impure sediment that lies beneath." Then, "having prescribed these bounds," men condemn woman's "efforts as tame and commonplace, because they lack earnestness and strength."[6]

That women were not truly integrated into intellectual life is shown by the Transcendentalist thinkers, an exceptionally progressive and enlightened group. Although Ralph Waldo Emerson seemed to encourage independent thinking and action regardless of sex—a doctrine that attracted Margaret Fuller—his essays were, perhaps unconsciously, addressed to a male audience. Almost all his examples in "Self-Reliance" are male, and he relentlessly reiterates *man* and *manly.* Lydia Child reported that in one otherwise beautiful lecture Emerson urged men "to *be* rather than *seem,* that they might . . . grow up into the full stature of spiritual manhood," but urged women "to simplicity and truthfulness, that they might become more *pleasing*" to men.[7] The male Transcendentalists accepted Fuller, but they were a little uncomfortable with her; Emerson wrote that her death at forty came at a "happy hour for herself."[8]

On the other hand, occupying a clearly defined sphere helped women writers to perfect their expression of experience that was distinctively female, to provide an alternative to the view and voice of the male writer. Kirkland, Fanny Fern, and Alcott (as well as Abigail Adams, writing personal letters) expressed themselves far more effectively than did Warren, Murray, and even Fuller, who were writing in the magisterial manner of their male contemporaries. Adopting a self-consciously "feminine" point of view, women brought out new, original aspects of American experience—the difficulties of housekeeping on the frontier (Kirkland) or the domestic feelings that wounded soldiers showed to sympathetic women (Alcott). Women

---

[6]"How Should Women Write?," *Southern Field and Fireside* 1 (January 1860), in *Hidden Hands: An Anthology of Women Writers, 1790–1870,* ed. Lucy M. Freibert and Barbara A. White (New Brunswick: Rutgers University Press, 1985), p. 370.

[7]Letter 34 of *Letters from New York,* in Fetterley, *Provisions,* p. 197.

[8]Letter to Carlyle, in *Woman and the Myth: Margaret Fuller's Life and Writings,* ed. Bell Gale Chevigny (Old Westbury, N.Y.: The Feminist Press, 1976), p. 415.

writers in general tend to emphasize practical, everyday details, because women have always been immersed in such things, but American women have shown a particular interest in household work. Because America had no traditional servant class (outside the slave states), it was "the only country where there is a class of women who may be described as *ladies* who do their own work."[9] From Bradstreet's loving inventory of the furniture she lost when her house burned, to Phelps's detailing of the calls upon a mother's time and energy, these women vividly re-create the daily concerns that take up the bulk of our lives. Style as well as subject brings these writers close to us today, making the experience they describe both lively and recognizable. Rejecting the authoritative or grandiloquent voice typical of male nineteenth-century American writing, they seem to speak to us directly and spontaneously.

In the twentieth century, when woman's separate sphere was no longer recognized and respected, the writers who occupied it were correspondingly devalued. Major American literature was defined in terms of Poe's and Hawthorne's romance, Emerson's and Thoreau's idealistic philosophy, Melville's tragedy of an isolated hero pitted against Nature in the form of a white whale. Domestic realism was dismissed as trivial and automatically suspected of effusive sentimentality. It was even considered less authentically American than the men's work, although it is hard to imagine anything more American than Stowe's appreciation of New England farmers. Authors such as Catharine Sedgwick, classed in her own day with James Fenimore Cooper as a founder of the American novel, dropped out of sight. Sigourney was dismissed as a writer of stock sentimental verse (as indeed she was), not remembered as the author of "The Father," a chilling story of male possessiveness in the manner of Poe. Critics took Fanny Fern's ironic pseudonym at face value and, without reading her work, assumed she was a coy sentimentalist.

The very popularity of the women writers counted against them, since the recognized great male writers of the period, such as Hawthorne and Melville, were greatly outsold by Warner and Stowe. Easily comprehensible meaning, overt appeals to the emotions, and direct political preaching were equated with artistic inferiority. As late as 1966, an editor of *Uncle Tom's Cabin* asked in puzzlement

[9]Harriet Beecher Stowe, "The Lady Who Does Her Own Work," *The Writings*, vol. 8 (Riverside ed., 1896; reprint New York: AMS Press, 1967), p. 86.

how "a book so seemingly artless, so lacking in apparent literary talent" could have endured.[10]

Of course there were many mid-nineteenth-century women who did not fit comfortably into the genteel feminine role. Black women, for whom it was a mocking irrelevancy, were forced to see through the myth of delicate, protected womanhood. In contrast to the fictitious ingenuous victim Charlotte Temple, Harriet Jacobs rationally chose to take a lover; instead of being "ruined," she benefited in terms of improved self-esteem (despite her expressions of guilt) and greater control of her children. Sojourner Truth demolished the idea that women require and lead protected lives by confronting it with the realities of an enslaved black woman's life. By a similar route, Sarah Grimké came to recognize the hollowness of the respect ostensibly paid to women in nineteenth-century America. Both she and Stanton saw that the idealization of "feminine" qualities and the domestic sphere had the effect of diminishing women and leaving them vulnerable to oppression.

It was not only the feminists, however, who resented male dominance. Even women who seemingly accepted their conventional role covertly expressed anger and protest. Fanny Fern delights in sniping at the lords of creation, in taking a stale antifeminist jibe and turning it around, in exposing to reality the sentimental clichés that women were supposed to accept as guiding truths. Phelps develops a painful contradiction between a conscientious woman's intellectual needs and her conventional obligations, and suggests that the problem is insoluble by offering a noticeably unconvincing solution. Kirkland jokes about her troubles in a crude frontier community, but makes it clear that they result from her husband's foolish scheme to get rich by speculating in land. This indirect hostility, often masked by facetiousness, stopping short of overt protest or rebellion, met emotional needs of many women readers and contributed to these authors' popularity.

This anthology offers a representative collection of women's contributions to American literature from the beginning to the Civil War, including both those who conformed to conventional expectations for women's writing and those who defied them. Much of the material is vividly personal—whether it was written to beloved family

[10]John William Ward, afterword to Harriet Beecher Stowe, *Uncle Tom's Cabin* (New York: New American Library, 1966), p. 480.

members or published in the forms that women made their own. There are actual letters, Abigail Adams's lively, passionate outpourings to her husband and the thoughtful analyses of self and womanhood that Eliza Southgate shared with her cousin Moses; letters home rewritten for publication by Kirkland and Alcott; Harriet Farley's fictitious letters home describing a country girl's new life in a mill town; Grimké's feminist tract presented as letters to a female associate. Autobiography ranges from the chatty reminiscences that Catharine Sedgwick wrote down for her grand-niece, to the rather formal, but outspoken, spiritual autobiography that Bradstreet composed for her children, to Sarah Kemble Knight's lively travel journal, to the public narratives, published to advance religion or abolish slavery, of Mary Rowlandson, Elizabeth Ashbridge, Jarena Lee, and Harriet Jacobs. Bradstreet's poetry, an intensely personal fusion of intellectuality and tenderness, piety and earthly love, contrasts with the more public, stylized eighteenth-century poems of Warren and Wheatley and the moving poetical oratory of Frances Harper. Sojourner Truth's spontaneous, down-to-earth eloquence is as wonderfully effective as the brilliantly built logical argument of Stanton.

Fiction is represented by examples of the three forms most characteristic of women's writing. Rowson's sentimental novel *Charlotte Temple* centers on sympathetic portrayal of a young woman's feelings; Stowe's "Love versus Law" develops regional character with humor and sympathy; and Phelps's "The Angel Over the Right Shoulder" appeals through its meticulous rendition of everyday domestic life. Because of my chronological limits, I have had to represent two major authors, Stowe and Alcott, by early and relatively minor pieces—although I would argue that each presages the vivid vernacular realism that was to characterize their greatest work. I regretfully omitted Rebecca Harding Davis's *Life in the Iron Mills* and Emily Dickinson's early poetry because they are readily available elsewhere.

Anne Dudley Bradstreet

1612 or 1613–1672

ANNE DUDLEY'S FATHER, Thomas, was a cultured man who encouraged her intellectual development and her writing. About 1619, he became manager of the estates of the Puritan Earl of Lincoln, so that she grew up in a noble household, with access to books and cultivated society. There she met Simon Bradstreet, a nonconformist minister's son and a Cambridge graduate, who came as an assistant to her father. She married him in 1628, and it was an ideally happy marriage. The Dudleys and the Bradstreets joined the group of Puritans that sailed for New England in 1630, with Dudley second in command. He continued to be a prominent leader in the colony, often serving as governor or deputy governor. Simon Bradstreet also came to hold important public posts, which required much travel away from home, and served as governor after Anne's death.

Life was bitterly hard in the Massachusetts Bay Colony: illness was constant and death frequent, and two years passed before the Dudleys and Bradstreets were able to build decent houses. They settled in Newtown (now Cambridge), but four years later moved to Ipswich, the most remote village in the colony. Nevertheless, its intellectual environment was stimulating. Some of the settlers had good libraries—the Bradstreets owned eight hundred books—and they included university graduates and a former member of the British Parliament. Here Anne Bradstreet began to write seriously, producing long poems on such subjects as the four ages and the four monarchies, which reflect learned reading and a keen interest in history and the science of her day. When she was pregnant with her sixth child, the family moved to Andover, then a rough frontier village.

When her brother-in-law went to England on political business in 1647, he brought along manuscripts of her poems, which were pub-

10

lished as *The Tenth Muse, Lately Sprung Up in America* (1650). Although she was somewhat embarrassed by the publication, she set about revising her poems for a second edition, which was to appear in 1678, after her death. The first three poems included here appeared in *The Tenth Muse,* and the following twelve were added in 1678; the rest remained in manuscript. From the beginning, Bradstreet's work reflected her experience as a woman: "The Four Ages of Man" includes a vivid description of the trials of pregnancy and infant care. Her style develops from the learned, sometimes contrived wit of metaphysical poetry to more simple, direct expression of feeling.

BIBLIOGRAPHY

Bradstreet, Anne. *The Works.* Edited by Jeannine Hensley. Foreword by Adrienne Rich. Cambridge: Harvard University Press, 1967.

———. *The Complete Works.* Edited by Joseph R. McElrath, Jr., and Allan P. Robb. Boston: Twayne, 1981.

Martin, Wendy. *An American Triptych: Anne Bradstreet, Emily Dickinson, Adrienne Rich.* Chapel Hill: University of North Carolina Press, 1984.

Stanford, Ann. *Anne Bradstreet: The Worldly Puritan.* New York: Burt Franklin, 1974.

White, Elizabeth Wade. *Anne Bradstreet: "The Tenth Muse."* New York: Oxford University Press, 1971.

The Prologue

1.

To sing of wars, of captains, and of kings,
Of cities founded, commonwealths begun,[1]
For my mean[2] pen are too superior things:

[1]Epics, such as Homer's *Iliad* and Virgil's *Aeneid,* dealt with war and were considered the highest form of literature; *The Aeneid* narrates the founding of Rome, originally a commonwealth.
[2]Humble.

Or how they all, or each their dates have run,
Let poets and historians set these forth,
My obscure lines shall not so dim their worth.

2.

But when my wondering eyes and envious heart
Great Bartas'[3] sugared lines do but read o'er,
Fool,[4] I do grudge the Muses did not part
'Twixt him and me, that overfluent store;
A Bartas can do what a Bartas will,
But simple I, according to my skill.

3.

From schoolboy's tongue, no Rhetoric we expect,
Nor yet a sweet consort from broken strings,
Nor perfect beauty, where's a main defect:
My foolish, broken, blemished Muse so sings;
And this to mend, alas, no art is able,
'Cause Nature made it so irreparable.

4.

Nor can I, like that fluent, sweet tongued Greek,
Who lisped at first, in future times speak plain.[5]
By art, he gladly found what he did seek,
A full requital of his striving pain:
Art can do much, but this maxim's most sure:
A weak or wounded brain admits no cure.

---

[3]Guillaume du Bartas, a sixteenth-century French Protestant writer much admired by the Puritans, wrote *Divine Weeks and Works,* an epic on the creation that provided an encyclopedia of natural history.

[4]Fool that I am.

[5]The great Greek orator Demosthenes cured himself of stuttering.

5.

I am obnoxious to each carping tongue
Who says my hand a needle better fits,
A poet's pen, all scorn I should thus wrong,
For such despite they cast on female wits:
If what I do prove well, it won't advance,
They'll say it's stolen, or else it was by chance.

6.

But sure the antique Greeks were far more mild,
Else of our sex why feigned they those nine,[6]
And poesy made Calliope's own child,
So 'mongst the rest, they placed the arts divine:
But this weak knot they will full soon untie,
The Greeks did nought but play the fool and lie.

7.

Let Greeks be Greeks, and women what they are,
Men have precedency, and still excel.
It is but vain unjustly to wage war;
Men can do best, and women know it well;
Preeminence in all and each is yours;
Yet grant some small acknowledgement of ours.

8.

And oh, ye high flown quills that soar the skies,[7]
And ever with your prey, still catch your praise,
If e're you deign these lowly lines your eyes,
Give thyme or parsley wreath, I ask no bays;[8]
This mean and unrefinèd ore of mine
Will make your glistering gold but more to shine.

---

[6]In Greek mythology, nine female Muses presided over the arts and sciences; Calliope was the muse of epic poetry.

[7]Quill pens, with a pun on flight feathers.

[8]A great poet was traditionally crowned with bay leaves (laurel).

In Honor of That High and Mighty Princess, Queen Elizabeth, of Happy Memory[1]

The Proem

Although, great Queen, thou now in silence lie,
Yet thy loud herald Fame doth to the sky
Thy wondrous worth proclaim in every clime,
And so has vowed, whilst there is world or time;
So great's thy glory and thine excellence,
The sound thereof rapts[2] every human sense,
That men account it no impiety,
To say thou wert a fleshly deity:
Thousands bring offerings (though out of date)
Thy world of honors to accumulate;
'Mongst hundred hecatombs of roaring verse,
Mine bleating stands before thy royal hearse:
Thou never didst, nor canst thou now disdain,
T' accept the tribute of a loyal brain;
Thy clemency did erst esteem as much
The acclamations of the poor, as rich,
Which makes me deem my rudeness is no wrong,
Though I resound thy praises 'mongst the throng.

[1] Queen Elizabeth had died in 1603.
[2] Seizes, engrosses completely.

The Poem

No Phoenix pen, nor Spenser's poetry,
No Speed's nor Camden's learned history,
Eliza's works, wars, praise, can e're compact;[3]
The world's the theater where she did act;
No memories, nor volumes can contain
The 'leven Olympiads[4] of her happy reign;
Who was so good, so just, so learn'd, so wise,
From all the kings on earth she won the prize;
Nor say I more than duly is her due,
Millions will testify that this is true.
She hath wiped off th' aspersion of her sex,
That women wisdom lack to play the rex;
Spain's monarch says not so, nor yet his host;[5]
She taught them better manners, to their cost.
The Salic law in force now had not been,
If France had ever hoped for such a queen;[6]
But can you, Doctors,[7] now this point dispute,
She's argument enough to make you mute;
Since first the sun did run his ne'er run race,
And earth had, once a year, a new old face,
Since time was time, and man unmanly man,
Come show me such a phoenix if you can;
Was ever people better ruled than hers?
Was ever land more happy, freed from stirs?[8]
Did ever wealth in England more abound?
Her victories in foreign coasts resound;
Ships more invincible than Spain's, her foe,
She wracked, she sacked, she sunk his Armado;
Her stately troops advanced to Lisbon's wall,

[3]Summarize. Edmund Spenser celebrated Elizabeth in his *Faerie Queene;* John Speed and William Camden, in their histories.

[4]An Olympiad was the four-year interval between celebrations of the Olympic Games in ancient Greece; Elizabeth reigned for forty-four years.

[5]Elizabeth defeated Philip II of Spain, who sent a mighty armada against her (line 46).

[6]The Salic Law barred females from inheriting land; in countries where it prevailed, such as France, women could not become monarchs.

[7]Scholars.

[8]Conflicts.

Don Anthony in's right there to install;
She frankly helped Frank's brave distressèd king,
The States united now her fame do sing;[9]
She their protectrix was, they well do know,
Unto our dread virago, what they owe:
Her nobles sacrificed their noble blood,
Nor men nor coin she spared to do them good;
The rude untamèd Irish she did quell,
Before her picture the proud Tyrone fell.[10]
Had ever prince such counsellors as she?
Herself Minerva, caused them so to be;
Such captains and such soldiers never seen,
As were the subjects of our Pallas queen:
Her seamen through all straits the world did round,
Terra incognita might know the sound;
Her Drake came laden home with Spanish gold,
Her Essex took Cadiz, their Herculean hold:[11]
But time would fail me, so my tongue would too,
To tell of half she did, or she could do.
Semiramis to her is but obscure,
More infamy than fame she did procure;
She built her glory but on Babel's walls,
World's wonder for a while, but yet it falls[12]
Fierce Tom'ris (Cyrus' headsman, Scythians' queen)

[9]Elizabeth supported Don Antonio, who contested Philip II's claim to the Portuguese throne; helped Henry IV of France, a Protestant sympathizer, subdue Catholic rebels backed by Spain; and helped the Protestant Dutch rebels against Philip II. The Dutch united their provinces (States) and declared their independence of Spain in 1581.

[10]The Earl of Tyrone led the Irish in rebellion against Elizabeth but was defeated.

[11]Sir Francis Drake captured many Spanish ships carrying gold; the Earl of Essex captured Cádiz for Elizabeth; Cádiz is near the Strait of Gibraltar, marked by the Pillars of Hercules.

[12]Semiramis, a legendary Assyrian queen, was supposed to have conquered many lands and founded the city of Babylon. In succeeding lines: Tomyris, Queen of the Massagetes (reputed to be a ferocious people), defeated the great Persian king Cyrus and abused his body after he was killed in battle; unescorted by a bodyguard, Elizabeth reviewed the troops assembled at Tilbury to repel an expected Spanish invasion and made them an inspiring speech; Dido, called Elissa, was the queen and founder of Carthage, who killed herself for love of Aeneas; Cleopatra's name means "glory of the father" (or "fatherland"); Zenobia, a notably able queen of Palmyra (in Syria), was conquered by the Roman emperor Aurelian.

Had put her harness off, had she but seen
Our Amazon i'th' Camp of Tilbury,
Judging all valor and all majesty
Within that princess to have residence,
And prostrate yielded to her excellence:
Dido, first foundress of proud Carthage walls,
Who living consummates her funerals,
A great Eliza, but compared with ours,
How vanisheth her glory, wealth, and powers;
Profuse proud Cleopatra, whose wrong name,
Instead of glory, proved her country's shame:
Of her what worth in story's to be seen,
But that she was a rich Egyptian queen;
Zenobia, potent empress of the East,
And of all these without compare the best,
Whom none but great Aurelius could quell,
Yet for our queen is no fit parallel:
She was a Phoenix Queen, so shall she be,
Her ashes not revived, more phoenix she;
Her personal perfections who would tell,
Must dip his pen i'th' Heliconian well;
Which I may not, my pride doth but aspire
To read what others write, and so admire.
Now say, have women worth, or have they none?
Or had they some, but with our queen is't gone?
Nay, masculines, you have thus taxed us long,
But she, though dead, will vindicate our wrong.
Let such as say our sex is void of reason,
Know 'tis a slander now, but once was treason.
But happy England, which had such a queen,
Yea happy, happy, had those days still been;[13]
But happiness lies in a higher sphere,
Then wonder not, Eliza moves not here.
Full fraught with honor, riches, and with days,
She set, she set, like Titan in his rays;
No more shall rise or set so glorious sun,

[13]Reversing Elizabeth's policy of religious toleration, her successor, James I, and even more his son Charles I (who succeeded him in 1625), tried to force the Puritans to conform to the Church of England.

Until the heavens' great revolution:[14]
If then new things, their old forms shall retain,
Eliza shall rule Albion once again.

Her Epitaph

Here sleeps the Queen, this is the royal bed
O'th' damask rose, sprung from the white and red,[15]
Whose sweet perfume fills the all-filling air.
This rose is withered, once so lovely fair.
On neither tree did grow such rose before,
The greater was our gain, our loss the more.

Another

Here lies the pride of queens, pattern of kings,
So blaze it, Fame, here's feathers for thy wings;
Here lies the envied, yet unparalleled prince,
Whose living virtues speak (though dead long since).
If many worlds, as that fantastic framed,[16]
In every one, be her great glory famed.

Of the Vanity of All Worldly Creatures

As he said, "vanity,"[1] so vain say I,
O vanity, O vain all under sky;
Where is the man can say, "Lo, I have found

[14]The Day of Judgment.

[15]Elizabeth's family, the House of Tudor, claimed to unite the royal Houses of Lancaster (represented by a red rose) and of York (represented by a white rose); a damask rose is deep pink.

[16]Bradstreet refers to current speculations about other worlds populated by intelligent beings.

[1]"Vanity of vanities, saith the Preacher, vanity of vanities; all is vanity" (Eccle-

On brittle earth, a consolation sound"?
What is't in honor, to be set on high?
No, they like beasts, and sons of men shall die;
And whilst they live, how oft doth turn their fate?
He's now a captive that was king of late.[2]
What is't in wealth, great treasures to obtain?
No, that's but labor, anxious care, and pain.
He heaps up riches, and he heaps up sorrow,
It's his today, but who's his heir tomorrow?
What then? Content in pleasures canst thou find?
More vain than all, that's but to grasp the wind.
The sensual senses for a time they please,
Meanwhile the conscience' rage, who shall appease?
What, is't in beauty? No, that's but a snare,
They're foul enough today, that once were fair.
What, is't in flowering youth, or manly age?
The first is prone to vice, the last to rage.
Where is it then? In wisdom, learning, arts?
Sure if on earth, it must be in those parts;
Yet these, the wisest man of men did find
But vanity, vexation of the mind;
And he that knows the most doth still bemoan,
He knows not all that here is to be known.
What is it then? To do as Stoics tell,
Nor laugh, nor weep, let things go ill or well?
Such Stoics are but stocks, such teaching vain:
While man is man, he shall have ease or pain.
If not in honor, beauty, age, nor treasure,
Nor yet in learning, wisdom, youth, nor pleasure,
Where shall I climb, sound, seek, search, or find
That *summum bonum* which may stay my mind?
There is a path no vulture's eye hath seen,[3]
Where lion fierce, nor lion's whelps have been,
Which leads unto that living crystal fount;

siastes 1:2). *Vanity* means *emptiness;* the Preacher is King Solomon, "the wisest man of men" (line 23), the supposed author of Ecclesiastes.
  [2]King Charles I had fallen into the hands of his Puritan enemies in 1647.
  [3]From here on, Bradstreet combines several Biblical texts (Job 28:7–22, Revelation 22:1–2, Matthew 13:46) to develop her interpretation of the *summum bonum:* religious faith and wisdom.

Who drinks thereof, the world doth naught account.
The depth and sea have said, " 'Tis not in me,"
With pearl and gold it shall not valued be:
For sapphire, onyx, topaz, who would change?
It's hid from eyes of men, they count it strange.
Death and destruction, the fame hath heard;
But where and what it is, from heaven's declared:
It brings to honor which shall ne'er decay,
It stores with wealth which time can't wear away.
It yieldeth pleasures far beyond conceit,
And truly beautifies without deceit.
Nor strength, nor wisdom, nor fresh youth shall fade,
Nor death shall see, but are immortal made,
This pearl of price, this tree of life, this spring,
Who is possessèd of, shall reign a king.
Nor change of state, nor cares shall ever see,
But wear his crown unto eternity,
This satiates the soul, this stays the mind,
And all the rest, but vanity we find.

Contemplations

Some time now past in the autumnal tide,
When Phoebus wanted but one hour to bed,
The trees all richly clad, yet void of pride,
Were gilded o'er by his rich golden head.
Their leaves and fruits seemed painted, but was true
Of green, of red, of yellow, mixèd hue,[1]
Rapt were my senses at this delectable view.

---

[1]An hour before setting, Phoebus, the sun, brings out the autumn foliage so that it seems painted, although these colors are real.

2

I wist not what to wish, yet sure thought I,
If so much excellence abide below,
How excellent is He that dwells on high,
Whose power and beauty by his works we know.
Sure he is goodness, wisdom, glory, light,
That hath this under world so richly dight:
More Heaven than Earth was here, no winter and no night.

3

Then on a stately oak I cast mine eye,
Whose ruffling top the clouds seemed to aspire;
How long since thou wast in thine infancy?
Thy strength, and stature, more thy years admire,
Hath hundred winters passed since thou wast born?
Or thousand since thou brakest thy shell of horn?[2]
If so, all these as nought, eternity doth scorn.

4

Then higher on the glistering Sun I gazed,
Whose beams was shaded by the leafy tree,
The more I looked, the more I grew amazed,
And softly said, "What glory's like to thee?"
Soul of this world, this universe's eye,
No wonder some made thee a deity:
Had I not better known, alas, the same had I.

5

Thou as a bridegroom from thy chamber rushes,
And as a strong man, joys to run a race;[3]
The morn doth usher thee, with smiles and blushes;
The earth reflects her glances in thy face.
Birds, insects, animals with vegative,

[2]Acorn
[3]Echoes Psalm 19:4–5.

Thy heat from death and dullness doth revive:
And in the darksome womb of fruitful nature dive.

6

Thy swift annual and diurnal course,
Thy daily straight and yearly oblique path,[4]
Thy pleasing fervor and thy scorching force,
All mortals here the feeling knowledge hath.
Thy presence makes it day, thy absence night,
Quaternal[5] seasons caused by thy might:
Hail creature, full of sweetness, beauty, and delight.

7

Art thou so full of glory that no eye
Hath strength, thy shining rays once to behold?
And is thy splendid throne erect so high,
As to approach it, can no earthly mould?
How full of glory then must thy Creator be,
Who gave this bright light luster unto thee?
Admired, adored for ever, be that Majesty.

8

Silent alone, where none or saw, or heard,
In pathless paths I led my wandering feet;
My humble eyes to lofty skies I reared
To sing some song, my mazèd Muse thought meet.
My great Creator I would magnify,
That nature had thus deckèd liberally:
But Ah, and Ah, again, my imbecility![6]

---

[4]Following the Ptolemaic system, according to which the sun circled the earth,
Bradstreet thinks of the sun passing straight across the sky every day, but facing the
earth at a changing angle over the seasons of the year.
[5]A set of four.
[6]Weakness.

9

I heard the merry grasshopper then sing,
The black-clad cricket bear a second part;
They kept one tune and played on the same string,
Seeming to glory in their little art.
Shall creatures abject thus their voices raise,
And in their kind resound their Maker's praise,
Whilst I, as mute, can warble forth no higher lays?

10

When present times look back to ages past,
And men in being fancy those are dead,
It makes things gone perpetually to last,
And calls back months and years that long since fled.
It makes a man more agèd in conceit[7]
Than was Methuselah,[8] or's grand-sire great,
While of their persons and their acts his mind doth treat.

11

Sometimes in Eden fair, he seems to be,
Sees glorious Adam there made lord of all,
Fancies the apple, dangle on the tree,
That turned his sovereign to a naked thrall.
Who like a miscreant's driven from that place,
To get his bread with pain and sweat of face,
A penalty imposed on his backsliding race.

[7]Imagination.
[8]Methuselah was supposed to have lived 969 years (Genesis 5:27). The following stanzas outline events narrated in Genesis: Adam's life in Eden and his fall (stanza 11), Eve's remorse for listening to Satan and forebodings about her first-born son, Cain (stanza 12), the rivalry between Cain and Abel, whose offering God preferred (stanza 13), Cain's murder of Abel and his consequent fear (stanza 14), Cain's punishment and building of the first city (stanza 15); see Genesis 1:26, 2:15–17, 3:1–7, 17–19, 23, 4:1–17.

12

Here sits our grandame in retired place,
And in her lap, her bloody Cain new-born;
The weeping imp oft looks her in the face,
Bewails his unknown hap and fate forlorn;
His mother sighs, to think of Paradise,
And how she lost her bliss, to be more wise,
Believing him that was, and is, Father of Lies.

13

Here Cain and Abel come to sacrifice,
Fruits of the earth, and fatlings each do bring;
On Abel's gift the fire descends from skies,
But no such sign on false Cain's offering;
With sullen hateful looks he goes his ways,
Hath thousand thoughts to end his brother's days,
Upon whose blood his future good he hopes to raise.

14

There Abel keeps his sheep, no ill he thinks;
His brother comes, then acts his fratricide;
The virgin earth, of blood her first draught drinks,
But since that time she often hath been cloyed;
The wretch with ghastly face and dreadful mind
Thinks each he sees will serve him in his kind,
Though none on earth but kindred near then could he find.

15

Who fancies not his looks now at the bar,
His face like death, his heart with horror fraught,
Nor malefactor ever felt like war,
When deep despair with wish of life hath fought,
Branded with guilt and crushed with treble woes,
A vagabond to Land of Nod he goes,
A city builds, that walls might him secure from foes.

16

Who thinks not oft upon the Fathers' ages,
Their long descent, how nephews' sons they saw,
The starry observations of those sages,
And how their precepts to their sons were law,
How Adam sighed to see his progeny
Clothed all in his black sinful livery,
Who neither guilt nor yet the punishment could fly.

17

Our life compare we with their length of days,
Who to the tenth of theirs doth now arrive?
And though thus short, we shorten many ways,
Living so little while we are alive;
In eating, drinking, sleeping, vain delight
So unawares comes on perpetual night,
And puts all pleasures vain unto eternal flight.

18

When I behold the heavens as in their prime,
And then the earth (though old) still clad in green,
The stones and trees, insensible of time,
Nor age nor wrinkle on their front are seen;
If winter come, and greenness then do fade,
A spring returns, and they more youthful made;
But man grows old, lies down, remains where once he's laid.

19

By birth more noble than those creatures all,
Yet seems by nature and by custom cursed,
No sooner born, but grief and care makes fall
That state obliterate he had at first:
Nor youth, nor strength, nor wisdom spring again,
Nor habitations long their names retain,
But in oblivion to the final day remain.

20

Shall I then praise the heavens, the trees, the earth
Because their beauty and their strength last longer?
Shall I wish there, or never to had birth,
Because they're bigger, and their bodies stronger?
Nay, they shall darken, perish, fade and die,
And when unmade, so ever shall they lie,
But man was made for endless immortality.

21

Under the cooling shadow of a stately elm,
Close sat I by a goodly river's side,
Where gliding streams the rocks did overwhelm;
A lonely place, with pleasures dignified.
I once that loved the shady woods so well,
Now thought the rivers did the trees excel,
And if the sun would ever shine, there would I dwell.

22

While on the stealing stream I fixed mine eye,
Which to the longed-for ocean held its course,
I marked, nor crooks, nor rubs⁹ that there did lie
Could hinder ought, but still augment its force:
"O happy flood," quoth I, "that holds thy race
Till thou arrive at thy beloved place,
Nor is it rocks or shoals that can obstruct thy pace.

23

Nor is't enough, that thou alone may'st slide,
But hundred brooks in thy clear waves do meet,
So hand in hand along with thee they glide
To Thetis' house, where all embrace and greet:
Thou emblem true of what I count the best,

⁹Bends, nor obstacles.

O could I lead my rivulets to rest,
So may we press to that vast mansion, ever blest."

24

Ye fish, which in this liquid region 'bide,
That for each season, have your habitation,
Now salt, now fresh, where you think best to glide
To unknown coasts to give a visitation,
In lakes and ponds you leave your numerous fry;
So nature taught, and yet you know not why,
You watery folk that know not your felicity.

25

Look how the wantons frisk to taste the air,
Then to the colder bottom straight they dive,
Eftsoon to Neptune's glassy hall repair
To see what trade the great ones there do drive,
Who forage o'er the spacious sea-green field,
And take the trembling prey before it yield,
Whose armor is their scales, their spreading fins their shield.

26

While musing thus with contemplation fed,
And thousand fancies buzzing in my brain,
The sweet-tongued Philomel[10] perched o'er my head,
And chanted forth a most melodious strain,
Which rapt me so with wonder and delight,
I judged my hearing better than my sight,
And wished me wings with her a while to take my flight.

[10]Philomel, the nightingale, is figurative here; nightingales were not native to New England.

27

"O merry bird," said I, "that fears no snares,
That neither toils nor hoards up in thy barn,
Feels no sad thoughts, nor cruciating[11] cares
To gain more good or shun what might thee harm;
Thy clothes ne'er wear, thy meat is everywhere,
Thy bed a bough, thy drink the water clear,
Reminds[12] not what is past, nor what's to come dost fear.

28

"The dawning morn with songs thou dost prevent,[13]
Sets hundred notes unto thy feathered crew,
So each one tunes his pretty instrument,
And warbling out the old, begin anew,
And thus they pass their youth in summer season,
Then follow thee into a better region,
Where winter's never felt by that sweet airy legion."

29

Man at the best a creature frail and vain,
In knowledge ignorant, in strength but weak,
Subject to sorrows, losses, sickness, pain,
Each storm his state, his mind, his body break;
From some of these he never finds cessation,
But day or night, within, without, vexation,
Troubles from foes, from friends, from dearest, nearest relation.

30

And yet this sinful creature, frail and vain,
This lump of wretchedness, of sin and sorrow,
This weather-beaten vessel wracked with pain,
Joys not in hope of an eternal morrow;
Nor all his losses, crosses and vexation,

[11]Excruciating.
[12]Recalls.
[13]Anticipate.

In weight, in frequency and long duration
Can make him deeply groan for that divine translation.[14]

31

The mariner that on smooth waves doth glide
Sings merrily and steers his bark with ease,
As if he had command of wind and tide,
And now becomes great master of the seas;
But suddenly a storm spoils all the sport,
And makes him long for a more quiet port,
Which 'gainst all adverse winds may serve for fort.

32

So he that saileth in this world of pleasure,
Feeding on sweets, that never bit of th' sour,
That's full of friends, of honor, and of treasure,
Fond fool, he takes this earth ev'n for heav'n's bower.
But sad affliction comes and makes him see
Here's neither honor, wealth, or safety;
Only above is found all with security.

33

O Time the fatal wrack of mortal things,
That draws oblivion's curtains over kings;
Their sumptuous monuments, men know them not,
Their names without a record are forgot,
Their parts, their ports, their pomp's all laid in th' dust;
Nor wit, nor gold, nor buildings scape time's rust;
But he whose name is graved in the white stone[15]
Shall last and shine when all of these are gone.

[14]Transformation from mortal to immortal being.
[15]One of the saved: "To him that overcometh will I give to eat of the hidden manna, and will give him a white stone, and in the stone a new name written, which no man knoweth saving he that receiveth it" (Revelation 2:17). This has a gloss in the Geneva Bible, the preferred version of the Puritans: "Such a stone signifieth here a token of God's favor and grace; also it was a sign that one was cleared in judgment."

The Flesh and the Spirit

In secret place where once I stood
Close by the banks of Lacrim flood,[1]
I heard two sisters reason on
Things that are past and things to come;
One Flesh was called, who had her eye
On worldly wealth and vanity;
The other Spirit, who did rear
Her thoughts unto a higher sphere:
Sister, quoth Flesh, what liv'st thou on,
Nothing but meditation?
Doth contemplation feed thee so
Regardlessly to let earth go?
Can speculation satisfy,
Notion without reality?
Dost dream of things beyond the moon,
And dost thou hope to dwell there soon?
Hast treasures there laid up in store
That all in th' world thou count'st but poor?
Art fancy sick, or turn'd a sot
To catch at shadows which are not?
Come, come, I'll show unto thy sense,
Industry hath its recompence.
What canst desire, but thou may'st see
True substance in variety?
Dost honor like? Acquire the same,
As some to their immortal fame:
And trophies to thy name erect
Which wearing time shall ne'er deject.
For riches dost thou long full sore?
Behold enough of precious store.
Earth hath more silver, pearls and gold,
Than eyes can see or hands can hold.
Affect'st thou pleasure? Take thy fill,
Earth hath enough of what you will.

---

[1]A river of tears (Latin *lacrimae);* related to the idea that life is a vale of tears.

Then let not go what thou may'st find
For things unknown, only in mind.
Spirit: Be still thou unregenerate part,
Disturb no more my settled heart,
For I have vowed (and so will do)
Thee as a foe, still to pursue.
And combat with thee will and must,
Until I see thee laid in th' dust.
Sisters we are, yea, twins we be,
Yet deadly feud 'twixt thee and me:
For from one father are we not,
Thou by old Adam wast begot,
But my arise is from above,
Whence my dear Father I do love.
Thou speak'st me fair, but hat'st me sore,
Thy flatt'ring shows I'll trust no more.
How oft thy slave, hast thou me made,
When I believed what thou hast said,
And never had more cause of woe
Than when I did what thou bad'st do.
I'll stop mine ears at these thy charms,
And count them for my deadly harms.
Thy sinful pleasures I do hate,
Thy riches are to me no bait,
Thine honors due, nor will I love;
For my ambition lies above.
My greatest honor it shall be
When I am victor over thee,
And triumph shall with laurel head,
When thou my captive shalt be led;
How I do live, thou need'st not scoff,
For I have meat thou know'st not of;
The hidden manna I do eat,
The word of life it is my meat.
My thoughts do yield me more content
Than can thy hours in pleasure spent.
Nor are they shadows which I catch,
Nor fancies vain at which I snatch,
But reach at things that are so high,
Beyond thy dull capacity;

Eternal substance I do see,
With which enrichèd I would be:
Mine eye doth pierce the heavens and see
What is invisible to thee.
My garments are not silk nor gold,
Nor such like trash which earth doth hold,
But royal robes I shall have on,
More glorious than the glistering sun;
My crown not diamonds, pearls, and gold,
But such as angels' heads enfold.
The city where I hope to dwell,[2]
There's none on earth can parallel;
The stately walls both high and strong
Are made of precious jasper stone;
The gates of pearl, both rich and clear,
And angels are for porters there;
The streets thereof transparent gold,
Such as no eye did e'er behold,
A crystal river there doth run,
Which doth proceed from the Lamb's throne:
Of life, there are the waters sure,
Which shall remain forever pure;
Nor sun, nor moon, they have no need,
For glory doth from God proceed:
No candle there, nor yet torchlight,
For there shall be no darksome night.
From sickness and infirmity,
For evermore they shall be free;
Nor withering age shall e'er come there,
But beauty shall be bright and clear;
This city pure is not for thee,
For things unclean there shall not be:
If I of Heaven may have my fill,
Take thou the world, and all that will.

[2]Bradstreet's description of the city follows the description of the heavenly New
Jerusalem in Revelation 21 and 22.

The Author to Her Book[1]

Thou ill-formed offspring of my feeble brain,
Who after birth did'st by my side remain,
Till snatched from thence by friends, less wise than true,
Who thee abroad, exposed to public view,
Made thee in rags, halting to th' press to trudge,
Where errors were not lessened (all may judge).
At thy return my blushing was not small,
My rambling brat (in print) should mother call,
I cast thee by as one unfit for light,
Thy visage was so irksome in my sight;
Yet being mine own, at length affection would
Thy blemishes amend, if so I could:
I washed thy face, but more defects I saw,
And rubbing off a spot, still made a flaw.
I stretched thy joints to make thee even feet,[2]
Yet still thou run'st more hobbling than is meet;
In better dress to trim thee was my mind,
But nought save homespun cloth i' th' house I find.
In this array, 'mongst vulgars[3] mayst thou roam,
In critics' hands, beware thou dost not come;
And take thy way where yet thou art not known;
If for thy father asked, say thou hadst none:
And for thy mother, she alas is poor,
Which caused her thus to send thee out of door.

[1]Bradstreet's brother-in-law took her poems to England, supposedly without her knowledge, where they were published in 1650. She therefore had no opportunity to correct errors of the press (line 6). Although she was embarrassed, she set about correcting her poems for a second edition.
[2]To make the meter (metrical feet) regular.
[3]Ignorant, undiscriminating readers.

Before the Birth of
One of Her Children

All things within this fading world hath end,
Adversity doth still our joys attend;
No ties so strong, nor friends so dear and sweet,
But with death's parting blow is sure to meet.
The sentence passed is most irrevocable,
A common thing, yet oh, inevitable;
How soon, my Dear, death may my steps attend,
How soon't may be thy lot to lose thy friend,
We both are ignorant; yet love bids me
These farewell lines to recommend to thee,
That when that knot's untied that made us one,
I may seem thine, who in effect am none.
And if I see not half my days that's due,[1]
What nature would, God grant to yours and you;
The many faults that well you know I have,
Let be interred in my oblivious grave;
If any worth or virtue were in me,
Let that live freshly in thy memory;
And when thou feel'st no grief, as I no harms,
Yet love thy dead, who long lay in thine arms:
And when thy loss shall be repaid with gains,
Look to my little babes, my dear remains.
And if thou love thyself, or loved'st me,
These O protect from step-dame's[2] injury.
And if chance to thine eyes shall bring this verse,
With some sad sighs honor my absent hearse;
And kiss this paper for thy love's dear sake,
Who with salt tears this last farewell did take.

---

[1]If I do not live to be thirty-five, half of the Biblically allotted span of three score
and ten years.
[2]Stepmother.

To My Dear and Loving Husband

If ever two were one, then surely we.
If ever man were loved by wife, then thee;
If ever wife was happy in a man,
Compare with me, ye women, if you can.
I prize thy love more than whole mines of gold,
Or all the riches that the East doth hold.
My love is such that rivers cannot quench,
Nor ought but love from thee, give recompence.
Thy love is such I can no way repay,
The heavens reward thee manifold, I pray.
Then while we love, in love let's so persevere,
That when we live no more, we may live ever.

A Letter to Her Husband,
Absent upon
Public Employment

My head, my heart, mine eyes, my life, nay, more,
My joy, my magazine of earthly store,[1]
If two be one, as surely thou and I,
How stayest thou there, whilst I at Ipswich lie?[2]
So many steps, head from the heart to sever,
If but a neck, soon should we be together:
I, like the earth this season, mourn in black,

[1] Storehouse of earthly treasure.
[2] The Bradstreets were living in Ipswich, north of Boston (line 17).

My sun is gone so far in's zodiac,[3]
Whom whilst I 'joyed, nor storms, nor frost I felt,
His warmth such frigid colds did cause to melt.
My chillèd limbs now numbèd lie forlorn;
Return, return, sweet Sol, from Capricorn;
In this dead time, alas, what can I more
Than view those fruits which through thy heat I bore?
Which sweet contentment yield me for a space,
True living pictures of their father's face.
O strange effect! now thou art southward gone,
I weary grow, the tedious day so long;
But when thou northward to me shalt return,
I wish my sun may never set, but burn
Within the Cancer of my glowing breast,
The welcome house of him, my dearest guest.
Where ever, ever stay, and go not thence,
Till nature's sad decree shall call thee hence;
Flesh of thy flesh, bone of thy bone,[4]
I here, thou there, yet both but one.

Another

Phoebus, make haste, the day's too long, be gone,
The silent night's the fittest time for moan;
But stay this once, unto my suit give ear,
And tell my griefs in either hemisphere:
And if the whirling of thy wheels don't drown,
The woeful accents of my doleful sound,
If in thy swift career thou canst make stay,

---

[3]Bradstreet compares her "sun's"—i.e., her husband's—travels to the apparent movement of the sun away from and toward the earth through the year, marked by the signs of the zodiac; Capricorn (line 12) is the sign for midwinter, Cancer (line 21) for early summer.
[4]Echoes Genesis 2:23–24.

I crave this boon, this errand by the way:
Commend me to the man more loved than life,
Show him the sorrows of his widowed wife,
My dumpish thoughts, my groans, my brackish tears,
My sobs, my longing hopes, my doubting fears;
And if he love, how can he there abide?
My interest's more than all the world beside.
He that can tell the stars or ocean sand,
Or all the grass that in the meads do stand,
The leaves in th' woods, the hail, or drops of rain,
Or in a cornfield number every grain,
Or every mote that in the sunshine hops,
May count my sighs, and number all my drops:
Tell him the countless steps that thou dost trace
That, once a day, thy spouse thou mayst embrace;
And when thou canst not treat by loving mouth,
Thy rays afar salute her from the south.
But for one month I see no day (poor soul)
Like those far situate under the pole,
Which day by day long wait for thy arise,
O how they joy when thou dost light the skies.
O Phoebus, hadst thou but thus long from thine
Restrained the beams of thy beloved shine,
At thy return, if so thou could'st or durst,
Behold a Chaos blacker than the first.
Tell him here's worse than a confused matter,
His little world's a fathom under water;[1]
Nought but the fervor of his ardent beams
Hath power to dry the torrent of these streams.
Tell him I would say more, but cannot well;
Oppressed minds, abruptest tales do tell.
Now post with double speed, mark what I say,
By all our loves conjure him not to stay.

[1]Chaos was the state of formless matter supposed to have existed before the creation of the ordered universe. Calling herself a "little world," Bradstreet carries on the creation imagery and draws on the Renaissance concept of a correspondence between the universe and the human body.

To Her Father with Some Verses

Most truly honored, and as truly dear,
If worth in me or ought I do appear,
Who can of right better demand the same
Than may your worthy self, from whom it came?
The principal might yield a greater sum,
Yet handled ill, amounts but to this crumb;
My stock's so small, I know not how to pay,
My bond remains in force unto this day;
Yet for part payment take this simple mite,
Where nothing's to be had, kings lose their right.
Such is my debt, I may not say, forgive;
But as I can, I'll pay it while I live:
Such is my bond, none can discharge but I,
Yet paying is not paid until I die.

In Reference to Her Children, 23 June 1659

I had eight birds hatch in one nest,
Four cocks there were, and hens the rest.
I nursed them up with pain and care,
Nor cost, nor labor did I spare,
Till at the last they felt their wing,
Mounted the trees, and learned to sing.
Chief of the brood then took his flight
To regions far, and left me quite:[1]
My mournful chirps I after send,
Till he return, or I do end:

[1] Her son Samuel was studying medicine in England from 1657–1661.

Leave not thy nest, thy dam and sire,
Fly back and sing amidst this choir.
My second bird did take her flight,
And with her mate flew out of sight;
Southward they both their course did bend,
And seasons twain they there did spend:
Till after blown by southern gales,
They norward steered with filléd sails.[2]
A prettier bird was nowhere seen,
Along the beach among the treen.
I have a third of color white,
On whom I placed no small delight;
Coupled with mate loving and true,
Hath also bid her dam adieu:
And where Aurora first appears,
She now hath perched to spend her years;[3]
One to the academy flew
To chat among that learned crew:[4]
Ambition moves still in his breast
That he might chant above the rest,
Striving for more than to do well,
That nightingales he might excel.
My fifth, whose down is yet scarce gone,
Is 'mongst the shrubs and bushes flown,
And as his wings increase in strength,
On higher boughs he'll perch at length.[5]
My other three still with me nest,[6]
Until they're grown; then as the rest,
Or here or there they'll take their flight,
As is ordained, so shall they light.
If birds could weep, then would my tears
Let others know what are my fears
Lest this my brood some harm should catch,

---

[2]Dorothy married and moved first to Connecticut and then to New Hampshire.
[3]Sarah married and moved to Ipswich, fifteen miles east of Andover, where Anne was then living.
[4]Simon, Jr., was at Harvard.
[5]Dudley (the seventh child, but the fifth to leave the nest) was at school in Ipswich.
[6]Hannah, Mercy, and John were still at home.

And be surprized for want of watch,
Whilst pecking corn and void of care,
They fall un'wares in fowler's snare:
Or whilst on trees they sit and sing,
Some untoward boy at them do fling.
Or whilst allured with bell and glass,
The net be spread, and caught alas.
Or lest by lime-twigs they be foiled,
Or by some greedy hawks be spoiled.
O would my young, ye saw my breast,
And knew what thoughts there sadly rest;
Great was my pain when I you bred,
Great was my care when I you fed,
Long did I keep you soft and warm,
And with my wings kept off all harm;
My cares are more, and fears than ever,
My throbs such now as 'fore were never:
Alas, my birds, you wisdom want,
Of perils you are ignorant;
Oft times in grass, on trees, in flight,
Sore accidents on you may light.
O to your safety have an eye,
So happy may you live and die:
Meanwhile my days in tunes I'll spend,
Till my weak lays with me shall end;
In shady woods I'll sit and sing,
And things that passed to mind I'll bring.
Once young and pleasant, as are you,
But former toys (no joys), adieu.
My age I will not once lament,
But sing, my time so near is spent.
And from the top bough take my flight
Into a country beyond sight,
Where old ones instantly grow young,
And there with seraphims set song:
No seasons cold, nor storms they see;
But spring lasts to eternity.
When each of you shall in your nest
Among your young ones take your rest,
In chirping language, oft them tell,

You had a dam that loved you well,
That did what could be done for young,
And nursed you up till you were strong,
And 'fore she once would let you fly,
She showed you joy and misery;
Taught what was good, and what was ill,
What would save life, and what would kill.
Thus gone, amongst you I may live,
And dead, yet speak, and counsel give:
Farewell, my birds; farewell, adieu,
I happy am, if well with you.

In Memory of My Dear Grandchild Elizabeth Bradstreet, Who Deceased August, 1665, Being a Year and Half Old[1]

Farewell dear babe, my heart's too much content,
Farewell sweet babe, the pleasure of mine eye,
Farewell fair flower that for a space was lent,
Then ta'en away unto eternity.
Blest babe, why should I once bewail thy fate,
Or sigh thy days so soon were terminate,
Sith thou art settled in an everlasting state.

[1]Anne Bradstreet's daughter-in-law Mercy, Samuel's wife, gave birth to four children, three of whom were the subjects of this and the following elegies. Mercy herself died on September 6, 1669, aged twenty-eight.

2.

By nature trees do rot when they are grown,
And plums and apples throughly ripe do fall,
And corn and grass are in their season mown,
And time brings down what is both strong and tall.
But plants new set to be eradicate,
And buds new blown, to have so short a date,
Is by His hand alone that guides nature and fate.

In Memory of My Dear Grandchild Anne Bradstreet, who Deceased June 20, 1669, Being Three Years and Seven Months Old

With troubled heart and trembling hand I write,
The heavens have changed to sorrow my delight.
How oft with disappointment have I met,
When I on fading things my hopes have set.
Experience might 'fore this have made me wise,
To value things according to their price.
Was ever stable joy yet found below?
Or perfect bliss without mixture of woe?
I knew she was but as a withering flower,
That's here today, perhaps gone in an hour;
Like as a bubble, or the brittle glass,
Or like a shadow turning as it was.
More fool then I to look on that was lent
As if mine own, when thus impermanent.
Farewell dear child, thou ne'er shall come to me,
But yet a while, and I shall go to thee;

Meantime my throbbing heart's cheered up with this:
Thou with thy Savior art in endless bliss.

On My Dear Grandchild
Simon Bradstreet,
Who Died on 16 November 1669,
Being but a Month and
One Day Old

No sooner come, but gone, and fallen asleep.
Acquaintance short, yet parting caused us weep;
Three flowers, two scarcely blown, the last i'th' bud,
Cropped by th' Almighty's hand; yet is He good.
With dreadful awe before Him let's be mute;
Such was His will, but why, let's not dispute;
With humble hearts and mouths put in the dust,
Let's say He's merciful, as well as just.
He will return, and make up all our losses,
And smile again, after our bitter crosses.
Go pretty babe, go rest with sisters twain;
Among the blest in endless joys remain.

To My Dear Children[1]

This book by any yet unread,
I leave for you when I am dead,
That being gone, here you may find

[1]During one of her illnesses, Bradstreet composed this spiritual autobiography for

What was your living mother's mind.
Make use of what I leave in love,
And God shall bless you from above.

My dear children,

I, knowing by experience that the exhortations of parents take most effect when the speakers leave to speak,[2] and those especially sink deepest which are spoke latest, and being ignorant whether on my death bed I shall have opportunity to speak to any of you, much less to all, thought it the best, whilst I was able, to compose some short matters (for what else to call them I know not) and bequeath to you, that when I am no more with you, yet I may be daily in your remembrance (although that is the least in my aim in what I now do), but that you may gain some spiritual advantage by my experience. I have not studied in this you read to show my skill, but to declare the truth, not to set forth myself, but the glory of God. If I had minded the former, it had been perhaps better pleasing to you, but seeing the last is the best, let it be best pleasing to you.

The method I will observe shall be this: I will begin with God's dealing with me from my childhood to this day.

In my young years, about six or seven as I take it, I began to make conscience of my ways, and what I knew was sinful, as lying, disobedience to parents, etc., I avoided it. If at any time I was overtaken with the like evils, it was as a great trouble, and I could not be at rest till by prayer I had confessed it unto God. I was also troubled at the neglect of private duties though too often tardy that way. I also found much comfort in reading the Scriptures, especially those places I thought most concerned my condition, and as I grew to have more understanding, so the more solace I took in them.

In a long fit of sickness which I had, on my bed I often communed with my heart and made my supplication to the most High, who set me free from that affliction.

But as I grew up to be about fourteen or fifteen, I found my heart

---

the guidance of her children. Hence she stresses the resolution of her spiritual doubts and the physical chastisements God inflicted on her to turn her from this world and remind her of her dependence on Him. In order to join a church, Puritans had to present a spiritual record such as this, including sin, repentance, turning to God, and conviction of salvation.

[2]Stop speaking.

more carnal, and sitting loose from God, vanity and the follies of youth take hold of me.

About sixteen, the Lord laid His hand sore upon me and smote me with the smallpox. When I was in my affliction, I besought the Lord and confessed my pride and vanity, and He was entreated of me and again restored me. But I rendered not to Him according to the benefit received.

After a short time I changed my condition and was married, and came into this country, where I found a new world and new manners, at which my heart rose. But after I was convinced it was the way of God, I submitted to it and joined to the church at Boston.

After some time I fell into a lingering sickness like a consumption, together with a lameness, which correction I saw the Lord sent to humble and try me and do me good, and it was not altogether ineffectual.

It pleased God to keep me a long time without a child, which was a great grief to me and cost me many prayers and tears before I obtained one; and after him gave me many more, of whom I now take the care, that as I have brought you into the world, and with great pains, weakness, cares, and fears brought you to this, I now travail in birth again of you till Christ be formed in you.

Among all my experiences of God's gracious dealings with me, I have constantly observed this, that He hath never suffered me long to sit loose from Him, but by one affliction or other hath made me look home, and search what was amiss; so usually thus it hath been with me that I have no sooner felt my heart out of order, but I have expected correction for it, which most commonly hath been upon my own person in sickness, weakness, pains, sometimes on my soul, in doubts and fears of God's displeasure and my sincerity towards Him; sometimes He hath smote a child with a sickness, sometimes chastened by losses in estate,[3] and these times (through His great mercy) have been the times of my greatest getting and advantage; yea, I have found them the times when the Lord hath manifested the most love to me. Then have I gone to searching and have said with David, "Lord, search me and try me, see what ways of wickedness are in me, and lead me in the way everlasting,"[4] and seldom or never but I have found either some sin I lay under which God would have

[3]Property.
[4]Psalm 139:23, 24 (paraphrased).

reformed, or some duty neglected which He would have performed, and by His help I have laid vows and bonds upon my soul to perform His righteous commands.

If at any time you are chastened of God, take it as thankfully and joyfully as in greatest mercies, for if ye be His, ye shall reap the greatest benefit by it. It hath been no small support to me in times of darkness when the Almighty hath hid His face from me that yet I have had an abundance of sweetness and refreshment after affliction and more circumspection in my walking after I have been afflicted. I have been with God like an untoward child, that no longer than the rod has been on my back (or at least in sight) but I have been apt to forget Him and myself, too. Before I was afflicted, I went astray, but now I keep Thy statutes.[5]

I have had great experience of God's hearing my prayers and returning comfortable answers to me, either in granting the thing I prayed for, or else in satisfying my mind without it, and I have been confident it hath been from Him, because I have found my heart through His goodness enlarged in thankfulness to Him.

I have often been perplexed that I have not found that constant joy in my pilgrimage and refreshing which I suppose most of the servants of God have, although He hath not left me altogether without the witness of His holy spirit, who hath oft given me His word and set to His seal that it shall be well with me. I have sometimes tasted of that hidden manna that the world knows not, and have set up my Ebenezer,[6] and have resolved with myself that against such a promise, such tastes of sweetness, the gates of hell shall never prevail; yet have I many times sinkings and droopings, and not enjoyed that felicity that sometimes I have done. But when I have been in darkness and seen no light, yet have I desired to stay myself upon the Lord, and when I have been in sickness and pain, I have thought if the Lord would but lift up the light of His countenance upon me, although He ground me to powder, it would be but light to me; yea, oft have I thought were I in hell itself and could there find the love of God toward me, it would be a heaven. And could I have been in heaven without the love of God, it would have been a hell to me,

---

[5]Close paraphrase of Psalm 119:67.

[6]In I Samuel 7:12, a monument set up to commemorate a victory of the Lord's people over the Philistines.

for in truth it is the absence and presence of God that makes heaven or hell.

Many times hath Satan troubled me concerning the verity of the Scriptures, many times by atheism: how I could know whether there was a God. I never saw any miracles to confirm me, and those which I read of, how did I know but they were feigned? That there is a God my reason would soon tell me by the wondrous works that I see, the vast frame of the heaven and the earth, the order of all things, night and day, summer and winter, spring and autumn, the daily providing for this great household upon the earth, the preserving and directing of all to its proper end. The consideration of these things would with amazement certainly resolve me that there is an Eternal Being. But how should I know He is such a God as I worship in Trinity, and such a Savior as I rely upon? Though this hath thousands of times been suggested to me, yet God hath helped me over. I have argued thus with myself. That there is a God, I see. If ever this God hath revealed himself, it must be in His word, and this must be it or none. Have I not found that operation by it that no human invention can work upon the soul, hath not judgments befallen divers who have scorned and contemned it, hath it not been preserved through all ages maugre all the heathen tyrants and all of the enemies who have opposed it? Is there any story but that which shows the beginnings of times, and how the world came to be as we see? Do we not know the prophecies in it fulfilled which could not have been so long foretold by any but God Himself?

When I have got over this block, then have I another put in my way, that admit this be the true God whom we worship, and that be his word, yet why may not the Popish religion be the right? They have the same God, the same Christ, the same word. They only interpret it one way, we another.

This hath sometimes stuck with me, and more it would, but the vain fooleries that are in their religion together with their lying miracles and cruel persecutions of the saints, which admit were they as they term them, yet not so to be dealt withal.

The consideration of these things and many the like would soon turn me to my own religion again.

But some new troubles I have had since the world has been filled with blasphemy and sectaries, and some who have been accounted sincere Christians have been carried away with them, that sometimes I have said, "Is there faith upon the earth?" and I have not known what to think; but then I have remembered the works of Christ that so it must be, and if it were possible, the very elect should be deceived. "Behold," saith our Savior, "I have told you before." That hath stayed my heart, and I can now say, "Return, O my Soul, to thy rest, upon this rock Christ Jesus will I build my faith, and if I perish, I perish"; but I know all the Powers of Hell shall never prevail against it. I know whom I have trusted, and whom I have believed, and that He is able to keep that I have committed to His charge.

Now to the King, immortal, eternal and invisible, the only wise God, be honor, and glory for ever and ever, Amen.

This was written in much sickness and weakness, and is very weakly and imperfectly done, but if you can pick any benefit out of it, it is the mark which I aimed at.

Upon My Son Samuel His Going for England, November 6, 1657

Thou mighty God of sea and land,
I here resign into Thy hand
The son of prayers, of vows, of tears,
The child I stayed for many years.
Thou heardst me then and gav'st him me;
Hear me again, I give him Thee.
He's mine, but more, O Lord, Thine own,
For sure Thy grace on him is shown.
No friend I have like Thee to trust,
For mortal helps are brittle dust.
Preserve, O Lord, from storms and wrack,
Protect him there and bring him back.
And if Thou shalt spare me a space
That I again may see his face,
Then shall I celebrate Thy praise
And bless Thee for't even all my days.

If otherwise I go to rest,
Thy will be done, for that is best.
Persuade my heart I shall him see
Forever happified with Thee.

Here Follows Some Verses upon the Burning of Our House, July 10, 1666

In silent night when rest I took
For sorrow near I did not look,
I wakened was with thundering noise
And piteous shrieks of dreadful voice.
That fearful sound of "Fire!" and "Fire!"
Let no man know, is my desire.
I, starting up, the light did spy,
And to my God my heart did cry
To strengthen me in my distress
And not to leave me succorless,
Then, coming out, beheld a space[1]
The flame consume my dwelling place.
And when I could no longer look,
I blest His name that gave and took,[2]
That laid my goods now in the dust,
Yea, so it was, and so 'twas just.
It was His own, it was not mine;
Far be it that I should repine.
He might of all justly bereft,
But yet sufficient for us left.
When by the ruins oft I passed,
My sorrowing eyes aside did cast

[1] For a short period of time.
[2] Echoes Job 1:21: "The Lord gave, and the Lord hath taken away; blessed be the name of the Lord."

And here and there the places spy
Where oft I sat and long did lie:
Here stood that trunk, and there that chest,
There lay that store I counted best.
My pleasant things in ashes lie,
And them behold no more shall I.
Under thy roof no guest shall sit,
Nor at thy table eat a bit.
No pleasant tale shall e'er be told,
Nor things recounted done of old.
No candle e'er shall shine in thee,
Nor bridegroom's voice e'er heard shall be.
In silence ever shalt thou lie
Adieu, Adieu, all's vanity.
Then straight I 'gin my heart to chide:
And did thy wealth on earth abide?
Didst fix thy hope on moldering dust?
The arm of flesh didst make thy trust?
Raise up thy thoughts above the sky
That dunghill mists away may fly.
Thou hast an house on high erect,
Framed by that mighty Architect,
With glory richly furnished,
Stands permanent, though this be fled.
It's purchasèd and paid for too
By Him who hath enough to do.
A price so vast as is unknown,
Yet by His gift is made thine own.
There's wealth enough, I need no more;
Farewell my pelf, farewell my store.
The world no longer let me love;
My hope and treasure lies above.

As Weary Pilgrim

As weary pilgrim, now at rest,
Hugs with delight his silent nest,
His wasted limbs now lie full soft
That miry steps have trodden oft,
Blesses himself to think upon
His dangers past and travails done.
The burning sun no more shall heat,
Nor stormy rains on him shall beat,
The briars and thorns no more shall scratch,
Nor hungry wolves at him shall catch.
He erring paths no more shall tread,
Nor wild fruits eat instead of bread.
For waters cold he doth not long,
For thirst no more shall parch his tongue.
No rugged stones his feet shall gall,
Nor stumps nor rocks cause him to fall.
All cares and fears he bids farewell,
And means in safety now to dwell.
A pilgrim I, on earth perplexed
With sins, with cares and sorrows vexed,
By age and pains brought to decay,
And my clay house moldering away.
Oh, how I long to be at rest
And soar on high among the blest.
This body shall in silence sleep,
Mine eyes no more shall ever weep,
No fainting fits shall me assail,
Nor grinding pains, my body frail.
With cares and fears ne'er cumbered be,
Nor losses know, nor sorrows see.
What though my flesh shall there consume,
It is the bed Christ did perfume,
And when a few years shall be gone,
This mortal shall be clothed upon.
A corrupt carcass down it lies,
A glorious body it shall rise.

In weakness and dishonor sown,
In power 'tis raised by Christ alone.
Then soul and body shall unite
And of their Maker have the sight.
Such lasting joys shall there behold
As ear ne'er heard, nor tongue e'er told.
Lord, make me ready for that day,
Then come, dear bridegroom,[1] come away.

[1]Christ is the bridegroom of the soul; see Mark 2:19.

Mary White Rowlandson

c.1635–c.1678

AFTER FIFTY YEARS of generally peaceful coexistence between Indians and English, the Algonquian chief Metacomet (called King Philip by the English) realized that the newcomers were taking possession of his people's homeland; he launched a series of raids against frontier settlements (King Philip's War, June 1675–August 1676). One of these was Lancaster, Massachusetts, a town of approximately fifty families, located about thirty miles west of Boston. The Indians slaughtered many of the inhabitants and took the rest prisoner, including Mary Rowlandson, the minister's wife, and her three children. She had been born in England, was the daughter of a prosperous landowner, and had married Joseph Rowlandson about 1656.

She was ransomed eleven weeks later and wrote a vivid account of her ordeal for her private use. It was not published until 1682, as *The Sovereignty and Goodness of God, Together with the Faithfulness of His Promises Displayed; Being a Narrative of the Captivity and Restoration of Mrs. Mary Rowlandson.* This book, the first autobiographical narrative of Indian captivity, combines religious edification with gripping exotic adventure. No wonder it was extremely popular with the Puritans: it went through three editions in its first year and was regularly reprinted into the nineteenth century. The Rowlandsons moved to Connecticut, where Joseph died in 1678; Mary must have survived him, because she was awarded a widow's pension. However, despite the fame of her book, we know nothing of her later life, not even the date of her death.

The narrative of Indian captivity was a sensational form of the standard Puritan spiritual autobiography. Inner temptations and illnesses such as Anne Bradstreet's are replaced by external trials imposed by unbelieving Indians (seen as agents of Satan); with God's grace, the soul withstands its testing and is finally saved; redemption by ransom implies spiritual redemption as well.

BIBLIOGRAPHY
Vaughan, Alden T., and Edward W. Clark. *Puritans among the Indians: Accounts of Captivity and Redemption 1676–1724.* Cambridge: Harvard University Press, 1981.

The Sovereignty and Goodness of God, Together with the Faithfulness of His Promises Displayed; Being a Narrative of the Captivity and Restoration of Mrs. Mary Rowlandson

On the tenth of February 1675[1] came the Indians with great numbers upon Lancaster. Their first coming was about sunrising. Hearing the noise of some guns, we looked out; several houses were burning and the smoke ascending to heaven. There were five persons taken in one house; the father and the mother and a sucking child, they knocked on the head; the other two they took and carried away alive. There were two others, who, being out of their garrison[2] upon some occasion, were set upon; one was knocked on the head, the other escaped. Another there was who running along was shot and wounded and fell down; he begged of them his life, promising them money (as they told me), but they would not hearken to him but knocked him in [the] head, stripped him naked, and split open his bowels. Another, seeing many of the Indians about his barn, ventured and went out, but was quickly shot down. There were three others belonging to the same garrison who were killed; the Indians, getting

---

[1] 1676, according to our present calendar.
[2] Fortified house.

up upon the roof of the barn, had advantage to shoot down upon them over their fortification. Thus these murderous wretches went on, burning and destroying before them.

At length they came and beset our own house, and quickly it was the dolefullest day that ever mine eyes saw. The house stood upon the edge of a hill. Some of the Indians got behind the hill, others into the barn, and others behind anything that could shelter them; from all which places they shot against the house so that the bullets seemed to fly like hail; and quickly they wounded one man among us, then another, and then a third. About two hours (according to my observation in that amazing time) they had been about the house before they prevailed to fire it (which they did with flax and hemp which they brought out of the barn, and there being no defense about the house, only two flankers[3] at two opposite corners and one of them not finished). They fired it once, and one ventured out and quenched it, but they quickly fired it again, and that took.

Now is that dreadful hour come that I have often heard of (in time of war as it was the case of others), but now mine eyes see it. Some in our house were fighting for their lives, others wallowing in their blood, the house on fire over our heads, and the bloody heathen ready to knock us on the head if we stirred out. Now might we hear mothers and children crying out for themselves and one another, "Lord, what shall we do?" Then I took my children (and one of my sisters, hers) to go forth and leave the house, but as soon as we came to the door and appeared, the Indians shot so thick that the bullets rattled against the house as if one had taken an handful of stones and threw them, so that we were fain to give back. We had six stout dogs belonging to our garrison, but none of them would stir, although another time, if any Indian had come to the door, they were ready to fly upon him and tear him down. The Lord hereby would make us the more to acknowledge His hand and to see that our help is always in Him. But out we must go, the fire increasing and coming along behind us roaring, and the Indians gaping before us with their guns, spears, and hatchets to devour us. No sooner were we out of the house, but my brother-in-law [John Divoll] (being before wounded, in defending the house, in or near the throat) fell down dead; whereat the Indians scornfully shouted, hallooed, and were presently upon him, stripping off his clothes. The bullets flying thick,

[3]Projecting fortifications.

one went through my side, and the same (as would seem) through the bowels and hand of my dear child in my arms. One of my elder sister's children, named William [Kerley], had then his leg broken, which the Indians perceiving, they knocked him on the head. Thus were we butchered by those merciless heathen, standing amazed, with the blood running down to our heels.

My eldest sister [Elizabeth] being yet in the house and seeing those woeful sights, the infidels hailing mothers one way and children another and some wallowing in their blood, and her elder son telling her that her son William was dead and myself was wounded, she said, "And, Lord, let me die with them." Which was no sooner said, but she was struck with a bullet and fell down dead over the threshold. I hope she is reaping the fruit of her good labors, being faithful to the service of God in her place. In her younger years she lay under much trouble upon spiritual accounts till it pleased God to make that precious scripture take hold of her heart, 2 Cor. 12:9, "And he said unto me, my grace is sufficient for thee." More than twenty years after I have heard her tell how sweet and comfortable that place was to her. But to return: the Indians laid hold of us, pulling me one way and the children another, and said, "Come go along with us." I told them they would kill me. They answered, if I were willing to go along with them they would not hurt me.

Oh, the doleful sight that now was to behold at this house! "Come, behold the works of the Lord, what desolation He has made in the earth."[4] Of thirty-seven persons who were in this one house, none escaped either present death or a bitter captivity save only one, who might say as he, Job I:15, "And I only am escaped alone to tell the news." There were twelve killed, some shot, some stabbed with their spears, some knocked down with their hatchets. When we are in prosperity, oh, the little that we think of such dreadful sights, and to see our dear friends and relations lie bleeding out their heart-blood upon the ground! There was one who was chopped into the head with a hatchet and stripped naked, and yet was crawling up and down. It is a solemn sight to see so many Christians lying in their blood, some here and some there, like a company of sheep torn by wolves, all of them stripped naked by a company of hell-hounds, roaring, singing, ranting and insulting, as if they would have torn our very hearts out. Yet the Lord by his almighty power preserved

[4]Psalm 46:8.

a number of us from death, for there were twenty-four of us taken alive and carried captive.

I had often before this said that if the Indians should come I should choose rather to be killed by them than taken alive, but when it came to the trial, my mind changed; their glittering weapons so daunted my spirit that I chose rather to go along with those (as I may say) ravenous beasts than that moment to end my days. And that I may the better declare what happened to me during that grievous captivity, I shall particularly speak of the several removes[5] we had up and down the wilderness.

The First Remove

Now away we must go with those barbarous creatures with our bodies wounded and bleeding and our hearts no less than our bodies. About a mile we went that night up upon a hill within sight of the town where they intended to lodge. There was hard by a vacant house (deserted by the English before, for fear of the Indians). I asked them whether I might not lodge in the house that night, to which they answered, "What, will you love English men still?" This was the dolefullest night that ever my eyes saw. Oh, the roaring and singing and dancing and yelling of those black creatures in the night, which made the place a lively resemblance of hell. And as miserable was the waste that was there made of horses, cattle, sheep, swine, calves, lambs, roasting pigs, and fowl (which they had plundered in the town), some roasting, some lying and burning, and some boiling to feed our merciless enemies, who were joyful enough though we were disconsolate. To add to the dolefulness of the former day and the dismalness of the present night, my thoughts ran upon my losses and sad bereaved condition. All was gone: my husband gone (at least separated from me, he being in the Bay,[6] and to add to my grief, the Indians told me they would kill him as he came homeward), my children gone, my relations and friends gone, our house and home

[5]Departures, moving from place to place. The word emphasizes that she is being removed further and further from Christianity and civilization. She was forced to travel about 150 miles.

[6]He had gone to Boston, capital of the Massachusetts Bay Colony, to request aid in defending Lancaster. He returned shortly after the raid to find his home burned and his family gone.

and all our comforts within door and without, all was gone except my life, and I knew not but the next moment that might go too. There remained nothing to me but one poor wounded babe, and it seemed at present worse than death that it was in such a pitiful condition bespeaking compassion, and I had no refreshing for it nor suitable things to revive it. Little do many think what is the savageness and brutishness of this barbarous enemy, ay, even those that seem to profess more than others among them when the English have fallen into their hands.

Those seven that were killed at Lancaster the summer before upon a Sabbath day and the one that was afterward killed upon a week day were slain and mangled in a barbarous manner by one-eye John and Marlborough's praying Indians which Capt. Mosely brought to Boston, as the Indians told me.[7]

The Second Remove[8]

But now, the next morning, I must turn my back upon the town and travel with them into the vast and desolate wilderness, I knew not whither. It is not my tongue or pen can express the sorrows of my heart and bitterness of my spirit that I had at this departure, but God was with me in a wonderful manner, carrying me along and bearing up my spirit that it did not quite fail. One of the Indians carried my poor wounded babe upon a horse; it went moaning all along, "I shall die, I shall die." I went on foot after it with sorrow that cannot be expressed. At length I took it off the horse and carried it in my arms till my strength failed, and I fell down with it. Then they set me upon a horse with my wounded child in my lap. And there being no furniture[9] upon the horse['s] back, as we were going down a steep hill, we both fell over the horse's head, at which they like inhuman creatures laughed and rejoiced to see it, though I thought we should there have ended our days, as overcome with so many difficulties. But the Lord renewed my strength still and carried

---

[7]Although converted to Christianity, many of the "praying Indians," especially at Marlborough, joined with King Philip. Captain Samuel Moseley, known for his rough treatment of Indians, brought some whom he accused of an attack on Lancaster into Boston in August 1675.

[8]To Princeton, Massachusetts.

[9]Saddle.

me along that I might see more of His power; yea, so much that I could never have thought of had I not experienced it.

After this it quickly began to snow, and when night came on, they stopped. And now down I must sit in the snow by a little fire and a few boughs behind me, with my sick child in my lap and calling much for water, being now (through the wound) fallen into a violent fever. My own wound also [was] growing so stiff that I could scarce sit down or rise up; yet so it must be that I must sit all this cold winter night upon the cold, snowy ground with my sick child in my arms, looking that every hour would be the last of its life, and having no Christian friend near me either to comfort or help me. Oh, I may see the wonderful power of God that my spirit did not utterly sink under my affliction! Still the Lord upheld me with His gracious and merciful spirit, and we were both alive to see the light of the next morning.

The Third Remove[10]

The morning being come, they prepared to go on their way. One of the Indians got up upon a horse, and they set me up behind him with my poor sick babe in my lap. A very wearisome and tedious day I had of it, what with my own wound and my child's being so exceeding sick in a lamentable condition with her wound. It may be easily judged what a poor feeble condition we were in, there being not the least crumb of refreshing that came within either of our mouths from Wednesday night to Saturday night except only a little cold water. This day in the afternoon, about an hour by sun, we came to the place where they intended, viz. an Indian town called Wenimesset, nor[th]ward of Quabaug. When we were come, oh, the number of pagans (now merciless enemies) that there came about me that I may say as David, Psal. 27:13, "I had fainted, unless I had believed," etc. The next day was the Sabbath. I then remembered how careless I had been of God's holy time, how many Sabbaths I had lost and misspent and how evilly I had walked in God's sight, which lay so close unto my spirit that it was easy for me to see how righteous it was with God to cut the thread of my life and cast me out of His presence forever. Yet the Lord still showed mercy to me

[10]To an Indian village near New Braintree (February 12–27).

and upheld me, and as He wounded me with one hand, so He healed me with the other.

This day there came to me one Robert Pepper (a man belonging to Roxbury), who was taken in Captain Beers his fight[11] and had been now a considerable time with the Indians and up with them almost as far as Albany to see King Philip, as he told me, and was now very lately come into these parts. Hearing, I say, that I was in this Indian town, he obtained leave to come and see me. He told me he himself was wounded in the leg at Captain Beers his fight and was not able some time to go, but, as they carried him, and as he took oaken leaves and laid to his wound, and through the blessing of God, he was able to travel again. Then I took oaken leaves and laid to my side, and, with the blessing of God, it cured me also. Yet before the cure was wrought, I may say, as it is in Psal. 38:5, 6, "My wounds stink and are corrupt, I am troubled, I am bowed down greatly, I go mourning all the day long." I sat much alone with a poor wounded child in my lap, which moaned night and day, having nothing to revive the body or cheer the spirits of her, but instead of that sometimes one Indian would come and tell me one hour that, "Your master will knock your child in the head." And then a second, and then a third, "Your master will quickly knock your child in the head."

This was the comfort I had from them. "Miserable comforters are ye all," as he said.[12] Thus nine days I sat upon my knees with my babe in my lap till my flesh was raw again; my child being even ready to depart this sorrowful world, they bade me carry it out to another wigwam (I suppose because they would not be troubled with such spectacles), whither I went with a heavy heart, and down I sat with the picture of death in my lap. About two hours in the night my sweet babe like a lamb departed this life on Feb. 18, 1675,[13] it being about six years and five months old. It was nine days from the first wounding in this miserable condition without any refreshing of one nature or other except a little cold water. I cannot but take notice how at another time I could not bear to be in the room where any dead person was, but now the case is changed; I must and could

[11]A skirmish with Connecticut River Indians at Watertown, Massachusetts, in August 1675.
[12]Job, in Job 16:2.
[13]I.e., 1676.

lie down by my dead babe side by side all the night after. I have thought since of the wonderful goodness of God to me in preserving me in the use of my reason and senses in that distressed time, that I did not use wicked and violent means to end my own miserable life.

In the morning, when they understood that my child was dead, they sent for me home to my master's wigwam. (By my master in this writing must be understood Quanopin, who was a sagamore and married [to] King Philip's wife's sister,[14] not that he first took me, but I was sold to him by another Narragansett Indian, who took me when first I came out of the garrison.) I went to take up my dead child in my arms to carry it with me, but they bid me let it alone. There was no resisting, but go I must and leave it. When I had been at my master's wigwam, I took the first opportunity I could get to go look after my dead child. When I came, I asked them what they had done with it. Then they told me it was upon the hill. Then they went and showed me where it was, where I saw the ground was newly digged, and there they told me they had buried it. There I left that child in the wilderness and must commit it and myself also in this wilderness condition to Him who is above all.

God having taken away this dear child, I went to see my daughter Mary, who was at this same Indian town at a wigwam not very far off, though we had little liberty or opportunity to see one another. She was about ten years old and taken from the door at first by a praying Indian and afterward sold for a gun. When I came in sight, she would fall a-weeping, at which they were provoked and would not let me come near her, but bade me be gone, which was a heart-cutting word to me. I had one child dead, another in the wilderness I knew not where; the third they would not let me come near to. "Me," as he said, "have ye bereaved of my children, Joseph is not, and Simeon is not, and ye will take Benjamin also, all these things are against me."[15] I could not sit still in this condition, but kept walking from one place to another. And as I was going along, my heart was even overwhelmed with the thoughts of my condition and that I should have children and a nation which I knew not ruled over them. Whereupon I earnestly entreated the Lord that He would consider my low estate and show me a token for good, and if it were

[14]Quanopin was married to Weetamoo, who was King Philip's sister-in-law and a powerful chief in her own right; sagamore, a subordinate chief.
[15]Genesis 42:36.

His blessed will, some sign and hope of some relief.

And indeed quickly the Lord answered in some measure my poor prayers; for, as I was going up and down mourning and lamenting my condition, my son [Joseph] came to me and asked me how I did. I had not seen him before since the destruction of the town, and I knew not where he was till I was informed by himself that he was amongst a smaller parcel of Indians whose place was about six miles off. With tears in his eyes he asked me whether his sister Sarah was dead and told me he had seen his sister Mary and prayed me that I would not be troubled in reference to himself. The occasion of his coming to see me at this time was this: there was, as I said, about six miles from us a small plantation of Indians, where it seems he had been during his captivity, and at this time there were some forces of the Indians gathered out of our company and some also from them (among whom was my son's master) to go to assault and burn Medfield.[16] In this time of the absence of his master his dame brought him to see me. I took this to be some gracious answer to my earnest and unfeigned desire.

The next day, *viz.* to this, the Indians returned from Medfield (all the company, for those that belonged to the other small company came through the town that now we were at). But before they came to us, oh, the outrageous roaring and whooping that there was! They began their din about a mile before they came to us. By their noise and whooping they signified how many they had destroyed, which was at that time twenty-three. Those that were with us at home were gathered together as soon as they heard the whooping, and every time that the other went over their number, these at home gave [such] a shout that the very earth rung again. And thus they continued till those that had been upon the expedition were come up to the sagamore's wigwam. And then, oh, the hideous insulting and triumphing that there was over some Englishmen's scalps that they had taken (as their manner is) and brought with them!

I cannot but take notice of the wonderful mercy of God to me in those afflictions in sending me a Bible. One of the Indians that came from Medfield fight [who] had brought some plunder came to me and asked me if I would have a Bible; he had got one in his basket. I was glad of it and asked him whether he thought the Indians would let me read. He answered, "Yes." So I took the Bible, and in that

---

[16]Medfield, Massachusetts, was burned on February 21, 1676.

melancholy time it came into my mind to read first the 28 chapter of Deut., which I did, and when I had read it, my dark heart wrought on this manner, that there was no mercy for me, that the blessings were gone and the curses come in their room, and that I had lost my opportunity. But the Lord helped me still to go on reading till I came to chapter 30, the seven first verses, where I found there was mercy promised again if we would return to him by repentance, and, though we were scattered from one end of the earth to the other, yet the Lord would gather us together and turn all those curses upon our enemies.[17] I do not desire to live to forget this scripture and what comfort it was to me.

Now the Indians began to talk of removing from this place, some one way and some another. There were now besides myself nine English captives in this place, all of them children except one woman. I got an opportunity to go and take my leave of them, they being to go one way and I another; I asked them whether they were earnest with God for deliverance. They told me they did as they were able, and it was some comfort to me that the Lord stirred up children to look to Him. The woman, *viz.* Goodwife[18] Joslin, told me she should never see me again and that she could find in her heart to run away; I wished her not to run away by any means, for we were near thirty miles from any English town and she very big with child and had but one week to reckon and another child in her arms, two years old, and bad rivers there were to go over, and we were feeble with our poor and coarse entertainment. I had my Bible with me; I pulled it out and asked her whether she would read. We opened the Bible and lighted on Psalm 27, in which psalm we especially took notice of that *ver. ult.,* "Wait on the Lord, be of good courage, and He shall strengthen thine heart, wait I say on the Lord."

[17]Chapter 28 of Deuteronomy promises rewards for obeying God, but pronounces dire curses upon the chosen people if they are disobedient. The first seven verses of Chapter 30 promise that the people will return to God and be restored to their country.
[18]Equivalent to modern *Mrs.*

The Fourth Remove[19]

And now I must part with that little company I had. Here I parted from my daughter Mary (whom I never saw again till I saw her in Dorchester, returned from captivity) and from four little cousins and neighbors, some of which I never saw afterward. The Lord only knows the end of them. Amongst them also was that poor woman before mentioned, who came to a sad end, as some of the company told me in my travel. She, having much grief upon her spirit about her miserable condition, being so near her time, she would be often asking the Indians to let her go home; they, not being willing to that and yet vexed with her importunity, gathered a great company together about her and stripped her naked and set her in the midst of them. And when they had sung and danced about her (in their hellish manner) as long as they pleased, they knocked her on [the] head and the child in her arms with her. When they had done that, they made a fire and put them both into it and told the other children that were with them that if they attempted to go home they would serve them in like manner. The children said she did not shed one tear, but prayed all the while. But to return to my own journey, we traveled about half a day or [a] little more and came to a desolate place in the wilderness where there were no wigwams or inhabitants before; we came about the middle of the afternoon to this place, cold and wet, and snowy, and hungry, and weary, and no refreshing for man but the cold ground to sit on and our poor Indian cheer.

Heartaching thoughts here I had about my poor children, who were scattered up and down among the wild beasts of the forest. My head was light and dizzy (either through hunger or hard lodging or trouble or all together), my knees feeble, my body raw by sitting double night and day, that I cannot express to man the affliction that lay upon my spirit, but the Lord helped me at that time to express it to Himself. I opened my Bible to read, and the Lord brought that precious scripture to me, Jer. 31:16, "Thus saith the Lord, 'Refrain thy voice from weeping and thine eyes from tears, for thy work shall be rewarded, and they shall come again from the land of the enemy.'" This was a sweet cordial to me when I was ready to faint; many and many a time have I sat down and wept sweetly over this scripture. At this place we continued about four days.

[19]To what is now Petersham, Massachusetts (February 28–March 3).

The Fifth Remove[20]

The occasion (as I thought) of their moving at this time was the English army, it being near and following them. For they went as if they had gone for their lives for some considerable way, and then they made a stop and chose some of their stoutest men and sent them back to hold the English army in play whilst the rest escaped. And then, like Jehu,[21] they marched on furiously with their old and with their young; some carried their old decrepit mothers; some carried one and some another. Four of them carried a great Indian upon a bier, but, going through a thick wood with him, they were hindered and could make no haste; whereupon they took him upon their backs and carried him, one at a time, till they came to Bacquaug River. Upon a Friday a little after noon we came to this river. When all the company was come up and were gathered together, I thought to count the number of them, but they were so many and, being somewhat in motion, it was beyond my skill. In this travel, because of my wound, I was somewhat favored in my load; I carried only my knitting work and two quarts of parched meal. Being very faint, I asked my mistress to give me one spoonful of the meal, but she would not give me a taste. They quickly fell to cutting dry trees to make rafts to carry them over the river, and soon my turn came to go over. By the advantage of some brush which they had laid upon the raft to sit upon, I did not wet my foot (when many of themselves at the other end were mid-leg deep) which cannot be but acknowledged as a favor of God to my weakened body, it being a very cold time. I was not before acquainted with such kind of doings or dangers. "When thou passeth through the waters, I will be with thee, and through the rivers they shall not overflow thee," Isai. 43:2. A certain number of us got over the river that night, but it was the night after the Sabbath before all the company was got over. On the Saturday they boiled an old horse's leg which they had got, and so we drank of the broth as soon as they thought it was ready, and when it was almost all gone, they filled it up again.

The first week of my being among them I hardly ate anything; the second week, I found my stomach grow very faint for want of some-

---

[20]To what is now Orange, Massachusetts (March 3–5). The English army was a contingent of Massachusetts and Connecticut troops under Captain Thomas Savage.
[21]King Jehu was known for driving "furiously" (II Kings 9:20).

thing; and yet it was very hard to get down their filthy trash. But the third week, though I could think how formerly my stomach would turn against this or that and I could starve and die before I could eat such things, yet they were sweet and savory to my taste. I was at this time knitting a pair of white cotton stockings for my mistress and had not yet wrought upon a Sabbath day. When the Sabbath came, they bade me go to work; I told them it was the Sabbath day and desired them to let me rest and told them I would do as much more tomorrow, to which they answered me they would break my face. And here I cannot but take notice of the strange providence of God in preserving the heathen. They were many hundreds, old and young, some sick and some lame, many had papooses at their backs. The greatest number at this time with us were squaws, and they traveled with all they had, bag and baggage, and yet they got over this river aforesaid. And on Monday they set their wigwams on fire, and away they went. On that very day came the English army after them to this river and saw the smoke of their wigwams, and yet this river put a stop to them. God did not give them courage or activity to go over after us; we were not ready for so great a mercy as victory and deliverance. If we had been, God would have found out a way for the English to have passed this river, as well as for the Indians with their squaws and children and all their luggage. "Oh that my people had hearkened to me, and Israel had walked in my ways, I should soon have subdued their enemies and turned my hand against their adversaries," Psal. 81:13, 14.

The Sixth Remove[22]

On Monday (as I said) they set their wigwams on fire and went away. It was a cold morning, and before us there was a great brook with ice on it; some waded through it up to the knees and higher, but others went till they came to a beaver dam, and I amongst them, where through the good providence of God I did not wet my foot. I went along that day mourning and lamenting, leaving farther my own country and traveling into the vast and howling wilderness, and I understood something of Lot's wife's temptation when she looked

[22]Near Northfield, Massachusetts.

back.[23] We came that day to a great swamp by the side of which we took up our lodging that night. When I came to the brow of the hill that looked toward the swamp, I thought we had been come to a great Indian town (though there were none but our own company). The Indians were as thick as the trees: it seemed as if there had been a thousand hatchets going at once. If one looked before one, there was nothing but Indians, and behind one nothing but Indians, and so on either hand, I myself in the midst, and no Christian soul near me, and yet how hath the Lord preserved me in safety. Oh, the experience that I have had of the goodness of God to me and mine!

The Seventh Remove[24]

After a restless and hungry night there, we had a wearisome time of it the next day. The swamp by which we lay was, as it were, a deep dungeon and an exceeding high and steep hill before it. Before I got to the top of the hill, I thought my heart and legs and all would have broken and failed me . . . What through faintness and soreness of body, it was a grievous day of travel to me. As we went along, I saw a place where English cattle had been. That was comfort to me, such as it was. Quickly after that we came to an English path, which so took with me that I thought I could have freely laid down and died. That day, a little after noon, we came to Squakeag, where the Indians quickly spread themselves over the deserted English fields, gleaning what they could find; some picked up ears of wheat that were crickled[25] down; some found ears of Indian corn; some found groundnuts, and others sheaves of wheat that were frozen together in the shock, and went to threshing of them out. Myself got two ears of Indian corn, and whilst I did but turn my back, one of them was stolen from me, which much troubled me. There came an Indian to them at that time with a basket of horse liver. I asked him to give me a piece. "What," says he, "can you eat horse liver?" I told him I would try if he would give a piece, which he did, and I laid it on the coals to roast, but before it was half ready they got half of it away

---

[23]Lot's wife looked back to her home in the wicked city of Sodom and was turned into a pillar of salt (Genesis 19:26).
[24]To another place near Northfield.
[25]Broken.

from me, so that I was fain to take the rest and eat it as it was with the blood about my mouth, and yet a savory bit it was to me: "For to the hungry soul every bitter thing is sweet."[26] A solemn sight methought it was to see fields of wheat and Indian corn forsaken and spoiled and the remainders of them to be food for our merciless enemies. That night we had a mess of wheat for our supper.

The Eighth Remove[27]

On the morrow morning we must go over the river, i.e. Connecticut, to meet with King Philip. Two canoesful they had carried over; the next turn I myself was to go, but as my foot was upon the canoe to step in, there was a sudden outcry among them, and I must step back. And instead of going over the river, I must go four or five miles up the river farther northward. Some of the Indians ran one way and some another. The cause of this rout was, as I thought, their espying some English scouts who were thereabout. In this travel up the river about noon the company made a stop and sat down, some to eat and others to rest them. As I sat amongst them musing of things past, my son, Joseph, unexpectedly came to me. We asked of each other's welfare, bemoaning our doleful condition and the change that had come upon us. We had husband and father, and children, and sisters, and friends, and relations, and house, and home, and many comforts of this life, but now we may say as Job, "Naked came I out of my mother's womb, and naked shall I return. The Lord gave, and the Lord hath taken away, blessed be the name of the Lord."[28] I asked him whether he would read; he told me he earnestly desired it. I gave him my Bible, and he lighted upon that comfortable scripture, Psal. 118:17, 18, "I shall not die but live and declare the works of the Lord: the Lord hath chastened me sore, yet he hath not given me over to death." "Look here, Mother," says he, "did you read this?" And here I may take occasion to mention one principal ground of my setting forth these lines: even as the psalmist says, to declare the works of the Lord and His wonderful power in

[26]Proverbs 27:7.
[27]To South Vernon, Vermont. Philip was returning from an unsuccessful attempt to get support from the Mohawks in northern New York.
[28]Job 1:21.

carrying us along, preserving us in the wilderness while under the enemy's hand and returning of us in safety again, and His goodness in bringing to my hand so many comfortable and suitable scriptures in my distress.

But to return, we traveled on till night, and in the morning we must go over the river to Philip's crew. When I was in the canoe, I could not but be amazed at the numerous crew of pagans that were on the bank on the other side. When I came ashore, they gathered all about me, I sitting alone in the midst. I observed they asked one another questions and laughed and rejoiced over their gains and victories. Then my heart began to fail and I fell a-weeping, which was the first time to my remembrance that I wept before them. Although I had met with so much affliction and my heart was many times ready to break, yet could I not shed one tear in their sight, but rather had been all this while in a maze and like one astonished. But now I may say as Psal. 137:1, "By the rivers of Babylon there we sat down; yea, we wept when we remembered Zion." There one of them asked me why I wept; I could hardly tell what to say, yet I answered they would kill me. "No," said he, "none will hurt you." Then came one of them and gave me two spoonfuls of meal to comfort me, and another gave me half a pint of peas, which was more worth than many bushels at another time. Then I went to see King Philip. He bade me come in and sit down and asked me whether I would smoke it (a usual compliment nowadays among saints and sinners), but this no way suited me. For though I had formerly used tobacco, yet I had left it ever since I was first taken. It seems to be a bait the devil lays to make men lose their precious time. I remember with shame how formerly when I had taken two or three pipes I was presently ready for another, such a bewitching thing it is. But I thank God He has now given me power over it; surely there are many who may be better employed than to lie sucking a stinking tobacco pipe.

Now the Indians gather their forces to go against Northampton. Overnight one went about yelling and hooting to give notice of the design, whereupon they fell to boiling of groundnuts and parching of corn (as many as had it) for their provision, and in the morning away they went. During my abode in this place Philip spoke to me to make a shirt for his boy, which I did, for which he gave me a shilling. I offered the money to my master, but he bade me keep it, and with it I bought a piece of horseflesh. Afterwards he asked me to make a cap for his boy, for which he invited me to dinner. I went, and he gave me a pancake about as big as two fingers; it was made of parched wheat, beaten and fried in bear's grease, but I thought I never tasted pleasanter meat in my life. There was a squaw who spoke to me to make a shirt for her *sannup*[29] for which she gave me a piece of bear. Another asked me to knit a pair of stockings, for which she gave me a quart of peas. I boiled my peas and bear together and invited my master and mistress to dinner, but the proud gossip,[30] because I served them both in one dish, would eat nothing except one bit that he gave her upon the point of his knife.

Hearing that my son was come to this place, I went to see him and found him lying flat upon the ground. I asked him how he could sleep so. He answered me that he was not asleep but at prayer and lay so that they might not observe what he was doing. I pray God he may remember these things now he is returned in safety. At this place (the sun now getting higher), what with the beams and heat of the sun and the smoke of the wigwams, I thought I should have been blind. I could scarce discern one wigwam from another. There was here one Mary Thurston of Medfield, who, seeing how it was with me, lent a hat to wear; but as soon as I was gone, the squaw who owned that Mary Thurston came running after me and got it away again. Here was the squaw that gave me one spoonful of meal. I put it in my pocket to keep it safe, yet notwithstanding, somebody stole it, but put five Indian corns in the room of it,[31] which corns were the greatest provision I had in my travel for one day.

The Indians, returning from Northampton, brought with them some horses, and sheep, and other things which they had taken. I desired them that they would carry me to Albany upon one of those horses and sell me for powder, for so they had sometimes discoursed. I was utterly hopeless of getting home on foot the way that I came. I could hardly bear to think of the many weary steps I had taken to come to this place.

[29]Husband.
[30]Companion; i.e., wife.
[31]Five kernels of corn in place of it.

The Ninth Remove[32]

But instead of going either to Albany or homeward, we must go five miles up the river and then go over it. Here we abode awhile. Here lived a sorry Indian who spoke to me to make him a shirt. When I had done it, he would pay me nothing. But he living by the riverside where I often went to fetch water, I would often be putting of him in mind and calling for my pay; at last he told me, if I would make another shirt for a papoose not yet born, he would give me a knife, which he did when I had done it. I carried the knife in, and my master asked me to give it him, and I was not a little glad that I had anything that they would accept of and be pleased with. When we were at this place, my master's maid came home; she had been gone three weeks into the Narragansett country to fetch corn where they had stored up some in the ground. She brought home about a peck and [a] half of corn. This was about the time that their great captain, Naananto, was killed in the Narragansett country. My son being now about a mile from me, I asked liberty to go and see him; they bade me go, and away I went. But quickly [I] lost myself, traveling over hills and through swamps, and could not find the way to him. And I cannot but admire at the wonderful power and goodness of God to me in that though I was gone from home and met with all sorts of Indians, and those I had no knowledge of, and there being no Christian soul near me, yet not one of them offered the least imaginable miscarriage to me.

I turned homeward again and met with my master; he showed me the way to my son. When I came to him, I found him not well, and withall he had a boil on his side which much troubled him. We bemoaned one another awhile, as the Lord helped us, and then I returned again. When I was returned, I found myself as unsatisfied as I was before. I went up and down mourning and lamenting, and my spirit was ready to sink with the thoughts of my poor children. My son was ill, and I could not but think of his mournful looks, and no Christian friend was near him to do any office of love for him either for soul or body. And my poor girl, I know not where she was nor whether she was sick or well, or alive or dead. I repaired under these thoughts to my Bible (my great comfort in that time) and that scripture came to my hand, "Cast thy burden upon the

---

[32]To the Ashuelot valley in New Hampshire, near present-day Keene.

Lord, and He shall sustain thee," Psal. 55:22.

But I was fain to go and look after something to satisfy my hunger, and going among the wigwams, I went into one and there found a squaw who showed herself very kind to me and gave me a piece of bear. I put it into my pocket and came home, but could not find an opportunity to broil it for fear they would get it from me, and there it lay all that day and night in my stinking pocket. In the morning I went to the same squaw, who had a kettle of groundnuts boiling; I asked her to let me boil my piece of bear in her kettle, which she did and gave me some groundnuts to eat with it, and I cannot but think how pleasant it was to me. I have sometime seen bear baked very handsomely among the English, and some like it, but the thoughts that it was bear made me tremble, but now that was savory to me that one would think was enough to turn the stomach of a brute creature.

One bitter cold day I could find no room to sit down before the fire. I went out and could not tell what to do, but I went into another wigwam where they were also sitting around the fire, but the squaw laid a skin for me, bid me sit down, gave me some groundnuts, bade me come again, and told me they would buy me if they were able, and yet these were strangers to me that I never saw before.

The Tenth Remove

That day a small part of the company removed about three-quarters of a mile, intending further the next day. When they came to the place where they intended to lodge and had pitched their wigwams, being hungry, I went again back to the place we were before at to get something to eat, being encouraged by the squaw's kindness who bade me come again when I was there. There came an Indian to look after me, who, when he had found me, kicked me all along. I went home and found venison roasting that night, but they would not give me one bit of it. Sometimes I met with favor and sometimes with nothing but frowns.

The Eleventh Remove[33]

The next day in the morning they took their travel, intending a day's journey up the river. I took my load at my back, and quickly we came to wade over the river and passed over tiresome and wearisome hills. One hill was so steep that I was fain to creep up upon my knees and to hold by the twigs and bushes to keep myself from falling backward. My head also was so light that I usually reeled as I went, but I hope all these wearisome steps that I have taken are but a forewarning of me to the heavenly rest. "I know, O Lord, that Thy judgments are right, and that Thou in faithfulness hast afflicted me," Psal. 119:71 [actually 75].

The Twelfth Remove

It was upon a Sabbath-day morning that they prepared for their travel. This morning I asked my master whether he would sell me to my husband; he answered me *nux*,[34] which did much rejoice my spirit. My mistress, before we went, was gone to the burial of a papoose, and, returning, she found me sitting and reading in my Bible. She snatched it hastily out of my hand and threw it out of doors; I ran out and catched it up and put it into my pocket and never let her see it afterward. Then they packed up their things to be gone and gave me my load. I complained it was too heavy, whereupon she gave me a slap in the face and bade me go. I lifted up my heart to God, hoping the redemption was not far off, and the rather because their insolency grew worse and worse.

But the thoughts of my going homeward (for so we bent our course) much cheered my spirit and made my burden seem light and almost nothing at all. But (to my amazement and great perplexity) the scale was soon turned, for when we had gone a little way, on a sudden my mistress gives out. She would go no further but turn back again and said I must go back again with her. And she called her *sannup* and would have had him gone back also, but he would not, but said he would go on and come to us again in three days. My spirit was upon this, I confess, very impatient and almost outra-

---

[33]Near Chesterfield, New Hampshire.
[34]Yes.

geous. I thought I could as well have died as went back; I cannot declare the trouble that I was in about it, but yet back again I must go. As soon as I had an opportunity, I took my Bible to read, and that quieting scripture came to my hand, Psal. 46:10, "Be still and know that I am God," which stilled my spirit for the present. But a sore time of trial, I concluded, I had to go through, my master being gone, who seemed to me the best friend that I had of an Indian both in cold and hunger, and quickly so it proved. Down I sat with my heart as full as it could hold, and yet so hungry that I could not sit neither. But, going out to see what I could find and walking among the trees, I found six acorns and two chestnuts, which were some refreshment to me. Towards night I gathered me some sticks for my own comfort that I might not lie a-cold, but when we came to lie down they bade me go out and lie somewhere else, for they had company (they said) come in more than their own. I told them I could not tell where to go; they bade me go look. I told them if I went to another wigwam they would be angry and send me home again. Then one of the company drew his sword and told me he would run me through if I did not go presently. Then was I fain to stoop to this rude fellow and to go out in the night, I knew not whither. Mine eyes have seen that fellow afterwards, walking up and down Boston under the appearance of a friend-Indian, and several others of the like cut.

I went to one wigwam, and they told me they had no room. Then I went to another, and they said the same; at last an old Indian bade me come to him, and his squaw gave me some groundnuts; she gave me also something to lay under my head, and a good fire we had. And through the good providence of God I had a comfortable lodging that night. In the morning another Indian bade me come at night, and he would give me six groundnuts, which I did. We were at this place and time about two miles from Connecticut River. We went in the morning to gather groundnuts, to the river, and went back again that night. I went with a good load at my back (for they, when they went though but a little way, would carry all their trumpery with them); I told them the skin was off my back, but I had no other comforting answer from them than this, that it would be no matter if my head were off too.

The Thirteenth Remove[35]

Instead of going toward the Bay, which was that I desired, I must go with them five or six miles down the river into a mighty thicket of brush, where we abode almost a fortnight. Here one asked me to make a shirt for her papoose, for which she gave me a mess of broth which was thickened with meal made of the bark of a tree, and to make it the better she had put into it about a handful of peas and a few roasted groundnuts. I had not seen my son a pretty while, and here was an Indian of whom I made inquiry after him and asked him when he saw him. He answered me that such a time his master roasted him and that himself did eat a piece of him as big as his two fingers and that he was very good meat. But the Lord upheld my spirit under this discouragement, and I considered their horrible addictedness to lying and that there is not one of them that makes the least conscience of speaking of truth. In this place on a cold night as I lay by the fire, I removed a stick that kept the heat from me; a squaw moved it down again, at which I looked up, and she threw a handful of ashes in mine eyes. I thought I should have been quite blinded and have never seen more, but lying down, the water run out of my eyes and carried the dirt with it, that by the morning I recovered my sight again. Yet upon this and the like occasions I hope it is not too much to say with Job, "Have pity upon me, have pity upon me, oh, ye my friends, for the hand of the Lord has touched me."[36]

And here I cannot but remember how many times sitting in their wigwams and musing on things past I should suddenly leap up and run out as if I had been at home, forgetting where I was and what my condition was. But when I was without and saw nothing but wilderness and woods and a company of barbarous heathens, my mind quickly returned to me, which made me think of that spoken concerning Samson, who said, "I will go out and shake myself as at other times, but he wist not that the Lord was departed from him."[37]

About this time I began to think that all my hopes of restoration would come to nothing. I thought of the English army and hoped for their coming and being taken by them, but that failed. I hoped

[35]To Hinsdale, New Hampshire.
[36]Job 19:21.
[37]Judges 16:20.

to be carried to Albany as the Indians had discoursed before, but that failed also. I thought of being sold to my husband, as my master spake, but instead of that my master himself was gone and I left behind, so that my spirit was now quite ready to sink. I asked them to let me go out and pick up some sticks, that I might get alone and pour out my heart unto the Lord. Then also I took my Bible to read, but I found no comfort here neither, which many times I was wont to find. So easy a thing it is with God to dry up the streams of scripture-comfort from us. Yet I can say that in all my sorrows and afflictions God did not leave me to have my impatience work towards Himself, as if His ways were unrighteous. But I knew that He laid upon me less than I deserved. Afterward, before this doleful time ended with me, I was turning the leaves of my Bible and the Lord brought to me some scriptures, which did a little revive me, as that Isai. 55:8, " 'For my thoughts are not your thoughts, neither are your ways my ways,' saith the Lord." And also that Psal. 37:5, "Commit thy way unto the Lord, trust also in Him, and He shall bring it to pass."

About this time they came yelping from Hadley, where they had killed three Englishmen and brought one captive with them, *viz.* Thomas Read. They all gathered about the poor man, asking him many questions. I desired also to go and see him, and when I came he was crying bitterly, supposing they would quickly kill him. Whereupon I asked one of them whether they intended to kill him; he answered me they would not. He being a little cheered with that, I asked him about the welfare of my husband; he told me he saw him such a time in the Bay, and he was well but very melancholy. By which I certainly understood (though I suspected it before) that whatsoever the Indians told me respecting him was vanity and lies. Some of them told me he was dead, and they had killed him. Some said he was married again, and that the governor wished him to marry and told him he should have his choice, and that all persuaded [him] I was dead. So like were these barbarous creatures to him who was a liar from the beginning.[38]

As I was sitting once in the wigwam here, Philip's maid came in with the child in her arms and asked me to give her a piece of my apron to make a flap for it. I told her I would not. Then my mistress bade me give it, but still I said no. The maid told me if I would not

[38]Satan.

give her a piece she would tear a piece off it. I told her I would tear her coat then; with that my mistress rises up and takes up a stick big enough to have killed me and struck me with it, but I stepped out, and she struck the stick into the mat of the wigwam. But while she was pulling of it out, I ran to the maid and gave her all my apron, and so that storm went over.

Hearing that my son was come to this place, I went to see him and told him his father was well but very melancholy. He told me he was as much grieved for his father as for himself; I wondered at his speech, for I thought I had enough upon my spirit in reference to myself to make me mindless of my husband and everyone else, they being safe among their friends. He told me also that a while before his master, together with other Indians, were going to the French for powder, but by the way the Mohawks met with them and killed four of their company, which made the rest turn back again, for which I desire that myself and he may bless the Lord. For it might have been worse with him had he been sold to the French than it proved to be in remaining with the Indians.

I went to see an English youth in this place, one John Gilbert of Springfield. I found him lying without doors upon the ground; I asked him how he did. He told me he was very sick of a flux with eating so much blood. They had turned him out of the wigwam and with him an Indian papoose almost dead (whose parents had been killed) in a bitter cold day without fire or clothes. The young man himself had nothing on but his shirt and waistcoat. This sight was enough to melt a heart of flint. There they lay quivering in the cold, the youth [curled] round like a dog, the papoose stretched out with his eyes, nose, and mouth full of dirt and yet alive and groaning. I advised John to go and get to some fire; he told me he could not stand, but I persuaded him still, lest he should lie there and die. And with much ado I got him to a fire and went myself home. As soon as I was got home, his master's daughter came after me to know what I had done with the Englishman; I told her I had got him to a fire in such a place. Now had I need to pray Paul's prayer, 2 Thess. 3:2, "That we may be delivered from unreasonable and wicked men." For her satisfaction I went along with her and brought her to him, but before I got home again, it was noised about that I was running away and getting the English youth along with me, that as soon as I came in they began to rant and domineer, asking me where I had been, and what I had been doing, and saying they would knock him on the head. I told them I had been seeing the English youth and that I would not run away. They told me I lied, and taking up a hatchet, they came to me and said they would knock me down if I stirred out again and so confined me to the wigwam. Now may I say with David, 2 Sam. 24:14, "I am in a great strait." If I keep in, I must die with hunger, and if I go out, I must be knocked in [the] head. This distressed condition held that day and half the next. And then the Lord remembered me, whose mercies are great.

Then came an Indian to me with a pair of stockings that were too big for him, and he would have me ravel them out and knit them fit for him. I showed myself willing and bid him ask my mistress if I might go along with him a little way; she said yes, I might, but I was not a little refreshed with that news that I had my liberty again. Then I went along with him, and he gave me some roasted groundnuts, which did again revive my feeble stomach.

Being got out of her sight, I had time and liberty again to look into my Bible, which was my guide by day and my pillow by night. Now that comfortable scripture presented itself to me, Isa. 54:7, "For a small moment have I forsaken thee, but with great mercies I will gather thee." Thus the Lord carried me along from one time to another and made good to me this precious promise and many others. Then my son came to see me, and I asked his master to let him stay awhile with me that I might comb his head and look over him, for he was almost overcome with lice. He told me when I had done that he was very hungry, but I had nothing to relieve him, but bid him go into the wigwams as he went along and see if he could get anything among them, which he did. And it seems [he] tarried a little too long, for his master was angry with him and beat him, and then sold him. Then he came running to tell me he had a new master, and that he had given him some groundnuts already. Then I went along with him to his new master, who told me he loved him and he should not want. So his master carried him away, and I never saw him afterward till I saw him at Pascataqua in Portsmouth.

That night they bade me go out of the wigwam again. My mistress's papoose was sick, and it died that night, and there was one benefit in it—that there was more room. I went to a wigwam, and they bade me come in and gave me a skin to lie upon and a mess of venison and groundnuts, which was a choice dish among them. On the morrow they buried the papoose, and afterward, both morning and evening, there came a company to mourn and howl with her, though I confess I could not much condole with them. Many sorrowful days I had in this place, often getting alone "like a crane, or a swallow, so did I chatter; I did mourn as a dove, mine eyes fail with looking upward. Oh, Lord, I am oppressed; undertake for me," Isai. 38:14. I could tell the Lord as Hezekiah, ver. 3, "Remember now, O Lord, I beseech Thee, how I have walked before Thee in truth."[39]

Now had I time to examine all my ways. My conscience did not accuse me of unrighteousness toward one or other, yet I saw how in my walk with God I had been a careless creature. As David said, "Against Thee, Thee only, have I sinned," and I might say with the poor publican, "God be merciful unto me a sinner."[40] On the Sabbath days I could look upon the sun and think how people were going to the house of God to have their souls refreshed and then home and their bodies also, but I was destitute of both and might say as the poor prodigal, "He would fain have filled his belly with the husks that the swine did eat, and no man gave unto him," Luke 15:16. For I must say with him, "Father I have sinned against heaven and in thy sight," ver. 21. I remembered how on the night before and after the Sabbath, when my family was about me and relations and neighbors with us, we could pray and sing, and then refresh our bodies with the good creatures of God, and then have a comfortable bed to lie down on. But instead of all this I had only a little swill for the body and then like a swine must lie down on the ground. I cannot express to man the sorrow that lay upon my spirit; the Lord knows it. Yet that comfortable scripture would often come to my mind, "For a small moment have I forsaken thee, but with great mercies will I gather thee."[41]

The Fourteenth Remove[42]

Now must we pack up and be gone from this thicket, bending our course toward the Bay towns, I having nothing to eat by the way this day but a few crumbs of cake that an Indian gave my girl the

[39]Isaiah 38:3.
[40]Psalm 51:4; Luke 18:13.
[41]Isaiah 54:7.
[42]The fourteenth to nineteenth Removes (April 20–28) retrace the path taken earlier. The Bay towns are the towns near Boston.

same day we were taken. She gave it me, and I put it in my pocket; there it lay till it was so moldy (for want of good baking) that one could not tell what it was made of; it fell all to crumbs and grew so dry and hard that it was like little flints, and this refreshed me many times when I was ready to faint. It was in my thoughts when I put it into my mouth that if ever I returned I would tell the world what a blessing the Lord gave to such mean food. As we went along, they killed a deer with a young one in her; they gave me a piece of the fawn, and it was so young and tender that one might eat the bones as well as the flesh, and yet I thought it very good. When night came on, we sat down. It rained, but they quickly got up a bark wigwam, where I lay dry that night. I looked out in the morning, and many of them had laid in the rain all night, [which] I saw by their reeking.[43] Thus the Lord dealt mercifully with me many times, and I fared better than many of them. In the morning they took the blood of the deer and put it into the paunch and so boiled it; I could eat nothing of that, though they ate it sweetly. And yet they were so nice[44] in other things that when I had fetched water and had put the dish I dipped the water with into the kettle of water which I brought, they would say they would knock me down, for they said it was a sluttish trick.

The Fifteenth Remove

We went on our travel. I having got one handful of groundnuts for my support that day, they gave me my load, and I went on cheerfully (with the thoughts of going homeward), having my burden more on my back than my spirit. We came to Baquaug River again that day, near which we abode a few days. Sometimes one of them would give me a pipe, another a little tobacco, another a little salt, which I would change for a little victuals. I cannot but think what a wolfish appetite persons have in a starving condition, for many times when they gave me that which was hot, I was so greedy that I should burn my mouth that it would trouble me hours after, and yet I should quickly do the same again. And after I was thoroughly hungry, I was never again satisfied. For though sometimes it fell out that I got

[43]Giving off steam.
[44]Fastidious.

enough and did eat till I could eat no more, yet I was as unsatisfied as I was when I began. And now could I see that scripture verified (there being many scriptures which we do not take notice of or understand till we are afflicted), Mic. 6:14, "Thou shalt eat and not be satisfied." Now might I see more than ever before the miseries that sin hath brought upon us. Many times I should be ready to run out against the heathen, but the scripture would quiet me again, Amos 3:6, "Shall there be evil in the city, and the Lord hath not done it?" The Lord help me to make a right improvement of His word and that I might learn that great lesson, Mic. 6:8, 9, "He hath showed thee (Oh Man) what is good, and what doth the Lord require of thee, but to do justly and love mercy and walk humbly with thy God? Hear ye the rod and who hath appointed it."

The Sixteenth Remove

We began this remove with wading over Baquag River; the water was up to the knees and the stream very swift and so cold that I thought it would have cut me in sunder. I was so weak and feeble that I reeled as I went along and thought there I must end my days at last after my bearing and getting through so many difficulties. The Indians stood laughing to see me staggering along, but in my distress the Lord gave me experience of the truth and goodness of that promise, Isai. 43:2, "When thou passest through the waters, I will be with thee, and through the rivers, they shall not overflow thee." Then I sat down to put on my stockings and shoes with the tears running down mine eyes and many sorrowful thoughts in my heart, but I got up to go along with them. Quickly there came up to us an Indian who informed them that I must go to Wachuset to my master, for there was a letter come from the council to the sagamores about redeeming the captives and that there would be another in fourteen days and that I must be there ready. My heart was so heavy before that I could scarce speak or go in the path and yet now so light that I could run. My strength seemed to come again and recruit my feeble knees and aching heart, yet it pleased them to go but one mile that night, and there we stayed two days. In that time came a company of Indians to us, near thirty, all on horseback. My heart skipped within me, thinking they had been Englishmen at the first sight of them, for they were dressed in English apparel, with hats, white neckcloths, and sashes about their waists, and ribbons upon their shoulders, but when they came near there was a vast difference between the lovely faces of Christians and the foul looks of those heathens which much dampened my spirit again.

The Seventeenth Remove

A comfortable remove it was to me because of my hopes. They gave me a pack, and along we went cheerfully, but quickly my will proved more than my strength. Having little or no refreshing, my strength failed me, and my spirits were almost quite gone. Now may I say with David, Psal. 119:22, 23, 24, "I am poor and needy, and my heart is wounded within me. I am gone like the shadow when it declineth: I am tossed up and down like the locust; my knees are weak through fasting, and my flesh faileth of fatness."

At night we came to an Indian town, and the Indians sat down by a wigwam discoursing, but I was almost spent and could scarce speak. I laid down my load and went into the wigwam, and there sat an Indian boiling of horses' feet (they being wont to eat the flesh first, and when the feet were old and dried and they had nothing else, they would cut off the feet and use them). I asked him to give me a little of his broth or water they were boiling in; he took a dish and gave me one spoonful of samp and bid me take as much of the broth as I would. Then I put some of the hot water to the samp and drank it up and my spirit came again. He gave me also a piece of the rough or ridding[45] of the small guts, and I broiled it on the coals; and now may I say with Jonathan, "See, I pray you, how mine eyes have been enlightened because I tasted a little of this honey," I Sam. 14:29. Now is my spirit revived again; though means be never so inconsiderable, yet if the Lord bestow His blessing upon them, they shall refresh both soul and body.

[45]Refuse.

The Eighteenth Remove

We took up our packs and along we went, but a wearisome day I had of it. As we went along I saw an Englishman stripped naked and lying dead upon the ground, but knew not who it was. Then we came to another Indian town where we stayed all night. In this town there were four English children, captives, and one of them my own sister's. I went to see how she did, and she was well, considering her captive condition. I would have tarried that night with her, but they that owned her would not suffer it. Then I went into another wigwam, where they were boiling corn and beans, which was a lovely sight to see, but I could not get a taste thereof. Then I went to another wigwam, where there were two of the English children. The squaw was boiling horses' feet; then she cut me off a little piece and gave one of the English children a piece also. Being very hungry, I had quickly eat up mine, but the child could not bite it, it was so tough and sinewy, but lay sucking, gnawing, chewing, and slabbering of it in the mouth and hand. Then I took it of the child and ate it myself, and savory it was to my taste. Then I may say [as] Job, chap. 6:7, "The things that my soul refused to touch are as my sorrowful meat." Thus the Lord made that pleasant and refreshing which another time would have been an abomination. Then I went home to my mistress' wigwam, and they told me I disgraced my master with begging, and if I did so anymore they would knock me in [the] head. I told them they had as good knock me in [the] head as starve me to death.

The Nineteenth Remove

They said when we went out that we must travel to Wachuset this day. But a bitter weary day I had of it, traveling now three days together without resting any day between. At last, after many weary steps, I saw Wachuset Hills, but many miles off. Then we came to a great swamp, through which we traveled up to the knees in mud and water, which was heavy going to one tired before. Being almost spent, I thought I should have sunk down at last and never got out, but I may say, as in Psal. 94:18, "When my foot slipped, Thy mercy, O Lord, held me up." Going along, having indeed my life but little spirit, Philip, who was in the company, came up and took me by the hand and said, "Two weeks more and you shall be mistress again." I asked him if he spake true. He answered, "Yes, and quickly you shall come to your master again, who has been gone from us three weeks." After many weary steps we came to Wachuset, where he was, and glad I was to see him. He asked me when I washed me. I told him not this month. Then he fetched me some water himself and bid me wash and gave me the glass to see how I looked and bid his squaw give me something to eat. So she gave me a mess of beans and meat and a little groundnut cake. I was wonderfully revived with this favor showed me, Psal. 106:46, "He made them also to be pitied of all those that carried them captives."

My master had three squaws, living sometimes with one and sometimes with another one. This old squaw at whose wigwam I was, my master had been [with] those three weeks. Another was Weetamoo, with whom I had lived and served all this while. A severe and proud dame she was, bestowing every day in dressing herself neat as much time as any of the gentry of the land, powdering her hair and painting her face, going with necklaces, with jewels in her ears, and bracelets upon her hands. When she had dressed herself, her work was to make girdles of wampum and beads. The third squaw was a younger one, by whom he had two papooses. By that time I was refreshed by the old squaw with whom my master was, Weetamoo's maid came to call me home, at which I fell a-weeping. Then the old squaw told me, to encourage me, that if I wanted victuals I should come to her, and that I should lie there in her wigwam. Then I went with the maid and quickly came again and lodged there. The squaw laid a mat under me and a good rug over me; the first time I had any such kindness showed me. I understood that Weetamoo thought that if she should let me go and serve with the old squaw, she would be in danger to lose not only my service but the redemption pay also. And I was not a little glad to hear this, being raised in my hopes that in God's due time there would be an end of this sorrowful hour. Then came an Indian and asked me to knit him three pairs of stockings, for which I had a hat and a silk handkerchief. Then another asked me to make her a shift, for which she gave me an apron.

Then came Tom and Peter[46] with the second letter from the council about the captives. Though they were Indians, I got them by the

[46]Christian Indians.

hand and burst out into tears; my heart was so full that I could not speak to them, but recovering myself, I asked them how my husband did and all my friends and acquaintances. They said they [were] all very well, but melancholy. They brought me two biscuits and a pound of tobacco. The tobacco I quickly gave away; when it was all gone, one asked me to give him a pipe of tobacco. I told him it was all gone. Then began he to rant and threaten. I told him when my husband came I would give some. "Hang [the] rogue," says he, "I will knock out his brains if he comes here." And then again in the same breath they would say that if there should come a hundred without guns they would do them no hurt, so unstable and like madmen they were, so that fearing the worst, I durst not send to my husband though there were some thoughts of his coming to redeem and fetch me, not knowing what might follow. For there was little more trust to them than to the master they served.

When the letter was come, the sagamores met to consult about the captives and called me to them to inquire how much my husband would give to redeem me. When I came, I sat down among them as I was wont to do, as their manner is. Then they bade me stand up and said they were the General Court.[47] They bid me speak what I thought he would give. Now knowing that all we had was destroyed by the Indians, I was in a great strait. I thought if I should speak of but a little, it would be slighted and hinder the matter; if of a great sum, I knew not where it would be procured. Yet at a venture, I said twenty pounds, yet desired them to take less; but they would not hear of that, but sent that message to Boston that for twenty pounds I should be redeemed. It was a praying Indian that wrote their letter for them. There was another praying Indian who told me that he had a brother that would not eat horse; his conscience was so tender and scrupulous (though as large as hell for the destruction of poor Christians). Then he said he read that scripture to him, 2 Kings, 6:25, "There was a famine in Samaria, and behold they besieged it, until an ass's head was sold for fourscore pieces of silver, and the fourth part of a kab of doves' dung for five pieces of silver." He expounded this place to his brother and showed him that it was lawful to eat that in a famine which is not at another time. "And now," says he, "he will eat horse with any Indian of them all."

[47]The highest legislative and judicial body in Massachusetts, before whom she would have had to stand.

There was another praying Indian who, when he had done all the mischief that he could, betrayed his own father into the English hands thereby to purchase his own life. Another praying Indian was at Sudbury fight,[48] though, as he deserved, he was afterward hanged for it. There was another praying Indian so wicked and cruel as to wear a string about his neck strung with Christians' fingers. Another praying Indian, when they went to Sudbury fight, went with them and his squaw also with him with her papoose at her back.

Before they went to that fight, they got a company together to pow-wow; the manner was as followeth. There was one that kneeled upon a deerskin with the company round him in a ring, who kneeled, and striking upon the ground with their hands and with sticks, and muttering or humming with their mouths; besides him who kneeled in the ring, there also stood one with a gun in his hand. Then he on the deerskin made a speech, and all manifested assent to it, and so they did many times together. Then they bade him with the gun go out of the ring, which he did, but when he was out, they called him in again. But he seemed to make a stand; then they called the more earnestly till he returned again. Then they all sang. Then they gave him two guns, in either hand one. And so he on the deerskin began again, and at the end of every sentence in his speaking, they all assented, humming or muttering with their mouths and striking upon the ground with their hands. Then they bade him with the two guns go out of the ring again, which he did a little way. Then they called him in again, but he made a stand; so they called him with greater earnestness, but he stood reeling and wavering as if he knew not whether he should stand or fall or which way to go. Then they called him with exceeding great vehemency, all of them, one and another. After a little while he turned in, staggering as he went, with his arms stretched out, in either hand a gun. As soon as he came in, they all sang and rejoiced exceedingly awhile. And then he upon the deerskin made another speech, unto which they all assented in a rejoicing manner, and so they ended their business and forthwith went to Sudbury fight.

To my thinking they went without any scruple[49] but that they should prosper and gain the victory. And they went out not so rejoicing, but they came home with as great a victory, for they said

---

[48]An attack on Sudbury, Massachusetts, April 18, 1676.
[49]Doubt.

they had killed two captains and almost an hundred men. One Englishman they brought along with them; and he said it was too true, for they had made sad work at Sudbury, as indeed it proved. Yet they came home without that rejoicing and triumphing over their victory which they were wont to show at other times but rather like dogs (as they say) which have lost their ears. Yet I could not perceive that it was for their own loss of men. They said they had not lost but above five or six, and I missed none except in one wigwam. When they went, they acted as if the devil had told them that they should gain the victory, and now they acted as if the devil had told them they should have a fall. Whither it were so or no, I cannot tell, but so it proved, for quickly they began to fall and so held on that summer till they came to utter ruin.

They came home on a Sabbath day, and the powwow that kneeled upon the deerskin came home (I may say without abuse) as black as the devil. When my master came home, he came to me and bid me make a shirt for his papoose of a holland lace pillowbeer.[50] About that time there came an Indian to me and bid me come to his wigwam at night, and he would give me some pork and groundnuts, which I did. And as I was eating, another Indian said to me, "He seems to be your good friend, but he killed two Englishmen at Sudbury, and there lie their clothes behind you." I looked behind me, and there I saw bloody clothes with bullet holes in them, yet the Lord suffered not this wretch to do me any hurt. Yea, instead of that, he many times refreshed me; five or six times did he and his squaw refresh my feeble carcass. If I went to their wigwam at any time, they would always give me something, and yet they were strangers that I never saw before. Another squaw gave me a piece of fresh pork and a little salt with it and lent me her pan to fry it in, and I cannot but remember what a sweet, pleasant and delightful relish that bit had to me to this day. So little do we prize common mercies when we have them to the full.

[50]Pillowcase with linen lace.

The Twentieth Remove[51]

It was their usual manner to remove when they had done any mischief, lest they should be found out, and so they did at this time. We went about three or four miles, and there they built a great wigwam big enough to hold a hundred Indians, which they did in preparation to a great day of dancing. They would say now amongst themselves that the governor would be so angry for his loss at Sudbury that he would send no more about the captives, which made me grieve and tremble. My sister being not far from the place where we now were, and hearing that I was here, desired her master to let her come and see me, and he was willing to it and would go with her. But she, being ready before him, told him she would go before and was come within a mile or two of the place. Then he overtook her and began to rant as if he had been mad and made her go back again in the rain so that I never saw her till I saw her in Charlestown. But the Lord requited many of their ill doings, for this Indian, her master, was hanged afterward at Boston.

The Indians now began to come from all quarters, against their merry dancing day. Among some of them came one Goodwife Kettle. I told her my heart was so heavy that it was ready to break. "So is mine, too,' said she. But yet [she] said, "I hope we shall hear some good news shortly." I could hear how earnestly my sister desired to see me, and I as earnestly desired to see her, and yet neither of us could get an opportunity. My daughter was also now about a mile off, and I had not seen her in nine or ten weeks as I had not seen my sister since our first taking. I earnestly desired them to let me go and see them; yea, I entreated, begged, and persuaded them but to let me see my daughter, and yet so hardhearted were they that they would not suffer it. They made use of their tyrannical power whilst they had it, but through the Lord's wonderful mercy their time was now but short.

On a Sabbath day, the sun being about an hour high in the afternoon, came Mr. John Hoar (the council permitting him and his own forward spirit inclining him) together with the two forementioned Indians, Tom and Peter, with their third letter from the council. When they came near, I was abroad; though I saw them not, they

---

[51]To an encampment at the southern end of Wachuset Lake, Princeton, Massachusetts (April 28–May 2).

presently called me in and bade me sit down and not stir. Then they catched up their guns and away they ran as if an enemy had been at hand, and the guns went off apace. I manifested some great trouble, and they asked me what was the matter. I told them I thought they had killed the Englishman (for they had in the meantime informed me that an Englishman was come). They said, "No." They shot over his horse and under, and before his horse, and they pushed him this way and that way at their pleasure, showing what they could do. Then they let them come to their wigwams. I begged of them to let me see the Englishman, but they would not; but there was I fain to sit their pleasure. When they had talked their fill with him, they suffered me to go to him. We asked each other of our welfare, and how my husband did and all my friends. He told me they were all well and would be glad to see me. Amongst other things which my husband sent me, there came a pound of tobacco, which I sold for nine shillings in money, for many of the Indians for want of tobacco smoked hemlock and ground ivy. It was a great mistake in any who thought I sent for tobacco, for through the favor of God that desire was overcome.

I now asked them whether I should go home with Mr. Hoar. They answered, "No," one and another of them. And it being night, we lay down with that answer. In the morning Mr. Hoar invited the sagamores to dinner, but when we went to get it ready, we found that they had stolen the greatest part of the provision Mr. Hoar had brought out of his bags in the night. And we may see the wonderful power of God in that one passage in that when there was such a great number of the Indians together and so greedy of a little good food and no English there but Mr. Hoar and myself, that there they did not knock us in the head and take what he had, there being not only some provision but also trading cloth, a part of the twenty pounds agreed upon. But instead of doing us any mischief, they seemed to be ashamed of the fact and said it were some *matchit*[52] Indian that did it. Oh, that we could believe that there is nothing too hard for God! God showed His power over the heathen in this as He did over the hungry lions when Daniel was cast into the den.[53] Mr. Hoar called them betime to dinner, but they ate very little, they

[52]Bad.
[53]Daniel 6:16–23.

being so busy in dressing themselves and getting ready for their dance, which was carried on by eight of them—four men and four squaws, my master and mistress being two. He was dressed in his Holland[54] shirt with great laces sewed at the tail of it; he had his silver buttons, his white stockings, his garters were hung round with shillings, and he had girdles of wampum upon his head and shoulders. She had a kersey coat[55] and [was] covered with girdles of wampum from the loins upward; her arms from her elbows to her hands were covered with bracelets; there were handfuls of necklaces about her neck and several sorts of jewels in her ears. She had fine red stockings and white shoes, her hair powdered and face painted red that was always before black. And all the dancers were after the same manner. There were two others singing and knocking on a kettle for their music. They kept hopping up and down one after another with a kettle of water in the midst, standing warm upon some embers, to drink of when they were dry. They held on till it was almost night, throwing out wampum to the standers by.

At night I asked them again if I should go home. They all as one said no except my husband would come for me. When we were lain down, my master went out of the wigwam, and by and by sent in an Indian called James the Printer,[56] who told Mr. Hoar that my master would let me go home tomorrow if he would let him have one pint of liquors. Then Mr. Hoar called his own Indians, Tom and Peter, and bid them go and see whether he would promise it before them three, and if he would, he should have it, which he did, and he had it. Then Philip, smelling the business, called me to him and asked me what I would give him to tell me some good news and speak a good word for me. I told him I could not tell what to give him. I would [give] anything I had and asked him what he would have. He said two coats and twenty shillings in money and half a bushel of seed corn and some tobacco. I thanked him for his love, but I knew the good news as well as the crafty fox.

My master, after he had had his drink, quickly came ranting into the wigwam again and called for Mr. Hoar, drinking to him and

[54]Linen.
[55]Wool petticoat.
[56]An Indian who assisted the Reverend John Eliot in printing the Bible in Algonquian.

saying he was a good man. And then again he would say, "Hang [the] rogue." Being almost drunk, he would drink to him, and yet presently say he should be hanged. Then he called for me. I trembled to hear him, yet I was fain to go to him, and he drank to me, showing no incivility. He was the first Indian I saw drunk all the while that I was amongst them. At last his squaw ran out, and he after her round the wigwam, with his money jingling at his knees, but she escaped him. But having an old squaw, he ran to her, and so through the Lord's mercy, we were no more troubled that night.

Yet I had not a comfortable night's rest, for I think I can say I did not sleep for three nights together. The night before the letter came from the council I could not rest, I was so full of fears and troubles, God many times leaving us most in the dark when deliverance is nearest. Yea, at this time I could not rest night nor day. The next night I was overjoyed, Mr. Hoar being come and that with such good tidings. The third night I was even swallowed up with the thoughts of things, *viz.* that ever I should go home again and that I must go, leaving my children behind me in the wilderness, so that sleep was now almost departed from mine eyes.

On Tuesday morning they called their General Court (as they call it) to consult and determine whether I should go home or no. And they all as one man did seemingly consent to it that I should go home, except Philip, who would not come among them.

But before I go any further, I would take leave to mention a few remarkable passages of providence which I took special notice of in my afflicted time.

1. Of the fair opportunity lost in the long march, a little after the fort fight, when our English army was so numerous, and in pursuit of the enemy, and so near as to take several and destroy them, and the enemy in such distress for food that our men might track them by their rooting in the earth for groundnuts while they were flying for their lives. I say that then our army should want provision and be forced to leave their pursuit and return homeward. And the very next week the enemy came upon our town like bears bereft of their whelps or so many ravenous wolves, rending us and our lambs to death. But what shall I say? God seemed to leave His people to themselves and order all things for His own holy ends. "Shall there be evil in the city and the Lord hath not done it? They are not grieved for the affliction of Joseph, therefore shall they go captive

with the first that go captive."[57] It is the Lord's doing, and it should be marvelous in our eyes.

2. I cannot but remember how the Indians derided the slowness and dullness of the English army in its setting out. For after the desolations at Lancaster and Medfield, as I went along with them, they asked me when I thought the English would come after them. I told them I could not tell. It may be they will come in May, said they. Thus did they scoff at us, as if the English would be a quarter of a year getting ready.

3. Which also I have hinted before: when the English army with new supplies were sent forth to pursue after the enemy, and they, understanding it, fled before them till they came to Baquaug River where they forthwith went over safely, that that river should be impassable to the English. I can but admire to see the wonderful providence of God in preserving the heathen for further affliction to our poor country. They could go in great numbers over, but the English must stop. God had an overruling hand in all those things.

4. It was thought if their corn were cut down they would starve and die with hunger, and all their corn that could be found was destroyed, and they driven from that little they had in store into the woods in the midst of winter. And yet how to admiration did the Lord preserve them for His holy ends and the destruction of many still amongst the English! Strangely did the Lord provide for them that I did not see (all the time I was among them) one man, woman, or child die with hunger. Though many times they would eat that that a hog or dog would hardly touch, yet by that God strengthened them to be a scourge to His people.

The chief and commonest food was groundnuts. They eat also nuts and acorns, artichokes, lily roots, groundbeans, and several other weeds and roots that I know not.

They would pick up old bones and cut them to pieces at the joints, and if they were full of worms and maggots, they would scald them over the fire to make the vermin come out and then boil them and drink up the liquor and then beat the great ends of them in a mortar and so eat them. They would eat horses' guts and ears, and all sorts of wild birds which they could catch; also bear, venison, beaver, tortoise, frogs, squirrels, dogs, skunks, rattlesnakes, yea, the very bark of trees, besides all sorts of creatures and provision which they

[57]Amos 3:6, 6:6–7.

plundered from the English. I can but stand in admiration to see the wonderful power of God in providing for such a vast number of our enemies in the wilderness, where there was nothing to be seen but from hand to mouth. Many times in a morning the generality of them would eat up all they had and yet have some further supply against they wanted. It is said, Psal. 81:13, 14, "Oh, that My people had hearkened to Me, and Israel had walked in My ways; I should soon have subdued their enemies and turned My hand against their adversaries." But now our perverse and evil carriages in the sight of the Lord have so offended Him that instead of turning His hand against them the Lord feeds and nourishes them up to be a scourge to the whole land.

5. Another thing that I would observe is the strange providence of God in turning things about when the Indians [were] at the highest and the English at the lowest. I was with the enemy eleven weeks and five days, and not one week passed without the fury of the enemy and some desolation by fire and sword upon one place or other. They mourned (with their black faces) for their own losses, yet triumphed and rejoiced in their inhuman and many times devilish cruelty to the English. They would boast much of their victories, saying that in two hours' time they had destroyed such a captain and his company at such a place, and such a captain and his company in such a place, and such a captain and his company in such a place, and boast how many towns they had destroyed; and then scoff and say they had done them a good turn to send them to heaven so soon. Again they would say this summer that they would knock all the rogues in the head, or drive them into the sea, or make them fly the country, thinking surely Agag-like, "The bitterness of death is past."[58] Now the heathen begins to think all is their own, and the poor Christians' hopes to fail (as to man), and now their eyes are more to God, and their hearts sigh heavenward and to say in good earnest, "Help Lord, or we perish." When the Lord had brought His people to this that they saw no help in anything but Himself, then He takes the quarrel into His own hand, and though they [the Indians] had made a pit in their own imaginations as deep as hell for the Christians that summer, yet the Lord hurled themselves into it. And the Lord had not so many ways before to preserve them, but now He hath as many to destroy them.

[58]See I Samuel, chapter 15.

But to return again to my going home, where we may see a remarkable change of providence. At first they were all against it except my husband would come for me, but afterwards they assented to it and seemed much to rejoice in it. Some asked me to send them some bread, others some tobacco, others shaking me by the hand, offering me a hood and scarf to ride in, not one moving hand or tongue against it. Thus hath the Lord answered my poor desire and the many earnest requests of others put up unto God for me. In my travels an Indian came to me and told me if I were willing, he and his squaw would run away and go home along with me. I told him no. I was not willing to run away, but desired to wait God's time that I might go home quietly and without fear. And now God hath granted me my desire. O, the wonderful power of God that I have seen and the experience that I have had! I have been in the midst of those roaring lions and savage bears that feared neither God nor man nor the devil, by night and day, alone and in company, sleeping all sorts together, and yet not one of them ever offered me the least abuse of unchastity to me in word or action. Though some are ready to say I speak it for my own credit, I speak it in the presence of God and to His glory. God's power is as great now and as sufficient to save as when He preserved Daniel in the lion's den or the three children in the fiery furnace.[59] I may well say as his Psal. 107:12, "Oh, give thanks unto the Lord for He is good, for His mercy endureth forever." Let the redeemed of the Lord say so whom He hath redeemed from the hand of the enemy, especially that I should come away in the midst of so many hundreds of enemies quietly and peaceably and not a dog moving his tongue.

So I took my leave of them, and in coming along my heart melted into tears more than all the while I was with them, and I was almost swallowed up with the thoughts that ever I should go home again. About the sun going down, Mr. Hoar, myself, and the two Indians came to Lancaster, and a solemn sight it was to me. There had I lived many comfortable years amongst my relations and neighbors, and now not one Christian to be seen nor one house left standing. We went on to a farmhouse that was yet standing, where we lay all night, and a comfortable lodging we had, though nothing but straw to lie on. The Lord preserved us in safety that night and raised us up again in the morning and carried us along, that before noon we

[59]See Daniel 3:13–30.

came to Concord. Now was I full of joy and yet not without sorrow—joy to see such a lovely sight, so many Christians together and some of them my neighbors. There I met with my brother [Josiah White] and my brother-in-law [Henry Kerley], who asked me if I knew where his wife was. Poor heart! He had helped to bury her and knew it not, she being shot down [when] the house was partly burned so that those who were at Boston at the desolation of the town and came back afterward and buried the dead did not know her. Yet I was not without sorrow to think how many were looking and longing, and my own children amongst the rest, to enjoy that deliverance that I had now received, and I did not know whether ever I should see them again.

Being recruited with food and raiment, we went to Boston that day, where I met with my dear husband, but the thoughts of our dear children, one being dead and the others we could not tell where, abated our comfort each to other. I was not before so much hemmed in with the merciless and cruel heathen but now as much with pitiful, tenderhearted, and compassionate Christians. In that poor and distressed and beggarly condition I was received in, I was kindly entertained in several houses; so much love I received from several (some of whom I knew and others I knew not) that I am not capable to declare it. But the Lord knows them all by name. The Lord reward them sevenfold into their bosoms of His spirituals for their temporals.[60]

The twenty pounds, the price of my redemption, was raised by some Boston gentlemen and Mrs. Usher, whose bounty and religious charity I would not forget to make mention of. Then Mr. Thomas Shepard of Charlestown received us into his house, where we continued eleven weeks, and a father and mother they were to us. And many more tenderhearted friends we met with in that place. We were now in the midst of love, yet not without much and frequent heaviness of heart for our poor children and other relations who were still in affliction. The week following after my coming in, the governor and council sent forth to the Indians again, and that not without success, for they brought in my sister and Goodwife Kettle.

Their not knowing where our children were was a sore trial to us still, and yet we were not without secret hopes that we should see them again. That which was dead lay heavier upon my spirit than

60 Worldly, material goods.

those which were alive and amongst the heathen, thinking how it suffered with its wounds and I was no way able to relieve it, and how it was buried by the heathen in the wilderness from among all Christians. We were hurried up and down in our thoughts; sometimes we should hear a report that they were gone this way, and sometimes that, and that they were come in in this place or that. We kept inquiring and listening to hear concerning them, but no certain news as yet. About this time the council had ordered a day of public thanksgiving, though I thought I had still cause of mourning, and, being unsettled in our minds, we thought we would ride toward the eastward to see if we could hear anything concerning our children. And as we were riding along (God is the wise disposer of all things), between Ipswich and Rowly we met with Mr. William Hubbard, who told us that our son Joseph was come in to Major Waldren's, and another with him which was my sister's son. I asked him how he knew it. He said the major himself told him so.

So along we went till we came to Newbury, and, their minister being absent, they desired my husband to preach the thanksgiving for them, but he was not willing to stay there that night but would go over to Salisbury to hear further and come again in the morning, which he did and preached there that day. At night when he had done, one came and told him that his daughter was come in at Providence. Here was mercy on both hands. Now hath God fulfilled that precious scripture which was such a comfort to me in my distressed condition. When my heart was ready to sink into the earth (my children being gone I could not tell whither), and my knees trembled under me, and I was walking through the valley of the shadow of death, then the Lord brought and now has fulfilled that reviving word unto me. Thus saith the Lord, "Refrain thy voice from weeping, and thine eyes from tears, for thy work shall be rewarded," saith the Lord, "and they shall come again from the land of the enemy."[61]

Now we were between them, the one on the east and the other on the west. Our son being nearest, we went to him first to Portsmouth, where we met with him and with the major also, who told us he had done what he could but could not redeem him under seven pounds, which the good people thereabouts were pleased to pay. The Lord reward the major and all the rest, though unknown to me, for their labor of love. My sister's son was redeemed for four pounds, which

[61]Jeremiah 31:16.

the council gave order for the payment of. Having now received one of our children, we hastened toward the other; going back through Newbury, my husband preached there on the Sabbath day, for which they rewarded him manyfold.

On Monday we came to Charlestown, where we heard that the governor of Rhode Island had sent over for our daughter to take care of her, being now within his jurisdiction, which should not pass without our acknowledgments. But she being nearer Rehoboth than Rhode Island, Mr. Newman went over and took care of her and brought her to his own house. And the goodness of God was admirable to us in our low estate in that he raised up [com]passionate friends on every side to us when we had nothing to recompense any for their love. The Indians were now gone that way, that it was apprehended dangerous to go to her; but the carts which carried provision to the English army, being guarded, brought her with them to Dorchester, where we received her safe. Blessed be the Lord for it, for great is His power, and He can do whatsoever seemeth Him good.

Her coming in was after this manner. She was traveling one day with the Indians with her basket at her back; the company of Indians were got before her and gone out of sight, all except one squaw. She followed the squaw till night, and then both of them lay down, having nothing over them but the heavens and under them but the earth. Thus she traveled three days together, not knowing whither she was going, having nothing to eat or drink but water and green hirtleberries. At last they came into Providence, where she was kindly entertained by several of that town. The Indians often said that I should never have her under twenty pounds. But now the Lord hath brought her in upon free cost and given her to me the second time. The Lord make us a blessing indeed, each to others. Now have I seen that scripture also fulfilled, Deut. 30:4, 7: "If any of thine be driven out to the outmost parts of heaven, from thence will the Lord thy God gather thee, and from thence will He fetch thee. . . . And the Lord thy God will put all these curses upon thine enemies, and on them which hate thee, which persecuted thee." Thus hath the Lord brought me and mine out of that horrible pit and hath set us in the midst of tenderhearted and compassionate Christians. It is the desire of my soul that we may walk worthy of the mercies received and which we are receiving.

Our family being now gathered together (those of us that were living), the South Church in Boston hired an house for us. Then we removed from Mr. Shepard's, those cordial friends, and went to Boston, where we continued about three-quarters of a year. Still the Lord went along with us and provided graciously for us. I thought it somewhat strange to set up housekeeping with bare walls, but as Solomon says, "Money answers all things,"[62] and that we had through the benevolence of Christian friends, some in this town and some in that and others, and some from England, that in a little time we might look and see the house furnished with love. The Lord hath been exceeding good to us in our low estate in that when we had neither house nor home nor other necessaries, the Lord so moved the hearts of these and those towards us that we wanted neither food nor raiment for ourselves or ours, Prov. 18:24, "There is a friend which sticketh closer than a brother." And how many such friends have we found and now living amongst! And truly such a friend have we found him to be unto us in whose house we lived, *viz.* Mr. James Whitcomb, a friend unto us near hand and afar off.

I can remember the time when I used to sleep quietly without workings in my thoughts whole nights together, but now it is other ways with me. When all are fast about me and no eye open but His who ever waketh, my thoughts are upon things past, upon the awful dispensation of the Lord toward us, upon His wonderful power and might in carrying of us through so many difficulties, in returning us in safety and suffering none to hurt us. I remember in the night season how the other day I was in the midst of thousands of enemies and nothing but death before me. It [was] then hard work to persuade myself that ever I should be satisfied with bread again. But now we are fed with the finest of the wheat, and, as I may say, with honey out of the rock. Instead of the husk, we have the fatted calf.[63] The thoughts of these things in the particulars of them, and of the love and goodness of God towards us, make it true of me what David said of himself, Psal. 6:5 [actually 6:6]. "I watered my couch with my tears." Oh, the wonderful power of God that mine eyes have seen, affording matter enough for my thoughts to run in, that when others are sleeping mine eyes are weeping!

I have seen the extreme vanity of this world. One hour I have been in health and wealth, wanting nothing, but the next hour in sickness

[62]Ecclesiastes 10:19.
[63]Psalm 81:16; Luke 15:23.

and wounds and death, having nothing but sorrow and affliction. Before I knew what affliction meant, I was ready sometimes to wish for it. When I lived in prosperity, having the comforts of the world about me, my relations by me, my heart cheerful, and taking little care for anything, and yet seeing many whom I preferred before myself under many trials and afflictions, in sickness, weakness, poverty, losses, crosses, and cares of the world, I should be sometimes jealous lest I should have my portion in this life, and that scripture would come to mind, Heb. 12:6, "For whom the Lord loveth he chasteneth and scourgeth every son whom He receiveth." But now I see the Lord had His time to scourge and chasten me. The portion of some is to have their afflictions by drops, now one drop and then another, but the dregs of the cup, the wine of astonishment, like a sweeping rain that leaveth no food, did the Lord prepare to be my portion. Affliction I wanted and affliction I had, full measure (I thought) pressed down and running over. Yet I see when God calls a person to anything and through never so many difficulties, yet He is fully able to carry them through and make them see and say they have been gainers thereby. And I hope I can say in some measure, as David did, "It is good for me that I have been afflicted."[64]

The Lord hath showed me the vanity of these outward things. That they are the vanity of vanities and vexation of spirit, that they are but a shadow, a blast, a bubble, and things of no continuance. That we must rely on God himself and our whole dependence must be upon Him. If trouble from smaller matters begin to arise in me, I have something at hand to check myself with and say, why am I troubled? It was but the other day that if I had had the world I would have given it for my freedom or to have been a servant to a Christian. I have learned to look beyond present and smaller troubles and to be quieted under them, as Moses said, Exod. 14:13, "Stand still and see the salvation of the Lord."

[64]Psalm 119:71.

Sarah Kemble Knight

1666–1727

SARAH KEMBLE KNIGHT was a Boston businesswoman who kept a shop and did legal work: drawing up documents and settling estates. Her husband, Richard, was apparently in the shipping business and was often away; so she managed a household that included her mother, her daughter, and several lodgers. Between October 2, 1704, and March 3, 1705, she traveled on horseback from Boston to New York and back in order to settle an estate on behalf of her cousin's widow. Such independent traveling was practically unheard of for a woman at this period, for reasons apparent from Knight's narrative. She kept notes during her journey and on her return wrote them up as a connected journal, probably intended only to be circulated among her friends; it was not published until 1825. In 1714, Knight moved to Connecticut, where she ran several farms, dealt in real estate, and kept an inn. Her lively, down-to-earth report contrasts with the seriousness of most American literature of her time.

BIBLIOGRAPHY
Knight, Sarah Kemble. *The Journal of Madam Knight.* Ed. George P. Winship. New York: P. Smith, 1935.

from The Private Journal of a Journey from Boston to New York in the Year 1704, Kept by Madam Knight

Tuesday, October the third, about eight in the morning, I with the post[1] proceeded forward without observing any thing remarkable; And about two, afternoon, arrived at the post's second stage, where the western post met him and exchanged letters. Here, having called for something to eat, the woman brought in a twisted thing like a cable, but something whiter, and laying it on the board, tugged for life to bring it into a capacity to spread; which having with great pains accomplished, she served in a dish of pork and cabbage, I suppose the remains of dinner. The sauce was of a deep purple, which I thought was boiled in her dye kettle; the bread was Indian, and everything on the table service agreeable to these. I, being hungry, got a little down; but my stomach was soon cloyed, and what cabbage I swallowed served me for a cud the whole day after.

Having here discharged the ordinary[2] for self and guide[3] (as I understood was the custom), about three, afternoon, went on with my third guide, who rode very hard; and having crossed Providence Ferry, we come to a river which they generally ride through. But I dare not venture; so the post got a lad and canoe to carry me to t'other side, and he rid through and led my horse. The canoe was very small and shallow, so that when we were in she seemed ready to take in water, which greatly terrified me and caused me to be very circumspect, sitting with my hands fast on each side, my eyes steady, not daring so much as to lodge my tongue a hair's breadth more on one side of my mouth than t'other, nor so much as think on Lot's wife,[4] for a wry thought would have overset our wherry. But [I] was soon put out of this pain, by feeling the canoe on shore, which I as

[1]Letter-carrier, who would travel regularly from one stage, or regular stopping place, to the next.
[2]Paid the tavern bill.
[3]In the absence of main roads, it was necessary to hire guides to show the way from one town to another.
[4]Lot's wife was turned into a pillar of salt for looking back as she left her home in Sodom (Genesis 19:26).

soon almost saluted with my feet; and rewarding my sculler, again mounted and made the best of our way forwards. The road here was very even and the day pleasant, it being now near sunset. But the post told me we had near fourteen miles to ride to the next stage (where we were to lodge.) I asked him of the rest of the road, foreseeing we must travel in the night. He told me there was a bad river we were to ride through, which was so very fierce a horse could sometimes hardly stem it. But it was but narrow, and we should soon be over. I cannot express the concern of mind this relation set me in: no thoughts but those of the dangerous river could entertain my imagination, and they were as formidable as various, still tormenting me with blackest ideas of my approaching fate—sometimes seeing myself drowning, otherwhiles drowned, and at the best like a holy sister just come out of a spiritual bath in dripping garments.[5]

Now was the glorious luminary, with his swift coursers arrived at his stage,[6] leaving poor me with the rest of this part of the lower world in darkness, with which we were soon surrounded. The only glimmering we now had was from the spangled skies, whose imperfect reflections rendered every object formidable. Each lifeless trunk, with its shattered limbs, appeared an armed enemy, and every little stump like a ravenous devourer. Nor could I so much as discern my guide, when at any distance, which added to the terror.

Thus, absolutely lost in thought, and dying with the very thoughts of drowning, I come up with the post, who I did not see till even with his horse: he told me he stopped for me; and we rode on very deliberately a few paces, when we entered a thicket of trees and shrubs, and I perceived by the horse's going, we were on the descent of a hill, which as we come nearer the bottom, 'twas totally dark with the trees that surrounded it. But I knew by the going of the horse we had entered the water, which my guide told me was the hazardous river he had told me of; and he, riding up close to my side, bid me not fear—we should be over immediately. I now rallied all the courage I was mistress of, knowing that I must either venture my fate of drowning or be left like the children in the wood.[7] So, as the post bid me, I gave reins to my nag, and sitting as steady as just

[5]A member of a nonconformist sect that baptized people as adults.

[6]The sun god and his horses have completed their journey across the sky; i.e., night has fallen.

[7]In an old ballad, two small children are taken into a wood to be killed; they are abandoned instead, but die during the night.

before in the canoe, in a few minutes got safe to the other side, which he told me was the Narragansett country.

Here we found great difficulty in traveling, the way being very narrow, and on each side the trees and bushes gave us very unpleasent welcomes with their branches and boughs, which we could not avoid, it being so exceeding dark. My guide, as before so now, put on harder than I, with my weary bones, could follow; so left me and the way behind him. Now returned my distressed apprehensions of the place where I was: the dolesome woods, my company next to none, going I knew not whither, and encompassed with terrifying darkness, the least of which was enough to startle a more masculine courage. Added to which the reflections, as in the afternoon of the day, that my call was very questionable,[8] which till then I had not so prudently as I ought considered. Now, coming to the foot of a hill, I found great difficulty in ascending, but being got to the top, was there amply recompensed with the friendly appearance of the kind conductress of the night,[9] just then advancing above the horizontal line. The raptures which the sight of that fair planet produced in me caused me, for the moment, to forget my present weariness and past toils, and inspired me for most of the remaining way with very diverting thoughts, some of which, with the other occurrences of the day, I reserved to note down when I should come to my stage. My thoughts on the sight of the moon were to this purpose:

> Fair Cynthia, all the homage that I may
> Unto a creature, unto thee I pay;
> In lonesome woods to meet so kind a guide,
> To me's more worth than all the world beside.
> Some joy I felt just now, when safe got o're
> Yon surly river to this rugged shore,
> Deeming rough welcomes from these clownish trees,
> Better than lodgings with Nereides.
> Yet swelling fears surprise; all dark appears—
> Nothing but light can dissipate those fears.
> My fainting vitals can't lend strength to say,
> But softly whisper, O I wish 'twere day.
> The murmur hardly warmed the ambient air,

[8]I.e., perhaps there was no good reason for me to be here.
[9]The moon.

Ere thy bright aspect rescues from despair:
Makes the old hag her sable mantle loose,
And a bright joy does through my soul diffuse.
The boisterous trees now lend a passage free,
And pleasant prospects thou giv'st light to see.

From hence we kept on, with more ease than before: the way
being smooth and even, the night warm and serene; and the tall and
thick trees at a distance, especially when the moon glared light
through the branches, filled my imagination with the pleasant delusion of a sumptuous city, filled with famous buildings and churches,
with their spiring steeples, balconies, galleries and I know not what:
grandeurs which I had heard of, and which the stories of foreign
countries had given me the idea of.

Here stood a lofty church—there is a steeple,
And there the grand parade—O see the people!
That famous castle there, were I but nigh,
To see the moat and bridge and walls so high—
They're very fine! says my deluded eye.

Being thus agreeably entertained without a thought of anything
but thoughts themselves, I on a sudden was roused from these pleasing imaginations by the post's sounding his horn, which assured me
he was arrived at the stage, where we were to lodge: and that music
was then most musical and agreeable to me.

Being come to Mr. Havens', I was very civilly received and cour-
teously entertained, in a clean comfortable house; and the good
woman was very active in helping off my riding clothes, and then
asked what I would eat. I told her I had some chocolate, if she would
prepare it; which with the help of some milk, and a little clean brass
kettle, she soon effected to my satisfaction. I then betook me to my
apartment, which was a little room parted from the kitchen by a
single board partition; where, after I had noted the occurrences of
the past day, I went to bed, which, though pretty hard, was yet neat
and handsome. But I could get no sleep, because of the clamor of
some of the town topers in the next room, who were entered into a
strong debate concerning the signification of the name of their country: viz., *Narragansett*. One said it was named so by the Indians
because there grew a brier there of a prodigious height and bigness,

the like hardly ever known, called by the Indians Narragansett; and quotes an Indian of so barbarous a name for his author, that I could not write it. His antagonist replied no—it was from a spring it had its name, which he well knew where it was, which was extreme cold in summer and as hot as could be imagined in the winter, which was much resorted to by the natives, and by them called Narragansett (hot and cold), and that was the original of their place's name—with a thousand impertinences not worth notice, which he uttered with such a roaring voice and thundering blows with the fist of wickedness on the table, that it pierced my very head. I heartily fretted, and wished them tongue-tied; but with as little success as a friend of mine once, who was (as she said) kept a whole night awake on a journey by a country lieutenant and a sergeant, ensign and a deacon, contriving how to bring a triangle into a square. They kept calling for t'other gill,[10] which while they were swallowing, was some intermission, but presently, like oil to fire, increased the flame. I set my candle on a chest by the bedside, and sitting up, fell to my old way of composing my resentments, in the following manner:

> I ask thy aid, O potent rum!
> To charm these wrangling topers dumb.
> Thou hast their giddy brains possessed—
> The man confounded with the beast—
> And I, poor I, can get no rest.
> Intoxicate them with thy fumes:
> O still their tongues till morning comes!

And I know not but my wishes took effect; for the dispute soon ended with t'other dram; and so good night!

Wednesday, October fourth. About four in the morning, we set out for Kingston (for so was the town called) with a French doctor in our company. He and the post put on very furiously, so that I could not keep up with them, only as now and then they'd stop till they see me. This road was poorly furnished with accommodations for travelers, so that we were forced to ride twenty-two miles by the post's account, but nearer thirty by mine, before we could bait so much as our horses, which I exceedingly complained of. But the post

[10]I.e., glass of wine or liquor.

encouraged me, by saying we should be well accommodated anon at Mr. Devill's, a few miles further. But I questioned whether we ought to go to the Devil to be helped out of affliction. However, like the rest of deluded souls that post to the infernal den, we made all possible speed to this Devill's habitation; where alighting, in full assurance of good accommodation, we were going in. But meeting his two daughters, as I supposed twins, they so nearly resembled each other, both in features and habit, and looked as old as the Devil himself and quite as ugly, we desired entertainment, but could hardly get a word out of them, till with our importunity, telling them our necessity, &c., they called the old sophister, who was as sparing of his words as his daughters had been, and no, or none, was the replies he made us to our demands. He differed only in this from the old fellow in t'other country: he let us depart. . . .

Saturday, October seventh, we set out early in the morning, and being something unacquainted with the way, having asked of it of some we met, they told us we must ride a mile or two and turn down a lane on the right hand; and by their direction we rode on, but not yet coming to the turning, we met a young fellow and asked him how far it was to the lane which turned down towards Guilford. He said we must ride a little further and turn down by the corner of Uncle Sam's lot. My guide vented his spleen at the lubber; and we soon after came into the road, and keeping still on, without anything further remarkable, about two o'clock, afternoon, we arrived at New Haven, where I was received with all possible respects and civility. Here I discharged Mr. Wheeler with a reward to his satisfaction, and took some time to rest after so long and toilsome a journey, and informed myself of the matters and customs of the place, and at the same time employed myself in the affair I went there upon.

They are governed by the same laws as we in Boston (or little differing) throughout this whole colony of Connecticut, and much the same way of church government, and many of them good, sociable people, and I hope religious too: but a little too much Independent[11] in their principles, and, as I have been told, were formerly in their zeal very rigid in their administrations towards[12] such

[11]Independents rejected the church discipline and organization accepted by most sects.

[12]I.e., treatment of.

as their laws made offenders, even to a harmless kiss or innocent merriment among young people. Whipping being a frequent and counted an easy punishment, about which, as other crimes, the judges were absolute in their sentences. . . .

There are great plenty of oysters all along by the sea side, as far as I rode in the colony, and those very good. And they generally lived very well and comfortably in their families. But too indulgent (especially the farmers) to their slaves: suffering too great familiarity from them, permitting them to sit at table and eat with them (as they say to save time), and into the dish goes the black hoof as freely as the white hand. They told me that there was a farmer lived near the town where I lodged who had some difference with his slave, concerning something the master had promised him and did not punctually perform, which caused some hard words between them; but at length they put the matter to arbitration and bound themselves to stand to the award of such as they named—which done, the arbitrators having heard the allegations of both parties, ordered the master to pay 40 shillings to black face and acknowledge his fault. And so the matter ended: the poor master very honestly standing to the award.

There are everywhere in the towns as I passed a number of Indians, the natives of the country, and are the most savage of all the savages of that kind that I had ever seen: little or no care taken (as I heard upon enquiry) to make them otherwise. They have in some places lands of their own, and governed by laws of their own making;—they marry many wives and at pleasure put them away, and on the least dislike or fickle humor, on either side, saying *stand away* to one another is a sufficient divorce. And indeed those uncomely *stand aways* are too much in vogue among the English in this indulgent colony, as their records plentifully prove, and that on very trivial matters, of which some have been told me, but are not proper to be related by a female pen, though some of that foolish sex have had too large a share in the story.

If the natives commit any crime on their own precincts among themselves, the English takes no cognizance of [it]. But if on the English ground, they are punishable by our laws. They mourn for their dead by blacking their faces and cutting their hair after an awkward and frightful manner; but can't bear you should mention the names of their dead relations to them: they trade most for rum, for which they'd hazard their very lives; and the English fit them generally as well, by seasoning it plentifully with water.

They give the title of merchant to every trader, who rate their goods according to the time and specie they pay in: viz. pay, money, pay as money, and trusting. *Pay* is grain, pork, beef, &c. at the prices set by the General Court that year; *money* is pieces of eight, royals, or Boston or Bay shillings (as they call them) or good hard money, as sometimes silver coin is termed by them; also wampum, viz., Indian beads which serves for change. *Pay as money* is provisions, as aforesaid, one third cheaper than as the assembly or General Court sets it; and *trust* as they and the merchant agree for time.

Now, when the buyer comes to ask for a commodity, sometimes before the merchant answers that he has it, he says, "Is your pay ready?" Perhaps the chap replies "Yes." "What do you pay in?" says the merchant. The buyer having answered, then the price is set; as suppose he wants a sixpenny knife, in pay it is 12 pence—in pay as money 8 pence, and hard money its own price, viz., 6 pence. It seems a very intricate way of trade and what Lex Mercatoria[13] had not thought of.

Being at a merchant's house, in comes a tall country fellow, with his alforges[14] full of tobacco—for they seldom loose their cud, but keep chewing and spitting as long as their eyes are open—he advanced to the middle of the room, makes an awkward nod, and spitting a large deal of aromatic tincture, he gave a scrape with his shovel-like shoe, leaving a small shovel full of dirt on the floor, made a full stop, hugging his own pretty body with his hands under his arms, stood staring round him like a cat let out of a basket. At last, like the creature Balaam rode on,[15] he opened his mouth and said: "Have you any ribbon for hatbands to sell, I pray?" The questions and answers about the pay being past, the ribbon is brought and opened. Bumpkin Simpers cries, "It's confounded gay, I vow." And beckoning to the door, in comes Joan Tawdry, dropping about fifty curtsies, and stands by him: he shows her the ribbon. "Law, You," says she, "It's right Gent;[16] do you take it, 'tis dreadful pretty." Then she enquires, "Have you any hood silk, I pray?" Which being brought and bought, "Have you any thread silk to sew it with," says she,

[13]Mercantile law; i.e., the legally recognized commercial system.
[14]Cheek-pouches (of a baboon).
[15]An ass. See Numbers 22:21–30.
[16]Genteel.

which being accommodated with, they departed. They generally stand after they come in a great while speechless, and sometimes don't say a word till they are asked what they want, which I impute to the awe they stand in of the merchants, who they are constantly almost indebted to, and must take what they bring without liberty to choose for themselves; but they serve them as well, making the merchants stay long enough for their pay.

We may observe here the great necessity and benefit both of education and conversation; for these people have as large a portion of mother wit, and sometimes a larger, than those who have been brought up in cities; but for want of improvements, render themselves almost ridiculous, as above. I should be glad if they would leave such follies, and am sure all that love clean houses (at least) would be glad on't too.

They are generally very plain in their dress, throughout all the colony, as I saw, and follow one another in their modes; that you may know where they belong, especially the women, meet them where you will.

Their chief red letter day is St. Election, which is annually observed according to Charter, to choose their Governor, a blessing they can never be thankful enough for, as they will find, if ever it be their hard fortune to lose it. The present Governor in Connecticut is the Honorable John Winthrop, Esq., a gentleman of an ancient and honorable family, whose father was Governor here some time before, and his grandfather had been Governor of the Massachusetts. This gentleman is a very courteous and affable person, much given to hospitality, and has by his good services gained the affections of the people as much as any who had been before him in that post.

December sixth. . . . The City of New York is a pleasant, well-compacted place, situated on a commodious river, which is a fine harbor for shipping. The buildings brick generally, very stately and high, though not altogether like ours in Boston. The bricks in some of the houses are of divers colors and laid in checkers, being glazed, look very agreeable. The inside of them are neat to admiration, the wooden work, for only the walls are plastered, and the summers and joists are planed and kept very white scoured, as so is all the partitions if made of boards. The fireplaces have no jambs (as ours have), but the backs run flush with the walls, and the hearth is of tiles and is as far out into the room at the ends as before the fire, which is generally five foot in the lower rooms; and the piece over where the mantel tree should be is made as ours with joiner's work, and as I suppose is fastened to iron rods inside. The house where the vendue[17] was had chimney corners like ours, and they and the hearths were laid with the finest tile that I ever see, and the staircases laid all with white tile, which is ever clean, and so are the walls of the kitchen, which had a brick floor. They were making great preparations to receive their governor, Lord Cornbury, from the Jerseys, and for that end raised the militia to guard him on shore to the fort.

They are generally of the Church of England and have a New England gentleman for their minister, and a very fine church set out with all customary requisites. There are also a Dutch and divers conventicles, as they call them, viz., Baptist, Quakers, &c. They are not strict in keeping the sabbath as in Boston and other places where I had been, but seem to deal with great exactness as far as I see or deal with. They are sociable to one another and courteous and civil to strangers and fare well in their houses. The English go very fashionable in their dress. But the Dutch, especially the middling sort, differ from our women, in their habit go loose,[18] wear French muches, which are like a cap and a headband in one, leaving their ears bare, which are set out with jewels of a large size and many in number. And their fingers hooped with rings, some with large stones in them of many colors, as were their pendants in their ears, which you should see very old women wear as well as young.

They have vendues very frequently and make their earnings very well by them, for they treat with good liquor liberally, and the customers drink as liberally and generally pay for't as well, by paying for that which they bid up briskly for, after the sack has gone plentifully about, though sometimes good pennyworths are got there. Their diversions in the winter is riding sleighs about three or four miles out of town, where they have houses of entertainment at a place called the Bowery, and some go to friends' houses, who handsomely treat them. Mr. Burroughs carried his spouse and daughter and myself out to one Madame Dowes, a gentlewoman that lived at a farmhouse, who gave us a handsome entertainment of five or six dishes and choice beer and metheglin,[19] cider, &c., all which she

[17]Auction.
[18]Uncorseted.
[19]An alcoholic drink made of fermented honey.

said was the produce of her farm. I believe we met 50 or 60 sleighs that day—they fly with great swiftness and some are so furious that they'll turn out of the path for none except a loaden cart. Nor do they spare for any diversion the place affords, and sociable to a degree, their tables being as free to their neighbors as to themselves.

Having here transacted the affair I went upon and some other that fell in the way, after about a fortnight's stay there I left New York with no little regret, and Thursday, December 21, set out for New Haven. . . .

Elizabeth Sampson
Sullivan Ashbridge

1713–1755

ELIZABETH SAMPSON was born in Cheshire, England. Her father, a ship's surgeon, was generally at sea; her deeply religious mother was "a pattern of virtue" to her. As a child, Elizabeth strove to be a model Christian, but she was also restless, independent-minded, and imprudent. At the age of fourteen, she eloped. Her husband died five months later, and her father barred her from his house. She stayed in Dublin with relatives of her mother's; they were Quakers, and she was repelled by their way of life. She considered converting to Catholicism, but recoiled when a priest required her to believe that non-Catholics would be damned. She decided to immigrate to Pennsylvania, where her mother's brother lived, and bound herself to go as an indentured servant, not understanding what that entailed.

In America she endured many trials from her master and her unregenerate husband (whose name, Sullivan, she never mentions in her *Account*), but finally found the religion that was right for her. She wrote her *Account* shortly after her third, happy, marriage to a Quaker, Aaron Ashbridge (1746), but it was not published until years after her death. She went on to become a well-known preacher.

BIBLIOGRAPHY
Ashbridge, Elizabeth. *Some Account of the Fore-Part of the Life of Elizabeth Ashbridge*. Nantwich, England: 1774.

from Some Account of the Fore-Part of the Life of Elizabeth Ashbridge

My life being attended with many uncommon occurrences, some of which I brought upon myself, which I believe were for my good, I have therefore thought proper to make some remarks on the dealings of Divine Goodness with me, having often had cause with David, to say, "It is good for me that I have been afflicted";[1] and I most earnestly desire that whosoever reads the following lines may take warning and shun the evils that through the deceitfulness of Satan I have been drawn into. . . .

In nine weeks from the time I left Dublin we arrived at New York, viz. on the 15 of the 7th month, 1732.[2] Now those to whom I had been instrumental to preserve life proved treacherous to me.—I was a stranger in a strange land.[3]

The captain got an indenture and demanded of me to sign it, at the same time threatening me if I refused it. I told him I could find means to satisfy him for my passage without being bound, but he told me I might take my choice: either to sign that or have the other in force which I signed in Ireland. I therefore in a fright signed the latter, and though there was no magistrate present it proved sufficient to make me a servant for four years. In two weeks time I was sold, and were it possible to convey in characters[4] a scene of the sufferings of my servitude, it would affect the most stony heart with pity for a young creature who had been so tenderly brought up. For though my father had no great estate yet he lived well, and I had been used to little but the school, though it had been better for me now if I had been brought up to greater hardships.

For a while I was pretty well used, but in a little time the scale turned, which was occasioned by a difference between my master

[1] Psalms 119:71.
[2] Quakers called the months "first month," "second month," etc. and the days of the week "first day," "second day," etc., because the conventional names are derived from those of pagan gods. According to British usage at this time, the year started in March, so the seventh month was September.
[3] Exodus 2:22.
[4] Writing.

and me, wherein I was innocent;[5] but from that time he set himself against me, and was so inhuman that he would not suffer me to have clothes to be decent in, making me to go barefoot in the snowy weather, and to be employed in the meanest drudgery, wherein I suffered the utmost hardships that my body was able to bear, and which the rest of my troubles had like to have been my ruin to all eternity, had not Almighty God interposed. My master would seem to be a religious man, often taking the Sacrament, so called, and used to pray every night in his family, except when his prayer book was lost, for he never prayed without it as I remember, but the difference was of such a kind, that I was sick of his religion. For though I had but little myself, I had an idea what sort of people they should be who professed much. But at length the enemy[6] by his insinuations made me believe there was no such a thing as religion, and that the convictions I had felt in my youth were nothing more than the prejudice of education, which convictions were at times so strong that I have gone and fallen on the ground, crying for mercy. But now I began to be hardened and for some months don't remember I felt any such thing, so that I was ready to conclude there was no God, and that all was priestcraft, I having a different opinion of those sort of men than what I had in my youth. And what corroborated with my atheistical opinion was this: my master's house used to be a place of great resort for the clergy, which gave me an opportunity of making my remarks on them; for sometimes those that came out of the country used to lodge there, and their evening diversions often was playing at cards and singing, and in a few moments after, praying and singing psalms to Almighty God. But I thought, if there be a God, he must be a pure Being and will not hear the prayers of polluted lips; for he hath in an abundant manner shown mercy to me, as will be shown in the sequel, which did not suffer me to doubt in this manner any longer. For when my feet were near the bottomless pit, he plucked me back.

I had to one woman and no other discovered[7] the occasion of this difference, and the nature of it, which two years before had happened betwixt my master and me, and by that means he heard of it,

---

[5]Probably she rejected sexual advances from him; see the reference to his wife in the following paragraph.

[6]Satan.

[7]Revealed.

and though he knew it to be true, he sent for the town whipper to correct me for it, and upon his appearing, I was called in and ordered to strip, without asking whether I deserved it or not, at which my heart was ready to burst, for I could as freely have given up my life as suffer such ignominy. And I then said, If there be a God, be graciously pleased to look down on one of the most unhappy creatures, and plead my cause, for thou knowest what I have said is the truth, and had it not been from a principle more noble than he was capable of, I would have told it before his wife. Then fixing my eyes on the barbarous man, in a flood of tears, I said to him, "Sir, if you have no pity on me, yet for my father's sake spare me from this shame" (for before this he had heard of my father several ways), "and if you think I deserve such punishment, do it yourself." He then took a turn about the room and bid the whipper go about his business, so I came off without a blow, which I thought something remarkable.

I now began to think my credit was gone, for they said several things of me which (I bless God) were not true; and here I suffered so much cruelty that I knew not how to bear it, and the enemy immediately came in and put me in a way how to get rid of it all, by tempting me to end my miserable life, which I joined with, and for that purpose went into the garret in order to hang myself, at which time I was convinced there was a God, for as my feet entered the place, horror seized me to that degree that I trembled much, and while I stood in amazement, it seemed as though I heard a voice say, "There is a hell beyond the grave," at which I was greatly astonished and convinced of an Almighty Power, to whom I prayed, saying, "God be merciful and enable me to bear whatsoever thou of thy providence shall bring or suffer to come upon me for my disobedience." I then went downstairs, but let none know what I had been about.

Soon after this I had a dream, and though some may ridicule dreams, yet this seems very significant to me; therefore I shall mention it.—I thought somebody knocked at the door, which when I had opened there stood a grave woman, holding in her right hand an oil lamp burning, who with a solid countenance fixed her eyes on me and said, "I am sent to tell thee, that if thou wilt return to the Lord thy God, he will have mercy on thee, and thy lamp shall not be put out in obscure darkness"; upon which the light flamed from the lamp in a very radiant manner and the vision left me. But oh!

alas, I did not give up to join with the heavenly vision, as I think I may call it; for, after all this, I was near being caught in another snare, which if I had, would probably have been my ruin, from which I was also preferred.[8]

I was accounted a fine singer and dancer, in which I took great delight, and once falling in company with some of the stage players, then at New York, they took a great fancy to me, as they said, and persuaded me to become an actress amongst them, and they would find means to get me from my servitude, and that I should live like a lady. The proposal took with me, and I used much pains to qualify myself for the stage, by reading plays, even when I should have slept; but after all this I found a stop in my mind, when I came to consider what my father would think when he heard of it, who had not only forgiven my disobedience in marriage, but had sent for me home, though my proud heart would not suffer me to return in so mean a condition I was then in, but rather chose bondage.

When I had served three years, I bought the remainder of my time, and got a genteel maintenance by my needle; but alas! I was not sufficiently punished by my former servitude but got into another, and that for life; for a few months after this, I married a young man, who fell in love with me for my dancing—a poor motive for a man to choose a wife, or a woman to choose a husband.

As to my part I fell in love for nothing I saw in him, and it seems unaccountable that I, who had refused several offers, both in this country and in Ireland, should at last marry a man I had no value for.

In a week after we were married, my husband, who was a school-master, removed from New York, and took me along with him to New England, and settled at a place called Westerley, in Rhode Island government. With respect to religion, he was much like myself, without any; for when he was in drink he would use the worst of oaths. I don't mention this to expose my husband, but to show the effect it had upon me, for I now saw myself ruined, as I thought, being joined to a man I had no love for, and who was a pattern of no good to me. I therefore began to think we were like two joining hands and going to destruction, which made me conclude that if I was not forsaken of God, to alter my course of life. But to love the Divine Being, and not to love my husband, I saw was an inconfi-

[8]Esteemed enough to be saved.

dency,[9] and seemed impossible; therefore I requested, with tears, that my affections might increase towards my husband, and I can say in truth that my love was sincere to him. I now resolved to do my duty towards God, and expecting that I must come to the knowledge of it by reading the Scriptures, I read them with a strong resolution of following their directions; but the more I read the more uneasy I grew, especially about baptism, for although I had reason to believe I was sprinkled in my infancy, because at the age of fourteen I passed under the bishop's hands for confirmation, as it is called, yet I could not find any precedent for that practice, and upon reading where it is said, he that believes and is baptized, etc.,[10] I observed that belief went before baptism, which I was not capable of when I was sprinkled, at which I grew very uneasy, and living in a neighborhood that were mostly Seventh Day Baptists, I conversed with them, and at length thinking it to be really my duty, I was baptized by one of their teachers, but did not join strictly with them, though I began to think the seventh-day[11] the true sabbath, and for some time kept it as such. My husband did not yet oppose me, for he saw I grew more affectionate to him, but I did not yet leave off singing and dancing so much, but I could divert him whenever he desired it.

Soon after this my husband and I concluded to go for England, and for that purpose went to Boston, where we found a ship bound for Liverpool, and agreed for our passage, expecting to sail in two weeks. But my time was not yet come, for there came one called a gentleman, who hired the ship to carry him and his attendants to Philadelphia and to take no other passengers. There being no other ship near sailing, we for that time gave it over.

We stayed several weeks at Boston, and I remained still dissatisfied as to religion, though I had reformed my conduct so as to be accounted by those that knew me a sober woman. But that was not sufficient; for even then I expected to find the sweets of such a change, and though several thought me religious, I dared not to think myself so, and what to do to be so, I seemed still an utter stranger to. I used to converse with people of all societies, as opportunity offered,

[9]Inconsistency (?).

[10]"He that believeth and is baptized shall be saved; but he that believeth not shall be damned" (Mark 16:16). She could not have been confirmed in the Church of England unless she had been baptized (as an infant). She now believes that baptism is effectual only for those old enough to understand.

[11]Saturday.

and, like many others, had got a deal of head knowledge, and several societies thought me of their opinion, but I joined strictly with none, resolving never to leave searching till I found the TRUTH. This was in the 22d year of my age.

While we were at Boston, I went one day to the Quakers' meeting, not expecting to find what I wanted, but from a motive of curiosity. At this meeting there was a woman spoke, at which I was a little surprised, for I had never heard one before. I looked on her with pity for her ignorance, and in contempt of her practice said to myself, "I am sure you're a fool, for if ever I should turn Quaker, which will never be, I could not be a preacher." In these and such like thoughts I sat while she was speaking. After she had done, there stood up a man, which I could better bear; he spoke well, as I thought, from good Joshua's resolutions, viz., "As for me and my house we will serve the Lord."[12] After a time of silence he went to prayer, which was attended with something so awful[13] and affecting that I was reduced to tears, yet a stranger to the cause.

Soon after this we left Boston, for my husband was given to ramble, which was very disagreeable to me; but I must submit. We went to Rhode Island, where he hired a place to keep a school. This place was mostly inhabited with Presbyterians, where I soon got acquainted with some of the most religious amongst them; for though I was poor, I was favored with respect amongst people of the best credit and had frequent discourses with them, but the more I was acquainted with their principles, the worse I liked them, so that I remained dissatisfied, and the old enemy of my happiness,[14] knowing I was resolved to abandon him, assaulted me afresh and laid a bait with which I had like to have been caught. For one day having been abroad, at my return home, I found the people, at whose house we had taken a room, had left some flax in an apartment through which I went to my own, at sight of which I was tempted to steal some to make some thread; and I went and took a small bunch in my hand, at which I was smote with remorse and immediately laid it down, saying, "Lord help me from such a vile act as this." But the twisting serpent did not leave me yet, his assaults were so strong and prevalent that I took it into my room; when I came there horror seized

[12]Joshua 24:15.
[13]Awe-inspiring.
[14]Satan.

me, and bursting into tears, I cried, "O God of mercy; enable me to resist this temptation," which he of his mercy did, and gave me power to say, "I will regard thy convictions." So I carried it back, and returning to my room, I was so filled with thanksgiving to God, and rapt into such a frame as I have not words to express, neither can any guess but those who have resisted temptation and tasted of the same sweet peace by experience.

Soon after this my husband hired[15] a place further up the island, where we were nearer a Church of England, to which place I used to go, for though I disliked some of their ways, yet I approved of them the best.

At this time a new exercise[16] fell upon me, and of such a sort as I had never heard of before, and while I was under it I thought myself alone.—It was in the 2nd month of the year.[17] I was sitting by a fire in company with several persons, amongst whom my husband was one; there arose a thunder gust, and with the noise that struck my ear, a voice attending, even as the sound of a mighty trumpet piercing through me with these words: "Oh, eternity! eternity! the endless term of long eternity!" at which I was exceedingly surprised and sat speechless as in a trance, and in a moment saw myself in such a state as made me despair of ever being happy. I seemed to behold a roll, wrote in black characters, at sight of which I heard a voice say, "These are thy sins"; and immediately followed another saying: "the Blood of Christ is not sufficient to wash them away, and this is shown thee that thou mayst confess thy damnation is just, and not in order that they should be forgiven thee."

All this while I sat speechless, but at last I got up trembling, and threw myself upon a bed. The company thought my indisposition proceeded only from the fright of the thunder, but oh! alas, it was of another kind, and from that time for several months I was in the utmost despair, for if I at any time did endeavor to hope or lay hold of a gracious promise, the old amuser would come in telling me it was now too late, that I had withstood the day of mercy, and that I should add to my sins by praying for pardon and provoke the Divine Vengeance to make a monument of wrath of me.

I now was like one already in torment. My sleep departed from

[15]Engaged himself for.
[16]Spiritual trial.
[17]April.

me, I ate little, became extremely melancholy, and took no delight in anything. Had this world been mine and the glory of it, I would gladly have given it for a glimpse of hope. My husband was shocked to see me so changed. I that once could divert him with a song, in which he took great delight—nay after I grew religious as to the outward form, and till I could do it no longer. But now my singing was turned into mourning, and my dancing into lamentations; for my nights and days were one continual scene of sorrow. I let none know my desperate condition. My husband used all means to divert my melancholy state, but all in vain; the wound was too deep to be healed with anything short of the true Balm of Gilead. I durst not go much alone for fear of evil spirits, but if I would, my husband would not suffer it, and if I took the Bible he would take it from me, saying, "How you are altered; you used to be agreeable company, but now I have no comfort of you." I endeavored to bear all with patience, expecting soon to bear more than man could inflict upon me.

At length I went to a priest to see if he could relieve me, but he was a stranger to my condition, and advised me to take the Sacrament and to use some innocent diversions, and sent me a book of prayers which he said was for my condition. But all was in vain. As to the Sacrament, I thought myself in a state very unfit to receive it worthily, and I then could not use my prayers, for I thought that if ever my prayers should be acceptable, I should be enabled to pray without a book, and diversions were burdensome, for as I said, my husband used all means tending that way to no purpose. Yet he with some others once persuaded me to the raising of a building, where much people were got, in hopes of diverting my grief. But instead of relief, it added to my sorrow; for to this place came an officer to summon a jury to inquire concerning the body of a man that had hanged himself, which as soon as I understood, it seemed to be attended with a voice, saying, "Thou shalt be the next monument of wrath, for thou art not worthy to die a natural death."

For two months after this, I was daily tempted to destroy myself, and sometimes the temptation was so strong I could scarce resist, through fear of which, when I went alone I used to throw off my apron and garters, and if I had a knife, to cast it from me, crying, "Lord keep me from taking away that life thou gave me, and which thou wouldst have made happy, if I had joined with the offers of thy grace and had regarded the convictions I've had from my youth—

the fault is my own, thou, O Lord, clear." And yet so great was my agony that I desired death, that I might know the worst of my torments; all this while I was so hardened that I could not shed a tear. But God in his own good time delivered my soul out of this thralldom.

For one night as I lay in my bed, my husband by me asleep, bemoaning my miserable condition, I had strength to cry, "O my God, had thou no mercy left? Look down I beseech thee for Christ's sake, who has promised that all manner of sin and blasphemy shall be forgiven. Therefore, Lord, if thou wilt graciously please to extend this promise to me, an unworthy creature trembling before thee, there is nothing thou shalt command, but I will obey." In an instant my heart tendered and dissolved into a flood of tears, abhorring my past offenses, and admiring the mercies of God; for I was made to hope in Christ my redeemer, and enabled to look upon him with an eye of faith, and saw fulfilled what I believed when the priest lent me his book, that if ever my prayers would be acceptable to God, I should be enabled to pray without form,[18] and so used it no more. Nevertheless I thought to join with some religious society, but met with none that I liked in everything. Yet the Church of England seemed nearest, upon which I joined with them and received the Sacrament, so called, and can say in truth that I did it with reverence and fear.

Being thus released from deep distress, I seemed like another creature, and went often alone without fear, and tears flowed abundantly from my eyes; and once as I was abhorring myself, in great humility of mind, I heard a gracious voice say, "I will not forsake thee, only obey what I shall make known unto thee." I then entered into covenant, saying, "My soul doth magnify thee, the God of mercy; if thou will vouchsafe thy Grace, the rest of my days shall be devoted to thee, and if it be thy will that I beg my bread, I will be content and submit to thy Providence."

I now began to think of my relations in Pennsylvania, whom I had not yet seen, and having a great desire to see them, I got leave of my husband to go, and also a certificate from the priest, in order that if I made any stay, I might be received as a member wherever I came. Then setting out, my husband bore me company to the Blazing Star Ferry, saw me safe over, and then returned. In the way near

[18]Without reading from a prayer book.

a place called Maidenhead, I fell from my horse and was disabled from traveling for some time and abode at the house of an honest Dutchman, who with his wife was very kind to me, and though they had much trouble in going to the doctor and waiting upon me, for I was several days unable to help myself yet would have nothing for it, which I thought very kind, and charged me, if ever I came that way again, to call and lodge there. I mention this because I shall have occasion to remark this place again.

I arrived next at Trent town [Trenton] Ferry, where I met with no small mortification upon hearing that my relations were Quakers, and, what was worst of all, my aunt was a preacher. I was sorry to hear of it, for I was exceedingly prejudiced against those people and have often wondered with what face they could call themselves Christians; and I began to repent my coming, sometimes having a mind to return back without seeing them. At last I concluded to go see them, since I was so far on my journey, though I expected little comfort from my visit. But see how God brings unforeseen things to pass, for by my going there I was brought to the knowledge of the TRUTH.

I went from Trent town to Philadelphia by water, and thence to my uncle's on horseback, where I met with a very kind reception; for though my own uncle was dead and my aunt married again, yet both she and her husband received me in a very kind manner. I had not been there three hours before I met with a shock, and my opinion began to alter with respect to these people; for seeing a book lie on the table and being much given to reading, I took it up, which my aunt observing, said, "Cousin, that is a Quaker's book, Samuel Crisp's *Two Letters*,"[19] and I suppose she thought I should not like it, at perceiving that I was not one. I made her no answer, but thought to myself, What can these people write about, for I have heard that they deny the Scripture, and have no other bible but George Fox's *Journal*,[20] and that they deny all the holy ordinances. For I resolved to read a little, and had not read two pages before my very heart burned within me, and tears came into my eyes, which I was afraid would be seen. I therefore walked with the book into the

[19]Samuel Crisp, *Two Letters . . . upon His Change from a Chaplain of the Church of England, to Join with the People Called Quakers* (written c. 1702, many editions).

[20]George Fox, founder of the Society of Friends (Quakers), recounted his spiritual experiences in his *Journal*.

garden, and the piece being small, read it through before I went in, and sometimes uttering these involuntary expressions: "My God, if ever I come to the true knowledge of the truth, must I be of this man's opinion, who has fought thee as I have done, and join with these people that I preferred the Papists to, but a [few] hours ago. Oh! Thou the God of my salvation and of my life, who hast in an abundant manner manifested thy long-suffering and tender mercy in redeeming me as from the lowest hell, a monument of thy grace. Lord, my soul beseeches thee to direct me in the right way, and keep me from error; and then according to my covenant, I'll think nothing too near to part with for thy name's sake, if these things be so. Oh! happy people thus beloved of God."

After I came a little to myself I washed my face, lest any in the house should perceive I had been weeping. At night I got very little sleep, for the old enemy began to suggest that I was one of those that wavered and was not steadfast in the faith, advancing several texts of Scripture against me, and them that mention, in the latter days there shall be those that will deceive the very elect,[21] and these people were them, and that I was in danger of being deluded. Here the subtle serpent transformed himself so hiddenly that I verily thought this to be a timely caution from a good angel, so resolved to beware of these deceivers, and for some weeks did not touch any of their books.

The next day, being the first of the week,[22] I wanted to have gone to church, which was distant about four miles, but being a stranger and having nobody to go with me was forced to give it up, and as most of the family was going to meeting, I went with them. But with this conclusion: not to like them. And so it was; for as they sat in silence, I looked over the meeting, thinking within myself, how like fools these people sit, how much better were it to stay at home and read the Bible, or some good book, than to come here and go to sleep; for I, being very sleepy, thought they were no better than me. Indeed, at length I fell asleep and had like to have fallen down, but this was the last time I ever fell asleep in a meeting, though often assaulted with it.

[21]"For there shall arise false Christs, and false prophets, and shall show great signs and wonders; insomuch that, if it were possible, they shall deceive the very elect" (Matthew 24:24).
[22]Sunday, which Quakers called "first-day."

I now began to be lifted up with spiritual pride and thought myself better than they, but through mercy this did not last long; for in a little time I was brought low, and saw that they were the people to whom I must join. It may seem strange that I, who had lived so long with one of this society in Dublin, should yet be so great a stranger to them. In answer, let it be considered that, during the time I was there, I never read one of their books or went to one meeting, and besides, I had heard such ridiculous stories of them as made me think they were the worst of any society of people. But God that knew the sincerity of my heart looked with pity on my weakness, and soon let me see my error; for in a few weeks there was an afternoon's meeting held at my uncle's, to which came that servant of the Lord William Hammons, who was then made instrumental in convincing me of the TRUTH more perfectly and helping me over some great doubts, though I believe no one did ever sit in greater opposition than I did when he first stood up. But I was soon brought down, for he preached the Gospel with such power that I was forced to give up and confess it was the TRUTH.

As soon as meeting was ended, I endeavored to get alone, for I was not fit to be seen, being so broken; yet afterwards the restless adversary assaulted me again in the manner following. The morning before this meeting I had been disputing with my uncle about Babylon, which was the subject this good man was upon and which he handled so clearly as to answer all my scruples beyond objection. Yet the crooked serpent farther alleged that the sermon I had heard did not proceed from Divine Revelation, but that my uncle and aunt had acquainted the Friend[23] of me, which being strongly suggested, I fell to accusing them of it, and of which they both cleared themselves, saying they had not seen him since my coming to these parts until he came to the meeting.

I then concluded he was a messenger sent from God to me, and with fervent cries desired I might be directed right. And now I laid aside all prejudice and set my heart to receive TRUTH, and the Lord in his own good time revealed to my soul not only the beauty there is in it, and that those should shine who continued faithful to it, but also the emptiness of all shadows, which in their way were glorious, but now the Son of Glory was come to put an end to them all and establish everlasting righteousness in the room thereof, which is a

[23]I.e., Hammons.

work in the soul. He likewise let me see that all I had gone through was to prepare me for this day, and that the time was near that he would require me to go forth and declare to others what the God of mercy had done for my soul; at which I was surprised and desired I might be excused, for fear I should bring dishonor to the TRUTH, and cause his holy Name to be evil spoken of.

All this while I did not let anybody know the condition I was in, nor did appear like a Friend,[24] and feared a discovery. I now began to think of returning to my husband, but found a restraint to stay where I was. I then hired a place to keep a school, and, hearing of a place for him, wrote desiring him to come to me, but let him know nothing how it was with me.

I loved to go to meetings, but did not like to be seen to go on weekdays, and therefore to shun it used to go from my school through the woods to them. But notwithstanding all my care, the neighbors that were not Friends soon began to revile, calling me Quaker, saying they supposed I intended to be a fool and turn preacher. I then received the same censure that I, a little above a year before, had passed on one of the handmaids of the Lord at Boston; and so weak was I, alas, I could not bear the reproach, and in order to change their opinions got in to greater excess in apparel than I had freedom to wear for some time before I became acquainted with Friends. In this condition I continued till my husband came, and then began the trial of my faith. Before he reached me, he heard I was turned Quaker, at which he stamped, saying, "I had rather have heard she had been dead, well as I love her, for if so all my comfort is gone." He then came to me, and had not seen me for four months; I got up and met him, saying, "My dear, I am glad to see thee," at which he fell in a great passion, and said, "The devil THEE thee, don't THEE me." I used all the mild means I could to pacify him, and at length got him fit to go and speak to my relations; but he was alarmed, and as soon as he got alone he said, "So I see your Quaker relations have made you one." I told him they had not, which was true, nor had I ever told them how it was with me. But he would have it that I was one, and therefore should not stay amongst them, and having found a place to his mind, hired it, and came directly back to fetch me, and in one afternoon walked near thirty miles to keep me from meeting, the next day being the first-

[24]Adopt Quaker dress.

day, and on the morrow took me to the aforesaid place, hired lodgings at a Church-man's house, who was one of the wardens and a bitter enemy to Friends, and would tell me a great deal of ridiculous stuff. But my judgment was too clearly convinced to believe. I still did not appear like a Friend, but they all believed I was one. When my husband and him used to be making their diversions and revilings, I used to sit in silence; but now and then an involuntary sigh would break from me, at which he would say to my husband, "There, did not I tell you your wife was a Quaker, and she will be a preacher soon," upon which my husband once in a great rage came up to me, and striking his hand over me said, "You had better be hanged on that day." I then, Peter like,[25] in a panic denied my being a Quaker, at which great horror seized upon me, and continued for near three months, so that I again feared that by denying the Lord who bought me the heavens were shut against me; for great darkness surrounded me, and I was again plunged in despair.

I used to walk much alone in the woods, where no eye saw, or ear heard me, and there lamented my miserable condition, and have often gone from morning till night without breaking my fast, with which I was brought so low that my life was a burden to me. The devil seemed to vaunt [that although] the sins [of] my youth were forgiven, yet now he was sure of me, for that I had committed the unpardonable sin, and hell would inevitably be my portion, and my torments would be greater than if I had hanged myself at the first.

In this doleful condition I had now to bewail my misery, and even in the night, when I could not sleep, under the painful distress of my mind. And if my husband perceived me weeping he used to revile me for it. At last, when he and his friends thought themselves too weak to overset me, though I feared it was already done, he went to the priest at Chester to advise what to do with me. This man knew I was a member of the Church, for I had shown him my certificate. His advice was to take me out of Pennsylvania and find some place where there was no Quakers, and there my opinion would wear off. To this my husband agreed, saying he did not care where he went, if he could but restore me to that liveliness of temper I was naturally of, and to that Church of which I was a member. I, on my part, had no spirit to oppose their proposals, neither much cared where I was; for I seemed to have nothing to hope for, but daily expected to be

---

[25]In fear of being arrested, Peter denied Christ three times (Mark 14:66–72).

made a spectacle of Divine Wrath, and I was possessed it would be by thunder.

The time of removal came, and I was not suffered to bid my relations farewell. My husband was poor and kept no horse, so I must travel on foot. We came to Wilmington, fifteen miles thence to Philadelphia, by water; here he took me to a tavern, where I soon became a spectacle and discourse of the company. My husband told them his wife was turned Quaker, and that he designed, if possible, to find out some place where there was none. Oh, thought I, I was once in condition of deserving that name, but now it was over with me. Oh, that I might, from a true hope, once more have an opportunity to confess to the TRUTH, though sure of all manner of cruelties, yet I would not regard it. These were my concerns while he was entertaining the company with my story, in which he told them that I had been a good dancer, but now he could neither get me to dance nor sing; upon which one of the company starts up, saying, "I'll go fetch my fiddle and we'll have a dance," at which my husband was pleased. The fiddle came, the sight of which put me in a sad condition, for fear, if I refused, my husband would be in a great passion. However I took up this resolution not to comply, whatever might be the consequence. He came to me and took me by the hand, saying, "Come, my dear, shake off that gloom, let's have a civil dance; you would now and then, when you were a good Church-woman and that is better than a stiff Quaker." I, trembling, desired to be excused. But he insisted on it, and knowing his temper to be exceeding choleric, I durst not say much, but would not consent. He then pulled me round the room till tears affected my eyes, at sight of which the musician stopped, and said, "I'll play no more, let your wife alone," of which I was glad. There was also a man in company who came from Freehold, in West Jersey, who said, "I see your wife is a Quaker, but if you'll take my advice, you need not go so far (for my husband designed to go to Staten Island); come and live amongst us and we'll soon cure her from her Quakerism, and we want both a school-master and mistress." To which he agreed, and a happy turn it was for me, as will be seen by and by, and the wonderful turn of Providence, who had not yet abandoned me, but raised a glimmering hope and afforded the answer of peace in refusing to dance, for which I was more rejoiced than if I were made a mistress of much riches; and in floods of tears, said, "Lord, I dread to ask, and yet without thy gracious pardon I am miserable; I therefore fall down before thy throne, imploring mercy at thy hand. O Lord, once more I beseech thee try my obedience, and then whatsoever thou commands, I will obey, and not fear to confess thee before men." Thus was my soul engaged before God in sincerity, and he of his tender mercy heard my cries, and in me has shown that he delights not in the death of a sinner, for he again set my soul at liberty and I could praise him.

I now again longed for an opportunity to confess to his TRUTH, which he showed me should come, though in what manner I did not see, but believed the words I had heard, which in a little time were fulfilled to me. My husband, as aforesaid, agreed to go to Freehold, and in our way thither came to Maidenhead, where I went to see the kind Dutchman, aforementioned, who made us welcome and invited us to stay a few days. While we were there, there was held a great meeting of the Presbyterians, not only of worship, but business also; for one of their preachers being charged with drunkenness was this day to have his trial before a great number of priests, and we went to it, of which I was afterwards glad; for here I perceived great divisions amongst the people about who should be their shepherd, and for which I greatly pitied their condition. I now saw beyond the men-made ministers, and what they preached for, and which all those at this meeting might have done, had not the prejudice of education, which is very prevalent, blinded their eyes. Some insisted to have the old offender restored; some to have a young man they had upon trial some weeks; a third party was for sending for one from New England. At length one stood up, and, addressing himself to the chief speaker, said, "Sir, when we have been at the expense, which will be no small matter, of fetching this gentleman from New England, perhaps he won't stay with us." "Don't you know how to make him?" "No, Sir." "I'll tell you then," said he, to which I gave good attention: "Give him a good salary, and I'll engage he'll stay." O, thought I, these mercenary creatures, they are actuated by one and the same thing, ever the love of money, and not the regard of souls. This, [so-]called reverend gentleman, whom these poor people almost adored, to my knowledge had left his flock on Long Island and moved to Philadelphia, where he could get more money. I myself had heard some of them on the Island say that they had almost impoverished themselves to keep him, but not being able to equal Philadelphia's invitation, he left them without a shepherd. This man therefore, knowing their ministry proceeded from one cause, might be purchased with the same thing.—Surely these and such like are the shepherds that regard the fleece more than the flock, and in whose mouth are lies, saying the Lord hath sent them, and that they were Christ's ambassadors, whose command to those he sent was "Freely ye have received, freely give."[26] I durst not say anything to my husband of the remarks I had made, but laid them up in my heart, and they did help to strengthen me in my resolutions.

Hence we set forward for Freehold, and coming through Stony Brook, my husband turning towards me said tauntingly, "There's one of Satan's Synagogues, don't you want to be in it? I hope I shall see you carried off [by] this new religion." I made no answer but went on. In a little time we came to a large run of water, over which was no bridge, and we being strangers knew no way to get over. But through we was obliged to go. My husband carried our clothes, which we had in bundles, and I pulled off my shoes and waded through in my stockings, which served somewhat to prevent the chill of the water from [freezing] me, it being very cold and a fall of snow, in the 12th month.[27] My heart was concerned in prayer that the Lord would sanctify all my afflictions to me, and give me patience to bear whatsoever should be suffered to come upon me.

We walked most part of a mile before we came to a house, which proved to be a sort of tavern. My husband called for some spirituous liquors, but I got some cider mulled, which when I had drank of 't, the cold being struck to my heart made me extremely sick, insomuch that when we were a little past the house I expected I should have fainted, and not being able to stand, fell down under a fence. Which my husband observing, tauntingly said, "What's the matter now? what, are you drunk? where's your religion now?" He knew better, and at that time I believed he pitied me, yet was suffered grievously to afflict me. In a little time I grew better, and going on came to another tavern, at which place we lodged. The next day I was indifferent well, and as we proceeded on our journey a young man with an empty cart overtook us, and I desired my husband to ask the young man to let us ride, which he did, and it was readily granted. I now thought myself well off, and took it as a great favor, for my proud heart was humbled, and I did not regard the looks of it, though the time had been that I would not have been seen in a cart. This

[26]Matthew 10:8.
[27]February.

cart belonged to a man at Shrewsbury and was to go through the place that we were going to, so we rode on. We soon had the care of the team to ourselves, from a failure in the driver, to the place where I was intended to have been made a prey on. But see how unforeseen things are brought to pass by a providential hand. It is said and answered, Shall we do evil that good may come? God forbid.[28] Yet hence good came to me. Here my husband would fain have me stay, while he went to see the team safe at home, but I told him no, since he had led me through the country like a vagabond, I would not stay behind him; so we went on, and lodged that night at the man's house who owned the cart. Next day on our return to Freehold, we met a man riding full speed, who stopped, and said to my husband, "Sir, are you a school-master?" and was answered yes. "I came to tell you," replied the stranger, "of the two new school houses, and each want a master and are two miles apart." How this stranger came to hear of us, who came but the night before, I never knew; but I was glad he was not one called a Quaker, lest my husband should have thought it had been a plot. I said to my husband, "My dear, look on me with pity. If thou hast any affections left for me, which I hope thou hast, for I am not conscious of having done anything to alienate them here, here is," continued I, "an opportunity to settle us both, and I am willing to do all in my power towards an honest livelihood."

My expressions took place, and after a little pause he consented to the young man's directions and made towards the place, and in our way we came to the house of a worthy Friend, whose wife was a preacher, though we did not know it. I was surprised to see the people so kind to us, who were strangers. We had not been long in the house before we were invited to lodge there that night, it being the last of the week. I said nothing, but waited to hear my master speak. He soon consented, saying, "My wife has had a tedious travel, and I pity her," at which kind expressions I was greatly affected, for they were now very seldom used to me.

The Friends' kindness could not have proceeded from my appearing in the garb of a Quaker, for I had not yet altered my dress; but the woman of the house, after we had concluded to stay, fixed her eyes on me and said, "I believe thou hast met with a deal of troubles," to which I made but little answer. My husband, observing

[28]Romans 6:1–2 (paraphrased).

they were of that sort of people he had so much endeavored to shun, would give us no opportunity for any discourse that night; but the next morning I let the Friend know a little how it was with me. Meeting time came, to which I longed to go, but durst not ask my husband leave, for fear of disturbing him, till we were settled; and then, thought I, if ever I am favored to be in this place, come life or death, I'll fight through, for my salvation is at stake. The Friends, getting ready for meeting, asked my husband if he would go, saying they knew who were to be his employers, and if they were at meeting, they would speak to them. He then consented to go. "Then," said the woman, "Friend, and wilt thou let thy wife go?" to which he denied, making several objections, all which she answered so prudently, that he could not be angry and at last he consented. With joy I went, for I had not been at one for near 4 months, and an heavenly meeting it was to me. I now renewed my covenant, and saw the word of the Lord made good, that I should have another opportunity to confess to his name, for which, "My soul did magnify the Lord, and my spirit did rejoice in the God of my salvation,"[29] who had brought strange things to pass. May I ever be preserved in humility, never forgetting his tender mercies to me.

Here, according to my desire, we settled; my husband got one school and I the other. We took a room at a Friend's house, a mile from each school, and eight miles from the meeting-house. Before the next first-day we were got to our new settlement, and now I concluded to let my husband see that I was determined to join with Friends. When the first-day came, I directed myself to him in this manner: "My dear, art thou willing to let me go to meeting?" at which he fell into a rage, saying, "No, you shan't." I then drew up a resolution and told him that as a dutiful wife ought, so was I ready to obey all his commands; but where they imposed on my conscience I no longer durst, for I had already done it too long, and had wronged myself by it, and though he was near and I loved him as a wife ought, yet God was nearer than all the world to me, and had made me sensible this was the way I ought to go, which I assured him was no small cross to my own will. Yet I had given up my heart, and hoped he that had called for it would enable me the residue of my life to keep it steadily devoted to him whatever I suffered, adding I hoped not to make him any worse a wife for it. But all I could say

[29]Luke 1:46–47.

was in vain. I had now put my hand to the plow and resolved not to look back, so went without leave, but expected to be immediately followed and forced back. He did not follow me as I expected, so I went to a neighbor's and got a girl to show me the way; and then went on rejoicing and praising God in my heart, who had thus far given me power and another opportunity to confess to the TRUTH.

Thus for some time I had to go eight miles on foot to meeting, which I never thought hard. My husband now bought a horse, but would not let me ride him; neither when my shoes were wore out would he let me have a new pair, thinking by that means to keep me from meetings. But this did not hinder me, for I have taken strings and tied round to keep them on. He now finding no hard usage could alter my resolution, neither threatening to beat me, nor denying it, for he several times struck me with sore blows which I endeavored to bear with patience, believing the time would come when he would see I was in the right, which accordingly [he] did. He once came up to me and took out his penknife, saying, "If you offer to go to meeting tomorrow, with this knife I'll cripple you, for you shall not be a Quaker." I made him no answer, but when morning came I set out as usual, and he was not suffered to hurt me.

In despair of recovering me himself, he now fled to the priest for help and told him that I had been a very religious woman in the way of the Church of England, was a member of it, and had a good certificate from Long Island, but now was bewitched and turned Quaker, which almost broke his heart. He therefore desired, as he was one who had the care of souls, he would come and pay me a visit and use his best endeavors to reclaim me, and he hoped by the blessing of God it would be done.

The priest consented to come, and the time was fixed, which was to be that day two weeks, for he said he could not come sooner. My husband came home extremely pleased, and told me of it, at which I smiled and said, "I hope to be enabled to give a reason for the hope that is in me," at the same time believing the priest would never trouble me, nor he never did. Before this appointed time came, it was required of me in a more public manner to confess to the world what I was, and to give up in prayer at the meeting. The sight of which and the power that attended it made me tremble, and I could not hold myself still. I now again desired death and could have freely given up my natural life as ransom. And what made it harder for me, I was not taken under the care of Friends; and what kept me from requesting it was for fear I should be overcome, and bring a scandal on the Society. I begged to be excused till I was joined, and then I would give up freely, to which I received this answer, as though I had heard a distinct voice: "I am a covenant-keeping God, and the words that I spoke to thee when I found thee in distress, even that I would never leave thee, nor forsake thee, if thou wouldst be obedient to what I should make known to thee, which I will assuredly make good; but if thou refuse, my Spirit shall not always strive. Fear not, I will make way for thee through all thy difficulties, which shall be many, for my name's sake; but be faithful, and I will give thee a crown of life." I then, being sure it was God that spoke, said, "Thy will, O God, be done; I am in thy hand, do with me according to thy word." And I gave up, but after it was over the enemy came in like a flood, telling me I had done what I ought not, and should now bring dishonor to this people. But this shock did not last long.

This day, as usual, I had gone on foot. My husband, as he afterwards told me, lying on the bed, these words ran through him, "Lord, where shall I fly to shun thee," at which he arose, and seeing it rain, got the horse and came to fetch me, and coming just as the meeting broke up, I got on horseback as quick as possible, lest he should hear what had happened. Nevertheless he had heard, and as soon as we were got into the woods he began, saying, "What do you mean thus to make my life unhappy? could you not be a Quaker without turning fool after this manner?" I answered in tears, saying, "My dear, look on me with pity, if thou hast any; can'st thou think that I in the bloom of my days would bear all that thou knowest of, and a great deal which thou knowest not of, if I did not believe it to be my duty?" This took hold of him, and he, taking my hand, said, "Well, I'll even give you up, for I see it don't avail to strive. If it be of God, I cannot overthrow it, and if it be of yourself it will soon fall"; and I saw the tears stand in his eyes, at which my heart was overcome with joy, and I would not have changed conditions with a queen. I already began to reap the fruit of my obedience, but my trials did not end here. The time being up that the priest was to come, but no priest appeared, my husband went to fetch him; but he would not come, saying he was busy and could not, which so displeased my husband that he'd never go near him more, and for some time went to no place of worship.

Now the unwearied adversary found out another scheme, and with it assaulted me so strong that I thought all I had gone through was but little to this. It came upon me in such an unexpected manner, I hearing a woman relate a book she had read, in which it was asserted that Christ was not the Son of God. As soon as she had spoke the words, if a man had spoke I could not more distinctly have heard these words, "No more he is, it's all a fancy, and the contrivance of man"; and an horror of great darkness fell upon me, which continued for three weeks. The exercise I was in I am not able to express, neither durst I let any one know how it was with me. I again sought desolate places, where I might make my moan, and have lain whole nights and don't know that my eyes have been shut to sleep. I again thought myself alone, but would never let go my faith in him, after saying in my heart, I'll believe till I die, and keep a hope that he who delivered me out of the paw of the bear and from the jaws of the devouring lion would in his own good time deliver me out of this temptation also, which he of his mercy did, and let me see this was for my good in order to prepare me for further service, which he had for me to do, and that it was necessary that his ministers should be dipped into all states, that thereby they might be abler to speak to all, for which my soul was thankful to him, the God of mercies, who had at several times redeemed me out of great distress. And I found the truth of his words that all things should work for good to those that loved and feared him, which I did with my whole heart, and I hope ever shall while I have a being.

This happened soon after my first appearance, and Friends had not been to talk with me, nor did they know what to do till I had appeared again, which was not for some time, when at the monthly meeting, four Friends came to pay me a visit, which I was glad of, and gave them such satisfaction that they left me well satisfied. I then joined with Friends; my husband went to no place of worship. One day he said, "I'd go to meeting, only I'm afraid I shall hear your clack, which I cannot bear." I used no persuasions, yet when meeting-time came he got the horse and took me behind him and went to meeting. But for several months, if he saw me offer to rise,[30] he would go out, till one time I got up before he was aware, and then, as he afterwards said, was ashamed to do it, and from that time never did nor hindered me from going to meeting; and though he, poor man, could not take up the Cross, yet his judgment was convinced, and sometimes in a flood of tears would say, "My dear, I've

[30]Stand up to speak.

seen the beauty there is in the TRUTH, and that thou art in the right, and I pray God preserve thee in it, but as for me the Cross is too heavy, I cannot bear it." I told him I hoped he that had given me strength would also favor him. "Oh!" said he, "I can't bear the reproach thou dost to be called turn-coat, and become a laughing stock to the world. But I'll no longer hinder thee from it"; which I looked on as a great favor that my way was thus far made easy, and a little hope remained that my prayers would be heard on his account.

In this place he had got linked in with some that he was afraid would make game of him, which indeed they already did, asking him when he designed to commence preacher, for that they saw he intended to turn Quaker, and seemed to love his wife better since she did than before. We were now got to a little house by ourselves, which though mean, and little to put in it, our bed being no better than chaff, yet I was truly content, and did not envy the rich their riches. The only desires I now had was my own persuasion, and to be blessed with the reformation of my husband. These men used to come to our house and there provoke my husband to sit up and drink sometimes till near day, while I have been sorrowing in a stable. As I once sat in this condition, I heard my husband say to his company, "I cannot bear any longer to afflict my poor wife in this manner, for whatever you may think of her, I do believe she is a good woman"; upon which he came to me and said, "Come in, my dear, God has given thee a deal of patience; I'll put an end to this practice." And so he did, for this was the last time they sat up at nights. My husband now thought if he was in any place where it was not known that he had been so bitter against Friends, he could do better than here; but I was much against his moving, fearing it would turn out to his hurt, having been for some months much altered for the better, establishing me in the TRUTH, and therefore would not have him be afflicted about that, and according to the measure of Grace received did what I could both by example and advice for his good; and my advice was for him to fight through it here, fearing he would grow weaker, and the enemy gain advantage over him, if he thus fled. But all I could say did not prevail against his moving, and hearing of a place at Burdon Town [Bordentown], [he] went there. But that did not suit. He then moved to Mount Holy [Holly], and there we settled. He got a good school and so did I, and here we might have done very well. We got our house pretty well furnished for poor folks. I now began to think I wanted but one thing to complete my happiness, viz. the reformation of my husband, which also I had too much reason to doubt, for it fell out according to my fears, and he grew worse here, and took to drinking, so that it seemed as though my life was to be a continual scene of sorrow; and most earnestly I prayed to Almighty God, to endue me with patience to bear my afflictions and submit to his providence, which I can say in truth I did without murmuring, or ever uttering an unsavory expression, to the best of my knowledge, except once when my husband coming home a little in drink, in which frame he was very fractious, and finding me at work by a candle, came to me, put it out, and fetching me a box on the ear said, "You don't earn your light," which unkind usage—for he had not struck me of two years before—went hard with me, and I uttered these rash expressions, "Thou art a vile man," and was a little angry, but soon recovered and was sorry for it. He struck me again, which I received without so much as a word in return, and [he] went on in a distracted manner, uttering several rash expressions that bespoke despair, as that he now believed he was predestined to damnation, and he did not care how soon God would strike him dead and the like. I durst say but little, but at length I broke out in these words, "Lord look down on my afflictions, and deliver me by some means or other." I was answered I should soon be, and so I was, but in such a manner as I verily believed it would have killed me.

In a little time he went to Burlington, where he got in drink and enlisted for a common soldier to go to Cuba, anno dom. 1740. I had drank many bitter cups, but this seemed to exceed them all; for indeed my very senses seemed shaken. I now a thousand times blamed myself for making such an undevised[31] request, fearing I had displeased God by it, and though he had granted it, it was in displeasure and suffered to be in this manner to punish me. But I can say I never desired his death more than my own, nay not so much. I have since had cause to believe his mind was benefited by the undertaking, which hope makes up for all I have suffered from him, being informed that he did in the army what he could not do at home, viz. suffer for the testimony of TRUTH. When they came to an engagement, he refused to fight, for which he was whipped and brought before the general, who asked him why he enlisted, if he would not fight. "I did it," said he, "in a drunken frolic, when the devil had the

---

[31]Thoughtless.

better of me, but my judgment is convinced that I ought not, neither will I, whatever I suffer. I have but one life and you may take that if you please, but I'll never take up arms." They used him with much cruelty to make him yield, but could not, by means whereof he was so disabled that the general sent him to the hospital at Chelsea, near London, where in nine months he died, and I hope made a good end, for which I prayed both night and day, till I heard of his death.

Thus I thought it my duty to say what I could in his favor, as I have been obliged to say so much of his hard usage to me, all which I hope did me good, and although he was so bad yet had several good properties, and I never thought him the worst of men. He was one I loved, and had he let religion have its perfect work, I should have thought myself happy in the lowest state of life; and I have cause to bless God, who enabled me in the station of a wife to do my duty, and now a widow, to submit to his will, always believing everything he doth to be right. May he in all stations of life so preserve me by the arm of Divine Power that I may never forget his tender mercies to me, the remembrance whereof doth often bow down my soul in humility before his throne, saying, Lord, what was I, that thou should'st have revealed to my soul the knowledge of the TRUTH, and done so much for me, who deserved thy displeasure rather. But in me thou hast shown thy long-suffering and tender mercy. May Thou, O God, be glorified, and I abased, for it is thy own works that praise thee, and, of a truth, to the humble soul makest everything sweet.

Mercy Otis Warren

1728–1814

By FAMILY SITUATION and personal inclination, Mercy Otis was at the center of political activity from the beginnings of trouble between England and her colonies through the establishment of the American republic. Her brother James and her husband were revolutionary leaders; she knew the Washingtons and was a close friend of the John Adamses. Her father, a judge and militia colonel in Barnstable, Massachusetts, had Mercy taught along with her two older brothers by their clergyman uncle. Later her brother James guided her reading; it was he who introduced her to the liberal political philosophy of John Locke. Her marriage to James's college friend James Warren proved to be long and happy; they had five sons.

James Otis took a leading role in defending colonial rights against British encroachments until he was incapacitated by a beating by thugs (1769). Mercy Warren took up his work in pamphlets and newspaper articles. At the suggestion of John Adams, she wrote a satiric poem on the Boston Tea Party, "The Squabble of the Sea Nymphs." She published three (or perhaps five) political tracts in dramatic form, including *The Adulateur* (1772, 1773), where James Otis appears as Brutus and Samuel Adams as Cassius, and *The Group* (1775), where American Tories expose themselves as fools and knaves. During the Revolution, James Warren served as paymaster general of the army and organized privateers to prey on British supply ships.

In 1790, Mercy Warren published *Poems, Dramatic and Miscellaneous,* which included two conventional tragedies on themes of freedom and patriotism. Her most substantial work is her three-volume *History of the Rise, Progress, and Termination of the American Revolution* (1805), partisan (on the liberal side), but con-

138

scientiously researched and vitalized by her personal acquaintance with many of the participants. Curiously, Warren's zeal for liberty, equality, and democracy did not seem to extend to women. In *The Group* she burlesques men who bully their wives, and in *The Ladies of Castile* she idealizes an actively patriotic woman over a conventionally passive one, but she never suggests that women should be included in government as voters or legislators.

BIBLIOGRAPHY
Warren, Mercy Otis. *History of the Rise, Progress, and Termination of the American Revolution.* 3 vols. Boston: 1805. Reprint. New York: AMS Press, 1970.
Warren, Mercy Otis. *The Poems and Plays.* Ed. Benjamin Franklin V. Delmar, N.Y.: Scholars' Facsimiles and Reprints, 1980.

To the Hon. J. Winthrop, Esq.[1]

Who, on the American determination, in 1774, to suspend all commerce with Britain (except for the real necessaries of life) requested a poetical list of the articles the ladies might comprise under that head.

Freedom may weep, and tyranny prevail,
And stubborn patriots either frown, or rail;
Let them of grave economy talk loud,
Prate prudent measures to the listening crowd;
With all the rhetoric of ancient schools,
Despise the mode, and fashion's modish fools;
Or show fair liberty, who used to smile,

[1] John Winthrop was Hollisian Professor of Mathematics and Natural Philosophy at Harvard; his wife, Hannah, was a close friend of Warren's. As a means of resistance to British restrictions on colonial trade (duties, laws forbidding the colonies to manufacture goods for export, to buy or sell where they wished, etc.), American patriots agreed to boycott all British goods that could possibly be dispensed with. The poem indicates that people differed on what was necessary.

The guardian goddess of Britannia's isle,
In sable weeds, anticipate the blow,
Aimed at Columbia by her royal foe;
And mark the period when inglorious kings
Deal round the curses that a Churchill[2] sings.

But what's the anguish of whole towns in tears,
Or trembling cities groaning out their fears?
The state may totter on proud ruin's brink,
The sword be brandished, or the bark may sink;
Yet shall Clarissa check her wanton pride,
And lay her female ornaments aside?
Quit all the shining pomp, the gay parade,
The costly trappings that adorn the maid?
What! all the aid of foreign looms refuse!
As beds of tulips stripped of richest hues,
Or the sweet bloom that's nipped by sudden frost,
Clarissa reigns no more a favorite toast.
For what is virtue, or the winning grace,
Of soft good humor, playing round the face;
Or what those modest antiquated charms,
That lured a Brutus to a Portia's arms;[3]
Or all the hidden beauties of the mind,
Compared with gauze, and tassels well combined?

This mighty theme produced a long debate,
On the best plan to save a sinking state;
The oratorial fair, as they inclined,
Freely discussed, and frankly spake their mind.

Lamira wished that freedom might succeed,
But to such terms what female ere agreed?
To British marts forbidden to repair,
(Where every luxury tempts the blooming fair)
Equals the rigor of those ancient times

---

[2]Charles Churchill, a contemporary British satirist, harshly attacked the government.

[3]Brutus and his wife, Portia, were shining examples of ancient Roman virtue and patriotism.

When Pharaoh, hardened as a G—— in crimes,
Plagued Israel's race, and taxed them by a law,
Demanding brick, when destitute of straw;
Miraculously led from Egypt's port,
They loved the fashions of the tyrant's court;
Sighed for the leeks, and waters of the Nile,[4]
As we for gewgaws from Britannia's isle;
That haughty isle, whose mercenary hand,
Spreads wide confusion round this fertile land,
Destroys the concord, and breaks down the shrine,
By virtue reared, to harmony divine.

Prudentia sighed—shall all our country mourn,
A powerful despot's lowering, haughty frown,
Whose hostile mandates, sent from venal courts,
Rob the fair vintage, and blockade our ports;
While troops of guards are planted on each plain,
Whose crimes contagious, youth and beauty stain?[5]
Fierce rancor blazoned on each breast's displayed,
And for a crest, a gorgon's snaky head.

The good, the wise, the prudent, and the gay,
Mingle their tears, and sighs for sighs repay;
Deep anxious thought each generous bosom fills,
How to avert the dread approaching ills;
Let us resolve on a small sacrifice,
And in the pride of Roman matrons rise;
Good as Cornelia, or a Pompey's wife,[6]
We'll quit the useless vanities of life.
Amidst loud discord, sadness, and dismay,
Hope spread her wing, and flit across the way:
Thanks to the sex, by heavenly hand designed,

[4]G_____, King George III. Although the Jews were oppressed in Egypt, they longed for its luxuries after Moses had led them into the wilderness, on their way toward liberty in the Promised Land. See Exodus 5:6–18, 16:1–3.

[5]Among other impositions, the "Intolerable Acts," passed by the British Parliament in 1774 as punishment for the Boston Tea Party, closed the port of Boston and ordered the quartering of soldiers in citizens' houses.

[6]Cornelia, the "Mother of the Gracchi," was famed for her patriotism. Pompey's wife, Julia, was generally admired for her good character and love for her husband.

Either to bless, or ruin all mankind.

A sharp debate ensued on wrong and right,
A little warm, 'tis true, yet all unite,
At once to end the great politic strife,
And yield up all but real wants of life.

But does Helvidius,[7] vigilant and wise,
Call for a schedule, that may all comprise?
'Tis so contracted, that a Spartan sage,[8]
Will sure applaud th' economizing age.

But if ye doubt, an inventory clear,
Of all she needs, Lamira offers here;
Nor does she fear a rigid Cato's[9] frown,
When she lays by the rich embroidered gown,
And modestly compounds for just enough—
Perhaps, some dozens of more flighty stuff;
With lawns and lustrings[10]—blond, and mecklin laces,
Fringes and jewels, fans and tweezer cases;
Gay cloaks and hats, of every shape and size,
Scarfs, cardinals, and ribbons of all dyes;
With ruffles stamped, and aprons of tambour,
Tippets and handkerchiefs, at least, three score;
With finest muslins that fair India boasts,
And the choice herbage from Chinesan coasts;[11]
(But while the fragrant hyson leaf regales,
Who'll wear the homespun produce of the vales?
For if 'twould save the nation from the curse
Of standing troops; or, name a plague still worse,
Few can this choice delicious draught give up,
Though all Medea's[12] poisons fill the cup.)

---

[7]Helvidius is a virtuous senator, no doubt representing an actual person, in Warren's propaganda play *The Defeat*.
[8]The ancient Spartans were known for austere living.
[9]Both Cato the Elder and his great-grandson Cato the Younger were noted for their simple living and condemnation of luxury.
[10]Glossy silk fabrics. Cardinals (3 lines down), short cloaks.
[11]Tea. Hyson (next line) is a type of tea.
[12]Medea, a sorceress in Greek mythology, was an expert poisoner.

Add feathers, furs, rich satins, and ducapes,[13]
And head dresses in pyramidial shapes;
Sideboards of plate, and porcelain profuse,
With fifty ditto's that the ladies use;
If my poor treacherous memory has missed,
Ingenious T——l shall complete the list.
So weak Lamira, and her wants so few,
Who can refuse?—they're but the sex's due.

   In youth, indeed, an antiquated page,
Taught us the threatenings of an Hebrew sage
'Gainst wimples, mantles, curls, and crisping pins,[14]
But rank not these among our modern sins:
For when our manners are well understood,
What in the scale is stomacher or hood?

   'Tis true, we love the courtly mien and air,
The pride of dress, and all the debonair;
Yet Clara quits the more dress'd negligee,
And substitutes the careless polanee;[15]
Until some fair one from Britannia's court,
Some jaunty dress, or newer taste import;
This sweet temptation could not be withstood,
Though for the purchase's paid her father's blood;
Though loss of freedom were the costly price,
Or flaming comets sweep the angry skies;
Or earthquakes rattle, or volcanoes roar;
Indulge this trifle, and she asks no more:
Can the stern patriot Clara's suit deny?
'Tis beauty asks, and reason must comply.

   But while the sex round folly's vortex play,
Say, if their lords are wiser far than they;
Few manly bosoms feel a nobler flame,
Some cog the die, and others win the game;
Trace their meanders to their tainted source,

[13]Strong silk fabrics.
[14]Isaiah 3:18–24.
[15]Polonaise, a relatively informal dress.

What's the grand pole star that directs their course?
Perhaps revenge, or some less glaring vice,
Their bold ambition, or their avarice,
Or vanity unmeaning, throw the bowl;
'Till pride and passion urge the narrow soul,
To claim the honors of that heavenly flame,
That warms the breast, and crowns the patriot's name.

But though your wives in fripperies are dressed,
And public virtue is the minion's jest,
America has many a worthy name,
Who shall, hereafter, grace the rolls of fame.
Her good Cornelias, and her Arrias fair,[16]
Who, death, in its most hideous forms, can dare,
Rather than live vain fickle fortune's sport,
Amidst the panders of a tyrant's court;
With a long list of generous, worthy men,
Who spurn the yoke, and servitude disdain;
Who nobly struggle in a vicious age,
To stem the torrent of despotic rage;
Who leagued, in solemn covenant unite,
And by the manes of good Hampden[17] plight,
That while the surges lash Britannia's shore,
Or wild Niagara's cataracts shall roar,
And Heaven looks down, and sanctifies the deed,
They'll fight for freedom, and for virtue bleed.

[16]Arria, like Cornelia, was a type of Roman virtue; when her husband hesitated to follow the emperor's order to commit suicide, she stabbed herself to give him courage.
[17]John Hampden led the resistance to King Charles I's imposition of an illegal tax in 1638.

To Fidelio[1]

Long absent on the great public cause, which agitated all America, in 1776.

The hilltops smile o'er all the blooming mead,
As I alone, on Clifford's[2] summit tread;
Traverse the rural walks, the gurgling rills,
Survey the beauties of th' adjacent hills;
Taste the delights of competence and health,
Each sober pleasure reason lends to wealth:
Yet o'er the lawn a whispering echo sighs,
Thy friend is absent—my fond heart replies—
Say—do not friendship's joys outweigh the whole?
'Tis social converse, animates the soul.
Thought interchanged, the heavenly spark improves,
And reason brightens by the heart it loves;
While solitude sits brooding o'er her cares,
She oft accelerates the ills she fears;
And though fond hope with silken hand displays,
The distant images of halcyon days,
Her sable brow contracts a solemn air,
That treads too near the threshold of despair;
'Till heaven benign the choicest blessings lend,
The balm of life, a kind and faithful friend:
This highest gift, by heaven indulged, I claim;
Ask, what is happiness?—My friend, I name:
Yet while the state, by fierce internal war,
Shook to the centre, asks his zealous care,
I must submit, and smile in solitude,
My fond affection, my self love subdued:
The times demand exertions of the kind,
A patriot zeal must warm the female mind.
Yet, gentle hope!—come, spread thy silken wing,

[1]Fidelio is James Warren, who spent most of the war years away from home, as paymaster of the army and a director of naval operations.
[2]The Warrens' country home in Plymouth.

And waft me forward to revolving spring;
Or ere the vernal equinox returns,
At worst, before the summer solstice burns,
May peace again erect her cheerful stand,
Disperse the ills which hover o'er the land;
May every virtuous noble minded pair,
Be far removed from the dread din of war;
Then each warm breast where generous friendships glow,
Where all the virtues of the patriot flow,
Shall taste each joy domestic life can yield,
Nor enter more the martial bloody field.

But, hark!—alas! the brave Montgomery dies,[3]
Oh, heaven forbid that such a sacrifice,
My country or my sex should yield again,
Or such rich blood pour o'er the purpled plain:
May guilty traitors satiate the grave,
But let the sword forever—spare the brave;
I weep his fall—I weep the hero slain,
And mingle sighs with his Janetta's pain:
Yet while I weep, and lend the pitying sigh,
I bow the knee, and lift my soul on high,
That virtue, struggling with assiduous pains,
May free this country from despotic chains:
Long life I ask, and blessings to descend,
And crown the efforts of my constant friend;
My early wish, and evening prayer the same,
That virtue, health, and peace, and honest fame,
May hover o'er thee, till time's latest hour,
Commissionate the dread resistless power;
Then gently lay thee by thy Marcia's[4] clay,
'Til both shall rise, and on a tide of day,
Be wafted on, and skim the ambient plains
Through lucid air, and see the God who reigns.

Where cherubims in borrowed lustre shine,

[3]General Richard Montgomery was killed in the American assault on Quebec in 1775. His wife, Janet, a friend of Warren's, was heartbroken.
[4]The wife of Cato the Younger.

We'll hand in hand our grateful homage join;
Beneath his throne, where listening angels stand,
With raptured seraphs wait his least command.

Clifford Farm, 1776

from An Address to the Inhabitants of the United States of America.[1]

At a period when every manly arm was occupied, and every trait of talent or activity engaged either in the cabinet or the field, apprehensive that amid the sudden convulsions, crowded scenes, and rapid changes that flowed in quick succession, many circumstances might escape the more busy and active members of society, I have been induced to improve the leisure Providence had lent, to record as they passed, in the following pages, the new and unexperienced events exhibited in a land previously blessed with peace, liberty, simplicity, and virtue. . . .

Connected by nature, friendship, and every social tie with many of the first patriots, and most influential characters on the continent; in the habits of confidential and epistolary intercourse with several gentlemen employed abroad in the most distinguished stations, and with others since elevated to the highest grades of rank and distinction,[2] I had the best means of information, through a long period that the colonies were in suspense, waiting the operation of foreign courts, and the success of their own enterprising spirit.

The solemnity that covered every countenance, when contemplating the sword uplifted and the horrors of civil war rushing to habi-

[1] This was the preface to Warren's history of the American Revolution.

[2] To list only the more conspicuous examples: her brother James was an important leader in the resistance to England in the 1760s; she corresponded with John Adams and Elbridge Gerry during their missions to Europe and with Presidents Washington, Adams, and Jefferson.

tations not inured to scenes of rapine and misery, even to the quiet cottage, where only concord and affection had reigned, stimulated to observation a mind that had not yielded to the assertion that all political attentions lay out of the road of female life.

It is true there are certain appropriate duties assigned to each sex; and doubtless it is the more peculiar province of masculine strength, not only to repel the bold invader of the rights of his country and of mankind, but in the nervous[3] style of manly eloquence, to describe the blood-stained field and relate the story of slaughtered armies.

Sensible of this, the trembling heart has recoiled at the magnitude of the undertaking, and the hand often shrunk back from the task; yet, recollecting that every domestic enjoyment depends on the unimpaired possession of civil and religious liberty, that a concern for the welfare of society ought equally to glow in every human breast, the work was not relinquished. The most interesting circumstances were collected, active characters portrayed, the principles of the times developed, and the changes marked; nor need it cause a blush to acknowledge, a detail was preserved with a view of transmitting it to the rising youth of my country,[4] some of them in infancy, others in the European world, while the most interesting events lowered over their native land. . . .

Not indifferent to the opinion of the world, nor servilely courting its smiles, no further apology is offered for the attempt, though many may be necessary, for the incomplete execution of a design, that had rectitude for its basis, and a beneficent regard for the civil and religious rights of mankind for its motive.

The liberal-minded will peruse with candor, rather than criticise with severity; nor will they think it necessary that any apology should be offered for sometimes introducing characters nearly connected with the author of the following annals; as they were early and zealously attached to the public cause, uniform in their principles, and constantly active in the great scenes that produced the revolution and obtained independence for their country, truth precludes that reserve which might have been proper on less important occasions, and forbids to pass over in silence the names of such as expired before the conflict was finished, or have since retired from public scenes. The historian has never laid aside the tenderness of the sex

[3]Sinewy, vigorous.
[4]Her own sons.

or the friend; at the same time, she has endeavored, on all occasions, that the strictest veracity should govern her heart, and the most exact impartiality be the guide of her pen.

If the work should be so far useful or entertaining, as to obtain the sanction of the generous and virtuous part of the community, I cannot but be highly gratified and amply rewarded for the effort, soothed at the same time with the idea that the motives were justifiable in the eye of Omniscience. Then, if it should not escape the remarks of the critic, or the censure of party, I shall feel no wound to my sensibility, but repose on my pillow as quietly as ever,—

> While all the distant din the world can keep,
> Rolls o'er my grotto, and but soothes my sleep.

Before this address to my countrymen is closed, I beg leave to observe, that as a new century has dawned upon us, the mind is naturally led to contemplate the great events that have run parallel with, and have just closed the last. From the revolutionary spirit of the times, the vast improvements in science, arts, and agriculture, the boldness of genius that marks the age, the investigation of new theories, and the changes in the political, civil, and religious characters of men, succeeding generations have reason to expect still more astonishing exhibitions in the next. In the meantime, Providence has clearly pointed out the duties of the present generation, particularly the paths which Americans ought to tread. The United States form a young republic, a confederacy which ought ever to be cemented by a union of interests and affection, under the influence of those principles which obtained their independence. These have indeed, at certain periods, appeared to be in the wane; but let them never be eradicated, by the jarring interests of parties, jealousies of the sister states, or the ambition of individuals! It has been observed, by a writer of celebrity, that "that people, government, and constitution is the freest, which makes the best provision for the enacting of expedient and salutary laws."[5] May this truth be evinced to all ages, by the wise and salutary laws that shall be enacted in the federal legislature of America!

May the hands of the executive of their own choice be strengthened more by the unanimity and affection of the people, than by the

---

[5]William Paley, *Moral and Political Philosophy,* 1785 (Warren's note).

dread of penal inflictions or any restraints that might repress free inquiry, relative to the principles of their own government and the conduct of its administrators! The world is now viewing America, as experimenting a new system of government, a FEDERAL RE-PUBLIC, including a territory to which the Kingdoms of Great Britain and Ireland bear little proportion. The practicability of supporting such a system has been doubted by some; if she succeeds, it will refute the assertion that none but small states are adapted to republican government; if she does not, and the union should be dissolved, some ambitious son of Columbia or some foreign adventurer, allured by the prize, may wade to empire through seas of blood, or the friends of monarchy may see a number of petty despots stretching their sceptres over the disjointed parts of the continent. Thus by the mandate of a single sovereign, the degraded subjects of one state, under the bannerets of royalty, may be dragged to sheathe their swords in the bosoms of the inhabitants of another.

The state of the public mind appears at present to be prepared to weigh these reflections with solemnity, and to receive with pleasure an effort to trace the origin of the American revolution, to review the characters that effected it, and to justify the principles of the defection and final separation from the parent state. With an expanded heart, beating with high hopes of the continued freedom and prosperity of America, the writer indulges a modest expectation that the following pages will be perused with kindness and candor: this she claims, both in consideration of her sex, the uprightness of her intentions, and the fervency of her wishes for the happiness of all the human race.

Abigail Smith Adams

1744-1818

ABIGAIL SMITH, daughter of a prosperous clergyman in Weymouth, Massachusetts, near Boston, was educated mainly by reading in her father's library and listening to intelligent conversation. She deplored her deficiency in formal education (apparent in the originals of her letters). In 1778 she wrote: "Every assistance and advantage which can be procured is afforded to the sons, whilst the daughters are wholly neglected in point of literature" (i.e., liberal studies: letter to John Thaxter, February 15). She married John Adams, a rising lawyer, in 1764. Despite separations brought about by his ever-increasing involvement in public affairs, their fifty-four-year marriage was singularly happy and devoted. The Adamses had six children, four of whom survived to adulthood: Abigail (Nabby), John Quincy, Charles, and Thomas.

For much of the time from 1774 to 1777, John Adams was away from home as a leading member of the Continental Congress. Abigail was left to run the family farm in Braintree (upon which their economic survival depended), raise the children (although she complained she was not sufficiently well-educated herself to educate them, August 14, 1776), and deal with such crises as epidemics of dysentery and threats of occupation by the British army. Her constant supportive letters to John helped him to carry on despite discouragements and criticism. In 1778, Congress sent him abroad to win support for the American cause in France and the Netherlands. After three months at home, he was sent late in 1779 to begin negotiations for peace with England. Both Adamses were unhappy about this prolonged separation—by 1784, John had been abroad for six years, with only one three-month interval—but they agreed to it out of patriotic duty. Abigail sustained herself with the thought that her management of their private affairs left him free for public service: "Here I can serve my partner, my family and myself, and enjoy the satisfaction of your serving your country" (June 3, 1776). She hesitated to join John abroad because of family obligations, her need to look after the Adams financial interests, and her reluctance to cross the ocean alone. In 1784, however, she and Nabby set out, and the family was reunited in London on August 7.

BIBLIOGRAPHY
Adams Family Correspondence. 4 vols. Edited by L. H. Butterfield (New York: Atheneum, 1965).
The Book of Abigail and John: Selected Letters of the Adams Family 1762–1784. Edited by L. H. Butterfield, Marc Friedlaender, and Mary-Jo Kline. Cambridge: Harvard University Press, 1975.

Selected Letters from the Adams Family Correspondence

My Friend[1]   Weymouth, April the 16, 1764
I think I write to you every day. Shall not I make my letters very cheap; don't you light your pipe with them? I care not if you do; 'tis a pleasure to me to write, yet I wonder I write to you with so little restraint, for as a critic I fear you more than any other person on earth, and 'tis the only character in which I ever did, or ever will fear you. What say you? Do you approve of that speech? Don't you think me a courageous being? Courage is a laudable, a glorious virtue in your sex, why not in mine? (For my part, I think you ought to applaud me for mine.)—Exit Rattle.

Solus your Diana.

And now pray tell me how you do, do you feel any venom work-

---

[1]Abigail's friend or dearest friend is John Adams.

ing in your veins, did you ever before experience such a feeling?[2]—
This letter will be made up with the questions I fancy—not set in
order before you neither.—How do you employ yourself? Do you
go abroad yet? Is it not cruel to bestow those favors upon others
which I should rejoice to receive, yet must be deprived of?

I have lately been thinking whether my Mamma—when I write
again I will tell you something. Did not you receive a letter today by
Hones?[3]

This is a right girl's letter, but I will turn to the other side and be
sober, if I can—but what is bred in the bone will never be out of the
flesh (as Lord M would have said).[4]

As I have a good opportunity to send some milk, I have not waited
for your *orders;* lest if I should miss this, I should not catch such an
other. If you want more balm, I can supply you.

Adieu, evermore remember me with the tenderest affection, which
is also borne unto you by your—   A. Smith

Abigail Adams to Isaac Smith, Jr.[1]

Dear Sir   Braintree, April the 20, 1771
I write you, not from the noisy busy town, but from my humble
cottage in Braintree, where I arrived last Saturday and here again
am to take up my abode.

> Where Contemplation plumes her ruffled wings
> And the free soul looks down to pity kings.

Suffer me to snatch you a few moments from all the hurry and tumult
of London and in imagination place you by me that I may ask you
ten thousand questions, and bear with me, Sir, tis the only recompence you can make for the loss of your company.

From my infancy I have always felt a great inclination to visit the
Mother Country, as 'tis called; and had nature formed me of the
other sex, I should certainly have been a rover. And although this

[2]JA had just been inoculated for smallpox.
[3]A servant in JA's family.
[4]Lord M., a character in Samuel Richardson's *Clarissa,* constantly repeated plat-
itudes.
[1]The Reverend Isaac Smith was AA's first cousin. He was in London and had
written her descriptions of the sights.

desire has greatly diminished, owing partly, I believe, to maturer years, but more to the unnatural treatment which this our poor America has received from her, I yet retain a curiosity to know whatever is valuable in her. I thank you, Sir, for the particular account you have already favored me with, but you always took pleasure in being communicatively good.

Women, you know, Sir, are considered as domestic beings; and although they inherit an equal share of curiosity with the other sex, yet but few are hardy enough to venture abroad and explore the amazing variety of distant lands. The natural tenderness and delicacy of our constitutions, added to the many dangers we are subject to from your sex, renders it almost impossible for a single lady to travel without injury to her character. And those who have a protector in an husband have, generally speaking, obstacles sufficient to prevent their roving, and instead of visiting other countries, are obliged to content themselves with seeing but a very small part of their own. To your sex we are most of us indebted for all the knowledge we acquire of distant lands. As to a knowledge of human nature, I believe it may as easily be obtained in this country as in England, France or Spain. Education alone I conceive constitutes the difference in manners. 'Tis natural, I believe, for every person to have a partiality for their own country. Don't you think this little spot of ours better calculated for happiness than any other you have yet seen or read of? Would you exchange it for England, France, Spain or Italy? Are not the people here more upon an equality in point of knowledge and of circumstances—there being none so immensely rich as to lord it over us, neither any so abjectly poor as to suffer for the necessaries of life, provided they will use the means. It has heretofore been our boasted privilege that we could sit under our own vine and apple trees in peace enjoying the fruits of *our own labor*[2]—but alas! the much dreaded change Heaven avert.[3] Shall we ever wish to change countries, to change conditions with the Africans and the Laplanders? For sure it were better never to have known

[2]"And Judah and Israel dwelt safely every man under his vine and under his fig tree . . ." (I Kings 4:25). AA substitutes New England apples for Middle Eastern figs. This was a favorite quotation of hers: see letters of March 31 and August 29, 1776.
[3]She foresees that the increasing strains between England and the American colonies will lead to war.

the blessings of liberty than to have enjoyed it, and then to have it ravished from us.

But where do I ramble? I only ask your ear a few moments longer. The Americans have been called a very religious people, would to Heaven they were so in earnest; but whatever they may have been, I am afraid 'tis now only a negative virtue, and that they are only a less vicious people. However I can quote Mr. Whitefield[4] as an authority that what has been said of us is not without foundation. The last sermon I heard him preach, he told us that he had been a very great traveler, yet he had never seen so much of the real appearance of religion in any country as in America, and from your description I imagine you join with him in sentiment. I think Dr. Shebbeare in his remarks upon the English nation[5] has some such observation as this: In London religion seems to be periodical, like an ague which only returns once in seven days, and then attacks the inhabitants with the cold fit only; the burning never succeeds in this country. Since which it seems they have found means to rid themselves entirely of the ague.—As to news, I have none to tell you, nor anything remarkable to entertain you with. But you, Sir, have every day new scenes opening to you, and you will greatly oblige me by a recital of whatever you find worthy notice. I have a great desire to be made acquainted with Mrs. Macaulay's own history.[6] One of my own sex so eminent in a tract so uncommon naturally raises my curiosity, and all I could ever learn relative to her is this: that she is a widow lady and sister to Mr. Sawbridge. I have a curiosity to know her education, and what first prompted her to engage in a study never before exhibited to the public by one of her own sex and country, though now to the honor of both so admirably performed by her. As you are now upon the spot, and have been introduced to her acquaintance, you will, I hope, be able to satisfy me with some account, in doing which you will confer an obligation upon your assured friend,   Abigail Adams

Dearest Friend   Braintree, July 16, 1775
     I have this afternoon had the pleasure of receiving your letter by

---

[4]George Whitefield, a famous English Methodist preacher, had toured the colonies and died in Massachusetts in 1770.

[5]John Shebbeare's *Letters on the English Nation* (1755).

[6]Catherine Sawbridge Macaulay, author of an eight-volume republican *History of England* (1763–83), the first such work by an English woman.

your friends Mr. Collins and Kaighn[1] and an English gentleman (his name I do not remember). It was next to seeing my dearest friend. Mr. Collins could tell me more particularly about you and your health than I have been able to hear since you left me. I rejoice in his account of your better health and of your spirits, though he says I must not expect to see you till next spring. I hope he does not speak the truth. I know (I think I do, for am not I your bosom friend?) your feelings, your anxieties, your exertions, &c. more than those before whom you are obliged to wear the face of cheerfulness.

I have seen your letters to Colonels Palmer and Warren.[2] I pity your embarrassments. How difficult the task to quench out the fire and the pride of private ambition, and to sacrifice ourselves and all our hopes and expectations to the public weal. How few have souls capable of so noble an undertaking—how often are the laurels worn by those who have had no share in earning them. But there is a future recompence of reward to which the upright man looks, and which he will most assuredly obtain, provided he perseveres unto the end.—The appointment of the Generals Washington and Lee gives universal satisfaction.[3] The people have the highest opinion of Lee's abilities, but you know the continuation of the popular breath depends much upon favorable events.

I had the pleasure of seeing both the generals and their aides decamp soon after their arrival and of being personally made known to them. They very politely express their regard for you. Major Mifflin[4] said he had orders from you to visit me at Braintree. I told him I should be very happy to see him there, and accordingly sent Mr. Thaxter[5] to Cambridge with a card to him and Mr. Reed to dine with me. Mrs. Warren and her son were to be with me. They very politely received the message and lamented that they were not able to upon account of expresses[6] which they were that day to get in readiness to send off.

I was struck with General Washington. You had prepared me to entertain a favorable opinion of him, but I thought the one half was

[1]Stephen Collins and John Kaighn (or Cain), Quakers from Philadelphia.
[2]Joseph Palmer and James Warren, the husband of Mercy Otis Warren.
[3]George Washington was named commander-in-chief of the American forces on June 15, 1775. Charles Lee was a major general.
[4]Major General Thomas Mifflin, Washington's aide-de-camp.
[5]John Thaxter, Jr., AA's cousin, who was studying law with JA.
[6]Urgent letters.

not told me. Dignity with ease and complacency,[7] the gentleman and soldier look agreeably blended in him. Modesty marks every line and feature of his face. Those lines of Dryden[8] instantly occurred to me:

> Mark his majestic fabric! he's a temple
> Sacred by birth, and built by hands divine;
> His soul's the deity that lodges there.
> Nor is the pile[9] unworthy of the God.

• • •

You have made often and frequent complaints that your friends do not write to you. I have stirred up some of them. Dr. Tufts, Col. Quincy, Mr. Tudor, Mr. Thaxter all have wrote you now, and a lady whom I am willing you should value preferable to all others save one.[10] May not I in my turn make complaints? All the letters I receive from you seem to be wrote in so much haste that they scarcely leave room for a social feeling. They let me know that you exist, but some of them contain scarcely six lines. I want some sentimental effusions of the heart. I am sure you are not destitute of them. Or are they all absorbed in the great public? Much is due to that, I know, but being part of the whole I lay claim to a larger share than I have had. You used to be more communicative on Sundays. I always loved a Sabbath day's letter, for then you had a greater command of your time—but hush to all complaints. . . .

Our little ones send duty to Papa. You would smile to see them all gather round Mamma upon the reception of a letter to hear from Papa, and Charles with open mouth, "What does Par say—did not he write no more?" And little Tom says, "I wish I could see Par." Upon Mr. Rice's going into the army, he asked Charles if he should get him a place; he catched at it with great eagerness and insisted upon going. We could not put him off; he cried and begged; no obstacle we could raise was sufficient to satisfy him, till I told him he must first obtain your consent. Then he insisted that I must write about it, and has been every day these three weeks insisting upon

[7]Willingness to oblige.
[8]John Dryden, author of plays featuring godlike heroes.
[9]Lofty building.
[10]Mercy Otis Warren.

my asking your consent. At last I have promised to write to you, and am obliged to be as good as my word.—I have now wrote you all I can collect from every quarter. 'Tis fit for no eye but yours, because you can make all necessary allowances. I cannot copy.

There are yet in Town[11] of the selectmen and some thousands of inhabitants, 'tis said.—I hope to hear from you soon. Do let me know if there is any prospect of seeing you. Next Wednesday is thirteen weeks since you went away.

I must bid you adieu. You have many friends, though they have not noticed you by writing. I am sorry they have been so negligent. I hope no share of that blame lays upon your most affectionate

Portia[12]

November 27, 1775

'Tis a fortnight tonight since I wrote you a line, during which I have been confined with the jaundice, rheumatism and a most violent cold; I yesterday took a puke, which has relieved me, and I feel much better today. Many, very many people who have had the dysentery are now afflicted both with the jaundice and rheumatism; some it has left in hectics, some in dropsies.

The great and incessant rains we have had this fall (the like cannot be recollected) may have occasioned some of the present disorders. The jaundice is very prevalent in the camp.[1] We have lately had a week of very cold weather, as cold as January, and a flight of snow, which I hope will purify the air of some of the noxious vapors. It has spoiled many hundreds of bushels of apples, which were designed for cider, and which the great rains had prevented people from making up. Suppose we have lost five barrels by it.

Col. Warren returned last week to Plymouth, so that I shall not hear anything from you till he goes back again, which will not be till the last of this month.

He damped my spirits greatly by telling me that the court had prolonged your stay another month.[2] I was pleasing myself with the

[11]Boston was occupied by the British army and besieged by the Americans under Washington.

[12]Portia, daughter of Cato the Younger and wife of Brutus, was famous for her virtue and devotion to her husband.

[1]Army camp.

[2]On November 11, the Massachusetts House of Representatives extended the terms

thoughts that you would soon be upon your return. 'Tis in vain to repine. I hope the public will reap what I sacrifice.

I wish I knew what mighty things were fabricating.[3] If a form of government is to be established here, what one will be assumed? Will it be left to our assemblies to choose one? and will not many men have many minds? and shall we not run into dissensions among ourselves?

I am more and more convinced that man is a dangerous creature, and that power, whether vested in many or a few, is ever grasping and like the grave cries give, give. The great fish swallow up the small, and he who is most strenuous for the rights of the people, when vested with power, is as eager after the prerogatives of government. You tell me of degrees of perfection to which human nature is capable of arriving, and I believe it, but at the same time lament that our admiration should arise from the scarcity of the instances.

The building up a great empire, which was only hinted at by my correspondent, may now, I suppose, be realized even by the unbelievers. Yet will not ten thousand difficulties arise in the formation of it? The reins of government have been so long slackened that I fear the people will not quietly submit to those restraints which are necessary for the peace and security of the community; if we separate from Britain, what code of laws will be established? How shall we be governed so as to retain our liberties? Can any government be free which is not administered by general stated laws? Who shall frame these laws? Who will give them force and energy? 'Tis true your resolutions as a body have hitherto had the force of laws. But will they continue to have?

When I consider these things and the prejudices of people in favor of ancient customs and regulations, I feel anxious for the fate of our monarchy or democracy or whatever is to take place. I soon get lost in a labyrinth of perplexities, but whatever occurs, may justice and righteousness be the stability of our times, and order arise out of confusion. Great difficulties may be surmounted by patience and perseverance.

I believe I have tired you with politics. As to news, we have not any at all. I shudder at the approach of winter when I think I am to

of the delegates to the Continental Congress from the end of December to the end of January.
[3]Being made.

remain desolate. Suppose your weather is warm yet. Mr. Mason and Thaxter[4] live with me and render some part of my time less disconsolate. Mr. Mason is a youth who will please you; he has spirit, taste and sense. His application to his studies is constant, and I am much mistaken if he does not make a very good figure in his profession.

I have with me now the only daughter of your brother; I feel a tenderer affection for her as she has lost a kind parent. Though too young to be sensible of her own loss, I can pity her. She appears to be a child of a very good disposition—only wants to be a little used to company.

Our little ones send duty to Papa and want much to see him. Tom says he won't come home till the battle is over—some strange notion he has got into his head. He has got a political creed to say to him when he returns.

I must bid you good night. 'Tis late for one who am much of an invalid. I was disappointed last week in receiving a packet by the post, and upon unsealing it found only four newspapers. I think you are more cautious than you need be. All letters, I believe, have come safe to hand. I have sixteen from you, and wish I had as many more. Adieu. Yours.

Braintree, March 31, 1776

I wish you would ever write me a letter half as long as I write you; and tell me if you may where your fleet are gone? What sort of defence Virginia can make against our common enemy? Whether it is so situated as to make an able defence? Are not the gentry lords and the common people vassals? Are they not like the uncivilized natives Britain represents us to be? I hope their riflemen, who have shown themselves very savage and even bloodthirsty, are not a specimen of the generality of the people.

I am willing to allow the colony great merit for having produced a Washington, but they have been shamefully duped by a Dunmore.[1]

I have sometimes been ready to think that the passion for liberty cannot be equally strong in the breasts of those who have been accustomed to deprive their fellow creatures of theirs. Of this I am

[4]John Thaxter, Jr., and Jonathan Mason, JA's law students.
[1]Lord Dunmore, royal governor of Virginia, had tried to suppress revolutionary activity.

certain: that it is not founded upon the generous and Christian principle of doing to others as we would that others should do unto us.

Do not you want to see Boston;[2] I am fearful of the smallpox, or I should have been in before this time. I got Mr. Crane to go to our house and see what state it was in. I find it has been occupied by one of the doctors of a regiment, very dirty, but no other damage has been done to it. The few things which were left in it are all gone. Crane has the key, which he never delivered up. I have wrote to him for it and am determined to get it cleaned as soon as possible and shut it up. I look upon it a new acquisition of property, a property which one month ago I did not value at a single shilling, and could with pleasure have seen it in flames.

The town in general is left in a better state than we expected, more owing to a precipitate flight than any regard to the inhabitants, though some individuals discovered[3] a sense of honor and justice and have left the rent of the houses in which they were for the owners and the furniture unhurt, or, if damaged, sufficient to make it good.

Others have committed abominable ravages. The mansion house of your President[4] is safe and the furniture unhurt, whilst both the house and the furniture of the Solicitor General have fallen a prey to their own merciless party. Surely the very fiends feel a reverential awe for virtue and patriotism, whilst they detest the parricide and traitor.

I feel very differently at the approach of spring to what I did a month ago. We knew not then whether we could plant or sow with safety, whether when we had toiled we could reap the fruits of our own industry, whether we could rest in our own cottages, or whether we should not be driven from the seacoasts to seek shelter in the wilderness, but now we feel as if we might sit under our own vine and eat the good of the land.

I feel a *gaieté de coeur* to which before I was a stranger. I think the sun looks brighter, the birds sing more melodiously, and Nature puts on a more cheerful countenance. We feel a temporary peace, and the poor fugitives are returning to their deserted habitations.

Though we felicitate ourselves, we sympathize with those who are

[2]The British army of occupation had evacuated Boston on March 17.
[3]Revealed.
[4]John Hancock, president of the Continental Congress. The Adamses believed that Samuel Quincy, the solicitor general, had collaborated with the English out of personal self-interest.

trembling lest the lot of Boston should be theirs. But they cannot be in similar circumstances unless pusillanimity and cowardice should take possession of them. They have time and warning given them to see the evil and shun it.—I long to hear that you have declared an independency—and by the way, in the new Code of Laws which I suppose it will be necessary for you to make, I desire you would remember the ladies, and be more generous and favorable to them than your ancestors. Do not put such unlimited power into the hands of the husbands. Remember, all men would be tyrants if they could. If particular care and attention is not paid to the ladies, we are determined to foment a rebellion, and will not hold ourselves bound by any laws in which we have no voice or representation.

That your sex are naturally tyrannical is a truth so thoroughly established as to admit of no dispute, but such of you as wish to be happy willingly give up the harsh title of master for the more tender and endearing one of friend. Why, then, not put it out of the power of the vicious and the lawless to use us with cruelty and indignity with impunity. Men of sense in all ages abhor those customs which treat us only as the vassals of your sex. Regard us then as beings placed by providence under your protection, and in imitation of the Supreme Being, make use of that power only for our happiness.[5]

Abigail Adams to Mercy Otis Warren

Braintree, April 27, 1776

I set myself down to comply with my friend's request, who I think seems rather low spirited.

I did write last week, but not meeting with an early conveyance, I thought the letter of but little importance and tossed it away. I acknowledge my thanks due to my friend for the entertainment she so kindly afforded me in the characters drawn in her last letter, and if coveting my neighbor's goods was not prohibited by the sacred law, I should be most certainly tempted to envy her the happy talent

[5]JA's reply to this exhortation (April 14, 1776) was facetious. AA summarizes it in her letter to Warren, following this. JA reserved his serious argument for a male friend, James Sullivan (May 26, 1776): people without property cannot be responsible, independent voters, because they will inevitably be influenced by the employer, husband, etc., upon whom they depend financially. Since married women's property belonged to their husbands, it followed that they should not vote.

she possesses above the rest of her sex, by adorning with her pen even trivial occurrences, as well as dignifying the most important. Cannot you communicate some of those graces to your friend and suffer her to pass them upon the world for her own that she may feel a little more upon an equality with you?—'Tis true I often receive large packages from Philadelphia. They contain, as I said before, more newspapers than letters, though they are not forgotten. It would be hard indeed if absence had not some alleviations.

I dare say he writes to no one unless to Portia oftener than to your friend,[1] because I know there is no one besides in whom he has an equal confidence. His letters to me have been generally short, but he pleads in excuse the critical state of affairs and the multiplicity of avocations and says further that he has been very busy, and writ near ten sheets of paper about some affairs which he does not choose to mention for fear of accident.

He is very saucy to me in return for a list of female grievances which I transmitted to him. I think I will get you to join me in a petition to Congress. I thought it was very probable our wise statesmen would erect a new government and form a new Code of Laws. I ventured to speak a word in behalf of our sex, who are rather hardly dealt with by the laws of England, which give such unlimited power to the husband to use his wife ill.

I requested that our legislators would consider our case, and as all men of delicacy and sentiment are averse to exercising the power they possess, yet as there is a natural propensity in human nature to domination, I thought the most generous plan was to put it out of the power of the arbitrary and tyrannic to injure us with impunity by establishing some laws in our favor upon just and liberal principles.

I believe I even threatened fomenting a rebellion in case we were not considered, and assured him we would not hold ourselves bound by any laws in which we had neither a voice, nor representation.

In return he tells me he cannot but laugh at my extraordinary Code of Laws. That he had heard their struggle had loosened the bands of government, that children and apprentices were disobedient, that schools and colleges were grown turbulent, that Indians slighted their guardians, and Negroes grew insolent to their masters.

[1]James Warren, Mercy's husband. He is also the friend of the second to last paragraph.

But my letter was the first intimation that another tribe more numerous and powerful than all the rest were grown discontented. This is rather too coarse a compliment, he adds, but that I am so saucy he won't blot it out.

So I have helped the sex abundantly, but I will tell him I have only been making trial of the disinterestedness of his virtue, and when weighed in the balance have found it wanting.

It would be bad policy to grant us greater power, say they, since under all the disadvantages we labor, we have the ascendancy over their hearts

And charm by accepting, by submitting sway.[2]

I wonder Apollo and the Muses could not have indulged me with a poetical genius. I have always been a votary to her charms, but never could ascend Parnassus myself.

I am very sorry to hear of the indisposition of your friend. I am afraid it will hasten his return, and I do not think he can be spared.

Though certain pains attend the cares of State
A good man owes his country to be great,
Should act abroad the high distinguished part
Or show at least the purpose of his heart.

Good night, my friend. You will be so good as to remember me to our worthy Friend Mrs. Winthrop when you see her and write soon to your   Portia

July 21, 1776, Boston

I have no doubt but that my dearest friend is anxious to know how his Portia does, and his little flock of children, under the operation of a disease once so formidable.[1]

[2]JA's concluding argument had been that men must retain their legal supremacy to protect themselves against women's emotional influence: "We have only the name of masters, and rather than give up this, which would completely subject us to the despotism of the petticoat, I hope General Washington and all our brave heroes would fight." AA slightly misquotes line 263 of Alexander Pope's "To a Lady: Of the Characters of Women."

[1]AA and the children had just been inoculated for smallpox—a serious operation in the eighteenth century, when actual smallpox was injected, rather than cowpox.

I have the pleasure to tell him that they are all comfortable, though some of them complaining. Nabby has been very ill, but the eruption begins to make its appearance upon her and upon Johnny. Tommy is so well that the doctor inoculated him again today, fearing it had not taken. Charly has no complaints yet, though his arm has been very sore.

I have been out to meeting this forenoon, but have so many disagreeable sensations this afternoon that I thought it prudent to tarry at home. The doctor says they are very good feelings. Mr. Cranch[2] has passed through the preparation, and the eruption is coming out cleverly[3] upon him without sickness at all. Mrs. Cranch is cleverly, and so are all her children. Those who are broke out are pretty full for the new method, as 'tis call'd, the Suttonian,[4] they profess to practice upon. I hope to give you a good account when I write next, but our eyes are very weak, and the doctor is not fond of either writing or reading for his patients. But I must transgress a little.

I received a letter from you by Wednesday post, 7 of July, and though I think it is a choice one in the literary way, containing many useful hints and judicious observations which will greatly assist me in the future instruction of our little ones, yet it lacked some essential ingredients to make it complete. Not one word respecting yourself, your health or your present situation. My anxiety for your welfare will never leave me but with my parting breath; 'tis of more importance to me than all this world contains besides. The cruel separation to which I am necessitated cuts off half the enjoyments of life; the other half are comprised in the hope I have that what I do and what I suffer may be serviceable to you, to our little ones and our country; I must beseech you therefore for the future never to omit what is so essential to my happiness.

Last Thursday,[5] after hearing a very good sermon, I went with the multitude into King's Street to hear the proclamation for independence read and proclaimed. Some field pieces with the train[6] were brought there, the troops appeared under arms, and all the inhabitants assembled there (the smallpox prevented many thousand from

[2]Richard Cranch, husband of AA's older sister.
[3]Nicely. In the next sentence, doing well.
[4]Named after Daniel Sutton, whose method required only a small puncture, rather than the usual gash, to infect the subject.
[5]July 18.
[6]Field guns and the wagons carrying them.

the country). When Col. Crafts read from the belcona[7] of the State House the proclamation, great attention was given to every word. As soon as he ended, the cry from the belcona was, "God Save our American States"; and then three cheers which rended the air, the bells rang, the privateers fired, the forts and batteries, the cannon were discharged, the platoons followed, and every face appeared joyful. Mr. Bowdoin then gave a sentiment,[8] "Stability and perpetuity to American independence." After dinner the king's arms were taken down from the State House, and every vestige of him from every place in which it appeared, and burnt in King Street. Thus ends royal authority in this state, and all the people shall say Amen.

I have been a little surprized that we collect no better accounts with regard to the horrid conspiricy at New York, and that so little mention has been made of it here.[9] It made a talk for a few days, but now seems all hushed in silence. The Tories say that it was not a conspiracy but an association, and pretend that there was no plot to assassinate the General. Even their hardened hearts feel —— the discovery. We have in George a match for a Borgia and a Catiline,[10] a wretch callous to every human feeling. Our worthy preacher told us that he believed one of our great sins, for which a righteous God has come out in judgment against us, was our bigoted attachment to so wicked a man. May our repentance be sincere.

Dearest Friend   Boston, August 29, 1776

I have spent the three days past almost entirely with you. The weather has been stormy, I have had little company, and I have amused myself in the closet[1] reading over the letters I have received from you since I have been here.

I have possession of my aunt's chamber, in which you know is a very convenient pretty closet with a window which looks into her flower garden. In this closet are a number of bookshelves, which are but poorly furnished; however, I have a pretty little desk or cabinet here where I write all my letters and keep my papers unmolested by

[7]Balcony.
[8]Slogan.
[9]A Tory plot for an uprising to assist British troops in capturing New York City, which may or may not have included an attempt to assassinate Washington.
[10]She compares King George III with the Borgias of Renaissance Italy and the ancient Roman Catiline, known as ruthless, unscrupulous politicians.
[1]Small private room.

anyone. I do not covet my neighbor's goods, but I should like to be the owner of such conveniences. I always had a fancy for a closet with a window which I could more peculiarly call my own.

Here, I say, I have amused myself in reading and thinking of my absent friend, sometimes with a mixture of pain, sometimes with pleasure, sometimes anticipating a joyful and happy meeting, whilst my heart would bound and palpitate with the pleasing idea, and with the purest affection I have held you to my bosom till my whole soul has dissolved in tenderness and my pen fallen from my hand.

How often do I reflect with pleasure that I hold in possession a heart equally warm with my own, and full as susceptible of the tenderest impressions, and who even now, whilst he is reading here, feels all I describe.

Forgive this reverie, this delusion, and since I am debarred real, suffer me to enjoy and indulge in ideal pleasures—and tell me they are not inconsistent with the stern virtue of a senator and a patriot.

I must leave my pen to recover myself and write in another strain. I feel anxious for a post day, and am full as solicitous for two letters a week and as uneasy if I do not get them, as I used to be when I got but one in a month or five weeks. Thus do I presume upon indulgence, and this is human nature, and brings to my mind a sentiment of one of your correspondents, viz., "That man is the only animal who is hungry with his belly full."

Last evening Dr. Cooper came in and brought me your favor from the post office of August 18, and Col. Whipple arrived yesterday morning and delivered me the two bundles you sent and a letter of the 12 of August. They have already afforded me much amusement, and I expect much more from them.

I am sorry to find from your last as well as from some others of your letters that you feel so dissatisfied with the office to which you are chosen.[2] Though in your acceptance of it, I know you was actuated by the purest motives, and I know of no person here so well qualified to discharge the important duties of it, yet I will not urge you to it. In accepting of it you must be excluded from all other employments. There never will be a salary adequate to the importance of the office or to support you and your family from penury. If you possess[ed] a fortune, I would urge you to it, in spite of all

[2]Probably the presidency of the Board of War and Ordnance, to which JA was elected in June.

the fleers and gibes of minds who themselves are incapable of acting a disinterested part, and have no conception that others can.

I have never heard any speeches about it, nor did I know that such insinuations had been thrown out.

Pure and disinterested virtue must ever be its own reward. Mankind are too selfish and too depraved to discover the pure gold from the baser metal.

I wish for peace and tranquillity. All my desires and all my ambition is to be esteemed and loved by my partner, to join with him in the education and instruction of our little ones, to set under our own vines in peace, liberty and safety.

Adieu, my dearest friend; soon, soon return to your most affectionate   Portia

Dearest of Friends   June 30, 1778[1]

Shall I tell my dearest that tears of joy filled my eyes this morning at the sight of his well known hand, the first line which has blessed my sight since his four months' absence, during which time I have never been able to learn a word from him or my dear son, till about ten days ago an English paper taken in a prize[2] and brought into Salem contained an account under the Paris News of your arrival at the abode of Dr. Franklin, and last week a carte[3] from Halifax brought Capt. Welch of the *Boston,* who informed that he left you well the eleventh of March, that he had letters for me but destroyed them when he was taken, and this is all the information I have ever been able to obtain. Our enemies have told us the vessel was taken and named the frigate which took her and that she was carried into Plymouth. I have lived a life of fear and anxiety ever since you left me; not more than a week after your absence, the horrid story of Doctor Franklin's assassination was received from France and sent by Mr. Purveyance of Baltimore to Congress and to Boston. Near two months before that was contradicted; then we could not hear a word from the *Boston,* and most people gave her up as taken or lost;

[1]JA, named by Congress to act with Benjamin Franklin as commissioner at the French court, had sailed on the *Boston* with his ten-year-old son John Quincy Adams and was now living in Franklin's household near Paris.

[2]Captured English ship.

[3]A ship commissioned to exchange prisoners of war. Hezekiah Welch, appointed captain of a ship that had been captured by the *Boston* and then recaptured by the British, had been carrying letters from JA to America.

thus has my mind been agitated like a troubled sea. You will easily conceive how grateful to me your favor of April 25 and those of our son were to me and mine, though I regret your short warning and the little time you had to write, by which means I know not how you fared upon your voyage, what reception you have met with (not even from the ladies, though you profess yourself an admirer of them), and a thousand circumstances which I wish to know, and which are always particularly interesting to [a] near connection. I must request you always to be minute and to write me by every conveyance. Some perhaps which may appear unlikely to reach [me] will be the first to arrive. I own I was mortified at so short a letter, but I quiet my heart with thinking there are many more upon their passage to me. I have wrote seven before this and some of them very long. Now I know you are safe I wish myself with you. Whenever you entertain such a wish, recollect that I would have willingly hazarded all dangers to have been your companion, but as that was not permitted,[4] you must console me in your absence by a recital of all your adventures, though methinks I would not have them in all respects too similar to those related of your venerable colleague, whose Mentor-like appearance, age and philosophy must certainly lead the polite scientific ladies of France to suppose they are embracing the God of Wisdom in a human form; but I, who own that I never yet "wished an angel whom I loved a man," shall be full as content if those divine honors are omitted.[5] The whole heart of my friend is in the bosom of his partner; more than half a score of years has so riveted [it] there that the fabric which contains it must crumble into dust ere the particles can be separated. I can hear of the brilliant accomplishment[s] of any of my sex with pleasure and rejoice in that liberality of sentiment which acknowledges them. At the same time I regret the trifling narrow contracted education of the females of my own country. I have entertained a superior opinion of the accomplishments of the French ladies ever since I read the *Letters* of Dr.

[4]AA had wanted to go with JA, taking the children, but he convinced her the trip would be too dangerous.

[5]Franklin, then seventy-two years old, was the darling of Parisian high society. He flirted with the ladies in a way that AA would not have approved for JA. Intellectual pursuits for women, particularly scientific investigation, were more acceptable in France than in England or America. She quotes Alexander Pope: "Back through the paths of pleasing sense I ran,/ Nor wished an angel whom I loved a man" ("Eloisa to Abelard," lines 69–70).

Shebbeare, who professes that he had rather take the opinion of an accomplished lady in matters of polite writing than the first wits of Italy and should think himself safer with her approbation than of a long list of literati, and he give[s] this reason for it: that women have in general more delicate sensations than men; what touches them is for the most part true in nature, whereas men, warped by education, judge amiss from previous prejudice and, referring all things to the model of the ancients, condemn that by comparison where no true similitude ought to be expected.

But in this country you need not be told how much female education is neglected, nor how fashionable it has been to ridicule female learning, though I acknowledge it my happiness to be connected with a person of a more generous mind and liberal sentiments. I cannot forbear transcribing a few generous sentiments which I lately met with upon this subject. If women, says the writer, are to be esteemed our enemies, methinks it is an ignoble cowardice thus to disarm them and not allow them the same weapons we use ourselves; but if they deserve the title of our friends, 'tis an inhuman tyranny to debar them of privileges of ingenious education, which would also render their friendship so much the more delightful to themselves and us. Nature is seldom observed to be niggardly of her choicest gifts to the sex: their senses are generally as quick as ours, their reason as nervous,[6] their judgment as mature and solid. Add but to these natural perfections the advantages of acquired learning, what polite and charming creatures would they prove, whilst their external beauty does the office of a crystal to the lamp, not shrouding but disclosing their brighter intellects. Nor need we fear to lose our empire over them by thus improving their native abilities, since where there is most learning, sense and knowledge, there is always observed to be the most modesty and rectitude of manners.

Braintree, October 25, 1778

The morning after I received your very short letter, I determined to have devoted the day in writing to my friend; but I had only just breakfasted when I had a visit from Monsieur Rivers, an officer on board the *Languedoc,* who speaks English well, the Captain of the *Zara,* and six or eight other officers from on board another ship. The first gentlemen dined with me and spent the day, so that I had

---

[6]Vigorous.

no opportunity of writing that day. The gentlemen officers have made me several visits, and I have dined twice on board at very elegant entertainments. Count d'Estaing has been exceeding polite to me. Soon after he arrived here, I received a message from him requesting that I would meet him at Col. Quincy's as it was inconvenient leaving his ship for any long time. I waited upon him and was very politely received. Upon parting, he requested that the family would accompany me on board his ship and dine with him the next Thursday with any friends we chose to bring, and his barge should come for us. We went accordingly to the invitation and were sumptuously entertained with every delicacy that this country produces and the addition of every foreign article that could render our feast splendid. Music and dancing for the young folks closed the day.

The temperance of these gentlemen, the peaceable quiet disposition both of officers and men, joined to many other virtues which they have exhibited during their continuance with us, is sufficient to make Europeans and Americans too blush at their own degeneracy of manners. Not one officer has been seen the least disguised with liquor since their arrival. Most that I have seen appear to be gentlemen of family and education. I have been the more desirous to take notice of them as I cannot help saying that they have been neglected in the town of Boston. Generals Heath and Hancock have done their part, but very few, if any, private families have any acquaintance with them.

Perhaps I feel more anxious to have them distinguished on account of the near and dear connection I have among them. It would gratify me much if I had it in my power to entertain every officer in the fleet.

In the very few lines I have received from you, not the least mention is made that you have ever received a line from me. I have not been so parsimonious as my friend; perhaps I am not so prudent, but I cannot take my pen with my heart overflowing and not give utterance to some of the abundance which is in it. Could you, after a thousand fears and anxieties, long expectation and painful suspenses, be satisfied with my telling you that I was well, that I wished you were with me, that my daughter sent her duty, that I had ordered some articles for you which I hoped would arrive &c. &c.—By Heaven, if you could you have changed hearts with some frozen Laplander or made a voyage to a region that has chilled every drop of your blood.—But I will restrain a pen already I fear too rash, nor shall it tell you how much I have suffered from this appearance of—inattention.

The articles sent by Capt. Tucker have arrived safe and will be of great service to me. Our money is very little better than blank paper; it takes 40 dollars to purchase a barrel of cider, 50 pounds lawful[1] for a hundred of sugar and 50 dollars for a hundred of flour, 4 dollars per day for a laborer and find him,[2] which will amount to 4 more. You will find by bills drawn before the date of this that I had taken the method which I was happy in finding you had directed me to. I shall draw for the rest as I find my situation requires. No article that can be named, foreign or domestic, but what costs more than double in hard money what it once sold for. In one letter I have given you an account of our local situation, and of *every thing* I thought you might wish to know. Four or five sheets of paper wrote to you by the last mail[3] were destroyed when she was taken. Duplicates are my aversion, though I believe I should set a value upon them if I was to receive them from a certain friend, a friend who never was deficient in testifying his regard and affection to his

Portia

My Dearest Friend   Braintree, December 15, 1783

I returned last evening from Boston, where I went at the kind invitation of my uncle and aunt, to celebrate our annual festival. Doctor Cooper being dangerously sick, I went to hear Mr. Clark, who is settled with Dr. Chauncey; this gentleman gave us an animated, elegant and sensible discourse, from Isaiah 55 chapter and 12th verse—"For ye shall go out with joy, and be led forth with peace; the mountains and the hills shall break forth before you into singing, and all the trees of the field shall clap their hands."

Whilst he ascribed glory and praise unto the most high, he considered the worthy, disinterested, and undaunted patriots as the instruments in the hand of providence for accomplishing what was marvelous in our eyes; he recapitulated the dangers they had passed through and the hazards they had run; the firmness which had in a particular manner distinguished some characters, not only early to engage in so dangerous a contest, but in spite of our gloomy pros-

[1]Lawful money.
[2]Furnish his meals.
[3]Ship carrying mail.

pects they persevered even unto the end, until they had obtained a peace safe and honorable: large as our designs, capacious as our wishes, and much beyond our expectations.

How did my heart dilate with pleasure when, as each event was particularized, I could trace my friend as a principal in them; could say, it was he, who was one of the first in joining the band of patriots who formed our first national council. It was he who, though happy in his domestic attachments, left his wife, his children, then but infants, even surrounded with the horrors of war, terrified and distressed the week after the memorable 17th of April.[1] Left them to the protection of that providence which has never forsaken them and joined, himself undismayed, to that respectable body, of which he was a member. Trace his conduct through every period, you will find him the same undaunted character, encountering the dangers of the ocean, risking captivity and a dungeon,[2] contending with wickedness in high places, jeoparding his life, endangered by the intrigues, revenge, and malice of a potent, though defeated nation.

These are not the mere eulogiums of conjugal affection, but certain facts and solid truths. My anxieties, my distress, at every period, bear witness to them; though now, by a series of prosperous events, the recollection is more sweet than painful.

Whilst I was in town, Mr. Dana[3] arrived very unexpectedly, for I had not received your letters by Mr. Thaxter. My uncle fortunately discovered him, as he came up into State Street, and instantly engaged him to dine with him, acquainting him that I was in town and at his house. The news soon reached my ears. Mr. Dana arrived, Mr. Dana arrived—from every person you saw. But how was I affected? The tears involuntary flowed from my eyes. Though God is my witness, I envied not the felicity of others, yet my heart swelled with grief, and the idea that I, I only, was left alone, recalled all the tender scenes of separation and overcame all my fortitude. I retired

[1] She probably means April 19, date of the battles of Lexington and Concord, the opening engagements of the Revolution.

[2] JA realistically feared that the British would find and capture the ship on which he would be sailing as an envoy to France in 1778; if caught, he would probably have been jailed in Newgate, tried for treason, and executed.

[3] Francis Dana had gone with JA in 1779 as secretary of legation on the mission to negotiate peace with Britain. Thaxter had accompanied Adams as private secretary.

and reasoned myself into composure sufficient to see him without a childish emotion.

He tarried but a short time, anxious, as you may well imagine, to reach Cambridge. He promised me a visit with his lady, in a few days, to which I look forward with pleasure.

I reached home last evening, having left Nabby in town to make her winter visit. I found Mr. Thaxter just arrived before me. It was a joyful meeting to both of us, though I could not prevail with him only for half an hour. His solicitude to see his parents was great, and though I wished his continuance with me, yet I checked not the filial flow of affection. Happy youth! who has parents still alive to visit, parents who can rejoice in a son returned to them after a long absence, untainted in his morals, improved in his understanding, with a character fair and unblemished.

But O, my dearest friend, what shall I say to you in reply to your pressing invitation?[4] I have already written to you in answer to your letters which were dated September 10th and reached me a month before those by Mr. Thaxter. I related to you all my fears respecting a winter's voyage. My friends[5] are all against it, and Mr. Gerry,[6] as you will see by the copy of his letter enclosed, has given his opinion upon well grounded reasons. If I should leave my affairs in the hands of my friends, there would be much to think of, and much to do, to place them in that method and order I would wish to leave them in.

Theory and practice are two very different things; and the object magnifies, as I approach nearer to it. I think if you were abroad in a private character, and necessitated to continue there, I should not hesitate so much at coming to you. But a mere American as I am, unacquainted with the etiquette of courts, taught to say the thing I mean and to wear my heart in my countenance, I am sure I should make an awkward figure, and then it would mortify my pride if I should be thought to disgrace you. Yet strip royalty of its pomp and power, and what are its votaries more than their fellow worms? I have so little of the ape about me that I have refused every public invitation to figure in the gay world and sequestered myself in this humble cottage, content with rural life and my domestic employments, in the midst of which I have sometimes smiled upon recol-

---

[4]JA wanted AA to join him in England.
[5]Family.
[6]Elbridge Gerry, a Massachusetts patriot and statesman and friend of the Adamses.

lecting that I had the honor of being allied to an ambassador. Yet I have for an example the chaste Lucretia, who was found spinning in the midst of her maidens when the brutal Tarquin plotted her destruction.[7]

I am not acquainted with the particular circumstances attending the renewal of your commission;[8] if it is modeled so as to give you satisfaction, I am content, and hope you will be able to discharge it so as to receive the approbation of your sovereign.

A friend of yours in Congress, some months ago, sent me an extract of a letter, requesting me to conceal his name, as he would not choose to have it known by what means he procured the copy. From all your letters I discovered that the treatment you had received, and the suspense you was in, was sufficiently irritating without anything further to add to your vexation. I therefore suppressed the extract, as I knew the author was fully known to you. But seeing a letter from Gen. Warren to you, in which this extract is alluded to, and finding by your late letters that your situation is less embarrassing, I enclose it, lest you should think it much worse than it really is. At the same time, I cannot help adding an observation which appears pertinent to me: that there is an ingredient necessary in a man's composition towards happiness, which people of feeling would do well to acquire—a certain respect for the follies of mankind. For there are so many fools whom the opinion of the world entitles to regard, whom accident has placed in heights of which they are unworthy, that he who cannot restrain his contempt or indignation at the sight will be too often quarreling with the disposal of things to relish that share which is allotted to himself.—And here my paper obliges me to close the subject, without room to say adieu.

[7]When some Roman aristocrats came home unexpectedly from the army camp to see what their wives were doing, most of the women were at parties; only Lucretia was found spinning with her handmaids. Her beauty and virtue inflamed the lust of Sextus Tarquinius, the king's son, who came back and raped her. As a result, she killed herself.

[8]Congress kept JA in suspense about his continuance as envoy and repeatedly changed the conditions of his service. Because JA tended to be testy and obstinate, he was often criticized.

Abigail Adams to Elizabeth Smith Shaw

> On board the ship *Active*[1]
> Latitude 34, Long. 35
My dear Sister   July 10?, 1784

This day three weeks I came on board this ship, and Heaven be praised, have hitherto had a favorable passage. Upon the banks of Newfoundland we had an easterly storm, I thought; but the sailors say it was only a breeze. We could not, however, sit without being held into our chairs, and everything that was moveable was in motion; plates, mugs, bottles, all crashing to pieces; the sea roaring and lashing the ship; and when, worn down with the fatigue of the violent and incessant motion, we were assisted into our cabins, we were obliged to hold ourselves in, with our utmost strength, without once thinking of closing our eyes; everything wet, dirty and cold, ourselves sick. You will not envy our situation, yet the returning sun, a smooth sea and a mild sky dispelled our fears and raised our languid heads.

> Ye too, ye Winds, I raise my voice to you
> In what far distant region of the sky
> Hushed in deep silence, sleep you when tis calm?

There is not an object in nature better calculated to raise in our minds sublime ideas of the Deity than the boundless ocean. Who can contemplate it, without admiration and wonder.

> And thou Majestic Main,
> A secret world of wonders in thyself
> Sound his stupendous praise; whose greater voice
> Or bids your roar, or bids your roarings fall.

I have contemplated it in its various appearances since I came to sea: smooth as a glass, then gently agitated with a light breeze, then lifting wave upon wave, moving on with rapidity, then rising to the skies, and in majestic force tossing our ship to and fro, alternately rising and sinking; in the night I have beheld it blazing and sparkling with ten thousand gems—until with the devout psalmist I have ex-

---

[1]AA was sailing, with Nabby, to join JA in England. Shaw was her sister.

claimed, "Great and marvelous are thy works, Lord God Almighty, in Wisdom hast thou made them all."[2]

It is very difficult to write at sea; in the serenest weather the vessel rolls and exceeds the moderate rocking of a cradle, and a calm gives one more motion than a side wind going at 7 and 8 knots an hour: I am now sitting in my *stateroom,* which is about 8 foot square, with two cabins[3] and a chair, which completely fills it, and I write leaning one arm upon my cabin, with a piece of board in my lap, whilst I steady myself by holding my other hand upon the opposite cabin; from this you will judge what accommodations we have for writing. The door of my room opens into the great cabin, where we sit, dine, and the gentlemen sleep: we cannot breathe with our door shut, so that, except when we dress and undress, we live in common. A sweet situation for a delicate lady, but necessity has no law; and we are very fortunate in our company.

We have six gentlemen passengers and a lad, brother to Mrs. Adams,[4] whom I find a very agreeable modest woman. There are two staterooms, one of which I occupy with my maid, the other Mrs. Adams and Nabby; when we first came on board, we suffered exceedingly from seasickness, which is a most disheartening disorder. This held us in some degree for ten days, and a more than ordinary motion will still affect us. The ship was very tight, and consequently very loathsome; in addition to this, our cargo was not of the most odoriferous kind, consisting of oil and potash, one of which leaked and the other fermented, so that we had that in concert with the sea smell. Our cook and steward is a lazy dirty Negro, with no more knowledge of his business than a savage. Until I was well enough to exert my authority, I was daily obliged to send my shoes upon deck to have them scraped: but the first time we were all able to go upon deck, I summoned my own man servant, who before had been as sick as any of us, and sent him down with all the boys I could muster, with scrapers, mops, brushes, infusions of vinegar &c., and in a few hours we found there *was boards for a floor.* When we returned, we scarcely knew our former habitation; since which I have taken upon me the whole direction of our cabin, taught the cook to dress his victuals, and have made several puddings with my

[2]Psalms 104:24, slightly misquoted.
[3]Berths.
[4]A physician's wife with whom AA already had a passing acquaintance.

own hands. We met with a great misfortune in the loss of our cow, which has deprived us of many conveniences; the poor creature was so bruised in the storm which we had that they were obliged to kill her the next day.

Our Captain is the very man one would wish to go to sea with, always upon deck a nights, never sleeps but six hours in the twenty-four, attentive to the clouds, to the wind and weather; anxious for his ship, constantly watchful of his sails and his rigging, humane and kind to his men, who are all quiet and still as a private family; nor do I recollect hearing him swear but once since I came on board, and that was at a vessel which spoke with us, and by imprudent conduct were in danger of running on board of us; to them he gave a broadside. Since that I have not wished to see a vessel near us. At a distance we have seen several sail. We came on board mere strangers to the passengers, but we have found them obliging and kind, polite and civil, particularly so a Dr. Clark, who has been as attentive to us as if we were all his sisters; we have profited by his care and advice during our seasickness, when he was nurse, as well as physician; doctors, you know, have an advantage over other gentlemen, and we soon grow fond of those who interest themselves in our welfare, and particularly so of those who show tenderness towards us in our sickness.

We have a Mr. Foster on board, who is a very agreeable man, whose manners are soft and modest; indeed we have not a disagreeable companion amongst them. All except one are married men. Dr. Clark is a great favorite of Nabby's. He found, I believe, that the mind wanted soothing and tenderness, as well as attention to the body.[5] Nobody said a word, nor do I know from anything but his manner of treating her, that he suspected it; but he has the art of diverting and amusing her, without seeming to try for it. She has behaved with a dignity and decorum worthy of her.

I have often, my dear sister, looked towards your habitation since I left America, and fancied you watching the wind and the weather, rejoicing when a favorable breeze was like to favor our passage, and lifting up a pious ejaculation to Heaven for the safety of your friends, then looking upon the children committed to your care with addi-

[5]Nabby was getting over a romantic attachment to Royall Tyler, which her parents had discouraged.

tional tenderness.[6] Aya, why drops the tear as I write? Why these tender emotions of a mother's breast: is it not folly to be thus agitated with a thought?—Nature, all powerful Nature! How is my dear brother? He too is kindly interested in my welfare, says, "Here they are and there they go. Well, when is it likely we shall hear from them?" Of a safe arrival I hope to inform you in ten days from the present; I will not seal my letter, but keep it open for that happy period, as I hope it will prove.

You must excuse every inaccuracy and be thankful if you can pick out my meaning. The confinement on board ship is as irksome as any circumstance I have yet met with; it is what we know there is no remedy for. The weather is so cold and damp that in the pleasantest day we can sit but a little while upon deck. There has been no time so warm but what we could bear our baize gowns over our double calico, and cloaks upon them, whilst you, I imagine, are panting under the midsummer heat. Tell Brother Shaw I could relish a fine plate of his sallet,[7] and when his hand is in a few of his peas; but not today; I would not have him send them, as I am now upon a low diet, for yesterday, my dear sister, I was seized with a severe fit of the rheumatism, which had threatened me for several days before, occasioned, I suppose, from the constant dampness of the ship. I was very sick, full of pain, a good deal of fever and very lame, so that I could not dress myself; but good nursing and a good physician, with rubbing and flannel, has relieved me.

[6]AA had left her youngest children, Charles and Tommy, with the Shaws.
[7]Salad.

Judith Sargent Murray

1751–1820

JUDITH SARGENT was born into a socially prominent and politically active family in Gloucester, Massachusetts. Allowed to share the lessons of her brother, whom a local minister was preparing for entrance into Harvard, she studied Latin, Greek, mathematics, and astronomy. She married John Stevens, a ship captain, and began to publish poems and essays in periodicals. She and her family were converted to Universalism by the Reverend John Murray, who was to found the Universalist Church in America. After Stevens's death, she married Murray (1788); and they had two children. In 1793, they moved to Boston.

From 1789 through 1794, Judith Murray published regularly in the *Massachusetts Magazine,* one of the most prestigious periodicals of the time; her later essays were collected as *The Gleaner* in 1798. She ranged freely over public issues such as liberal religion, Federalist politics, and the need to develop a national literature, but she took a particular interest in the advancement of women. "On the Equality of the Sexes," originally written in 1779, is the first systematic feminist manifesto in American literature. In later essays, Murray further enlarged on the capacities of women, argued for giving them a substantial education, and urged that they be trained for economic self-sufficiency (although she did not specify how this could be attained). Believing that America should develop a native drama, she praised the plays of Royall Tyler and Mercy Otis Warren and wrote two of her own, which were produced but not successful.

BIBLIOGRAPHY

The Massachusetts Magazine (March, April, and May 1790).

Murray, Judith Sargent. *The Gleaner: A Miscellaneous Production*. Vol. 2. (Boston: L. Thomas and E. T. Andrews, 1798).

On the Equality of the Sexes

That minds are not alike, full well I know,
This truth each day's experience will show;
To heights surprising some great spirits soar,
With inborn strength mysterious depths explore;
5   Their eager gaze surveys the path of light,
Confessed[1] it stood to Newton's piercing sight.
    Deep science, like a bashful maid retires,
And but the *ardent* breast her worth inspires;
By perseverance the coy fair is won.
10   And Genius, led by Study, wears the crown.
    But some there are who wish not to improve,
Who never can the path of knowledge love,
Whose soul's almost with the dull body one,
With anxious care each mental pleasure shun;
15   Weak is the leveled, enervated mind,
And but while here to vegetate designed.
The torpid spirit mingling with its clod,
Can scarcely boast its origin from God;
Stupidly dull—they move progressing on—
20   They eat, and drink, and all their work is done.
While others, emulous of sweet applause,
Industrious seek for each event a cause,
Tracing the hidden springs whence knowledge flows,
Which nature all in beauteous order shows.
25   Yet cannot I their sentiments imbibe,

[1]Revealed.

Who this distinction to the sex ascribe,
As if a woman's form must needs enroll,
A weak, a servile, an inferior soul;
And that the guise of man must still proclaim,
30   Greatness of mind, and him, to be the same:
Yet as the hours revolve fair proofs arise,
Which the bright wreath of growing fame supplies;
And in past times some men have *sunk* so *low,*
That female records nothing *less* can show.

35   But imbecility[2] is still confined,
And by the lordly sex to us consigned;
They rob us of the power t' improve,
And then declare we only trifles love;
Yet haste the era, when the world shall know,
40   That such distinctions only dwell below;
The soul unfettered, to no sex confined,
Was for the abodes of cloudless day designed.
    Meantime we emulate their manly fires,
Though erudition all their thoughts inspires,
45   Yet nature with *equality* imparts,
And *noble passions,* swell e'en *female hearts.*

Is it upon mature consideration we adopt the idea that nature is thus partial in her distributions? Is it indeed a fact that she hath yielded to one-half of the human species so unquestionable a mental superiority? I know that to both sexes elevated understandings, and the reverse, are common. But, suffer me to ask in what the minds of females are so notoriously deficient or unequal. May not the intellectual powers be ranged under these four heads—imagination, reason, memory and judgment? The province of imagination hath long since been surrendered up to us, and we have been crowned undoubted sovereigns of the regions of fancy. Invention is perhaps the most arduous effort of the mind; this branch of imagination hath been particularly ceded to us, and we have been time out of mind invested with that creative faculty. Observe the variety of fashions (here I bar the contemptuous smile) which distinguish and adorn the female world; how continually are they changing, insomuch that they almost render the wise man's assertion problematical, and we

[2]Weakness.

are ready to say, *there is something new under the sun.*[3] Now what a playfulness, what an exuberance of fancy, what strength of inventive imagination, doth this continual variation discover? Again, it hath been observed that if the turpitude of the conduct of our sex hath been ever so enormous, so extremely ready are we, that the very first thought presents us with an apology so plausible as to produce our actions even in an amiable light. Another instance of our creative powers is our talent for slander; how ingenious are we at inventive scandal! what a formidable story can we in a moment fabricate merely from the force of a prolific imagination! how many reputations, in the fertile brain of a female, have been utterly despoiled! how industrious are we at improving a hint! suspicion how easily do we convert into conviction, and conviction, embellished by the power of eloquence, stalks abroad to the surprise and confusion of unsuspecting innocence. Perhaps it will be asked if I furnish these facts as instances of excellency in our sex. Certainly not; but as proofs of a creative faculty, of a lively imagination. Assuredly, great activity of mind is thereby discovered, and was this activity properly directed, what beneficial effects would follow. Is the needle and kitchen sufficient to employ the operations of a soul thus organized? I should conceive not. Nay, it is a truth that those very departments leave the intelligent principle vacant, and at liberty for speculation. Are we deficient in reason? we can only reason from what we know, and if an opportunity of acquiring knowledge hath been denied us, the inferiority of our sex cannot fairly be deduced from thence. Memory, I believe, will be allowed us in common, since every one's experience must testify that a loquacious old woman is as frequently met with as a communicative old man; their subjects are alike drawn from the fund of other times, and the transactions of their youth or of maturer life entertain, or perhaps fatigue you, in the evening of their lives. "But our judgment is not so strong—we do not distinguish so well."—Yet it may be questioned, from what doth this superiority, in this determining faculty of the soul, proceed? May we not trace its source in the difference of education, and continued advantages? Will it be said that the judgment of a male of two years old is more sage than that of a female's of the same age? I believe the reverse is generally observed to be true. But from that period what partiality! how is the one exalted, and the other depressed, by

[3]See Ecclesiastes 1:9.

the contrary modes of education which are adopted! the one is taught to aspire, and the other is early confined and limited. As their years increase, the sister must be wholly domesticated, while the brother is led by the hand through all the flowery paths of science. Grant that their minds are by nature equal, yet who shall wonder at the *apparent* superiority, if indeed custom becomes *second nature*; nay, if it taketh place of nature, and that it doth the experience of each day will evince. At length arrived at womanhood, the uncultivated fair one feels a void, which the employments allotted her are by no means capable of filling. What can she do? to books she may not apply; or if she doth, *to those only of the novel kind,* lest she merit the appellation of a *learned lady;* and what ideas have been affixed to this term, the observation of many can testify. Fashion, scandal, and sometimes what is still more reprehensible, are then called in to her relief; and who can say to what lengths the liberties she takes may proceed. Meantime she herself is most unhappy; she feels the want of a cultivated mind. Is she single, she in vain seeks to fill up time from sexual employments or amusements. Is she united to a person whose soul nature made equal to her own, education hath set him so far above her that in those entertainments which are productive of such rational felicity, she is not qualified to accompany him. She experiences a mortifying consciousness of inferiority, which embitters every enjoyment. Doth the person to whom her adverse fate hath consigned her possess a mind incapable of improvement, she is equally wretched, in being so closely connected with an individual whom she cannot but despise. Now, was she permitted the same instructors as her brother (with an eye however to their particular departments), for the employment of a rational mind an ample field would be opened. In astronomy she might catch a glimpse of the immensity of the Deity, and thence she would form amazing conceptions of the august and supreme Intelligence. In geography she would admire Jehovah in the midst of his benevolence: thus adapting this globe to the various wants and amusements of its inhabitants. In natural philosophy she would adore the infinite majesty of heaven, clothed in condescension; and as she traversed the reptile world, she would hail the goodness of a creating God. A mind thus filled would have little room for the trifles with which our sex are, with too much justice, accused of amusing themselves; and they would thus be rendered fit companions for those, who should one day wear them as their crown.[4] Fashions, in their variety, would then give place to conjectures which might perhaps conduce to the improvement of the literary world; and there would be no leisure for slander or detraction. Reputation would not then be blasted, but serious speculations would occupy the lively imaginations of the sex. Unnecessary visits would be precluded, and that custom would only be indulged by way of relaxation, or to answer the demands of consanguinity and friendship. Females would become discreet, their judgments would be invigorated, and their partners for life being circumspectly chosen, an unhappy Hymen would then be as rare as is now the reverse.

Will it be urged that those acquirements would supersede our domestic duties? I answer that every requisite in female economy is easily attained; and, with truth I can add, that when once attained, they require no further *mental attention*. Nay, while we are pursuing the needle or the superintendency of the family, I repeat that our minds are at full liberty for reflection; that imagination may exert itself in full vigor; and that if a just foundation is early laid, our ideas will then be worthy of rational beings. If we were industrious, we might easily find time to arrange them upon paper, or should avocations press too hard for such an indulgence, the hours allotted for conversation would at least become more refined and rational. Should it still be vociferated, "Your domestic employments are sufficient"—I would calmly ask, is it reasonable that a candidate for immortality, for the joys of heaven, an intelligent being, who is to spend an eternity in contemplating the works of Deity, should at present be so degraded as to be allowed no other ideas than those which are suggested by the mechanism of a pudding or the sewing the seams of a garment? Pity that all such censurers of female improvement do not go one step further and deny their future existence; to be consistent they surely ought.

Yes, ye lordly, ye haughty sex, our souls are by nature *equal* to yours; the same breath of God animates, enlivens, and invigorates us; and that we are not fallen lower than yourselves, let those witness who have greatly towered above the various discouragements by which they have been so heavily oppressed; and though I am unacquainted with the list of celebrated characters on either side, yet from the observations I have made in the contracted circle in which

4"A virtuous woman is a crown to her husband" (Proverbs 12:4).

I have moved, I dare confidently believe, that from the commencement of time to the present day, there hath been as many females, as males, who, by the *mere force of natural powers,* have merited the crown of applause; who, *thus unassisted,* have seized the wreath of fame. I know there are who assert, that as the animal powers of the one sex are superior, of course their mental faculties also must be stronger; thus attributing strength of mind to the transient organization of this earth-born tenement. But if this reasoning is just, man must be content to yield the palm to many of the brute creation, since by not a few of his brethren of the field, he is far surpassed in bodily strength. Moreover, was this argument admitted, it would prove too much, for ocular demonstration evinceth, that there are many robust masculine ladies, and effeminate gentlemen. Yet I fancy that Mr. Pope, though clogged with an enervated body, and distinguished by a diminutive stature, could nevertheless lay claim to greatness of soul;[5] and perhaps there are many other instances which might be adduced to combat so unphilosophical an opinion. Do we not often see, that when the clay-built tabernacle is well nigh dissolved, when it is just ready to mingle with the parent soil, the immortal inhabitant aspires to, and even attaineth heights the most sublime, and which were before wholly unexplored. Besides, were we to grant that animal strength proved anything, taking into consideration the accustomed impartiality of nature, we should be induced to imagine that she had invested the female mind with superior strength as an equivalent for the bodily powers of man. But waving this however palpable advantage, for *equality only,* we wish to contend.[6]

I am aware that there are many passages in the sacred oracles which seem to give the advantage to the other sex; but I consider all these as wholly metaphorical. Thus David was a man after God's own heart, yet see him enervated by his licentious passions! behold him following Uriah to the death, and shew me wherein could consist the immaculate Being's complacency. Listen to the curses which Job bestoweth upon the day of his nativity, and tell me where is his perfection, where his patience—*literally* it existed not. David and Job were types of him who was to come; and the superiority of man,

---

[5]Alexander Pope, the greatest English poet of the eighteenth century, was a hunchback.

[6]Originally this essay was published in two installments, the first ending here.

as exhibited in scripture, being also emblematical, all arguments deduced from thence, of course fall to the ground.[7] The exquisite delicacy of the female mind proclaimeth the exactness of its texture, while its nice sense of honor announceth its innate, its native grandeur. And indeed, in one respect, the preeminence seems to be tacitly allowed us, for after an education which limits and confines, and employments and recreations which naturally tend to enervate the body and debilitate the mind; after we have from early youth been adorned with ribbons and other gewgaws, dressed out like the ancient victims previous to a sacrifice, being taught by the care of our parents in collecting the most showy materials that the ornamenting our exterior ought to be the principal object of our attention; after, I say, fifteen years thus spent, we are introduced into the world, amid the united adulation of every beholder. Praise is sweet to the soul; we are immediately intoxicated by large draughts of flattery, which, being plentifully administered, is to the pride of our hearts the most acceptable incense. It is expected that with the other sex we should commence immediate war, and that we should triumph over the machinations of the most artful. We must be constantly upon our guard; prudence and discretion must be our characteristics; and we must rise superior to, and obtain a complete victory over those who have been long adding to the native strength of their minds by an unremitted study of men and books, and who have, moreover, conceived from the loose characters which they have seen portrayed in the extensive variety of their reading, a most contemptible opinion of the sex. Thus unequal, we are, notwithstanding, forced to the combat, and the infamy which is consequent upon the smallest deviation in our conduct, proclaims the high idea which was formed of our native strength; and thus, indirectly at least, is the preference acknowledged to be our due. And if we are allowed an equality of acquirement, let serious studies equally employ our minds, and we will bid our souls arise to equal strength. We will meet upon even ground, the despot man; we will rush with alacrity to the combat, and, crowned by success, we shall then answer the exalted expectations which are formed. Though sensibility, soft compassion, and gentle commiseration are inmates in the female bosom, yet

[7]See I Samuel 13:14; II Samuel, chapter 11; Job, chapter 3. Both David and Job were thought to have prefigured Christ; hence, according to Murray's interpretation, their goodness was figurative rather than actual (as is man's superiority over woman).

against every deep-laid art, altogether fearless of the event, we will
set them in array; for assuredly the wreath of victory will encircle
the spotless brow. If we meet an equal, a sensible[8] friend, we will
reward him with the hand of amity, and through life we will be
assiduous to promote his happiness; but from every deep-laid scheme
for our ruin, retiring into ourselves, amid the flowery paths of science,[9] we will indulge in all the refined and sentimental pleasures of
contemplation. And should it still be urged that the studies thus
insisted upon would interfere with our more peculiar department, I
must further reply that *early hours,* and close application, will do
wonders; and to her who is from the first dawn of reason taught to
fill up time rationally, both the requisites will be easy. I grant that
niggard fortune is too generally unfriendly to the mind, and that
much of that valuable treasure, time, is necessarily expended upon
the wants of the body; but it should be remembered, that in embarrassed circumstances our companions have as little leisure for literary
improvement as is afforded to us; for most certainly their provident
care is at least as requisite as our exertions. Nay, we have even more
leisure for sedentary pleasures, as our avocations are more retired,
much less laborious, and, as hath been observed, by no means require that avidity of attention which is proper to the employments
of the other sex. In high life, or, in other words, where the parties
are in possession of affluence, the objection respecting time is wholly
obviated, and of course falls to the ground; and it may also be repeated that many of those hours which are at present swallowed up
in fashion and scandal might be redeemed, were we habituated to
useful reflections. But in one respect, O ye arbiters of our fate! we
confess that the superiority is undubitably yours; you are by nature
formed for our protectors; we pretend not to vie with you in bodily
strength; upon this point we will never contend for victory. Shield
us then, we beseech you, from external evils, and in return we will
transact *your* domestic affairs. Yes, *your,* for are you not equally
interested in those matters with ourselves? Is not the elegancy of
neatness as agreeable to your sight as to ours, is not the well favored
viand equally delightful to your taste; and doth not your sense of
hearing suffer as much from the discordant sounds prevalent in an

[8]Sensitive.
[9]Knowledge.

ill regulated family, produced by the voices of children and many *et ceteras?*

Constantia.[10]

By way of supplement to the foregoing pages, I subjoin the following extract from a letter, wrote to a friend in the December of 1780.

And now assist me, O thou genius of my sex, while I undertake the arduous task of endeavoring to combat that vulgar, that almost universal error, which hath, it seems, enlisted even Mr. P—— under its banners. The superiority of your sex hath, I grant, been time out of mind esteemed a truth incontrovertible; in consequence of which persuasion, every plan of education hath been calculated to establish this favorite tenet. Not long since, weak and presuming as I was, I amused myself with selecting some arguments from nature, reason, and experience against this so generally received idea. I confess that to sacred testimonies I had not recourse. I held them to be merely metaphorical, and thus regarding them, I could not persuade myself that there was any propriety in bringing them to decide in this *very important debate.* However, as you, sir, confine yourself entirely to the sacred oracles, I mean to bend the whole of my artillery against those supposed proofs, which you have from thence provided, and from which you have formed an intrenchment *apparently* so invulnerable. And first, to begin with our great progenitors; but here, suffer me to premise that it is for mental strength I mean to contend, for with respect to animal powers, I yield them undisputed to that sex which enjoys them in common with the lion, the tiger, and many other beasts of prey; therefore your observations respecting the *rib, under the arm, at a distance from the head, &c. &c.* in no sort militate against my view. Well, but the woman was first in the transgression. Strange how blind *self love* renders you men; were you not wholly absorbed in a partial admiration of your own abilities, you would long since have acknowledged the force of what I am now going to urge. It is true some ignoramuses have, absurdly enough, informed us that the beauteous fair of paradise was seduced from her obedience by a malignant demon *in the guise of a baleful serpent;* but we, who are better informed, know that the fallen spirit pre-

---

[10]Murray's pen name.

sented himself to her view, *a shining angel still;* for thus, saith the critics in the Hebrew tongue, ought the word to be rendered. Let us examine her motive—Hark! the seraph declares that she shall attain a perfection of knowledge; for is there aught which is not comprehended under one or other of the terms *good* and *evil?* It doth not appear that she was governed by any one sensual appetite, but merely by a desire of adorning her mind; a laudable ambition fired her soul, and a thirst for knowledge impelled the predilection so fatal in its consequences. Adam could not plead the same deception; assuredly he was not deceived; nor ought we to admire his superior strength, or wonder at his sagacity, when we so often confess that example is much more influential than precept. His gentle partner stood before him, a melancholy instance of the direful effects of disobedience; he saw her not possessed of that wisdom which she had fondly hoped to obtain, but he beheld the once blooming female disrobed of that innocence which had heretofore rendered her so lovely. To him then deception became impossible, as he had proof positive of the fallacy of the argument which the deceiver had suggested. What then could be his inducement to burst the barriers, and to fly directly in the face of that command, which *immediately* from the mouth of Deity *he* had received, since, I say, he could not plead that fascinating stimulus, the accumulation of knowledge, as indisputable conviction was so visibly portrayed before him. What mighty cause impelled him to sacrifice myriads of beings yet unborn, and by one impious act, which *he saw* would be productive of such fatal effects, entail undistinguished ruin upon a race of beings, which he was yet to produce. Blush, ye vaunters of fortitude; ye boasters of resolution; ye haughty lords of the creation; blush when ye remember that he was influenced by no other motive than a bare pusillanimous attachment to a woman! by sentiments so exquisitely soft that all his sons have, from that period, when they have designed to degrade them, described as highly feminine. Thus it should seem that all the arts of the grand deceiver (since means adequate to the purpose are, I conceive, invariably pursued) were requisite to mislead our general mother, while the father of mankind forfeited his own, and relinquished the happiness of posterity, merely in compliance with the blandishments of a female. The subsequent subjection the apostle Paul explains as a figure; after enlarging upon the subject, he adds, *"This is a great mystery; but I speak concerning Christ and the* church."[11] Now we know with what consummate wisdom the unerring father of eternity hath formed his plans; all the types which he hath displayed, he hath permitted *materially* to fail, in the very virtue for which *they* were famed. The reason for this is obvious, we might otherwise mistake his economy, and render that honor to the creature which is due only to the creator. I know that Adam was a figure of him who was to come. The grace contained in this figure is the reason of my rejoicing, and while I am very far from prostrating before the shadow, I yield joyfully in all things the preeminence to the second federal head. Confiding faith is prefigured by Abraham, yet he exhibits a contrast to affiance, when he says of his fair companion, she is my sister. Gentleness was the characteristic of Moses, yet he hesitated not to reply to Jehovah himself; with unsaintlike tongue he murmured at the waters of strife, and with rash hands he brake the tables, which were inscribed by the finger of divinity. David, dignified with the title of the man after God's own heart, and yet how stained was his life. Solomon was celebrated for wisdom, but folly is wrote in legible characters upon his almost every action. Lastly, let us turn our eyes to man in the aggregate. He is manifested as the figure of strength, but that we may not regard him as anything more than a figure, his soul is formed in no sort superior, but every way equal to the mind of her, who is the emblem of weakness, and whom he hails the gentle companion of his better days.

On the Domestic Education of Children

I hate severity to trembling youth,
Mildness should designate each useful truth;
My soul detests the rude unmanly part,
Which swells with bursting sighs the little heart.
What can an infant do to merit blows?
See, from his eyes a briny torrent flows.

[11]Ephesians 5:32.

Behold the pretty mourner! pale his cheek,
His tears are fruitless, and he dare not speak.
Lowly he bends beneath yon tyrant's rod;
Unfeeling pedagogue—who like some god
Fabled of old, of bloody savage mind,
To scourge, and not to mend the human race, designed.

It would be well if every gentle method to form the young untutored mind was essayed, previous to a harsher mode of procedure. Do blows ever produce a salutary effect upon a gentle or a generous disposition? It can hardly be presumed that they do; and if not upon the bosom, the feelings of which urbanity hath arranged, is it not more than probable that they tend to make an obstinate being still more perverse? Yet the reins of government I would not consign to children; the young idea I would direct, nor would I permit the dawn of life to pass uncultured by; nevertheless, to barbarous hands I would not yield the tender plant. Behold the pallid countenance of the little culprit, the tender sorrow, the imploring tear, the beseeching eye, the knee bent for forgiveness—and can the offences of a child be other than venial? But it is in vain—the inhuman preceptor continues obdurate—he retains his purpose, and the wretched sufferer receives those blows which only the malefactor can merit! Is there not some reason to suppose that, by a repetition of ignominious punishments, we shall eradicate from the young mind all sense of shame, thus throwing down a very essential barrier and finally opening the floodgates of vice?

But what shall we substitute instead of those violent and coercive measures? I proceed to give an example. Martesia is blessed with a numerous offspring of both sexes—some of her young folks have discovered dispositions not a little refractory—caprice hath shown its head, and a number of little petulancies early displayed themselves; yet that weapon known by the name of a rod was never so much as heard of among them, nor do they know the meaning of a blow. How then doth Martesia manage, for it is certain that her salutary efforts have well nigh eradicated from her little circle every perverse humor. Her family is a well regulated Commonwealth, the moving spring of which is emulation, *a laudable kind of emulation, which never partakes of envy, save when virtue acknowledgeth the hue of vice.* She hath in her gift various posts of honor; these she distributes according to the merit of the pretender; they are conferred upon those who have made any improvement, and the whole company join to invest the distinguished candidate with his new dignity. Martesia makes it a rule never to appear ruffled before her children, and she is particularly careful to keep every irregular passion from their observation. That she is tenderly concerned for them, and takes a very deep interest in their happiness, is a truth which she daily inculcates. She wishes also to implant in their young minds the most elevated opinion of her understanding; and she conceives that they cannot be too early impressed with an idea of her possessing superior abilities. The advantages which she will derive from this plan are obvious; her authority will be the more readily acknowledged, and her decisions will obtain the requisite weight. By reiterated petitions she is seldom persecuted, for, as the little claimants are sensible of her attachment and cannot call her judgment in question, they are not accustomed to repeat their requests. Yet, notwithstanding they are taught to believe Martesia ever under the government of reason, should a persevering spirit be found clamorously urgent, the pursuit, however, cannot be long continued, since but one answer will be given; which answer, though mild, is always peremptory and conclusive. To render prevalent in the minds of her children, sentiments of humanity and benevolence, is with Martesia an essential object. A *dignified* condescension to inferiors she also inculcates, and she early endeavors, by judicious advances, to bring them acquainted with that part of the economy of the Deity which hath made our obligations to each other reciprocal: Thus solicitous to enforce the idea of their dependence, even upon the meanest domestic, she exacts from her servants no extraordinary marks of humility toward them, for her view is to choke, if possible, the first buddings of unbecoming pride.

Doth she discover the smallest disposition to cruelty, or are her children deficient in divine sensibility, she is anxiously studious to exterminate the unhappy propensity and to awaken, or to *create,* the finer feelings of the soul. To this end she hath ever at hand a number of well chosen tales, calculated to promote the interests of virtue, to excite commiseration, and suited to their tender years. Meantime she is sparing of reproaches, and would, if possible, avoid imparting to them a consciousness of the discovery which she hath made. Her rewards are always exactly and impartially proportioned—*the degree of merit she critically examines*—and as this is her invariable rule, a murmur in the little society can never arise, and they are constantly convinced of the propriety of her decisions. The highest honor by which they can be distinguished is the investiture of a commission to convey to some worthy, but destitute, family a dinner, a garment, or a piece of money; and this office being always adjudged according to the magnitude of any particular action, it often happens that the most insensible are found in this department. Thus they are accustomed to acts of benevolence—they learn to feel, and become humane by habit.

The greatest felicity which our little family can experience is in the presence of Martesia. They are free from every restraint—pursue, unmolested, their amusements—and of their innocent mirth she not seldom partakes. It is in the pleasure which they derive from her smiles, her approbation, and her society, that she founds the basis of all her punishments.—When coercive measures are judged indispensable, if the fault is trivial, it remains a profound secret to all but Martesia and the little aggressor: But on the maternal countenance hangs a cloud—cold and distant looks take place of benign complacency; nor doth returning tenderness manifest tokens of reconciliation until full atonement is made for the error. If the offence is of a more heinous dye, it is immediately published throughout the house; from Martesia the culprit receiveth not the smallest attention; not a look, nor a word; while he or she is regarded by everyone with studied indifference. Should the transgression be considered as capital, the criminal is forthwith excluded the parental presence—not even a domestic conceives him worthy of notice—and it is with difficulty that he can obtain the assistance of which he stands in need. At length his little heart is almost broke—he petitions for favor, he sueth for forgiveness. No mediator presents, for Martesia reserves to herself the merit of obliging. Well, the concessions of the pretty offender are sufficiently humble—it is judged that his sufferings are adequate to his fault—Martesia is appeased, and the offense is cancelled. And it is to be observed that, when once the penitent is admitted into favor, his crime is entirely obliterated—it can no more be held up to view. Martesia, however, seldom hath occasion to exercise the last mentioned severity. Perverseness she hath at length well nigh subdued—and among her little flock a refractory spirit is now hardly known. To behold her in the midst of the sweetly smiling circle is truly charming.

When, for the completion of their education, she is obliged to part with her boys, with a firmness becoming her character she will submit; and should their preceptor pursue her plan, they will undoubtedly be rendered useful members of society; while her girls, continuing under such auspices, cannot be other than worthy and amiable women.

Constantia

A Letter to the Gleaner,
from *The Gleaner*, Number 65

Sir,

As you have assumed an office (whether properly qualified or not) the duties of which point out a cognizance of, and an effort to correct, as well the petty deviation, as those enormities which essentially involve the peace of society, I take the liberty to address you on a subject that, although little attended to, is frequently productive of real inconvenience. That few people possess the power of *pleasing,* the experience of every day incontrovertibly pronounces. I could make a thousand reflections, all very much to the purpose; but I will confine myself to a single instance, being fully convinced that it will present both my design and its illustration.

Embracing the long days of this uncommonly fine season, I determined on a jaunt, from which I calculated on receiving a prodigious deal of pleasure; but to my great disappointment, I was so tormented by the *civilities* with which I was hourly persecuted that I was kept in a continual state of vexation. I will confess to you, Mr. Gleaner, that the necessity of refusing any request, importunately urged, agonizes me beyond description; and I have frequently done violence to my most favorite wishes, and broke in upon plans that have been regularly arranged for a whole year, merely because I had not the firmness to withstand the solicitations of those who did not care three brass farthings what became of me or my views.

But, to begin my journey—I set out, escorted by my brother, a modest, docile young man, altogether as unequal to opposition as myself; we had taken places in the stage, a front seat in which is generally thought the least eligible; but, as it was my wish to inhale the perfumed breeze and to indulge myself with viewing the beauty of the surrounding prospects, I had stipulated for one of those seats. I was not, however, permitted to occupy it; my remonstrances were ineffectual; *the travelers too well understood what belonged to politeness* to let me remain in a situation exposed to dust, wind, and sun; and I was compelled to take my quarters in a back seat, where I was absolutely nearly suffocated in the want of air, and had nothing in view but the number of very *civil persons* who had thus contrived, with a politeness on which they plumed themselves very highly, to intercept every other prospect. After many days, during which I was persecuted with a multiplicity of attentions, all of a nature similar to that which placed me in the rear of the carriage, we arrived at a village in the neighborhood of Philadelphia, whither I had been drawn by my desire of visiting a female friend, who had passed some weeks at my father's. My friend is one of the few who is versed in all those delicate and minute attentions, which soothe and assist, while they neither oppress nor embarrass; but, alas! by hard necessity she is dependent on a set of beings whose ideas bear no more affinity to hers than darkness to light; and unfortunately she possesses no power to influence their movements.

I am naturally fond of tranquillity, and that I might be indulged in my own way, I had no sooner reached the abode of my friend than, avowedly for the purpose of contributing to my felicity, a numerous family, in all its branches, was thrown into confusion; a redundancy of apologies poured from every mouth, and they expressed, in the most moving terms, their regrets that their abilities were not proportioned to my superabounding merit. The children, too, were in dishabille—Mary's slip[1] happened to be the worst she had; Catharine's holiday shoes were immediately ordered out; and the eldest son, that he might exhibit his parts[2] to the best advantage, was directed to pin on those ruffles which were sewed to tape and carefully reserved to ornament his person on those gala days which occasionally occurred in the family. But a new scene of disorder was thus opened: one of those said ruffles was unfortunately lost, in search of which the whole house was engaged, and everything turned topsy turvy; yet, although each individual largely shared the perplexity produced by this accident, the search proved ineffectual, and Master Johnny was reduced to the necessity of sitting down to supper with only one solitary ruffle! The good man of the house was thus furnished with an admirable opportunity of expatiating on female *nonsicallities* and *primosities*,[3] and his satirical remarks were only suspended for the purpose of helping to load my plate. I was importuned to consider myself at home, and I was accused of a want of complacency in those viands, which it was *evident* they had *with*

---

[1]Pinafore.
[2]Abilities.
[3]Nonsensicallities (?) and primnesses.

infinite labor collected for the sole purpose of gratifying my ladyship.

Supper over, I flattered myself, fatigued as I was, that I should at length be permitted to make my escape to the chamber of repose; but, ah me! I found to my inexpressible chagrin that we were then only beginning the fifth act of the drama; the whole family were drawn out, and peremptorily ordered to sing for my *amusement;* and their tedious chansons, love ditties, and ballads were chanted in rotation, encored and repeated in concert, until, at the instance of my sympathizing friend, I was permitted to retire. On the ensuing day, scorched by the intense rays of a meridian sun, I was dragged over grounds that evinced nothing so much as the ill taste of the owner, and returned to take my seat at the dinner table, where the incidents which occurred seemed but a continuation of the scene opened the preceding evening.

A round of visits succeeded, all of which were in the same style. I recollect one afternoon, a timely shower having given a peculiar sweetness to the evening breeze, being on one of these same visits, I anticipated the pleasure of my walk homeward, distant about two miles; but this very shower, from which I had promised myself so much, proved a new source of vexation. The lady of the house, fearful that I might take cold after the rain, insisted on my accepting a cloak; it was to no purpose I assured her it would be particularly inconvenient to me; she was not to be outdone in good breeding; the cloak was produced—it was a *thick satin, lined, and full trimmed with a rich dark sable!* I glowed spontaneously at its approach! but notwithstanding all my resistance, I was arrayed in this cloak; and I returned to my temporary home in a profuse perspiration. I might, Mr. Gleaner, proceed in my narration; but I have nearly got to the bottom of my paper. If I am properly encouraged, you may hear from me again; and, in the meantime, I take the liberty to add, that I have conceived *true politeness to consist in making people easy, and in permitting our connections to enjoy themselves in their own way.* I am, good Mr. Vigillius,[4] your most obedient humble servant, and constant reader,

Harriot B____

---

[4] "The Gleaner's" name.

Phillis Wheatley

c.1753–1784

PHILLIS WHEATLEY arrived in Boston when she was about seven years old; she got her first name from the slave ship she came on, and her second from the man who bought her, John Wheatley, a prosperous merchant. John's wife, Susannah, and grown daughter, Mary, took a keen interest in the precocious child: they gave her only light work, educated her, and encouraged her writing. Phillis got a better education than most white girls of her time, including English and Latin literature, history, and geography, as well as Bible study. An able and enthusiastic student, she began writing poems at twelve; she soon demonstrated easy command of the conventions of neoclassical poetry. Her favorite secular book was Alexander Pope's translation of Homer. The Wheatleys were devout, and Phillis first attracted attention by her poem on the death of George Whitefield, the famous Methodist preacher, in 1770. Her poems and letters were published in newspapers, magazines, and separate broadsides in the colonies and in England. She was accepted as a guest in the homes of prominent Bostonians and even called on George Washington at his headquarters in Cambridge in 1776.

When the Wheatleys' son went to England in 1773, he took Phillis with him to restore her health and to meet influential people who admired her poetry and would help her to get it published in book form in England (the project having failed in Boston). She spent six happy weeks there, made much of by pious aristocrats, such as the Earl of Dartmouth, who gave her money to buy books, and the Countess of Huntington, who accepted the dedication of her book. *Poems on Various Subjects, Religious and Moral* appeared in 1773 and became widely known through the colonies. On her return to Boston that year, her master belatedly freed her, apparently prompted by his English friends. But freedom did not bring happiness. The Wheatleys died or moved away, and Phillis felt the loss of their patronage. She married John Peters, a free black, in 1778 and bore three children, all of whom died young. The Peters family had constant financial worries. Phillis twice issued proposals for a second volume of poems, but could not get a publisher. Ultimately she became a drudge in a cheap boardinghouse. In 1784 she died, and her last surviving child was buried with her.

BIBLIOGRAPHY
Wheatley, Phillis. *The Poems*. Revised and enlarged ed. Edited by Julian D. Mason, Jr. Chapel Hill, N.C.: University of North Carolina Press, 1989.

To Mæcenas[1]

Mæcenas, you, beneath the myrtle shade,
Read o'er what poets sung, and shepherds played.
What felt those poets but you feel the same?
Does not your soul possess the sacred flame?
Their noble strains your equal genius shares
In softer language, and diviner airs.

While Homer paints, lo! circumfused in air,
Celestial gods in mortal forms appear;
Swift as they move hear each recess rebound,
Heaven quakes, earth trembles, and the shores resound.
Great Sire of verse, before my mortal eyes,
The lightnings blaze across the vaulted skies,
And, as the thunder shakes the heavenly plains,
A deep-felt horror thrills through all my veins.
When gentler strains demand thy graceful song,

[1]Maecenas, patron of Virgil and Horace, is the type of the generous, discriminating patron of poets.

The lengthening line moves languishing along.
When great Patroclus courts Achilles' aid,[2]
The grateful tribute of my tears is paid;
Prone on the shore he feels the pangs of love,
And stern Pelides tenderest passions move.

    Great Maro's[3] strain in heavenly numbers flows,
The Nine[4] inspire, and all the bosom glows.
O could I rival thine and Virgil's page,
Or claim the Muses with the Mantuan Sage;
Soon the same beauties should my mind adorn,
And the same ardors in my soul should burn:
Then should my song in bolder notes arise,
And all my numbers pleasingly surprize;
But here I sit, and mourn a groveling mind,
That fain would mount, and ride upon the wind.

    Not you, my friend, these plaintive strains become,
Not you, whose bosom is the Muses' home;
When they from towering Helicon retire,
They fan in you the bright immortal fire,
But I less happy, cannot raise the song,
The faltering music dies upon my tongue.

    The happier Terence[5] all the choir inspired,
His soul replenished, and his bosom fired;
But say, ye Muses, why this partial grace,
To one alone of Afric's sable race;
From age to age transmitting thus his name
With the first glory in the rolls of fame?

    Thy virtues, great Maecenas! shall be sung
In praise of him, from whom those virtues sprung:

    [2]Characters in Homer's *Iliad;* Pelides (line 20) is Achilles.
    [3]Maro is a name of Virgil, who was the Mantuan Sage (line 24).
    [4]The nine Muses, who presided over the arts, especially poetry. They lived on
Mount Helicon (line 33).
    [5]He was an African by birth (Wheatley's note). Publius Terentius Afer (?195–
159 B.C.) was brought from North Africa as a young slave; he was soon educated
and freed, and he became a famous comic poet.

While blooming wreaths around thy temples spread,
I'll snatch a laurel from thine honored head,
While you indulgent smile upon the deed.

   As long as Thames in streams majestic flows,
Or Naiads in their oozy beds repose,
While Phoebus reigns above the starry train,
While bright Aurora purples o'er the main,
So long, great Sir, the muse thy praise shall sing,
So long thy praise shall make Parnassus ring:
Then grant, Maecenas, thy paternal rays,
Hear me propitious, and defend my lays.

On Being Brought from Africa to America

'Twas mercy brought me from my pagan land,
Taught my benighted soul to understand
That there's a God, that there's a Savior too:
Once I redemption neither sought nor knew.
Some view our sable race with scornful eye,
"Their color is a diabolic dye."
Remember, Christians, Negroes, black as Cain,[1]
May be refined, and join th' angelic train.

---

[1]Cain was marked by God after murdering his brother, Abel. Some interpreters identified this mark with the physical characteristics of black people.

To the Right Honorable William, Earl of Dartmouth, His Majesty's Principal Secretary of State for North America, & C.[1]

Hail, happy day, when, smiling like the morn,
Fair Freedom rose New England to adorn:
The northern clime beneath her genial ray,
Dartmouth, congratulates thy blissful sway:
Elate with hope her race no longer mourns,
Each soul expands, each grateful bosom burns,
While in thine hand with pleasure we behold
The silken reins, and Freedom's charms unfold.
Long lost to realms beneath the northern skies
She shines supreme, while hated faction dies:
Soon as appeared the Goddess long desired,
Sick at the view, she languished and expired;
Thus from the splendors of the morning light
The owl in sadness seeks the caves of night.

No more, America in mournful strain
Of wrongs, and grievance unredressed complain,
No longer shalt thou dread the iron chain,
Which wanton Tyranny with lawless hand
Had made, and with it meant t' enslave the land.

Should you, my lord, while you peruse my song,
Wonder from whence my love of Freedom sprung,
Whence flow these wishes for the common good,
By feeling hearts alone best understood,
I, young in life, by seeming cruel fate
Was snatched from Afric's fancied happy seat:

---

[1]Lord Dartmouth, appointed secretary in charge of the American colonies in August 1772, replaced the stern Lord Hillsborough. Americans hoped that Dartmouth would be more sympathetic to their grievances.

What pangs excruciating must molest,
What sorrows labor in my parent's breast?
Steeled was that soul and by no misery moved
That from a father seized his babe beloved:
Such, such my case. And can I then but pray
Others may never feel tyrannic sway?

    For favors past, great Sir, our thanks are due,
And thee we ask thy favors to renew,
Since in thy power, as in thy will before,
To soothe the griefs, which thou did'st once deplore.
May heavenly grace the sacred sanction give
To all thy works, and thou forever live
Not only on the wings of fleeting Fame,
Though praise immortal crowns the patriot's name,
But to conduct to heaven's refulgent fane,
May fiery coursers sweep th' ethereal plain,
And bear thee upwards to that blest abode,
Where, like the prophet, thou shalt find thy God.[2]

On the Death of General Wooster[1]

Madam:

    I received your favor by Mr. Dennison enclosing a paper containing the character of the truly worthy General Wooster. It was with the most sensible regret that I heard of his fall in battle, but the pain of so afflicting a dispensation of Providence must be greatly alleviated to you and all his friends in the consideration that he fell a martyr in the Cause of Freedom—

[2]The prophet Elijah was carried up into heaven in a fiery chariot (II Kings 2:11).
[1]General David Wooster died on May 2, 1777, as a result of wounds suffered in a Revolutionary War battle. This letter is addressed to his widow. Wheatley knew Wooster personally.

From this the muse rich consolation draws
He nobly perished in his country's cause,
His country's cause that ever fired his mind,
Where martial flames, and Christian virtues joined.
How shall my pen his warlike deeds proclaim
Or paint them fairer on the list of Fame—
Enough, great Chief—now wrapped in shades around—
Thy grateful country shall thy praise resound;
Though not with mortals' empty praise elate,
That vainest vapor to th' immortal state,
Inly serene the expiring hero lies
And thus (while heavenward roll his swimming eyes):
Permit, great power, while yet my fleeting breath
And spirits wander to the verge of Death—
Permit me yet to paint fair freedom's charms;
For her the continent shines bright in arms,
By thy high will, celestial prize she came—
For her we combat on the field of Fame;
Without her presence vice maintains full sway,
And social love and virtue wing their way.
O still propitious be thy guardian care
And lead Columbia through the toils of war.
With thine own hand conduct them and defend
And bring the dreadful contest to an end—
For ever grateful let them live to thee
And keep them ever virtuous, brave, and free—
But how, presumptuous, shall we hope to find
Divine acceptance with th' Almighty mind—
While yet (O deed ungenerous!) they disgrace
And hold in bondage Afric's blameless race?
Let virtue reign—And thou accord our prayers
Be victory ours, and generous freedom theirs.
The hero prayed—the wondering spirit fled
And sought the unknown regions of the dead—
'Tis thine, fair partner of his life, to find
His virtuous path and follow close behind—
A little moment steals him from thy sight,
He waits thy coming to the realms of light,
Freed from his labors in the ethereal Skies,
Where in succession endless pleasures rise!

You will do me a great favor by returning to me by the first opportunity those books that remain unsold[2] and remitting the money for those that are sold—I can easily dispose of them here for 12/Lm.°[3] each—I am greatly obliged to you for the care you show me, and your condescension in taking so much pains for my interest—I am extremely sorry not to have been honored with a personal acquaintance with you—if the foregoing lines meet with your acceptance and approbation I shall think them highly honored. I hope you will pardon the length of my letter, when the reason is apparent—fondness of the subject and—the highest respect for the deceased—I sincerely sympathize with you in the great loss you and your family sustain and am sincerely

Your friend and very humble servant,
Phillis Wheatley

Queen Street
Boston, July—
15th 1778

To Samson Occom[1]

The following is an extract of a Letter from Phillis, a Negro Girl of Mr. Wheatley's, in Boston, to the Rev. Samson Occom, which we are desired to insert as a specimen of her ingenuity.—It is dated 11th February, 1774.[2]

"Reverend and honored Sir,

[2]Copies of her *Poems on Various Subjects* (1773).

[3]Twelve shillings lawful money.

[1]Occum, a Mohegan Indian, was a Presbyterian minister. He was a friend of the Wheatleys, interested in many of the same causes, and stayed in their home when he was preaching in Boston. He corresponded with Phillis and sold her book in Connecticut. He had written a protest against ministers who held slaves while preaching Christianity and liberty.

[2]The letter was published in the *Connecticut Gazette* and several other newspapers in New England.

I have this day received your obliging kind epistle, and am greatly satisfied with your reasons respecting the Negroes, and think highly reasonable what you offer in vindication of their natural rights: Those that invade them cannot be insensible that the divine light is chasing away the thick darkness which broods over the land of Africa; and the chaos which has reigned so long, is converting into beautiful order, and reveals more and more clearly, the glorious dispensation of civil and religious liberty, which are so inseparably united, that there is little or no enjoyment of one without the other: otherwise, perhaps, the Israelites had been less solicitous for their freedom from Egyptian slavery; I do not say they would have been contented without it, by no means, for in every human breast, God has implanted a principle, which we call love of freedom; it is impatient of oppression, and pants for deliverance; and by the leave of our modern Egyptians I will assert, that the same principle lives in us. God grant deliverance in His own way and time, and get him honor upon all those whose avarice impels them to countenance and help forward the calamities of their fellow creatures. This I desire not for their hurt, but to convince them of the strange absurdity of their conduct, whose words and actions are so diametrically opposite. How well the cry for liberty, and the reverse disposition for the exercise of oppressive power over others agree,—I humbly think it does not require the penetration of a philosopher to determine."—

Susanna Haswell Rowson

1762–1824

SUSANNA HASWELL, whose father was a lieutenant in the Royal Navy and whose mother died shortly after her birth, was born in England. Lieutenant Haswell became a customs officer in America and brought Charlotte to Massachusetts when she was five. She read widely as a child and became a favorite of James Otis, Mercy Otis Warren's brilliant brother, who called her his "Little Scholar." When the Revolution started, however, the Haswells were sent back to England, arriving penniless in 1778. Susanna got a job as a governess. In 1786, she married William Rowson, an unsuccessful actor, musician, and businessman, and published her first novel. *Charlotte: A Tale of Truth* (later titled *Charlotte Temple*) followed in 1791. When William Rowson's hardware business failed, he and Susanna joined an acting company bound for America, arriving in Philadelphia in 1793. She played major character roles and wrote songs and plays, including the patriotic musical *Slaves in Algiers* (1794). The Rowsons moved to Boston, and in 1797 Susanna left the stage to open the Young Ladies' Academy, which soon became successful and remained so until she retired in 1822. She wrote some of the textbooks, which included feminist features such as observations on the status of women in different countries in her geography text. She published a total of eight novels, besides editing and writing for magazines. For many years, she supported herself and her husband, as well as his sister, his illegitimate son, and two adopted children.

Charlotte Temple, the first American best-seller, was read and loved up into the twentieth century. Like many women's novels of the period, it is a sentimental tale of seduction, although it is distinguished by an unusually sympathetic presentation of its ruined heroine. The following chapters, which show how Charlotte yielded despite her essential virtue and relate the immediate consequences of her fall, convey the flavor of the novel.

BIBLIOGRAPHY
Davidson, Cathy N. *Revolution and the Word: The Rise of the Novel in America.* New York: Oxford University Press, 1986.
Rowson, Susanna. *Charlotte Temple.* Introduction by Cathy N. Davidson. New York: Oxford University Press, 1986.

from Charlotte Temple

Montraville, a British army lieutenant about to be sent to America to fight in the Revolution, fell in love with Charlotte Temple, a fifteen-year-old schoolgirl. Meeting her on the way to a party, to which her French teacher had taken her in violation of school rules, he slipped her a letter and bribed the teacher, Mademoiselle La Rue, to further his courtship.

CHAPTER VII

NATURAL SENSE OF PROPRIETY INHERENT IN THE FEMALE BOSOM

"I cannot think we have done exactly right in going out this evening, Mademoiselle," said Charlotte, seating herself when she entered her apartment: "nay I am sure it was not right; for I expected to be very happy, but was sadly disappointed."

"It was your own fault then," replied Mademoiselle: "for I am sure my cousin omitted nothing that could serve to render the evening agreeable."

"True," said Charlotte: "but I thought the gentlemen were very free in their manner: I wonder you would suffer them to behave as they did."

"Prithee don't be such a foolish little prude," said the artful French woman, affecting anger: "I invited you to go in hopes it would divert you, and be an agreeable change of scene; however if your delicacy was hurt by the behavior of the gentlemen, you need not go again; so there let it rest."

"I do not intend to go again," said Charlotte, gravely taking off her bonnet, and beginning to prepare for bed: "I am sure if Madame Du Pont[1] knew we had been out to-night she would be very angry; and it is ten to one but she hears of it by some means or other."

"Nay, Miss," said La Rue, "perhaps your mighty sense of propriety may lead you to tell her yourself; and in order to avoid the censure you would incur, should she hear of it by accident, throw the blame on me: but I confess I deserve it: it will be a very kind return for that partiality which led me to prefer you before any of the rest of the ladies; but perhaps it will give you pleasure," continued she, letting fall some hypocritical tears, "to see me deprived of bread, and for an action which by the most rigid could only be esteemed an inadvertency, lose my place and character, and be drove again into the world, where I have already suffered all the evils attendant on poverty."

This was touching Charlotte in the most vulnerable part: she rose from her seat, and taking Mademoiselle's hand—"You know, my dear La Rue," said she, "I love you too well to do anything that would injure you in my governess's opinion: I am only sorry we went out this evening."

"I don't believe it, Charlotte," said she, assuming a little vivacity; "for if you had not gone out you would not have seen the gentleman who met us crossing the field, and I rather think you were pleased with his conversation."

"I had seen him once before," replied Charlotte, "and thought him an agreeable man; and you know one is always pleased to see a person with whom one has passed several cheerful hours. But," said she pausing and drawing the letter from her pocket, while a general suffusion of vermillion tinged her neck and face, "he gave me this letter; what shall I do with it?"

"Read it to be sure," returned Mademoiselle.

"I am afraid I ought not," said Charlotte: "my mother has often

[1] Headmistress of Charlotte's school.

told me I should never read a letter given me by a young man without first giving it to her."

"Lord bless you, my dear girl!" cried the teacher smiling, "have you a mind to be in leading strings all your lifetime. Prithee open the letter, read it, and judge for yourself; if you show it your mother the consequence will be you will be taken from school, and a strict guard kept over you, so you will stand no chance of ever seeing the smart young officer again."

"I should not like to leave school yet," replied Charlotte, "till I have attained a greater proficiency in my Italian and music. But you can if you please, Mademoiselle, take the letter back to Montraville, and tell him I wish him well but cannot with any propriety enter into a clandestine correspondence with him." She laid the letter on the table, and began to undress herself.

"Well," said La Rue, "I vow you are an unaccountable girl: have you no curiosity to see the inside now? for my part I could no more let a letter addressed to me lie unopened so long, than I could work miracles: he writes a good hand," continued she, turning the letter to look at the superscription.

" 'Tis well enough," said Charlotte, drawing it towards her.

"He is a genteel young fellow," said La Rue carelessly, folding up her apron at the same time; "but I think he is marked with the small pox."

"Oh you are greatly mistaken," said Charlotte eagerly; "he has a remarkable clear skin and fine complexion."

"His eyes, if I could judge by what I saw," said La Rue, "are grey, and want expression."

"By no means," replied Charlotte; "they are the most expressive eyes I ever saw."

"Well, child, whether they are grey or black is of no consequence: you have determined not to read his letter, so it is likely you will never either see or hear from him again."

Charlotte took up the letter, and Mademoiselle continued—

"He is most probably going to America; and if ever you should hear any account of him it may possibly be that he is killed; and though he loved you ever so fervently, though his last breath should be spent in a prayer for your happiness, it can be nothing to you: you can feel nothing for the fate of the man whose letters you will not open, and whose sufferings you will not alleviate by permitting him to think you would remember him when absent, and pray for his safety."

Charlotte still held the letter in her hand: her heart swelled at the conclusion of Mademoiselle's speech, and a tear dropped upon the wafer that closed it.

"The wafer is not dry yet," said she, "and sure there can be no great harm—" She hesitated. La Rue was silent. "I may read it, Mademoiselle, and return it afterward."

"Certainly," replied Mademoiselle.

"At any rate I am determined not to answer it," continued Charlotte, as she cut the paper round the wafer.

Here let me stop to make one remark, and trust me my very heart aches while I write it; but certain I am that when once a woman has stifled the sense of shame in her own bosom, when once she has lost sight of the basis on which reputation, honor, everything that should be dear to the female heart, rests, she grows hardened in guilt, and will spare no pains to bring down innocence and beauty to the shocking level with herself: and this proceeds from that diabolical spirit of envy, which repines at seeing another in the full possession of that respect and esteem which she can no longer hope to enjoy.

Mademoiselle eyed the unsuspecting Charlotte, as she perused the letter, with a malignant pleasure. She saw that the contents had awakened new emotions in her youthful bosom: she encouraged her hopes, calmed her fears, and before they parted for the night it was determined that she should meet Montraville the ensuing evening.

CHAPTER IX

WE KNOW NOT WHAT
A DAY MAY BRING FORTH

Various were the sensations which agitated the mind of Charlotte during the day preceding the evening in which she was to meet Montraville. Several times did she almost resolve to go to her governess,[2] show her the letter, and be guided by her advice: but Charlotte had taken one step in the ways of imprudence, and when that is once done there are always innumerable obstacles to prevent the erring

[2]The headmistress.

person returning to the path of rectitude: yet these objections, however forcible they may appear in general, exist chiefly in the imagination.

Charlotte feared the anger of her governess: she loved her mother, and the very idea of incurring her displeasure gave her the greatest uneasiness: but there was a more forcible reason still remaining: should she show the letter to Madame Du Pont, she must confess the means by which it came into her possession, and what would be the consequence? Mademoiselle would be turned out of doors.

"I must not be ungrateful," said she. "La Rue is very kind to me; besides I can, when I see Montraville, inform him of the impropriety of our continuing to see or correspond with each other, and request him to come no more to Chichester."

However prudent Charlotte might be in these resolutions, she certainly did not take a proper method to confirm herself in them. Several times in the course of the day she indulged herself in reading over the letter, and each time she read it, the contents sunk deeper in her heart. As evening drew near, she caught herself frequently consulting her watch. "I wish this foolish meeting was over," said she, by way of apology to her own heart, "I wish it was over; for when I have seen him, and convinced him my resolution is not to be shaken, I shall feel my mind much easier."

The appointed hour arrived. Charlotte and Mademoiselle eluded the eye of vigilance; and Montraville, who had waited their coming with impatience, received them with rapturous and unbounded acknowledgments for their condescension: he had wisely brought Belcour with him to entertain Mademoiselle while he enjoyed an uninterrupted conversation with Charlotte.

Belcour was a man whose character might be comprised in a few words; and as he will make some figure in the ensuing pages, I shall here describe him. He possessed a genteel fortune, and had a liberal education; dissipated, thoughtless, and capricious, he paid little regard to the moral duties, and less to religious ones: eager in the pursuit of pleasure, he minded not the miseries he inflicted on others, so that his own wishes, however extravagant, were gratified. Self, darling self, was the idol he worshiped, and to that he would have sacrificed the interest and happiness of all mankind. Such was the friend of Montraville: will not the reader be ready to imagine that the man who could regard such a character must be actuated by the same feelings, follow the same pursuits, and be equally unworthy with the person to whom he thus gave his confidence?

But Montraville was a different character: generous in his disposition, liberal in his opinions, and good natured almost to a fault; yet eager and impetuous in the pursuit of a favorite object, he stayed not to reflect on the consequence which might follow the attainment of his wishes; with a mind ever open to conviction, had he been so fortunate as to possess a friend who would have pointed out the cruelty of endeavoring to gain the heart of an innocent artless girl, when he knew it was utterly impossible for him to marry her, and when the gratification of his passion would be unavoidable infamy and misery to her, and a cause of never ceasing remorse to himself: had these dreadful consequences been placed before him in a proper light, the humanity of his nature would have urged him to give up the pursuit: but Belcour was not this friend; he rather encouraged the growing passion of Montraville; and being pleased with the vivacity of Mademoiselle, resolved to leave no argument untried which he thought might prevail on her to be the companion of their intended voyage, and he made no doubt but her example, added to the rhetoric of Montraville, would persuade Charlotte to go with them.

Charlotte had, when she went out to meet Montraville, flattered herself that her resolution was not to be shaken, and that conscious of the impropriety of her conduct in having a clandestine intercourse with a stranger, she would never repeat the indiscretion.

But alas! poor Charlotte, she knew not the deceitfulness of her own heart, or she would have avoided the trial of her stability.

Montraville was tender, eloquent, ardent, and yet respectful. "Shall I not see you once more," said he, "before I leave England? Will you not bless me by an assurance that when we are divided by a vast expanse of sea I shall not be forgotten?"

Charlotte sighed.

"Why that sigh, my dear Charlotte? Could I flatter myself that a fear for my safety, or a wish for my welfare occasioned it, how happy would it make me."

"I shall ever wish you well, Montraville," said she, "but we must meet no more."

"Oh, say not so, my lovely girl: reflect that when I leave my native land, perhaps a few short weeks may terminate my existence; the perils of the ocean—the dangers of war—"

"I can hear no more," said Charlotte, in a tremulous voice. "I must leave you."

"Say you will see me once again."

"I dare not," said she.

"Only for one-half hour to-morrow evening: 'tis my last request. I shall never trouble you again, Charlotte."

"I know not what to say," cried Charlotte, struggling to draw her hands from him: "let me leave you now."

"And will you come to-morrow?" said Montraville.

"Perhaps I may," said she.

"Adieu then. I will live upon that hope till we meet again."

He kissed her hand. She sighed an adieu, and catching hold of Mademoiselle's arm, hastily entered the garden gate.

CHAPTER X

WHEN WE HAVE EXCITED CURIOSITY, IT IS BUT AN ACT OF GOOD NATURE TO GRATIFY IT.

Montraville was the youngest son of a gentleman of fortune: but his family being numerous, he was obliged to bring up his sons to genteel professions, by the exercise of which they might hope to raise themselves into notice.

"My daughters," said he, "have been educated like gentlewomen; and should I die before they are settled, they must have some provision made to place them above the snares and temptations which vice ever holds out to the elegant, accomplished female, when oppressed by the frowns of poverty and the sting of dependence: my boys, with only moderate incomes, when placed in the church, at the bar, or in the field, may exert their talents, make themselves friends, and raise their fortunes on the basis of merit."

When Montraville chose the profession of arms, his father presented him with a commission, and made him a handsome provision for his private purse. "Now, my boy," said he; "go! seek glory in the field of battle. You have received from me all I shall ever have it in my power to bestow: it is certain I have interest to gain you promotion; but be assured that interest shall never be exerted unless by your future conduct you deserve it. Remember therefore your success in life depends entirely on yourself. There is one thing I think it my duty to caution you against; the precipitancy with which young men frequently rush into matrimonial engagements, and by their thoughtlessness draw many a deserving woman into scenes of poverty and distress. A soldier has no business to think of a wife till his rank is such as to place him above the fear of bringing into the world a train of helpless innocents, heirs only to penury and affliction. If indeed, a woman, whose fortune is sufficient to preserve you in that state of independence I would teach you to prize, should generously bestow herself on a young soldier, whose chief hope of future prosperity depended on his success in the field; if such a woman should offer, every barrier is removed, and I should rejoice in an union which would promise so much felicity. But mark me, boy, if on the contrary you rush into a precipitate union with a girl of little or no fortune, take the poor creature from a comfortable home and kind friends, and plunge her into all the evils a narrow income and increasing family can inflict, I will leave you to enjoy the blessed fruits of your rashness; for by all that is sacred, neither my interest nor fortune shall ever be exerted in your favor. I am serious," continued he, "therefore imprint this conversation on your memory, and let it influence your future conduct. Your happiness will always be dear to me, and I wish to warn you of a rock on which the peace of many an honest fellow has been wrecked; for believe me the difficulties and dangers of the longest winter campaign are much easier to be borne than the pangs that would seize your heart when you beheld the woman of your choice, the children of your affection, involved in penury and distress, and reflected that it was your own folly and precipitancy had been the prime cause of their sufferings."

As this conversation passed but a few hours before Montraville took leave of his father, it was deeply impressed on his mind: when therefore Belcour came with him to the place of assignation with Charlotte, he directed him to enquire of the French woman what were Miss Temple's expectations in regard to fortune.

Mademoiselle informed him, that though Charlotte's father possessed a genteel independence, it was by no means probable that he could give his daughter more than a thousand pounds; and in case she did not marry to his liking, it was possible he might not give her a single *sou;* nor did it appear the least likely that Mr. Temple would agree to her union with a young man on the point of embarking for the seat of war.

Montraville therefore concluded it was impossible he should ever marry Charlotte Temple; and what end he proposed to himself by continuing the acquaintance he had commenced with her he did not at that moment give himself time to enquire.

CHAPTER XI

CONFLICT OF LOVE AND DUTY

Almost a week was now gone, and Charlotte continued every evening to meet Montraville, and in her heart every meeting was resolved to be the last; but alas! when Montraville at parting would earnestly entreat one more interview, that treacherous heart betrayed her; and forgetful of its resolution, pleaded the cause of the enemy so powerfully, that Charlotte was unable to resist. Another and another meeting succeeded; and so well did Montraville improve each opportunity, that the heedless girl at length confessed no idea could be so painful to her as that of never seeing him again.

"Then we will never be parted," said he.

"Ah, Montraville," replied Charlotte, forcing a smile, "how can it be avoided? My parents would never consent to our union; and even could they be brought to approve of it, how should I bear to be separated from my kind, my beloved mother?"

"Then you love your parents more than you do me, Charlotte?"

"I hope I do," said she, blushing and looking down, "I hope my affection for them will ever keep me from infringing the laws of filial duty."

"Well, Charlotte," said Montraville, gravely, and letting go her hand, "since that is the case, I find I have deceived myself with fallacious hopes. I had flattered my fond heart that I was dearer to Charlotte than anything in the world besides. I thought that you would for my sake have braved the danger of the ocean, that you would, by your affection and smiles, have softened the hardships of war, and had it been my fate to fall, your tenderness would cheer the hour of death, and smooth my passage to another world. But farewell, Charlotte! I see you never loved me. I shall now welcome the friendly ball that deprives me of the sense of my misery."

"Oh stay, unkind Montraville," cried she, catching hold of his arm, as he pretended to leave her, "stay, and to calm your fears I will here protest that was it not for the fear of giving pain to the best of parents, and returning their kindness with ingratitude, I would follow you through every danger, and in studying to promote your happiness, ensure my own. But I can not break my mother's heart, Montraville; I must not bring the grey hairs of my doting grandfather with sorrow to the grave, or make my beloved father perhaps curse the hour that gave me birth." She covered her face with her hands, and burst into tears.

"All these distressing scenes, my dear Charlotte," cried Montraville, "are merely the chimeras of a disturbed fancy. Your parents might perhaps grieve at first, but when they heard from your own hand that you was with a man of honor, and that it was to ensure your felicity by a union with him, to which you feared they would never have given their assent, that you left their protection, they will, be assured, forgive an error which love alone occasioned, and when we return from America, receive you with open arms and tears of joy."

Belcour and Mademoiselle heard this last speech, and conceiving it a proper time to throw in their advice and persuasions, approached Charlotte, and so well seconded the entreaties of Montraville, that finding Mademoiselle intended going with Belcour, and feeling her own treacherous heart too much inclined to accompany them, the hapless Charlotte, in an evil hour, consented that the next evening they should bring a chaise to the end of the town, and that she would leave her friends, and throw herself entirely on the protection of Montraville. "But should you," said she, looking earnestly at him, her eyes full of tears, "should you, forgetful of your promises, and repenting the engagements you here voluntarily enter into, forsake and leave me on a foreign shore—"

"Judge not so meanly of me," said he. "The moment we reach our place of destination, Hymen shall sanctify our love; and when I shall forget your goodness, may heaven forget me!"

"Ah," said Charlotte, leaning on Mademoiselle's arm, as they walked up the garden together, "I have forgot all that I ought to have remembered, in consenting to this intended elopement."

"You are a strange girl," said Mademoiselle: "you never know your own mind two minutes at a time. Just now you declared Montraville's happiness was what you prized most in the world; and now I suppose you repent having ensured that happiness by agreeing to accompany him abroad."

"Indeed I do repent," replied Charlotte, "from my soul; but while discretion points out the impropriety of my conduct, inclination urges me on to ruin."

"Ruin! fiddlesticks!" said Mademoiselle; "am not I going with you? and do I feel any of these qualms?"

"You do not renounce a tender father and mother," said Charlotte.

"But I hazard my dear reputation," replied Mademoiselle, bridling.

"True," replied Charlotte, "but you do not feel what I do." She then bade her good night: but sleep was a stranger to her eyes, and the tear of anguish watered her pillow.

CHAPTER XII

> *Nature's last, best gift:*
> *Creature in whom excell'd, whatever could*
> *To sight or thought be nam'd!*
> *Holy, divine! good, amiable, and sweet!*
> *How thou art fall'n!*—[3]

When Charlotte left her restless bed, her languid eye and pale cheek discovered to Madame Du Pont the little repose she had tasted.

"My dear child," said the affectionate governess, "what is the cause of the languor so apparent in your frame? Are you not well?"

"Yes, my dear Madame, very well," replied Charlotte, attempting to smile, "but I know not how it was I could not sleep last night, and my spirits are depressed this morning."

"Come cheer up, my love," said the governess; "I believe I have brought a cordial to revive them. I have just received a letter from your good mama, and here is one for yourself."

Charlotte hastily took the letter: it contained these words—

"As tomorrow is the anniversary of the happy day that gave my beloved girl to the anxious wishes of a maternal heart, I have requested your governess to let you come home and spend it with us; and as I know you to be a good affectionate child, and make

[3] John Milton, *Paradise Lost* 9:896–900 (inaccurately quoted).

it your study to improve in those branches of education which you know will give most pleasure to your delighted parents, as a reward for your diligence and attention I have prepared an agreeable surprise for your reception. Your grandfather, eager to embrace the darling of his aged heart, will come in the chaise for you; so hold yourself in readiness to attend him by nine o'clock. Your dear father joins in every tender wish for your health and future felicity which warms the heart of my dear Charlotte's affectionate mother.

"L. TEMPLE."

"Gracious heaven!" cried Charlotte, forgetting where she was, and raising her streaming eyes as in earnest supplication.

Madame Du Pont was surprised. "Why these tears, my love?" said she. "Why this seeming agitation? I thought the letter would have rejoiced instead of distressing you."

"It does rejoice me," replied Charlotte, endeavoring at composure, "but I was praying for merit to deserve the unremitted attentions of the best of parents."

"You do right," said Madame Du Pont, "to ask the assistance of heaven that you may continue to deserve their love. Continue, my dear Charlotte, in the course you have ever pursued, and you will ensure at once their happiness and your own."

"Oh!" cried Charlotte, as her governess left her, "I have forfeited both forever! Yet let me reflect:—the irrevocable step is not yet taken: it is not too late to recede from the brink of a precipice, from which I can only behold the dark abyss of ruin, shame, and remorse!"

She arose from her seat and flew to the apartment of La Rue. "Oh Mademoiselle!" said she, "I am snatched by a miracle from destruction! This letter has saved me: it has opened my eyes to the folly I was so near committing. I will not go, Mademoiselle; I will not wound the hearts of those dear parents who make my happiness the whole study of their lives."

"Well," said Mademoiselle, "do as you please, Miss; but pray understand that my resolution is taken, and it is not in your power to alter it. I shall meet the gentlemen at the appointed hour, and shall not be surprised at any outrage which Montraville may commit when he finds himself disappointed. Indeed I should not be astonished was he to come immediately here and reproach you for your instability in the hearing of the whole school: and what will be the consequence? you will bear the odium of having formed the resolution of eloping, and every girl of spirit will laugh at your want of fortitude to put it in execution, while prudes and fools will load you with reproach and contempt. You will have lost the confidence of your parents, incurred their anger, and the scoffs of the world; and what fruit do you expect to reap from this piece of heroism (for such no doubt you think it is) you will have the pleasure to reflect that you have deceived the man who adores you, and whom in your heart you prefer to all other men, and that you are separated from him forever."

This eloquent harangue was given with such volubility, that Charlotte could not find an opportunity to interrupt her, or to offer a single word till the whole was finished, and then found her ideas so confused that she knew not what to say.

At length she determined that she would go with Mademoiselle to the place of assignation, convince Montraville of the necessity of her adhering to her resolution of remaining behind; assure him of her affection, and bid him adieu.

Charlotte formed this plan in her mind and exulted in the certainty of its success. "How shall I rejoice," said she, "in this triumph of reason over inclination, and when in the arms of my affectionate parents, lift up my soul in gratitude to heaven as I look back on the dangers I have escaped!"

The hour of assignation arrived: Mademoiselle put what money and valuables she possessed in her pocket, and advised Charlotte to do the same; but she refused; "my resolution is fixed;" said she; "I will sacrifice love to duty."

Mademoiselle smiled internally, and they proceeded softly down the back stairs and out of the garden gate. Montraville and Belcour were ready to receive them.

"Now," said Montraville, taking Charlotte in his arms, "you are mine forever."

"No," said she, withdrawing from his embrace; "I am come to take an everlasting farewell."

It would be useless to repeat the conversation that here ensued; suffice it to say, that Montraville used every argument that had formerly been successful, Charlotte's resolution began to waver, and he drew her almost imperceptibly toward the chaise.

"I can not go," said she: "cease, dear Montraville, to persuade. I must not: religion, duty, forbid."

"Cruel Charlotte!" said he, "if you disappoint my ardent hopes, by all that is sacred this hand shall put a period to my existence. I can not—will not live without you."

"Alas! my torn heart!" said Charlotte, "how shall I act?"

"Let me direct you," said Montraville, lifting her into the chaise.

"Oh! my dear, forsaken parents!" cried Charlotte.

The chaise drove off. She shrieked, and fainted into the arms of her betrayer.

Chapters XIII and XIV describe the pathetic distress of Charlotte's grandfather and parents when they discover that she has eloped.

CHAPTER XV

EMBARKATION

It was with the utmost difficulty that the united efforts of Mademoiselle and Montraville could support Charlotte's spirits during their short ride from Chichester to Portsmouth, where a boat waited to take them immediately on board the ship in which they were to embark for America.

As soon as she became tolerably composed, she entreated pen and ink to write to her parents. This she did in the most affecting, artless manner, entreating their pardon and blessing, and describing the dreadful situation of her mind, the conflict she suffered in endeavoring to conquer this unfortunate attachment, and concluded with saying her only hope of future comfort consisted in the (perhaps delusive) idea she indulged of being once more folded in their protecting arms, and hearing the words of peace and pardon from their lips.

The tears streamed incessantly while she was writing, and she was frequently obliged to lay down her pen: but when the task was completed, and she had committed the letter to the care of Montraville to be sent to the post office, she became more calm, and indulging the delightful hope of soon receiving an answer that would seal her pardon, she in some measure assumed her usual cheerfulness.

But Montraville knew too well the consequences that must unavoidably ensue should this letter reach Mr. Temple: he therefore wisely resolved to walk on the deck, tear it in pieces, and commit the fragments to the care of Neptune, who might or might not, as it suited his convenience, convey them on shore.

All Charlotte's hopes and wishes were now concentered in one, namely that the fleet might be detained at Spithead till she could receive a letter from her friends:[4] but in this she was disappointed, for the second morning after she went on board the signal was made, the fleet weighed anchor, and in a few hours (the wind favorable) they bid adieu to the white cliffs of Albion.

In the meantime every enquiry that could be thought of was made by Mr. and Mrs. Temple; for many days did they indulge the fond hope that she was merely gone off to be married, and that when the indissoluble knot was once tied, she would return with the partner she had chosen, and entreat their blessing and forgiveness.

"And shall we not forgive her?" said Mr. Temple.

"Forgive her!" exclaimed the mother. "Oh yes, whatever be her errors, is she not our child? and though bowed to the earth even with shame and remorse, is it not our duty to raise the poor penitent, and whisper peace and comfort to her desponding soul? would she but return, with rapture would I fold her to my heart, and bury every remembrance of her faults in the dear embrace."

But still day after day passed on, and Charlotte did not appear, nor were any tidings to be heard of her: yet each rising morning was welcomed by some new hope—the evening brought with it disappointment. At length hope was no more; despair usurped her place; and the mansion which was once the mansion of peace, became the habitation of pale dejected melancholy.

The cheerful smile that was wont to adorn the face of Mrs. Temple was fled, and had it not been for the support of unaffected piety, and a consciousness of having ever set before her child the fairest example, she must have sunk under this heavy affliction.

"Since," said she, "the severest scrutiny cannot charge me with any breach of duty to have deserved this severe chastisement, I will bow before the power who inflicts it with humble resignation to his will; nor shall the duty of a wife be totally absorbed in the feelings of the mother; I will endeavor to appear more cheerful, and by appearing in some measure to have conquered my own sorrow, alleviate the sufferings of my husband, and rouse him from that torpor into which this misfortune has plunged him. My father too demands my care and attention: I must not, by a selfish indulgence of my own grief,

[4]Family.

forget the interest those two dear objects take in my happiness or misery: I will wear a smile on my face, though the thorn rankles in my heart; and if by so doing I in the smallest degree contribute to restore their peace of mind, I shall be amply rewarded for the pain the concealment of my own feelings may occasion."

Thus argued this excellent woman: and in the execution of so laudable a resolution we shall leave her, to follow the fortunes of the hapless victim of imprudence and evil counsellors.

CHAPTER XVI

Necessary Digression

On board of the ship on which Charlotte and Mademoiselle were embarked was an officer of large unencumbered fortune and elevated rank, and whom I shall call Crayton.

He was one of those men, who, having traveled in their youth, pretend to have contracted a peculiar fondness for everything foreign, and to hold in contempt the productions of their own country; and this affected partiality extended even to the women.

With him therefore the blushing modesty and unaffected simplicity of Charlotte passed unnoticed; but the forward pertness of La Rue, the freedom of her conversation, the elegance of her person, mixed with a certain engaging *je ne sais quoi,* perfectly enchanted him.

The reader no doubt has already developed the character of La Rue: designing, artful and selfish, she had accepted the devoirs of Belcour because she was heartily weary of the retired life she led at the school, wished to be released from what she deemed a slavery, and to return to that vortex of folly and dissipation which had once plunged her into the deepest misery;[5] but her plan, she flattered herself, was now better formed: she resolved to put herself under the protection of no man till she had first secured a settlement;[6] but the clandestine manner in which she left Madame Du Pont's prevented her putting this plan into execution, though Belcour solemnly protested he would make her a handsome settlement the moment they

[5]She had eloped with a young officer from the convent where she was being educated, lived with several men, and been reduced to abject poverty before she managed to get a teaching position in Madame Du Pont's school.
[6]Legal assignment of money to a mistress (or wife).

arrived at Portsmouth. This he afterward contrived to evade by a pretended hurry of business; La Rue readily conceiving he never meant to fulfill his promise, determined to change her battery and attack the heart of Colonel Crayton. She soon discovered the partiality he entertained for her nation; and having imposed on him a feigned tale of distress, representing Belcour as a villain who had seduced her from her friends under promise of marriage, and afterward betrayed her, pretending great remorse for the errors she had committed, and declaring whatever her affection might have been, it was now entirely extinguished, and she wished for nothing more than an opportunity to leave a course of life which her soul abhorred; but she had no friends to apply to, they had all renounced her, and guilt and misery would undoubtedly be her future portion through life.

Crayton was possessed of many amiable qualities, though the peculiar trait in his character, which we have already mentioned, in a great measure threw a shade over them. He was beloved for his humanity and benevolence by all who knew him, but he was easy and unsuspicious himself, and easily became a dupe to the artifice of others.

He was, when very young, united to an amiable Parisian lady, and perhaps it was his affection for her that laid the foundation for the partiality he ever retained for the whole nation. He had by her one daughter, who entered into the world but a few hours before her mother left it. This lady was universally beloved and admired, being endowed with all the virtues of her mother without the weakness of the father: she was married to Major Beauchamp, and was at this time in the same fleet with her father, attending her husband to New York.

Crayton was melted by the affected contrition and distress of La Rue: he would converse with her for hours, read to her, play cards with her, listen to all her complaints, and promise to protect her to the utmost of his power. La Rue easily saw his character; her sole aim was to awaken a passion in his bosom that might turn out to her advantage, and in this aim she was but too successful, for before the voyage was finished, the infatuated Colonel gave her from under his hand a promise of marriage on their arrival at New York, under forfeiture of five thousand pounds.

And how did our poor Charlotte pass her time during a tedious and tempestuous passage? naturally delicate, the fatigue and sickness which she endured rendered her so weak as to be almost entirely confined to her bed: yet the kindness and attention of Montraville in some measure contributed to alleviate her sufferings, and the hope of hearing from her friends soon after her arrival, kept up her spirits, and cheered many a gloomy hour.

But during the voyage a great revolution took place, not only in the fortune of La Rue but in the bosom of Belcour: whilst in the pursuit of his amour with Mademoiselle, he had attended little to the interesting[7] unobtrusive charms of Charlotte, but when, cloyed by possession, and disgusted with the art and dissimulation of one, he beheld the simplicity and gentleness of the other, the contrast became too striking not to fill him at once with surprise and admiration. He frequently conversed with Charlotte; he found her sensible, well informed, but diffident and unassuming. The languor which the fatigue of her body and perturbation of her mind spread over her delicate features, served only in his opinion to render her more lovely: he knew that Montraville did not design to marry her, and he formed a resolution to endeavor to gain her himself whenever Montraville should leave her.

Let not the reader imagine Belcour's designs were honorable. Alas! when once a woman has forgot the respect due to herself, by yielding to the solicitations of illicit love, they lose all the consequence, even in the eyes of the man whose art has betrayed them, and for whose sake they have sacrificed every valuable consideration.

The heedless Fair, who stoops to guilty joys,
A man may pity—but he must despise.

Nay, every libertine will think he has a right to insult her with his licentious passions; and should the unhappy creature shrink from the insolent overture, he will sneeringly taunt her with pretence of modesty.

[7]Touching.

CHAPTER XVII

A WEDDING

On the day before their arrival at New York, after dinner, Crayton arose from his seat, and placing himself by Mademoiselle, thus addressed the company—

"As we are now nearly arrived at our destined port, I think it but my duty to inform you, my friends, that this lady," (taking her hand) "has placed herself under my protection. I have seen and severely felt the anguish of her heart, and through every shade which cruelty or malice may throw over her, can discover the most amiable qualities. I thought it but necessary to mention my esteem for her before our disembarkation, as it is my fixed resolution, the morning after we land, to give her an undoubted title to my favor and protection by honorably uniting my fate to hers. I would wish every gentleman here, therefore, to remember that her honor henceforth is mine, and," continued he, looking at Belcour, "should any man presume to speak in the least disrespectfully of her, I shall not hesitate to pronounce him a scoundrel."

Belcour cast at him a smile of contempt, and bowing profoundly low, wished Mademoiselle much joy in the proposed union; and assuring the Colonel that he need not be in the least apprehensive of any one throwing the least odium on the character of his lady, shook him by the hand with ridiculous gravity, and left the cabin.

The truth was, he was glad to be rid of La Rue, and so he was but freed from her, he cared not who fell a victim to her infamous arts.

The inexperienced Charlotte was astonished at what she heard. She thought La Rue had, like herself, only been urged by the force of her attachment to Belcour, to quit her friends, and follow him to the seat of war: how wonderful, then, that she should resolve to marry another man. It was certainly extremely wrong. It was indelicate. She mentioned her thoughts to Montraville. He laughed at her simplicity, called her a little idiot, and patting her on the cheek, said she knew nothing of the world. "If the world sanctifies such things, 'tis a very bad world, I think," said Charlotte. "Why I always understood they were to have been married when they arrived at New York. I am sure Mademoiselle told me Belcour promised to marry her."

"Well, and suppose he did?"

"Why he should be obliged to keep his word, I think."

"Well, but I suppose he has changed his mind," said Montraville, "and then, you know, the case is altered."

Charlotte looked at him attentively for a moment. A full sense of her own situation rushed upon her mind. She burst into tears, and remained silent. Montraville too well understood the cause of her tears. He kissed her cheek, and bidding her not make herself uneasy, unable to bear the silent but keen remonstrance, hastily left her.

The next morning by sunrise they found themselves at anchor before the city of New York. A boat was ordered to convey the ladies on shore. Crayton accompanied them; and they were shown to a house of public entertainment. Scarcely were they seated, when the door opened, and the Colonel found himself in the arms of his daughter, who had landed a few minutes before him. The first transport of meeting subsided, Crayton introduced his daughter to Mademoiselle La Rue, as an old friend of her mother's (for the artful French woman had really made it appear to the credulous Colonel that she was in the same convent with his first wife, and though much younger, received many tokens of her esteem and regard).

"If, Mademoiselle," said Mrs. Beauchamp, "you were the friend of my mother, you must be worthy the esteem of all good hearts."

"Mademoiselle will soon honor our family," said Crayton, "by supplying the place that valuable woman filled; and as you are married, my dear, I think you will not blame—"

"Hush, my dear Sir," replied Mrs. Beauchamp: "I know my duty too well to scrutinize your conduct. Be assured, my dear father, your happiness is mine. I shall rejoice in it, and sincerely love the person who contributes to it. But tell me," continued she, turning to Charlotte, "who is this lovely girl? Is she your sister, Mademoiselle?"

A blush deep as the glow of the carnation suffused the cheeks of Charlotte.

"It is a young lady," replied the Colonel, "who came in the same vessel with us from England." He then drew his daughter aside, and told her in a whisper that Charlotte was the mistress of Montraville.

"What a pity!" said Mrs. Beauchamp, softly, casting a most compassionate glance at her. "But surely her mind is not depraved. The goodness of her heart is depicted in her ingenuous countenance."

Charlotte caught the word *pity*. "And am I already fallen so low?" said she. A sigh escaped her, and a tear was ready to start, but Montraville appeared, and she checked the rising emotion. Mademoiselle went with the Colonel and his daughter to another apartment. Charlotte remained with Montraville and Belcour. The next morning the Colonel performed his promise, and La Rue became in due form Mrs. Crayton, exulted in her good fortune, and dared to look with an eye of contempt on the unfortunate but far less guilty Charlotte.

CHAPTER XVIII

Reflections

"And am I indeed fallen so low," said Charlotte, "as to be only pitied? Will the voice of approbation no more meet my ear? and shall I never again possess a friend whose face will wear a smile of joy whenever I approach? Alas! how thoughtless, how dreadfully imprudent have I been! I know not which is most painful to endure, the sneer of contempt, or the glance of compassion, which is depicted in the various countenances of my own sex: they are both equally humiliating. Ah! my dear parents, could you now see the child of your affections, the daughter whom you so dearly loved, a poor solitary being, without society, here wearing out her heavy hours in deep regret and anguish of heart, no kind friend of her own sex to whom she can unbosom her griefs, no beloved mother, no woman of character will appear in my company, and low as your Charlotte is fallen, she can not associate with infamy."

These were the painful reflections which occupied the mind of Charlotte. Montraville had placed her in a small house a few miles from New York: he gave her one female attendant, and supplied her with what money she wanted; but business and pleasure so entirely occupied his time, that he had little to devote to the woman whom he had brought from all her connections and robbed of innocence. Sometimes indeed he would steal out at the close of the evening and pass a few hours with her; and then so much was she attached to him, that all her sorrows were forgotten while blessed with his society: she would enjoy a walk by moonlight, or sit by him in a little arbor at the bottom of the garden, and play on the harp, accompanying it with her plaintive, harmonious voice. But often, very often, did he promise to renew his visits, and, forgetful of his promise, leave her to mourn her disappointment. What painful hours of expectation would she pass; she would sit at a window which looked toward a field he used to cross, counting the minutes and straining her eyes to catch the first glimpse of his person, till, blinded with tears of disappointment, she would lean her head on her hands and give free vent to her sorrows: then catching at some new hope, she would again renew her watchful position, till the shades of evening enveloped every object in a dusky cloud: she would then renew her complaints, and with a heart bursting with disappointed love and wounded sensibility, retire to a bed which remorse had strewed with thorns, and court in vain that comforter of weary nature (who seldom visits the unhappy) to come and steep her senses in oblivion.

Who can form an adequate idea of the sorrow that preyed upon the mind of Charlotte? The wife whose breast glows with affection to her husband, and who in return meets only indifference, can but faintly conceive her anguish. Dreadfully painful is the situation of such a woman, but she has many comforts of which our poor Charlotte was deprived. The duteous, faithful wife, though treated with indifference, has one solid pleasure within her own bosom: she can reflect that she has not deserved neglect—that she has ever fulfilled the duties of her station with the strictest exactness; she may hope, by constant assiduity and unremitted attention, to recall her wanderer, and be doubly happy in his returning affection; she knows he can not leave her to unite himself to another: he can not cast her out to poverty and contempt; she looks around her and sees the smile of friendly welcome, or the tear of affectionate consolation on the face of every person whom she favors with her esteem, and from all these circumstances she gathers comfort: but the poor girl by thoughtless passion led astray, who in parting with her honor has forfeited the esteem of the very man to whom she has sacrificed everything dear and valuable in life, feels his indifference is the fruit of her own folly, and laments her want of power to recall his lost affection; she knows there is no tie but honor, and that, in a man who has been guilty of seduction, is but very feeble: he may leave her in a moment to shame and want; he may marry and forsake her forever; and should he, she has no redress, no friendly soothing companion to pour into her wounded mind the balm of consolation, no benevolent hand to lead her back to the path of rectitude; she has disgraced her friends, forfeited the good opinion of the world, and undone herself: she feels herself a poor solitary being in the midst of surrounding multitudes; shame bows her to the earth, remorse tears her distracted mind, and guilt, poverty, and disease, close the dreadful scene: she sinks unnoticed to oblivion. The finger of contempt may point out to some passing daughter of youthful mirth the humble bed where lies this frail sister of mortality; and will she, in the unbounded gaiety of her heart, exult in her own unblemished fame, and triumph over the silent ashes of the dead? Oh no! has she a heart of sensibility she will stop and thus address the unhappy victim of folly—

"Thou had'st thy faults, but sure thy sufferings have expatiated [sic: expiated] them: thy errors brought thee to an early grave; but thou wert a fellow creature—thou hast been unhappy—then be those errors forgotten."

Then as she stoops to pluck the noxious weed from off the sod, a tear will fall and consecrate the spot to Charity.

For ever honored be the sacred drop of humanity; the angel of mercy shall record its source, and the soul from whence it sprang shall be immortal.

My dear Madam, contract not your brow into a frown of disapprobation. I mean not to extenuate the faults of those unhappy women who fall victims to guilt and folly; but surely when we reflect how many errors we are ourselves subject to, how many secret faults lie hid in the recesses of our hearts, which we should blush to have brought into open day (and yet those faults require the lenity and pity of a benevolent judge, or awful would be our prospect of futurity), I say, my dear Madam, when we consider this, we surely may pity the faults of others.

Believe me, many an unfortunate female, who has once strayed into the thorny paths of vice, would gladly return to virtue was any generous friend to endeavor to raise and reassure her; but alas! it cannot be, you say; the world would deride and scoff. Then let me tell you, Madam, 'tis a very unfeeling world, and does not deserve half the blessings which a bountiful Providence showers upon it.

Oh, thou benevolent giver of all good! how shall we erring mortals dare to look up to thy mercy in the great day of retribution if we now uncharitably refuse to overlook the errors, or alleviate the miseries of our fellow creatures?

Montraville continued to lose interest in Charlotte and fell truly in love with and married a beautiful heiress. Pregnant and destitute, Charlotte begged for help from Mrs. La Rue Crayton, who spurned her. At last one of Charlotte's letters reached her parents, but by the time her father arrived to bring her home, Charlotte was dying. Her newborn daughter grew up to be a consolation to the family. Montraville suffered from remorse all his days, and La Rue relapsed into bad conduct that led her to destitution and death.

Jarena Lee

1783–c.1849 or later

JARENA LEE was born in 1783 in Cape May. It is not clear whether she was born free or became so when slaves were emancipated in New Jersey in 1804. At seven, she was taken sixty miles away from her parents to serve as a maid. Shortly afterward, according to her spiritual autobiography, she had her first religious experience, an attack of acute remorse for telling a lie to her mistress. At twenty-one, she was convinced of her sinfulness by a Presbyterian minister and was so cast down that she was tempted to commit suicide. She was converted to religion by the Reverend Richard Allen, founder of the African Methodist Episcopal Church. As her religious fervor increased, she felt a call to preach, but was rebuffed by Allen. She resigned herself to marriage to Joseph Lee, pastor of a church near Philadelphia, and confinement to private spiritual counseling. After five or six years, her husband died, leaving her with two small children. Again she felt the call to preach, like "a fire shut up in my bones." At last she rose up in church and did so, and so impressed Allen that he supported her vocation.

For the rest of her life, she traveled and preached in churches, courthouses, schools, private homes, and camp meetings. She went as far north as Canada, as far west as Ohio, and as far south as Maryland. There, in slave territory, she had a narrow escape when some white bullies tried to get hold of her free papers. On a typical year she traveled 2,325 miles and preached 187 sermons. Allen got her a church in Philadelphia, her home, but it appears that the congregation would not accept a female preacher. She was very successful on the road, however, and was generally accepted by blacks and whites in the communities she visited, although she kept meeting ministers and elders who sneered at her work and barred her from

231

their churches. She published the account of her call to preach in 1836, and again in 1849, augmented by the journal she kept of her career. She supported herself by the sale of these books and donations. Avowing that she had only three months of regular schooling, she hints that she had help in correcting her work for publication.

BIBLIOGRAPHY

Lee, Jarena. *Religious Experience and Journal of Mrs. Jarena Lee. Giving an Account of Her Call to Preach the Gospel.* Philadelphia, 1849.

Shockley, Ann Allen, ed. *Afro-American Women Writers: 1746–1933.* New York: New American Library, 1989.

from Religious Experience and Journal of Mrs. Jarena Lee

My Call to Preach the Gospel

Between four and five years after my sanctification,[1] on a certain time, an impressive silence fell upon me, and I stood as if someone was about to speak to me, yet I had no such thought in my heart.— But to my utter surprise there seemed to sound a voice which I thought I distinctly heard, and most certainly understood, which said to me, "Go preach the Gospel!" I immediately replied aloud, "No one will believe me." Again I listened, and again the same voice seemed to say—"Preach the Gospel; I will put words in your mouth, and will turn your enemies to become your friends."

At first I supposed that Satan had spoken to me, for I had read that he could transform himself into an angel of light for the purpose of deception. Immediately I went into a secret place, and called upon the Lord to know if he had called me to preach, and whether I was

---

[1]Progressing "from a state of darkness, or of nature," the soul must experience "first, conviction for sin. Second, justification from sin. Third, the entire sanctification of the soul to God" (*Religious Experience* 9).

deceived or not; when there appeared to my view the form and figure of a pulpit, with a Bible lying thereon, the back of which was presented to me as plainly as if it had been a literal fact.

In consequence of this, my mind became so exercised, that during the night following, I took a text and preached in my sleep. I thought there stood before me a great multitude, while I expounded to them the things of religion. So violent were my exertions and so loud were my exclamations, that I awoke from the sound of my own voice, which also awoke the family of the house where I resided. Two days after I went to see the preacher in charge of the African Society, who was the Rev. Richard Allen, the same before named in these pages, to tell him that I felt it my duty to preach the gospel. But as I drew near the street in which his house was, which was in the city of Philadelphia, my courage began to fail me; so terrible did the cross[2] appear, it seemed that I should not be able to bear it. Previous to my setting out to go to see him, so agitated was my mind, that my appetite for my daily food failed me entirely. Several times on my way there, I turned back again; but as often I felt my strength again renewed, and I soon found that the nearer I approached to the house of the minister, the less was my fear. Accordingly, as soon as I came to the door, my fears subsided, the cross was removed, all things appeared pleasant—I was tranquil.

I now told him, that the Lord had revealed it to me, that I must preach the gospel. He replied, by asking, in what sphere I wished to move in? I said, among the Methodists. He then replied, that a Mrs. Cook, a Methodist lady, had also some time before requested the same privilege; who, it was believed, had done much good in the way of exhortation, and holding prayer meetings; and who had been permitted to do so by the verbal license of the preacher in charge at the time. But as to women preaching, he said that our Discipline knew nothing at all about it—that it did not call for women preachers. This I was glad to hear, because it removed the fear of the cross—but no sooner did this feeling cross my mind, than I found that a love of souls had in a measure departed from me; that holy energy which burned within me, as a fire, began to be smothered. This I soon perceived.

O how careful ought we to be, lest through our by-laws of church government and discipline, we bring into disrepute even the word of

[2]Burden laid on her by God.

life. For as unseemly as it may appear nowadays for a woman to preach, it should be remembered that nothing is impossible with God. And why should it be thought impossible, heterodox, or improper for a woman to preach? seeing the Savior died for the woman as well as for the man.

If the man may preach, because the Savior died for him, why not the woman? seeing he died for her also. Is he not a whole Savior, instead of a half one? as those who hold it wrong for a woman to preach would seem to make it appear.

Did not Mary *first* preach the risen Savior,[3] and is not the doctrine of the resurrection the very climax of Christianity—hangs not all our hope on this, as argued by St. Paul? Then did not Mary, a woman, preach the gospel? for she preached the resurrection of the crucified Son of God.

But some will say that Mary did not expound the Scripture; therefore, she did not preach, in the proper sense of the term. To this I reply, it may be that the term *preach* in those primitive times, did not mean exactly what it is now *made* to mean; perhaps it was a great deal more simple then, than it is now—if it were not, the unlearned fishermen could not have preached the gospel at all, as they had no learning.

To this it may be replied, by those who are determined not to believe that it is right for a woman to preach, that the disciples, though they were fishermen and ignorant of letters too, were inspired so to do. To which I would reply, that though they were inspired, yet that inspiration did not save them from showing their ignorance of letters, and of man's wisdom; this the multitude soon found out, by listening to the remarks of the envious Jewish priests. If then, to preach the gospel, by the gift of heaven, comes by inspiration solely, is God straitened; must he take the man exclusively? May he not, did he not, and can he not inspire a female to preach the simple story of the birth, life, death, and resurrection of our Lord, and accompany it too with power to the sinner's heart? As for me, I am fully persuaded that the Lord called me to labor according to what I have received, in his vineyard. If he has not, how could he consistently bear testimony in favor of my poor labors, in awakening and converting sinners?

[3]When Christ rose from the dead, He appeared first to Mary Magdalene, who told His disciples (Matthew 16:9–11).

In my wanderings up and down among men, preaching according to my ability, I have frequently found families who told me that they had not for several years been to a meeting, and yet, while listening to hear what God would say by his poor female instrument, have believed with trembling—tears rolling down their cheeks, the signs of contrition and repentance towards God. I firmly believe that I have sown seed, in the name of the Lord, which shall appear with its increase at the great day of accounts, when Christ shall come to make up his jewels.

At a certain time, I was beset with the idea, that soon or late I should fall from grace and lose my soul at last. I was frequently called to the throne of grace about this matter, but found no relief; the temptation pursued me still. Being more and more afflicted with it, till at a certain time, when the spirit strongly impressed it on my mind to enter into my closet[4] and carry my case once more to the Lord; the Lord enabled me to draw nigh to him, and to his mercy seat, at this time, in an extraordinary manner; for while I wrestled with him for the victory over this disposition to doubt whether I should persevere, there appeared a form of fire, about the size of a man's hand, as I was on my knees; at the same moment there appeared to the eye of faith a man robed in a white garment, from the shoulders down to the feet; from him a voice proceeded, saying: "Thou shalt never return from the cross." Since that time I have never doubted, but believe that God will keep me until the day of redemption. Now I could adopt the very language of St. Paul, and say that nothing could have separated me from the love of God, which is in Christ Jesus.[5] Since that time, 1807, until the present, 1833, I have not even doubted the power and goodness of God to keep me from falling, through the sanctification of the spirit and belief of the truth.

. . .

But to return to the subject of my call to preach. Soon after this, as above related, the Rev. Richard Williams was to preach at Bethel Church, where I with others were assembled. He entered the pulpit, gave out the hymn, which was sung, and then addressed the throne

[4]Small private room.
[5]Romans 8:35, slightly altered.

of grace; took his text, passed through the exordium, and commenced to expound it. The text he took is in Jonah, 2d chap. 9th verse,—"Salvation is of the Lord." But as he proceeded to explain, he seemed to have lost the spirit; when in the same instant, I sprang, as by altogether supernatural impulse, to my feet, when I was aided from above to give an exhortation on the very text which my brother Williams had taken.

I told them I was like Jonah; for it had been then nearly eight years since the Lord had called me to preach his gospel to the fallen sons and daughters of Adam's race, but that I had lingered like him, and delayed to go at the bidding of the Lord, and warn those who are as deeply guilty as were the people of Nineveh.[6]

During the exhortation, God made manifest his power in a manner sufficient to show the world that I was called to labor according to my ability, and the grace given unto me, in the vineyard of the good husbandman.[7]

I now sat down, scarcely knowing what I had done, being frightened. I imagined that for this indecorum, as I feared it might be called, I should be expelled from the church. But instead of this, the Bishop[8] rose up in the assembly, and related that I had called upon him eight years before, asking to be permitted to preach and that he had put me off; but that he now as much believed that I was called to that work, as any of the preachers present. These remarks greatly strengthened me, so that my fears of having given an offence, and made myself liable as an offender, subsided, giving place to a sweet serenity, a holy joy of a peculiar kind, untasted in my bosom until then.

The next Sabbath day, while sitting under the word of the gospel, I felt moved to attempt to speak to the people in a public manner, but I could not bring my mind to attempt it in the church. I said, Lord, anywhere but here. Accordingly, there was a house not far off which was pointed out to me; to this I went. It was the house of a sister belonging to the same society with myself. Her name was Anderson. I told her I had come to hold a meeting in her house, if she would call in her neighbors. With this request she immediately com-

[6]God ordered Jonah to preach repentance to the wicked citizens of Nineveh, but Jonah tried to evade the mission.

[7]Allusion to Christ's parable of the workers in the vineyard, Matthew 20:1–16.

[8]Allen had become the first Bishop of the African Methodist Episcopal Church when it was organized nationally (1816).

plied. My congregation consisted of but five persons. I commenced by reading and singing a hymn; when I arose I found my hand resting on the Bible, which I had not noticed till that moment. It now occurred to me to take a text. I opened the Scripture, as it happened, at the 141st Psalm, fixing my eye on the third verse, which reads: "Set a watch, O Lord, before my mouth, keep the door of my lips." My sermon, such as it was, applied wholly to myself, and I added an exhortation. Two of my congregation wept much, as the fruit of my labor this time. In closing, I said to the few, that if anyone would open a door, I would hold a meeting the next sixth-day evening: when one answered that her house was at my service. Accordingly I went, and God made manifest his power among the people. Some wept, while others shouted for joy. One whole seat of females, by the power of God, as the rushing of a wind, were all bowed to the floor, at once, and screamed out. Also a sick man and woman in one house, the Lord convicted them both; one lived, and the other died. God wrought a judgment—some were well at night, and died in the morning. At this place I continued to hold meetings about six months. During that time I kept house with my little son, who was very sickly. About this time I had a call to preach at a place about thirty miles distant, among the Methodists, with whom I remained one week, and during the whole time, not a thought of my little son came into my mind; it was hid from me, lest I should have been diverted from the work I had to do, to look after my son. Here by the instrumentality of a poor colored woman, the Lord poured forth his spirit among the people. Though, as I was told, there were lawyers, doctors, and magistrates present, to hear me speak, yet there was mourning and crying among sinners, for the Lord scattered fire among them of his own kindling. The Lord gave his hand-maiden power to speak for his great name, for he arrested the hearts of the people, and caused a shaking amongst the multitude, for God was in the midst.

I now returned home, found all well; no harm had come to my child, although I left it very sick. Friends had taken care of it, which was of the Lord. I now began to think seriously of breaking up housekeeping, and forsaking all to preach the everlasting Gospel. I felt a strong desire to return to the place of my nativity, at Cape May, after an absence of about fourteen years. To this place, where the heaviest cross was to be met with, the Lord sent me, as Saul of Tarsus was sent to Jerusalem, to preach the same gospel which he had neglected and despised before his conversion.[9] I went by water, and on my passage was much distressed by seasickness, so much so that I expected to have died, but such was not the will of the Lord respecting me. After I had disembarked, I proceeded on as opportunities offered, toward where my mother lived. When within ten miles of that place, I appointed an evening meeting. There were a goodly number came out to hear. The Lord was pleased to give me light and liberty among the people.[10] After meeting, there came an elderly lady to me and said, she believed the Lord had sent me among them; she then appointed me another meeting there two weeks from that night. The next day I hastened forward to the place of my mother, who was happy to see me, and the happiness was mutual between us. With her I left my poor sickly boy, while I departed to do my Master's will. In this neighborhood I had an uncle, who was a Methodist, and who gladly threw open his door for meetings to be held there. At the first meeting which I held at my uncle's house, there was, with others who had come from curiosity to hear the woman preacher, an old man, who was a Deist, and who said he did not believe the colored people had any souls—he was sure they had none. He took a seat very near where I was standing, and boldly tried to look me out of countenance. But as I labored on in the best manner I was able, looking to God all the while, though it seemed to me I had but little liberty, yet there went an arrow from the bent bow of the gospel, and fastened in his till then obdurate heart. After I had done speaking, he went out, and called the people around him, said that my preaching might seem a small thing, yet he believed I had the worth of souls at heart. This language was different from what it was a little time before, as he now seemed to admit that colored people had souls, as it was to these I was chiefly speaking; and unless they had souls, whose good I had in view, his remark must have been without meaning. He now came into the house, and in the most friendly manner shook hands with me, saying he hoped God had spared him to some good purpose. This man was a great slave holder, and had been very cruel; thinking nothing of knocking down a slave with a fence stake, or whatever might come to hand. From this time it was said of him that he became greatly altered in

[9]Acts of the Apostles, chapter 21–22.
[10]God inspired her with what to say and the ability to pour it out freely, without inhibitions. Cf. "life and liberty," below.

his ways for the better. At that time he was about seventy years old, his head as white as snow; but whether he became a converted man or not, I never heard.

The week following, I had an invitation to hold a meeting at the Court House of the County, when I spoke from the 53d chap. of Isaiah, 3d verse. It was a solemn time, and the Lord attended the word; I had life and liberty, though there were people there of various denominations. Here again I saw the aged slaveholder, who notwithstanding his age, walked about three miles to hear me. . . .

From this place I next went to Dennis Creek meeting house, where at the invitation of an elder, I spoke to a large congregation of various and conflicting sentiments, when a wonderful shock of God's power was felt, shown everywhere by groans, by sighs, and loud and happy amens. I felt as if aided from above. My tongue was cut loose, the stammerer spoke freely;[11] the love of God, and of his service, burned with a vehement flame within me—his name was glorified among the people.

I had my little son with me, and was very much straitened for money—and not having means to procure my passage home, I opened a school and taught eleven scholars, for the purpose of raising a small sum. For many weeks I knew not what to do about returning home, when the Lord came to my assistance as I was rambling in the fields meditating upon his goodness, and made known to me that I might go to the city of Philadelphia, for which place I soon embarked with a very kind captain. We had a perilous passage—a dreadful storm arose, and before leaving the Delaware Bay, we had a narrow escape from being run down by a large ship. But the good Lord held us in the hollow of his hand, and in the afternoon of November 12, 1821, we arrived at the city.

• • •

I now returned to Philadelphia, where I stayed a short time, and went to Salem, West Jersey. I met with many troubles on my journey, especially from the elder, who, like many others, was averse to a woman's preaching. And here let me tell that elder, if he has not gone to heaven, that I have heard that as far back as Adam Clarke's time, his objections to female preaching were met by the answer—"If an ass reproved Ba-

[11]Probably an allusion to Moses, Exodus 4:10–12.

laam, and a barn-door fowl reproved Peter, why should not a woman reprove sin?"[12] I do not introduce this for its complimentary classification of women with donkeys and fowls, but to give the reply of a poor woman, who had once been a slave. To the first companion she said—"Maybe a speaking woman is like an ass—but I can tell you one thing, the ass seen the angel when Balaam didn't."

Notwithstanding the opposition, we had a prosperous time at Salem. I had some good congregations, and sinners were cut to the heart. After speaking in the meeting house, two women came up into the pulpit, and falling upon my neck cried out "What shall I do to be saved?" One said she had disobeyed God, and he had taken her children from her—he had called often after her, but she did not hearken. I pointed her to the all-atoning blood of Christ, which is sufficient to cleanse from all sin, and left her, after prayer, to his mercy. From this place I walked twenty-one miles, and preached with difficulty to a stiff-necked and rebellious people, who I soon left without any animosity for their treatment. They might have respected my message, if not the poor weak servant who brought it to them with so much labor.

"If they persecute you in one city, flee into another," was the advice I had resolved to take, and I hastened to Greenwich, where I had a lively congregation, had unusual life and liberty in speaking, and the power of God was there. We also had a solemn time in the meeting house on Sabbath day morning, and in a dwelling house in the evening; a large company assembled, when the spirit was with us, and we had a mighty shaking among the dry bones.[13]

On second day morning, I took stage and rode seven miles to Woodstown, and there I spoke to a respectable congregation of white and colored, in a school house. I was desired to speak in the colored meeting house, but the minister could not reconcile his mind to a woman preacher—he could not unite in fellowship with me even to shaking hands as Christians ought. I had visited that place before, when God made manifest his power "through the foolishness of preaching," and

---

[12]Balaam disobeyed God by going along with the king's emissaries to curse Israel. God sent an angel to stand in his path, who was invisible to Balaam but visible to the ass he was riding. The ass refused to proceed, and Balaam, not understanding, beat her to make her go on. Thereupon God gave her the power to speak and reprove Balaam, who then saw the angel and repented (Numbers 22:20–34). Jesus told Peter that he would deny Him three times before the cock crowed; Peter did, and realized his disloyalty only when he heard the cock (Matthew 26:34, 75).

[13]Reference to Ezekiel 37:7.

owned the poor old woman. One of the brothers appointed a meeting in his own house, and after much persuasion this minister came also. I did not feel much like preaching, but spoke from Acts VIII, 35. I felt my inability, and was led to complain of weakness—but God directed the arrow to the hearts of the guilty—and my friend the minister got happy, and often shouted "Amen," and "As it is, sister." We had a wonderful display of the spirit of God among us, and we found it good to be there. There is nothing too hard for the Lord to do. I committed the meeting into the hands of the elder, who afterwards invited me to preach in the meeting house. He had said he did not believe that ever a soul was converted under the preaching of a woman—but while I was laboring in his place, conviction seized a woman, who fell to the floor crying for mercy. This meeting held till 12 or 1 o'clock. O how precious is the sound of Jesus' name! I never felt a doubt at this time of my acceptance with God, but rested my soul on his every promise. The elder shook hands, and we parted. . . .

From here I proceeded to Christine, where we worshipped in a dwelling house, and I must say was well treated by some of my colored friends. I then returned to Wilmington, where in a few days I had a message to return again to C. My friends said I should have the Meeting House, for which Squire Luden interested himself, and the appointment was published. When the people met at the proper time, the doors remained locked. Amid cries of "shame" we left the church steps—but a private house was opened a short distance up the road, and though disappointed in obtaining egress [ingress] to a church, the Lord did not disappoint his people, for we were fed with the bread of life, and had a happy time. Mr. and Mrs. Lewelen took me to their house, and treated me, not as one of their hired servants, but as a companion, for which I shall ever feel grateful. Mr. Smith, a doctor, also invited me to call upon them—he was a Presbyterian, but we prayed and conversed together about Jesus and his love, and parted without meddling with each other's creeds. Oh, I long to see the day when Christians will meet on one common platform—Jesus of Nazareth—and cease their bickerings and contentions about non-essentials—when "our Church" shall be less debated, but "our Jesus" shall be all in all.

Eliza Southgate Bowne

1783–1809

ELIZA SOUTHGATE'S FATHER was a doctor and judge; her maternal uncle, the distinguished Federalist statesman Rufus King. She grew up in Scarborough, Maine, the third of twelve children. At fourteen, she was sent to Susanna Rowson's school (then located in Medford, Massachusetts); she greatly enjoyed and appreciated her opportunity to learn there, although in retrospect, as her letter of May 1801 shows, she doubted the value of her education. In 1803 she married Walter Bowne, a prominent New York businessman. They had two children. The marriage seems to have been very happy, but it ended when she died of tuberculosis at the age of twenty-five.

While all of Eliza Southgate Bowne's letters demonstrate lively intelligence, most of them simply tell the news or report on her activities. Her letters to her mother are affectionate, but restricted by the dutifulness expected of an eighteenth-century daughter. Only in her letters to her first cousin, Moses Porter, did she address significant issues and candidly express her thoughts and feelings about them. Unfortunately, he died of yellow fever in 1802, just as he was about to complete his legal education.

BIBLIOGRAPHY

Bowne, Eliza Southgate. *A Girl's Life Eighty Years Ago: Selections from the Letters of Eliza Southgate Bowne.* Edited by and with an introduction by Clarence Cook. New York: Charles Scribner's Sons, 1887. Reprint New York: Arno Press, 1974.

from the Letters of Eliza Southgate Bowne to her Cousin Moses Porter

Fall, 1800 (?)

To Moses Porter.

My most charming Cousin! Most kind and condescending friend—teach me how I may express the grateful sense I have of the obligations I owe you; your many and long letters have chased away the spleen,[1] they have rendered me cheerful and happy, and I almost forgot I was so far from home.—O shame on you! Moses, you know I hate this formality among friends, you know how gladly I would throw all these fashionable forms from our correspondence; but you still oppose me, you adhere to them with as much scrupulosity as to the ten commandments, and for aught I know you believe them equally essential to the salvation of your soul. But, Eliza, you have not answered my last letter! True, and if I had not have answered it would you never have written me again—and I confess that I believe you would not—yet I am mortified and displeased that you value my letters so little, that the exertions to continue the correspondence must all come from me, that if I relax my zeal in the smallest degree it may drop to the ground without your helping hand to raise it. I do think you are a charming fellow,—would not write because I am in debt, well, be it so, my ceremonious friend,—I submit, and though I transgress by sending a half sheet more than you ever did, yet I assure you 'twas to convince you of the violence of my anger which could *induce* me to forget the rules of politeness. I am at Wiscassett. I have seen Rebecca every day, she is handsome as ever, and we both of us were in constant expectation of seeing you for two or three days; you did not come and we were disappointed.

I leave here for Bath next week. I have had a ranting time, and if I did not feel so offended, I would tell you more about it.

As I look around me I am surprised at the happiness which is so generally enjoyed in families, and that marriages which have not love for a foundation on more than one side at most, should produce so much apparent harmony. I may be censured for declaring it as my

[1]Depression, "the blues."

opinion that not one woman in a hundred marries for love. A woman of taste and sentiment will surely see but a very few whom she could love, and it is altogether uncertain whether either of them will particularly distinguish her.[2] If they should, surely she is very fortunate, but it would be one of fortune's random favors and such as we have no right to expect. The female mind, I believe, is of a very pliable texture; if it were not, we should be wretched indeed. Admitting as a known truth that few women marry those whom they would prefer to all the world if they could be viewed by them with equal affection, or rather that there are often others whom they could have preferred if they had felt that affection for them which would have induced them to offer themselves,—admitting this as a truth not to be disputed,—is it not a subject of astonishment that happiness is not almost banished from this connection? Gratitude is undoubtedly the foundation of the esteem we commonly feel for a husband. One that has preferred us to all the world, one that has thought us possessed of every quality to render him happy, surely merits our gratitude. If his character is good—if he is not displeasing in his person or manners—what objection can we make that will not be thought frivolous by the greater part of the world?—yet I think there are many other things necessary for happiness, and the world should never compel me to marry a man because I could not give satisfactory reasons for not liking him. I do not esteem marriage absolutely essential to happiness, and that it does not always bring happiness we must every day witness in our acquaintance. A single life is considered too generally as a reproach; but let me ask you, which is the most despicable—she who marries a man she scarcely thinks *well* of—to avoid the reputation of an old maid—or she who, with more delicacy, than marry one she could not highly esteem, preferred to live single all her life, and had wisdom enough to despise so mean a sacrifice to the opinion of the rabble, as the woman who marries a man she has not much love for—must make. I wish not to alter the laws of na-

---

[2]Throughout this and the following paragraph, ESB is responding to the dicta of Dr. John Gregory, the well-intentioned but conservative author of a very popular and influential work, *A Father's Legacy to His Daughters* (1774). Gregory declared that a woman of delicacy hesitates to admit even to herself that she loves, that it is unlikely that a woman of sense and taste will be courted by one of the few men she can esteem, that women's enforced passivity is not a hardship because Nature has given them greater flexibility of taste and gratitude for a man's preference is a sufficient basis for marriage.

ture—neither will I quarrel with the rules which custom has established and rendered indispensably necessary to the harmony of society. But every being who has contemplated human nature on a large scale will certainly justify me when I declare that the inequality of privilege between the sexes is very sensibly felt by us females, and in no instance is it greater than in the liberty of choosing a partner in marriage; true, we have the liberty of refusing those we don't like, but not of selecting those we do. This is undoubtedly as it should be. But let me ask you, what must be that love which is altogether voluntary, which we can withhold or give, which sleeps in dullness and apathy till it is requested to brighten into life? Is it not a cold, lifeless dictate of the head,—do we not weigh all the conveniences and inconveniences which will attend it? And after a long calculation, in which the heart never was consulted, we determine whether it is most prudent to love or not.

How I should despise a soul so sordid, so mean! How I abhor the heart which is regulated by mechanical rules, which can say "thus far will I go and no farther," whose feelings can keep pace with their convenience, and be awakened at stated periods,—a mere piece of clockwork which always moves right! How far less valuable than that being who has a soul to govern her actions, and though she may not always be coldly prudent, yet she will sometimes be generous and noble; and that the other never can be. After all, I must own that a woman of delicacy never will suffer her esteem to ripen into love unless she is convinced of a return. Though our first approaches to love may be involuntary, yet I should be sorry if we had no power of controlling them if occasion required. There is a happy conformity or pliability in the female mind which seems to have been a gift of nature to enable them to be happy with so few privileges,—and another thing, they have more gratitude in their dispositions than men, and there is a something particularly gratifying to the heart in being beloved, if the object is worthy; it produces a something like, and "Pity melts the heart to love."[3] Added to these there is a self-love which does more than all the rest. Our vanity ('tis an ugly word but I can't find a better) is gratified by the distinguished preference given us. There must be an essential difference in the dispositions of men and women. I am astonished when I think of it—yet—But I have written myself into sunshine—'tis always my way when any-

---

[3] John Dryden, "Alexander's Feast," line 96 (slightly misquoted).

thing oppresses me, when any chain of thoughts particularly occupies my mind, and I feel dissatisfied at anything which I have not the power to alter,—to sit down and unburthen them on paper; it never fails to alleviate me, and I generally give full scope to the feelings of the moment, and as I write all disagreeable thoughts evaporate, and I end contented that things shall remain as they are. When I began this it absolutely appeared to me that no woman, or rather not one in a hundred, married the man she should prefer to all the world—not that I ever could suppose that at the time she married him she did not prefer him to all others,—but that she would have preferred another if he had professed to love her as well as the one she married. Indeed, I believe no woman of delicacy suffers herself to think she could love anyone before she had discovered an affection for her. For my part I should never ask the question of myself—do I love such a one, if I had reason to think he loved me—and I believe there are many who love that never confessed it to themselves. My pride, my delicacy, would all be hurt if I discovered such *unasked* for love, even in my own bosom. I would strain every nerve and rouse every faculty to quell the first appearance of it. There is no danger, however. I could never love without being beloved, and I am confident in my own mind that no person whom I could love would ever think me sufficiently worthy to love me. But I congratulate myself that I am at liberty to refuse those I don't like, and that I have firmness enough to brave the sneers of the world and live an old maid, if I never find one I can love.

Sunday, Scarborough, May—, 1801.

When one commences an action with a full conviction they shall not acquit themselves with honor, they are sure not to succeed; impressed with this idea, I write you. I positively declare I have felt a great reluctance ever since we concluded on the plan. I am aware of the construction you may put on this, but call it *affectation* or what you will, I assure you it proceeds from different motives. When I first proposed this correspondence, I thought only of the amusement and instruction it would afford *me*. I almost forgot that I should have any part to perform. Since, however, I have reflected on the scheme as it was about to be carried into execution, I have felt a degree of diffidence which has almost induced me to hope you would *forget* the engagement. Fully convinced of my inability to afford pleasure or instruction to an enlarged mind, I rely wholly on your candor and generosity to pardon the errors which will cloud my best efforts. When I reflect on the severity of your criticisms in general, I shrink at the idea of exposing to you what will never stand the test. Yet did I not imagine you would throw aside the *critic* and assume the *friend,* I should never dare, with all my vanity (and I am not deficient), give you so fine an opportunity to exercise your favorite propensity. I know you will laugh at all this, but I must confess it appears rather a folly, first to request your correspondence and then with so much diffidence and false delicacy, apparently to extort a compliment, talk about my inability and the like. You will not think I intend a compliment when I say I have ever felt a disagreeable restraint when conversing before you. Often, when, with all the confidence I possess, I have brought forward an opinion, said all my imagination could suggest in support of it, and viewed with pleasure the little fabric, which I imagined to be founded on truth and justice, with one word you would crush to the ground that which had cost me so many to erect. These things I think in time will humble my vanity; I wish sincerely that they may.

Yet I believe I possess decent talents and should have been quite another being had they been properly cultivated. But as it is, I can never get over some little prejudices which I have imbibed long since, and which warp all the faculties of my mind. I was pushed onto the stage of action without one principle to guide my actions,—the impulse of the moment was the only incitement. I have never committed any grossly imprudent action, yet I have been folly's darling child. I trust they were rather errors of the head than the heart, for we have all a kind of inherent power to distinguish between right and wrong, and if before the heart becomes contaminated by the maxims of society it is left to act from impulse, though it have no fixed principle, yet it will not materially err. Possessing a gay lively disposition, I pursued pleasure with ardor. I wished for admiration, and took the means which would be most likely to obtain it. I found the mind of a female, if such a thing existed, was thought not worth cultivating. I disliked the trouble of thinking for myself and therefore adopted the sentiments of others—fully convinced to adorn my person and acquire a few little accomplishments was sufficient to secure me the admiration of the society I frequented. I cared but little about the mind. I learned to flutter about with a thoughtless gaiety—a mere feather which every breath had power to move. I left school with a head full of something, tumbled in without order or connection. I returned home with a determination to put it in more order; I set about the great work of culling the best part to make a few sentiments out of—to serve as a little ready change in my commerce with the world. But I soon lost all patience (a virtue I do not possess in an eminent degree), for the greater part of my ideas I was obliged to throw away without knowing where I got them or what I should do with them; what remained I pieced as ingeniously as I could into a few patchwork opinions,—they are now almost worn threadbare, and as I am about quilting a few more, I beg you will send me any spare ideas you may chance to have that will answer my turn. By this time I suppose you have found out what you have a right to expect from this correspondence, and probably at this moment lay down the letter with a long sage-like face to ponder on my egotism.—'Tis a delightful employment, I will leave you to enjoy it while I eat my dinner: And what is the result, Cousin? I suppose a few exclamations on the girl's vanity to think no subject could interest me but where herself was concerned, or the barrenness of her head that could write on no other subject. But she is a *female,* say you, with a *manly contempt.* Oh you Lords of the world, what are you that your unhallowed lips should dare profane the fairest part of creation! But honestly I wish to say something by way of apology, but don't seem to know what,—it is true I have a kind of natural affection for myself, I find no one more ready to pardon my faults or find excuses for my failings—it is natural to love our friends. . . .

Scarborough, June 1, 1801.

As to the qualities of mind peculiar to each sex, I agree with you that sprightliness is in favor of females and profundity of males. Their education, their pursuits would create such a quality even though nature had not implanted it. The business and pursuits of men require deep thinking, judgment, and moderation, while, on the other hand, females are under no necessity of dipping deep, but merely "skim the surface," and we too commonly spare ourselves the exertion which deep researches require, unless they are absolutely necessary to our pursuits in life. We rarely find one giving themselves up to profound investigation for amusement merely. Necessity is the nurse of all the great qualities of the mind; it explores all the hidden treasures and by its stimulating power they are "polished into brightness." Women who have no such incentives to action suffer all the strong energetic qualities of the mind to sleep in obscurity; sometimes a ray of genius gleams through the thick clouds with which it is enveloped, and irradiates for a moment the darkness of mental night; yet, like a comet that shoots wildly from its sphere, it excites our wonder, and we place it among the phenomenons of nature, without searching for a natural cause. Thus it is [that] the qualities with which nature has endowed us, as a support amid the misfortunes of life and a shield from the allurements of vice, are left to moulder in ruin. In this dormant state they become enervated and impaired, and at last die for *want of exercise*. The little airy qualities which produce sprightliness are left to flutter about like feathers in the wind, the sport of every breeze.

Women have more fancy, more lively imaginations than men. That is easily accounted for: a person of correct judgment and accurate discernment will never have that flow of ideas which one of a different character might,—every object has not the power to introduce into his mind such a variety of ideas; he rejects all but those closely connected with it. On the other hand, a person of small discernment will receive every idea that arises in the mind, making no distinction between those nearly related and those more distant; they are all equally welcome, and consequently such a mind abounds with fanciful, out-of-the-way ideas. Women have more imagination, more sprightliness, because they have less discernment. I never was of opinion that the pursuits of the sexes ought to be the same; on the contrary, I believe it would be destructive to happiness: there would a degree of rivalry exist, incompatible with the harmony we wish to establish. I have ever thought it necessary that each should have a separate sphere of action,—in such a case there could be no clashing unless one or the other should leap their respective bounds. Yet to cultivate the qualities with which we are endowed can never be called infringing the prerogatives of man. Why, my dear Cousin, were we furnished with such powers, unless the improvement of them would conduce to the happiness of society? Do you suppose the mind of woman the only work of God that was "made in vain?" The cultivation of the powers we possess, I have ever thought a privilege (or I may say duty) that belonged to the human species, and not man's exclusive prerogative. Far from destroying the harmony that ought to subsist, it would fix it on a foundation that would not totter at every jar. Women would be under the same degree of subordination that they now are; enlighten and expand their minds, and they would perceive the necessity of such a regulation to preserve the order and happiness of society. Yet you require that their conduct should be always guided by that reason which you refuse them the power of exercising. I know it is generally thought that in such a case women would assume the right of commanding. But I see no foundation for such a supposition,—not a blind submission to the will of another which neither honor nor reason dictates. It would be criminal in such a case to submit, for we are under a prior engagement to conduct in all things according to the dictates of reason. I had rather be the meanest reptile that creeps the earth, or cast upon the wide world to suffer all the ills "that flesh is heir to,"[1] than live a slave to the despotic will of another.

I am aware of the censure that will ever await the female that attempts the vindication of her sex, yet I dare to brave that censure that I know to be undeserved. It does not follow (O what a pen!) that every female who vindicates the capacity of the sex is a disciple of Mary Wollstonecraft.[2] Though I allow her to have said many things which I cannot but approve, yet the very foundation on which she builds her work will be apt to prejudice us so against her that we will not allow her the merit she really deserves,—yet, prejudice set aside, I confess I admire many of her sentiments, notwithstanding I believe should anyone adopt her principles, they would conduct in the same manner, and upon the whole her life is the best comment on her writings. Her style is nervous[3] and commanding, her sentiments appear to carry conviction along with them, but they will not bear analyzing. I wish to say something on your *natural refinement*, but I shall only have room to touch upon it if I begin, "therefore I'll leave it till another time."

Last evening Mr. Samuel Thatcher spent with us; we had a fine "dish of conversation" served up with great taste, fine sentiments dressed with elegant language and seasoned with wit. He is really excellent company—a little enthusiastic or so—but that is no matter. In compassion I entreat you to come over here soon and make me some pens. I have got one that I have been whittling this hour and at last have got it to make a stroke (it liked to have given me the lie). I believe I must give up all pretension to *profundity,* for I am

[1]*Hamlet,* Act 3, scene 1, line 63.
[2]Mary Wollstonecraft's eloquent *A Vindication of the Rights of Woman* (1792) was very radical. Her emotional life was chaotic; she lived with two men to whom she was not married and attempted suicide for frustrated love.
[3]Vigorous.

much more at home in my female character. This argumentative
style is not congenial to my taste. I hate anything that requires order
or connection. I never could do anything by rule,—when I get a
subject I am incapable of reasoning upon, I play with it as with a
rattle, for what else should I do with it? But I have kept along quite
in a direct line; I caught myself "upon the wing" two or three times,
but I had power to check my nonsense. I send you my sentiments on
this subject as they really exist with me. I believe they are not the
mere impulse of the moment, but founded on what I think truth. I
could not help laughing at that part of your letter where you said
the seal of my letter deprived you of some of the most interesting
part of it. I declare positively I left a blank place on purpose for it,
that you might not lose one precious word, and now you have the
impudence to tell me that the most interesting part was the blank
paper.[4] It has provoked my ire to such a degree that I positively
declare I never will send you any more blank paper than I possibly
can avoid, to "spite you."

. . . I have just read your last and picture something in it that at first
I did not pay much attention to. You say all you have said on the
subject of education was merely the thought of the moment, "written
not to be received but laughed at." What shall I think?—That you
think me too contemptible to know your real sentiments? I should
be very unwilling to admit such a suspicion, yet what can you
mean?—with the greatest apparent seriousness, you speak of the *sincerity* with which you conduct this correspondence. Was that likewise meant to be laughed at? I had flattered myself, when I
commenced this correspondence, to reap both instruction and
amusement from an undisguised communication of sentiments. I had
likewise hoped you would not think it too great a condescension to
speak to me with that openness you would to a male friend. However, I shall begin to think it is contrary to the nature of things that
a gentleman should speak his real sentiments to a lady, yet in our
correspondence I wished and expected to step aside from the world,
speak to each other in the plain language of sincerity. I have much
to say on this subject, but unfortunately my ideas never begin to
flow until I have filled up my paper. Do not imagine from what I

---

[4]ESB is joking: there are obviously words missing from her earlier letter, where
he tore the paper in breaking her seal.

have said that the most disagreeable truths will offend me. I promise not to feel hurt at any thing you write, if 'tis your real sentiment. But, Cousin, don't trifle with me. Do not make me think so contemptibly of myself as you will by not allowing me your confidence; promise to speak as you think and I will never scold you again.

ELIZA.

Portland, May 23, 1802[1]

... Were I a man, I should think it cowardly to bury myself in solitude,—nay, I should be unwilling to confess I felt myself unable to preserve my virtue where there were temptations to destroy it; there is no merit in being virtuous when there is no struggle to preserve that virtue. 'Tis in the midst of temptations and allurements that the active and generous virtues must be exerted in their full force. One virtuous action where there were temptations and delusions to surmount would give more delight to my own heart, more real satisfaction than a whole life spent in mere negative goodness; he must be base indeed who can voluntarily act wrong when no allurement draws him from the path of virtue. You say you never dipped much into the pleasures of *high life* and therefore should have but little to regret on that score. In the choice of life one ought to consult their own dispositions and inclinations, their own powers and talents. We all have a preference to some particular mode of life, and we surely ought to endeavor to arrive at that which will more probably ensure us most happiness. I have often thought what profession I should choose were I a man. I might then think very differently from what I do now, yet I have always thought if I felt conscious of possessing brilliant talents, the *law* would be my choice. Then I might hope to arrive at an eminence which would be gratifying to my feelings. I should then hope to be a public character, respected and admired,—but unless I was convinced I possessed the talents which would distinguish me as a speaker I would be anything rather than a lawyer;—from the dry sameness of such employments as the business of an office all my feelings would revolt, but to be an eloquent speaker would be the delight of my heart. I thank Heaven I was *born* a woman. I have now only patiently to wait till some clever fellow shall take a fancy to me and place me in a situation; I

[1] A consideration of the advantages and disadvantages of rural retirement prompts ESB to think about the differences between women's and men's lives.

am determined to make the best of it, let it be what it will. We ladies, you know, possess that "sweet pliability of temper" that disposes us to enjoy any situation, and we must have no choice in these things till we find what is to be our destiny; then we must consider it the best in the world. But remember, I desire to be thankful I am not a man. I should not be content with moderate abilities—nay, I should not be content with mediocrity in anything, but as a woman I am equal to the generality of my sex, and I do not feel that great desire of fame I think I should if I was a man. Should you hereafter become an inhabitant of Boyford I make no doubt you will be very happy, because you will weigh all the advantages and disadvantages. Yet I do not think you qualified for the laborious life farmers generally lead, and it requires a little fortune to live an independent farmer without labor. Rebecca would do charmingly, I know you are imagining her the partner of all your joys and cares,—of all your harmony and content, when you charm yourself with your description of rural happiness. With her you imagined you could quit the world and almost live happily in a desert. So may it be,—I know none but a lover could paint the sweets of retirement with such enthusiasm . . .

Catharine Maria Sedgwick

(1789-1867)

CATHARINE MARIA SEDGWICK was born into an upper-class family in Stockbridge, Massachusetts. Her father, Theodore, was a prominent Federalist politician, a friend of George Washington and Alexander Hamilton; he served in both houses of Congress and rose to be Speaker of the House of Representatives. His constant absences from home may have contributed to her mother's clinical depression. Catharine was brought up largely by her older sister, Eliza, and Elizabeth Freeman, called "Mumbet," their black housekeeper. Freeman had been a slave, but when she was abused by her mistress and appealed to Theodore Sedgwick, he successfully argued in court that the Massachusetts state constitution prohibited slavery. All the Sedgwicks were ardent abolitionists.

Raised in the strict Calvinism of rural Massachusetts, Catharine left the church in 1821 and became a Unitarian. According to family legend, an aunt told her after her conversion: "Come and see me as often as you can, dear, for you know, after this world, we shall never meet again." Catharine's first book, *A New England Tale* (1882), aimed to help others escape from Calvinism. She wrote five other novels, of which the best is *Hope Leslie* (1827), a story set in Puritan New England that shows unusual sympathy for Indian culture. She was one of the most successful authors of her day, widely recognized as one of the founders of a distinctively American literature, and a personal friend of most of the leading contemporary writers. Nathaniel Hawthorne and Herman Melville met in her home in 1850; Margaret Fuller cited her as "a fine example of the independent and beneficent existence that intellect and character can give to Woman, no less than Man."

Catharine, the only one of the Sedgwick children who did not marry, often wrote about female celibacy. Throughout her writings, she protested against the popular belief "that a woman's single life must be useless or undignified—that she is but an adjunct of man" (Preface to *Married or Single,* 1857); yet she also missed being the center of a family of her own. Nevertheless, she enjoyed a rich emotional life with brothers and sisters, nieces and nephews. She generally lived with her brothers' families in Stockbridge, Lenox, or New York City. It was for Alice, daughter of her favorite niece, that Sedgwick started writing her "Recollections of Childhood" in 1853. Although these gloss over the acute difficulties of the family, they present a faithful picture of life in rural New England, the life that she drew on for her best fiction.

BIBLIOGRAPHY

Foster, Edward Halsey. *Catharine Maria Sedgwick.* New York: Twayne, 1974.

Sedgwick, Catharine M. *Life and Letters.* Edited by Mary E. Dewey. New York: Harper and Brothers, 1871.

from Recollections of Childhood

How trivial, too, are the recollections of childhood! The next notch on my memory is of being sent over to Mrs. Caroline Dwight, to borrow a boy's dress of Frank Dwight's, which was to be the model of your "father Charles's"[1] first male attire. Then come thronging recollections of my childhood, its joys and sorrows—"Papa's going away," and "Papa's coming home"; the dreadful clouds that came over our sunny home when mamma was sick—my love of Mumbet, that noble woman, the main pillar of our household—distinctly the faces of the favorite servants, *Grippy,* Sampson Derby, Sampson the cook, a runaway slave, "Lady Prime," and various others who, to my mind's eye, are still young, vigorous, and alert! Not Agrippa, for

[1]Actually her great uncle, Charles Sedgwick.

him I saw through the various stages of manhood to decrepit old age. Grippy is one of the few who will be immortal in our village annals. He enlisted in the army of the Revolution, and, being a very well-trained and adroit servant, he was taken into the personal service of the noble Pole, Kosciusko.[2] Unlike most heroes, he always remained a hero to his valet Grippy, who many a time has charmed our childhood with stories of his soldier-master. One I remember, of which the catastrophe moved my childish indignation. Kosciusko was absent from camp, and Agrippa, to amuse his fellow-servants, dressed in his master's most showy uniform, and blacked with shining black-ball his legs and feet to resemble boots. Just as he was in full exhibition, his master returned, and, resolved to have his own fun out of the joke, he bade "Grip" follow him, and took him to the tents of several officers, introducing him as an African prince. Poor Grippy, who had as mortal an aversion practically as our preachers of temperance have theoretically to every species of spirituous liquor, was received at each new introduction by a soldier's hospitality, and compelled, by a nod from his master, to taste each abhorrent cup, brandy, or wine, or "Hollands," or whatever (to Grippy poisonous) potion it might chance to be, till, when his master was sated with the joke, he gave him a kick, and sent him staggering away. I think Grippy was fully compensated by the joke for the ignominy of its termination. He had a fund of humor and mother-wit, and was a sort of Sancho Panza in the village, always trimming[3] other men's follies with a keen perception, and the biting wit of wisdom. Grippy was a capital subaltern, but a very poor officer. As a servant he was faultless, but in his own domain at home a tyrant. Mumbet (mamma Bet), on the contrary, though absolutely perfect in service, was never servile. Her judgment and will were never subordinated by mere authority; but when she went to her own little home, like old Eli,[4] she was the victim of her affections, and was weakly indulgent to her riotous and ruinous descendants.

I believe, my dear Alice, that the people who surround us in our childhood, whose atmosphere infolds us, as it were, have more to do with the formation of our characters than all our didactic and

[2]Thaddeus Kosciusko was a Polish general who came to fight in the American Revolution.
[3]Censuring.
[4]Eli, a virtuous priest in Israel, was unable to control his sinful sons (I Samuel, chapter 2).

preceptive education. Mumbet had a clear and nice perception of justice, and a stern love of it, an uncompromising honesty in word and deed, and conduct of high intelligence, that made her the unconscious moral teacher of the children she tenderly nursed. She was a remarkable exception to the general character of her race. Injustice and oppression have confounded their moral sense; cheated as they have been of their liberty, defrauded at wholesale of time and strength, what wonder that they allow themselves petty reprisals—a sort of predatory warfare in the households of their masters and employers—for, though they now among us be free,[5] they retain the vices of a degraded and subjected people.

I do not believe that any amount of temptation could have induced Mumbet to swerve from truth. She knew nothing of the compromises of bigotry. Truth was her nature—the offspring of courage and loyalty. In my childhood I clung to her with instinctive love and faith, and the more I know and observe of human nature, the higher does she rise above others, whatever may have been their instruction or accomplishment. In her the image of her Maker was cast in material so hard and pure that circumstances could not alter its outline or cloud its lustre. This may seem rhodomontade to you, my child. "Why," you may exclaim, "my aunt could say nothing more of Washington, and this woman was once a slave, born a slave, and always a servant!" Yes, so she was, and yet I will remember that during her last sickness, when I daily visited her in her little hut— her then independent home—I said then, and my sober after judgment ratified it, that I felt awed as if I had entered the presence of Washington. Even protracted suffering and mortal sickness, with old age, could not break down her spirit. When Dr. F. said to her, with the proud assurance of his spiritual office, "Are you not afraid to meet your God?" "No, sir," she replied, "I am not afeard. I have tried to do my duty, and I am *not* afeard!" This was truth, and she spoke it with calm dignity. Creeds crumble before such a faith.

Speaking to me of the mortal nature of her disease, she said, "It is the last stroke, and it is the best stroke."

Her expressions of feeling were simple and comprehensive. When she suddenly lost a beloved grandchild, the only descendant of whom she had much hope—she was a young mother, and died without an

---

[5]In the 1780s, Massachusetts courts ruled that the state constitution prohibited slavery.

instant's warning—I remember Mumbet walking up and down the room with her hands knit together and great tears rolling down her cheeks, repeating, as if to send back into her soul its swelling sorrow, "Don't say a word; it's God's will!" And when I was sobbing over my dead mother, she said, "We must be quiet. Don't you think I am grieved? Our hair has grown white together." Even at this distance of time I remember the effect on me of her still, solemn sadness. Elsewhere, my dear, you will see notices of the memorable things in her life, and I need not here repeat them.[6] Her virtues are recorded, with a truth that few epitaphs can boast, on the stone we placed over her grave. Your "father Charles" wrote the inscription.

My dear Alice, I wish I could give you a true picture, and a vivid one, of my *fragmentary* childhood—how different from the thoughtful, careful (whether judicious or injudicious) education of the present day.

Education in the common sense I had next to none, but there was much chance seed dropped in the fresh furrow, and some of it was good seed, and some of it, I may say, fell on good ground. My father was absorbed in political life, but his affections were at home. My mother's life was eaten up with calamitous sicknesses. My sisters were just at that period when girls' eyes are dazzled with their own glowing future. I had constantly before me examples of goodness, and from all sides admonitions to virtue, but no regular instruction. I went to the district schools, or, if any other school a little more select or better chanced, I went to that. But no one dictated my studies or overlooked my progress. I remember feeling an intense ambition to be at the head of my class, and generally being there. Our minds were not weakened by too much study; reading, spelling, and Dwight's Geography were the only paths of knowledge into which we were led. Yes, I did go in a slovenly way through the first four rules of arithmetic, and learned the names of the several parts of speech, and could parse glibly. But my life in Stockbridge was a most happy one. I enjoyed unrestrained the pleasures of a rural childhood; I went with herds of school-girls nutting, and berrying, and bathing by moonlight, and wading by daylight in the lovely Housatonic that flows through my father's meadows. I saw its beauty then; I loved it as a playfellow; I loved the hills and mountains that

6Sedgwick had published an article on Mumbet in an unidentified periodical.

I roved over. My father was an observer and lover of nature, my sister Frances a romantic, passionate devotee to it, and if I had no natural perception or relish of its loveliness, I caught it from them, so that my heart was early knit to it, and I at least early studied and early learned this picture language, so rich and universal.

From my earliest recollection to this day of our Lord, 13th October, 1853, nature has been an ever fresh and growing beauty and enjoyment to me; and now, when so many of my dearest friends are gone, when few, even of my contemporaries, are left, when new social pleasures have lost their excitement, the sun coming up over these hills and sinking behind them—the springing and the dying year—all changes and aspects of nature are more beautiful to me than ever. They have more solemnity, perhaps, but it is because they have more meaning. If they speak in a lower tone to my dimmed eye-sight, it is a gentler and tenderer one.

What would the children now, who are steeped to the lips in "ologies," think of a girl of eight spending a whole summer working a wretched sampler which was not even a tolerable specimen of its species! But even as early as that, my father, whenever he was at home, kept me up and at his side till nine o'clock in the evening, to listen to him while he read aloud to the family Hume, or Shakespeare, or Don Quixote, or Hudibras![7] Certainly I did not understand them, but some glances of celestial light reached my soul, and I caught from his magnetic sympathy some elevation of feeling, and that love of reading which has been to me "education."

I remember a remark of Gibbon's[8] which corresponds with my own experience. He says that the love of reading with which an aunt inspired him was worth all the rest of his education, and what must that "rest" have been in the balance against the pauperism of my instruction!

I was not more than twelve years old—I think but ten—when, during one winter, I read Rollin's *Ancient History*. The walking to our school-house was often bad, and I took my lunch (how well I remember the bread and butter, and "nut-cakes," and cold sausage, and nuts, and apples, that made the miscellaneous contents of that

[7]David Hume's *History of Great Britain* (1754–1761), William Shakespeare's plays, Miguel de Cervantes's *Don Quixote* (1605–1615), Samuel Butler's satirical poem *Hudibras* (1663–1678).

[8]Edward Gibbon, a dedicated scholar, wrote *The Decline and Fall of the Roman Empire* (1776–1788). He attended Oxford University.

enchanting lunchbasket!), and in the interim between the morning and afternoon school I crept under my desk (the desks were so made as to afford little close recesses under them) and read, and munched, and forgot myself in Cyrus's greatness![9]

It was in those pleasant winters that Crocker brought, at the close of the afternoon school, "old Rover" to the school-house door for me to ride home. The gallant, majestic old veteran was then super-annuated, and treated with all the respect that waits on age. I believe this was the hardest service he rendered, but this made his life not quite a sinecure, for it was my custom and delight to take up my favorite school friends, one after another, and "ride" them home, putting old Rover to his utmost speed, and I think the poor old horse caught something of our youthful spirits, for he galloped over the plain with us, distancing the boys, who were fond of running at his heels, hurrahing and throwing up their hats.

I was a favorite with my school-mates, partly, I fear, because I had what the phrenologists term an excessive love of approbation, and partly that I had, more than the rest, the means of gratifying them. On Saturday it was usual to appoint two of the girls to sweep the school-house and set it in order, and these two chose a third. I was usually distinguished by the joint vote of my compatriots, and why? I had unlimited credit at the "store," where my father kept an open account, and, while the girls swept, I provided a lunch of Mal-aga wine and raisins, or whatever was to be had that suited the "sweet tooth" of childhood. I well remember my father's consterna-tion when he looked over the semi-annual bill, and found it dotted with these charges, "per daughter Catharine," in country fashion. He was much more amazed than displeased, but I remember he cut me off from thereafter being in that mode "glorious" by a "my dear little girl, this must not be in future." What would our Temperance zealots[10] say to so slight a rebuke on such an occasion! But it was effectual, and left no stinging sense of wrong, which a harsher visi-tation of an unconscious error would have done.

Oh, how different was my miscellaneous childhood from the driv-ing study and the elaborate accomplishments of children of my class of the present day! I have all my life felt the want of more systematic

---

[9]Charles Rollin's *Ancient History* (1730–1738) narrated the career of the Persian king Cyrus the Great (sixth century B.C.).

[10]Temperance was a major reformist cause in nineteenth-century America.

training, but there were peculiar circumstances in my condition that in some degree supplied these great deficiencies, and these were blessings ever to be remembered with gratitude. I was reared in an atmosphere of high intelligence. My father had uncommon mental vigor. So had my brothers. Their daily habits, and pursuits, and pleasures were intellectual, and I naturally imbibed from them a kindred taste. Their "talk was *not* of beeves,"[11] nor of making money; that now universal passion had not entered into men and possessed them as it does now, or, if it had, it was not in the sanctuary of our home—there the money-changers did not come. My father was richer than his neighbors. His income supplied abundantly the wants of a very careless family and an unmeasured hospitality, but nothing was ever given to mere style, and nothing was wasted on vices. I know we were all impressed with a law that no prodigalities were to be permitted, and that we were all to spend conscientiously; but our consciences were not very tender, I think, and when I look back upon the freedom of our expenditures, I wonder that the whole concern was not ruined. I don't remember that I had a silk frock before I was fourteen years old. I wore stuffs in winter (such fabrics as in the present advanced condition of manufactures a factory-girl would scarcely wear; one villainous stuff I particularly recall for school wear, called "bird's-eye"), and calicoes, and muslinets, and muslins for summer; but, thus limited in quality and variety, I was allowed any number; and I remember one winter, when I was about nine or ten, being particularly unfortunate in scorching my "bird's-eye," I bought, at my own discretion, three or four new dresses in the course of the winter. And in the article of shoes, the town-bought morocco slippers were few and far between, but I was permitted to order a pair of calf-skin shoes as often as I fancied I wanted them, and our village shoemaker told me in after life that his books showed fifteen pairs made for me in one year! No disrespect either to his fabrication or his leather; the shoes were burnt, or water-soaked, or run down at the heel—sad habits occasioned by the want of female supervision. My dear mother, most neat and orderly, was often ill or absent, my sisters were married, my father took no cognizance of such matters, and I had a natural carelessness which a lifetime of consciousness of its inconvenience and struggle against it has not overcome. You, dear Alice, are brought up with all the advantages of order in both your

[11]I.e., of farming business (even though they lived in the country).

parents. But, missing this, I look back with satisfaction to the perfect freedom that set no limit to expansion.

No bickering or dissension was ever permitted. Love was the habit, the life of the household rather than the law, or rather it was the law of our nature. Neither the power of despots nor the universal legislation of our republic can touch this element, for as God is love, so love is God, is life, is light. We were born with it—it was our inheritance. But the duty and the virtue of guarding all its manifestations, of never failing in its demonstrations, of preserving its interchanges and smaller duties, was most vigilantly watched, most peremptorily insisted on. A querulous tone, a complaint, a slight word of dissension, was met by that awful frown of my father's. Jove's thunder was to a pagan believer but as a summer day's drifting cloud to it. It was not so dreadful because it portended punishment—it was punishment; it was a token of a suspension of the approbation and love that were our life.

Have I given you an idea of the circumstances and education that made a family of seven children all honorable men and women—all, I think I may say without exaggeration, having noble aspirations and strong affections, with the fixed principle that these were holy and inviolable?

I have always considered country life with outlets to the great world as an essential advantage in education. Besides all the teaching and inspiration of Nature, and the development of the faculties from the necessity of using them for daily exigencies, one is brought into close social relations with all conditions of people. There are no barriers between you and your neighbors. There are grades and classes in our democratic community seen and acknowledged. These must be everywhere, as Scott truly says, "except among the Hottentots," but with us one sees one's neighbor's private life unveiled. The highest and the lowest meet in their joys and sorrows, at weddings and funerals, in sicknesses and distresses of all sorts. Not merely as alms-bearers, but the richest and highest go to the poorest to "watch" with them in sickness, and perform the most menial offices for them; and though your occupations, your mode of life may be very different from the artisan's, your neighbor, you meet him on an apparent equality, and talk with him as members of one family. In my youth there was something more of the old valuation than now. My mother's family was of the old established gentry of Western Massachusetts, connected by blood and friendship with the families of the

"River-gods," as the Hawleys, Worthingtons, and Dwights of Connecticut River were then designated. My father had attained an elevated position in political life, and his income was ample and liberally expended. He was born too soon to relish the freedoms of democracy, and I have seen his brow lower when a free-and-easy mechanic[12] came to the *front* door, and upon one occasion I remember his turning off the "east steps" (I am *sure* not kicking, but the demonstration was unequivocal) a grown-up lad who kept his hat on after being told to take it off (would the President of the United States dare do as much now!); but, with all this tenacious adherence to the habits of the elder time, no man in life was kindlier than my father. One of my contemporaries, now a venerable missionary, told me last summer an anecdote, perhaps worth preserving, as characterizing the times and individuals. He was a gentle boy, the son of a shoemaker, and then clerk to the clerk of the court. The boy had driven his master to Lenox, and all the way this gentleman, conscious that his dignity must be preserved by vigilance, had maintained silence. When they came to their destination, he ordered the boy to take his trunk into the house. As he set it down in the entry, my father, then judge of the Supreme Judicial Court, was coming downstairs, bringing his trunk himself. He set it down, accosted the boy most kindly, and gave him his cordial hand. The lad's feelings, chilled by his master's haughtiness, at once melted, and took an impression of my father's kindness that was never effaced.

There were upon the Bench, at the time my father was placed on it, some men of crusty, oppressive manners. The Bar were not treated as *gentlemen,* and were in a state of antagonism, and some of them had even determined to leave their profession. My father's kind, courteous, considerate manners were said by his contemporaries to have produced an entire change in the relation of the Bench and Bar. His children, from instinct, from the example of their parents, and the principles of their home, had that teaching whose value Scott so well expressed in the "Fortunes of Nigel."[13] "For ourselves," he says (and what does he not say better than another man—not to say any other!), "we can assure the reader—and perhaps, if we have ever been able to afford him amusement, it is owing in a great degree to this cause—that we never found ourselves in company with the stu-

---

[12]Manual worker.
[13]Walter Scott, the novelist, published *The Fortunes of Nigel* in 1822.

pidest of all possible companions in a post-chaise, or with the most arrant cumber-corner that ever occupied a place in a mail-coach, without finding that, in the course of our conversation with him, we had some ideas suggested to us, either grave or gay, or some information communicated in the course of our journey which we should have regretted not to have learned, and which we should have been sorry to have immediately forgotten."

It was the same principle by which Napoleon made himself the focus of every man's light; and in our humble, obscure village life, we profited by this "free-trade" school of ideas. There were no sacrifices made of personal dignity or purity; nor, if there was in condition or character a little elevation above the community we lived in, was it preserved by arrogant vigilance or jealous proscription.

Three of my brothers were my seniors. I have no recollections of the eldest during my childhood; he was away at school and at college, but with Harry and Robert I had intimate companionship, and I think as true and loving a friendship as ever existed between brothers and sister. Charles was the youngest of the family, and so held a peculiar relation to us all as junior, and in some sort dependent, and the natural depositary of our petting affections. I hardly know why, but I believe it was because my father could not bear to send him away from him, that his means of education were far inferior to his brothers'. He did not go to college, and, except a year or two's residence at Dr. Backus's, in Connecticut, I think he had no teaching beyond that of our common schools. He had extreme modesty, and a habit of self-sacrifice and self-negation that I fear we all selfishly accepted. I do not think it ever occurred to him that he was quite equal to his brothers in mental gifts, and it was not till we had all got fairly into life that we recognized in him rare intellectual qualities. His *heart* was always to us the image of God.

But all my brothers were beloved, and I can conceive of no truer image of the purity and happiness of the equal loves of Heaven than that which unites brothers and sisters. It has been my chiefest blessing in life, and, but that I look to its continuance hereafter, I should indeed be wretched.

My brother Harry was, I think, intellectually superior to any of us. He had a wider horizon, more mental action, and I think he was the only one of us that had the elements of greatness. But he had great defects of mind, which, cooperating with the almost total loss of his eyesight, led to the great calamity of his life.[14] He had that absence of mind and fixidity of thought so dangerous where the tendencies are all to what the Germans call subjectivity. Never was there a more loving, generous disposition than his, nor tenderer domestic affections.

But my particular and paramount love in childhood was for your uncle Robert. We were bound together from our infancy, and I remember instances of tenderness while he was yet a little boy that are still bright as diamonds when so much has faded from my memory, or is dim to its eye.

Once, when ransacking the barn with my brothers for eggs, I somehow slipped under a mass of hay, and was so oppressed by it, and so scared, that I could scarcely make a sound. Robert heard my faint cries, but could not find me, and he ran to call my father, who, with some friends who happened to be with him, soon extricated me. From their caresses and conversation I inferred that my danger of suffocation had been imminent, and I looked henceforward upon my favorite brother as my preserver. How brightly are some points in our childhood's path illuminated, while all along, before and behind, the track is dim or lost in utter darkness! We can not always recall the feeling that fixed these bright passages in our memory. They are the shrines for our hearts' saints, and there the light never goes out.

Robert was, more than any other, my protector and companion. Charles was as near my own age, but he was younger, and a feeling of dependence—of most loving dependence—on Robert began then, which lasted through his life. I remember once when I was ill, and not more than five years old, his refusing to go out and play with "the boys," and lying down by me to soothe and amuse me. How early we are impressed by love and disinterestedness! These are small matters, my dear child, but they are the cement of household loves.

Manners are now so changed, and education so pressed, that you would be surprised by various rustic duties then performed by the sons of a man in my father's position. In the progress of civilization, offices and exercises similar to these will come to be considered a healthy part of a high education. They do the mind and heart good— the mind by forming and developing observation, the first faculty Nature unfolds, and the heart by awakening and cultivating sym-

---

[14]He became insane in later life.

pathies with the laboring classes.

It was the duty of our boys to drive the cows to pasture in the morning, and to fetch them at night, and our pastures being a mile distant, this was rather onerous. . . .

Lenox, Aug., 1854—Another year is gone, and I am admonished that few *can* remain to me, and this day, at 12 M., alone in my little parlor, your dear father and mother here on their annual visit, having just finished telling a fairy tale to you, and Will, and Lucy Pike, I have taken my pen to note some changes in the condition of our village since I was young. I remember the making of the turnpike through Stockbridge—I think it must have been about forty years ago—and that was a great event then, for it enabled us to have a stage-coach three days in the week from Boston to Albany, and three from Albany to Boston. In due time came the daily coach, arriving, after driving the greater part of the night, the middle of the second day from Boston.

It then seemed there could be nothing in advance of this. Your uncle Theodore has the honor of being the first person who conceived the possibility of a railroad over the mountains to Connecticut River. He proposed it in the Legislature, and argued so earnestly for it, that it became a very common reproach to him that he was crazy. Basil Hall,[15] when he was in Stockbridge, ridiculed the idea, and said to your uncle, "If you had it, what would you carry over it?" He did not live to be confuted, nor your uncle to witness the triumph of his opinion, but I have lived this very summer to travel to the Mississippi by rail!

The daily coach was a great advance on my earliest experience, when a mongrel vehicle, half wagon, half coach, drawn by horses that seemed to me like Time to the Lover,[16] came once a week from New York, letting the light from the outer world into our little valley, and bringing us letters from "papa." Now, at 3 P.M., we read the paper issued the same morning at New York.

We had one clergyman in Stockbridge, of sound New England orthodoxy, a Hopkinsian Calvinist.[17] Heaven forbid, dear Alice, that you should ever inquire into the splitting of these theological hairs! Sixty years he preached to us, and in all that time, though there may

---

[15]A British naval officer and scientist, who toured the United States and published *Travels in North America* (1829).

[16]I.e., slow.

[17]A particularly strict form of Calvinism.

have been at some obscure dwelling a Methodist or Baptist ranter, the "pious" of the town all stood by the Doric faith. The law then required each town to support a clergyman, and his salary was paid by taxation. The conscience was left free; he who preferred to dissent from the prevailing religion could, on assigning his reasons, "sign off"; but I believe he was required to transfer his allegiance to some other ministry. Now the clergy are supported by the voluntary system, and a man may revert to heathenism (some do!), and no man call him to account. I have elsewhere and repeatedly described our good pastor of sixty years—stern as an old Israelite in his faith, gentle and kindly in his life as "my Uncle Toby."[18] I dreaded him, and certainly did not understand him in my youth. He was then only the dry, sapless embodiment of polemical divinity. It was in my mature age and his old age that I discovered his Christian features, and found his unsophisticated nature as pure and gentle as a good little child's. He stood up in the pulpit for sixty years, and logically proved the whole moral creation of God (for this he thought limited to earth, and the stars made to adorn man's firmament) left by him to suffer eternally for Adam's transgression, except a handful *elected* to salvation, and yet no scape-grace, no desperate wretch within his ken died without some hope for his eternal state springing up in the little doctor's merciful heart. Some contrite word, some faint aspiration, a last slight expression of faith on the death-bed, a look, was enough to save this kind heart from despair of any fellow-creature.

Dr. West belonged to other times than ours. His three-cornered beaver, and Henry Ward Beecher's Cavalier hat, fitly denote the past and present clerical dynasties;[19] the first formal, elaborate, fixed; the last easy, comfortable, flexible, and assuming nothing superior to the mass.

. . .

One of the periods most marked in my childhood, and best remembered, because it was out of the general current of my life, was a summer when I was seven or eight years old, passed under the care of my cousin Sabrina Parsons, in Bennington, Vermont, at the house

---

[18]A kindly, inoffensive character in Laurence Sterne's *Tristram Shandy* (1760–1767).
[19]Henry Ward Beecher was an eminent liberal preacher of the mid-nineteenth century.

of the Rev. Mr. Swift, the husband of my father's eldest sister. There were a dozen children, more or less, some grown, some still young—the kindest and cheerfulest people in the world. I was an object of general affection and indulgence. I remember distinctly, and I see it now with my mind's eye, a cherry-tree of fantastic shape that my cousin Persis, my contemporary, and I were in the habit of running up like kittens, to the dismay of my tender, sickly aunt, who would invariably raise her bedroom window and call out, "Girls, come down! you'll break your necks!" I am now the old crone, and, alas! I now should probably mar the sport of idle, fearless girls in the same way. No, dear Alice, I don't honestly think I should. I should be more like to try to climb the cherry-tree with them.

When I lived at my uncle's was the period of the most bitter hostility between the Federalists and Democrats. The whole nation, from Maine to Georgia, was then divided into these two great parties. The Federalists stood upright, and with their feet firmly planted on the rock of aristocracy, but that rock itself was bedded in sands, or rather was a boulder from the Old World, and the tide of democracy was surely and swiftly undermining it. The Federalists believed that all sound principles, truth, justice, and patriotism, were identified with the upper classes. They were sincere republicans, but I think they began to fear a republic could only continue to exist in Utopia. They were honest and noble men. The Democrats had among them much native sagacity; they believed in themselves, some from conceit, some from just conviction; they had less education, intellectual and moral, than their opponents—little refinement, intense desire to grasp the power and place that had been denied to them, and a determination to work out the theories of the government. All this, my dear Alice, as you may suppose, is an afterthought with me. Then I entered fully, and with the faith and ignorance of childhood, into the prejudices of the time. I thought every Democrat was grasping, dishonest, and vulgar, and would have in good faith adopted the creed of a stanch old parson, who, in a Fast-day sermon, said, "I don't say that every Democrat is a horse-thief, but I do say that every horse-thief is a Democrat!"

While I was at Bennington, I know not to commemorate what occasion, small gold eagles were struck, and presented to the ladies of conspicuous Federal families. My grownup cousins had them. They were sewn into the center of large bows they wore on their bonnets. I remember well pining in my secret soul that one was not given to me, and thinking that my father's position entitled me, though a child, to the distinction. One memorable Sunday, while my uncle was making the "long prayer," and I was standing on the bench in the clergyman's great square pew, my cousin Sally's bow got awry; the eagle "stooped" under its folds; and I, to save her from the ignominy of not showing her colors, walked around three sides of the pew, and disturbed not only my pious cousin's devotions, but many others', by the pother I made in rectifying the bow. I remember my good uncle, on being told of the exploit, instead of reproving me for my misdemeanor, heartily joined in the laugh.

After all, I believe there was a deal of good humor and village fun mingled in with the animosities. The village street, according to my recollection, extended a long way, some mile and a half, from a hill at one end to a plain at the other. There was a superannuated, particolored horse, that had been turned out to find his own living by wayside grazing, with now and then a chance handful of oats from charity, who was used as a walking advertiser. He came regularly from the hill, the Democratic quarter, placarded over with jibes and jokes on the Federalists of the plain, and returned with such missives as their wit could furnish. . . .

My dear Alice, would you like to know what were the books of my childhood? You, of the present time, for whom the press daily turns out its novelties, for whom Miss Edgeworth has written her charming stories, and Scott has simplified history,[20] will look upon my condition as absolute inanition.

The books that I remember (there were, perhaps, besides, a dozen little story-books) are Berquin's "Children's Friend," translated from the French, I think, in four volumes—I know I can remember the form and shade of color of the book, the green edges of the leaves, the look of my favorite pages. Then there was the "Looking-glass," an eclectic, which contained that most pathetic story of "Little Jack." Then there was a little thin book called "Economy of Human Life," made up of some small pieces of Mrs. Barbauld's. That was quite above my comprehension, and I thought it very unmeaning and tedious. There was a volume of Rowe's "Letters from the Dead to the Living," which had a strange charm for me. I do not think that

[20]Maria Edgeworth's pleasing juvenile fiction (1796–1825) and Walter Scott's histories and historical novels.

I believed them to have been actually written by the departed, but there was a little mystification about it that excited my imagination. And last and most delightful were the fables, tales, and ballads in a large volume of "Elegant Extracts." I have sometimes questioned whether the keen relish which this scarcity of juvenile reading kept up, and the sound digestion it promoted, did not overbalance your advantage in the abundance and variety that certainly extinguishes some minds, and debilitates others with over-excitement.

All books but such as had an infusion of religion were proscribed on Sunday, and of course the literature for that day was rather circumscribed. We were happily exempted from such confections as Mrs. Sherwood's—sweetened slops and water-gruels that impair the mental digestion. We lived as people in a new country live—on bread and meat—the Bible and good old sermons, reading these over and over again. I remember, when very young, a device by which I extended my Sunday horizon; I would turn over the leaves of a book, and if I found "God" or "Lord," no matter in what connection, I considered the book sanctified—the *taboo* removed!

Both my sisters were very religious. They were educated when the demonstration of religion and its offices made much more a part of life than now—when almost all of women's intellectual life took that tinge. They were both born with tendencies to the elevated and unseen; their religion was their pursuit, their daily responsibility, their aim, and end, and crowning affection.

They both began with the strict faith. Sister Eliza suffered from the horrors of Calvinism. She was so true, so practical, that she could not evade its realities; she believed its monstrous doctrines, and they made her gloomy; but for the last fifteen years of her life she was redeemed from this incubus; her faith softened into a true comprehension of the filial relation to God, and I have often heard her say that it was impossible for her to describe the happiness of her redemption from the cruel doctrines of Geneva.

Sister Frances's imagination saved her from a like suffering. However deep the slough into which she was cast, she would spread her wings and rise up into a pure atmosphere, bright with God's presence. She was one of those who believe without believing; her faith was governed by her moods; when she was bilious and unhappy—very rarely—she sank down again into the slough.

Thank God, their sweet spirits are now both expatiating in truth which is light!

My sisters were both married when I was still a child. I was but seven when my sister Eliza was married, and I remember that wedding evening as the first tragedy of my life. She was my mother-sister. I had always slept with her, and been her assigned charge. The wedding was in our "west room." I remember where the bride and groom stood, and how he looked to me like some cruel usurper. I remember my father's place, and the rest is a confused impression of a room full of friends and servants—I think Mumbet stood by me. When the long consecrating prayer was half through, I distinctly remember the consciousness that my sister was going away from me struck me with the force of a blow, and I burst into loud sobs and crying. After the service, my father took me in his arms, and tried to quiet and soothe me, but I could be neither comforted nor quieted, so I stole out into the "east room," where Mumbet, Grippy, all the servants did their best to suggest consolations. Then came my new brother-in-law—how well I remember recoiling from him and hating him when he said, "I'll let your sister stay with you this summer." He let her! I was undressed and put into bed, and I cried myself to sleep and waked crying the next morning, and so, from that time to this, weddings in my family have been to me days of sadness, and yet, by some of them, I have gained treasures that no earthly balance or calculation can weigh or estimate! . . .

Journal

"New York, May 18, 1828. Again the spring is here, the season of life and loveliness, the beautiful emblem of our resurrection unto life eternal. I have seen the country again arrayed in its green robe, with its budding honors thick upon it, the brimful streams, all Nature steeped in perfume, as if the gates of Paradise were thrown open, and the air ringing with the wild notes of every bird upon the wing. Even the poor little prisoners that are hanging beside the walls in our pent-up yards open their throats to pour out the hymn of the season, and Poll Parrot jabbers, laughs, and screams a wild note of joy. I will not say, with the ungracious poet, that I turn from what

Spring brings to what she can not bring,[21] but alas! I find there is no longer that capacity for swelling, springing, brightening joy that I once felt. Memory has settled her shadowy curtain over too much of the space of thought, and Hope, that once to my imagination tempted me with her arch, and laughing, and promising face, to snatch away the veil with which she but half hid the future—Hope now seems to turn from me; and if I now and then catch some glimpses of her averted face, she looks so serious, so admonitory, that I almost believe that her sister Experience, with an eye of apprehension, and lips that never smile, has taken her place. All is not right with me, I know. I still build on sandy foundations; I still hope for perfection, where perfection is not given. The best sources of earthly happiness are not within my grasp—those of contentment I have neglected. I have suffered for the whole winter a sort of mental paralysis, and at times I have feared the disease extended to my affections. It is difficult for one who began life as I did, the primary object of affection to many, to come by degrees to be first to none, and still to have my love remain in its entire strength, and craving such returns to have no substitute. How absurd, how groundless your complaints! would half a dozen voices exclaim, if I ever ventured to *make* this complaint. I do not. Each one has his own point of sight. Others are not conscious—at least I believe they are not—of any diminution in their affections for me, but others have taken my place, naturally and of right, I allow it. It is the necessity of a solitary condition, an unnatural state. He who gave us our nature has set the solitary in families, and has, by an array of motives, secured this sweet social compact to his children. From my own experience I would not advise anyone to remain unmarried, for my experience has been a singularly happy one. My feelings have never been embittered by those slights and taunts that the repulsive and neglected have to endure; there has been no period of my life to the present moment when I might not have allied myself respectably, and to those sincerely attached to me, if I would. I have always felt myself to be an object of attention, respect, and regard, and, though not *first* to any, I am, like Themistocles,[22] *second* to a great many.

---

[21]Either William Shakespeare (Sonnet 98) or Thomas Gray ("Sonnet on the Death of Richard West," 1742); neither poet can take pleasure in the spring, because he misses a person he loves.
[22]An ancient Greek statesman.

My fortune is not adequate to an independent establishment, but it is ample for ease to myself and liberality to others. In the families of all my brothers I have an agreeable home. My sisters are all kind and affectionate to me, my brothers generous and invariably kind; their children all love me. My dear Kate, my adopted child, is, though far from perfect even in my doting eyes, yet such as to perfectly satisfy me, if I did not crave perfection for one I so tenderly love. I have troops of friends, some devotedly attached to me, and yet the result of all this very happy experience is that there is no equivalent for those blessings which Providence has placed first, and ordained that they should be purchased at the dearest sacrifice. I have not set this down in a spirit of repining, but it is well, I think, honestly to expose our own feelings—they may serve for examples or beacons. While I live I do not mean this shall be read, and after, my individual experience may perhaps benefit some one of all my tribe. I ought, I know, to be grateful and humble, and I do hope, through the grace of God, to rise more above the world, to attain a higher and happier state of feeling, to order my house for that better world where self may lose something of its engrossing power."

• • •

"New York, December 17, 1835. More than a fortnight has elapsed since I came to this city—a fortnight of my short remainder of life passed away without exertion and without fruit. I have been met by everyone with congratulations about my book,[23] which has, I think, proved more generally acceptable than anything I have before written. My *author* existence has always seemed something accidental, extraneous, and independent of my inner self. My books have been a pleasant occupation and excitement in my life. The notice, and friends, or acquaintance they have procured me, have relieved me from the danger of ennui and blue devils, that are most apt to infest a single person. But they constitute no portion of my happiness—that is, of such as I derive from the dearest relations of life. When I feel that my writings have made any one happier or better, I feel an emotion of gratitude to Him who has made me the medium of any blessing to my fellow-creatures. And I do feel that I am but the instrument."

[23]Probably *The Linwoods* (1835), a historical novel, which was highly praised.

Sarah Moore Grimké

1792–1873

SARAH GRIMKÉ, daughter of the chief judge of the South Carolina Supreme Court, grew up in one of the first families of Charleston. Already in her childhood, the sight of whippings convinced her that slavery was wrong. She began to realize the restrictions on women when the early education in classics, mathematics, and legal theory encouraged by her father and brother was replaced by training in ladylike accomplishments. She took over the raising of her sister Angelina, twelve years younger than she and the last of the fourteen Grimké children. Yielding to social pressure, Sarah became a typical southern belle, but she would periodically repudiate her frivolous life-style and turn to religious devotion.

When she accompanied her dying father to visit a doctor in Philadelphia, she became acquainted with the Society of Friends and was impressed by their belief that all people, men and women, should interpret the Scriptures for themselves. She studied Quaker doctrines and finally insisted on moving to Philadelphia to become a preacher. Angelina joined her there. Through Angelina, Sarah became involved in the anti-slavery cause; they became the first female abolitionist agents. They attracted large crowds, not only because they were eloquent speakers, but because they were former slaveholders, and even more because they were the first respectable women to address "promiscuous"—that is, mixed sex—audiences. They emphasized the particular sufferings of female slaves and noticed a parallel between the powerless situations of slaves and women—a parallel that became more vivid to them as they were vilified for immodesty in presuming to address men. The opposition culminated in a Pastoral Letter from the Council of Congregationalist Ministers of Massachusetts, which was read from Congregational pulpits

274

throughout the state. Sarah replied in a series of letters addressed to Mary Parker, president of the Boston Female Anti-Slavery Society, published first in *The New England Spectator* and then as *Letters on the Equality of the Sexes and the Condition of Woman* (1838).

Both sisters retired into domesticity after Angelina married the abolitionist leader Theodore Weld (1838). However, Sarah continued to write, and they both participated in the campaign for woman suffrage. In 1870 Sarah and Angelina, aged respectively seventy-eight and sixty-five, led forty-two women through a snowstorm to make a protest by voting illegally.

BIBLIOGRAPHY

Grimké, Sarah Moore. *Letters on the Equality of the Sexes and Other Essays.* Edited by Elizabeth Ann Bartlett. New Haven: Yale University Press, 1988.

Lerner, Gerda. *The Grimké Sisters from South Carolina: Pioneers for Woman's Rights and Abolition.* New York: Schocken Books, 1971.

from Letters on the Equality of the Sexes and the Condition of Women

LETTER II

WOMAN SUBJECT ONLY TO GOD

Newburyport, 7th mo.[1] 17, 1837

My Dear Sister,

In my last, I traced the creation and the fall of man and woman from that state of purity and happiness which their beneficent Creator designed them to enjoy. As they were one in transgression, their chastisement was the same. "So God drove out *the man,* and he

---

[1] July. Quakers avoided the conventional names for the months because they are of pagan origin.

placed at the East of the garden of Eden a cherubim and a flaming sword, which turned every way to keep the way of the tree of life" [Gen. 3:24]. We now behold them expelled from Paradise, fallen from their original loveliness, but still bearing on their foreheads the image and superscription of Jehovah; still invested with high moral responsibilities, intellectual powers, and immortal souls. They had incurred the penalty of sin, they were shorn of their innocence, but they stood on the same platform side by side, acknowledging *no superior* but their God. Notwithstanding what has been urged, woman I am aware stands charged to the present day with having brought sin into the world. I shall not repel the charge by any counter assertions, although, as was before hinted, Adam's ready acquiescence with his wife's proposal does not savor much of that superiority *in strength of mind* which is arrogated by man. Even admitting that Eve was the greater sinner, it seems to me man might be satisfied with the dominion he has claimed and exercised for nearly six thousand years, and that more true nobility would be manifested by endeavoring to raise the fallen and invigorate the weak, than by keeping woman in subjection. But I ask no favors for my sex. I surrender not our claim to equality. All I ask of our brethren is, that they will take their feet from off our necks, and permit us to stand upright on that ground which God designed us to occupy. If he has not given us the rights which have, as I conceive, been wrested from us, we shall soon give evidence of our inferiority, and shrink back into that obscurity, which the high-souled magnanimity of man has assigned us as our appropriate sphere.

As I am unable to learn from sacred writ when woman was deprived by God of her equality with man, I shall touch upon a few points in the Scriptures which demonstrate that no supremacy was granted to man. When God had destroyed the world, except Noah and his family, by the deluge, he renewed the grant formerly made to man, and again gave him dominion over every beast of the earth, every fowl of the air, over all that moveth upon the earth, and over all the fishes of the sea; into his hands they were delivered. But was woman, bearing the image of her God, placed under the dominion of her fellow man? Never! Jehovah could not surrender his authority to govern his own immortal creatures into the hands of a being whom he knew, and whom his whole history proved, to be unworthy of a trust so sacred and important. God could not do it, because it is a direct contravention of his law, "Thou shalt worship the Lord thy

God, and *him only* shalt thou serve" [Matt. 4:10]. If Jehovah had appointed man as the guardian or teacher of woman, he would certainly have given some intimation of this surrender of his own prerogative. But so far from it, we find the commands of God invariably the same to man and woman; and not the slightest intimation is given in a single passage of the Bible, that God designed to point woman to man as her instructor. The tenor of his language always is, "Look unto ME, and be ye saved, all the ends of the earth, for I am God, and there is none else" [Isai. 45:22].

The lust of dominion was probably the first effect of the fall; and as there was no other intelligent being over whom to exercise it, woman was the first victim of this unhallowed passion. We afterwards see it exhibited by Cain in the murder of his brother, by Nimrod in his becoming a mighty hunter of men, and setting up a kingdom over which to reign.[2] Here we see the origin of that Upas of slavery, which sprang up immediately after the fall, and has spread its pestilential branches over the whole face of the known world. All history attests that man has subjected woman to his will, used her as a means to promote his selfish gratification, to minister to his sensual pleasures, to be instrumental in promoting his comfort; but never has he desired to elevate her to that rank she was created to fill. He has done all he could to debase and enslave her mind; and now he looks triumphantly on the ruin he has wrought, and says, the being he has thus deeply injured is his inferior.

Woman has been placed by John Quincy Adams, side by side with the slave, whilst he was contending for the right side of petition.[3] I thank him for ranking us with the oppressed; for I shall not find it difficult to show, that in all ages and countries, not even excepting enlightened republican America, woman has more or less been made a *means* to promote the welfare of man, without due regard to her own happiness, and the glory of God as the end of her creation.

During the *patriarchal* ages, we find men and women engaged in the same employments. Abraham and Sarah both assisted in preparing the food which was to be set before the three men who visited them in the plains of Mamre [Gen. 18]; but although their occupa-

---

[2] Genesis 4:8, 10:8–10.
[3] John Quincy Adams, then a Representative in Congress, successfully defended the right of petition against a "gag rule" that automatically tabled abolitionist petitions (1836–1844).

tions were similar, Sarah was not permitted to enjoy the society of the holy visitant; and as we learn from Peter, that she "obeyed Abraham, calling him Lord" [I Peter 3:6], we may presume he exercised dominion over her. We shall pass on now to Rebecca [Gen. 24]. In her history, we find another striking illustration of the low estimation in which woman was held. Eleazur is sent to seek a wife for Isaac. He finds Rebecca going down to the well to fill her pitcher. He accosts her; and she replies with all humility, "Drink, my lord." How does he endeavor to gain her favor and confidence? Does he approach her as a dignified creature, whom he was about to invite to fill an important station in his master's family, as the wife of his only son? No. He offered incense to her vanity, and "he took a golden earring of half a shekel weight, and two bracelets for her hands of ten shekels weight of gold," and gave them to Rebecca.

The cupidity of man soon led him to regard woman as property, and hence we find them sold to those who wished to marry them, as far as appears, without any regard to those sacred rights which belong to woman, as well as to man, in the choice of a companion. That women were a profitable kind of property, we may gather from the description of a virtuous woman in the last chapter of Proverbs [Prov. 31:10–31]. To work willingly with her hands, to open her hands to the poor, to clothe herself with silk and purple, to look well to her household, to make fine linen and sell it, to deliver girdles to the merchant, and not to eat the bread of idleness, seems to have constituted, in the view of Solomon, the perfection of a woman's character and achievements. "The spirit of that age was not favorable to intellectual improvement; but as there were wise men who formed exceptions to the general ignorance, and were destined to guide the world into more advanced states, so there was a corresponding proportion of wise women; and among the Jews, as well as other nations, we find a strong tendency to believe that women were in more immediate connection with heaven than men."—L. M. Child's Con. of Woman.[4] If there be any truth in this tradition, I am at a loss to imagine in what the superiority of man consists.

Thine in the bonds of womanhood,

Sarah M. Grimké.

---

[4]Lydia Maria Child, a feminist and abolitionist, wrote *History of the Condition of Women, in Various Ages and Nations* (1835), a major source for Grimké.

LETTER III

THE PASTORAL LETTER OF THE GENERAL ASSOCIATION OF CONGREGATIONAL MINISTERS OF MASSACHUSETTS

Haverhill, 7th Mo. 1837

Dear Friend,

When I last addressed thee, I had not seen the Pastoral Letter of the General Association.[1] It has since fallen into my hands, and I must digress from my intention of exhibiting the condition of women in different parts of the world, in order to make some remarks on this extraordinary document. I am persuaded that when the minds of men and women become emancipated from the thraldom of superstition and "traditions of men," the sentiments contained in the Pastoral Letter will be recurred to with as much astonishment as the opinions of Cotton Mather and other distinguished men of his day, on the subject of witchcraft;[2] nor will it be deemed less wonderful, that a body of divines should gravely assemble and endeavor to prove that woman has no right to "open her mouth for the dumb," than it now is that judges should have sat on the trials of witches, and solemnly condemned nineteen persons and one dog to death for witchcraft.

But to the letter. It says, "We invite your attention to the dangers which at present seem to threaten the FEMALE CHARACTER with widespread and permanent injury." I rejoice that they have called the attention of my sex to this subject, because I believe if woman investigates it, she will soon discover that danger is impending, though from a totally different source from that which the Association apprehends,—danger from those who, having long held the reins of *usurped* authority, are unwilling to permit us to fill that sphere which God created us to move in, and who have entered into league to crush the immortal mind of woman. I rejoice, because I am persuaded that the rights of woman, like the rights of slaves, need only be examined to be understood and asserted, even by some of those who are now endeavoring to smother the irrepressible desire for

[1]This Pastoral Letter (July 28, 1837) condemned women for speaking in public for abolition or any other cause.

[2]Cotton Mather, an eminent clergyman and writer, and the Puritan authorities in general believed the hysterical witnesses who testified against so-called witches in Salem (1692).

mental and spiritual freedom which glows in the breast of many, who hardly dare to speak their sentiments.

"The appropriate duties and influence of women are clearly stated in the New Testament. Those duties are unobtrusive and private, but the sources of *mighty power*. When the mild, *dependent*, softening influence of woman upon the sternness of man's opinions is fully exercised, society feels the effects of it in a thousand ways." No one can desire more earnestly than I do, that woman may move exactly in the sphere which her Creator has assigned her; and I believe her having been displaced from that sphere has introduced confusion into the world. It is, therefore, of vast importance to herself and to all the rational creation, that she should ascertain what are her duties and her privileges as a responsible and immortal being. The New Testament has been referred to, and I am willing to abide by its decisions, but must enter my protest against the false translation of some passages by the MEN who did that work, and against the perverted interpretation by the MEN who undertook to write commentaries thereon. I am inclined to think, when we are admitted to the honor of studying Greek and Hebrew, we shall produce some various readings of the Bible a little different from those we now have.

The Lord Jesus defines the duties of his followers in his Sermon on the Mount. He lays down grand principles by which they should be governed, without any reference to sex or condition.—"Ye are the light of the world. A city that is set on a hill cannot be hid. Neither do men light a candle and put it under a bushel, but on a candlestick, and it giveth light unto all that are in the house. Let your light so shine before men, that they may see your good works, and glorify your Father which is in Heaven" [Matt. 5:14–16]. I follow him through all his precepts, and find him giving the same directions to women as to men, never even referring to the distinction now so strenuously insisted upon between masculine and feminine virtues: this is one of the anti-Christian "traditions of men" which are taught instead of the "commandments of God." Men and women were CREATED EQUAL; they are both moral and accountable beings, and whatever is *right* for man to do, is *right* for woman.

But the influence of woman, says the Association, is to be private and unobtrusive; her light is not to shine before man like that of her brethren; but she is passively to let the lords of the creation, as they call themselves, put the bushel over it, lest peradventure it might appear that the world has been benefitted by the rays of *her* candle. So that her quenched light, according to their judgment, will be of more use than if it were set on the candlestick. "Her influence is the source of mighty power." This has ever been the flattering language of man since he laid aside the whip as a means to keep woman in subjection. He spares her body; but the war he has waged against her mind, her heart, and her soul, has been no less destructive to her as a moral being. How monstrous, how anti-Christian, is the doctrine that woman is to be dependent on man! Where, in all the sacred Scriptures, is this taught? Alas! she has too well learned the lesson, which MAN has labored to teach her. She has surrendered her dearest RIGHTS, and been satisfied with the privileges which man has assumed to grant her; she has been amused with the show of power, whilst man has absorbed all the reality into himself. He has adorned the creature whom God gave him as a companion with baubles and gewgaws, turned her attention to personal attractions, offered incense to her vanity, and made her the instrument of his selfish gratification, a plaything to please his eye and amuse his hours of leisure. "Rule by obedience and by submission sway,"[3] or in other words, study to be a hypocrite, pretend to submit, but gain your point, has been the code of household morality which woman has been taught. The poet has sung, in sickly strains, the loveliness of woman's dependence upon man, and now we find it reechoed by those who profess to teach the religion of the Bible. God says, "Cease ye from man whose breath is in his nostrils, for wherein is he to be accounted of?"[4] Man says, depend upon me. God says, "HE will teach us of his ways." Man says, believe it not, I am to be your teacher. This doctrine of dependence upon man is utterly at variance with the doctrine of the Bible. In that book I find nothing like the softness of woman, nor the sternness of man: both are equally commanded to bring forth the fruits of the Spirit, love, meekness, gentleness, &c.

But we are told, "the power of woman is in her dependence, flowing from a consciousness of that weakness which God has given her for her protection." If physical weakness is alluded to, I cheerfully concede the superiority; if brute force is what my brethren are claiming, I am willing to let them have all the honor they desire; but if they mean to intimate, that mental or moral weakness belongs to

---

[3]Alexander Pope, "Epistle II. To a Lady" (1735), line 263 (inaccurately quoted).
[4]Isaiah 2:22.

woman, more than to man, I utterly disclaim the charge. Our powers of mind have been crushed, as far as man could do it, our sense of morality has been impaired by his interpretation of our duties; but no where does God say that he made any distinction between us, as moral and intelligent beings.

"We appreciate," say the Association, "the *unostentatious* prayers and efforts of woman in advancing the cause of religion at home and abroad, in leading religious inquirers TO THE PASTOR for instruction." Several points here demand attention. If public prayers and public efforts are necessarily ostentatious, then "Anna the prophetess (or preacher), who departed not from the temple, but served God with fastings and prayers night and day," "and spake of Christ to all them that looked for redemption in Israel," was ostentatious in her efforts.[5] Then, the apostle Paul encourages women to be ostentatious in their efforts to spread the gospel, when he gives them directions how they should appear, when engaged in praying, or preaching in the public assemblies. Then, the whole association of Congregational ministers are ostentatious, in the efforts they are making in preaching and praying to convert souls.

But woman may be permitted to lead religious inquirers to the PASTORS for instruction. Now this is assuming that all pastors are better qualified to give instruction than woman. This I utterly deny; I have suffered too keenly from the teaching of man, to lead anyone to him for instruction. The Lord Jesus says,—"Come unto me and learn of me" [Matt. 11:29]. He points his followers to no man; and when woman is made the favored instrument of rousing a sinner to his lost and helpless condition, she has no right to substitute any teacher for Christ; all she has to do is, to turn the contrite inquirer to the "Lamb of God which taketh away the sins of the world" [John 1:29]. More souls have probably been lost by going down to Egypt for help, and by trusting in man in the early stages of religious experience, than by any other error. Instead of the petition being offered to God,—"Lead me in thy truth, and TEACH me, for thou art the God of my salvation" [Psalms 25:5],—instead of relying on the precious promises—"What man is he that feareth the Lord? him shall HE TEACH in the way that he shall choose" [Psalms 25:12—"I will instruct thee and TEACH thee in the way which thou shalt go—I will guide thee with mine eye" [Psalms 27:11]—the young convert is di-

[5] Luke 2:36–38.

rected to go to man, as if he were in the place of God, and his instructions essential to an advancement in the path of righteousness. That woman can have but a poor conception of the privilege of being taught of God, what he alone can teach, who would turn the "religious inquirer aside" from the fountain of living waters, where he might slake his thirst for spiritual instruction, to those broken cisterns which can hold no water, and therefore cannot satisfy the panting spirit. The business of men and women, who are ORDAINED OF GOD to preach the unsearchable riches of Christ to a lost and perishing world, is to lead souls to Christ, and not to Pastors for instruction.

The General Association say that, "when woman assumes the place and tone of man as a public reformer, our care and protection of her seem unnecessary; we put ourselves in self-defence against her, and her character becomes unnatural." Here again the unscriptural notion is held up, that there is a distinction between the duties of men and women as moral beings; that what is virtue in man, is vice in woman; and women who dare to obey the command of Jehovah, "Cry aloud, spare not, lift up thy voice like a trumpet, and show my people their transgression" [Isai. 58:1], are threatened with having the protection of the brethren withdrawn. If this is all they do, we shall not even know the time when our chastisement is inflicted; our trust is in the Lord Jehovah, and in him is everlasting strength. The motto of woman, when she is engaged in the great work of public reformation should be,—"The Lord is my light and my salvation; whom shall I fear? The Lord is the strength of my life; of whom shall I be afraid?" [Psalms 27:1]. She must feel, if she feels rightly, that she is fulfilling one of the important duties laid upon her as an accountable being, and that her character, instead of being "unnatural," is in exact accordance with the will of Him to whom, and to no other, she is responsible for the talents and the gifts confided to her. As to the pretty simile, introduced into the "Pastoral Letter," "If the vine whose strength and beauty is to lean upon the trellis work, and half conceal its clusters, thinks to assume the independence and the overshadowing nature of the elm," &c., I shall only remark that it might well suit the poet's fancy, who sings of sparkling eyes and coral lips, and knights in armor clad; but it seems to me utterly inconsistent with the dignity of a Christian body, to endeavor to draw such an anti-scriptural distinction between men and women. Ah! how many of my sex feel in the dominion, thus unrighteously exercised over them, under the gentle appellation of *protection,* that what they have leaned upon has proved a broken reed at best, and oft a spear.

Thine in the bonds of womanhood,

Sarah M. Grimké

LETTER IV

SOCIAL INTERCOURSE OF THE SEXES

Andover, 7th Mo. 27, 1837

My Dear Friend,

Before I proceed with the account of that oppression which woman has suffered in every age and country from her *protector,* man, permit me to offer for your consideration, some views relative to the social intercourse of the sexes. Nearly the whole of this intercourse is, in my apprehension, derogatory to man and woman, as moral and intellectual beings. We approach each other, and mingle with each other, under the constant pressure of a feeling that we are of different sexes; and, instead of regarding each other only in the light of immortal creatures, the mind is fettered by the idea which is early and industriously infused into it, that we must never forget the distinction between male and female. Hence our intercourse, instead of being elevated and refined, is generally calculated to excite and keep alive the lowest propensities of our nature. Nothing, I believe, has tended more to destroy the true dignity of woman, than the fact that she is approached by man in the character of a female. The idea that she is sought as an intelligent and heaven-born creature, whose society will cheer, refine and elevate her companion, and that she will receive the same blessings she confers, is rarely held up to her view. On the contrary, man almost always addresses himself to the weakness of woman. By flattery, by an appeal to her passions, he seeks access to her heart; and when he has gained her affections, he uses her as the instrument of his pleasure—the minister of his temporal comfort. He furnishes himself with a housekeeper, whose chief business is in the kitchen or the nursery. And whilst he goes abroad and enjoys the means of improvement afforded by collision of intellect with cultivated minds, his wife is condemned to draw nearly all her instruction from books, if she has time to peruse them; and if not, from her meditations, whilst engaged in those domestic duties which are necessary for the comfort of her lord and master.

Surely no one who contemplates, with the eye of a Christian philosopher, the design of God in the creation of woman, can believe that she is now fulfilling that design. The literal translation of the word "help-meet" is a helper like unto himself; it is so rendered in the Septuagint, and manifestly signifies a companion. Now I believe it will be impossible for woman to fill the station assigned her by God, until her brethren mingle with her as an equal, as a moral being; and lose, in the dignity of her immortal nature, and in the fact of her bearing like himself the image and superscription of her God, the idea of her being a female. The apostle beautifully remarks, "As many of you as have been baptized into Christ, have put on Christ. There is neither Jew nor Greek, there is neither bond nor free, there is neither *male* nor *female;* for ye are all one in Christ Jesus" [Gal. 3:28]. Until our intercourse is purified by the forgetfulness of sex,—until we rise above the present low and sordid views which entwine themselves around our social and domestic interchange of sentiment and feelings, we never can derive that benefit from each other's society which it is the design of our Creator that we should. Man has inflicted an unspeakable injury upon woman, by holding up to her view her animal nature, and placing in the background her moral and intellectual being. Woman has inflicted an injury upon herself by submitting to be thus regarded; and she is now called upon to rise from the station where *man,* not God, has placed her, and claim those sacred and inalienable rights, as a moral and responsible being, with which her Creator has invested her.

What but these views, so derogatory to the character of woman, could have called forth the remark contained in the Pastoral Letter? "We especially deplore the intimate acquaintance and promiscuous conversation of *females* with regard to things 'which ought not to be named,' by which that modesty and delicacy, which is the charm of domestic life, and which constitutes the true influence of woman, is consumed." How wonderful that the conceptions of man relative to woman are so low, that he cannot perceive that she may converse on any subject connected with the improvement of her species, without swerving in the least from that modesty which is one of her greatest virtues! Is it designed to insinuate that woman should possess a greater degree of modesty than man? This idea I utterly reprobate. Or is it supposed that woman cannot go into scenes of misery, the necessary result of those very things, which the Pastoral Letter says ought not to be named, for the purpose of moral reform, without becoming contaminated by those with whom she thus mingles?

This is a false position; and I presume has grown out of the never-forgotten distinction of male and female. The woman who goes forth, clad in the panoply of God, to stem the tide of iniquity and misery, which she beholds rolling through our land, goes not forth to her labor of love as a female. She goes as the dignified messenger of Jehovah, and all she does and says must be done and said irrespective of sex. She is in duty bound to communicate with all who are able and willing to aid her in saving her fellow creatures, both men and women, from that destruction which awaits them.

So far from woman losing anything of the purity of her mind by visiting the wretched victims of vice in their miserable abodes, by talking with them, or of them, she becomes more and more elevated and refined in her feelings and views. While laboring to cleanse the minds of others from the malaria of moral pollution, her own heart becomes purified, and her soul rises to nearer communion with her God. Such a woman is infinitely better qualified to fulfil the duties of a wife and a mother than the woman whose *false delicacy* leads her to shun her fallen sister and brother, and shrink from *naming those sins* which she knows exist, but which she is too fastidious to labor by deed and by word to exterminate. Such a woman feels, when she enters upon the marriage relation, that God designed that relation not to debase her to a level with the animal creation, but to increase the happiness and dignity of his creatures. Such a woman comes to the important task of training her children in the nurture and admonition of the Lord, with a soul filled with the greatness of the beings committed to her charge. She sees in her children creatures bearing the image of God; and she approaches them with reverence, and treats them at all times as moral and accountable beings. Her own mind being purified and elevated, she instills into her children that genuine religion which induces them to keep the commandments of God. Instead of ministering with ceaseless care to their sensual appetites, she teaches them to be temperate in all things. She can converse with her children on any subject relating to their duty to God, can point their attention to those vices which degrade and brutify human nature, without in the least defiling her own mind or theirs. She views herself, and teaches her children to regard themselves, as moral beings; and in all their intercourse with their fellow men, to lose the animal nature of man and woman, in the recognition of that immortal mind wherewith Jehovah has blessed and enriched them.

Thine in the bonds of womanhood,

Sarah M. Grimké

LETTER VIII

ON THE CONDITION OF WOMEN IN THE UNITED STATES

Brookline, 1837

My Dear Sister,

I have now taken a brief survey of the condition of woman in various parts of the world. I regret that my time has been so much occupied by other things, that I have been unable to bestow that attention upon the subject which it merits, and that my constant change of place has prevented me from having access to books, which might probably have assisted me in this part of my work. I hope that the principles I have asserted will claim the attention of some of my sex, who may be able to bring into view, more thoroughly than I have done, the situation and degradation of woman. I shall now proceed to make a few remarks on the condition of women in my own country.

During the early part of my life, my lot was cast among the butterflies of the *fashionable* world; and of this class of women, I am constrained to say, both from experience and observation, that their education is miserably deficient; that they are taught to regard marriage as the one thing needful, the only avenue to distinction; hence to attract the notice and win the attentions of men, by their external charms, is the chief business of fashionable girls. They seldom think that men will be allured by intellectual acquirements, because they find that where any mental superiority exists, a woman is generally shunned and regarded as stepping out of her "appropriate sphere," which, in their view, is to dress, to dance, to set out to the best possible advantage her person, to read the novels which inundate the press, and which do more to destroy her character as a rational creature than anything else. Fashionable women regard themselves, and are regarded by men, as pretty toys or as mere instruments of pleasure; and the vacuity of mind, the heartlessness, the frivolity which is the necessary result of this false and debasing estimate of women, can only be fully understood by those who have mingled in the folly and wickedness of fashionable life; and who have been called from such pursuits by the voice of the Lord Jesus, inviting their weary and heavy laden souls to come unto Him and learn of Him, that they may find something worthy of their immortal spirit and their intellectual powers; that they may learn the high and holy purposes of their creation, and consecrate themselves unto the service of God; and not, as is now the case, to the pleasure of man.

There is another and much more numerous class in this country, who are withdrawn by education or circumstances from the circle of fashionable amusements, but who are brought up with the dangerous and absurd idea that *marriage* is a kind of preferment; and that to be able to keep their husband's house, and render his situation comfortable, is the end of her being. Much that she does and says and thinks is done in reference to this situation; and to be married is too often held up to the view of girls as the sine qua non of human happiness and human existence. For this purpose more than for any other, I verily believe the majority of girls are trained. This is demonstrated by the imperfect education which is bestowed upon them, and the little pains taken to cultivate their minds after they leave school, by the little time allowed them for reading and by the idea being constantly inculcated that, although all household concerns should be attended to with scrupulous punctuality at particular seasons, the improvement of their intellectual capacities is only a secondary consideration, and may serve as an occupation to fill up the odds and ends of time. In most families, it is considered a matter of far more consequence to call a girl off from making a pie or a pudding, than to interrupt her whilst engaged in her studies. This mode of training necessarily exalts, in their view, the animal above the intellectual and spiritual nature, and teaches women to regard themselves as a kind of machinery, necessary to keep the domestic engine in order, but of little value as the *intelligent* companions of men.

Let no one think, from these remarks, that I regard a knowledge of housewifery as beneath the acquisition of women. Far from it: I believe that a complete knowledge of household affairs is an indispensable requisite in a woman's education,—that by the mistress of a family, whether married or single, doing her duty thoroughly and *understandingly,* the happiness of the family is increased to an incalculable degree, as well as a vast amount of time and money saved.

All I complain of is, that our education consists so almost exclusively in culinary and other manual operations. I do long to see the time when it will no longer be necessary for women to expend so many precious hours in furnishing "a well spread table," but that their husbands will forego some of their accustomed indulgences in this way, and encourage their wives to devote some portion of their time to mental cultivation, even at the expense of having to dine sometimes on baked potatoes, or bread and butter.

I believe the sentiment expressed by the author of "Live and let Live,"[1] is true:

Other things being equal, a woman of the highest mental endowments will always be the best housekeeper, for domestic economy, is a science that brings into action the qualities of the mind, as well as the graces of the heart. A quick perception, judgment, discrimination, decision and order are high attributes of mind, and are all in daily exercise in the well ordering of a family. If a sensible woman, an intellectual woman, a woman of genius, is not a good housewife, it is not because she is either, or all of those, but because there is some deficiency in her character, or some omission of duty which should make her very humble, instead of her indulging in any secret self-complacency on account of a certain superiority, which only aggravates her fault.

The influence of women over the minds and character of *children* of both sexes, is allowed to be far greater than that of men. This being the case by the very ordering of nature, women should be prepared by education for the performance of their sacred duties as mothers and as sisters. A late American writer,[2] speaking on this subject, says in reference to an article in the *Westminster Review:*

I agree entirely with the writer in the high estimate which he places on female education, and have long since been satisfied, that the subject not only merits, but *imperiously demands* a thorough reconsideration. The whole scheme must, in my opinion, be reconstructed. The great elements of usefulness and duty are too little

[1]Catharine Maria Sedgwick, *Live and Let Live: or Domestic Service Illustrated* (1837).
[2]Thomas S. Grimké, Sarah's older brother.

attended to. Women ought, in my view of the subject, to approach to the best education now given to men (I except mathematics and the classics), far more I believe than has ever yet been attempted. Give me a host of educated, pious mothers and sisters, and I will do more to revolutionize a country, in moral and religious taste, in manners and in social virtues and intellectual cultivation, than I can possibly do in double or treble the time, with a similar host of educated men. I cannot but think that the miserable condition of the great body of the people in all ancient communities, is to be ascribed in a very great degree to the degradation of women.

There is another way in which the general opinion, that women are inferior to men, is manifested that bears with tremendous effect on the laboring class, and indeed on almost all who are obliged to earn a subsistence, whether it be by mental or physical exertion—I allude to the disproportionate value set on the time and labor of men and of women. A man who is engaged in teaching can always, I believe, command a higher price for tuition than a woman—even when he teaches the same branches, and is not in any respect superior to the woman. This I know is the case in boarding and other schools with which I have been acquainted, and it is so in every occupation in which the sexes engage indiscriminately. As for example, in tailoring, a man has twice, or three times as much for making a waistcoat or pantaloons as a woman, although the work done by each may be equally good. In those employments which are peculiar to women, their time is estimated at only half the value of that of men. A woman who goes out to wash, works as hard in proportion as a wood sawyer or a coal heaver, but she is not generally able to make more than half as much by a day's work. The low remuneration which women receive for their work has claimed the attention of a few philanthropists, and I hope it will continue to do so until some remedy is applied for this enormous evil. I have known a widow, left with four or five children to provide for, unable to leave home because her helpless babes demand her attention, compelled to earn a scanty subsistence, by making coarse shirts at $12^1/_2$ cents apiece, or by taking in washing, for which she was paid by some wealthy persons $12^1/_2$ cents per dozen. All these things evince the low estimation in which woman is held. There is yet another and more disastrous consequence arising from this unscriptural notion—women being educated, from earliest childhood, to regard themselves as inferior creatures, have not that self-respect which conscious equality would engender, and hence when their virtue is assailed, they yield to temptation with facility, under the idea that it rather exalts than debases them, to be connected with a superior being.

There is another class of women in this country, to whom I cannot refer without feelings of the deepest shame and sorrow. I allude to our female slaves. Our southern cities are whelmed beneath a tide of pollution; the virtue of female slaves is wholly at the mercy of irresponsible tyrants, and women are bought and sold in our slave markets to gratify the brutal lust of those who bear the name of Christians. In our slave States, if amid all her degradation and ignorance, a woman desires to preserve her virtue unsullied, she is either bribed or whipped into compliance, or if she dares resist her seducer, her life by the laws of some of the slave States may be, and has actually been sacrificed to the fury of disappointed passion. Where such laws do not exist, the power which is necessarily vested in the master over his property, leaves the defenceless slave entirely at his mercy, and the sufferings of some females on this account, both physical and mental, are intense. Mr. Gholson, in the House of Delegates of Virginia, in 1832, said, "He really had been under the impression that he owned his slaves. He had lately purchased four women and ten children, in whom he thought he had obtained a great bargain; for he supposed they were his own property, *as were his brood mares.*" But even if any laws existed in the United States, as in Athens formerly, for the protection of female slaves, they would be null and void, because the evidence of a colored person is not admitted against a white in any of our Courts of Justice in the slave States. "In Athens, if a female slave had cause to complain of any want of respect to the laws of modesty, she could seek the protection of the temple, and demand a change of owners; and such appeals were never discountenanced, or neglected by the magistrate." In Christian America, the slave has no refuge from unbridled cruelty and lust.

S. A. Forrall, speaking of the state of morals at the South, says, "Negresses when young and likely, are often employed by the planter, or his friends, to administer to their sensual desires. This frequently is a matter of speculation, for if the offspring, a mulatto, be a handsome female, 800 or 1,000 dollars may be obtained for her in the New Orleans market. It is an occurrence of no uncommon nature to see a Christian father sell his own daughter, and the brother his own sister." The following is copied by the *New York Evening Star* from the *Picayune,* a paper published in New Orleans. "A very beautiful girl, belonging to the estate of John French, a deceased gambler at New Orleans, was sold a few days since for the round sum of $7,000. An ugly-looking bachelor named Gouch, a member of the Council of one of the Principalities, was the purchaser. The girl is a brunette; remarkable for her beauty and intelligence, and there was considerable contention, who should be the purchaser. She was, however, persuaded to accept Gouch, he having made her princely promises." I will add but one more from the numerous testimonies respecting the degradation of female slaves and the licentiousness of the South. It is from the *Circular of the Kentucky Union,* for the moral and religious improvement of the colored race. "To the female character among our black population, we cannot allude but with feelings of the bitterest shame. A similar condition of moral pollution and utter disregard of a pure and virtuous reputation, is to be found *only without the pale of Christendom.* That such a state of society should exist in a Christian nation, claiming to be the most enlightened upon earth, without calling forth any *particular attention* to its existence, though ever before our eyes and *in our* families, is a moral phenomenon at once unaccountable and disgraceful." Nor does the colored woman suffer alone: the moral purity of the white woman is deeply contaminated. In the daily habit of seeing the virtue of her enslaved sister sacrificed without hesitancy or remorse, she looks upon the crimes of seduction and illicit intercourse without horror, and although not personally involved in the guilt, she loses that value for innocence in her own, as well as the other sex, which is one of the strongest safeguards to virtue. She lives in habitual intercourse with men whom she knows to be polluted by licentiousness, and often is she compelled to witness in her own domestic circle those disgusting and heart-sickening jealousies and strifes which disgraced and distracted the family of Abraham.[3] In addition to all this, the female slaves suffer every species of degradation and cruelty which the most wanton barbarity can inflict; they are indecently divested of their clothing, sometimes tied up and severely whipped, sometimes pros-

---

[3]Sarah, Abraham's wife, grew jealous of his slave-mistress, Hagar, and her son, and persuaded Abraham to send them out into the desert (Genesis 21:9–14).

trated on the earth, while their naked bodies are torn by the scorpion lash.

> The whip on WOMAN's shrinking flesh!
> Our soil yet reddening with the stains
> Caught from her scourging warm and fresh.[4]

Can any American woman look at these scenes of shocking licentiousness and cruelty, and fold her hands in apathy and say, "I have nothing to do with slavery?" *She cannot and be guiltless.*

I cannot close this letter, without saying a few words on the benefits to be derived by men, as well as women, from the opinions I advocate relative to the equality of the sexes. Many women are now supported, in idleness and extravagance, by the industry of their husbands, fathers, or brothers, who are compelled to toil out their existence at the counting house, or in the printing office, or some other laborious occupation, while the wife and daughters and sisters take no part in the support of the family, and appear to think that their sole business is to spend the hard bought earnings of their male friends.[5] I deeply regret such a state of things, because I believe that if women felt their responsibility for the support of themselves or their families, it would add strength and dignity to their characters, and teach them more true sympathy for their husbands than is now generally manifested,—a sympathy which would be exhibited by actions as well as words. Our brethren may reject my doctrine, because it runs counter to common opinions, and because it wounds their pride; but I believe they would be "partakers of the benefit" resulting from the Equality of the Sexes, and would find that woman, as their equal, was unspeakably more valuable than woman as their inferior, both as a moral and an intellectual being.

Thine in the bonds of womanhood,

Sarah M. Grimké

---

[4]John Greenleaf Whittier, "Stanzas," lines 18–20.
[5]Relatives.

LETTER XV

MAN EQUALLY GUILTY WITH WOMAN IN THE FALL

Uxbridge, 10th Mo. 20, 1837

My Dear Sister,

It is said that "modern Jewish women light a lamp every Friday evening, half an hour before sunset, which is the beginning of their Sabbath, in remembrance of their original mother, who first extinguished the lamp of righteousness,—to remind them of their obligation to rekindle it." I am one of those who always admit, to its fullest extent, the popular charge that woman brought sin into the world. I accept it as a powerful reason why woman is bound to labor with double diligence for the regeneration of that world she has been intrumental in ruining.

But, although I do not repel the imputation, I shall notice some passages in the sacred Scriptures where this transaction is mentioned, which prove, I think, the identity and equality of man and woman, and that there is no difference in their guilt in the view of that God who searcheth the heart and trieth the reins of the children of men. In Isai. 43:27, we find the following passage—"Thy first father hath sinned, and thy teachers have transgressed against me"—which is synonymous with Rom. 5:12. "Wherefore, as by ONE MAN sin entered into the world, and death by sin, &c." Here man and woman are included under one term, and no distinction is made in their criminality. The circumstances of the fall are again referred to in 2 Cor. 11:3—"But I fear lest, by any means, as the serpent *beguiled* Eve through his subtility, so your mind should be beguiled from the simplicity that is in Christ." Again, 1st Tim. 2:14—"Adam *was not deceived;* but the woman being *deceived,* was in the transgression." Now, whether the fact that Eve was beguiled and deceived is a proof that her crime was of deeper dye than Adam's, who was not deceived, but was fully aware of the consequences of sharing in her transgression, I shall leave the candid reader to determine.

My present object is to show that, as woman is charged with all the sin that exists in the world, it is her solemn duty to labor for its extinction; and that this she can never do effectually and extensively until her mind is disenthralled of those shackles which have been riveted upon her by a *"corrupt public opinion, and a perverted interpretation of the holy Scriptures."* Woman must feel that she is the equal, and is designed to be the fellow laborer of her brother, or she will be studying to find out the *imaginary* line which separates the sexes and divides the duties of men and women into two distinct classes, a separation not even hinted at in the Bible, where we are expressly told, "there is neither male nor female, for ye are all one in Christ Jesus" [Gal. 3:28].

My views on this subject are so much better embodied in the language of a living author than I can express them, that I quote the passage entire: "Woman's rights and man's rights are *both* contained in the *same* charter, and held by the *same* tenure. *All rights* spring out of the *moral* nature: they are both the root and the offspring of *responsibilities*. The physical constitution is the mere *instrument* of the *moral* nature; sex is a mere *incident* of this constitution, a provision necessary to this *form* of existence; its *only* design, not to give, nor to take away, nor in any respect to modify or even *touch* rights or responsibilities in any sense, except so far as the peculiar offices of each sex may afford less or more *opportunity* and ability for the exercise of rights, and the discharge of responsibilities; but merely to continue and enlarge the human department of God's government. Consequently, I know nothing of *man's* rights, or *woman's* rights; *human* rights are all that I recognise. The doctrine, that the *sex of the body* presides over and administers upon the rights and responsibilities of the moral, immortal nature, is to my mind a doctrine kindred to blasphemy, *when seen in its intrinsic nature.* It breaks up utterly the *relations* of the two natures, and reverses their functions; exalting the animal nature into a monarch, and humbling the moral into a slave; making the former a proprietor, and the latter its property."

To perform our duties, we must comprehend our rights and responsibilities; and it is because we do not understand, that we now fall so far short in the discharge of our obligations. Unaccustomed to think for ourselves, and to search the sacred volume to see how far we are living up to the design of Jehovah in our creation, we have rested satisfied with the sphere marked out for us by man, never detecting the fallacy of that reasoning which forbids woman to exercise some of her noblest faculties, and stamps with the reproach of indelicacy those actions by which women were formerly dignified and exalted in the church.

I should not mention this subject again, if it were not to point out to my sisters what seems to me an irresistible conclusion from the literal interpretation of St. Paul, without reference to the context, and the peculiar circumstances and abuses which drew forth the expressions, "I suffer not a woman to teach"—"Let your women keep silence in the church," [I Cor. 14:34], i.e. congregation. It is manifest that, if the apostle meant what his words imply, when taken in the strictest sense, then women have no right to *teach* Sabbath or day schools, or to open their lips to sing in the assemblies of the people; yet young and delicate women are engaged in all these offices; they are expressly trained to exhibit themselves and raise their voices to a high pitch in the choirs of our places of worship. I do not intend to sit in judgment on my sisters for doing these things; I only want them to see, that they are as really infringing a *supposed* divine command, by instructing their pupils in the Sabbath or day schools, and by singing in the congregation, as if they were engaged in preaching the unsearchable riches of Christ to a lost and perishing world. Why, then, are we permitted to break this injunction in some points, and so sedulously warned not to overstep the bounds set for us by our *brethren* in another? Simply, as I believe, because in the one case we subserve *their* views and *their* interests, and act *in subordination to them;* whilst in the other, we come in contact with their interests, and claim to be on an equality with them in the highest and most important trust ever committed to man, namely, the ministry of the world. It is manifest that if women were permitted to be ministers of the gospel, as they unquestionably were in the primitive ages of the Christian church, it would interfere materially with the present organized system of spiritual power and ecclesiastical authority, which is now vested solely in the hands of men. It would either show that all the paraphernalia of theological seminaries, &c. &c. to prepare men to become evangelists, is wholly unnecessary, or it would create a necessity for similar institutions in order to prepare women for the same office; and this would be an encroachment on that learning which our kind brethren have so ungenerously monopolized. I do not ask anyone to believe my statements, or adopt my conclusions, because they are mine; but I do earnestly entreat my sisters to lay aside their prejudices, and examine these subjects *for themselves,* regardless of the "traditions of men," because they are intimately connected with their duty and their usefulness in the present important crisis.

All who know anything of the present system of benevolent and religious operations, know that women are performing an important part in them in *subserviency to men,* who guide our labors and are often the recipients of those benefits of education we toil to confer, and which we rejoice they can enjoy, although it is their mandate which deprives us of the same advantages. Now, whether our brethren have defrauded us intentionally or unintentionally, the wrong we suffer is equally the same. For years, they have been spurring us up to the performance of our duties. The immense usefulness and the vast influence of woman have been eulogized and called into exercise, and many a blessing has been lavished upon us, and many a prayer put up for us, because we have labored by day and by night to clothe and feed and educate young men, whilst our own bodies sometimes suffer for want of comfortable garments, and our minds are left in almost utter destitution of that improvement which we are toiling to bestow upon the brethren.

> Full many a gem of purest ray serene,
> The dark unfathomed caves of ocean bear;
> Full many a flower is born to blush unseen
> And waste its sweetness on the desert air.[1]

If the sewing societies, the avails of whose industry are now expended in supporting and educating young men for the ministry, were to withdraw their contributions to these objects, and give them where they are *more needed,* to the advancement of their *own sex* in useful learning, the next generation might furnish sufficient proof that in intelligence and ability to master the whole circle of sciences, woman is not inferior to man; and instead of a sensible woman being regarded as she now is, as a *lusus naturae,* they would be quite as common as sensible men. I confess, considering the high claim men in this country make to great politeness and deference to women, it does seem a little extraordinary that we should be urged to work for the brethren. I should suppose it would be more in character with "the generous promptings of chivalry, and the poetry of romantic gallantry," for which Catharine E. Beecher[2] gives them credit, for them to form societies to educate their sisters, seeing our inferior capacities require more cultivation to bring them into use, and qualify us to be helps meet for them. However, though I think this would

---

[1]Thomas Gray, "Elegy Written in a Country Churchyard" (1751), lines 53–56.
[2]Catharine E. Beecher (1800–1878), a prominent conservative writer on women.

be but a just return for all our past kindnesses in this way, I should be willing to balance our accounts, and begin a new course. Henceforth, let the benefit be reciprocated, or else let each sex provide for the education of their own poor, whose talents ought to be rescued from the oblivion of ignorance. Sure I am, the young men who are now benefitted by the handiwork of their sisters will not be less honorable if they occupy half their time in earning enough to pay for their own education, instead of depending on the industry of women, who not unfrequently deprive themselves of the means of purchasing valuable books which might enlarge their stock of useful knowledge, and perhaps prove a blessing to the family by furnishing them with instructive reading. If the minds of women were enlightened and improved, the domestic circle would be more frequently refreshed by intelligent conversation, a means of edification now deplorably neglected, for want of that cultivation which these intellectual advantages would confer.

Duties of Women

One of the duties which devolve upon women in the present interesting crisis is to prepare themselves for more extensive usefulness, by making use of those religious and literary privileges and advantages that are within their reach, if they will only stretch out their hands and possess them. By doing this, they will become better acquainted with their rights as moral beings, and with their responsibilities growing out of those rights; they will regard themselves, as they really are, FREE AGENTS, immortal beings, amenable to no tribunal but that of Jehovah, and bound not to submit to any restriction imposed for selfish purposes, or to gratify that love of power which has reigned in the heart of man from Adam down to the present time. In contemplating the great moral reformations of the day, and the part which they are bound to take in them, instead of puzzling themselves with the harassing, because unnecessary inquiry, how far they may go without overstepping the bounds of propriety which separate male and female duties, they will only inquire, "Lord, what wilt thou have us to do?" They will be enabled to see the simple truth, that God has made no distinction between men and women as moral beings; that the distinction now so much insisted upon between male and female virtues is as absurd as it is unscriptural, and has been the fruitful source of much mischief—granting to man a license for the exhibition of brute force and conflict on the battlefield; for sternness, selfishness, and the exercise of irresponsible power in the circle of home—and to woman a permit to rest on an arm of flesh, and to regard modesty and delicacy, and all the kindred virtues, as peculiarly appropriate to her. Now to me it is perfectly clear, that WHATSOEVER IT IS MORALLY RIGHT FOR A MAN TO DO, IT IS MORALLY RIGHT FOR A WOMAN TO DO; and that confusion must exist in the moral world, until woman takes her stand on the same platform with man, and feels that she is clothed by her Maker with the *same rights,* and, of course, that upon her devolve the *same duties.*

It is not my intention, nor indeed do I think it is in my power, to point out the precise duties of women. To him who still teacheth by his Holy Spirit as never man taught, I refer my beloved sisters. There is a vast field of usefulness before them. The signs of the times give portentous evidence that a day of deep trial is approaching; and I urge them, by every consideration of a Savior's dying love, by the millions of heathen in our midst, by the sufferings of woman in almost every portion of the world, by the fearful ravages which slavery, intemperance, licentiousness and other iniquities are making of the happiness of our fellow creatures, to come to the rescue of a ruined world, and to be found co-workers with Jesus Christ.

> Ho! to the rescue, ho!
>   Up every one that feels—
> 'Tis a sad and fearful cry of woe
>   From a guilty world that steals.
> Hark! hark! how the horror rolls,
>   Whence can this anguish be?
> 'Tis the groan of a trammel'd people's souls,
>   *Now bursting* to be free.

And here, with all due deference for the office of the ministry, which I believe was established by Jehovah himself, and designed by Him to be the means of spreading light and salvation through a crucified Savior to the ends of the earth, I would entreat my sisters not to *compel* the ministers of the present day to give their names to great moral reformations. The practice of making ministers life members or officers of societies, when their hearts have not been touched with a live coal from the altar, and animated with love for the work we are engaged in, is highly injurious to them, as well as to the cause. They often satisfy their consciences in this way, without doing anything to promote the anti-slavery, or temperance, or other reformations; and we please ourselves with the idea that we have done something to forward the cause of Christ, when, in effect, we have been sewing pillows like the false prophetesses of old under the armholes of our clerical brethren. Let us treat the ministers with all tenderness and respect, but let us be careful how we cherish in their hearts the idea that they are of more importance to a cause than other men. I rejoice when they take hold heartily. I love and honor some ministers with whom I have been associated in the anti-slavery ranks, but I do deeply deplore, for the sake of the cause, the prevalent notion that the clergy must be had, either by persuasion or by bribery. They will not need persuasion or bribery, if their hearts are with us; if they are not, we are better without them. It is idle to suppose that the kingdom of heaven cannot come on earth without their co-operation. It is the Lord's work, and it must go forward with or without their aid. As well might the converted Jews have despaired of the spread of Christianity without the co-operation of Scribes and Pharisees.

Let us keep in mind that no abolitionism is of any value, which is not accompanied with deep, heartfelt repentance; and that, whenever a minister sincerely repents of having, either by his apathy or his efforts, countenanced the fearful sin of slavery, he will need no inducement to come into our ranks; so far from it, he will abhor himself in dust and ashes for his past blindness and indifference to the cause of God's poor and oppressed: and he will regard it as a privilege to be enabled to do something in the cause of human rights. I know the ministry exercise vast power; but I rejoice in the belief that the spell is broken which encircled them, and rendered it all but blasphemy to expose their errors and their sins. We are beginning to understand that they are but men, and that their station should not shield them from merited reproof.

I have blushed for my sex when I have heard of their entreating ministers to attend their associations, and open them with prayer. The idea is inconceivable to me, that Christian women can be engaged in doing God's work, and yet cannot ask his blessing on their efforts except through the lips of a man. I have known a whole town scoured to obtain a minister to open a female meeting, and their refusal to do so spoken of as quite a misfortune. Now, I am not glad that the ministers do wrong; but I am glad that my sisters have been sometimes compelled to act for themselves: it is exactly what they need to strengthen them, and prepare them to act independently. And to say the truth, there is something really ludicrous in seeing a minister enter the meeting, open it with prayer, and then take his departure. However, I only throw out these hints for the consideration of women. I believe there are solemn responsibilities resting upon us, and that in this day of light and knowledge, we cannot plead ignorance of duty. The great moral reformations now on the wheel are only practical Christianity; and if the ministry is not prepared to labor with us in these righteous causes, let us press forward, and they will follow on to know the Lord.

Conclusion

I have now, my dear sister, completed my series of letters. I am aware, they contain some new views; but I believe they are based on the immutable truths of the Bible. All I ask for them is the candid and prayerful consideration of Christians. If they strike at some of our bosom sins, our deep-rooted prejudices, our long cherished opinions, let us not condemn them on that account, but investigate them fearlessly and prayerfully, and not shrink from the examination; because, if they are true, they place heavy responsibilities upon women. In throwing them before the public, I have been actuated solely by the belief that, if they are acted upon, they will exalt the character and enlarge the usefulness of my own sex, and contribute greatly to the happiness and virtue of the other. That there is a root of bitterness continually springing up in families and troubling the repose of both men and women, must be manifest to even a superficial observer; and I believe it is the mistaken notion of the inequality of the sexes. As there is an assumption of superiority on the one part, which is not sanctioned by Jehovah, there is an incessant struggle on the other to rise to that degree of dignity which God designed women to possess in common with men, and to maintain those rights and exercise those privileges which every woman's common sense, apart from the prejudices of education, tells her are inalienable; they are a part of her moral nature, and can only cease when her immortal mind is extinguished.

One word more. I feel that I am calling upon my sex to sacrifice what has been, what is still dear to their hearts, the adulation, the flattery, the attentions of trifling men. I am asking them to repel these insidious enemies whenever they approach them; to manifest by their conduct that, although they value highly the society of pious and intelligent men, they have no taste for idle conversation and for that silly preference which is manifested for their personal accommodation, often at the expense of great inconvenience to their male companions. As an illustration of what I mean, I will state a fact.

I was traveling lately in a stagecoach. A gentleman who was also a passenger was made sick by riding with his back to the horses. I offered to exchange seats, assuring him it did not affect me at all unpleasantly; but he was too polite to permit a lady to run the risk of being discommoded. I am sure he meant to be very civil, but I really thought it was a foolish piece of civility. This kind of attention encourages selfishness in woman, and is only accorded as a sort of quietus, in exchange for those *rights* of which we are deprived. Men and women are equally bound to cultivate a spirit of accommodation; but I exceedingly deprecate her being treated like a spoiled child, and sacrifices made to her selfishness and vanity. In lieu of these flattering but injurious attentions, yielded to her as an inferior, as a mark of benevolence and courtesy, I want my sex to claim nothing from their brethren but what their brethren may justly claim from them, in their intercourse as Christians. I am persuaded woman can do much in this way to elevate her own character. And that we may become duly sensible of the dignity of our nature, only a little lower than the angels, and bring forth fruit to the glory and honor of Emanuel's name, is the fervent prayer of

Thine in the bonds of womanhood,

Sarah M. Grimké

Sojourner Truth

c.1797–1883

ORIGINALLY NAMED ISABELLA, Sojourner Truth was born a slave to a Dutch family in New York State and had several owners. She wanted to marry Robert, a slave on a neighboring estate (insofar as slaves were allowed to marry), but his master ordered him to marry one of his own slaves, so as to retain property in the children. So Isabella married a man on her own place, whose two previous wives had been sold away from him. When her master failed to keep his promise to free her, she ran away with her infant daughter, one of the two children remaining to her. She became legally free in 1827, when slaves in New York were emancipated. Meanwhile, however, her master had illegally sold or sent her five-year-old son into slavery in Alabama. She persuaded a lawyer to force him to reclaim the child.

After working for some years as a maid, Isabella felt a call to preach and to change her name to Sojourner Truth. In 1843 she became a traveling preacher, exhorting the people to embrace Christ and renounce sin. Later she took up the cause of abolition and then of women's rights. She risked her life at abolitionist meetings and could quiet a pro-slavery mob with her fearless dignity and pointed remarks. Since Sojourner never learned to read or write, she studied the Bible by having someone read and reread a sentence to her until she felt she understood its meaning. During the Civil War, she worked with newly freed blacks, exhorting them to support themselves instead of living on government handouts, finding them jobs, and campaigning to get the government to grant them land in the West. (She thought this plan would have succeeded if mothers, concerned for future generations, had had the vote.) After the war, when many leaders pushed the women's cause aside in order to concentrate on black rights, Sojourner Truth continued to campaign for woman suffrage, pointing out that half the recently freed slaves were women.

Since Sojourner Truth was illiterate, her words survive as recorded by contemporaries she impressed, such as Frances Gage and Harriet Beecher Stowe. Gage describes the 1851 Woman's Rights Convention in Akron, Ohio.

BIBLIOGRAPHY

Gilbert, Olive. *Narrative of Sojourner Truth*. Battle Creek, Mich.: Published for the Author, 1878. Reprint New York: Arno, 1968.

History of Woman Suffrage. Edited by Elizabeth Cady Stanton, Susan B. Anthony, and Matilda Joslyn Gage. New York: Fowler & Wells, 1881. Reprint New York: Arno, 1969.

Stowe, Harriet Beecher. *The Writings*. Vol. 4. Riverside ed., 1896. Reprint New York: AMS Press, 1967.

Reminiscences by Frances D. Gage: Sojourner Truth

The leaders of the movement trembled on seeing a tall, gaunt black woman in a gray dress and white turban, surmounted with an uncouth sunbonnet, march deliberately into the church, walk with the air of a queen up the aisle, and take her seat upon the pulpit steps. A buzz of disapprobation was heard all over the house, and there fell on the listening ear, "An abolition affair!" "Woman's rights and niggers!" "I told you so!" "Go it, darkey!"

I chanced on that occasion to wear my first laurels in public life as president of the meeting. At my request order was restored, and the business of the Convention went on. Morning, afternoon, and evening exercises came and went. Through all these sessions old Sojourner, quiet and reticent as the "Libyan Statue,"[1] sat crouched against the wall on the corner of the pulpit stairs, her sunbonnet

---

[1]See Stowe's character sketch, following this.

shading her eyes, her elbows on her knees, her chin resting upon her broad, hard palms. At intermission she was busy selling the "Life of Sojourner Truth," a narrative of her own strange and adventurous life.[2] Again and again, timorous and trembling ones came to me and said, with earnestness, "Don't let her speak, Mrs. Gage, it will ruin us. Every newspaper in the land will have our cause mixed up with abolition and niggers, and we shall be utterly denounced." My only answer was, "We shall see when the time comes."

The second day the work waxed warm. Methodist, Baptist, Episcopal, Presbyterian, and Universalist ministers came in to hear and discuss the resolutions presented. One claimed superior rights and privileges for man, on the ground of "superior intellect"; another, because of the "manhood of Christ; if God had desired the equality of woman, He would have given some token of His will through the birth, life, and death of the Savior." Another gave us a theological view of the "sin of our first mother."

There were very few women in those days who dared to "speak in meeting"; and the august teachers of the people were seemingly getting the better of us, while the boys in the galleries, and the sneerers among the pews, were hugely enjoying the discomfiture, as they supposed, of the "strong-minded." Some of the tender-skinned friends were on the point of losing dignity, and the atmosphere betokened a storm. When, slowly from her seat in the corner rose Sojourner Truth, who, till now, had scarcely lifted her head. "Don't let her speak!" gasped half a dozen in my ear. She moved slowly and solemnly to the front, laid her old bonnet at her feet, and turned her great speaking eyes to me. There was a hissing sound of disapprobation above and below. I rose and announced "Sojourner Truth," and begged the audience to keep silence for a few moments.

The tumult subsided at once, and every eye was fixed on this almost Amazon form, which stood nearly six feet high, head erect, and eyes piercing the upper air like one in a dream. At her first word there was a profound hush. She spoke in deep tones, which, though not loud, reached every ear in the house, and away through the throng at the doors and windows.

"Wall, chilern, whar dar is so much racket dar must be somethin' out o' kilter. I tink dat 'twixt de niggers of de Souf and de womin at

---

[2]As was customary, she supported herself in part by selling her autobiography, which was written down for her by a white friend, Olive Gilbert, and published in 1850.

de Norf, all talkin' 'bout rights, de white men will be in a fix pretty soon. But what's all dis here talkin' 'bout?

"Dat man ober dar say dat womin needs to be helped into carriages, and lifted ober ditches, and to hab de best place everywhar. Nobody eber helps me into carriages, or ober mud-puddles, or gibs me any best place!" And raising herself to her full height, and her voice to a pitch like rolling thunder, she asked, "And a'n't I a woman? Look at me! Look at my arm!" And she bared her right arm to the shoulder, showing her tremendous muscular power. "I have ploughed, and planted, and gathered into barns, and no man could head me! And a'n't I a woman? I could work as much and eat as much as a man—when I could get it—and bear de lash as well! And a'n't I a woman? I have borne thirteen chilern, and seen 'em mos' all sold off to slavery, and when I cried out with my mother's grief, none but Jesus heard me! And a'n't I a woman?

"Den dey talks 'bout dis ting in de head; what dis dey call it?" ("Intellect," whispered someone near.) "Dat's it, honey. What's dat got to do wid womin's rights or nigger's rights? If my cup won't hold but a pint, and yourn holds a quart, wouldn't ye be mean not to let me have my little half-measure full?" And she pointed her significant finger, and sent a keen glance at the minister who had made the argument. The cheering was long and loud.

"Den dat little man in black dar, he say women can't have as much rights as men, 'cause Christ wan't a woman! Whar did your Christ come from?" Rolling thunder couldn't have stilled that crowd, as did those deep, wonderful tones, as she stood there with outstretched arms and eyes of fire. Raising her voice still louder, she repeated, "Whar did your Christ come from? From God and a woman! Man had nothin' to do wid Him." Oh, what a rebuke that was to that little man.

Turning again to another objector, she took up the defense of Mother Eve. I can not follow her through it all. It was pointed, and witty, and solemn; eliciting at almost every sentence deafening applause; and she ended by asserting: "If de fust woman God ever made was strong enough to turn de world upside down all alone, dese women togedder (and she glanced her eye over the platform) ought to be able to turn it back, and get it right side up again! And now dey is asking to do it, de men better let 'em." Long-continued cheering greeted this. " 'Bleeged to ye for hearin' on me, and now ole Sojourner han't got nothin' more to say."

Amid roars of applause, she returned to her corner, leaving more than one of us with streaming eyes, and hearts beating with gratitude. She had taken us up in her strong arms and carried us safely over the slough of difficulty, turning the whole tide in our favor. I have never in my life seen anything like the magical influence that subdued the mobbish spirit of the day, and turned the sneers and jeers of an excited crowd into notes of respect and admiration. Hundreds rushed up to shake hands with her, and congratulate the glorious old mother, and bid her God-speed on her mission of "testifyin' agin concerning the wickedness of this 'ere people."

Sojourner Truth, the Libyan Sibyl[1]
by Harriet Beecher Stowe

Many years ago, the few readers of radical abolitionist papers must often have seen the singular name of Sojourner Truth announced as a frequent speaker at anti-slavery meetings, and as traveling on a sort of self-appointed agency through the country. I had myself often remarked the name, but never met the individual. On one occasion, when our house was filled with company, several eminent clergymen being our guests, notice was brought up to me that Sojourner Truth was below and requested an interview. Knowing nothing of her but her singular name, I went down, prepared to make the interview short, as the pressure of many other engagements demanded.

When I went into the room, a tall, spare form arose to meet me. She was evidently a full-blooded African, and, though now aged and

[1]Sojourner Truth visited Stowe's home in 1853, probably because she wanted to meet the author of *Uncle Tom's Cabin* (1852). Stowe published this account of her visit in *The Atlantic Monthly* in April 1863. "The Libyan Sibyl" refers to a statue by William Wetmore Story, which was inspired by Stowe's description of Sojourner. The statue, intended to represent a specifically African type of beauty, attracted much attention at the time.

worn with many hardships, still gave the impression of a physical development which in early youth must have been as fine a specimen of the torrid zone as Cumberworth's celebrated statuette of the Negro Woman at the Fountain. Indeed, she so strongly reminded me of that figure, that, when I recall the events of her life, as she narrated them to me, I imagine her as a living, breathing impersonation of that work of art.

I do not recollect ever to have been conversant with anyone who had more of that silent and subtle power which we call personal presence than this woman. In the modern spiritualistic phraseology, she would be described as having a strong sphere. Her tall form, as she rose up before me, is still vivid to my mind. She was dressed in some stout, grayish stuff, neat and clean, though dusty from travel. On her head she wore a bright Madras handkerchief, arranged as a turban, after the manner of her race. She seemed perfectly self-possessed and at her ease,—in fact, there was almost an unconscious superiority, not unmixed with a solemn twinkle of humor, in the odd, composed manner in which she looked down on me. Her whole air had at times a gloomy sort of drollery which impressed one strangely.

"So this is *you?*" she said.

"Yes," I answered.

"Well, honey, de Lord bless ye! I jes' thought I'd like to come an' have a look at ye. You's heerd o' me, I reckon?" she added.

"Yes, I think I have. You go about lecturing, do you not?"

"Yes, honey, that's what I do. The Lord has made me a sign unto this nation, an' I go round a-testifyin', an' showin' on 'em their sins agin my people."

So saying, she took a seat, and, stooping over and crossing her arms on her knees, she looked down on the floor, and appeared to fall into a sort of reverie. Her great gloomy eyes and her dark face seemed to work with some undercurrent of feeling; she sighed deeply, and occasionally broke out,—

"O Lord! O Lord! O the tears, an' the groans, an' the moans! O Lord!"

I should have said that she was accompanied by a little grandson of ten years,—the fattest, jolliest woolly-headed little specimen of Africa that one can imagine. He was grinning and showing his glistening white teeth in a state of perpetual merriment, and at this moment broke out into an audible giggle, which disturbed the reverie into which his relative was falling.[2]

She looked at him with an indulgent sadness, and then at me.

"Laws, ma'am, *he* don't know nothin' about it,—*he* don't. Why, I've seen them poor critturs, beat an' 'bused an' hunted, brought in all torn,—ears hangin' all in rags, where the dogs been a-bitin' of 'em!"

This set off our little African Puck into another giggle, in which he seemed perfectly convulsed.

She surveyed him soberly, without the slightest irritation.

"Well, you may bless the Lord you *can* laugh; but I tell you, 'twa'n't no laughin' matter."

By this time I thought her manner so original that it might be worthwhile to call down my friends; and she seemed perfectly well pleased with the idea. An audience was what she wanted,—it mattered not whether high or low, learned or ignorant. She had things to say, and was ready to say them at all times, and to anyone.

I called down Dr. Beecher,[3] Professor Allen, and two or three other clergymen, who, together with my husband and family, made a roomful. No princess could have received a drawing-room with more composed dignity than Sojourner her audience. She stood among them, calm and erect, as one of her own native palm-trees waving alone in the desert. I presented one after another to her, and at last said,—

"Sojourner, this is Dr. Beecher. He is a very celebrated preacher."

"*Is* he?" she said, offering her hand in a condescending manner, and looking down on his white head. "Ye dear lamb, I'm glad to see ye! De Lord bless ye! I loves preachers. I'm a kind o' preacher myself."

"You are?" said Dr. Beecher. "Do you preach from the Bible?"

"No, honey, can't preach from de Bible,—can't read a letter."

"Why, Sojourner, what do you preach from, then?"

Her answer was given with a solemn power of voice, peculiar to herself, that hushed everyone in the room.

"When I preaches, I has just one text to preach from, an' I always preaches from this one. *My* text is, 'WHEN I FOUND JESUS.' "

"Well, you couldn't have a better one," said one of the ministers.

She paid no attention to him, but stood and seemed swelling with her own thoughts, and then began this narration:—

[2] In 1863 this grandson enlisted in the Massachusetts 54th Regiment, a black unit that distinguished itself for heroism.

[3] Lyman Beecher, Harriet's father.

"Well, now, I'll jest have to go back, an' tell ye all about it. Ye
see, we was all brought over from Africa, father an' mother an' I,
an' a lot more of us; an' we was sold up an' down, an' hither an'
yon; an' I can 'member when I was a little thing, not bigger than
this 'ere," pointing to her grandson, "how my ole mammy would sit
out o' doors in the evenin', an' look up at the stars an' groan. She'd
groan an' groan, an' says I to her,—

" 'Mammy, what makes you groan so?'

"An' she'd say,—

" 'Matter enough, chile! I'm groanin' to think o' my poor children:
they don't know where I be, an' I don't know where they be; they
looks up at the stars, an' I looks up at the stars, but I can't tell where
they be.

" 'Now,' she said, 'chile, when you're grown up, you may be sold
away from your mother an' all your ole friends, an' have great troubles come on ye; an' when you has these troubles come on ye, ye jes'
go to God, an' He'll help ye.'

"An' says I to her,—

" 'Who is God anyhow, mammy?'

"An' says she,—

" 'Why, chile, you jes' look up *dar!* It's Him that made all *dem!*'

"Well, I didn't mind much 'bout God in them days. I grew up
pretty lively an' strong, an' could row a boat, or ride a horse, or
work round, an' do 'most anything.

"At last I got sold away to a real hard massa an' missis. Oh, I tell
you, they *was* hard! 'Peard like I couldn't please 'em, nohow. An'
then I thought o' what my old mammy told me about God; an' I
thought I'd got into trouble, sure enough, an' I wanted to find God,
an' I heerd someone tell a story about a man that met God on a
threshin'-floor, an' I thought, 'Well an' good, I'll have a threshin'-
floor, too.' So I went down in the lot, an' I threshed down a place
real hard, an' I used to go down there every day an' pray an' cry
with all my might, a-prayin' to the Lord to make my massa an' missis
better, but it didn't seem to do no good; an' so says I, one day,—

" 'O God, I been a-askin' ye, an' askin' ye, for all this long time,
to make my massa an' missis better, an' you don't do it, an' what
can be the reason? Why, maybe you *can't*. Well, I shouldn't wonder
ef you couldn't. Well, now, I tell you, I'll make a bargain with you.
Ef you'll help me to git away from my massa an' missis, I'll agree to
be good; but ef you don't help me, I really don't think I can be.

Now,' says I, 'I want to git away; but the trouble's jest here: ef I try to git away in the night, I can't see; an' ef I try to git away in the daytime, they'll see me, an' be after me.'

"Then the Lord said to me, 'Git up two or three hours afore daylight, an' start off.'

"An' says I, 'Thank 'ee, Lord! that's a good thought.'

"So up I got, about three o'clock in the mornin', an' I started an' traveled pretty fast, till, when the sun rose, I was clear away from our place an' our folks, an' out o' sight. An' then I begun to think I didn't know nothin' where to go. So I kneeled down, and says I,—

" 'Well, Lord, you've started me out, an' now please to show me where to go.'

"Then the Lord made a house appear to me, an' He said to me that I was to walk on till I saw that house, an' then go in an' ask the people to take me. An' I traveled all day, an' didn't come to the house till late at night; but when I saw it, sure enough, I went in, an' I told the folks that the Lord sent me; an' they was Quakers, an' real kind they was to me. They jes' took me in, an' did for me as kind as ef I'd been one of 'em; an' after they'd giv me supper, they took me into a room where there was a great, tall, white bed; an' they told me to sleep there. Well, honey, I was kind o' skeered when they left me alone with that great white bed; 'cause I never had been in a bed in my life. It never came into my mind they could mean me to sleep in it. An' so I jes' camped down under it on the floor, an' then I slep' pretty well. In the mornin', when they came in, they asked me ef I hadn't been asleep; an' I said, 'Yes, I never slep' better.' An' they said, 'Why, you haven't been in the bed!' An' says I, 'Laws, you didn't think o' sech a thing as my sleepin' in dat ar *bed,* did you? I never heerd o' sech a thing in my life.'

"Well, ye see, honey, I stayed an' lived with 'em. An' now jes' look here: instead o' keepin' my promise an' bein' good, as I told the Lord I would, jest as soon as everything got a-goin' easy, *I forgot all about God.*

"Pretty well don't need no help; an' I gin up prayin'. I lived there two or three years, an' then the slaves in New York were all set free, an' ole massa came to our house to make a visit, an' he asked me ef I didn't want to go back an' see the folks on the ole place. An' I told him I did. So he said, ef I'd jes' git into the wagon with him, he'd carry me over. Well, jest as I was goin' out to git into the wagon, *I met God!* an' says I, 'O God, I didn't know as you was so great!'

An' I turned right round an' come into the house, an' set down in my room; for 't was God all around me. I could feel it burnin', burnin', burnin' all around me, an' goin' through me; an' I saw I was so wicked, it seemed as ef it would burn me up. An' I said, 'Oh, somebody, somebody, stand between God an' me, for it burns me!' Then, honey, when I said so, I felt as it were somethin' like an *amberill* [umbrella] that came between me an' the light, an' I felt it was *somebody*,—somebody that stood between me an' God; an' it felt cool, like a shade; an' says I, 'Who's this that stands between me an' God? Is it old Cato?' He was a pious old preacher; but then I seemed to see Cato in the light, an' he was all polluted an' vile, like me; an' I said, 'Is it old Sally?' an' then I saw her, an' she seemed jes' so. An' then says I, '*Who* is this?' An' then, honey, for a while it was like the sun shinin' in a pail o' water, when it moves up an' down; for I begun to feel 't was somebody that loved me; an' I tried to know him. An' I said, 'I know you! I know you! I know you!'—an' then I said, 'I don't know you! I don't know you! I don't know you!' An' when I said, 'I know you, I know you,' the light came; an' when I said, 'I don't know you, I don't know you,' it went, jes' like the sun in a pail o' water. An' finally somethin' spoke out in me an' said, '*This is Jesus!*' an' I spoke out with all my might, an' says I, '*This is Jesus!* Glory be to God!' An' then the whole world grew bright, an' the trees they waved an' waved in glory, an' every little bit o' stone on the ground shone like glass; an' I shouted an' said, 'Praise, praise, praise to the Lord!' An' I begun to feel sech a love in my soul as I never felt before,—love to all creatures. An' then, all of a sudden, it stopped, an' I said, 'Dar's de white folks, that have abused you an' beat you an' abused your people,—think o' them!' But then there came another rush of love through my soul, an' I cried out loud, 'Lord, Lord, I can love *even de white folks!*'

"Honey, I jes' walked round an' round in a dream. Jesus loved me! I knowed it,—I felt it. Jesus was my Jesus. Jesus would love me always. I didn't dare tell nobody; 't was a great secret. Everything had been got away from me that I ever had; an' I thought that ef I let white folks know about this, maybe they'd get *Him* away,—so I said, 'I'll keep this close. I won't let anyone know.' "

"But, Sojourner, had you never been told about Jesus Christ?"

"No, honey. I hadn't heerd no preachin',—been to no meetin'. Nobody hadn't told me. I'd kind o' heerd of Jesus, but thought he was like Gineral Lafayette, or some o' them. But one night there was a Methodist meetin' somewhere in our parts, an' I went; an' they got up an' begun for to tell der 'speriences; an' de fust one begun to speak. I started, 'cause he told about Jesus. 'Why,' says I to myself, 'dat man's found him, too!' An' another got up an' spoke, an' I said, 'He's found him, too!' An' finally I said, 'Why, they all know him!' I was so happy! An' then they sung this hymn" (here Sojourner sang, in a strange, cracked voice, but evidently with all her soul and might, mispronouncing the English, but seeming to derive as much elevation and comfort from bad English as from good) . . .

I put in this whole hymn, because Sojourner, carried away with her own feeling, sang it from beginning to end with a triumphant energy that held the whole circle around her intently listening. She sang with the strong barbaric accent of the native African, and with those indescribable upward turns and those deep gutturals which give such a wild, peculiar power to the negro singing,—but, above all, with such an overwhelming energy of personal appropriation that the hymn seemed to be fused in the furnace of her feelings and come out recrystallized as a production of her own.

It is said that Rachel[4] was wont to chant the Marseillaise in a manner that made her seem, for the time, the very spirit and impersonation of the gaunt, wild, hungry, avenging mob which rose against aristocratic oppression; and in like manner Sojourner, singing this hymn, seemed to impersonate the fervor of Ethiopia, savage, hunted of all nations, but burning after God in her tropic heart, and stretching her scarred hands towards the glory to be revealed.

"Well, den, ye see, after a while I thought I'd go back an' see de folks on de ole place. Well, you know, de law had passed dat de cullud folks was all free; an' my old missis, she had a daughter married about dis time who went to live in Alabama,—an' what did she do but give her my son, a boy about de age of dis yer, for her to take down to Alabama? When I got back to de ole place, they told me about it, an' I went right up to see ole missis, an' says I,—

" 'Missis, have you been an' sent my son away down to Alabama?'

" 'Yes, I have,' says she; 'he's gone to live with your young missis.'

" 'Oh, missis,' says I, 'how could you do it?'

" 'Poh!' says she, 'what a fuss you make about a little nigger! Got more of 'em now than you know what to do with.'

"I tell you, I stretched up. I felt as tall as the world!

[4]A nineteenth-century French actress, perhaps the greatest of her day.

" 'Missis,' says I, *I'll have my son back agin!'*

"She laughed.

" '*You* will, you nigger? How you goin' to do it? You ha'n't got no money.'

" 'No, missis, but *God* has, an' you'll see He'll help me!' An' I turned round, an' went out.

"Oh, but I *was* angry to have her speak to me so haughty an' so scornful, as ef my chile wasn't worth anything. I said to God, 'O Lord, render unto her double!' It was a dreadful prayer, an' I didn't know how true it would come.

"Well, I didn't rightly know which way to turn; but I went to the Lord, an' I said to Him, 'O Lord, ef I was as rich as you be, an' you was as poor as I be, I'd help you,—you *know* I would; and, oh, do help me!' An' I felt sure then that He would.

"Well, I talked with people, an' they said I must git the case before a grand jury. So I went into the town, when they was holdin' a court, to see ef I could find any grand jury. An' I stood round the court-house, an' when they was a-comin' out I walked right up to the grandest-lookin' one I could see, an' says I to him,—

" 'Sir, be you a grand jury?'

"An' then he wanted to know why I asked, an' I told him all about it; an' he asked me all sorts of questions, an' finally he says to me,—

" 'I think, ef you pay me ten dollars, that I'd agree to git your son for you.' An' says he, pointin' to a house over the way, 'You go long an' tell your story to the folks in that house, an' I guess they'll give you the money.'

"Well, I went, an' I told them, an' they gave me twenty dollars; an' then I thought to myself, 'Ef ten dollars will git him, twenty dollars will git him *sartin.'* So I carried it to the man all out, an' said,—

" 'Take it all,—only be sure an' git him.'

"Well, finally they got the boy brought back; an' then they tried to frighten him, an' to make him say that I wasn't his mammy, an' that he didn't know me; but they couldn't make it out. They gave him to me, an' I took him an' carried him home; an' when I came to take off his clothes, there was his poor little back all covered with scars an' hard lumps, where they'd flogged him.

"Well, you see, honey, I told you how I prayed the Lord to render unto her double. Well, it came true; for I was up at ole missis' house not long after, an' I heerd 'em readin' a letter to her how her daughter's husband had murdered her,—how he'd thrown her down an' stamped the life out of her when he was in liquor; an' my ole missis, she giv' a screech an' fell flat on the floor. Then says I, 'O Lord, I didn't mean all that! You took me up too quick.'

"Well, I went in an' tended that poor critter all night. She was out of her mind,—a-cryin,' an' callin' for her daughter; an' I held her poor ole head on my arms, an' watched for her as ef she'd been my babby. An' I watched by her, an' took care on her all through her sickness after that, an' she died in my arms, poor thing!"

"Well, Sojourner, did you always go by this name?"

"No, 'deed! My name was Isabella; but when I left the house of bondage, I left everything behind. I wa'n't goin' to keep nothin' of Egypt on me,[5] an' so I went to the Lord an' asked Him to give me a new name. And the Lord gave me Sojourner, because I was to travel up an' down the land, showin' the people their sins, an' bein' a sign unto them. Afterwards I told the Lord I wanted another name, 'cause everybody else had two names; and the Lord gave me Truth, because I was to declare the truth to the people.

"Ye see, some ladies have given me a white satin banner," she said, pulling out of her pocket and unfolding a white banner, printed with many texts, such as, "Proclaim liberty throughout all the land unto all the inhabitants thereof," and others of like nature. "Well," she said, "I journeys round to camp-meetin's, an' wherever folks is, an' I sets up my banner, an' then I sings, an' then folks always comes up round me, an' then I preaches to 'em. I tells 'em about Jesus, an' I tells 'em about the sins of this people. A great many always comes to hear me; an' they're right good to me, too, an' say they want to hear me agin."

We all thought it likely; and as the company left her, they shook hands with her, and thanked her for her very original sermon; and one of the ministers was overhead to say to another, "There's more of the gospel in that story than in most sermons."

Sojourner stayed several days with us, a welcome guest. Her conversation was so strong, simple, shrewd, and with such a droll flavoring of humor, that the Professor[6] was wont to say of an evening, "Come, I am dull, can't you get Sojourner up here to talk a little?" She would come up into the parlor, and sit among pictures and ornaments, in her simple stuff gown, with her heavy traveling-shoes,

---

[5]She compares her slavery to the bondage of the Jews in Egypt, as narrated in Exodus.

[6]Harriet's husband, Calvin Stowe, a professor at Bowdoin.

the central object of attention both to parents and children, always ready to talk or to sing, and putting into the common flow of conversation the keen edge of some shrewd remark.

"Sojourner, what do you think of Women's Rights?"

"Well, honey, I's ben to der meetings, an' harked a good deal. Dey wanted me fur to speak. So I got up. Says I, 'Sisters, I ain't clear what you'd be after. Ef women want any rights more'n dey's got, why don't dey jes' *take 'em,* an' not be talkin' about it?' Some on 'em came round me, an' asked why I didn't wear bloomers.[7] An' I told 'em I had bloomers enough when I was in bondage. You see," she said, "dey used to weave what dey called nigger-cloth, an' each one of us got jes' sech a strip, an' had to wear it width-wise. Them that was short got along pretty well, but as for me"—She gave an indescribably droll glance at her long limbs and then at us, and added, "Tell *you,* I had enough of bloomers in them days."

Sojourner then proceeded to give her views of the relative capacity of the sexes, in her own way.

"S'pose a man's mind holds a quart, an' a woman's don't hold but a pint; ef her pint is *full,* it's as good as his quart."

Sojourner was fond of singing an extraordinary lyric, commencing,—

> "I'm on my way to Canada,
> That cold but happy land;
> The dire effects of slavery
> I can no longer stand.
> O righteous Father,
> Do look down on me,
> And help me on to Canada,
> Where colored folks are free!"[8]

The lyric ran on to state that, when the fugitive crosses the Canada line,

> "The Queen comes down unto the shore,

[7] A form of rational dress for women, popularized by Amelia Bloomer from 1851, that replaced the voluminous skirts of the period with a short skirt and trousers.

[8] After the passage of the Fugitive Slave Law (1850), which increased the power of slaveholders to pursue and seize their "property," many blacks felt safe only if they got to Canada.

With arms extended wide,
To welcome the poor fugitive
Safe on to Freedom's side."

In the truth thus set forth she seemed to have the most simple faith.

But her chief delight was to talk of "glory," and to sing hymns whose burden was,—

"O glory, glory, glory,
Won't you come along with me?"

and when left to herself she would often hum these with great delight, nodding her head.

On one occasion I remember her sitting at a window singing, and fervently keeping time with her head, the little black Puck of a grandson meanwhile amusing himself with ornamenting her red-and-yellow turban with green dandelion curls, which shook and trembled with her emotions, causing him perfect convulsions of delight.

"Sojourner," said the Professor to her one day when he heard her singing, "you seem to be very sure about heaven."

"Well, I be," she answered triumphantly.

"What makes you so sure there is any heaven?"

"Well, 'cause I got such a hankerin' arter it in here," she said, giving a thump on her breast with her usual energy.

There was at the time an invalid in the house, and Sojourner, on learning it, felt a mission to go and comfort her. It was curious to see the tall, gaunt, dusky figure stalk up to the bed, with such an air of conscious authority, and take on herself the office of consoler with such a mixture of authority and tenderness. She talked as from above, and at the same time if a pillow needed changing, or any office to be rendered, she did it with a strength and handiness that inspired trust. One felt as if the dark, strange woman were quite able to take up the invalid in her bosom and bear her as a lamb, both physically and spiritually. There was both power and sweetness in that great warm soul and that vigorous frame.

At length Sojourner, true to her name, departed. She had her mission elsewhere. Where now she is, I know not; but she left deep memories behind her.

Caroline Stansbury Kirkland

1801–1864

CAROLINE STANSBURY was the eldest of eleven children in a cultured family in New York City; her mother was a writer. Caroline got an unusually good education at one of the several schools run by her aunt, and went on to teach at one located in upstate New York. There she met William Kirkland, a classics tutor at Hamilton College, whom she married in 1828. They opened a girls' school in Geneva, New York, but in 1835 moved west to run the Detroit Female Seminary. Infected by the current dream of becoming rich through land speculation, they bought 1,300 acres of Michigan woodland and marsh and set out to found a city. They settled in the tiny hamlet of Pinckney, sixty miles west of Detroit. Caroline recorded their experiences, in slightly fictionalized form, in *A New Home—Who'll Follow?* (1839). The book was enthusiastically received by readers and critics, including Margaret Fuller.

After five years at Pinckney, the Kirklands gave up their project, returning to New York poorer than they had set out. Caroline established herself as a writer, dealing particularly with the development of civilized communities on the frontier. After William's death (1846), she had to support herself and their four children. She wrote sketches and stories, managed and taught in girls' schools, and edited high-quality gift books and magazines. She advocated economic and legal rights for women, satirized the contemporary tendency to disparage women writers, and opposed slavery.

A New Home graphically renders the experience of educated Eastern ladies who were uprooted from the culture they knew to follow their men west, usually against their wishes. Brought up to believe their mission in life was to make a refined home, they keenly felt the roughness and privation of life on the frontier.

BIBLIOGRAPHY
  Kirkland, Caroline. *A New Home—Who'll Follow? or, Glimpses of Western Life*. New York: C. S. Francis, 1855.

from A New Home—Who'll Follow?

CHAPTER I[1]

Our friends in the "settlements"[2] have expressed so much interest in such of our letters to them as happened to convey any account of the peculiar features of western life, and have asked so many questions, touching particulars which we had not thought worthy of mention, that I have been for some time past contemplating the possibility of something like a detailed account of our experiences. And I have determined to give them to the world, in a form not very different from that in which they were originally recorded for our private delectation; nothing doubting that a veracious history of actual occurrences, an unvarnished transcript of real characters, and an impartial record of everyday forms of speech (taken down in many cases from the lips of the speaker) will be pronounced "graphic" by at least a fair proportion of the journalists of the day.

It is true there are but meager materials for anything that might be called a story. I have never seen a cougar—nor been bitten by a rattlesnake. The reader who has patience to go with me to the close of my desultory sketches, must expect nothing beyond a meandering recital of commonplace occurrences—mere gossip about everyday people, little enhanced in value by any fancy or ingenuity of the writer; in short, a very ordinary pen-drawing; which, deriving no interest from coloring, can be valuable only for its truth.

A home on the outskirts of civilization—habits of society which allow the maid and her mistress to do the honors in complete equal-

---

[1]Each chapter has one to three epigraphs reflecting Kirkland's wide reading in American, English, and French literature; they are omitted here.
[2]Settled communities in the East.

ity, and to make the social tea visit in loving conjunction—such a distribution of the duties of life as compels all, without distinction, to rise with the sun or before him—to breakfast with the chickens—then, "Count the slow clock, and dine exact at noon"—[3] to be ready for tea at four, and for bed at eight—may certainly be expected to furnish some curious particulars for the consideration of those whose daily course almost reverses this primitive arrangement—who "call night day and day night," and who are apt occasionally to forget, when speaking of a particular class, that "those creatures" are partakers with themselves of a common nature.

I can only wish, like other modest chroniclers, my respected prototypes, that so fertile a theme had fallen into worthier hands. If Miss Mitford, who has given us such charming glimpses of Aberleigh, Hilton Cross, and the Loddon, had, by some happy chance, been translated to Michigan, what would she not have made of such materials as Tinkerville, Montacute, and the Turnip?[4]

When my husband purchased two hundred acres of wild land on the banks of this to-be-celebrated stream, and drew with a piece of chalk on the bar-room table at Danforth's[5] the plan of a village, I little thought I was destined to make myself famous by handing down to posterity a faithful record of the advancing fortunes of that favored spot.

"The madness of the people" in those days of golden dreams took more commonly the form of city-building; but there were a few who contented themselves with planning villages, on the banks of streams which certainly never could be expected to bear navies, but which might yet be turned to account in the more homely way of grinding or sawing—operations which must necessarily be performed somewhere, for the well-being of those very cities. It is of one of these humble attempts that it is my lot to speak, and I make my confession at the outset, warning any fashionable reader, who may have taken up my book, that I intend to be "decidedly low."

Whether the purchaser of *our* village would have been as moderate under all possible circumstances, I am not prepared to say, since,

---

[3] Alexander Pope, epistle to Miss Blount "On Her Leaving the Town after the Coronation" (1714), line 18.

[4] Mary Russell Mitford, particularly known for her sketches of English village life, e.g. *Our Village* (1832). Montacute is Kirkland's pseudonym for Pinckney; Tinkerville and the Turnip, for the neighboring village and river.

[5] The primitive tavern in the settlement.

never having enjoyed a situation under government, his resources have not been unlimited; and for this reason any remark which may be hazarded in the course of these my lucubrations touching the more magnificent plans of wealthier aspirants, must be received with some grains of allowance. "Il est plus aisé d'être sage pour les autres, que de l'être pour soi-même."[6] . . .

CHAPTER X

At length came the joyful news that our moveables had arrived in port;[1] and provision was at once made for their transportation to the banks of the Turnip. But many and dire were the vexatious delays, thrust by the cruel Fates between us and the accomplishment of our plans; and it was not till after the lapse of several days that the most needful articles were selected and bestowed in a large wagon which was to pioneer the grand body. In this wagon had been reserved a seat for myself, since I had far too great an affection for my chairs and tables to omit being present at their debarkation at Montacute, in order to ensure their undisturbed possession of the usual complement of legs. And there were the children to be packed this time—little roly-poly things, whom it would have been in vain to have marked, "this side up," like the rest of the baggage.

A convenient space must be contrived for my plants, among which were two or three tall geraniums and an enormous calla ethiopica. Then D'Orsay[2] must be accommodated, of course; and, to crown all, a large basket of live fowls; for we had been told that there were none to be purchased in the vicinity of Montacute. Besides these, there were all our travelling trunks, and an enormous square box crammed with articles which we then, in our greenness, considered indispensable. We have since learned better.

After this enumeration, which yet is only partial, it will not seem strange that the guide and director of our omnibus was to ride "On horseback after we." He acted as a sort of adjutant—galloping forward to spy out the way, or provide accommodations for the troop—pacing close to the wheels to modify our arrangements, to console

[6]"It is easier to be wise for others than for oneself."
[1]Detroit.
[2]Her greyhound.

one of the imps who had bumped his pate, or to give D'Orsay a gentle hint with the riding-whip, when he made demonstrations of mutiny—and occasionally falling behind to pick up a stray handkerchief or parasol.

The roads near Detroit were inexpressibly bad. Many were the chances against our toppling load's preserving its equilibrium. To our inexperience, the risks seemed nothing less than tremendous—but the driver so often reiterated, "that a'n't nothin' " in reply to our despairing exclamations, and, what was better, so constantly proved his words by passing the most frightful inequalities (Michiganicé,[3] "sidlings") in safety, that we soon became more confident, and ventured to think of something else besides the ruts and mud-holes.

Our stopping-places after the first day were of the ordinary new country class—the very coarsest accommodations by night and by day, and all at the dearest rate. When everybody is buying land, and scarce anybody cultivating it, one must not expect to find living either good or cheap: but, I confess, I was surprised at the dearth of comforts which we observed everywhere. Neither milk, eggs, nor vegetables were to be had, and those who could not live on hard salt ham, stewed dried apples, and bread raised with "salt risin," would necessarily run some risk of starvation.

One word as to this and similar modes of making bread, so much practised throughout this country. It is my opinion that the sin of bewitching snow-white flour by means of either of those abominations, "salt risin," "milk emptins," "bran east," or any of their odious compounds, ought to be classed with the turning of grain into whiskey, and both made indictable offences. To those who know of no other means of producing the requisite sponginess in bread than the wholesome hop-yeast of the brewer, I may be allowed to explain the mode to which I have alluded with such hearty reprobation. Here follows the recipe:—

To make milk emptins. Take *quantum suf.* of good sweet milk—add a teaspoonful of salt and some water, and set the mixture in a warm place till it ferments, then mix your bread with it; and if you are lucky enough to catch it just in the right moment before the fermentation reaches the putrescent stage, you may make tolerably good rolls, but if you are five minutes too late, you will have to open your doors and windows while your bread is baking.—*Verbum sap.*

---

[3]In Michiganese (facetious).

"Salt risin" is made with water slightly salted and fermented like the other; and becomes putrid rather sooner, and "bran east" is on the same plan. The consequences of letting these mixtures stand too long will become known to those whom it may concern, when they shall travel through the remoter parts of Michigan; so I shall not dwell upon them here—but I offer my counsel to such of my friends as may be removing westward, to bring with them some form of portable yeast (the old-fashioned dried cakes which mothers and aunts can furnish are as good as any)—and also full instructions for perpetuating the same; and to plant hops as soon as they get a corner to plant them in.

> And may they better reck the rede,
> Than ever did th' adviser.

The last two days of our slow journey were agreeably diversified with sudden and heavy showers, and intervals of overpowering sunshine. The weather had all the changefulness of April, with the torrid heat of July. Scarcely would we find shelter from the rain which had drenched us completely—when the sunshine would tempt us forth: and by the time all the outward gear was dried, and matters in readiness for a continuation of our progress, another threatening cloud would drive us back, though it never really rained till we started.

We had taken a newly opened and somewhat lonely route this time, in deference to the opinion of those who ought to have known better, that this road from having been less traveled, would not be quite so *deep*[4] as the other. As we went farther into the wilderness, the difficulties increased. The road had been but little "worked" (the expression in such cases) and in some parts was almost in a state of nature. Where it wound round the edge of a marsh, where in future times there will be a bridge or drain, the wheels on one side would be on the dry ground, while the others were sinking in the long wet grass of the marsh—and in such places it was impossible to discern inequalities which yet might overturn us in an instant. In one case of this sort, we were obliged to dismount the "live lumber"—as the man who helped us through phrased it, and let the loaded wagon pass on, while we followed in an empty one which was fortunately at hand—and it was, in my eyes, little short of a miracle that our

[4]Covered with deep mud.

skillful friend succeeded in piloting safely the top-heavy thing which seemed thrown completely off its center half a dozen times.

At length we came to a dead stand. Our driver had received special cautions as to a certain *mash*[5] that "lay between us and our home"— to "keep to the right"—to "follow the travel" to a particular point, and then "turn up stream": but whether the very minuteness and reiteration of the directions had puzzled him, as is often the case, or whether his good genius had for once forsaken him, I know not. We had passed the deep center of the miry slough when, by some un-lucky hair's breadth swerving, in went our best horse—our sorrel— our "Prince,"—the "off haus,"[6] whose value had been speered three several times since we left Detroit, with magnificent offers of a "swop"! The noble fellow, unlike the tame beasties that are used to such occurrences, showed his good blood by kicking and plunging, which only made his case more desperate. A few moments more would have left us with a "single team,"[7] when his master succeeded in cutting the traces with his penknife. Once freed, Prince soon made his way out of the bog-hole and pranced off, far up the green swell-ing hill which lay before us—out of sight in an instant—and there we sat in the marsh.

There is but one resource in such cases. You must mount your remaining horse, if you have one, and ride on till you find a farmer and one, two, or three pairs of oxen—and all this accomplished, you may generally hope for a release in time.

The interval seemed a *leetle* tedious, I confess. To sit for three mortal hours in an open wagon, under a hot sun, in the midst of a swamp, is not pleasant. The expanse of inky mud which spread around us was hopeless, as to any attempt at getting ashore. I crept cautiously down the tongue, and tried one or two of the tempting green tufts, which looked as if they *might* afford foothold; but alas! they sank under the slightest pressure. So I was fain to regain my low chair, with its abundant cushions, and lose myself in a book. The children thought it fine fun for a little while, but then they began to want a drink. I never knew children who did not, when there was no water to be had.

[5]Marsh.
[6]Off horse; i.e., the horse on the right, further from the driver. Following phrase: Speered: inquired about.
[7]I.e., only one horse.

There ran through the very midst of all this black puddling as clear a stream as ever rippled, and the wagon stood almost in it!—but how to get at it? The basket which had contained, when we left the city, a store of cakes and oranges, which the children thought inexhaustible, held now nothing but the napkins which had enveloped those departed joys, and those napkins, suspended corner-wise, and soaken long and often in the crystal water, served for business and pleasure, till Papa came back.

"They're coming! They're coming!" was the cry, and with one word, over went Miss Alice, who had been reaching as far as she could, trying how large a portion of her napkin she could let float in the water.

Oh, the shrieks and the exclamations! how hard Papa rode, and how hard Mamma scolded! but the little witch got no harm beyond a thorough wetting and a few streaks of black mud, and felt herself a heroine for the rest of the day.

CHAPTER XII

The log-house which was to be our temporary home was tenanted at this time; and we were obliged to wait while the incumbent could build a framed one,[1] the materials for which had been growing in the woods not long before; I was told it would take but a short time, as it was already framed.

What was my surprise, on walking that way to ascertain the progress of things, to find the materials still scattered on the ground, and the place quite solitary.

"Did not Mr. Ketchum[2] say Green's house was framed?" said I to the *dame du palais,* on my return; "the timbers are all lying on the ground, and nobody at work."

"Why, la! so they be all framed, and Green's gone to —— for the sash. They'll be ready to raise tomorrow."

It took me some time to understand that *framing* was nothing more than cutting the tenons and mortices ready for putting the timbers together, and that these must be *raised* before there could

---

[1] A regular wooden house, a timber frame covered with boards.
[2] The family lived with the Ketchums until they could move into their own house. Following phrase: *Dame du palais,* lady of the palace (facetious).

be a frame. And that "sash," which I in my ignorance supposed could be but for one window, was a *generic* term.

The "raising" took place the following afternoon, and was quite an amusing scene to us cockneys,[3] until one man's thumb was frightfully mashed, and another had a severe blow upon the head. A jug of whiskey was pointed out by those who understood the matter as the true cause of these disasters, although the Fates got the blame.

"Jem White always has such bad luck!" said Mr. Ketchum, on his return from the raising, "and word spake never more," for that night at least; for he disappeared behind the mysterious curtain, and soon snored most sonorously.

The many raisings which have been accomplished at Montacute without that ruinous ally, strong drink, since the days of which I speak, have been free from accidents of any sort; Jem White having carried his "bad luck" to a distant country, and left his wife and children to be taken care of by the public.

Our cottage bore about the same proportion to the articles we had expected to put into it that the "lytell hole" did to the fiend whom Virgilius cajoled into its narrow compass; and the more we reflected, the more certain we became that without the magic powers of necromancy, one half of our moveables at least must remain in the open air. To avoid such necessity, Mr. Clavers[4] was obliged to return to Detroit and provide storage for sundry unwieldly boxes which could by no art of ours be conjured into our cot.

While he was absent, Green had enclosed his new house; that is to say, put on the roof and the siding, and laid one floor, and forthwith he removed thither without door, window, or chimney, a course by no means unusual in Michigan.

As I was by this time, truth to speak, very nearly starved, I was anxious to go as soon as possible to a place where I could feel a little more at home; and so completely had my nine days at Ketchums' brought down my ideas, that I anticipated real satisfaction in a removal to this hut in the wilderness. I would not wait for Mr. Clavers' return, but insisted on setting up for myself at once.

But I should in vain attempt to convey to those who know nothing of the woods, any idea of the difficulties in my way. If one's courage did not increase, and one's invention brighten under the stimulus of

[3] I.e., city people.
[4] Kirkland's pseudonym.

such occasions, I should have given up at the outset, as I have often done with far less cause.

It was no easy matter to get a "lady" to clean the place, and ne'er had place more need of the tutelary aid of the goddess of scrubbing brushes. Then this lady must be provided with the necessary utensils, and here arose dilemma upon dilemma. Mrs. Ketchum rendered what aid she could, but there was little superfluous in her house.

And then, such racing and chasing, such messages and requisitions! Mrs. Jennings "couldn't do nothin" without a mop, and I had not thought of such a thing, and was obliged to sacrifice on the spot sundry nice towels, a necessity which made all the housekeeping blood in my veins tingle.

After one day's experience of this sort, I decided to go myself to the scene of action, so as to be at hand for these trying occasions; and I induced Mr. Ketchum to procure a wagon and carry to our new home the various articles which we had piled in a hovel on his premises.

Behold me then seated on a box, in the midst of as anomalous a congregation of household goods as ever met under one roof in the backwoods, engaged in the seemingly hopeless task of calling order out of chaos, attempting occasionally to throw out a hint for the instruction of Mrs. Jennings, who uniformly replied by requesting me not to fret, as she knew what she was about.

Mr. Jennings, with the aid of his sons, undertook the release of the pent-up myriads of articles which crammed the boxes, many of which, though ranked when they were put in as absolutely essential, seemed ridiculously superfluous when they came out. The many observations made by the spectators as each new wonder made its appearance, though at first rather amusing, became after a while quite vexatious; for the truth began to dawn upon me that the common sense was all on their side.

"What on airth's them gimcracks for?" said my lady, as a nest of delicate japanned tables were set out upon the uneven floor.

I tried to explain to her the various convenient uses to which they were applicable; but she looked very scornfully after all and said, "I guess they'll do better for kindlins than anything else here." And I began to cast a disrespectful glance upon them myself, and forthwith ordered them upstairs, and wondering in my own mind how I could have thought a log house would afford space for such superfluities.

All this time there was a blazing fire in the chimney to accommodate Mrs. Jennings in her operations, and while the doors and windows were open we were not sensible of much discomfort from it. Supper was prepared and eaten—beds spread on the floor, and the children stowed away. Mrs. Jennings and our other "helps" had departed, and I prepared to rest from my unutterable weariness, when I began to be sensible of the suffocating heat of the place. I tried to think it would grow cooler in a little while, but it was absolutely insufferable to the children as well as myself, and I was fain to set both doors open, and in this exposed situation passed the first night in my western home, alone with my children and far from any neighbor.

If I could live a century, I think that night will never fade from my memory. Excessive fatigue made it impossible to avoid falling asleep, yet the fear of being devoured by wild beasts, or poisoned by rattlesnakes, caused me to start up after every nap with sensations of horror and alarm, which could hardly have been increased by the actual occurrence of all I dreaded. Many wretched hours passed in this manner. At length sleep fairly overcame fear, and we were awakened only by a wild storm of wind and rain which drove in upon us and completely wetted everything within reach.

A doleful morning was this—no fire on the hearth—streams of water on the floor—and three hungry children to get breakfast for. I tried to kindle a blaze with matches, but alas, even the straw from the packing-boxes was soaked with the cruel rain; and I was distributing bread to the hungry, hopeless of anything more, when Mr. Jennings made his appearance.

"I was thinking you'd begin to be sick o' your bargain by this time," said the good man, "and so I thought I'd come and help you a spell. I reckon you'd ha' done better to have waited till the old man got back."

"What old man?" asked I, in perfect astonishment.

"Why, *your* old man to be sure," said he laughing. I had yet to learn that in Michigan, as soon as a man marries he becomes "the old man," though he may yet be in his minority. Not long since I gave a young bride the how d' do in passing, and the reply was, "I'm pretty well, but my old man's sick a-bed."

But to return. Mr. Jennings kindled a fire, which I took care should be a moderate one; and I managed to make a cup of tea to dip our bread in, and then proceeded to find places for the various articles which strewed the floor. Some auger-holes bored in the logs received large and long pegs, and these served to support boards which were made to answer the purpose of shelves. It was soon found that the multiplicity of articles which were to be accommodated on these shelves would fill them a dozen times.

"Now to my thinkin," said my good genius, Mr. Jennings, "that 'ere soup t'reen, as you call it, and them little ones, and these here great glass-dishes, and all *sich,* might jist as well go up chamber for all the good they'll ever do you here."

This could not be gainsaid; and the good man proceeded to exalt them to another set of extempore shelves in the upper story; and so many articles were included in the same category, that I began to congratulate myself on the increase of clear space below, and to fancy we should soon begin to look very comfortable.

My ideas of comfort were by this time narrowed down to a well-swept room with a bed in one corner, and cooking apparatus in another—and this in some fourteen days from the city! I can scarcely, myself, credit the reality of the change.

It was not till I had occasion to mount the ladder that I realized that all I had gained on the confusion below was most hopelessly added to the confusion above, and I came down with such a sad and thoughtful brow, that my good aid-de-camp perceived my perplexity.

"Hadn't I better go and try to get some of the neighbors' *gals* to come and help you for a few days?" said he.

I was delighted with the offer, and gave him carte-blanche as to terms, which I afterwards found was a mistake, for where sharp bargains are the grand aim of everybody, those who express anything like indifference on the subject are set down at once as having more money than they know what to do with; and as this was far from being my case, I found reason to regret having given room for the conclusion.

The damsel made her appearance before a great while—a neat-looking girl with "scarlet hair and belt to match"; and she immediately set about "reconciling" as she called it, with a good degree of energy and ingenuity. I was forced to confess that she knew much better than I how to make a log house comfortable.

She began by turning out of doors the tall cupboard, which had puzzled me all the morning, observing very justly, "Where there ain't no room for a thing, why, there ain't"; and this decision cut the Gordian knot of all my plans and failures in the disposal of the ungainly convenience. It did yeoman's service long afterwards as a corn-crib.

When the bedsteads were to be put up, the key was among the missing; and after we had sent far and wide and borrowed a key, or the substitute for one, no screws could be found, and we were reduced to the dire necessity of trying to keep the refractory posts in their places by means of ropes. Then there were candles, but no candlesticks. This seemed at first rather inconvenient, but when Mr. Jennings had furnished blocks of wood with auger-holes bored in them for sockets, we could do nothing but praise the ingenuity of the substitute.

My rosy-haired Phillida, who rejoiced in the euphonious appellation of Angeline, made herself entirely at home, looking into my trunks, &c., and asking the price of various parts of my dress. She wondered why I had not my hair cut off, and said she reckoned I would before long, as it was all the fashion about there.

"When d'ye expect *Him?*" said the damsel, with an air of sisterly sympathy, and ere I could reply becomingly, a shout of "tiny joy" told me that Papa had come.

I did not cry for sorrow this time.

CHAPTER XV

Several lots had already been purchased in Montacute, and some improvement marked each succeeding day. The mill had grown to its full stature, the dam was nearly completed; the tavern began to exhibit promise of its present ugliness, and all seemed prosperous as our best dreams, when certain rumors were set afloat touching the solvency of our disinterested friend Mr. Mazard.[1] After two or three days' whispering, a tall black-browed man who "happened in" from Gullsborough, the place which had for some time been honored as the residence of the Dousterswivel[2] of Montacute, stated boldly that Mr. Mazard had absconded; or, in Western language, "cleared." It seemed passing strange that he should run away from the large house which was going on under his auspices; the materials all on the ground and the work in full progress. Still more unaccountable did

[1]The agent who had contracted to build Montacute.
[2]Herman Dousterswivel, a swindler in Walter Scott's *The Antiquary* (1816).

it appear to us that his workmen should go on so quietly, without so much as expressing any anxiety about their pay.

Mr. Clavers had just been telling me of these things, when the long genius above mentioned presented himself at the door of the loggery. His *abord*[3] was a singular mixture of coarseness and an attempt at being civil; and he sat for some minutes looking round and asking various questions before he touched the mainspring of his visit.

At length, after some fumbling in his pocket, he produced a dingy sheet of paper, which he handed to Mr. Clavers.

"There; I want you to read that, and tell me what you think of it."

I did not look at the paper, but at my husband's face, which was blank enough. He walked away with the tall man, "and I saw no more of them at that time."

Mr. Clavers did not return until late in the evening, and it was then I learned that Mr. Mazard had been getting large quantities of lumber and other materials on his account, and as his agent; and that the money which had been placed in the agent's hands for the purchase of certain lands to be flowed[4] by the mill-pond, had gone into government coffers in payment for sundry eighty-acre lots, which were intended for his, Mr. Mazard's, private behoof and benefit. These items present but a sample of our amiable friend's trifling mistakes. I will not fatigue the reader by dwelling on the subject. The results of all this were most unpleasant to us. Mr. Clavers found himself involved to a large amount; and his only remedy seemed to be to prosecute Mr. Mazard. A consultation with his lawyer, however, convinced him that, even by this most disagreeable mode, redress was out of the question, since he had, through inadvertence, rendered himself liable for whatever that gentleman chose to buy or engage in his name. All that could be done was to get out of the affair with as little loss as possible, and to take warning against land-sharks in future.

An immediate journey to Detroit became necessary, and I was once more left alone, and in no overflowing spirits. I sat,

Revolving in *my* altered soul

[3]Approach.
[4]Flooded.

The various turns of fato below,

when a tall damsel, of perhaps twenty-eight or thirty, came in to make a visit. She was tastefully attired in a blue gingham dress, with broad cuffs of black morocco, and a black cambric apron edged with orange worsted lace. Her oily black locks were cut quite short round the ears, and confined close to her head by a black ribbon, from one side of which depended, almost in her eye, two very long tassels of black silk, intended to do duty as curls. Prunelle[5] slippers with high heels and a cotton handkerchief tied under the chin finished the costume, which I have been thus particular in describing, because I have observed so many that were nearly similar.

The lady greeted me in the usual style, with a familiar nod, and seated herself at once in a chair near the door.

"Well, how do you like Michi*gan?*"

This question received the most polite answer which my conscience afforded; and I asked the lady in my turn, if she was one of my neighbors?

"Why, massy,[6] yes!" she replied; "don't you know me? I tho't everybody know'd me. Why, I'm the school ma'am, Simeon Jenkins's sister, Cleory Jenkins."

Thus introduced, I put all my civility in requisition to entertain my guest, but she seemed quite independent, finding amusement for herself and asking questions on every possible theme.

"You're doing your own work now, a'n't ye?"

This might not be denied; and I asked if she did not know of a girl whom I might be likely to get.

"Well, I don't know, I'm looking for a place where I can board and do chores myself. I have a good deal of time before school, and after I get back; and I didn't know but I might suit ye for a while."

I was pondering on this proffer, when the sallow damsel arose from her seat, took a short pipe from her bosom (not "Pan's reedy pipe," reader), filled it with tobacco, which she carried in her "work pocket," and, reseating herself, began to smoke with the greatest gusto, turning ever and anon to spit at the hearth.

Incredible again? alas, would it were not true! I have since known

---

[5]Prunella, a strong cloth used for academic gowns and upper parts of women's shoes.
[6]Mercy (?).

a girl of seventeen, who was attending a neighbor's sick infant, smoke the live-long day, and take snuff besides; and I can vouch for it, that a large proportion of the married women in the interior of Michigan use tobacco in some form, usually that of the odious pipe.

I took the earliest decent opportunity to decline the offered help, telling the school-ma'am plainly that an inmate who smoked would make the house uncomfortable to me.

"Why, law!" said she, laughing; "that's nothing but pride now: folks is often too proud to take comfort. For my part, I couldn't do without my pipe to please nobody."

Mr. Simeon Jenkins, the brother of this independent young lady, now made his appearance on some trifling errand; and his sister repeated to him what I had said.

Mr. Jenkins took his inch of cigar from his mouth and asked if I really disliked tobacco smoke, seeming to think it scarcely possible.

"Don't your old man smoke?" said he.

"No, indeed," said I, with more than my usual energy; "I should hope he never would."

"Well," said neighbor Jenkins, "I tell you what, I'm *boss* at home; and if my old woman was to stick up that fashion, I'd keep the house so blue she couldn't see to snuff the candle."

His sister laughed long and loud at this sally, which was uttered rather angrily, and with an air of most manful bravery; and Mr. Jenkins, picking up his end of cigar from the floor, walked off with an air evidently intended to be as expressive as the celebrated and oft-quoted nod of Lord Burleigh in *The Critic*.[7]

Miss Jenkins was still arguing on the subject of her pipe, when a gentleman approached whose dress and manner told me that he did not belong to our neighborhood. He was a red-faced, jolly-looking person, evidently "well to do in the world," and sufficiently consequential for any meridian. He seated himself quite unceremoniously—for who feels ceremony in a log house?—said he understood Mr. Clavers was absent—then hesitated; and, as Miss Jenkins afterwards observed, "hummed and hawed," and seemed as if he would fain say something, but scarce knew how.

At length Miss Cleora took the hint—a most necessary point of delicacy, where there is no withdrawing room. She gave her parting

---

[7]In Richard Brinsley Sheridan's *The Critic* (1779), Lord Burleigh says nothing, but nods with great expressiveness.

nod, and disappeared; and the old gentleman proceeded.

He had come to Montacute with the view of settling his son, "a wild chap," he said, a lawyer by profession, and not very fond of work of any sort; but as he himself had a good deal of land in the vicinity, he thought his son might find employment in attending to it, adding such professional business as might occur.

"But what I wished particularly to say, my dear madam," said he, "regards rather my son's wife than himself. She is a charming girl, and accustomed to much indulgence; and I have felt afraid that a removal to a place so new as this might be too trying to her. I knew you must be well able to judge of the difficulties to be encountered here, and took the liberty of calling on that account."

I was so much pleased with the idea of having a neighbor whose habits might in some respects accord with my own, that I fear I was scarcely impartial in the view which I gave Mr. Rivers, of the possibilities of Montacute. At least, I communicated only such as rises before my own mind, while watching perhaps a glorious sunset reflected in the glassy pond; my hyacinths in all their glory; the evening breeze beginning to sigh in the tree tops; the children just coming in after a fine frolic with D'Orsay on the grass; and Papa and Prince returning up the lane. At such times, I always conclude that Montacute is, after all, a dear little world; and I am probably quite as near the truth, as when,

> —on some cold rainy day,
> When the birds cannot show a dry feather;

when Arthur comes in with a pound of mud on each foot, D'Orsay at his heels, bringing in as much more; little Bell crying to go out to play; Charlie prodigiously fretful with his prospective tooth; and some gaunt marauder from "up north," or "out west," sits talking on "business," and covering my andirons with tobacco juice; I determine sagely that a life in the woods is worse than no life at all. One view is, I insist, as good as the other; but I told Mr. Rivers he must make due allowance for my desire to have his fair daughter-in-law for a neighbor, with which he departed; and I felt that my gloom had essentially lightened in consequence of his visit.

CHAPTER XVII

It was on one of our superlatively doleful ague days, when a cold drizzling rain had sent mildew into our unfortunate bones; and I lay in bed burning with fever, while my stronger half sat by the fire, taking his chill with his great-coat, hat, and boots on, that Mr. Rivers came to introduce his young daughter-in-law. I shall never forget the utterly disconsolate air which, in spite of the fair lady's politeness, would make itself visible in the pauses of our conversation. She *did* try not to cast a curious glance round the room. She fixed her eyes on the fire-place—but there were the clay-filled sticks, instead of a chimney-piece—the half consumed wooden *crane,* which had, more than once, let our dinner fall—the Rocky Mountain hearth, and the reflector baking biscuits for tea—so she thought it hardly polite to appear to dwell too long there. She turned towards the window: there were the shelves, with our remaining crockery, a grotesque assortment! and, just beneath, the unnameable iron and tin affairs that are reckoned among the indispensables, even of the half-civilized state. She tried the other side, but there was the ladder, the flour-barrel, and a host of other things—rather odd parlor furniture—and she cast her eyes on the floor, with its gaping cracks, wide enough to admit a massasauga[1] from below, and its inequalities, which might trip any but a sylph. The poor thing looked absolutely confounded, and I exerted all the energy my fever had left me to try to say something a little encouraging.

"Come tomorrow morning, Mrs. Rivers," said I, "and you shall see the aspect of things quite changed; and I shall be able to tell you a great deal in favor of this wild life."

She smiled faintly, and tried not to look miserable, but I saw plainly that she was sadly depressed, and I could not feel surprised that she should be so. Mr. Rivers spoke very kindly to her, and filled up all the pauses in our forced talk with such cheering observations as he could muster.

He had found lodgings, he said, in a farmhouse, not far from us, and his son's house would, ere long, be completed, when we should be quite near neighbors.

I saw tears swelling in the poor girl's eyes as she took leave, and I longed to be well for her sake. In this newly-formed world, the

[1] Rattlesnake.

earlier settler has a feeling of hostess-ship toward the newcomer. I speak only of women—men look upon each one, newly arrived, merely as an additional business-automaton—a somebody more with whom to try the race of enterprise, i. e., money-making.

The next day Mrs. Rivers came again, and this time her husband was with her. Then I saw at a glance why it was that life in the wilderness looked so peculiarly gloomy to her. Her husband's face showed but too plainly the marks of early excess; and there was at intervals, in spite of an evident effort to play the agreeable, an appearance of absence, of indifference, which spoke volumes of domestic history. He made innumerable inquiries touching the hunting and fishing facilities of the country around us, expressed himself enthusiastically fond of those sports, and said the country was a living death without them, regretting much that Mr. Clavers was not of the same mind.

Meanwhile I had begun to take quite an interest in his little wife. I found that she was as fond of novels and poetry as her husband was of field-sports. Some of her flights of sentiment went quite beyond my sobered-down views. But I saw we should get on admirably, and so we have done ever since. I did not mistake that pleasant smile and that soft sweet voice. They are even now as attractive as ever. And I had a neighbor.

Before the winter had quite set in, our little nest was finished, or as nearly finished as anything in Michigan; and Mr. and Mrs. Rivers took possession of their new dwelling, on the very same day that we smiled our adieux to the loggery.

Our new house was merely the beginning of a house, intended for the reception of a front-building, Yankee fashion, whenever the owner should be able to enlarge his borders. But the contrast with our sometime dwelling made even this humble cot seem absolutely sumptuous. The children could do nothing but admire the conveniences it afforded. Robinson Crusoe exulted not more warmly in his successive acquisitions[2] than did Alice in "a kitchen, a real kitchen! and a pantry to put the dishes!" while Arthur found much to praise in the wee bedroom which was allotted as his sanctum in the "hic, hæc, hoc" hours.[3] Mrs. Rivers, who was fresh from the "settlements," often curled her pretty lip at the deficiencies in her little mansion, but we had learned

[2]Crusoe, shipwrecked on a desert island, rejoiced as he improved his living conditions by finding and making things (Daniel Defoe, *Robinson Crusoe*, 1719).
[3]When he was studying Latin.

to prize anything which was even a shade above the wigwam, and dreamed not of two parlors or a piazza.

Other families removed to Montacute in the course of the winter. Our visiting list was considerably enlarged, and I used all my influence with Mrs. Rivers to persuade her that her true happiness lay in making friends of her neighbors. She was very shy, easily shocked by those sins against Chesterfield[4] which one encounters here at every turn, did not conceal her fatigue when a neighbor happened in after breakfast to make a three hours' call, forgot to ask those who came at one o'clock to take off their things and stay to tea, even though the knitting needles might peep out beneath the shawl. For these and similar omissions I lectured her continually, but with little effect. It was with the greatest difficulty I could persuade her to enter any house but ours, although I took especial care to be impartial in my own visiting habits, determined at all sacrifice to live down the impression that I felt *above* my neighbors. In fact, however we may justify certain exclusive habits in populous places, they are strikingly and confessedly ridiculous in the wilderness. What can be more absurd than a feeling of proud distinction, where a stray spark of fire, a sudden illness, or a day's contretemps, may throw you entirely upon the kindness of your humblest neighbor? If I treat Mrs. Timson with neglect today, can I with any face borrow her broom tomorrow? And what would become of me, if in revenge for my declining her invitation to tea this afternoon, she should decline coming to do my washing on Monday?

It was as a practical corollary to these my lectures, that I persuaded Mrs. Rivers to accept an invitation that we received for the wedding of a young girl, the sister of our cooper, Mr. Whitefield. I attired myself in white, considered here as the extreme of festal elegance, to do honor to the occasion; and called for Mrs. Rivers in the ox-cart at two o'clock.

I found her in her ordinary neat home-dress; and it required some argument on my part to induce her to exchange it for a gay chally[5] with appropriate ornaments.

"It really seemed ridiculous," she said, "to *dress* for such a place! and besides, my dear Mrs. Clavers, I am afraid we shall be suspected of a desire to outshine."

[4]The Earl of Chesterfield practiced and preached impeccable manners, as in his letters to his son (1774).
[5]Challis, a printed fabric.

I assured her we were in more danger of that other and far more dangerous suspicion of undervaluing our rustic neighbors.

"I s'pose they didn't think it worthwhile to put on their best gowns for country-folks!"

I assumed the part of Mentor on this and many similar occasions; considering myself by this time quite an old resident, and of right entitled to speak for the natives.

Mrs. Rivers was a little disposed to laugh at the ox-cart; but I soon convinced her that, with its cushion of straw overspread with a buffalo robe, it was far preferable to a more ambitious carriage.

"No letting down of steps, no ruining one's dress against a muddy wheel! no gay horses tipping one into the gutter!"

She was obliged to acknowledge the superiority of our vehicle, and we congratulated ourselves upon reclining *à la* Lalla Rookh and Lady Mary Wortley Montague.[6] Certainly a cart is next to a palanquin.

The pretty bride was in white cambric, worn over pink glazed muslin. The prodigiously stiff under-dress with its large cords (not more than three or four years behind the fashion) gave additional slenderness to her taper waist, bound straitly with a sky-blue zone. The fair hair was decorated, not covered, with a cap, the universal adjunct of full dress in the country, placed far behind the ears, and displayed the largest puffs,[7] set off by sundry gilt combs. The unfailing high-heeled prunelle shoe gave the finishing-touch, and the whole was scented, *à l'outrance,*[8] with essence of lemon.

After the ceremony, which occupied perhaps one minute, fully twice as long as is required by our State laws, tea was served, absolutely handed on a salver, and by the master of the house, a respectable farmer. Mountains of cake followed. I think either pile might have measured a foot in height, and each piece would have furnished a meal for a hungry schoolboy. Other things were equally abundant, and much pleasant talk followed the refreshments. I returned home highly delighted, and tried to persuade my companion to look on the rational side of the thing, which she scarcely seemed disposed to do, so *outré* did the whole appear to her. I, who had begun to claim for myself the dignified character of a cosmopolite, a philosophical observer of men and things,

[6]Both Lalla Rookh, a fictitious Indian princess (in Thomas Moore's *Lalla Rookh,* 1817), and Montagu, a real eighteenth-century Englishwoman, traveled in the East, reclining in palanquins.
[7]Of hair.
[8]Excessively.

consoled myself for this derogatory view of Montacute gentility by thinking, "All city people are so cockneyish!"

CHAPTER XLIII

Mr. Simeon Jenkins entered at an early stage of his career upon the arena of public life, having been employed by his honored mother to dispose of a basket full of hard-boiled eggs on election day, before he was eight years old. He often dwells with much unction upon this his debût, and declares that even at that dawning period he had cut his eye-teeth.

"There wasn't a feller there," Mr. Jenkins often says, "that could find out which side I was on, for all they tried hard enough. They thought I was soft, but I let 'em know I was as much baked as any on 'em. 'Be you a dimocrat?' says one. 'Buy some eggs and I'll tell ye,' says I; and by the time he'd bought his eggs, I could tell well enough which side *he* belonged to, and I'd hand him out a ticket according, for I had blue ones in one end o' my basket, and white ones in the other, and when night come, and I got off the stump to go home, I had eighteen shillin and four-pence in my pocket."

From this auspicious commencement may be dated Mr. Jenkins's glowing desire to serve the public. Each successive election-day saw him at his post. From eggs he advanced to pies, from pies to almanacs, whiskey, powder and shot, foot-balls, playing-cards, and at length, for ambition ever "did grow with what it fed on,"[1] he brought into the field a large turkey, which was tied to a post and stoned to death at twenty-five cents a throw. By this time the still youthful aspirant had become quite the man of the world; could smoke twenty-four segars[2] per diem, if anybody else would pay for them; play cards in old Hurler's shop from noon till daybreak, and rise winner; and all this with suitable trimmings of gin and hard words. But he never lost sight of the main chance. He had made up his mind to serve his country, and he was all this time convincing his fellow-citizens of the disinterested purity of his sentiments.

"Patriotism!" he would say, "patriotism is the thing! any man that's too proud to serve his country ain't fit to live. Some thinks so much

[1]Paraphrase of William Shakespeare, *Hamlet* I, ii, lines 144–45.
[2]Cigars.

o' themselves that if they can't have jist what they think they're fit for, they won't take nothin; but for my part, *I* call myself an American citizen; and any office that's in the gift o' the people will suit *me*. I'm up to anything. And as there ain't no other man about here—no suitable man, I mean—that's got a horse, why I'd be willing to be constable, if the people's a mind to, though it would be a dead loss to me in my business to be sure; but I could do anything for my country. Hurra for patriotism! them's my sentiments."

It can scarcely be doubted that Mr. Jenkins became a very popular citizen, or that he usually played a conspicuous part at the polls. Offices began to fall to his share, and though they were generally such as brought more honor than profit, office is office, and Mr. Jenkins did not grumble. Things were going on admirably.

> The spoils of office glitter in his eyes,
> He climbs, he pants, he grasps them—

or thought he was just going to grasp them, when, presto! he found himself in the minority; the wheel of fortune turned, and Mr. Jenkins and his party were left undermost. Here was a dilemma! His zeal in the public service was ardent as ever, but how could he get a chance to show it unless his party was in power? His resolution was soon taken. He called his friends together, mounted a stump which had fortunately been left standing not far from the door of his shop, and then and there gave "reasons for my ratting" in terms sublime enough for any meridian.

"My friends and feller-citizens," said this self-sacrificing patriot, "I find myself conglomerated in such a way, that my feelins suffers severely. I'm sitivated in a peculiar sitivation. O' one side, I see my dear friends, pussonal friends—friends, that's stuck to me like wax, through thick and thin—never shinnyin off and on, but up to the scratch, and no mistake. O' t' other side I behold my country, my bleedin country, the land that fetch'd me into this world o' trouble. Now, since things be as they be, and can't be no otherways as I see, I feel kind o' screwed into an auger-hole to know what to do. If I hunt over the history of the universal world from the creation of man to the present day, I see that men has always had difficulties; and that some has took one way to get shut of 'em, and some another. My candid and unrefragable opinion is, that rather than remain useless, buckled down to the shop, and indulging in selfishness, it is my solemn dooty to change my ticket. It is severe, my friends, but dooty is dooty. And now, if any man calls me a turn-coat," continued the orator, gently spitting in his hands, rubbing them together, and rolling his eyes round the assembly, "all I say is, let him say it so that I can hear him."

The last argument was irresistible, if even the others might have brooked discussion, for Mr. Jenkins stands six feet two in his stockings, when he wears any, and gesticulates with a pair of arms as long and muscular as Rob Roy's.[3] So, though the audience did not cheer him, they contented themselves with dropping off one by one, without calling in question the patriotism of the rising statesman.

The very next election saw Mr. Jenkins justice of the peace, and it was in this honorable capacity that I have made most of my acquaintance with him, though we began with threatenings of a storm. He called to take the acknowledgment of a deed, and I, anxious for my country's honor, for I too am something of a patriot in my own way, took the liberty of pointing out to his notice a trifling slip of the pen; videlicet, "Justas of Piece," which manner of writing those words I informed him had gone out of fashion.

He reddened, looked at me very sharp for a moment, and then said he thanked me: but subjoined,

"Book-learning is a good thing enough where there ain't too much of it. For my part, I've seen a good many that know'd books that didn't know much else. The proper cultivation and edication of the human intellect has been the comprehen*sive* study of the human understanding from the original creation of the universal world to the present day, and there has been a good many ways tried besides book-learning. Not but what that's very well in its place."

And the justice took his leave with somewhat of a swelling air. But we are excellent friends, notwithstanding this hard rub; and Mr. Jenkins favors me now and then with half an hour's conversation, when he has had leisure to read up for the occasion in an odd volume of the Cyclopedia, which holds an honored place in a corner of his shop. He ought in fairness to give me previous notice, that I might study the dictionary a little, for the hard words with which he arms himself for these "keen encounters" often push me to the very limits of my English.

I ought to add that Mr. Jenkins has long since left off gambling, drinking, and all other vices of that class, except smoking; in this

---

[3] A brawny outlaw in Walter Scott's *Rob Roy* (1817).

point he professes to be incorrigible. But as his wife, who is one of the nicest women in the world, and manages him admirably, pretends to like the smell of tobacco, and takes care never to look at him when he disfigures her well-scoured floor, I am not without hopes of his thorough reformation.

Margaret Fuller Ossoli

1810–1850

MARGARET FULLER, daughter of Timothy Fuller, a lawyer and politician, and Margaret Crane, a traditionally self-sacrificing woman, was born near Cambridge, Massachusetts, the second oldest of nine children. Recognizing Margaret's gifts, Timothy took charge of her upbringing. He gave her a rigorous "masculine" education, which made her a prodigy of learning, but also imposed such strain that she suffered from night terrors in childhood and headaches throughout her life. On her father's death in 1835, Margaret assumed responsibility for the family. She gave up an exciting trip to Europe in order to earn money for them and guide her younger brothers and sisters. She taught school, feeling increasingly frustrated because she lacked time for her own intellectual development.

She returned to Boston in 1839 and became part of the Transcendentalist circle led by Ralph Waldo Emerson, a close friend. Fuller found a liberating acceptance in this movement, which not only sanctioned but encouraged self-development in accordance with individual vision. For five years she conducted a series of "Conversations," in which intellectual women gathered once a week to discuss fundamental questions concerning art, philosophy, and woman's role. These seminars aimed to help women think clearly, deeply, and systematically; but they must also have functioned like modern consciousness-raising groups. Fuller's conversation was superior to her writing. Contemporaries found her force of mind and personality overwhelming and testified that she led them to insight and purpose; she was able to inspire both female and male friends to be their best selves.

From 1840 to 1842, Fuller edited *The Dial*, the Transcendentalist journal, in which she published the essay that she later developed into *Woman in the Nineteenth Century* (1845). Horace Greeley engaged her as a reviewer for the *New York Herald Tribune* and sent her to Europe as a foreign correspondent. She became deeply involved in the Italian struggle for independence. She accepted Giovanni Angelo, marchese d'Ossoli, a younger and less intellectual man, as a lover and bore their son; it is uncertain when or if they married. The family sailed for America in 1850, but were shipwrecked just off the coast.

Woman in the Nineteenth Century is based on the Transcendentalist belief that individuals should develop their powers to the fullest extent in accordance with the ideal they have independently formed. Only Fuller made explicit that women as well as men must strive for this self-development and self-reliance.

BIBLIOGRAPHY

Chevigny, Bell Gale. *The Woman and the Myth: Margaret Fuller's Life and Writings*. Old Westbury, N.Y.: The Feminist Press, 1976.

Ossoli, Margaret Fuller. *Woman in the Nineteenth Century, and Kindred Papers*. Introduction by Horace Greeley (1855). New York: Source Book Press, 1970.

from Woman in the Nineteenth Century

. . . Though the national independence be blurred by the servility of individuals; though freedom and equality have been proclaimed only to leave room for a monstrous display of slave-dealing and slave-keeping; though the free American so often feels himself free, like the Roman, only to pamper his appetites and his indolence through the misery of his fellow-beings; still it is not in vain that the verbal statement has been made, "All men are born free and equal." There it stands, a golden certainty wherewith to encourage the good, to shame the bad. The New World may be called clearly to perceive that it incurs the utmost penalty if it reject or oppress the sorrowful brother. And, if men are deaf, the angels hear. But men cannot be deaf. It is inevitable that an external freedom, an independence of the encroachments of other men, such as has been achieved for the nation, should be so also for every member of it. That which has once been clearly conceived in the intelligence cannot fail, sooner or later, to be acted out. . . .

We have waited here long in the dust; we are tired and hungry; but the triumphal procession must appear at last.

Of all its banners, none has been more steadily upheld, and under none have more valor and willingness for real sacrifices been shown, than that of the champions of the enslaved African. And this band it is, which, partly from a natural following out of principles, partly because many women have been prominent in that cause, makes, just now, the warmest appeal in behalf of Woman.

Though there has been a growing liberality on this subject, yet society at large is not so prepared for the demands of this party, but that its members are, and will be for some time, coldly regarded as the Jacobins of their day.

"Is it not enough," cries the irritated trader, "that you have done all you could to break up the national union, and thus destroy the prosperity of our country, but now you must be trying to break up family union, to take my wife away from the cradle and the kitchen-hearth to vote at polls, and preach from a pulpit? Of course, if she does such things, she cannot attend to those of her own sphere. She is happy enough as she is. She has more leisure than I have,—every means of improvements, every indulgence."

"Have you asked her whether she was satisfied with these *indulgences?*"

"No, but I know she is. She is too amiable to desire what would make me unhappy, and too judicious to wish to step beyond the sphere of her sex. I will never consent to have our peace disturbed by any such discussions."

" 'Consent—you?' it is not consent from you that is in question—it is assent from your wife."

"Am not I the head of my house?"

"You are not the head of your wife. God has given her a mind of her own."

"I am the head, and she the heart."

"God grant you play true to one another, then! I suppose I am to be grateful that you did not say she was only the hand. If the head represses no natural pulse of the heart, there can be no question as to your giving your consent. Both will be of one accord, and there needs but to present any question to get a full and true answer. There is no need of precaution, of indulgence, nor consent. But our doubt is whether the heart *does* consent with the head, or only obeys its decrees with a passiveness that precludes the exercise of its natural powers, or a repugnance that turns sweet qualities to bitter, or a doubt that lays waste the fair occasions of life. It is to ascertain the truth that we propose some liberating measures."

Thus vaguely are these questions proposed and discussed at present. But their being proposed at all implies much thought, and suggests more. Many women are considering within themselves what they need that they have not, and what they can have if they find they need it. Many men are considering whether women are capable of being and having more than they are and have, *and* whether, if so, it will be best to consent to improvement in their condition.

This morning, I open the Boston *Daily Mail,* and find in its "poet's corner" a translation of Schiller's "Dignity of Woman."[1] In the advertisement of a book on America, I see in the table of contents this sequence, "Republican Institutions. American Slavery. American Ladies."

I open the *Deutsche Schnellpost,* published in New York, and find at the head of a column, *Juden und Frauen-emancipation in Ungarn*—"Emancipation of Jews and Women in Hungary."

The past year has seen action in the Rhode Island legislature, to secure married women rights over their own property, when men showed that a very little examination of the subject could teach them much; an article in the *Democratic Review* on the same subject more largely considered, written by a woman, impelled, it is said, by glaring wrong to a distinguished friend, having shown the defects in the existing laws, and the state of opinion from which they spring; and an answer from the revered old man, J. Q. Adams,[2] in some respects the Phocion of his time, to an address made him by some ladies. To this last I shall again advert in another place.

These symptoms of the times have come under my view quite ac-

---

[1]Friedrich Schiller (1759–1805), German poet and dramatist.
[2]John Quincy Adams (1767–1848), former president and son of Abigail Adams. Following phrase: Phocion was an ancient Greek statesman noted for integrity.

cidentally: one who seeks, may, each month or week, collect more.

The numerous party, whose opinions are already labeled and adjusted too much to their mind to admit of any new light, strive, by lectures on some model-woman of bride-like beauty and gentleness, by writing and lending little treatises, intended to mark out with precision the limits of Woman's sphere, and Woman's mission, to prevent other than the rightful shepherd from climbing the wall, or the flock from using any chance to go astray.

Without enrolling ourselves at once on either side, let us look upon the subject from the best point of view which today offers; no better, it is to be feared, than a high house-top. A high hill-top, or at least a cathedral-spire, would be desirable.

It may well be an Anti-Slavery party that pleads for Woman, if we consider merely that she does not hold property on equal terms with men; so that, if a husband dies without making a will, the wife, instead of taking at once his place as head of the family, inherits only a part of his fortune, often brought him by herself, as if she were a child, or ward only, not an equal partner.

We will not speak of the innumerable instances in which profligate and idle men live upon the earnings of industrious wives; or if the wives leave them, and take with them the children, to perform the double duty of mother and father, follow from place to place, and threaten to rob them of the children, if deprived of the rights of a husband, as they call them, planting themselves in their poor lodgings, frightening them into paying tribute by taking from them the children, running into debt at the expense of these otherwise so overtasked helots. Such instances count up by scores within my own memory. I have seen the husband who had stained himself by a long course of low vice, till his wife was wearied from her heroic forgiveness, by finding that his treachery made it useless, and that if she would provide bread for herself and her children, she must be separate from his ill fame—I have known this man come to install himself in the chamber of a woman who loathed him, and say she should never take food without his company. I have known these men steal their children, whom they knew they had no means to maintain, take them into dissolute company, expose them to bodily danger, to frighten the poor woman, to whom, it seems, the fact that she alone had borne the pangs of their birth, and nourished their infancy, does not give an equal right to them. I do believe that this mode of kidnapping—and it is frequent enough in all classes of society—will be by the next age viewed as it is by Heaven now, and that the man who avails himself of the shelter of men's laws to steal from a mother her own children, or arrogate any superior right in them, save that of superior virtue, will bear the stigma he deserves, in common with him who steals grown men from their mother-land, their hopes, and their homes.

I said, we will not speak of this now; yet I *have* spoken, for the subject makes me feel too much. I could give instances that would startle the most vulgar and callous; but I will not, for the public opinion of their own sex is already against such men, and where cases of extreme tyranny are made known, there is private action in the wife's favor. But she ought not to need this, nor, I think, can she long. Men must soon see that as, on their own ground, Woman is the weaker party, she ought to have legal protection, which would make such oppression impossible. But I would not deal with "atrocious instances," except in the way of illustration, neither demand from men a partial redress in some one matter, but go to the root of the whole. If principles could be established, particulars would adjust themselves aright. Ascertain the true destiny of Woman; give her legitimate hopes, and a standard within herself; marriage and all other relations would by degrees be harmonized with these.

But to return to the historical progress of this matter. Knowing that there exists in the minds of men a tone of feeling toward women as toward slaves, such as is expressed in the common phrase, "Tell that to women and children"; that the infinite soul can only work through them in already ascertained limits; that the gift of reason, Man's highest prerogative, is allotted to them in much lower degree; that they must be kept from mischief and melancholy by being constantly engaged in active labor, which is to be furnished and directed by those better able to think, &c., &c.,—we need not multiply instances, for who can review the experience of last week without recalling words which imply, whether in jest or earnest, these views, or views like these,—knowing this, can we wonder that many reformers think that measures are not likely to be taken in behalf of women, unless their wishes could be publicly represented by women?

"That can never be necessary," cry the other side. "All men are privately influenced by women; each has his wife, sister, or female friends, and is too much biased by these relations to fail of representing their interests; and, if this is not enough, let them propose and enforce their wishes with the pen. The beauty of home would be destroyed, the delicacy of the sex be violated, the dignity of halls of legislation degraded, by an attempt to introduce them there. Such duties are inconsistent with those of a mother"; and then we have ludicrous pictures of ladies in hysterics at the polls, and senate-chambers filled with cradles.

But if, in reply, we admit as truth that Woman seems destined by nature rather for the inner circle, we must add that the arrangements of civilized life have not been, as yet, such as to secure it to her. Her circle, if the duller, is not the quieter. If kept from "excitement," she is not from drudgery. Not only the Indian squaw carries the burdens of the camp, but the favorites of Louis XIV accompany him in his journeys, and the washerwoman stands at her tub, and carries home her work at all seasons, and in all states of health. Those who think the physical circumstances of Woman would make a part in the affairs of national government unsuitable, are by no means those who think it impossible for negresses to endure field-work, even during pregnancy, or for seamstresses to go through their killing labors.[3]

As to the use of the pen, there was quite as much opposition to Woman's possessing herself of that help to free agency as there is now to her seizing on the rostrum or the desk;[4] and she is likely to draw, from a permission to plead her cause that way, opposite inferences to what might be wished by those who now grant it.

As to the possibility of her filling with grace and dignity any such position, we should think those who had seen the great actresses, and heard the Quaker preachers of modern times, would not doubt that Woman can express publicly the fullness of thought and creation, without losing any of the peculiar beauty of her sex. What can pollute and tarnish is to act thus from any motive except that something needs to be said or done. Woman could take part in the processions, the songs, the dances of old religion; no one fancied her delicacy was impaired by appearing in public for such a cause.

As to her home, she is not likely to leave it more than she now does for balls, theaters, meetings for promoting missions, revival

[3]Louis XIV insisted that his mistresses accompany him on his continual journeys through France, despite the hardships of seventeenth-century travel and even when they were in advanced pregnancy. Fuller tellingly classes these apparently privileged aristocrats with working women who were more obviously victimized. Seamstresses' labors were "killing" because they had to work almost continuously to earn starvation wages.

[4]The speaker's platform or the pulpit.

meetings, and others to which she flies, in hope of an animation for her existence commensurate with what she sees enjoyed by men. Governors of ladies'-fairs are no less engrossed by such a charge, than the governor of a state by his; presidents of Washingtonian societies no less away from home than presidents of conventions. If men look straitly to it, they will find that, unless their lives are domestic, those of the women will not be. A house is no home unless it contain food and fire for the mind as well as for the body. The female Greek, of our day, is as much in the street as the male to cry, "What news?"[5] We doubt not it was the same in Athens of old. The women, shut out from the market-place, made up for it at the religious festivals. For human beings are not so constituted that they can live without expansion. If they do not get it in one way, they must in another, or perish.

As to men's representing women fairly at present, while we hear from men who owe to their wives not only all that is comfortable or graceful, but all that is wise, in the arrangement of their lives, the frequent remark, "You cannot reason with a woman,"—when from those of delicacy, nobleness, and poetic culture, falls the contemptuous phrase "women and children," and that in no light sally of the hour, but in works intended to give a permanent statement of the best experiences,[6]—when not one man, in the million, shall I say? no, not in the hundred million, can rise above the belief that Woman was made *for Man*.—when such traits as these are daily forced upon the attention, can we feel that Man will always do justice to the interests of Woman? Can we think that he takes a sufficiently discerning and religious view of her office and destiny *ever* to do her justice, except when prompted by sentiment,—accidentally or transiently, that is, for the sentiment will vary according to the relations in which he is placed? The lover, the poet, the artist, are likely to view her nobly. The father and the philosopher have some chance of liberality; the man of the world, the legislator for expediency, none.

Under these circumstances, without attaching importance, in

[5]Athenians of New Testament times did "nothing else, but either to tell, or to hear some new thing" (Acts 17:21). In ancient Athens, women hardly went out except in connection with religious festivals.

[6]Cf. Ralph Waldo Emerson, "The American Scholar": "Free should the scholar be,—free and brave. . . . It is a shame to him if his tranquillity, . . . arise from the presumption that like children and women, his is a protected class."

themselves, to the changes demanded by the champions of Woman, we hail them as signs of the times. We would have every arbitrary barrier thrown down. We would have every path laid open to Woman as freely as to Man. Were this done, and a slight temporary fermentation allowed to subside, we should see crystallizations more pure and of more various beauty. We believe the divine energy would pervade nature to a degree unknown in the history of former ages, and that no discordant collision, but a ravishing harmony of the spheres, would ensue.

Yet, then and only then will mankind be ripe for this, when inward and outward freedom for Woman as much as for Man shall be acknowledged as a *right,* not yielded as a concession. As the friend of the negro assumes that one man cannot by right hold another in bondage, so should the friend of Woman assume that Man cannot by right lay even well-meant restrictions on Woman. If the negro be a soul, if the woman be a soul, appareled in flesh, to one Master only are they accountable. There is but one law for souls, and, if there is to be an interpreter of it, he must come not as man, or son of man, but as son of God.

Were thought and feeling once so far elevated that Man should esteem himself the brother and friend, but nowise the lord and tutor, of Woman,—were he really bound with her in equal worship,—arrangements as to function and employment would be of no consequence. What Woman needs is not as a woman to act or rule, but as a nature to grow, as an intellect to discern, as a soul to live freely and unimpeded, to unfold such powers as were given her when we left our common home. If fewer talents were given her, yet if allowed the free and full employment of these, so that she may render back to the giver his own with usury, she will not complain; nay, I dare to say she will bless and rejoice in her earthly birth-place, her earthly lot. Let us consider what obstructions impede this good era, and what signs give reason to hope that it draws near.

I was talking on this subject with Miranda, a woman, who, if any in the world could, might speak without heat and bitterness of the position of her sex.[7] Her father was a man who cherished no sentimental reverence for Woman, but a firm belief in the equality of the sexes. She was his eldest child, and came to him at an age when he needed a companion. From the time she could speak and go alone,

[7]Miranda's education is an idealized version of Fuller's own.

he addressed her not as a plaything, but as a living mind. Among the few verses he ever wrote was a copy addressed to this child, when the first locks were cut from her head; and the reverence expressed on this occasion for that cherished head, he never belied. It was to him the temple of immortal intellect. He respected his child, however, too much to be an indulgent parent. He called on her for clear judgment, for courage, for honor and fidelity; in short, for such virtues as he knew. In so far as he possessed the keys to the wonders of this universe, he allowed free use of them to her, and, by the incentive of a high expectation, he forbade, so far as possible, that she should let the privilege lie idle.

Thus this child was early led to feel herself a child of the spirit. She took her place easily, not only in the world of organized being, but in the world of mind. A dignified sense of self-dependence was given as all her portion, and she found it a sure anchor. Herself securely anchored, her relations with others were established with equal security. She was fortunate in a total absence of those charms which might have drawn to her bewildering flatteries, and in a strong electric nature, which repelled those who did not belong to her, and attracted those who did. With men and women her relations were noble,—affectionate without passion, intellectual without coldness. The world was free to her, and she lived freely in it. Outward adversity came, and inward conflict; but that faith and self-respect had early been awakened which must always lead, at last, to an outward serenity and an inward peace.

Of Miranda I had always thought as an example, that the restraints upon the sex were insuperable only to those who think them so, or who noisily strive to break them. She had taken a course of her own, and no man stood in her way. Many of her acts had been unusual, but excited no uproar. Few helped, but none checked her; and the many men who knew her mind and her life, showed to her confidence as to a brother, gentleness as to a sister. And not only refined, but very coarse men approved and aided one in whom they saw resolution and clearness of design. Her mind was often the leading one, always effective.

When I talked with her upon these matters, and had said very much what I have written, she smilingly replied: "And yet we must admit that I have been fortunate, and this should not be. My good father's early trust gave the first bias, and the rest followed, of course. It is true that I have had less outward aid, in after years, than most women; but that is of little consequence. Religion was early awakened in my soul,—a sense that what the soul is capable to ask it must attain, and that, though I might be aided and instructed by others, I must depend on myself as the only constant friend. This self-dependence, which was honored in me, is deprecated as a fault in most women. They are taught to learn their rule from without, not to unfold it from within.

"This is the fault of Man, who is still vain, and wishes to be more important to Woman than, by right, he should be."

"Men have not shown this disposition toward you," I said.

"No; because the position I early was enabled to take was one of self-reliance. And were all women as sure of their wants as I was, the result would be the same. But they are so overloaded with precepts by guardians, who think that nothing is so much to be dreaded for a woman as originality of thought or character, that their minds are impeded by doubts till they lose their chance of fair, free proportions. The difficulty is to get them to the point from which they shall naturally develop self-respect, and learn self-help.

"Once I thought that men would help to forward this state of things more than I do now. I saw so many of them wretched in the connections they had formed in weakness and vanity. They seemed so glad to esteem women whenever they could.

" 'The soft arms of affection,' said one of the most discerning spirits, 'will not suffice for me, unless on them I see the steel bracelets of strength.'

"But early I perceived that men never, in any extreme of despair, wished to be women. On the contrary, they were ever ready to taunt one another, at any sign of weakness, with,

'Art thou not like the women, who,'—

The passage ends various ways, according to the occasion and rhetoric of the speaker. When they admired any woman, they were inclined to speak of her as 'above her sex.' Silently I observed this, and feared it argued a rooted scepticism, which for ages had been fastening on the heart, and which only an age of miracles could eradicate. Ever I have been treated with great sincerity; and I look upon it as a signal instance of this, that an intimate friend of the other sex said, in a fervent moment, that I 'deserved in some star to be a man.' He was much surprised when I disclosed my view of my position and hopes, when I declared my faith that the feminine side, the side of love, of beauty, of holiness, was now to have its full chance, and that, if either were better, it was better now to be a woman; for even the slightest achievement of good was furthering an especial work of our time. He smiled incredulously. 'She makes the best she can of it,' thought he. 'Let Jews believe the pride of Jewry, but I am of the better sort, and know better.'

"Another used as highest praise, in speaking of a character in literature, the words 'a manly woman.'

"So in the noble passage of Ben Jonson:[8]

> 'I meant the day-star should not brighter ride,
>   Nor shed like influence from its lucent seat;
> I meant she should be courteous, facile, sweet,
>   Free from that solemn vice of greatness, pride;
> I meant each softest virtue there should meet,
>   Fit in that softer bosom to abide,
> Only a learned and a *manly* soul
>   I purposed her, that should with even powers
> The rock, the spindle, and the shears control
> Of destiny, and spin her own free hours.' "

"Methinks," said I, "you are too fastidious in objecting to this. Jonson, in using the word 'manly,' only meant to heighten the picture of this, the true, the intelligent fate, with one of the deeper colors."

"And yet," said she, "so invariable is the use of this word where a heroic quality is to be described, and I feel so sure that persistence and courage are the most womanly no less than the most manly qualities, that I would exchange these words for others of a larger sense, at the risk of marring the fine tissue of the verse. Read, 'A heavenward and instructed soul,' and I should be satisfied. Let it not be said, wherever there is energy or creative genius, 'She has a masculine mind.' "

This by no means argues a willing want of generosity toward Woman. Man is as generous towards her as he knows how to be.

Wherever she has herself arisen in national or private history, and

[8]Ben Jonson (1572–1637), English poet.

nobly shone forth in any form of excellence, men have received her, not only willingly, but with triumph. Their encomiums, indeed, are always, in some sense, mortifying; they show too much surprise. "Can this be you?" he cries to the transfigured Cinderella; "well, I should never have thought it, but I am very glad. We will tell every one that you have *'surpassed your sex.'* "

In everyday life, the feelings of the many are stained with vanity. Each wishes to be lord in a little world, to be superior at least over one; and he does not feel strong enough to retain a life-long ascendency over a strong nature. Only a Theseus could conquer before he wed the Amazonian queen. Hercules wished rather to rest with Dejanira, and received the poisoned robe as a fit guerdon.[9] The tale should be interpreted to all those who seek repose with the weak.

But not only is Man vain and fond of power, but the same want of development, which thus affects him morally, prevents his intellectually discerning the destiny of Woman. The boy wants no woman, but only a girl to play ball with him, and mark his pocket handkerchief.

Thus, in Schiller's "Dignity of Woman," beautiful as the poem is, there is no "grave and perfect man," but only a great boy to be softened and restrained by the influence of girls. Poets—the elder brothers of their race—have usually seen further; but what can you expect of everyday men, if Schiller was not more prophetic as to what women must be? Even with Richter,[10] one foremost thought about a wife was that she would "cook him something good." But as this is a delicate subject, and we are in constant danger of being accused of slighting what are called "the functions," let me say, in behalf of Miranda and myself, that we have high respect for those who "cook something good," who create and preserve fair order in houses, and prepare therein the shining raiment for worthy inmates, worthy guests. Only these "functions" must not be a drudgery, or enforced necessity, but a part of life. Let Ulysses drive the beeves home, while Penelope there piles up the fragrant loaves; they are

[9]Theseus, a legendary king of Athens, defeated and married Hippolyta, queen of the Amazons. Deianira, wife of the hero Hercules, unintentionally poisoned him because she foolishly took the advice of his enemy.

[10]Johann Paul Friedrich Richter ("Jean Paul," 1763–1825), idealistic and sentimental German novelist.

both well employed if these be done in thought and love, willingly.[11] But Penelope is no more meant for a baker or weaver solely, than Ulysses for a cattle-herd.

The sexes should not only correspond to and appreciate, but prophesy to one another. In individual instances this happens. Two persons love in one another the future good which they aid one another to unfold. This is imperfectly or rarely done in the general life. Man has gone but little way; now he is waiting to see whether Woman can keep step with him; but, instead of calling out, like a good brother, "You can do it, if you only think so," or impersonally, "Any one can do what he tries to do"; he often discourages with school-boy brag: "Girls can't do that; girls can't play ball." But let any one defy their taunts, break through and be brave and secure, they rend the air with shouts. . . .

It is not the transient breath of poetic incense that women want; each can receive that from a lover. It is not life-long sway; it needs but to become a coquette, a shrew, or a good cook, to be sure of that. It is not money, nor notoriety, nor the badges of authority which men have appropriated to themselves. If demands, made in their behalf, lay stress on any of these particulars, those who make them have not searched deeply into the need. The want is for that which at once includes these and precludes them; which would not be forbidden power, lest there be temptation to steal and misuse it; which would not have the mind perverted by flattery from a worthiness of esteem; it is for that which is the birthright of every being capable of receiving it,—the freedom, the religious, the intelligent freedom of the universe to use its means, to learn its secret, as far as Nature has enabled them, with God alone for their guide and their judge. . . .

Centuries have passed since, but civilized Europe is still in a transition state about marriage; not only in practice but in thought. It is idle to speak with contempt of the nations where polygamy is an institution, or seraglios a custom, while practices far more debasing haunt, well-nigh fill, every city and every town, and so far as union of one with one is believed to be the only pure form of marriage, a great majority of societies and individuals are still doubtful whether the earthly bond must be a meeting of souls, or only supposes a

---

[11]In Homer's *Odyssey,* even aristocrats like King Ulysses and his wife, Penelope, performed manual labor.

contract of convenience and utility. Were Woman established in the rights of an immortal being, this could not be. She would not, in some countries, be given away by her father, with scarcely more respect for her feelings than is shown by the Indian chief, who sells his daughter for a horse, and beats her if she runs away from her new home. Nor, in societies where her choice is left free, would she be perverted, by the current of opinion that seizes her, into the belief that she must marry, if it be only to find a protector, and a home of her own. Neither would Man, if he thought the connection of permanent importance, form it so lightly. He would not deem it a trifle, that he was to enter into the closest relations with another soul, which, if not eternal in themselves, must eternally affect his growth. Neither, did he believe Woman capable of friendship, would he, by rash haste, lose the chance of finding a friend in the person who might, probably, live half a century by his side. Did love, to his mind, stretch forth into infinity, he would not miss his chance of its revelations, that he might the sooner rest from his weariness by a bright fireside, and secure a sweet and graceful attendant "devoted to him alone." Were he a step higher, he would not carelessly enter into a relation where he might not be able to do the duty of a friend, as well as a protector from external ill, to the other party, and have a being in his power pining for sympathy, intelligence and aid, that he could not give.

What deep communion, what real intercourse is implied in sharing the joys and cares of parentage, when any degree of equality is admitted between the parties! It is true that, in a majority of instances, the man looks upon his wife as an adopted child, and places her to the other children in the relation of nurse or governess, rather than that of parent. Her influence with them is sure; but she misses the education which should enlighten that influence, by being thus treated. It is the order of nature that children should complete the education, moral and mental, of parents, by making them think what is needed for the best culture of human beings, and conquer all faults and impulses that interfere with their giving this to these dear objects, who represent the world to them. Father and mother should assist one another to learn what is required for this sublime priesthood of Nature. But, for this, a religious recognition of equality is required.

Where this thought of equality begins to diffuse itself, it is shown in four ways.

First;—The household partnership. In our country, the woman looks for a "smart but kind" husband; the man for a "capable, sweet-tempered" wife. The man furnishes the house; the woman regulates it. Their relation is one of mutual esteem, mutual dependence. Their talk is of business; their affection shows itself by practical kindness. They know that life goes more smoothly and cheerfully to each for the other's aid; they are grateful and content. The wife praises her husband as a "good provider"; the husband, in return, compliments her as a "capital housekeeper." This relation is good so far as it goes.

Next comes a closer tie, which takes the form either of mutual idolatry or of intellectual companionship. The first, we suppose, is to no one a pleasing subject of contemplation. The parties weaken and narrow one another; they lock the gate against all the glories of the universe, that they may live in a cell together. To themselves they seem the only wise; to all others, steeped in infatuation; the gods smile as they look forward to the crisis of cure; to men, the woman seems an unlovely siren; to women, the man an effeminate boy.

The other form of intellectual companionship has become more and more frequent. Men engaged in public life, literary men, and artists have often found in their wives companions and confidants in thought no less than in feeling. And, as the intellectual development of Woman has spread wider and risen higher, they have, not unfrequently, shared the same employment; as in the case of Roland and his wife, who were friends in the household and in the nation's councils, read, regulated home affairs, or prepared public documents together, indifferently.[12] It is very pleasant, in letters begun by Roland and finished by his wife, to see the harmony of mind, and the difference of nature; one thought, but various ways of treating it.

This is one of the best instances of a marriage of friendship. It was only friendship, whose basis was esteem; probably neither party knew love, except by name. Roland was a good man, worthy to esteem, and be esteemed; his wife as deserving of admiration as able to do without it.

Madame Roland is the fairest specimen we yet have of her class;

---

[12]Jeanne Roland de la Platière worked closely with her husband, a moderate political leader during the French Revolution; both were distinguished for idealistic patriotism. When she was guillotined, she exclaimed, "Oh liberty, what crimes are committed in thy name!"

as clear to discern her aim, as valiant to pursue it, as Spenser's Britomart;[13] austerely set apart from all that did not belong to her, whether as Woman or as mind. She is an antetype of a class to which the coming time will afford a field—the Spartan matron, brought by the culture of the age of books to intellectual consciousness and expansion. Self-sufficingness, strength, and clearsightedness were, in her, combined with a power of deep and calm affection. She, too, would have given a son or husband the device for his shield, "Return with it or upon it";[14] and this, not because she loved little, but much. The page of her life is one of unsullied dignity. Her appeal to posterity is one against the injustice of those who committed such crimes in the name of Liberty. She makes it in behalf of herself and her husband. I would put beside it, on the shelf, a little volume, containing a similar appeal from the verdict of contemporaries to that of mankind, made by Godwin in behalf of his wife, the celebrated, the by most men detested, Mary Wollstonecraft.[15] In his view, it was an appeal from the injustice of those who did such wrong in the name of virtue. Were this little book interesting for no other cause, it would be so for the generous affection evinced under the peculiar circumstances. This man had courage to love and honor this woman in the face of the world's sentence, and of all that was repulsive in her own past history. He believed he saw of what soul she was, and that the impulses she had struggled to act out were noble, though the opinions to which they had led might not be thoroughly weighed. He loved her, and he defended her for the meaning and tendency of her inner life. It was a good fact.

Mary Wollstonecraft, like Madame Dudevant (commonly known as George Sand)[16] in our day, was a woman whose existence better proved the need of some new interpretation of Woman's Rights than anything she wrote. Such beings as these, rich in genius, of most tender sympathies, capable of high virtue and a chastened harmony,

[13]A woman warrior in Edmund Spenser's *Faerie Queene* (1589–1596).

[14]Spartan matrons, proverbial for their patriotism, were said to have told their sons going into battle to return victorious (with their shields) or dead (carried on them).

[15]Mary Wollstonecraft, author of *A Vindication of the Rights of Woman* (1792), was virtuous and idealistic, but violated contemporary sexual norms. In the memoirs that he published after her death, her husband, William Godwin, justified her conduct; but it shocked contemporary readers.

[16]Aurore Dudevant (1804–1876), who published novels as George Sand, shocked her contemporaries by wearing men's dress and having many affairs.

ought not to find themselves, by birth, in a place so narrow, that, in breaking bonds, they become outlaws. Were there as much room in the world for such, as in Spenser's poem for Britomart, they would not run their heads so wildly against the walls, but prize their shelter rather. They find their way, at last, to light and air, but the world will not take off the brand it has set upon them. The champion of the Rights of Woman found, in Godwin, one who would plead that cause like a brother. He who delineated with such purity of traits the form of Woman in the Marguerite, of whom the weak St. Leon could never learn to be worthy,[17]—a pearl indeed whose price was above rubies,—was not false in life to the faith by which he had hallowed his romance. He acted, as he wrote, like a brother. This form of appeal rarely fails to touch the basest man:—"Are you acting toward other women in the way you would have men act towards your sister?" George Sand smokes, wears male attire, wishes to be addressed as "Mon frère"—perhaps, if she found those who were as brothers indeed, she would not care whether she were brother or sister. We rejoice to see that she, who expresses such a painful contempt for men in most of her works, as shows she must have known great wrong from them, depicts, in *La Roche Mauprat,* a man raised by the workings of love from the depths of savage sensualism to a moral and intellectual life. It was love for a pure object, for a steadfast woman, one of those who, the Italian said, could make the "stair to heaven."

This author, beginning like the many in assault upon bad institutions, and external ills, yet deepening the experience through comparative freedom, sees at last that the only efficient remedy must come from individual character. These bad institutions, indeed, it may always be replied, prevent individuals from forming good character, therefore we must remove them. Agreed; yet keep steadily the higher aim in view. Could you clear away all the bad forms of society, it is vain, unless the individual begins to be ready for better. There must be a parallel movement in these two branches of life. And all the rules left by Moses availed less to further the best life than the living example of one Messiah.

Still the mind of the age struggles confusedly with these problems, better discerning as yet the ill it can no longer bear, than the good by which it may supersede it. But women like Sand will speak now

[17]Marguerite is the noble heroine of Godwin's novel *St. Leon* (1799).

and cannot be silenced; their characters and their eloquence alike foretell an era when such as they shall easier learn to lead true lives. But though such forebode, not such shall be parents of it. Those who would reform the world must show that they do not speak in the heat of wild impulse; their lives must be unstained by passionate error; they must be severe lawgivers to themselves. They must be religious students of the divine purpose with regard to man, if they would not confound the fancies of a day with the requisitions of eternal good. Their liberty must be the liberty of law and knowledge. But as to the transgressions against custom which have caused such outcry against those of noble intention, it may be observed that the resolve of Eloisa to be only the mistress of Abelard, was that of one who saw in practice around her the contract of marriage made the seal of degradation.[18] Shelley feared not to be fettered, unless so to be was to be false. Wherever abuses are seen, the timid will suffer; the bold will protest. But society has a right to outlaw them till she has revised her law; and this she must be taught to do, by one who speaks with authority, not in anger or haste.

• • •

The fourth and highest grade of marriage union is the religious, which may be expressed as pilgrimage toward a common shrine. This includes the others: home sympathies and household wisdom, for these pilgrims must know how to assist each other along the dusty way; intellectual communion, for how sad it would be on such a journey to have a companion to whom you could not communicate your thoughts and aspirations as they sprang to life; who would have no feeling for the prospects that open, more and more glorious as we advance; who would never see the flowers that may be gathered by the most industrious traveler! It must include all these.

• • •

The influence has been such, that the aim certainly is, now, in

[18]Héloise (d. 1164) loved and was pregnant by Peter Abelard, but refused his offer of marriage—actually, to avoid interfering with his career in the Church rather than to protest the degraded state of medieval marriage. Following sentence: The Romantic poet Percy Bysshe Shelley disapproved of conventional marriage.

arranging school instruction for girls, to give them as fair a field as boys. As yet, indeed, these arrangements are made with little judgment or reflection; just as the tutors of Lady Jane Grey,[19] and other distinguished women of her time, taught them Latin and Greek, because they knew nothing else themselves, so now the improvement in the education of girls is to be made by giving them young men as teachers, who only teach what has been taught themselves at college, while methods and topics need revision for these new subjects, which could better be made by those who had experienced the same wants. Women are, often, at the head of these institutions; but they have, as yet, seldom been thinking women, capable of organizing a new whole for the wants of the time, and choosing persons to officiate in the departments. And when some portion of instruction of a good sort is got from the school, the far greater proportion which is infused from the general atmosphere of society contradicts its purport. Yet books and a little elementary instruction are not furnished in vain. Women are better aware how great and rich the universe is, not so easily blinded by narrowness or partial views of a home circle. "Her mother did so before her" is no longer a sufficient excuse. Indeed, it was never received as an excuse to mitigate the severity of censure, but was adduced as a reason, rather, why there should be no effort made for reformation.

Whether much or little has been done, or will be done,—whether women will add to the talent of narration the power of systematizing,—whether they will carve marble, as well as draw and paint,— is not important. But that it should be acknowledged that they have intellect which needs developing—that they should not be considered complete, if beings of affection and habit alone—is important.

Yet even this acknowledgment, rather conquered by Woman than proffered by Man, has been sullied by the usual selfishness. Too much is said of women being better educated, that they may become better companions and mothers *for men*. They should be fit for such companionship, and we have mentioned, with satisfaction, instances where it has been established. Earth knows no fairer, holier relation than that of a mother. It is one which, rightly understood, must both promote and require the highest attainments. But a being of infinite scope must not be treated with an exclusive view to any one relation. Give the soul free course, let the organization, both of body and

[19] A learned young woman of the sixteenth century.

mind, be freely developed, and the being will be fit for any and every relation to which it may be called. The intellect, no more than the sense of hearing, is to be cultivated merely that Woman may be a more valuable companion to Man, but because the Power who gave a power, by its mere existence signifies that it must be brought out toward perfection. . . .

There are two aspects of Woman's nature, represented by the ancients as Muse and Minerva. . . .

The especial genius of Woman I believe to be electrical in movement, intuitive in function, spiritual in tendency. She excels not so easily in classification, or recreation, as in an instinctive seizure of causes, and a simple breathing out of what she receives, that has the singleness of life, rather than the selecting and energizing of art.

More native is it to her to be the living model of the artist than to set apart from herself any one form in objective reality; more native to inspire and receive the poem, than to create it. In so far as soul is in her completely developed, all soul is the same; but in so far as it is modified in her as Woman, it flows, it breathes, it sings, rather than deposits soil, or finishes work; and that which is especially feminine flushes, in blossom, the face of earth, and pervades, like air and water, all this seeming solid globe, daily renewing and purifying its life. Such may be the especially feminine element spoken of as Femality. But it is no more the order of nature that it should be incarnated pure in any form, than that the masculine energy should exist unmingled with it in any form.

Male and female represent the two sides of the great radical dualism. But, in fact, they are perpetually passing into one another. Fluid hardens to solid, solid rushes to fluid. There is no wholly masculine man, no purely feminine woman.

History jeers at the attempts of physiologists to bind great original laws by the forms which flow from them. They make a rule; they say from observation what can and cannot be. In vain! Nature provides exceptions to every rule. She sends women to battle, and sets Hercules spinning;[20] she enables women to bear immense burdens, cold, and frost; she enables the man, who feels maternal love, to nourish his infant like a mother. Of late she plays still gayer pranks. Not only she deprives organizations, but organs, of a necessary end.

[20]Hercules was once a slave of Queen Omphale, who set him to woman's work, spinning.

She enables people to read with the top of the head, and see with the pit of the stomach. Presently she will make a female Newton, and a male siren.

Man partakes of the feminine in the Apollo, Woman of the masculine as Minerva.

What I mean by the Muse is that unimpeded clearness of the intuitive powers, which a perfectly truthful adherence to every admonition of the higher instincts would bring to a finely organized human being. It may appear as prophecy or as poesy. It enabled Cassandra to foresee the results of actions passing round her;[21] the Seeress to behold the true character of the person through the mask of his customary life. (Sometimes she saw a feminine form behind the man, sometimes the reverse.) It enabled the daughter of Linnæus to see the soul of the flower exhaling from the flower.[22] It gave a man, but a poet-man, the power of which he thus speaks: "Often in my contemplation of nature, radiant intimations, and as it were sheaves of light, appear before me as to the facts of cosmogony, in which my mind has, perhaps, taken especial part." He wisely adds, "But it is necessary with earnestness to verify the knowledge we gain by these flashes of light." And none should forget this. Sight must be verified by light before it can deserve the honors of piety and genius. Yet sight comes first, and of this sight of the world of causes, this approximation to the region of primitive motions, women I hold to be especially capable. Even without equal freedom with the other sex, they have already shown themselves so; and should these faculties have free play, I believe they will open new, deeper and purer sources of joyous inspiration than have as yet refreshed the earth.

Let us be wise, and not impede the soul. Let her work as she will. Let us have one creative energy, one incessant revelation. Let it take what form it will, and let us not bind it by the past to man or woman, black or white. Jove sprang from Rhea, Pallas from Jove. So let it be.

If it has been the tendency of these remarks to call Woman rather to the Minerva side,—if I, unlike the more generous writer, have spoken from society no less than the soul,—let it be pardoned! It is love that has caused this—love for many incarcerated souls, that

[21]Cassandra, in Homer's *Iliad,* could predict the future.
[22]According to Fuller's note, the daughter of Carolus Linnaeus, an eighteenth-century botanist, could see the soul of a flower.

might be freed, could the idea of religious self-dependence be established in them, could the weakening habit of dependence on others be broken up.

Proclus[23] teaches that every life has, in its sphere, a totality or wholeness of the animating powers of the other spheres; having only, as its own characteristic, a predominance of some one power. Thus Jupiter comprises, within himself, the other twelve powers, which stand thus: The first triad is *demiurgic or fabricative,* that is, Jupiter, Neptune, Vulcan; the second, *defensive,* Vesta, Minerva, Mars; the third, *vivific,* Ceres, Juno, Diana; and the fourth, Mercury, Venus, Apollo, *elevating and harmonic.* In the sphere of Jupiter, energy is predominant—with Venus, beauty; but each comprehends and apprehends all the others.

When the same community of life and consciousness of mind begin among men, humanity will have, positively and finally, subjugated its brute elements and Titanic childhood; criticism will have perished; arbitrary limits and ignorant censure be impossible; all will have entered upon the liberty of law, and the harmony of common growth.

Then Apollo will sing to his lyre what Vulcan forges on the anvil, and the Muse weave anew the tapestries of Minerva.

It is, therefore, only in the present crisis that the preference is given to Minerva. The power of continence must establish the legitimacy of freedom, the power of self-poise the perfection of motion.

Every relation, every gradation of nature is incalculably precious, but only to the soul which is poised upon itself, and to whom no loss, no change, can bring dull discord, for it is in harmony with the central soul.

If any individual live too much in relations, so that he becomes a stranger to the resources of his own nature, he falls, after a while, into a distraction, or imbecility, from which he can only be cured by a time of isolation, which gives the renovating fountains time to rise up. With a society it is the same. Many minds, deprived of the traditionary or instinctive means of passing a cheerful existence, must find help in self-impulse, or perish. It is therefore that, while any elevation, in the view of union, is to be hailed with joy, we shall not decline celibacy as the great fact of the time. It is one from which no vow, no arrangement, can at present save a thinking mind. For

[23]Proclus (A.D. 410–485), a neo-Platonic philosopher.

now the rowers are pausing on their oars; they wait a change before they can pull together. All tends to illustrate the thought of a wise cotemporary. Union is only possible to those who are units. To be fit for relations in time, souls, whether of Man or Woman, must be able to do without them in the spirit.

It is therefore that I would have Woman lay aside all thought, such as she habitually cherishes, of being taught and led by men. I would have her, like the Indian girl, dedicate herself to the Sun, the Sun of Truth, and go nowhere if his beams did not make clear the path.[24] I would have her free from compromise, from complaisance, from helplessness, because I would have her good enough and strong enough to love one and all beings, from the fullness, not the poverty of being.

Men, as at present instructed, will not help this work, because they also are under the slavery of habit. I have seen with delight their poetic impulses. A sister is the fairest ideal, and how nobly Wordsworth, and even Byron, have written of a sister!

There is no sweeter sight than to see a father with his little daughter. Very vulgar men become refined to the eye when leading a little girl by the hand. At that moment, the right relation between the sexes seems established, and you feel as if the man would aid in the noblest purpose, if you ask him in behalf of his little daughter. Once, two fine figures stood before me, thus. The father of very intellectual aspect, his falcon eye softened by affection as he looked down on his fair child; she the image of himself, only more graceful and brilliant in expression. I was reminded of Southey's Kehama;[25] when, lo, the dream was rudely broken! They were talking of education, and he said,

"I shall not have Maria brought too forward. If she knows too much, she will never find a husband; superior women hardly ever can."

"Surely," said his wife, with a blush, "you wish Maria to be as good and wise as she can, whether it will help her to marriage or not."

"No," he persisted, "I want her to have a sphere and a home, and someone to protect her when I am gone."

---

[24]Fuller refers to a story she told earlier of an Indian woman who lived unmarried because she believed herself betrothed to the Sun.

[25]Robert Southey's *Curse of Kehama* (1810) is a poetic tale of fatherly devotion.

It was a trifling incident, but made a deep impression. I felt that the holiest relations fail to instruct the unprepared and perverted mind. If this man, indeed, could have looked at it on the other side, he was the last that would have been willing to have been taken himself for the home and protection he could give, but would have been much more likely to repeat the tale of Alcibiades with his phials.

But men do *not* look at both sides, and women must leave off asking them and being influenced by them, but retire within themselves, and explore the ground-work of life till they find their peculiar secret. Then, when they come forth again, renovated and baptized, they will know how to turn all dross to gold, and will be rich and free though they live in a hut, tranquil if in a crowd. Then their sweet singing shall not be from passionate impulse, but the lyrical overflow of a divine rapture, and a new music shall be evolved from this many-chorded world.

Grant her, then, for a while, the armor and the javelin. Let her put from her the press of other minds, and meditate in virgin loneliness. The same idea shall reappear in due time as Muse, or Ceres, the all-kindly, patient Earth-Spirit.

Harriet Beecher Stowe

1811–1896

HARRIET BEECHER was born in Connecticut, the seventh of the nine children of Lyman and Roxana Beecher; Roxana died when Harriet was five, and her father, the leading Calvinist churchman of his day, dominated her childhood. The whole family was eminent; her brother Henry Ward was an outstanding pulpit orator, her sister Catharine a leader in women's education, her half-sister Isabella a leader in the crusade for woman suffrage. At thirteen Harriet went to study at Catharine's new Hartford Female Seminary, where she soon became a teacher. When their father became president of Lane Theological Seminary in Cincinnati, Ohio, Catharine went with him to establish the Western Female Institute, and Harriet to teach there. There, too, Harriet began to publish stories and sketches, the best of which, including "Love Versus Law," she collected in *The Mayflower* (1843).

She married Calvin Stowe, a professor at Lane, in 1836, and was soon immersed in child-rearing (four children in four years, and then three more), running a household on a meager income, keeping up her melancholy husband's spirits, and pursuing her writing career, now necessary to help support the family. When Calvin got a position on the faculty of Bowdoin College, they moved to Maine. There she wrote *Uncle Tom's Cabin* (1851–1852)—burdened by domestic cares, but driven by indignation at the Fugitive Slave Law. This book, one of the great best-sellers of all time, won her international fame. She continued to write voluminously for the next thirty-five years— stories, essays, tracts, and nine more novels.

Stowe began her career as a regionalist writing about her native place and returned to this setting in her later novels. In her first published work, "A New England Sketch" (1834), she explicitly rejected exotic romance in favor of a realistic portrayal of New England character. Her appreciation of its humorous angularity and rigid uprightness gives life to "Love Versus Law" and was to be deployed later in Miss Ophelia of *Uncle Tom's Cabin*.

BIBLIOGRAPHY
Crozier, Alice C. *The Novels of Harriet Beecher Stowe.* New York: Oxford, 1969.
Stowe, Harriet Beecher. *The Writings.* Vol. 14. Riverside edition, 1896. Reprint New York: AMS Press, 1967.
Wilson, Forrest. *Crusader in Crinoline: The Life of Harriet Beecher Stowe.* Philadelphia: J. B. Lippincott Co., 1941.

Love Versus Law

How many kinds of beauty there are! How many even in the human form! There are the bloom and motion of childhood, the freshness and ripe perfection of youth, the dignity of manhood, the softness of woman—all different, yet each in its kind perfect.

But there is none so peculiar, none that bears more the image of the heavenly, than the beauty of Christian old age. It is like the loveliness of those calm autumn days, when the heats of summer are past, when the harvest is gathered into the garner, and the sun shines over the placid fields and fading woods, which stand waiting for their last change. It is a beauty more strictly moral, more belonging to the soul, than that of any other period of life. Poetic fiction always paints the old man as a Christian; nor is there any period where the virtues of Christianity seem to find a more harmonious development. The aged man, who has outlived the hurry of passion—who has withstood the urgency of temptation—who has concentrated the religious impulses of youth into habits of obedience and love—who, having served his generation by the will of God, now leans in helplessness on Him whom once he served, is, perhaps, one of the most faultless representations of the beauty of holiness that this world affords.

Thoughts something like these arose in my mind as I slowly turned my footsteps from the graveyard of my native village, where I had been wandering after years of absence. It was a lovely spot—a soft slope of ground close by a little stream, that ran sparkling through the cedars and junipers beyond it, while on the other side arose a green hill, with the white village laid like a necklace of pearls upon its bosom.

There is no feature of the landscape more picturesque and peculiar than that of the graveyard,—that "city of the silent," as it is beautifully expressed by the Orientals,—standing amid the bloom and rejoicing of nature, its white stones glittering in the sun, a memorial of decay, a link between the living and the dead.

As I moved slowly from mound to mound, and read the inscriptions, which purported that many a money-saving man, and many a busy, anxious housewife, and many a prattling, half-blossomed child, had done with care or mirth, I was struck with a plain slab, bearing the inscription, *"To the memory of Deacon Enos Dudley, who died in his hundredth year."* My eye was caught by this inscription, for in other years I had well known the person it recorded. At this instant, his mild and venerable form arose before me as erst it used to rise from the deacon's seat, a straight, close slip just below the pulpit. I recollected his quiet and lowly coming into meeting, precisely ten minutes before the time, every Sunday,—his tall form a little stooping,—his best suit of butternut-colored Sunday clothes, with long flaps and wide cuffs, on one of which two pins were always to be seen stuck in with the most reverent precision. When seated, the top of the pew came just to his chin, so that his silvery, placid head rose above it like the moon above the horizon. His head was one that might have been sketched for a St. John—bald at the top and around the temples adorned with a soft flow of bright fine hair,—

> That down his shoulders reverently spread,
> As hoary frost with spangles doth attire
> The naked branches of an oak half dead.

He was then of great age, and every line of his patient face seemed to say, "And now, Lord, what wait I for?" Yet still, year after year, was he to be seen in the same place, with the same dutiful punctuality.

The services he offered to his God were all given with the exactness of an ancient Israelite. No words could have persuaded him of the propriety of meditating when the choir was singing, or of sitting down, even through infirmity, before the close of the longest prayer that ever was offered. A mighty contrast was he to his fellow officer, Deacon Abrams, a tight, little, tripping, well-to-do man, who used to sit beside him with his hair brushed straight up like a little blaze, his coat buttoned up trig[1] and close, his psalm-book in hand, and his quick gray eyes turned first on one side of the broad aisle, and then on the other, and then up into the gallery, like a man who came to church on business, and felt responsible for everything that was going on in the house.

A great hindrance was the business talent of this good little man to the enjoyments of us youngsters, who, perched along in a row on a low seat in front of the pulpit, attempted occasionally to diversify the long hour of sermon by sundry small exercises of our own, such as making our handkerchiefs into rabbits, or exhibiting, in a sly way, the apples and gingerbread we had brought for a Sunday dinner, or pulling the ears of some discreet meeting-going dog, who now and then would soberly pitapat through the broad aisle. But woe be to us during our contraband sports, if we saw Deacon Abrams's sleek head dodging up from behind the top of the deacon's seat. Instantly all the apples, gingerbread, and handkerchiefs vanished, and we all sat with our hands folded, looking as demure as if we understood every word of the sermon, and more too.

There was a great contrast between these two deacons in their services and prayers, when, as was often the case, the absence of the pastor devolved on them the burden of conducting the duties of the sanctuary. That God was great and good, and that we all were sinners, were truths that seemed to have melted into the heart of Deacon Enos, so that his very soul and spirit were bowed down with them. With Deacon Abrams it was an undisputed fact, which he had settled long ago, and concerning which he felt that there could be no reasonable doubt, and his bustling way of dealing with the matter seemed to say that he knew *that* and a great many things besides.

Deacon Enos was known far and near as a very proverb for peace-

[1]Neat.

fulness of demeanor and unbounded charitableness in covering and excusing the faults of others. As long as there was any doubt in a case of alleged evil doing, Deacon Enos guessed "the man did not mean any harm, after all"; and when transgression became too barefaced for this excuse, he always guessed "it wa'n't best to say much about it; nobody could tell what they might be left to."

Some incidents in his life will show more clearly these traits. A certain shrewd landholder, by the name of Jones, who was not well reported of in the matter of honesty, sold to Deacon Enos a valuable lot of land, and received the money for it; but, under various pretenses, deferred giving the deed. Soon after, he died; and, to the deacon's amazement, the deed was nowhere to be found, while this very lot of land was left by will to one of his daughters.

The deacon said "it was very extraor'nary: he always knew that Seth Jones was considerable sharp about money, but he did not think he would do such a right up-and-down wicked thing." So the old man repaired to Squire Abel to state the case, and see if there was any redress. "I kinder hate to tell of it," said he; "but, Squire Abel, you know Mr. Jones was—was—what he was, even if he is dead and gone!" This was the nearest approach the old gentleman could make to specifying a heavy charge against the dead. On being told that the case admitted of no redress, Deacon Enos comforted himself with half soliloquizing,—"Well, at any rate, the land has gone to those two girls, poor lone critters; I hope it will do them some good. There is Silence—we won't say much about her; but Sukey is a nice, pretty girl." And so the old man departed, leaving it as his opinion that, since the matter could not be mended, it was just as well not to say anything about it.

Now, the two girls here mentioned (to wit, Silence and Sukey) were the eldest and the youngest of a numerous family, the offspring of three wives of Seth Jones, of whom these two were the sole survivors. The elder, Silence, was a tall, strong, black-eyed, hard-featured woman, verging upon forty, with a good, loud, resolute voice, and what the Irishman would call "a dacent notion of using it." Why she was called Silence was a standing problem to the neighborhood; for she had more faculty and inclination for making a noise than any person in the whole township. Miss Silence was one of those persons who have no disposition to yield any of their own rights. She marched up to all controverted matters, faced down all opposition, held her way lustily and with good courage, making men, women, and children turn out for her, as they would for a mail stage. So evident was her innate determination to be free and independent that, though she was the daughter of a rich man, and well portioned, only one swain was ever heard of who ventured to solicit her hand in marriage; and he was sent off with the assurance that, if he ever showed his face about the house again, she would set the dogs on him.

But Susan Jones was as different from her sister as the little graceful convolvulus from the great rough stick that supports it. At the time of which we speak she was just eighteen; a modest, slender, blushing girl, as timid and shrinking as her sister was bold and hardy. Indeed, the education of poor Susan had cost Miss Silence much painstaking and trouble, and, after all, she said "the girl would make a fool of herself; she never could teach her to be up and down with people, as she was."

When the report came to Miss Silence's ears that Deacon Enos considered himself as aggrieved by her father's will, she held forth upon the subject with great strength of courage and of lungs. "Deacon Enos might be in better business than in trying to cheat orphans out of their rights—she hoped he would go to law about it, and see what good he would get by it—a pretty church member and deacon, to be sure! getting up such a story about her poor father, dead and gone!"

"But, Silence," said Susan, "Deacon Enos is a good man: I do not think he means to injure anyone; there must be some mistake about it."

"Susan, you are a little fool, as I have always told you," replied Silence; "you would be cheated out of your eye teeth if you had not me to take care of you."

But subsequent events brought the affairs of these two damsels in closer connection with those of Deacon Enos, as we shall proceed to show.

It happened that the next-door neighbor of Deacon Enos was a certain old farmer, whose crabbedness of demeanor had procured for him the name of Uncle Jaw.[2] This agreeable surname accorded very well with the general characteristics both of the person and manner of its possessor. He was tall and hard-favored, with an expression of countenance much resembling a northeast rainstorm—a drizzling, settled sulkiness, that seemed to defy all prospect of clearing off, and to take comfort in its own disagreeableness. His voice

[2]Jaw means to abuse or scold.

seemed to have taken lessons of his face, in such admirable keeping was its sawing, deliberate growl with the pleasing physiognomy before indicated. By nature he was endowed with one of those active, acute, hair-splitting minds, which can raise forty questions for dispute on any point of the compass; and had he been an educated man, he might have proved as clever a metaphysician as ever threw dust in the eyes of succeeding generations. But being deprived of these advantages, he nevertheless exerted himself to quite as useful a purpose in puzzling and mystifying whomsoever came in his way. But his activity particularly exercised itself in the line of the law, as it was his meat, and drink, and daily meditation, either to find something to go to law about or to go to law about something he had found. There was always some question about an old rail fence that used to run "a leetle more to the left hand," or that was built up "a leetle more to the right hand," and so cut off a strip of his "medder land," or else there was some outrage of Peter Somebody's turkeys getting into his mowing, or Squire Moses's geese were to be shut up in the town pound, or something equally important kept him busy from year's end to year's end. Now, as a matter of private amusement, this might have answered very well; but then Uncle Jaw was not satisfied to fight his own battles, but must needs go from house to house, narrating the whole length and breadth of the case, with all the "says he's" and "says I's," and the "I tell'd him's" and "he tell'd me's," which do either accompany or flow therefrom. Moreover, he had such a marvelous facility of finding out matters to quarrel about, and of letting everyone else know where they, too, could muster a quarrel, that he generally succeeded in keeping the whole neighborhood by the ears.

And as good Deacon Enos assumed the office of peacemaker for the village, Uncle Jaw's efficiency rendered it no sinecure. The deacon always followed the steps of Uncle Jaw, smoothing, hushing up, and putting matters aright with an assiduity that was truly wonderful.

Uncle Jaw himself had a great respect for the good man, and, in common with all the neighborhood, sought unto him for counsel, though, like other seekers of advice, he appropriated only so much as seemed good in his own eyes.

Still he took a kind of pleasure in dropping in of an evening to Deacon Enos's fire, to recount the various matters which he had taken or was to take in hand; at one time to narrate "how he had been over the milldam, telling old Granny Clark that she could get the law of Seth Scran about that pasture lot," or else "how he had told Ziah Bacon's widow that she had a right to shut up Bill Scranton's pig every time she caught him in front of her house."

But the grand "matter of matters," and the one that took up the most of Uncle Jaw's spare time, lay in a dispute between him and Squire Jones, the father of Susan and Silence; for it so happened that his lands and those of Uncle Jaw were contiguous. Now, the matter of dispute was on this wise: On Squire Jones's land there was a mill, which mill Uncle Jaw averred was "always a-flooding his medder land." As Uncle Jaw's "medder land" was by nature half bog and bulrushes, and therefore liable to be found in a wet condition, there was always a happy obscurity as to where the water came from, and whether there was at any time more there than belonged to his share. So, when all other subject matters of dispute failed, Uncle Jaw recreated himself with getting up a lawsuit about his "medder land"; and one of these cases was in pendency when, by the death of the squire, the estate was left to Susan and Silence, his daughters. When, therefore, the report reached him that Deacon Enos had been cheated out of his dues, Uncle Jaw prepared forthwith to go and compare notes. Therefore, one evening, as Deacon Enos was sitting quietly by the fire, musing and reading with his big Bible open before him, he heard the premonitory symptoms of a visitation from Uncle Jaw on his door-scraper; and soon the man made his appearance. After seating himself directly in front of the fire, with his elbows on his knees, and his hands spread out over the coals, he looked up in Deacon Enos's mild face with his little inquisitive gray eyes, and remarked, by way of opening the subject, "Well, deacon, old Squire Jones is gone at last. I wonder how much good all his land will do him now?"

"Yes," replied Deacon Enos, "it just shows how all these things are not worth striving after. We brought nothing into the world, and it is certain we can carry nothing out."[3]

"Why, yes," replied Uncle Jaw, "that's all very right, deacon; but it was strange how that old Squire Jones did hang on to things. Now, that mill of his, that was always soaking off water into these medders of mine—I took and tell'd Squire Jones just how it was, pretty nigh twenty times, and yet he would keep it just so; and now he's dead and gone, there is that old gal Silence is full as bad and makes more

[3]Paraphrase of Job 1:21.

noise; and she and Suke have got the land; but, you see, I mean to work it yet."

Here Uncle Jaw paused to see whether he had produced any sympathetic excitement in Deacon Enos; but the old man sat without the least emotion, quietly contemplating the top of the long kitchen shovel. Uncle Jaw fidgeted in his chair, and changed his mode of attack for one more direct. "I heard 'em tell, Deacon Enos, that the squire served you something of an unhandy sort of trick about that 'ere lot of land."

Still Deacon Enos made no reply; but Uncle Jaw's perseverance was not so to be put off, and he recommenced. " 'Squire Abel, you see, he tell'd me how the matter was, and he said he did not see as it could be mended; but I took and tell'd him, " 'Squire Abel,' says I, 'I'd bet pretty nigh 'most anything, if Deacon Enos would tell the matter to me, that I could find a hole for him to creep out at; for,' says I, 'I've seen daylight through more twistical cases than that afore now.' "

Still Deacon Enos remained mute; and Uncle Jaw, after waiting a while, recommenced with, "But, railly, deacon, I should like to hear the particulars."

"I have made up my mind not to say anything more about that business," said Deacon Enos, in a tone which, though mild, was so exceedingly definite that Uncle Jaw felt that the case was hopeless in that quarter; he therefore betook himself to the statement of his own grievances.

"Why, you see, deacon," he began, at the same time taking the tongs, and picking up all the little brands, and disposing them in the middle of the fire,—"you see, two days arter the funeral (for I didn't railly like to go any sooner), I stepped up to hash over the matter with old Silence; for as to Sukey, she ha'n't no more to do with such things than our white kitten. Now, you see, Squire Jones, just afore he died, he took away an old rail fence of his'n that lay between his land and mine, and began to build a new stone wall; and when I come to measure, I found he had took and put a'most the whole-width of the stone wall on to my land, when there ought not to have been more than half of it come there. Now, you see, I could not say a word to Squire Jones, because, jest before I found it out, he took and died; and so I thought I'd speak to old Silence, and see if she meant to do anything about it, 'cause I knew pretty well she wouldn't; and I tell you, if she didn't put it on to me! We had a regular pitched battle—the old gal, I thought she would 'a' screamed herself to death!

I don't know but she would, but just then poor Sukey came in, and looked so frightened and scarey—Sukey is a pretty gal, and looks so trembling and delicate, that it's kinder a shame to plague her, and so I took and come away for that time."

Here Uncle Jaw perceived a brightening in the face of the good deacon, and felt exceedingly comforted that at last he was about to interest him in his story.

But all this while the deacon had been in a profound meditation concerning the ways and means of putting a stop to a quarrel that had been his torment from time immemorial, and just at this moment a plan had struck his mind which our story will proceed to unfold.

The mode of settling differences which had occurred to the good man was one which has been considered a specific in reconciling contending sovereigns and states from early antiquity, and the deacon hoped it might have a pacifying influence even in so unpromising a case as that of Miss Silence and Uncle Jaw.

In former days, Deacon Enos had kept the district school for several successive winters, and among his scholars was the gentle Susan Jones, then a plump, rosy little girl, with blue eyes, curly hair, and the sweetest disposition in the world. There was also little Joseph Adams, the only son of Uncle Jaw, a fine, healthy, robust boy, who used to spell the longest words, make the best snowballs and popular whistles, and read the loudest and fastest in the "Columbian Orator" of any boy at school.

Little Joe inherited all his father's sharpness, with a double share of good humor; so that, though he was forever effervescing in the way of one funny trick or another, he was a universal favorite, not only with the deacon, but with the whole school.

Master Joseph always took little Susan Jones under his especial protection, drew her to school on his sled, helped her out with all the long sums in her arithmetic, saw to it that nobody pillaged her dinner basket, or knocked down her bonnet, and resolutely whipped or snowballed any other boy who attempted the same gallantries. Years passed on, and Uncle Jaw had sent his son to college. He sent him because, as he said, he had "a right to send him; just as good a right as Squire Abel or Deacon Abrams to send their boys, and so he would send him." It was the remembrance of his old favorite Joseph, and his little pet Susan, that came across the mind of Deacon Enos, and which seemed to open a gleam of light in regard to the future. So, when Uncle Jaw had finished his prelection, the deacon, after some meditation, came out with, "Railly, they say that your son is going to have the valedictory in college."

Though somewhat startled at the abrupt transition, Uncle Jaw found the suggestion too flattering to his pride to be dropped; so, with a countenance grimly expressive of his satisfaction, he replied, "Why, yes—yes—I don't see no reason why a poor man's son ha'n't as much right as any one to be at the top, if he can get there."

"Just so," replied Deacon Enos.

"He was always the boy for larning, and for nothing else," continued Uncle Jaw; "put him to farming, couldn't make nothing of him. If I set him to hoeing corn or hilling potatoes, I'd always find him stopping to chase hoptoads, or off after chip-squirrels. But set him down to a book, and there he was! That boy larnt reading the quickest of any boy that ever I saw: it wasn't a month after he began his *a-b abs,* before he could read in the 'Fox and the Brambles,' and in a month more he could clatter off his chapter in the Testament as fast as any of them; and you see, in college, it's jest so—he has ris right up to be first."

"And he is coming home week after next," said the deacon meditatively.

The next morning, as Deacon Enos was eating his breakfast, he quietly remarked to his wife, "Sally, I believe it was week after next you were meaning to have your quilting?"

"Why, I never told you so: what alive makes you think that, Deacon Dudley?"

"I thought that was your calculation," said the good man quietly.

"Why no; to be sure, I *can* have it, and maybe it's the best of any time, if we can get Black Dinah to come and help about the cakes and pies. I guess we will, finally."

"I think it's likely you had better," replied the deacon, "and we will have all the young folks here."

And now let us pass over all the intermediate pounding, and grinding, and chopping, which for the next week foretold approaching festivity in the kitchen of the deacon. Let us forbear to provoke the appetite of a hungry reader by setting in order before him the mince pies, the cranberry tarts, the pumpkin pies, the doughnuts, the cookies, and other sweet cakes of every description, that sprang into being at the magic touch of Black Dinah, the village priestess on all these solemnities. Suffice it to say that the day had arrived, and the auspicious quilt was spread.

The invitation had not failed to include the Misses Silence and Susan Jones—nay, the good deacon had pressed gallantry into the matter so far as to be the bearer of the message himself; for which he was duly rewarded by a broadside from Miss Silence, giving him what she termed a piece of her mind in the matter of the rights of widows and orphans; to all which the good old man listened with great benignity from the beginning to the end, and replied with,—"Well, well, Miss Silence, I expect you will think better of this before long; there had best not be any hard words about it." So saying, he took up his hat and walked off, while Miss Silence, who felt extremely relieved by having blown off steam, declared that "it was of no more use to hector old Deacon Enos than to fire a gun at a bag of cotton wool. For all that, though, she shouldn't go to the quilting; nor more should Susan."

"But, sister, why not?" said the little maiden; "I think I *shall* go." And Susan said this in a tone so mildly positive that Silence was amazed.

"What upon 'arth ails you, Susan?" said she, opening her eyes with astonishment; "haven't you any more spirit than to go to Deacon Enos's when he is doing all he can to ruin us?"

"I like Deacon Enos," replied Susan; "he was always kind to me when I was a little girl, and I am not going to believe that he is a bad man now."

When a young lady states that she is not going to believe a thing, good judges of human nature generally give up the case; but Miss Silence, to whom the language of opposition and argument was entirely new, could scarcely give her ears credit for veracity in the case; she therefore repeated over exactly what she said before, only in a much louder tone of voice, and with much more vehement forms of asseveration—a mode of reasoning which, if not strictly logical, has at least the sanction of very respectable authorities among the enlightened and learned.

"Silence," replied Susan, when the storm had spent itself, "if it did not look like being angry with Deacon Enos, I would stay away to oblige you; but it would seem to everyone to be taking sides in a quarrel, and I never did, and never will, have any part or lot in such things."

"Then you'll just be trod and trampled on all your days, Susan," replied Silence; "but, however, if *you* choose to make a fool of yourself, I don't;" and so saying, she flounced out of the room in great wrath. It so happened, however, that Miss Silence was one of those who have so little economy in disposing of a fit of anger, that it was all used up before the time of execution arrived. It followed of consequence that, having unburdened her mind freely both to Deacon Enos and to Susan, she began to feel very much more comfortable and good-natured; and consequent upon that came divers reflections upon the many gossiping opportunities and comforts of a quilting; and then the intrusive little reflection, "What if she should go, after all; what harm would be done?" and then the inquiry, "Whether it was not her duty to go and look after Susan, poor child, who had no mother to watch over her?" In short, before the time of preparation arrived, Miss Silence had fully worked herself up to the magnanimous determination of going to the quilting. Accordingly, the next day, while Susan was standing before her mirror, braiding up her pretty hair, she was startled by the apparition of Miss Silence coming into the room as stiff as a changeable silk and a high horn comb could make her; and "grimly determined was her look."

"Well, Susan," said she, "if you will go to the quilting this afternoon, I think it is my duty to go and see to you."

What would people do if this convenient shelter of duty did not afford them a retreat in cases when they are disposed to change their minds? Susan suppressed the arch smile that, in spite of herself, laughed out at the corners of her eyes, and told her sister that she was much obliged to her for her care. So off they went together. Silence in the meantime held forth largely on the importance of standing up for one's rights, and not letting one's self be trampled on. The afternoon passed on, the elderly ladies quilted and talked scandal, and the younger ones discussed the merits of the various beaux who were expected to give vivacity to the evening entertainment. Among these the newly arrived Joseph Adams, just from college, with all his literary honors thick about him, became a prominent subject of conversation. It was duly canvassed whether the young gentleman might be called handsome, and the affirmative was carried by a large majority, although there were some variations and exceptions; one of the party declaring his whiskers to be in too high a state of cultivation, another maintaining that they were in the exact line of beauty, while a third vigorously disputed the point whether he wore whiskers at all. It was allowed by all, however, that he had been a great beau in the town where he had passed his college days. It was also inquired into whether he were matrimonially engaged;

and the negative being understood, they diverted themselves with predicting to one another the capture of such a prize; each prophecy being received with such disclaimers as "Come now!" "Do be still!" "Hush your nonsense!" and the like.

At length the long-wished-for hour arrived, and one by one the lords of creation began to make their appearance; and one of the last was this much admired youth.

"That is Joe Adams." "That is he!" was the busy whisper, as a tall, well-looking young man came into the room with the easy air of one who had seen several things before, and was not to be abashed by the combined blaze of all the village beauties.

In truth, our friend Joseph had made the most of his residence in N., paying his court no less to the Graces than the Muses. His fine person, his frank, manly air, his ready conversation, and his faculty of universal adaptation had made his society much coveted among the *beau monde* of N.; and though the place was small, he had become familiar with much good society.

We hardly know whether we may venture to tell our fair readers the whole truth in regard to our hero. We will merely hint, in the gentlest manner in the world, that Mr. Joseph Adams, being undeniably first in the classics and first in the drawing-room, having been gravely commended in his class by his venerable president, and gayly flattered in the drawing-room by the elegant Miss This and Miss That, was rather inclining to the opinion that he was an uncommonly fine fellow, and even had the assurance to think that, under present circumstances, he could please without making any great effort—a thing which, however true it were in point of fact, is obviously improper to be thought of by a young man. Be that as it may, he moved about from one to another, shaking hands with all the old ladies, and listening with the greatest affability to the various comments on his growth and personal appearance, his points of resemblance to his father, mother, grandfather, and grandmother, which are always detected by the superior acumen of elderly females.

Among the younger ones he at once, and with full frankness, recognized old schoolmates, and partners in various whortleberry, chestnut, and strawberry excursions, and thus called out an abundant flow of conversation. Nevertheless, his eye wandered occasionally around the room, as if in search of something not there. What could it be? It kindled, however, with an expression of sudden brightness as he perceived the tall and spare figure of Miss Silence;

whether owing to the personal fascinations of that lady, or to other causes, we leave the reader to determine.

Miss Silence had predetermined never to speak a word again to Uncle Jaw or any of his race; but she was taken by surprise at the frank, extended hand and friendly "How do ye do?" It was not in woman to resist so cordial an address from a handsome young man, and Miss Silence gave her hand, and replied with a graciousness that amazed herself. At this moment, also, certain soft blue eyes peeped forth from a corner, just "to see if he looked as he used to." Yes, there he was! the same dark, mirthful eyes that used to peer on her from behind the corners of the spelling-book at the district school; and Susan Jones gave a deep sigh to those times, and then wondered why she happened to think of such nonsense.

"How is your sister, little Miss Susan?" said Joseph.

"Why, she is here—have you not seen her?" said Silence; "there she is, in that corner."

Joseph looked, but could scarcely recognize her. There stood a tall, slender blooming girl, that might have been selected as a specimen of that union of perfect health with delicate fairness so characteristic of the young New England beauty.

She was engaged in telling some merry story to a knot of young girls, and the rich color that, like a bright spirit, constantly went and came in her cheeks; the dimples, quick and varying as those of a little brook; the clear, mild eye; the clustering curls, and, above all, the happy, rejoicing smile, and the transparent frankness and simplicity of expression which beamed like sunshine about her, all formed a combination of charms that took our hero quite by surprise; and when Silence, who had a remarkable degree of directness in all her dealings, called out, "Here Susan, is Joe Adams, inquiring after you!" our practiced young gentleman felt himself color to the roots of his hair, and for a moment he could scarce recollect that first rudiment of manners, "to make his bow like a good boy." Susan colored also; but, perceiving the confusion of our hero, her countenance assumed an expression of mischievous drollery, which, helped on by the titter of her companions, added not a little to his confusion.

"Deuce take it!" thought he, "what's the matter with me?" and, calling up his courage, he dashed into the formidable circle of fair ones, and began chattering with one and another, calling by name with or without introduction, remembering things that never happened, with a freedom that was perfectly fascinating.

"Really, how handsome he has grown!" thought Susan; and she colored deeply when once or twice the dark eyes of our hero made the same observation with regard to herself, in that quick, intelligible dialect which eyes alone can speak. And when the little party dispersed, as they did very punctually at nine o'clock, our hero requested of Miss Silence the honor of attending her home—an evidence of discriminating taste which materially raised him in the estimation of that lady. It was true, to be sure, that Susan walked on the other side of him, her little white hand just within his arm; and there was something in that light touch that puzzled him unaccountably, as might be inferred from the frequency with which Miss Silence was obliged to bring up the ends of conversation with, "What did you say?" "What were you going to say?" and other persevering forms of inquiry, with which a regular-trained matter-of-fact talker will hunt down a poor fellow mortal who is in danger of sinking into a comfortable reverie.

When they parted at the gate, however, Silence gave our hero a hearty invitation to "come and see them any time," which he mentally regarded as more to the point than anything else that had been said. As Joseph soberly retraced his way homeward, his thoughts, by some unaccountable association, began to revert to such topics as the loneliness of man by himself, the need of kindred spirits, the solaces of sympathy, and other like matters.

That night Joseph dreamed of trotting along with his dinner basket to the old brown schoolhouse, and vainly endeavoring to overtake Susan Jones, whom he saw with her little pasteboard sunbonnet a few yards in front of him; then he was teetering with her on a long board, her bright little face glancing up and down, while every curl around it seemed to be living with delight; and then he was snowballing Tom Williams for knocking down Susan's doll's house, or he sat by her on a bench, helping her out with a long sum in arithmatic; but, with the mischievous fatality of dreams, the more he ciphered and expounded, the longer and more hopeless grew the sum; and he awoke in the morning pshawing at his ill luck, after having done a sum over half a dozen times, while Susan seemed to be looking on with the same air of arch drollery that he saw on her face the evening before.

"Joseph," said Uncle Jaw, the next morning at breakfast, "I s'pose Squire Jones's daughters were not at the quilting."

"Yes, sir, they were," said our hero; "they were both there."

"Why, you don't say so!"

"They certainly were," persisted the son.

"Well, I thought the old gal had too much spunk for that; you see there is a quarrel between the deacon and them gals."

"Indeed!" said Joseph. "I thought the deacon never quarreled with anybody."

"But, you see, old Silence there, she will quarrel with *him*; railly, that cretur is a tough one;" and Uncle Jaw leaned back in his chair, and contemplated the quarrelsome propensities of Miss Silence with the satisfaction of a kindred spirit. "But I'll fix her yet," he continued; "I see how to work it."

"Indeed, father, I did not know that you had anything to do with their affairs."

"Hain't I? I should like to know if I hain't!" replied Uncle Jaw triumphantly. "Now, see here, Joseph: you see, I mean you shall be a lawyer: I'm pretty considerable of a lawyer myself—that is, for one not college larnt; and I'll tell you how it is;" and thereupon Uncle Jaw launched forth into the case of the medder land and the mill, and concluded with, "Now, Joseph, this 'ere is a kinder whetstone for you to hone up your wits on."

In pursuance, therefore, of this plan of sharpening his wits in the manner aforesaid, our hero, after breakfast, went, like a dutiful son, directly towards Square Jones's, doubtless for the purpose of taking ocular survey of the meadow land, mill, and stone wall; but, by some unaccountable mistake lost his way, and found himself standing before the door of Squire Jones's house.

The old squire had been among the aristocracy of the village, and his house had been the ultimate standard of comparison in all matters of style and garniture. Their big front room, instead of being strewn with lumps of sand, duly streaked over twice a week, was resplendent with a carpet of red, yellow, and black stripes, while a towering pair of long-legged brass andirons, scoured to a silvery white, gave an air of magnificence to the chimney, which was materially increased by the tall brass-headed shovel and tongs, which, like a decorous, starched married couple, stood bolt upright in their places on either side. The sanctity of the place was still further maintained by keeping the window shutters always closed, admitting only so much light as could come in by a round hole at the top of the shutter; and it was only on occasions of extraordinary magnificence that the room was thrown open to profane eyes.

Our hero was surprised, therefore, to find both the doors and windows of this apartment open, and symptoms evident of its being in daily occupation. The furniture still retained its massive, clumsy stiffness, but there were various tokens that lighter fingers had been at work there since the notable days of good Dame Jones. There was a vase of flowers on the table, two or three books of poetry, and a little fairy work-basket, from which peeped forth the edges of some worked ruffling; there was a small writing-desk, and last, not least, in a lady's collection, an album, with leaves of every color of the rainbow, containing inscriptions, in sundry strong masculine hands, "To Susan," indicating that other people had had their eyes open as well as Mr. Joseph Adams. "So," said he to himself, "this quiet little beauty has had admirers, after all;" and consequent upon this came another question (which was none of his concern, to be sure), whether the little lady were or were not engaged; and from these speculations he was aroused by a light footstep, and anon the neat form of Susan made its appearance.

"Good-morning, Miss Jones," said he, bowing.

Now, there is something very comical in the feeling, when little boys and girls, who have always known each other as plain Susan or Joseph, first meet as "Mr." or "Miss" So-and-so. Each one feels half disposed, half afraid, to return to the old familiar form, and awkwardly fettered by the recollection that they are no longer children. Both parties had felt this the evening before, when they met in company; but now that they were alone together, the feeling became still stronger; and when Susan had requested Mr. Adams to take a chair, and Mr. Adams had inquired after Miss Susan's health, there ensued a pause, which, the longer it continued, seemed the more difficult to break, and during which Susan's pretty face slowly assumed an expression of the ludicrous, till she was as near laughing as propriety would admit; and Mr. Adams, having looked out at the window, and up at the mantlepiece, and down at the carpet, at last looked at Susan; their eyes met; the effect was electrical; they both smiled, and then laughed outright, after which the whole difficulty of conversation vanished.

"Susan," said Joseph, "do you remember the old schoolhouse?"

"I thought that was what you were thinking of," said Susan; "but, really, you have grown and altered so that I could hardly believe my eyes last night."

"Nor I mine," said Joseph, with a glance that gave a very complimentary turn to the expression.

Our readers may imagine that after this the conversation proceeded to grow increasingly confidential and interesting; that from the account of early life, each proceeded to let the other know something of intervening history, in the course of which each discovered a number of new and admirable traits in the other, such things being matters of very common occurrence. In the course of the conversation Joseph discovered that it was necessary that Susan should have two or three books then in his possession; and as promptitude is a great matter in such cases, he promised to bring them "tomorrow."

For some time our young friends pursued their acquaintance without a distinct consciousness of anything except that it was a very pleasant thing to be together. During the long, still afternoons, they rambled among the fading woods, now illuminated with the radiance of the dying year, and sentimentalized and quoted poetry; and almost every evening Joseph found some errand to bring him to the house; a book for Miss Susan, or a bundle of roots and herbs for Miss Silence, or some remarkably fine yarn for her to knit— attentions which retained our hero in the good graces of the latter lady, and gained him the credit of being "a young man that knew how to behave himself." As Susan was a leading member in the village choir, our hero was directly attacked with a violent passion for sacred music, which brought him punctually to the singing-school, where the young people came together to sing anthems and fuguing tunes, and to eat apples and chestnuts.

It cannot be supposed that all these things passed unnoticed by those wakeful eyes that are ever upon the motions of such "bright, particular stars;" and as is usual in such cases, many things were known to a certainty which were not yet known to the parties themselves. The young belles and beaux whispered and tittered, and passed the original jokes and witticisms common in such cases, while the old ladies soberly took the matter in hand when they went out with their knitting to make afternoon visits, considering how much money Uncle Jaw had, how much his son would have, and what all together would come to, and whether Joseph would be a "smart man," and Susan a good housekeeper, with all the "ifs, ands, and buts" of married life.

But the most fearful wonders and prognostics crowded around the point "what Uncle Jaw would have to say to the matter." His lawsuit with the sisters being well understood, as there was every reason it should be, it was surmised what two such vigorous belligerents as himself and Miss Silence would say to the prospect of a matrimonial conjunction. It was also reported that Deacon Enos Dudley had a claim to the land which constituted the finest part of Susan's portion, the loss of which would render the consent of Uncle Jaw still more doubtful. But all this while Miss Silence knew nothing of the matter, for her habit of considering and treating Susan as a child seemed to gain strength with time. Susan was always to be seen to, and watched, and instructed, and taught; and Miss Silence could not conceive that one who could not even make pickles, without her to oversee, could think of such a matter as setting up housekeeping on her own account. To be sure, she began to observe an extraordinary change in her sister; remarked that "lately Susan seemed to be getting sort o' crazy-headed"; that she seemed not to have any "faculty" for anything; that she had made gingerbread twice, and forgot the ginger one time, and put in mustard the other; that she shook the salt-cellar out in the tablecloth, and let the cat into the pantry half a dozen times; and that when scolded for these sins of omission or commission, she had a fit of crying, and did a little worse than before. Silence was of opinion that Susan was getting to be "weakly and naarvy," and actually concocted an unmerciful pitcher of wormwood and boneset, which she said was to keep off the "shaking weakness" that was coming over her. In vain poor Susan protested that she was well enough; Miss Silence knew better; and one evening she entertained Mr. Joseph Adams with a long statement of the case in all its bearings, and ended with demanding his opinion, as a candid listener, whether the wormwood and boneset sentence should not be executed.

Poor Susan had that very afternoon parted from a knot of young friends who had teased her most unmercifully on the score of attentions received, till she began to think the very leaves and stones were so many eyes to pry into her secret feelings; and then to have the whole case set in order before the very person, too, whom she most dreaded. "Certainly he would think she was acting like a fool; perhaps he did not mean anything more than friendship, after all; and she would not for the world have him suppose that she cared a copper more for him than for any other friend, or that she was in love, of all things." So she sat very busy with her knitting-work, scarcely knowing what she was about, till Silence called out,—

"Why, Susan, what a piece of work you are making of that stocking heel! What in the world are you doing to it?"

Susan dropped her knitting, and making some pettish answer, escaped out of the room.

"Now, did you ever?" said Silence, laying down the seam she had been cross-stitching; "what *is* the matter with her, Mr. Adams?"

"Miss Susan is certainly indisposed," replied our hero gravely. "I must get her to take your advice, Miss Silence."

Our hero followed Susan to the front door, where she stood looking out at the moon, and begged to know what distressed her.

Of course it was "nothing," the young lady's usual complaint when in low spirits; and to show that she was perfectly easy, she began an unsparing attack on a white rosebush near by.

"Susan!" said Joseph, laying his hand on hers, and in a tone that made her start. She shook back her curls, and looked up to him with such an innocent, confiding face!

Ah, my good reader, you may go on with this part of the story for yourself. We are principled against unveiling the "sacred mysteries," the "thoughts that breathe and words that burn,"[4] in such little moonlight interviews as these. You may fancy all that followed; and we can only assure all who are doubtful that, under judicious management, cases of this kind may be disposed of without wormwood or boneset. Our hero and heroine were called to sublunary realities by the voice of Miss Silence, who came into the passage to see what upon earth they were doing. That lady was satisfied by the representations of so friendly and learned a young man as Joseph that nothing immediately alarming was to be apprehended in the case of Susan; and she retired. From that evening Susan stepped about with a heart many pounds lighter than before.

"I'll tell you what, Joseph," said Uncle Jaw, "I'll tell you what, now: I hear 'em tell that you've took and courted that 'ere Susan Jones. Now, I jest want to know if it's true."

There was an explicitness about this mode of inquiry that took our hero quite by surprise, so that he could only reply,—

"Why, sir, supposing I had, would there be any objection to it in your mind?"

"Don't talk to me," said Uncle Jaw. "I jest want to know if it's true."

Our hero put his hands in his pockets, walked to the window and whistled.

[4]Thomas Gray, "The Progress of Poesy" (1754), line 110.

" 'Cause if you have," said Uncle Jaw, "you may jest uncourt as fast as you can; for Squire Jones's daughter won't get a single cent of my money, I can tell you that."

"Why, father, Susan Jones is not to blame for anything that her father did; and I'm sure she is a pretty girl enough."

"I don't care if she is pretty. What's that to me? I've got you through college, Joseph; and a hard time I've had of it, a-delvin' and slavin'; and here you come, and the very first thing you do you must take and court that 'ere Squire Jones's daughter, who was always putting himself up above me. Besides, I mean to have the law on that estate yet; and Deacon Dudley, he will have the law, too; and it will cut off the best piece of land the girl has; and when you get married, I mean you shall have something. It's jest a trick of them gals at me; but I guess I'll come up with 'em yet. I'm just a-goin' down to have a 'regular hash' with old Silence, to let her know she can't come round me that way."

"Silence," said Susan, drawing her head into the window, and looking apprehensive, "there is Mr. Adams coming here."

"What, Joe Adams? Well, and what if he is?"

"No, no, sister, but it is his father—it is Uncle Jaw."

"Well, s'pose 'tis, child—what scares you? S'pose I'm afraid of him? If he wants more than I gave him last time, I'll put it on." So saying, Miss Silence took her knitting work and marched down into the sitting-room, and sat herself bolt upright in an attitude of defiance, while poor Susan, feeling her heart beat unaccountably fast, glided out of the room.

"Well, good-morning, Miss Silence," said Uncle Jaw, after having scraped his feet on the scraper, and scrubbed them on the mat nearly ten minutes, in silent deliberation.

"Morning, sir," said Silence, abbreviating the "good."

Uncle Jaw helped himself to a chair directly in front of the enemy, dropped his hat on the floor, and surveyed Miss Silence with a dogged air of satisfaction, like one who is sitting down to a regular, comfortable quarrel, and means to make the most of it.

Miss Silence tossed her head disdainfully, but scorned to commence hostilities.

"So, Miss Silence," said Uncle Jaw deliberately, "you don't think you'll do anything about that 'ere matter."

"What matter?" said Silence, with an intonation resembling that of a roasted chestnut when it bursts from the fire.

"I really thought, Miss Silence, in that 'ere talk I had with you about Squire Jones's cheatin' about that 'ere—"

"Mr. Adams," said Silence, "I tell you, to begin with, I'm not a-going to be sauced in this 'ere way by you. You hain't got common decency, nor common sense, nor common anything else, to talk so to me about my father; I won't bear it, I tell you."

"Why, Miss Jones," said Uncle Jaw, "how you talk. Well, to be sure, Squire Jones is dead and gone, and it is as well not to call it cheatin', as I was tellin' Deacon Enos when he was talking about that 'ere lot—that 'ere lot, you know, that he sold the deacon, and never let him have the deed on't."

"That's a lie," said Silence, starting on her feet; "that's an up and down black lie! I tell you that, now, before you say another word."

"Miss Silence, railly, you seem to be getting touchy," said Uncle Jaw; "well, to be sure, if the deacon can let that pass, other folks can; and maybe the deacon will, because Squire Jones was a church member, and the deacon is 'mazin' tender about bringin' out anything against professors;[5] but railly, now, Miss Silence, I didn't think you and Susan were going to work it so cunning in this here way."

"I don't know what you mean, and what's more, I don't care," said Silence, resuming her work, and calling back the bolt-upright dignity with which she began.

There was a pause of some moments, during which the features of Silence worked with suppressed rage, which was contemplated by Uncle Jaw with undisguised satisfaction.

"You see, I s'pose, I shouldn't 'a' minded your Susan's setting out to court my Joe, if it hadn't a' been for them things."

"Courting your son! Mr. Adams, I should like to know what you mean by that. I'm sure nobody wants your son, though he's a civil, likely fellow enough; yet with such an old dragon for a father, I'll warrant he won't get anybody to court him, nor be courted by him neither."

"Railly, Miss Silence, you ain't hardly civil, now."

"Civil! I should like to know who could be civil. You know, now, as well as I do, that you are saying all this out of clear, sheer ugliness; and that's what you keep a-doing all round the neighborhood."

"Miss Silence," said Uncle Jaw, "I don't want no hard words with you. It's pretty much known round the neighborhood that your Su-

---

[5]Those who have openly declared their religious belief.

san thinks she'll get my Joe, and I s'pose you was thinking that perhaps it would be the best way of settling up matters; but you see, now, I took and tell'd my son I railly didn't see as I could afford it; I took and tell'd him that young folks must have something considerable to start with; and that, if Susan lost that 'ere piece of ground, as is likely she will, it would be cutting off quite too much of a piece; so you see, I don't want you to take no encouragement about that."

"Well, I think this is pretty well!" exclaimed Silence, provoked beyond measure or endurance. "You old torment! think I don't know what you're at! I and Susan courting your son? I wonder if you ain't ashamed of yourself, now! I should like to know what I or she have done, now, to get that notion into your head?"

"I didn't s'pose you 'spected to get him yourself," said Uncle Jaw, "for I guess by this time you've pretty much gin up trying, hain't ye? But Susan does, I'm pretty sure."

"Here, Susan! Susan! you—come down!" called Miss Silence, in great wrath, throwing open the chamber door; "Mr. Adams wants to speak with you." Susan, fluttering and agitated, slowly descended into the room, where she stopped, and looked hesitatingly, first at Uncle Jaw and then at her sister, who, without ceremony, proposed the subject matter of the interview as follows:—

"Now, Susan, here's this man pretends to say that you've been a-courting and snaring to get his son; and I just want you to tell him that you hain't never had no thought of him, and that you won't have, neither."

This considerate way of announcing the subject had the effect of bringing the burning color into Susan's face, as she stood like a convicted culprit, with her eyes bent on the floor.

Uncle Jaw, savage as he was, was always moved by female loveliness, as wild beasts are said to be mysteriously swayed by music, and looked on the beautiful, downcast face with more softening than Miss Silence, who, provoked that Susan did not immediately respond to the question, seized her by the arm, and eagerly reiterated,—

"Susan! why don't you speak, child?"

Gathering desperate courage, Susan shook off the hand of Silence, and straightened herself up with as much dignity as some little flower lifts up its head when it has been bent down by raindrops.

"Silence," she said, "I never would have come down if I had thought it was to hear such things as this. Mr. Adams, all I have to say to you is, that your son has sought me, and not I your son. If you wish to know any more, he can tell you better than I."

"Well, I vow! she is a pretty gal," said Uncle Jaw, as Susan shut the door.

This exclamation was involuntary; then recollecting himself, he picked up his hat, and saying, "Well, I guess I may as well get along hum," he began to depart; but turning round before he shut the door, he said, "Miss Silence, if you should conclude to do anything about that 'ere fence, just send word over and let me know."

Silence, without deigning any reply, marched up into Susan's little chamber, where our heroine was treating resolution to a good fit of crying.

"Susan, I did not think you had been such a fool," said the lady. "I do want to know, now, if you've railly been thinking of getting married, and to that Joe Adams of all folks!"

Poor Susan! such an interlude in all her pretty, romantic little dreams about kindred feelings and a hundred other delightful ideas, that flutter like singing birds through the fairy land of first love. Such an interlude! to be called on by gruff human voices to give up all the cherished secrets that she had trembled to whisper even to herself. She felt as if love itself had been defiled by the coarse, rough hands that had been meddling with it; so to her sister's soothing address Susan made no answer, only to cry and sob still more bitterly than before.

Miss Silence, if she had a great stout heart, had no less a kind one, and seeing Susan take the matter so bitterly to heart, she began gradually to subside.

"Susan, you poor little fool, you," she said, at the same time giving her a hearty slap, as expressive of earnest sympathy, "I really do feel for you; that good-for-nothing fellow has been a-cheatin' you, I do believe."

"Oh, don't talk any more about it, for mercy's sake," said Susan; "I am sick of the whole of it."

"That's you, Susan! Glad to hear you say so! I'll stand up for you, Susan; if I catch Joe Adams coming here again with his palavering face, I'll let him know!"

"No, no! Don't for mercy's sake, say anything to Mr. Adams— don't!"

"Well, child, don't claw hold of a body so! Well, at any rate, I'll just let Joe Adams know that we hain't nothing more to say to him."

"But I don't wish to say that; that is—I don't know—indeed, sister Silence, don't say anything about it."

"Why not? You ain't such a natural, now, as to want to marry him, after all, hey?"

"I don't know what I want, nor what I don't want; only, Silence, do now, if you love me, do promise not to say anything at all to Mr. Adams—don't."

"Well, then, I won't," said Silence; "but, Susan, if you railly was in love all this while, why hain't you been and told me? Don't you know that I'm as much as a mother to you, and you ought to have told me in the beginning?"

"I don't know, Silence! I couldn't—I don't want to talk about it."

"Well, Susan, you ain't a bit like me," said Silence—a remark evincing great discrimination, certainly, and with which the conversation terminated.

That very evening our friend Joseph walked down towards the dwelling of the sisters, not without some anxiety for the result, for he knew by his father's satisfied appearance that war had been declared. He walked into the family room and found nobody there but Miss Silence, who was sitting grim as an Egyptian sphinx, stitching very vigorously on a meal bag, in which interesting employment she thought proper to be so much engaged as not to remark the entrance of our hero. To Joseph's accustomed "Good-evening, Miss Silence," she replied merely by looking up with a cold nod, and went on with her sewing. It appeared that she had determined on a literal version of her promise not to say anything to Mr. Adams.

Our hero, as we have before stated, was familiar with the crooks and turns of the female mind, and mentally resolved to put a bold face on the matter, and give Miss Silence no encouragement in her attempt to make him feel himself unwelcome. It was rather a frosty autumnal evening, and the fire on the hearth was decaying. Mr. Joseph bustled about most energetically, throwing down the tongs and shovel and bellows, while he pulled the fire to pieces, raked out ashes and brands, and then, in a twinkling, was at the woodpile, from whence he selected a massive backlog and forestick, with accompaniments, which were soon roaring and crackling in the chimney.

"There, now, that does look something like comfort," said our hero; and drawing forward the big rocking-chair, he seated himself in it, and rubbed his hands with an air of great complacency. Miss Silence looked not up, but stitched so much the faster, so that one might distinctly hear the crack of the needle and the whistle of the thread all over the apartment.

"Have you a headache tonight, Miss Silence?"

"No!" was the gruff answer.

"Are you in a hurry about those bags?" said he, glancing at a pile of unmade ones which lay by her side.

No reply. "Hang it all!" said our hero to himself, "I'll make her speak."

Miss Silence's needlebook and brown thread lay on a chair beside her. Our friend helped himself to a needle and thread, and taking one of the bags, planted himself bolt upright opposite to Miss Silence, and pinning his work to his knee, commenced stitching at a rate fully equal to her own. Miss Silence looked up and fidgeted, but went on with her work faster than before; but the faster she worked, the faster and steadier worked our hero, all in "marvelous silence." There began to be an odd twitching about the muscles of Miss Silence's face; our hero took no notice, having pursed his features into an expression of unexampled gravity, which only grew more intense as he perceived, by certain uneasy movements, that the adversary was beginning to waver. As they were sitting, stitching away, their needles whizzing at each other like a couple of locomotives engaged in conversation, Susan opened the door.

The poor child had been crying for the greater part of her spare time during the day, and was in no very merry humor; but the moment that her astonished eyes comprehended the scene, she burst into a fit of almost inextinguishable merriment, while Silence laid down her needle, and looked half amused and half angry. Our hero, however, continued his business with inflexible perseverance, unpinning his work and moving the seam along, and going on with increased velocity. Poor Miss Silence was at length vanquished, and joined in the loud laugh which seemed to convulse her sister. Whereupon our hero unpinned his work, and folding it up, looked up at her with all the assurance of impudence triumphant, and remarked to Susan,—

"Your sister had such a pile of these pillowcases to make, that she was quite discouraged, and engaged me to do half a dozen of them; when I first came in she was so busy she could not even speak to me."

"Well, if you ain't the beater for impudence!" said Miss Silence.

"The beater for industry—so I thought," rejoined our hero.

Susan, who had been in a highly tragical state of mind all day, and who was meditating on nothing less sublime than an eternal separation from her lover, which she had imagined, with all the affecting attendants and consequents, was entirely revolutionized by the unexpected turn thus given to her ideas, while our hero pursued the opportunity he had made for himself, and exerted his powers of entertainment to the utmost, till Miss Silence, declaring that if she had been washing all day she should not have been more tired than she was with laughing, took up her candle, and good-naturedly left our young people to settle matters between themselves. There was a grave pause of some length when she had departed, which was broken by our hero, who, seating himself by Susan, inquired very seriously if his father had made proposals of marriage to Miss Silence that morning.

"No, you provoking creature!" said Susan, at the same time laughing at the absurdity of the idea.

"Well, now, don't draw on your long face again, Susan," said Joseph; "you have been trying to lengthen it down all the evening, if I would have let you. Seriously, now, I know that something painful passed between my father and you this morning, but I shall not inquire what it was. I only tell you, frankly, that he has expressed his disapprobation of our engagement, forbidden me to go on with it, and"—

"And, consequently, I release you from all engagements and obligations to me, even before you ask it," said Susan.

"You are extremely accommodating," replied Joseph; "but I cannot promise to be as obliging in giving up certain promises made to me, unless, indeed, the feelings that dictated them should have changed."

"Oh, no—no, indeed," said Susan earnestly; "you know it is not that; but if your father objects to me"—

"If my father objects to you, he is welcome not to marry you," said Joseph.

"Now, Joseph, do be serious," said Susan.

"Well, then, seriously, Susan, I know my obligations to my father, and in all that relates to his comfort I will ever be dutiful and submissive, for I have no college-boy pride on the subject of submission; but in a matter so individually my own as the choice of a wife, in a matter that will most likely affect my happiness years and years after he has ceased to be, I hold that I have a right to consult my own inclinations, and, by your leave, my dear little lady, I shall take that liberty."

"But, then, if your father is made angry, you know what sort of a man he is; and how could I stand in the way of all your prospects?"

"Why, my dear Susan, do you think I count myself dependent upon my father, like the heir of an English estate, who has nothing to do but sit still and wait for money to come to him? No! I have energy and education to start with, and if I cannot take care of myself, and you too, then cast me off and welcome"; and, as Joseph spoke, his fine face glowed with a conscious power, which unfettered youth never feels so fully as in America. He paused a moment, and resumed: "Nevertheless, Susan, I respect my father; whatever others may say of him, I shall never forget that I owe to his hard earnings the education that enables me to do or be anything, and I shall not wantonly or rudely cross him. I do not despair of gaining his consent; my father has a great partiality for pretty girls, and if his love of contradiction is not kept awake by open argument, I will trust to time and you to bring him round; but, whatever comes, rest assured, my dearest one, I have chosen for life, and cannot change."

The conversation, after this, took a turn which may readily be imagined by all who have been in the same situation, and will, therefore, need no further illustration.

"Well, deacon, railly I don't know what to think now; there's my Joe, he's took and been a-courting that 'ere Susan," said Uncle Jaw.

This was the introduction to one of Uncle Jaw's periodical visits to Deacon Enos, who was sitting with his usual air of mild abstraction, looking into the coals of a bright November fire, while his busy helpmate was industriously rattling her knitting needles by his side.

A close observer might have suspected that this was no news to the good deacon, who had given a great deal of good advice, in private, to Master Joseph of late; but he only relaxed his features into a quiet smile, and ejaculated, "I want to know!"

"Yes; and railly, deacon, that 'ere gal is a rail pretty un. I was a-tellin' my folks that our new minister's wife was a fool to her."

"And so your son is going to marry her?" said the good lady; "I knew that long ago."

"Well—no—not so fast; ye see there's two to that bargain yet. You see, Joe, he never said a word to me, but took and courted the gal out of his own head; and when I come to know, says I, 'Joe,' says I, 'that 'ere gal won't do for me;' and I took and tell'd him, then, about that 'ere old fence, and all about that old mill, and them medders of mine; and I tell'd him, too, about that 'ere lot of Susan's; and I should like to know, now, deacon, how that lot business is a-going to turn out."

"Judge Smith and Squire Moseley say that my claim to it will stand," said the deacon.

"They do?" said Uncle Jaw with much satisfaction; "s'pose, then, you'll sue, won't you?"

"I don't know," replied the deacon meditatively.

Uncle Jaw was thoroughly amazed; that anyone should have doubts about entering suit for a fine piece of land, when sure of obtaining it, was a problem quite beyond his powers of solving.

"You say your son has courted the girl," said the deacon after a long pause; "that strip of land is the best part of Susan's share; I paid down five hundred dollars on the nail for it; I've got papers here that Judge Smith and Squire Moseley say will stand good in any court of law."

Uncle Jaw pricked up his ears and was all attention, eyeing with eager looks the packet; but, to his disappointment, the deacon deliberately laid it into his desk, shut and locked it, and resumed his seat.

"Now, railly," said Uncle Jaw, "I should like to know the particulars."

"Well, well," said the deacon, "the lawyers will be at my house to-morrow evening, and if you have any concern about it, you may as well come along."

Uncle Jaw wondered all the way home at what he could have done to get himself into the confidence of the old deacon, who, he rejoiced to think, was a-going to "take" and go to law like other folks.

The next day there was an appearance of some bustle and preparation about the deacon's house; the best room was opened and aired; an ovenful of cake was baked; and our friend Joseph, with a face full of business, was seen passing to and fro, in and out of the house, from various closetings with the deacon. The deacon's lady bustled about the house with an air of wonderful mystery, and even gave her directions about eggs and raisins in a whisper, lest they should possibly let out some eventful secret.

The afternoon of that day Joseph appeared at the house of the sisters, stating that there was to be company at the deacon's that evening, and he was sent to invite them.

"Why, what's got into the deacon's folks lately," said Silence, "to have company so often? Joe Adams, this 'ere is some 'cut up' of yours. Come, what are you up to now?"

"Come, come, dress yourselves and get ready," said Joseph; and, stepping up to Susan, as she was following Silence out of the room, he whispered something into her ear, at which she stopped short and colored violently.

"Why, Joseph, what do you mean?"

"It is so," said he.

"No, no, Joseph; no, I can't, indeed I can't."

"But you can, Susan."

"Oh, Joseph, don't."

"Oh, Susan, do."

"Why, how strange, Joseph!"

"Come, come, my dear, you keep me waiting. If you have any objections on the score of propriety, we will talk about them tomorrow"; and our hero looked so saucy and so resolute that there was no disputing further; so, after a little more lingering and blushing on Susan's part, and a few kisses and persuasions on the part of the suitor, Miss Susan seemed to be brought to a state of resignation.

At a table in the middle of Uncle Enos's north front room were seated the two lawyers, whose legal opinion was that evening to be fully made up. The younger of these, Squire Moseley, was a rosy, portly, laughing little bachelor, who boasted that he had offered himself, in rotation, to every pretty girl within twenty miles round, and, among others, to Susan Jones, notwithstanding which he still remained a bachelor, with a fair prospect of being an old one; but none of these things disturbed the boundless flow of good nature and complacency with which he seemed at all times full to overflowing. On the present occasion he appeared to be particularly in his element, as if he had some law business in hand remarkably suited to his turn of mind; for, on finishing the inspection of the papers, he started up, slapped his graver brother on the back, made two or three flourishes round the room, and then seizing the old deacon's hand, shook it violently, exclaiming,—

"All's right, deacon, all's right! Go it! go it! hurrah!"

When Uncle Jaw entered, the deacon, without preface, handed him a chair and the papers, saying,—

"These papers are what you wanted to see. I just wish you would read them over."

Uncle Jaw read them deliberately over. "Didn't I tell ye so, deacon? The case is as clear as a bell: now ye will go to law, won't you?"

"Look here, Mr. Adams; now you have seen these papers, and heard what's to be said, I'll make you an offer. Let your son marry Susan Jones, and I'll burn these papers and say no more about it, and there won't be a girl in the parish with a finer portion."

Uncle Jaw opened his eyes with amazement, and looked at the old man, his mouth gradually expanding wider and wider, as if he hoped, in time, to swallow the idea.

"Well, now, I swan!" at length he ejaculated.

"I mean just as I say," said the deacon.

"Why, that's the same as giving the gal five hundred dollars out of your own pocket, and she ain't no relation neither."

"I know it," said the Deacon; "but I have said I will do it."

"What upon 'arth for?" said Uncle Jaw.

"To make peace," said the deacon, "and to let you know that when I say it is better to give up one's rights than to quarrel, I mean so. I am an old man; my children are dead,"—his voice faltered,—"my treasures are laid up in heaven; if I can make the children happy, why, I will. When I thought I had lost the land, I made up my mind to lose it, and so I can now."

Uncle Jaw looked fixedly on the old deacon, and said,—

"Well, deacon, I believe you. I vow, if you hain't got something ahead in t'other world, I'd like to know who has—that's all; so, if Joe has no objections, and I rather guess he won't have—"

"The short of the matter is," said the squire, "we'll have a wedding; so come on"; and with that he threw open the parlor door, where stood Susan and Joseph in a recess by the window, while Silence and the Rev. Mr. Bissel were drawn up by the fire, and the deacon's lady was sweeping up the hearth, as she had been doing ever since the party arrived.

Instantly Joseph took the hand of Susan, and led her to the middle of the room; the merry squire seized the hand of Miss Silence, and placed her as bridesmaid, and before any one knew what they were about, the ceremony was in actual progress, and the minister, having been previously instructed, made the two one with extraordinary celerity.

"What! what! what!" said Uncle Jaw. "Joseph! Deacon!"

"Fair bargain, sir," said the squire. "Hand over your papers, deacon."

The deacon handed them, and the squire, having read them aloud, proceeded, with much ceremony, to throw them into the fire; after which, in a mock solemn oration, he gave a statement of the whole affair, and concluded with a grave exhortation to the new couple on the duties of wedlock, which unbent the risibles even of the minister himself.

Uncle Jaw looked at his pretty daughter-in-law, who stood half smiling, half blushing, receiving the congratulations of the party, and then at Miss Silence, who appeared full as much taken by surprise as himself.

"Well, well, Miss Silence, these 'ere young folks have come round us slick enough," said he. "I don't see but we must shake hands upon it." And the warlike powers shook hands accordingly, which was a signal for general merriment.

As the company were dispersing, Miss Silence laid hold of the good deacon, and by main strength dragged him aside. "Deacon," said she, "I take back all that 'ere I said about you, every word on't."

"Don't say any more about it, Miss Silence," said the good man; "it's gone by, and let it go."

"Joseph!" said his father, the next morning, as he was sitting at breakfast with Joseph and Susan, "I calculate I shall feel kinder proud of this 'ere gal! and I'll tell you what, I'll jest give you that nice little delicate Stanton place that I took on Stanton's mortgage: it's a nice little place, with green blinds, and flowers, and all them things, just right for Susan."

And accordingly, many happy years flew over the heads of the young couple in the Stanton place, long after the hoary hairs of their kind benefactor, the deacon, were laid with reverence in the dust. Uncle Jaw was so far wrought upon by the magnanimity of the good old man as to be very materially changed for the better. Instead of quarreling in real earnest all around the neighborhood, he confined himself merely to battling the opposite side of every question with his son, which, as the latter was somewhat of a logician, afforded a pretty good field for the exercise of his powers; and he was heard to declare at the funeral of the old deacon, that, "after all, a man got as much, and maybe more, to go along as the deacon did, than to be all the time fisting and jawing; though I tell you what it is," said he, afterwards, " 't ain't everyone that has the deacon's faculty, anyhow."

Sara Willis Eldredge Farrington Parton, "Fanny Fern"

1811–1872

SARA WILLIS grew up in Boston, where her father, a grim Presbyterian, published a religious newspaper. She was devoted to her mother, who, she believed, would have distinguished herself in literature had she not been so harried by domestic cares. One of her brothers, Nathaniel P. Willis, became a rich and prominent newspaper editor. Sara was educated at Catharine Beecher's Hartford Female Seminary, where Catharine and Harriet Beecher remembered her as mischievous but bright and lovable. She married Charles Eldredge, who died young and left her penniless with two little girls. Neither his family nor hers would support them. After trying vainly to support herself, she agreed to a marriage of convenience with Samuel Farrington. When this proved disastrous, she scandalized her family by leaving him and was thrown entirely on her own resources. She discovered that she could not earn a living wage by sewing, and then thought of journalism. She hoped for help from her brother, but he told her she had no talent. Fortunately, she persisted, publishing her first sketch in 1851. After a few years of exploitation, she was running regular columns in a series of newspapers, attracted a large and devoted readership, and became the most highly paid newspaper writer in America. She adopted the pseudonym Fanny Fern, which she also used in her personal life. In 1856 she married James Parton, a well-known biographer. She continued writing columns all her life; her last one appeared two days after her death from cancer.

Fanny Fern's earlier essays often conformed to stereotyped expectations that women's writing was sentimental, as she gushed over sacred maternal devotion ("Mother's Room") or over the grave of a child she had never seen ("Little Benny"). But she soon developed a brisk satiric tone; she delighted in puncturing male pomposity, exposing male selfishness, and setting forth the trials of wives and housekeepers. She moved from humorous complaints to serious attacks on the double standard and on economic exploitation of women. In her novel *Ruth Hall* (1855) she shocked contemporary readers by exposing her family's callous treatment of her (vengeance was not consistent with womanly gentleness) and by admiringly presenting a self-assertive heroine; nevertheless it was, like all her works, a best-seller.

BIBLIOGRAPHY

Fanny Fern, *Ruth Hall and Other Writings*. Edited, with introduction by Joyce W. Warren. New Brunswick, N.J.: Rutgers University Press, 1986.

Aunt Hetty on Matrimony

"Now girls," said Aunt Hetty, "put down your embroidery and worsted work; do something sensible, and stop building air-castles, and talking of lovers and honeymoons. It makes me sick; it is perfectly antimonial.[1] Love is a farce; matrimony is a humbug; husbands are domestic Napoleons, Neroes, Alexanders,—sighing for other hearts to conquer, after they are sure of yours. The honeymoon is as short-lived as a lucifer-match; after that you may wear your wedding-dress at the wash tub, and your night-cap to meeting, and your husband wouldn't know it. You may pick up your own pocket-handkerchief, help yourself to a chair, and split your gown across the back reaching over the table to get a piece of butter, while he is laying in his breakfast as if it was the last meal he should eat this side of Jordan. When he gets through he will aid your digestion,—while you are sipping your first cup of coffee,—by inquiring what you'll have for dinner; whether the cold lamb was all ate yesterday; if the charcoal is all out, and what you gave for the last green tea you bought. Then

---

[1] Nauseating. Antimony was used in a common emetic.

he gets up from the table, lights his cigar with the last evening's paper, that you have not had a chance to read; gives two or three whiffs of smoke,—which are sure to give you a headache for the forenoon,—and, just as his coat-tail is vanishing through the door, apologizes for not doing 'that errand' for you yesterday,—thinks it doubtful if he can to-day,—"so *pressed with business.*" Hear of him at eleven o'clock, taking an ice-cream with some ladies at a confectioner's, while you are new-lining his old coat-sleeves. Children by the ears all day, can't get out to take the air, feel as crazy as a fly in a drum; husband comes home at night, nods a "How d'ye do, Fan," boxes Charley's ears, stands little Fanny in the corner, sits down in the easiest chair in the warmest corner, puts his feet up over the grate, shutting out all the fire, while the baby's little pug nose grows blue with the cold; reads the newspaper all to himself, solaces his inner man with a hot cup of tea, and, just as you are laboring under the hallucination that he will ask you to take a mouthful of fresh air with him, he puts on his dressing-gown and slippers, and begins to reckon up the family expenses! after which he lies down on the sofa, and you keep time with your needle, while he sleeps till nine o'clock. Next morning, ask him to leave you a "little money,"—he looks at you as if to be sure that you are in your right mind, draws a sigh long enough and strong enough to inflate a pair of bellows, and asks you "what you want with it, and if a half a dollar won't do?"— Gracious king! as if those little shoes, and stockings, and petticoats could be had for half a dollar! Oh girls! set your affections on cats, poodles, parrots or lap dogs; but let matrimony alone. It's the hardest way on earth of getting a living—you never know when your work is done. Think of carrying eight or nine children through the measles, chicken pox, rash, mumps, and scarlet fever, some of 'em twice over; it makes my head ache to think of it. Oh, you may scrimp and save, and twist and turn, and dig and delve, and economise *and die,* and your husband will marry again, take what you have saved to dress his second wife with, and she'll take your portrait for a fireboard, and,—but, what's the use of talking? I'll warrant every one of you'll try it, the first chance you get! there's a sort of bewitchment about it, somehow. I wish one half the world warn't fools, and the other half idiots, I do. Oh, dear!"

Olive Branch
December 6, 1851

The Tear of a Wife

"The tear of a loving girl is like a dew-drop on a rose; but on the cheek of a wife, is a drop of poison to her husband."

It is "an ill wind that blows *nobody* any good." Papas will be happy to hear that twenty-five dollar pocket-handkerchiefs can be dispensed with *now,* in the bridal *trousseau.* Their "occupation's gone"! Matrimonial tears "are poison." There is no knowing what you will do, girls, with that escape-valve shut off; but that is no more to the point, than—whether you have anything to smile at or not; one thing is settled—*you mustn't cry!* Never mind back aches, and side aches, and head aches, and dropsical complaints, and smoky chimneys, and old coats, and young babies! *Smile! It flatters your husband.* He wants to be *considered* the source of your happiness; whether he was baptized *Nero* or *Moses!* Your mind *never* being supposed to be occupied with any other subject than himself, of course a tear is a tacit reproach. Besides, you miserable little whimperer, what have you to cry for? A-i-n-t y-o-u m-a-r-r-i-e-d? Isn't that the *summum bonum*—the height of feminine ambition? You *can't* get beyond *that!* It's the *jumping-off place!* You've arriv!—got to the end of your journey! Stage puts up *there!* You've nothing to do but retire on your laurels, and spend the rest of your life endeavoring to be thankful that you are Mrs. John Smith! *"Smile!" you simpleton!*

Olive Branch
Aug. 28, 1852

Soliloquy of a Housemaid

Oh dear, dear! Wonder if my mistress knows I'm made of flesh and blood? I've been upstairs five times, in fifteen minutes, to hand her things about four feet from her rocking-chair! *Ain't I tired?* Wish I could be rich once, just to show ladies how to treat their servants! *Such* a rheumatiz as I've got in my shoulders, going up on that shed in the rain. It's "Sally do this," and "Sally do that," till I wish I hadn't been baptized at all; and I might as well go *farther* back while I'm about it, and say I don't know what I was born for! Didn't master say some AWFUL words about those eggs? Oh, I can't stand it—haven't heart enough left to swear by.

Now, instead of ordering me round like a dray-horse, if they'd look up *smiling like,* now and then, or ask me how my rheumatiz did; or even say good morning, Sally—or show some sort of interest in a fellow-cretur, I should know whether it was worthwhile to try to live or not. A soft word would ease the wheels of my treadmill amazingly, and wouldn't *kill them,* anyhow!

Look at my clothes; all at sixes and sevens; can't get time to sew on a string or button, except at night, and then I'm so sleepy I can't but tell whether I'm the candle or the candle's *me!* They call "Sunday a day of rest," too, I guess!—more company, more care, more confusion than any day in the week! If I own a soul, I haven't heard how to take care of it, for many a long day. Wonder if my master and mistress calculate to *pay* me for *that,* if I lose it? It's a question in *my* mind. Land of Goshen! I ain't sure I've got a mind!—there's that bell again!

True Flag
September 11, 1852

Children's Rights

Men's rights! Women's rights! I throw down the gauntlet for children's rights! Yes, little pets, Fanny Fern's about "takin' notes," and she'll "print 'em," too, if you don't get your dues. She has seen you seated by a pleasant window, in a railroad car, with your bright eyes dancing with delight at the prospect of all the pretty things you were going to see, forcibly ejected by some overgrown Napoleon, who fancied your place and thought, in his wisdom, that children had no taste for anything but sugar-candy. Fanny Fern knew better. She knew that the pretty trees and flowers, and bright blue sky, gave your little souls a thrill of delight, though you could not tell why; and she knew that great big man's soul was a great deal smaller than yours, to sit there and read a stupid political paper, when such a glowing landscape was before him, that he might have feasted his eyes upon. And she longed to wipe away the big tear that you didn't dare to let fall; and she understood how a little girl or boy, that didn't get a ride every day in the year, should not be quite able to swallow that great big lump in the throat, as he or she sat jammed down in a dark, crowded corner of the car, instead of sitting by that pleasant window.

Yes; and Fanny has seen you sometimes, when you've been muffled up to the tip of your little nose in woollen wrappers, in a close, crowded church, nodding your little drowsy heads, and keeping time to the sixth-lie and seventh-lie of some pompous theologian, whose preaching would have been high Dutch to you, had you been wide awake.

And she has seen you sitting, like little automatons, in a badly-ventilated school-room, with your nervous little toes at just such an angle, for hours; under the tuition of a Miss Nancy Nipper, who didn't care a rush-light[1] whether your spine was as crooked as the letter S or not, if the Great Mogul Committee, who marched in once a month to make the "grand tour," voted her a "model school-marm."

Yes, and that ain't all. She has seen you sent off to bed, just at the witching hour of candle-light, when some entertaining guest was in the middle of a delightful story, that you, poor, miserable "little pitcher," was doomed never to hear the end of! Yes, and she has seen "the line and plummet"[2] laid to you so rigidly, that you were driven to deceit and evasion; and then seen you punished for the very sin your tormentors helped you to commit. And she has seen your ears boxed just as hard for tearing a hole in your best pinafore, or breaking a China cup, as for telling as big a lie as Ananias and Sapphira did.[3]

---

[1] A flimsy candle.
[2] Line with a weight attached, used to determine perpendicularity; in this case, rigid adherence to truth.
[3] Ananias and Sapphira tried to cheat the Church by lying about money they had received, and were struck dead for their lie (Acts of the Apostles, chapter 5).

And when, by patient labor, you had reared an edifice of tiny blocks,—fairer in its architectural proportions, to your infantile eye, than any palace in ancient Rome,—she has seen it ruthlessly kicked into a shattered ruin by somebody in the house whose dinner hadn't digested!

Never mind. I wish I was mother to the whole of you! Such glorious times as we'd have! Reading pretty books, that had no big words in 'em; going to school where you could sneeze without getting a rap on the head for not asking leave first; and going to church on the quiet, blessed Sabbath, where the minister—like our dear Savior—sometimes remembered to "take little children in his arms, and bless them."[4]

Then, if you asked me a question, I wouldn't pretend not to hear; or lazily tell you I "didn't know," or turn you off with some fabulous evasion, for your memory to chew for a cud till you were old enough to see how you had been fooled. And I'd never wear such a fashionable gown that you couldn't climb on my lap whenever the fit took you; or refuse to kiss you, for fear you'd ruffle my curls, or my collar, or my temper,—not a bit of it; and then you should pay me with your merry laugh, and your little confiding hand slid ever trustingly in mine.

O, I tell you, my little pets, Fanny is sick of din, and strife, and envy, and uncharitableness!—and she'd rather, by ten thousand, live in a little world full of fresh, guileless, loving little children, than in this great museum full of such dry, dusty, withered hearts.

Olive Branch
January 29, 1853

---

[4]See Mark 10:16.

Sewing Machines

There's "nothing new under the sun;"—so I've read, somewhere; either in Ecclesiastes[1] or *Uncle Tom's Cabin;* but at any rate, I was forcibly reminded of the profound wisdom of the remark upon seeing a great flourish of trumpets in the papers about a "Sewing Machine," that had been *lately invented.*[2]

Now if *I* know anything of history, that discovery dates back as far as the Garden of Eden. If *Mrs. Adam* wasn't *the first sewing machine, I'll give up guessing.* Didn't she go right to work making aprons, before she had done receiving her bridal calls from the beasts and beastesses? Certainly she did, and I honor her for it, too.

Well—do you suppose all her pretty little descendants who ply their "busy fingers in the upper lofts of tailors, and hatters, and vestmakers, and 'finding' establishments," are going to be superseded by that dumb old thing? Do you suppose their young and enterprising patrons prefer the creaking of a crazy machine to the music of their young voices? Not by a great deal!

It's something, I can tell you, for them to see their pretty faces light up, when they pay off their wages of a Saturday night (small fee enough! too often, God knows!) Pity that the *shilling heart* so often accompanies the *guinea means.*

Oh, launch out, gentlemen! Don't *always* look at things with a *business* eye. Those fragile forms are young, to toil so unremittingly. God made no distinction of *sex* when he said—"The laborer is worthy of his hire."[3] Man's cupidity puts that interpretation upon it.

Those young operatives in your employ pass, in their daily walks, forms youthful as their own, "clothed in purple and fine linen," who *"toil not, neither do they spin."*[4] Oh, teach them not to look after their "satin and sheen," purchased at such a fearful cost, with a discouraged sigh!

For one, I can never pass such a "fallen angel" with a "stand aside" feeling. A neglected youth, an early orphanage, poverty, beauty, coarse fare, the weary day of toil lengthened into night,—a mere

[1]Ecclesiastes 1:9.
[2]Invented by Elias Howe in 1845.
[3]Luke 10:7.
[4]Matthew 6:28. FF is alluding to prostitutes.

pittance its reward. Youth, health, young blood, and the practised wile of the ready tempter! *Oh, where's the marvel?*

Think of all this, when you poise that hardly earned dollar, on your business finger. What if it were your own delicate sister? Let a LITTLE heart creep into that shrewd bargain. 'Twill be an investment in the Bank of Heaven, that shall return to you four-fold.

True Flag
January 29, 1853

Mrs. Adolphus Smith Sporting the "Blue Stocking"

Well, I think I'll finish that story for the editor of the "Dutchman." Let me see; where did I leave off? The setting sun was just gilding with his last ray—"Ma, I want some bread and molasses"—(yes, dear) gilding with his last ray the church spire—"Wife, where's my Sunday pants?" *(Under the bed, dear)* the church spire of Inverness, when a—"There's nothing under the bed, dear, but your lace cap"—(Perhaps they are in the coal hod in the closet) when a horseman was seen approaching—"Ma'am, the *pertators* is out; not one for dinner"—(Take some turnips) approaching, covered with dust, and—"Wife! the baby has swallowed a button"—(*Reverse him,* dear—take him by the heels) and waving in his hand a banner, on which was written—"Ma! I've torn my pantaloons"—liberty or death! The inhabitants rushed *en masse*—"Wife! *will* you leave off scribbling? (Don't be disagreeable, Smith, I'm just getting inspired) to the public square, where De Begnis, who had been secretly—"Butcher wants to see you, ma'am"—secretly informed of the traitors'—"Forgot *which* you said, ma'am, sausages or mutton chop"—movements, gave orders to fire; not less than twenty—"My gracious! Smith, you haven't been *reversing* that child all this time; he's as black as your coat; and that boy of *yours* has torn up the first sheet of my manuscript. There!

it's no use for a married woman to cultivate her intellect.—Smith, hand me those twins.

Fern Leaves, Second Series
1854[1]

Fresh Leaves

This little volume has just been laid upon our table.[1] The publishers have done all they could for it, with regard to outward adorning. No doubt it will be welcomed by those who admire this lady's style of writing: we confess ourselves not to be of that number. We have never seen Fanny Fern, nor do we desire to do so. We imagine her, from her writings, to be a muscular, black-browed, grenadier-looking female, who would be more at home in a boxing gallery than in a parlor,—a vociferous, demonstrative, strong-minded horror,—a woman only by virtue of her dress. Bah! the very thought sickens us. We have read, or, rather, tried to read, her halloo-there effusions. When we take up a woman's book we expect to find gentleness, timidity, and that lovely reliance on the patronage of our sex which constitutes a woman's greatest charm. We do not wish to be startled by bold expressions, or disgusted with exhibitions of masculine weaknesses. We do not desire to see a woman wielding the scimitar blade of sarcasm. If she be, unfortunately, endowed with a gift so dangerous, let her—as she values the approbation of our sex— fold it in a napkin. Fanny's strong-minded nose would probably turn up at this inducement. Thank heaven! there are still women who *are* women—who know the place Heaven assigned them, and keep it— who do not waste floods of ink and paper, brow-beating men and stirring up silly women;—who do not teach children that a game of

---

[1]FF's essays were gathered into volumes of *Fern Leaves.*

[1]*Fresh Leaves,* the third collection of FF's newspaper sketches (1857). This is a parody of a conventional male critic's review of a woman's book.

romps is of as much importance as Blair's Philosophy;—who have not the presumption to advise clergymen as to their duties, or lecture doctors, and savants;—who live for something else than to astonish a gaping, idiotic crowd. Thank heaven! there are women writers who do not disturb our complacence or serenity; whose books lull one to sleep like a strain of gentle music; who excite no antagonism, or angry feeling. Woman never was intended for an irritant: she should be oil upon the troubled waters of manhood—soft and amalgamating, a necessary but unobtrusive ingredient;—never challenging attention—never throwing the gauntlet of defiance to a beard, but softly purring beside it lest it bristle and scratch.

The very fact that Fanny Fern has, in the language of her admirers, "elbowed her way through unheard of difficulties," shows that she is an antagonistic, pugilistic female. One must needs, forsooth, get out of her way, or be pushed one side, or trampled down. How much more womanly to have allowed herself to be doubled up by adversity, and quietly laid away on the shelf of fate, than to have rolled up her sleeves, and gone to fisticuffs with it. Such a woman may conquer, it is true, but her victory will cost her dear; it will neither be forgotten nor forgiven—let her put that in her apron pocket.

As to Fanny Fern's grammar, rhetoric, and punctuation, they are beneath criticism. It is all very well for her to say, those who wish commas, semi-colons and periods must look for them in the printer's case, or that she who finds ideas must not be expected to find rhetoric or grammar; for our part, we should be gratified if we had even found any ideas!

We regret to be obliged to speak thus of a lady's book: it gives us great pleasure, when we can do so conscientiously, to pat lady writers on the head; but we owe a duty to the public which will not permit us to recommend to their favorable notice an aspirant who has been unwomanly enough so boldly to contest every inch of ground in order to reach them—an aspirant at once so high-stepping and so ignorant, so plausible, yet so pernicious. We have a conservative horror of this pop-gun, torpedo female; we predict for Fanny Fern's "Leaves" only a fleeting autumnal flutter.

New York Ledger
October 10, 1857

A Word on the Other Side

Heaven give our sex patience to read such trash as the following: "If irritation should occur, a woman must expect to hear from her husband a strength and vehemence of language far more than the occasion requires."

Now, with my arms akimbo, I ask, *why* a woman should "expect" it? Is it because her husband claims to be her intellectual superior? Is it because he is his wife's natural protector? Is it because an unblest marriage lot is more tolerable to her susceptible organization and monotonous life, than to his hardier nature relieved by outdoor occupations? Is it because the thousand diversions which society winks at and excuses in his case, are stamped in hers as guilty and unhallowed? Is it because maternity has never gasped out in his hearing its sacred agony? Is it because no future wife is to mourn in that man's imitative boy his father's low standard of a husband's duty?

Oh, away with such one-sided moralizing; that the law provides no escape from a brutal husband, who is breaking his wife's heart, unless he also attempts breaking her head, should be, and, I thank God, is, by every magnanimous and honorable man—and, alas, they are all too few—a wife's strongest defence. I have no patience with those who would reduce woman to a mere machine, to be twitched this way and twitched that, and jarred, and unharmonized at the dogged will of a stupid brute. (This does not sound pretty, I know; but when a woman is irritated, men "must expect to hear a strength and vehemence of language far more than the occasion requires!") I have no patience with those who preach one code of morality for the wife, and another for the husband. If the marriage vow allows him to absent himself from his house under cover of darkness, scorning to give account of himself, it also allows it to her. There is no sex designated in the fifth commandment.[1] *"Thou* shalt not," and *"thou,"* and *"thou!"* There is no excuse that I have ever yet heard offered for a man's violation of it, that should not answer equally for his wife. What is right for him is just as right for her. It is right for neither. The weakness of their cause who plead for license in this

---

[1] "Honor thy father and thy mother." The seventh commandment, "Thou shalt not commit adultery," would seem more relevant here.

sin, was never better shown than in a defence lately set up in this city, viz., that "without houses of infamy our wives and daughters would not be safe."

Oh, most shallow reasoner, *how safe* are our "wives and daughters" with them? Let our medical men, versed in the secrets of family histories, answer! Let weeping wives, who mourn over little graves, tell you!

But while women submit to have their wifely honor insulted, and their lives jeopardized by the legalized or un-legalized brutality of husbands, just so long they will have to suffer it, and I was going to say, just so long they *ought*. Let not those women who have too little self-respect to take their lives in their hands, and say to a dissolute husband, this you can never give, and this you shall not therefore take away—whine about "their lot." "But the children?" Aye—the children—shame that the law should come between them and a good mother![2] Still—better let her leave them, than remain to bring into the world their puny brothers and sisters. Does she shrink from the toil of self-support? What toil, let me ask, could be more hopeless, more endless, *more degrading* than that from which she turns away?

There are all phases of misery. A case has recently come under my notice, of a wife rendered feeble by the frequently recurring cares and pains of maternity, whose husband penuriously refuses to obtain medical advice or household help, when her tottering step and trembling hands tell more eloquently than words of mine could do her total unfitness for family duties. And this when he has a good business—when, as a mere matter of policy, it were dollars in his short-sighted pocket to hoard well her strength, who, in the pitying language of Him who will most surely avenge her cause, "hath done what she could."[3]

Now I ask *you,* and *you,* and *you,* if this woman should lay down her life on the altar of that man's selfishness? I ask you if he is not her murderer, as truly, but not as mercifully, as if our most righteous, woman-protecting law saw him place the glittering knife at her throat? I ask you if she has not as God-given a right to her life, as he has to his? I ask you if, through fear of the world, she should stay there to die? I ask you if that world could be sterner, its eye

---

[2]Husbands usually got custody of the children, regardless of the circumstances.
[3]Mark 14:8 (Christ, speaking of Mary Magdalene).

colder, its heart flintier, its voice harsher, than that from which she turns—all honor to her self-sacrificing nature—*sorrowing* away?

Perhaps you ask would I have a woman, for every trifling cause, "leave her husband and family?" Most emphatically, *No*. But there are aggravated cases for which the law provides no remedy—from which it affords no protection; and that hundreds of suffering women bear their chains because they have not courage to face a scandal-loving world, to whom it matters not a pin that their every nerve is quivering with suppressed agony, is no proof to the contrary of what I assert. What I say is this: in such cases, let a woman who *has the self-sustaining power* quietly take her fate in her own hands, and right herself. Of course she will be misjudged and abused. *It is for her to choose whether she can better bear this at hands from which she has a rightful claim for love and protection, or from a nine-days-wonder-loving public.* These are bold words; but they are needed words—words whose full import I have well considered, and from the responsibility of which I do not shrink.

New York Ledger
October 24, 1857

A Law More Nice Than Just
Number II

After all, having tried it I affirm that nothing reconciles a woman quicker to her femininity than an experiment in male apparel, although I still maintain that she should not be forbidden by law to adopt it when necessity requires; at least, not till the practice is amended by which a female clerk, who performs her duty equally well with a male clerk, receives less salary, simply because she is a woman.

To have to jump on to the cars when in motion, and scramble yourself on to the platform as best you may without a helping hand; to be nudged roughly in the ribs by the conductor with, "your fare, sir?" to have your pretty little toes trod on, and no healing "beg your pardon," applied to the smart; to have all those nice-looking men who used to make you such crushing bows, and give you such insinuating smiles, pass you without the slightest interest in your coat tails, and perhaps push you against the wall or into the gutter, with a word tabooed by the clergy. In fine, to dispense with all those delicious little politenesses (for men are great bears to each other) to which one has been accustomed, and yet feel no inclination to take advantage of one's corduroys and secure an equivalent by making interest with the "fair sex," stale to you as a thrice-told tale. Isn't *that* a situation?

To be subject to the promptings of that unstifleable feminine desire for adornment, which is right and lovely within proper limits, and yet have no field for your operations. To have to conceal your silken hair, and yet be forbidden a becoming moustache, or whiskers, or beard—(all hail beards, I say!). To choke up your nice throat with a disguising cravat; to hide your bust (I trust no Miss Nancy is blushing) under a baggy vest. To have nobody ask you to ice cream, and yet be forbidden, by your horrible disgust of tobacco, to smoke. To have a gentleman ask you "the time sir?" when you are new to the geography of your watch-pocket. To accede to an invitation to test your "heft," by sitting down in one of those street-weighing chairs, and have one of the male bystanders, taking hold of your foot, remark, "Halloo, sir, you must not rest these upon the ground while you are being weighed"; and go grinning away in your coat-sleeve at your truly feminine faux pas.

And yet—and yet—to be able to step over the ferry-boat chain when you are in a distracted hurry, like any other fellow, without waiting for that tedious unhooking process, and quietly to enjoy your triumph over scores of impatient-waiting crushed petticoats behind you; to taste that nice lager beer "on draught"; to pick up contraband bits of science in a Medical Museum, forbidden to crinoline, and hold conversations with intelligent men, who supposing you to be a man, consequently talk sense to you. That is worth while.

Take it all in all, though, I thank the gods I am a woman. I had rather be loved than make love; though I could beat the makers of it, out and out, if I did not think it my duty to refrain out of regard to their feelings, and the final disappointment of the deluded women! But—oh, dear, I want to do such a quantity of "improper" things, that there is not the slightest real harm in doing. I want to see and know a thousand things which are forbidden to flounces—custom only can tell why—I can't. I want the free use of my ankles, for this summer at least, to take a journey; I want to climb and wade, and tramp about, without giving a thought to my clothes; without carrying about with me a long procession of trunks and boxes, which are the inevitable penalty of femininity as at present appareled. I hate a Bloomer,[1] such as we have seen—words are weak to say how much; I hate myself as much in a man's dress; and yet I want to run my fingers through my cropped hair some fine morning without the bore of dressing it; put on some sort of loose blouse affair—it must be pretty, though—and a pair of Turkish trousers—*not* Bloomers—and a cap, or hat—and start; nary a trunk—"nary" a bandbox. Wouldn't that be fine? But propriety scowls and says, "ain't you ashamed of yourself, Fanny Fern?" *Yes, I am,* Miss Nancy. I *am* ashamed of myself, that I haven't the courage to carry out what would be so eminently convenient, and right, and proper under the circumstances. I am ashamed of myself that I sit like a fool on the piazza of some hotel every season, gazing at some distant mountain, which every pulse and muscle of my body, and every faculty of my soul, are urging me to climb, that I may "see the kingdoms of the earth and the glory of them."[2] I *am* ashamed of myself that you, Miss Nancy, with your uplifted forefinger and your pursed-up mouth, should keep me out of a dress in which only I can hope to do such things. Can't I make a compromise with you, Miss Nancy? for I'm getting restless, as these lovely summer days pass on. I'd write you such long accounts of beautiful things, Miss Nancy—things which God made for female as well as male eyes to see; and I should come home so strong and healthy, Miss Nancy—a freckle or two, perhaps—but who cares? O-h-n-o-w, Miss Nancy, d-o—Pshaw! you cross old termagant! May Lucifer fly away wid ye.

New York Ledger
July 17, 1858

---

[1]Some feminists were wearing "Bloomers," a relatively convenient costume consisting of a short skirt worn over baggy trousers, popularized by Amelia Bloomer. Women wearing this costume were ridiculed and reviled.
[2]Matthew 4:8

Independence

"Fourth of July." Well—I don't feel patriotic. Perhaps I might if they would stop that deafening racket. Washington was very well, if he *couldn't* spell, and I'm glad we are all free; but as a woman—I shouldn't know it, didn't some orator tell me. Can I go out of an evening without a hat[1] at my side? Can I go out with one on my head without danger of a station-house? Can I clap my hands at some public speaker when I am nearly bursting with delight? Can I signify the contrary when my hair stands on end with vexation? Can I stand up in the cars "like a gentleman" without being immediately invited "to sit down"? Can I get into an omnibus without having my sixpence taken from my hand and given to the driver? Can I cross Broadway without having a policeman tackled to my helpless elbow? Can I go to see anything *pleasant,* like an execution or a dissection? Can I drive that splendid "Lantern,"[2] distancing—like his owner— all competitors? Can I have the nomination for "Governor of Vermont," like our other contributor, John G. Saxe? Can I be a Senator, that I may hurry up that millennial International Copyright Law?[3] Can I *even* be President? Bah—you know I can't. *"Free!"* Humph!

New York Ledger
July 30, 1859

---

[1] I.e., a man (women wore bonnets). Next sentence: it was illegal for women to dress as men.

[2] Lantern, a famous trotting horse, belonged to the editor of the *Ledger,* FF's employer.

[3] Before the international copyright agreement was signed (1886), books published in one country could be freely pirated in other countries. As a woman, FF could not participate in lawmaking.

A Reasonable Being

If there's anything I hate, it is "a reasonable being." Says the lazy mother to her restless child whom she has imprisoned within doors and whose active mind seeks solutions of passing remarks, "Don't bother, Tommy; do be *reasonable,* and not tease with your questions." Says the husband to his sick or overtasked wife, when she cries from mere mental or physical exhaustion, "How I hate tears; do be a reasonable being." Says the conservative father to his son, whom he would force into some profession or employment for which nature has utterly disqualified him, "Are you wiser than your father? do be a reasonable being." Says the mother to sweet sixteen, whom she would marry to a sixty-five-year-old money-bag, "Think what a thing it is to have a fine establishment; do be a reasonable being."

As near as I can get at it, to be a reasonable being, is to laugh when your heart aches; it is to give confidence and receive none; it is faithfully to keep your own promises, and never mind such a trifle as having promises broken to you. It is never to have or to promulgate a dissenting opinion. It is either to be born a fool, or in lack of that to become a hypocrite, trying to become a "reasonable being."

New York Ledger
February 16, 1861

A Bit of Injustice

As a general thing there are few people who speak approbatively of a woman who has a smart business talent or capability. No matter how isolated or destitute her condition, the majority would consider it more "feminine" would she unobtrusively gather up her thimble, and, retiring into some out-of-the-way place, gradually scoop out her coffin with it, than to develop that smart turn for business which would lift her at once out of her troubles; and which, in a man so situated, would be applauded as exceedingly praiseworthy. The most curious part of it is, that they who are loudest in their abhorrence of this "unfeminine" trait, are they who are the most intolerant of dependent female relatives. "Anywhere, out of this world," would be their reply, if applied to by the latter for a straw for the drowning. "Do something for yourself," is their advice in general terms; but, above all, you are to do it quietly, unobtrusively; in other words, die as soon as you like on sixpence a day, but don't trouble *us!* Of such cold-blooded comfort, in sight of a new-made grave, might well be born "the *smart business woman.*" And, in truth, so it often is. Hands that never toiled before, grow rough with labor; eyes that have been tearless for long, happy years, drop agony over the slow lagging hours; feet that have been tenderly led and cared for, stumble as best they may in the new, rough path of self-denial. But out of this bitterness groweth sweetness. *No crust so tough as the grudged bread of dependence.* Blessed the "smart business woman" who, in a self-sustained crisis like this, after having through much tribulation reached the goal, is able to look back on the weary track and see the sweet flower of faith and trust in her kind still blooming.

New York Ledger
June 8, 1861

A Chapter for Parents

There is one great defect in the present system of family education. Not that there is only one; but we wish to call attention at present to the practice of obliging the *girls* of a family, in almost every instance in which self-denial is involved, to give way to the boys. "Remember he is your brother," is the appeal to tender little hearts, which, though often swelling under a sense of injustice, naturally give way under this argument. This might be all very well, were the boys also taught reciprocity in this matter, but as this unfortunately is not often the case, a monstrous little tyrant is produced whose

overbearing exactions and hourly selfishnesses are disgusting to witness. As years roll on, Augustus's handkerchiefs are hemmed at half
a wink from his lordship that he wishes it done, and his breakfast
kept hot for him, though he change his breakfast hour as often as
the disgusted cook leaves her place; while his sister's faintest intimation of her desire for his escort of an evening is met with a yawn,
and an allusion to "the fellows" who are always "expecting him." It
is easy to see what delightful ideas of reciprocity in mutual good
offices Augustus will carry into the conjugal state, if he ever marries.
His bride soon finds this out to her dismay, and half a dozen babies,
and her wakeful nights and careworn days, are no excuse for not
always placing his clean linen on a chair by his bed when needed,
"to save him the trouble of opening his bureau drawers." "Before he
was married" his handkerchiefs were always laid in a pile in the
northeast corner of his drawer, duly perfumed, and with the exquisite word *"Augustus"* embroidered in the corner.—And *now!* "Before
he was married" he was always consulted about the number of plums
in his pudding.—And *now!* "Before he was married" he was never
bothered to wait upon a woman of an evening unless he chose.—
And *now!* "Before he was married" he had his breakfast any time
between seven in the morning and three in the afternoon.—And *now!*

And so the poor weary woman hears the changes rung upon the
newly-discovered virtues and perfections of his family, till she heartily wishes he had never left them. It never once occurs meanwhile to
the domestic Nero to look at the *other* side of the question. How
should it? when all his life at home was one ovation to his vanity
and selfishness. "He could never bear contradiction! dear Augustus
couldn't;" so he must never be contradicted. His friends must either
agree with him or be silent, "because a contrary course always vexed
him." Now we beg all mothers, who are thus educating domestic
tyrants in their nurseries, to have some regard for the wife of his
future, waiting for him somewhere, all unconscious, poor thing! of
her fate; even if they have none on his sisters and themselves.

The most interesting story we read, was one which did *not* end as
usual, with the marriage of the children of the family, but followed
them into homes of their own, where the results of affectionate and
at the same time *judicious* home-training manifested themselves in
their beautiful, unselfish lives. It would do no harm, if mothers would
sometimes ask themselves, when looking at their boys, what sort of
husband am I educating for somebody? It is very common to think

what sort of *wife* a *daughter* may make. Surely the former question, although so seldom occurring, is no less important.

New York Ledger
August 29, 1863

Whose Fault Is It?

No, so and so —— street. I have lived in New York twelve years, but I never heard of *that* street. However, I hunted it up, and piloted by different policemen on the route, finally reached it. It was a warm day; there were slaughter-houses, with pools of blood in front, round which gambolled pigs and children; there were piles of garbage in the middle of the street, composed of cabbage stumps, onion-skins, potato-parings, old hats, and meat-bones, cemented with cinders, and penetrated by the sun's rays, emitting the most beastly odors. Uncombed, unwashed girls, and ragged, fighting lads swarmed on every door step, and emerged from narrow, slimy alleys. Weary, worn-looking mothers administered hasty but well-aimed slaps at draggled, neglected children, while fathers smoked, and drank, and swore, and *lazed* generally.

It was a little piece of hell. I grew sick, physically and mentally, as I staggered, rather than walked along. How *can* human beings sleep, and eat, and drink in this pestiferous atmosphere? I asked. How *can* those children ever get a chance to grow up anything but penitentiary inmates? How *can* those tired mothers take heart, day by day, to drag along their miserable existence? And yet this horrible street is only one of many to be seen in New York.

There must be horrible blame somewhere for such a state of things on this beautiful island. How far these poor creatures are responsible for the moral deterioration consequent upon such a state of things, is a question I could not solve with all my thinking. For one, I cannot believe self-respect to be possible where cleanliness of person and habitation is wholly unknown. No wonder that on the warm days these little bare-legged children, the color of whose skins is a matter of mystery, so many layers of dirt conceal them, swarm up into our parks, and lay trespassing but delighted hands on the dandelion and clover blossoms. I thank God that every ragged, dirty child I see there has unchallenged *his* share at least of the blue sky and the sunshine in those places, all too few as they are. Alas! if some of the money spent on corporation-dinners, on Fourth of July fireworks, and on public balls, where rivers of champagne are worse than wasted, were laid aside for the cleanliness and purification of these terrible localities which slay more victims than the war is doing, and whom nobody thinks of numbering.

New York Ledger
June 25, 1864

Harriet Farley Donlevy

1813–1907

THE YOUNG WOMEN who worked in the Lowell textile mills from the 1820s into the 1840s were a remarkable labor force. The factory owners who recruited them from New England farms to work in a new industry took pains to provide them with respectable, subsidized boardinghouses, better pay than was available in any other occupation open to women, and working conditions that were fair for the time. Although the working day ran from ten to twelve hours, the women would have worked about as hard at home on the farm and would not have been paid for it. They were highly superior workers; almost all were literate, and many had been schoolteachers. And they avidly seized opportunities to improve themselves. They took courses, borrowed from libraries, and attended lectures at the local Lyceum, which featured speakers such as Ralph Waldo Emerson. A Harvard professor who spoke there described them all reading assiduously before his lecture and taking more careful notes on it than his students did. The women also started writing groups, which led in 1840 to *The Lowell Offering,* a magazine written, and from 1842 edited, entirely by mill girls. *The Offering* seems to have received some financial support from the factory owners and was accused of catering to them by presenting too rosy a picture of life in the mills, a charge Harriet Farley answers in her editorial.

Harriet, sixth child of a Congregational minister and a woman who became insane after bearing ten children, contributed to her family's support from the age of fourteen. After doing piecework at home and teaching school, she went to work in the Lowell textile mills in 1837. With some other workers, she became co-editor of *The Lowell Offering* in 1842; she also wrote many of the articles, including "Letters from Susan" and "Two Suicides," both published

423

in 1844. As workers began to protest militantly against worsening conditions, *The Lowell Offering* seemed too bland; and, losing touch with its readership, it ceased publication in 1845. Farley edited a successor, *The New England Offering,* from 1847 to 1850; then she moved to New York City and contributed to *Godey's Lady's Book.* She gave up writing after her marriage (1854), because her husband disapproved.

BIBLIOGRAPHY

Eisler, Benita, ed. *The Lowell Offering: Writings by New England Mill Women (1840–1845).* Philadelphia: J. B. Lippincott Co., 1977.

Letters from Susan

LETTER FIRST

March—, ——.

Dear Mary: When I left home I told you that I would write in a week, and let you have my first impressions of Lowell. I will keep my promise; though, if I should defer my letter a while longer, I think I could make it much more interesting. But you know I promised to be very minute, and there is always sufficient minutiæ to fill up a letter.

I arrived here safe and sound, after being well jolted over the rocks and hills of New Hampshire; and when (it was then evening) a gentleman in the stage first pointed out Lowell to me, with its lights twinkling through the gloom, I could think of nothing but Passampscot swamp, when brilliantly illuminated by "lightning-bugs." You, I know, will excuse all my "up-country" phrases, for I have not yet got the rust off; and to you, and all my old-fashioned friends, I shall always be *rusty.* My egotism I will not apologize for—it is what you request.

To return to my adventures—for it all appears very romantic to me. The driver carried me to the "corporation," as it is called; and which, so far as I now can describe it, is a number of short parallel streets with high brick blocks on either side. There are some blocks with blinds to them, and some are destitute. Some of the doors have bells, others have not. Contiguous to these *boardinghouses* are the *mills,* of which I will tell you more by and by.

I told the driver to carry me to N. —, and there he left me; where there was not a soul that I knew, if cousin Sarah was gone. I inquired, of an Irish girl who came to the door, if Sarah G. Pollard boarded there. She said that she had gone to Manchester, to work with an overseer who was an old acquaintance. The girl did not invite me in, and there I stood like "a statter," as Aunt Hitty says. I did not feel disposed to make inquiries of the girl, I was so unaccustomed to her brogue. Just then—that is, just as my heart was sinking ten fathoms below zero—a pleasant-looking woman came into the entry; and, in a very motherly way, invited me into her own room; took off my things, ordered away my trunk and bandbox, brought camphor for my head, for it ached with my ride, and told me all about cousin Sarah. She said that I had better not think of following her to Manchester, and promised to do all for me that she could. This was Mrs. C., "the boarding woman"—a widow, with several children, whom she keeps at school, and maintains well, by her own industry and good management.

I had expected coldness, or at least entire indifference, in this city, and the cordiality of the good landlady filled my heart with gratitude. I have since inquired if she were not unusually kind; but, though she is a very good woman, the girls here say that she is not more so to me than to any other new boarder; and that the boarding-women are always "dreadful good" to a new boarder. Every girl, let her be ever so rusty, or rather rustic, fills one of the many niches prepared here for so many, and some, you know, are like nest-eggs, and bring many more. But we will not be so uncharitable as to suppose there is nothing but policy in all this, for there is surely something to excite a woman's sympathies in the sight, which is not uncommon here, of a lonely friendless helpless stranger.

You can hardly think how my heart beat when I heard the bells ring for the girls to come to supper, and then the doors began to slam, and then Mrs. C. took me into the dining-room, where there were three common-sized dining tables, and she seated me at one of them, and then the girls thickened around me, until I was almost dizzy.

At the table where I sat they were very still, for the presence of a stranger is usually "a damper" upon them. But there was quite noise enough at the other tables, and what was wanted in wit was made up in merriment. After a while one or two of my boon companions "opened their mouths and spoke," and I have already found that those who make themselves most conspicuous in the presence of strangers, and would soonest attract their attention, are those who do themselves, and those with whom they are connected, the least credit.

I remember that I must be very minute—so I will inform you that we had tea, flapjacks, and plum-cake for supper. There was also bread, butter, and crackers, upon the table; but I saw no one touch them.

After supper the tables were cleared in a trice. Some of the girls came in with their sewing, some went to their own rooms, and some went "out upon the street"—that is, they went to some meeting, or evening school, or they were shopping, or visiting upon some other corporation, all of which is "going upon the street," in factory parlance.

I retained my seat with the girls in the great keeping-room, for Mrs. C. had company in her own sanctum, and I did not know where else to go. Some book-pedlers, shoe-pedlers, essence-pedlers, and candy-boys came in, and made very strenuous exertions to attract our attention. By most of the girls they were treated with cool civility, but there were some little noisy self-conceited misses who detained them, under the pretence of examining goods for purchase, but who were slily joking at the expense of the pedler, and collecting material for future merriment. Sometimes the joke was turned upon themselves, and it was seldom that both parties separated in good humor.

At ten o'clock Mrs. C. came in, and told us that it was time for us all to go to bed. Some begged for time to "read this story out"; others just for "a few minutes to finish this seam." She refused them good-naturedly, but those were most cunning who wanted to warm their feet, and detained her by telling queer stories of what they had seen and heard upon "the street"—and she unconsciously gave them the few minutes she had at first refused.

I was shown up three flight of stairs, into what is called "the long attic"—where they put all poor stranger girls—the most objectionable places being always left for newcomers. There were three beds in it, only two of which were occupied, for this is always the room for vacancies. My baggage had already been carried up by "the boys," as the boarders call Mrs. C'.s sons; and I looked woefully at the strange girl who was to be my "chum." She took no notice of me, and went to sleep as composedly as if I had been still among the White Mountains; but the two girls in the further bed kept whispering together something about "the old man." I was very nervous, and almost wished "the old boy"[1] had them both; but, when the house was still, a strange fear came over me, such as is created in children by telling them about "the old man."

I heard the bells strike the midnight hour long before I went to sleep, and then I dreamed about "the old man."

As soon as day broke I was awakened by one of the girls jumping out of bed, and beginning to crow. That awakened the others, and they bestirred themselves. One sung,

> Morning bells I hate to hear,
> Ringing dolefully, loud, and drear, &c.

Then the other struck up, with a loud voice,

> Now isn't it a pity,
>   Such a pretty girl as I,
> Should be sent to the factory
>   To pine away and die.

I dressed myself and followed them downstairs, where I found my place at the table, and our early breakfast was all ready for us. It consisted of hot cakes and coffee—there was also "hash" upon the table, for those who wanted it.

When the girls had all gone to work, I asked Mrs. C. what I should do. She replied that she would go herself and see if I could have a place, for she was well acquainted with many of the overseers, and thought she could "get me in."

She went in for me, but no overseer would take me, even upon her recommendation, until they had seen me themselves. One promised, however, to give me work if he liked the looks of me, and she

¹Satan.

considers this place as if already engaged, for she says she knows he will like me when he sees me.

You may ask how Mrs. C. could recommend me. She was so well acquainted with cousin Sarah that she had often heard her speak of me, and she says that she is never deceived, either, in her estimate of a good honest country girl.

The overseer said he should not want me until next week, and I felt rather unpleasant at the thought of paying my board while earning nothing. But Mrs. C. said she had some quilts to make, and if I would assist her a little she would give me my board. So I can run round, and see all the lions and lionesses, and get quite an idea of my location, before I go into the mill. O, how I dread to be cooped up there, day after day.

You will ask what I have already seen. I have been out upon a long street, called Central Street, and another long street, at right angles with it, called Merrimack Street. There are stores filled with beautiful goods upon either side, and some handsome public buildings. There is a great hotel called the Merrimack House, which is much larger than any that I ever saw before, and near it is the Railroad Depot. I waited, one day, to see the cars come in from Boston. They moved, as you know, very swiftly, but not so much like "a streak of lightning" as I had anticipated. If all country girls are like me, their first impressions of a city are far below their previous conceptions, and they think there is more difference than there really is. Little as I know of it now, I see that the difference is more apparent than real. There are the same passions at work beneath another surface.

When I went out with Mrs. C. she made me put on one of her girls' bonnets, because mine did not turn up behind and out at the ears, and she said it was O. S.,[2] instead of O. K. Well, as I walked along, and saw all the beautifully dressed ladies, I thought, within myself, that, with bonnets and dresses of an old style, they too would not be passable.

You must know that they dress very much here—at least, it so appears to us, who have just come off of the hills, and been accustomed to put on our woollen gowns in the morning, and our better woollen gowns in the "arternoon." Here they wear velvets, and furs, and plumes, and bugles, and *all*. I should wish to know a great deal

[2] Out of style (?).

to be dressed so, for I should think there was a great deal to be expected of one who made such pretensions.

I told Mrs. C. that the city ladies were not so pale as I expected. She said that many of them were painted, and that *rouge* was becoming more fashionable every year. She says that even some of the factory girls use it, and pointed out several highly dressed girls whose cheeks were truly of "a carmine tint."

I have attended meeting the only Sabbath I have been here. It seems as though everyone went to meeting, the streets are so full on Sundays, but it is not so. Yet Lowell is a church-going place, and they say that they have good meetings and ministers.

I went to the Congregational meeting, for that, you know, is the one I have always been accustomed to attend. The meeting-house is one of the oldest in the city, and not beautiful, though a good respectable looking building. The congregation was very tastefully dressed. I thought, as I looked at some of the ladies, that old Parson Trevor would preach to them from Matthew xxvi. 18. "Top not come down."

In the afternoon I went to the Methodist meeting. This, you are aware, is, with us, "the ragged meeting";[3] but here—my paper is full, and I can only say ribbons, bows, plumes, ruffles, fringes, wimples, and crimples, "ruffs, puffs, and farthingales." Yet the preaching was of a higher order than I had anticipated.

Next Sunday I shall go to *see* the Episcopalians, and Catholics, of whom we have always heard so little that is good. Yet there was a strange, and not unhallowed, sensation excited in my breast when I first saw a church with a spire surmounted by a cross, that symbol of our holy religion; and the dark stone church which was first built here revived the impressions which were created by our juvenile literature, which you know a few years since was wholly English.

Yours affectionately,
Susan

---

[3]Generally in New England, the Methodist congregation would be of lower class than the Congregationalists.

LETTER SECOND

Lowell, April—, ——.

Dear Mary: In my last I told you I would write again, and say more of my life here; and this I will now attempt to do.

I went into the mill to work a few days after I wrote to you. It looked very pleasant at first, the rooms were so light, spacious, and clean, the girls so pretty and neatly dressed, and the machinery so brightly polished or nicely painted. The plants in the windows, or on the overseer's bench or desk, gave a pleasant aspect to things. You will wish to know what work I am doing. I will tell you of the different kinds of work.

There is, first, the carding-room, where the cotton flies most, and the girls get the dirtiest. But this is easy, and the females are allowed time to go out at night before the bell rings—on Saturday night at least, if not on all other nights. Then there is the spinning-room, which is very neat and pretty. In this room are the spinners and doffers. The spinners watch the frames; keep them clean, and the threads mended if they break. The doffers take off the full bobbins, and put on the empty ones. They have nothing to do in the long intervals when the frames are in motion, and can go out to their boardinghouses, or do anything else that they like. In some of the factories the spinners do their own doffing, and when this is the case they work no harder than the weavers. These last have the hardest time of all—or can have, if they choose to take charge of three or four looms, instead of the one pair which is the allotment. And they are the most constantly confined. The spinners and dressers have but the weavers to keep supplied, and then their work can stop. The dressers never work before breakfast, and they stay out a great deal in the afternoons. The drawers-in, or girls who draw the threads through the harnesses, also work in the dressing-room, and they all have very good wages—better than the weavers who have but the usual work. The dressing-rooms are very neat, and the frames move with a gentle undulating motion which is really graceful. But these rooms are kept very warm, and are disagreeably scented with the "sizing," or starch, which stiffens the "beams," or unwoven webs. There are many plants in these rooms, and it is really a good greenhouse for them. The dressers are generally quite tall girls, and must have pretty tall minds too, as their work requires much care and attention.

I could have had work in the dressing-room, but chose to be a weaver; and I will tell you why. I disliked the closer air of the dressing-room, though I might have become accustomed to that. I could not learn to dress so quickly as I could to weave, nor have work of my own so soon, and should have had to stay with Mrs. C. two or three weeks before I could go in at all, and I did not like to be "lying upon my oars" so long. And, more than this, when I get well learned I can have extra work, and make double wages, which you know is quite an inducement with some.

Well, I went into the mill, and was put to learn with a very patient girl—a clever old maid. I should be willing to be one myself if I could be as good as she is. You cannot think how odd everything seemed to me. I wanted to laugh at everything, but did not know what to make sport of first. They set me to threading shuttles, and tying weaver's knots, and such things, and now I have improved so that I can take care of one loom. I could take care of two if I only had eyes in the back part of my head, but I have not got used to "looking two ways of a Sunday" yet.

At first the hours seemed very long, but I was so interested in learning that I endured it very well; and when I went out at night the sound of the mill was in my ears, as of crickets, frogs, and jewsharps, all mingled together in strange discord. After that it seemed as though cotton-wool was in my ears, but now I do not mind at all. You know that people learn to sleep with the thunder of Niagara in their ears, and a cotton mill is no worse, though you wonder that we do not have to hold our breath in such a noise.

It makes my feet ache and swell to stand so much, but I suppose I shall get accustomed to that too. The girls generally wear old shoes about their work, and you know nothing is easier; but they almost all say that when they have worked here a year or two they have to procure shoes a size or two larger than before they came. The right hand, which is the one used in stopping and starting the loom, becomes larger than the left; but in other respects the factory is not detrimental to a young girl's appearance. Here they look delicate, but not sickly; they laugh at those who are much exposed and get pretty brown; but I, for one, had rather be brown than pure white. I never saw so many pretty looking girls as there are here. Though the number of men is small in proportion, there are many marriages here, and a great deal of courting. I will tell you of this last sometime.

You wish to know minutely of our hours of labor. We go in at five o'clock; at seven we come out to breakfast; at half-past seven we return to our work, and stay until half-past twelve. At one, or quarter-past one four months in the year, we return to our work, and stay until seven at night. Then the evening is all our own, which is more than some laboring girls can say, who think nothing is more tedious than a factory life.

When I first came here, which was the last of February, the girls ate their breakfast before they went to their work. The first of March they came out at the present breakfast hour, and the twentieth of March they ceased to "light up" the rooms, and come out between six and seven o'clock.

You ask if the girls are contented here: I ask you, if you know of *any one* who is perfectly contented. Do you remember the old story of the philosopher, who offered a field to the person who was contented with his lot; and, when one claimed it, he asked him why, if he was so perfectly satisfied, he wanted his field. The girls here are not contented; and there is no disadvantage in their situation which they do not perceive as quickly, and lament as loudly, as the sternest opponents of the factory system do. They would scorn to say they were contented, if asked the question; for it would compromise their Yankee spirit—their pride, penetration, independence, and love of "freedom and equality" to say that they were *contented* with such a life as this. Yet, withal, they are cheerful. I never saw a happier set of beings. They appear blithe in the mill, and out of it. If you see one of them with a very long face, you may be sure that it is because she has heard bad news from home, or because her beau has vexed her. But if it is a Lowell trouble, it is because she has failed in getting off as many "sets" or "pieces" as she intended to have done; or because she had a sad "break-out" or "break-down" in her work, or something of that sort.

You ask if the work is not disagreeable. Not when one is accustomed to it. It tried my patience sadly at first, and does now when it does not run well; but, in general, I like it very much. It is easy to do, and does not require very violent exertion, as much of our farm work does.

You also ask how I get along with the girls here. Very well indeed; only we came near having a little flurry once. You know I told you I lodged in the "long attic." Well, a little while ago, there was a place vacated in a pleasant lower chamber. Mrs. C. said that it was my "chum's" turn to go downstairs to lodge, unless she would waive her claim in favor of me. You must know that here they get up in the world by getting down, which is what the boys in our debating society used to call a paradox. Clara, that is the girl's name, was not at all disposed to give up her rights, but maintained them staunchly. I had nothing to do about it—the girls in the lower room liked me, and disliked Clara, and were determined that it should not be at all pleasant weather there if she did come. Mrs. C. was in a dilemma. Clara's turn came first. The other two girls in the chamber were sisters, and would not separate, so they were out of the question. I wanted to go, and knew Clara would not be happy with them. But I thought what was my duty to do. She was not happy now, and would not be if deprived of her privilege. She had looked black at me for several days, and slept with her face to the wall as many nights. I went up to her and said, "Clara, take your things down into the lower chamber, and tell the girls that *I will not come*. It is your turn now, and mine will come in good time."

Clara was mollified in an instant. "No," said she; "I will not go now. They do not wish me to come, and I had rather stay here." After this we had quite a contest—I trying to persuade Clara to go, and she trying to persuade me, and I *"got beat."* So now I have a pleasanter room, and am quite a favorite with all the girls. They have given me some pretty plants, and they go out with me whenever I wish it, so that I feel quite happy.

You think we must live very nice here to have plum-cake, &c. The plum-cake, and crackers, and such things as the bakers bring upon the corporations, are not as nice as we have in the country, and I presume are much cheaper. I seldom eat anything that is not cooked in the family. I should not like to tell you the stories they circulate here about the bakers, unless I *knew* that they were true. Their brown bread is the best thing that I have tasted of their baking.

You see that I have been quite *minute* in this letter, though I hardly liked your showing the former to old Deacon Gale, and 'Squire Smith, and those old men. It makes me feel afraid to write you all I should like to, when I think so many eyes are to pore over my humble sheet. But if their motives are good, and they can excuse all defects, why I will not forbid.

'Squire Smith wishes to know what sort of men our superintendents are. I know very well what he thinks of them, and what their reputation is up our way. I am not personally acquainted with any of them; but, from what I hear, I have a good opinion of them. I suppose they are not faultless, neither are those whom they superintend; but they are not the overbearing tyrants which many suppose them to be. The abuse of them which I hear is so very low that I think it must be unjust and untrue; and I do frequently hear them spoken of as *men*—whole-hearted, full-souled men. Tell 'Squire Smith they are not what he would be in their places—that they treat their operatives better than he does his "hired girls," and associate with them on terms of as much equality. But I will tell you who are almost universally unpopular: the "runners," as they are called, or counting-room boys. I suppose they are little whipper-snappers who will grow better as they grow older.

My paper is filling up, and I must close by begging your pardon for speaking of the Methodists as having lost their simplicity of attire. It was true, nevertheless, for I have not seen one of the old "Simon Pure" Methodist bonnets since I have been here. But they may be as consistent as other denominations. [How] few of us follow in the steps of the primitive Christians.

Yours as ever,
Susan

LETTER THIRD

Lowell, July—, ——.

Dear Mary: You complain that I do not keep my promise of being a good correspondent, but if you could know how sultry it is here, and how fatigued I am by my work this warm weather, you would not blame me. It is now that I begin to dislike these hot brick pavements and glaring buildings. I want to be at home—to go down to the brook over which the wild grapes have made a natural arbor, and to sit by the cool spring around which the fresh soft brakes cluster so lovingly. I think of the time when, with my little bare feet, I used to follow in aunt Nabby's footsteps through the fields of corn—stepping high and long till we came to the bleaching ground; and I remember—but I must stop, for I know you wish me to write of what I am now doing, as you already know of what I have done.

Well; I go to work every day—not earlier than I should at home, nor do I work later, but I mind the confinement more than I should in a more unpleasant season of the year. I have extra work now—I take care of three looms; and when I wrote you before I could not well take care of two. But help is very scarce now, and they let us do as much work as we please, and I am highly complimented upon my "powers of execution." Many of the girls go to their country homes in the summer. The majority of the operatives are country girls. These have always the preference, because, in the fluctuations to which manufactures are liable, there would be much less distress among a population who could resort to other homes, than if their entire interest was in the city. And in the summer these girls go to rest, and recruit themselves for another "yearly campaign"—not a bad idea in them either. I shall come home next summer; I have been here too short a time to make it worth while now. I wish they would have a *vacation* in "dog days"—stop the mills, and *make* all the girls rest; and let their "men-folks" do up their "ditching," or whatever else it is they now do Sundays.

But these mills are not such dreadful places as you imagine them to be. You think them dark damp holes; as close and black as—as the Black Hole at Calcutta. Now, dear M., it is no such thing. They are high, spacious, well-built edifices, with neat paths around them and beautiful plots of greensward. These are kept fresh by the "force-pumps" belonging to every corporation. And some of the corporations have beautiful flower gardens connected with the factories. One of the overseers with whom I am acquainted gave me a beautiful bouquet the other morning, which was radiant with all the colors of the rainbow, and fragrant with the sweet perfume of many kinds of mints and roses. He has a succession of beautiful blossoms from spring till "cold weather." He told me that he could raise enough to bring him fifty dollars if he chose to sell them; and this from a little bit of sand not larger than our front yard, which you know is small for a country house. But it is so full—here a few dollars have brought on a fresh soil, and "patience has done its perfect work." What might not be accomplished in the country with a little industry and taste.

But I have said enough of the outside of our mills—now for the inside. The rooms are high, very light, kept nicely whitewashed, and extremely neat; with many plants in the window seats, and white cotton curtains to the windows. The machinery is very handsomely made and painted, and is placed in regular rows; thus, in a large mill, presenting a beautiful and uniform appearance. I have sometimes stood at one end of a row of green looms, when the girls were gone from between them, and seen the lathes moving back and forth, the harnesses up and down, the white cloth winding over the rollers, through the long perspective; and I have thought it beautiful.

Then the girls dress so neatly, and are so pretty. The mill girls are the prettiest in the city. You wonder how they can keep neat. Why not? There are no restrictions as to the number of pieces to be washed in the boarding-house. And, as there is plenty of water in the mill, the girls can wash their laces and muslins and other nice things themselves, and no boarding woman ever refuses the conveniences for starching and ironing. You say too that you do not see how we can have so many conveniences and comforts at the price we pay for board. You must remember that the boardinghouses belong to the companies, and are let to the tenants far below the usual city rent— sometimes the rent is remitted. Then there are large families, so that there are the profits of many individuals. The country farmers are quite in the habit of bringing their produce to the boardinghouses for sale, thus reducing the price by the omission of the market-man's profit. So you see there are many ways by which we get along so well.

You ask me how the girls behave in the mill, and what are the punishments. They behave very well while about their work, and I have never heard of punishments, or scoldings, or anything of that sort. Sometimes an overseer finds fault, and sometimes offends a girl by refusing to let her stay out of the mill, or some deprivation like that; and then, perhaps, there are tears and pouts on her part, but, in general, the tone of intercourse between the girls and overseers is very good—pleasant, yet respectful. When the latter are fatherly sort of men, the girls frequently resort to them for advice and assistance about other affairs than their work. Very seldom is this confidence abused; but, among the thousands of overseers who have lived in Lowell, and the tens of thousands of girls who have in time been here, there are legends still told of wrong suffered and committed. "To err is human,"[4] and when the frailties of humanity are exhibited by a factory girl, it is thought of far worse than are the errors of any other persons.

The only punishment among the girls is dismission from their places. They do not, as many think, withhold their wages; and as for corporal punishment—mercy on me! To strike a female would cost any overseer his place. If the superintendents did not take the

[4]Alexander Pope, *An Essay on Criticism* (1711), line 525.

affair into consideration, the girls would turn out,[5] as they did at the Temperance celebration, "Independent Day"; and if they didn't look as pretty, I am sure they would produce as deep an impression.

By the way, I almost forgot to tell you that we had a "Fourth of July" in Lowell, and a nice one it was too. The Temperance celebration was the chief dish in the entertainment. The chief, did I say? It was almost the whole. It was the great turkey that Scroggs sent for Bob Cratchet's Christmas dinner.[6] But, perhaps you don't read Dickens, so I will make no more "classical allusions." In the evening we had the Hutchinsons, from our own Granite State, who discoursed sweet music *so sweetly.* They have become great favorites with the public. It is not on account of their fine voices only, but their pleasant modest manners—the perfect sense of propriety which they exhibit in all their demeanor; and I think they are not less popular *here* because they sing the wrongs of the slave and the praises of cold water.

But, dear Mary, I fear I have tired you with this long letter, and yet I have not answered half your questions. Do you wish to hear anything more about the overseers? Once for all, then, there are many very likely,[7] intelligent, public-spirited men among them. They are interested in the good movements of the day; teachers in the Sabbath schools; and some have represented the city in the State Legislature. They usually marry among the factory girls, and do not connect themselves with their inferiors either. Indeed, in almost all the matches here the female is superior in education and manner, if not in intellect, to her partner.

The overseers have good salaries, and their families live very prettily. I observe that in almost all cases the mill girls make excellent wives. They are good managers, orderly in their households, and "neat as waxwork." It seems as though they were so delighted to have houses of their own to take care of, that they would never weary of the labor and the care.

The boarding women you ask about. They are usually widows or single women from the country; and many questions are always asked, and references required, before a house is given to a new

[5]Strike.
[6]In Charles Dickens's *A Christmas Carol* (1843), the miser Ebenezer Scrooge (not Scroggs) reforms and gives his downtrodden clerk Bob Cratchit a fine turkey.
[7]Good-looking.

applicant. It is true that mistakes are sometimes made, and *the wrong person gets into the pew,* but

> "Things like this you know must be,"
> Where'er there is a factory.

I see I have given you rhyme; it is not all quotation, nor *entirely original.*

I think it requires quite a complication of good qualities to make up a good boarding woman. "She looks well to the ways of her household," and must be even more than all that King Solomon describes in the last chapter of Proverbs.[8] She not only in winter "riseth while it is yet night, and giveth meat to her household, a portion to her maidens," but she sitteth up far into the night, and seeth that her maidens are asleep, and that their lamps are gone out. Perhaps she doth not "consider a field to buy it," but she considereth every piece of meat, and bushel of potatoes, and barrel of flour, and load of wood, and box of soap, and every little thing, whether its quantity, quality, and price are what discretion would recommend her to purchase. "She is not afraid of the snow for her household," for she maketh them wear rubber overshoes, and thick cloaks and hoods, and seeth that the paths are broken out. "Her clothing is silk and purple," and she looketh neat and comely. It may be that her husband sitteth *not* "in the gates," for it is too often the case that he hath abandoned her, or loafeth in the streets. "She openeth her mouth with wisdom, and in her tongue is the law of kindness." Her maidens go to her for counsel and sympathy, if a decayed tooth begins to jump, or a lover proves faithless; and to keep twoscore young maidens in peace with themselves, each other, and her own self, is no slight task. The price of such a woman is, indeed, *above rubies.* "Give her of the fruit of her hands, and let her own works praise her."

I have now told you of mill girls, overseers and their wives, and boardinghousekeepers, and I feel that I have won forgiveness for neglecting you so long. You think that I have too high an opinion of our superintendents. I hope not. I do think that many of them are chosen as combining, in their characters, many excellent qualities. Some of them may be as selfish as you suppose. But we must remem-

---

[8]What follows is an adaptation of Proverbs 31: 10–27.

ber that they owe a duty to their employers, as well as to those they employ. They are agents of the companies, as well as superintendents of us. Where those duties conflict, I hope the sympathies of the man will always be with the more dependent party.

Country people are very suspicious. I do not think them perfect. A poet will look at a wood-cutter and say, "there is an honest man;" and as likely as not the middle of his load is rotten punk, and crooked sticks make many interstices, while all looks well without. A rustic butcher slays an animal that is dying of disease, and carries his meat to the market. The butcher and the woodman meet, and say all manner of harsh things against the *"grandees"* of the city, and quote such poetry as,

> "God made the country—
> Man made the town," &c.[9]

It is true that, with the same disposition for villainy, the man of influence must do the most harm. But, where there is most light, may there not be most true knowledge? And, even if there is no more principle, may there not be, with more cultivation of mind, a feeling of honor and of self-respect which may be of some benefit in its stead?

But I have written till I am fairly wearied. Good-bye.

Yours always,
Susan

LETTER FOURTH

Dear Mary: You say that you wish to come to Lowell, and that some others of my old acquaintance wish to come, if I think it advisable; and, as I have but a few moments to write, I will devote all my letter to this subject.

There are girls here for every reason, and for no reason at all. I will speak to you of my acquaintances in the family here. One, who sits at my right hand at table, is in the factory because she hates her mother-in-law.[10] She has a kind father, and an otherwise excellent

[9]William Cowper, *The Task* (1785), Bk. I, line 749 (slightly misquoted).
[10]Stepmother.

home, but, as she and her mama agree about as well as cat and mouse, she has come to the factory. The one next her has a wealthy father, but, like many of our country farmers, he is very penurious, and he wishes his daughters to maintain themselves. The next is here because there is no better place for her, unless it is a Shaker settlement. The next has a "well-off" mother, but she is a very pious woman, and will not buy her daughter so many pretty gowns and collars and ribbons and other etceteras of "Vanity Fair" as she likes; so she concluded to "help herself." The next is here because her parents and family are wicked infidels, and she cannot be allowed to enjoy the privileges of religion at home. The next is here because she must labor somewhere, and she has been ill treated in so many families that she has a horror of domestic service. The next has left a good home because her lover, who has gone on a whaling voyage, wishes to be married when he returns, and she would like more money than her father will give her. The next is here because her home is in a lonesome country village, and she cannot bear to remain where it is so dull. The next is here because her parents are poor, and she wishes to acquire the means to educate herself. The next is here because her beau came, and she did not like to trust him alone among so many pretty girls. And so I might go on and give you the variety of reasons, but this is enough for the present.

I cannot advise you to come. You must act according to your own judgment. Your only reasons are a desire to see a new place, a city, and to be with me. You have now an excellent home, but, dear M., it may not seem the same to you after you have been here a year or two—for it is not advisable to come and learn a new occupation unless you can stay as long as that. The reasons are that you may become unaccustomed to your present routine of home duties, and lose your relish for them, and also for the very quiet pleasures of our little village. Many, who are dissatisfied here, have also acquired a dissatisfaction for their homes, so that they cannot be contented anywhere, and wish they had never seen Lowell.

But tell Hester that I advise her to come. She has always lived among relatives who have treated her as a slave, and yet they would not allow her to go away and be a slave in any other family. I think I can make her happier here, and I see no better way for her to do than to break all those ties at once, by leaving her cheerless drudgery and entering the mill.

I don't know what to say to Miriam, so many pleasant and unpleasant things are mingled in her lot now. There she lives with Widow Farrar, and everything about them looks so nice and comfortable that people think she must be happy. The work is light, but everything must be just as the old lady says, and she has strange vagaries at times. Miriam has to devote a great deal of time to her whims and fancies which is not spent in labor. Yet she would find it unpleasant to leave her nice large chamber, with its bureau and strip carpet and large closets, for the narrow accommodations of a factory boardinghouse. And the fine great garden, in which she now takes so much pleasure, would be parted from with much sadness. But then her wages are so low that she says she can lay aside nothing and still dress herself suitably, for she is always expected to receive and help entertain the old lady's company. When the widow dies, Miriam will have nothing, unless she leaves her a legacy, which, on account of the many needy relatives, is not to be expected. So you had better tell her to make all arrangements for coming here, and then if the old lady will retain her by "raising her salary," tell her to stay with her.

As for Lydia, I think she had better not come. I know how disagreeable her home is in many respects, but it is her home after all. She has to be up at four o'clock in the morning, and to be "on her feet," as she says, till nine o'clock at night, unless she sits down for an hour to patch the boys' clothes or keep her father's accounts. She has to be everybody's waiter, and says that all seem to think she was born for that occupation. Then she has no accommodations but a little crowded attic, which she shares with old Jenny and three or four little ones, and she has told me that she never knew what it was to have a dollar of her own to spend as she might like. Yet there she is an important personage in the family, while here it would be quite different. She enjoys excellent health, and her varied employment appears to suit her. It might be very different here in that respect also. She has nothing of her own now, but she is sure of care and comforts in case of sickness, and necessaries always. When her father dies, or when she marries, she will probably have something of *her own*. "But," you will reply, "her father may live as long as she will, and she may never marry." True; but tell her to consider all things, and, before she decides to leave home, to request her father to pay her a stated sum as wages. If he will give her a dollar a week, I should advise her to stay with him and her mother. Here she would have as many of the comforts and accommodations of life as there, but perhaps no more. She could dress better here, but not better compared with others. This is something to consider.

Nancy wishes also to come, because her trade does not suit her. If she is losing her health by a sedentary employment, I certainly advise her to change it. I think she could do well here, and then she has a voice like a nightingale. It would gain for her notice and perhaps emolument.

But I have hardly room to say good-bye.

Yours, as ever,
Susan

Editorial: Two Suicides

One more unfortunate,
Weary of breath,
Rashly importunate,
Gone to her death!

Take her up tenderly,
Lift her with care;
Fashion'd so slenderly,
Young and so fair!

Touch her not scornfully;
Think of her mournfully,
Gently and humanly;

. . . . .

Perishing gloomily,
Spurned by contumely,
Cold inhumanity,
Burning insanity,
Into her rest.

Hood's Magazine.[1]

Within a few weeks the papers of the day have announced the deaths of two young female operatives by their own hands—one in Lowell, the other in an adjacent manufacturing town. With the simple announcement, these papers have left the affair to their readers—appending to one, however, the remark that the unfortunate had neither friends nor home; to the other the assertion that reports injurious to her fair fame had been circulated—reports which, after her death, were ascertained to be false. And how have the community received this intelligence? Apparently with much indifference; but where we hear an expression of opinion it is one of horror. The human being who has dared, herself, to wrench away the barrier which separated her from the Giver of her life, and who will judge her for this rash act, is spoken of as a reckless contemner of His laws, both natural and revealed. People are shocked that any human being should dare imbrue her hands in blood, and rush, all stained and gory, before her God. But He who placed us here, and commanded that we should stay until He willed to call us hence, has enforced His law by one written on our own hearts—a horror of death inwrought into our nature, so that we violate our own sensibilities by disobeying His will; unless, indeed, our feelings have become so distorted and perverted that they are untrue to their original action. So possible is a discord in this "harp of thousand strings," and so improbable is a violation of its harmony while perfectly attuned, that many have supposed this last discordant note, which rings from the ruined lyre, a proof that its perfect unison had been previously destroyed, though unobserved by all around.

We may easily conceive of the feelings of those who give away their lives in some noble cause—we can imagine how the higher feelings of the soul bear it away from all subordinate doubts and fears, and the greatest boon we can ever give is laid upon the altar, a holy sacrifice. We can in some degree enter into the feelings of the martyrs of old, and can perhaps imperfectly apprehend the philosophy of a Cato or a Cleopatra;[2] but when one in the very prime of

[1]Thomas Hood, "The Bridge of Sighs" (1843), on a "fallen" woman who drowned herself, lines 1–8, 15–17, 95–99.

[2]Cato, a Roman patriot, and Cleopatra, Queen of Egypt, committed suicide to avoid being captured by their enemies.

womanhood, with no philosophy to support her, and no great misfortune to impel her to the deed, yields up her life, we feel that the soul itself must have become distorted and diseased.

When we reflect upon the shudder which the thought of death occasions in our season of health and prosperity—when we find that it requires all our strength of soul to look upon it, and prepare our minds for its always possible approach—when, in a healthy and natural state of feeling, it needs all the consolation and hopes of religion to reconcile us to this last event, then we may think how heavy has been the weight which has pressed upon some poor spirit till, crushed and mutilated, it has writhed from beneath its influence, into the dark abyss of despair. How heavily must life weigh upon her who flees to death for refuge!—who waits not for the grim tyrant, but rushes impetuously into his loathsome embrace! There must have been a fearful change in the nature of her, whose natural reluctance to pain is so wholly overcome that no bodily agony is dreaded if but the prison bars of this clay tenement be loosened—and, when the innate delicacy of her nature is so far forgotten that the body, itself, is yielded up to the cold eye, and unshrinking hand, of the dissector—for this must always follow. Let us contemplate all this, and feel assured that, though reason may have been left, though it may even have been actively manifest in the preparations for this dreadful *finale,* that something was gone even more essential to vitality than reason itself—that "the life of life was o'er"—that the something, which gives zest to being, was taken away—that the *vitativeness* of the phrenologist[3] no longer acted and harmonized with the other faculties of the brain.

In the first instance, were the causes mental or physical which led to the deed? We believe in this, and indeed in all cases, that both operated upon the individual. There was action and reaction, and it is impossible that the mind should be so deeply affected without injury to the body: as, on the contrary, oppression of any part of the physical system must depress and weaken the mind. We will not make a long sermon, for we have a short text. "She had no parents or home." She was alone in the world—she had no kindred to support and cheer her in life's toilsome journey, and no place of refuge to which she might retreat, when weary and faint with the tedious pilgrimage. She was alone; and none came forward to cheer her with

[3]In phrenological theory, the desire to live, regarded as a mental faculty.

their companionship—she had no home, and saw no prospect of one. Life, before her, was a dreary waste, and her path more rugged than any other. It was uncheered. There was not the voice of sympathy to sustain her, nor the necessity of acting for others to arouse her energies. When her spirits drooped there were none to revive them—then they sank still lower, and there was nothing to sustain them. Mere acquaintance seldom strives to remove the dark cloud which may rest upon another's brow. Perhaps they think it habitual, and that nothing may remove it—perhaps that, if it is not so, they have not the power to drive it away. They are so distrustful that they strive not to lighten that which they might possibly remove. Perhaps their own hearts are saddened, and they flee rather to the gay hearted, that they may be infected by their joyousness. They shrink from the sad one lest sympathy should reveal that which in their own hearts had better be concealed.

Mere acquaintance strove not to comfort her, and "she had no parents or home." O, how soothingly might a mother's voice have fallen upon her ear!—her words, like healing balm, might have sunk into her heart, and her kind glance have been the charm to drive away the demon. But, *she had no home*. She rose at early dawn, and toiled till night. Day after day brought the same wearisome round of duties; and, as she looked forward, she saw no prospect of a brighter future. It would take long years to procure an independence by her slight savings, and mayhap, with her sinking energies, she hardly gained a maintenance. Her spirits were gone, but life remained; and vitality seemed fixed upon her as a curse. The physical laws of her nature had not been violated, and nature still resisted the spirit's call for death. Perhaps it was frenzy, perhaps despondency, but—the rest is a short item in the common newspaper.

The other had friends and home—at least, we learn nothing to the contrary. She probably had a father, mother, sister, or brother.

> And there was a nearer one
> Still, and a dearer one
> Yet, than all other.[4]

She, too, had toiled daily and hourly, but not hopelessly. There was one near whose smile was her joy, and whose voice was her strength.

[4]"The Bridge of Sighs," lines 40–42 (inaccurately quoted).

She had turned from all others to devote herself more entirely to him. All other affections were absorbed in this. She was affianced to him, and, in anticipation of the time when they twain should become one, her soul had made his its stay. But, when Calumny had sent its blasting simoon over this fair prospect, how changed the scene! That which was so bright is, O how dark! How susceptible must have been that heart which the consciousness of innocence could not sustain! How keen must have been those sufferings which could only find relief in the sleep of the grave?

And here may it not be well to add one word against the sin of detraction?—of rashly and wantonly speaking ill where there is no proof of error—of lightly repeating the gossip of the day, which may or may not be true—of carelessly passing opinions upon those of whom no close acquaintance justifies us in passing this judgment. People may talk of *village* gossip; but in no place is an evil report more quickly circulated, and apparently believed, than in a factory. One fiendish-minded girl can start a calumny which will soon ruin the good name of another, unless she be unusually fortunate in friends, or circumstances are peculiarly favorable; or her whole past life has been as remarkable for the wisdom of the serpent as the harmlessness of the dove.[5] But enough!—this evil is already curing itself, and "it is only a factory story" is considered as an intimation to inquire further.

But we return from our digression to the theme which suggested it. Morbid dejection and wounded sensibility have, in these instances, produced that insanity which prompted suicide. Is it not an appropriate question to ask here whether, or not, there was any thing in their mode of life which tended to this dreadful result?

We have been accused of representing unfairly the relative advantages and disadvantages of factory life. We are thought to give the former too great prominence, and the latter too little, in the pictures we have drawn. Are we guilty?

We should be willing to resign our own individual contributions to the harshest critic, and say to him, *Judge ye!* And, with regard to the articles of our contributors, we have never published anything which our own experience had convinced us was unfair. But, if in our sketches there is too much light, and too little shade, let our excuse be found in the circumstances which have brought us before

[5]See Matthew 10:16.

the public. We have not thought it necessary to state, or rather to constantly reiterate, that our life was a toilsome one—for we supposed that would be universally understood, after we had stated how many hours in a day we tended our machines. We have not thought a constant repetition of the fact necessary, that our life was one of confinement, when it was known that we work in one spot of one room. We have not thought it necessary to enlarge upon the fact that there was ignorance and folly among a large population of young females, away from their homes and indiscriminately collected from all quarters. These facts have always been so generally understood that the worth, happiness and intelligence, which really exists, have been undervalued. But, are the operatives here as happy as females in the prime of life, in the constant intercourse of society, in the enjoyment of all necessaries and many comforts—with money at their own command; and the means of gratifying their peculiar tastes in dress, &c.—are they as happy as they would be, with all this, in some other situations? We sometimes fear they are not.

And was there anything, we ask again, in the situation of these young women which influenced them to this melancholy act? In factory labor it is sometimes an advantage, but also sometimes the contrary, that the mind is thrown back upon itself—it is forced to depend upon its own resources for a large proportion of the time of the operative. Excepting by sight, the females hold but little companionship with each other. This is why the young girls rush so furiously together when they are set at liberty. This is why the sedate young woman who loves contemplation, and enjoys her own thoughts better than any other society, prefers this to any other employment. But, when a young woman is naturally of a morbid tone of mind, or when afflictions have created such a state, that employment which forces the thoughts back upon an unceasing reminiscence of its own misery is not the right one. This is not the life suited to a misanthrope or an unfortunate, although they, in their dejection, might think otherwise. However much of a materialist, and little of a sentimentalist, we may appear, we still believe that fresh bracing air, frequent bathings, and carefully prepared food may do much in reconciling us to the sorrows and disappointments of life. The beneficial influence of social intercourse and varied employment has never been questioned.

Last summer a young woman of this city, who was weary of her monotonous life, but saw no hope of redemption, opened her heart to a benevolent lady who was visiting us upon a philanthropic mission. "And now," said she, as she concluded her tale of grievances, "what shall I do?" She could do nothing but dig, and was ashamed to beg.[6] The lady was appalled by a misery for which there was no relief. There was no need of pecuniary aid, or she might have appealed to the benevolent. She could give her kind and soothing words, but these would have no permanent power to reconcile her to her lot. "I can tell you of nothing," she replied, "but *to throw yourself into the canal.*"

There is something better than this—and we are glad that so noble a spirit is manifested by our operatives, for there *is* something noble in their general cheerfulness and contentment. "They also serve who only stand and wait."[7] They serve, even more acceptably, who labor patiently and wait.   H.F.

---

[6]"I cannot dig; to beg I am ashamed" (Luke 16:3).
[7]John Milton, "Sonnet: On His Blindness" (1652), line 14.

Harriet Ann Jacobs,
"Linda Brent"

c.1813–1897

HARRIET ANN JACOBS was born to slave parents in Edenton, North Carolina. Her grandmother, however, had been freed in middle age, owned her house, and made her living as a baker. After her mother died, six-year-old Harriet went to live with her mistress. This woman treated her kindly and taught her to read and write; nevertheless, instead of freeing Harriet at her death, she bequeathed her to three-year-old Mary Matilda Norcom. Meanwhile, Mary's father, Dr. James Norcom, had been harassing Harriet sexually since she was fourteen. She took the only means of resistance open to her by becoming the mistress of a different white man, the lawyer Samuel Tredwell Sawyer, to whom she bore two children. Although Jacobs wanted to run away from Norcom, she would not leave her children.

However, it occurred to her that if she were out of reach, Norcom might be willing to sell her children to their father. She escaped and went into hiding, first with a sympathetic white woman and then with her grandmother. For almost seven years, she lived in a tiny crawlspace under the roof of her grandmother's house. Sawyer did buy the children and sent the girl North, although he never emancipated them. Jacobs finally escaped to New York City (1842), where she worked as a nursemaid for a sympathetic family, that of the editor Nathaniel Parker Willis (Fanny Fern's brother). In 1849 she worked with Frederick Douglass and other anti-slavery activists in Rochester, New York. Then she went back to work for the Willises. Meanwhile, first Norcom and then his daughter (Jacobs's legal owner) came North to pursue her; she was not secure until Mrs. Willis bought her—a galling concession to the slavery system.

Jacobs's abolitionist friends had been urging her to publish her story, but she was reluctant to tell the world her sexual experiences.

However, she now felt she had a duty to publicize them in order to awaken Northern women to the situation of women slaves. With the help of an established white author, Lydia Maria Child—who condensed and rearranged, but did not significantly alter her narrative—Jacobs published *Incidents in the Life of a Slave Girl* in 1861. In order to protect herself and those who helped her, she changed all the proper names: she appears as Linda Brent, the Norcoms as the Flints, and Sawyer as Mr. Sands.

BIBLIOGRAPHY

Jacobs, Harriet A. *Incidents in the Life of a Slave Girl,* edited by Lydia Maria Child. Edited by Jean Fagan Yellin. Cambridge: Harvard University Press, 1987.

from Incidents in the Life of a Slave Girl

V

THE TRIALS OF GIRLHOOD

During the first years of my service in Dr. Flint's family, I was accustomed to share some indulgences with the children of my mistress. Though this seemed to me no more than right, I was grateful for it, and tried to merit the kindness by the faithful discharge of my duties. But I now entered on my fifteenth year—a sad epoch in the life of a slave girl. My master began to whisper foul words in my ear. Young as I was, I could not remain ignorant of their import. I tried to treat them with indifference or contempt. The master's age, my extreme youth, and the fear that his conduct would be reported to my grandmother, made him bear this treatment for many months. He was a crafty man, and resorted to many means to accomplish his purposes. Sometimes he had stormy, terrific ways, that made his victims tremble; sometimes he assumed a gentleness that he thought must surely subdue. Of the two, I preferred his stormy moods, although they left me trembling. He tried his utmost to corrupt the pure principles my grandmother had instilled. He peopled my young mind with unclean images, such as only a vile monster could think of. I turned from him with disgust and hatred. But he was my master. I was compelled to live under the same roof with him—where I saw a man forty years my senior daily violating the most sacred commandments of nature.[1] He told me I was his property; that I must be subject to his will in all things. My soul revolted against the mean tyranny. But where could I turn for protection? No matter whether the slave girl be as black as ebony or as fair as her mistress. In either case, there is no shadow of law to protect her from insult, from violence, or even from death; all these are inflicted by fiends who bear the shape of men. The mistress, who ought to protect the helpless victim, has no other feelings towards her but those of jealousy and rage. The degradation, the wrongs, the vices, that grow out of slavery, are more than I can describe. They are greater than you would willingly believe. Surely, if you credited one-half the truths that are told you concerning the helpless millions suffering in this cruel bondage, you at the north would not help to tighten the yoke. You surely would refuse to do for the master, on your own soil, the mean and cruel work which trained bloodhounds and the lowest class of whites do for him at the south.[2]

Everywhere the years bring to all enough of sin and sorrow; but in slavery the very dawn of life is darkened by these shadows. Even the little child who is accustomed to wait on her mistress and her children will learn, before she is twelve years old, why it is that her mistress hates such and such a one among the slaves. Perhaps the child's own mother is among those hated ones. She listens to violent outbreaks of jealous passion, and cannot help understanding what is the cause. She will become prematurely knowing in evil things. Soon she will learn to tremble when she hears her master's footfall. She will be compelled to realize that she is no longer a child. If God has bestowed beauty upon her, it will prove her greatest curse. That

---

[1]Norcom was actually about thirty-five years older than Jacobs.

[2]The Fugitive Slave Law (1850) forbid anyone anywhere in the United States to help a fugitive slave in any way and empowered federal officers to require all citizens to aid in enforcing the law.

which commands admiration in the white woman only hastens the degradation of the female slave. I know that some are too much brutalized by slavery to feel the humiliation of their position; but many slaves feel it most acutely, and shrink from the memory of it. I cannot tell how much I suffered in the presence of these wrongs, nor how I am still pained by the retrospect. My master met me at every turn, reminding me that I belonged to him, and swearing by heaven and earth that he would compel me to submit to him. If I went out for a breath of fresh air, after a day of unwearied toil, his footsteps dogged me. If I knelt by my mother's grave, his dark shadow fell on me even there. The light heart which nature had given me became heavy with sad forebodings. The other slaves in my master's house noticed the change. Many of them pitied me; but none dared to ask the cause. They had no need to inquire. They knew too well the guilty practices under that roof; and they were aware that to speak of them was an offence that never went unpunished.

I longed for someone to confide in. I would have given the world to have laid my head on my grandmother's faithful bosom, and told her all my troubles. But Dr. Flint swore he would kill me if I was not as silent as the grave. Then, although my grandmother was all in all to me, I feared her as well as loved her. I had been accustomed to look up to her with a respect bordering upon awe. I was very young, and felt shamefaced about telling her such impure things, especially as I knew her to be very strict on such subjects. Moreover, she was a woman of a high spirit. She was usually very quiet in her demeanor; but if her indignation was once roused, it was not very easily quelled. I had been told that she once chased a white gentleman with a loaded pistol, because he insulted one of her daughters. I dreaded the consequences of a violent outbreak; and both pride and fear kept me silent. But though I did not confide in my grandmother, and even evaded her vigilant watchfulness and inquiry, her presence in the neighborhood was some protection to me. Though she had been a slave, Dr. Flint was afraid of her. He dreaded her scorching rebukes. Moreover, she was known and patronized by many people; and he did not wish to have his villainy made public. It was lucky for me that I did not live on a distant plantation, but in a town not so large that the inhabitants were ignorant of each other's affairs. Bad as are the laws and customs in a slaveholding community, the doctor, as a professional man, deemed it prudent to keep up some outward show of decency.

O, what days and nights of fear and sorrow that man caused me! Reader, it is not to awaken sympathy for myself that I am telling you truthfully what I suffered in slavery. I do it to kindle a flame of compassion in your hearts for my sisters who are still in bondage, suffering as I once suffered.

I once saw two beautiful children playing together. One was a fair white child; the other was her slave, and also her sister. When I saw them embracing each other, and heard their joyous laughter, I turned sadly away from the lovely sight. I foresaw the inevitable blight that would fall on the little slave's heart. I knew how soon her laughter would be changed to sighs. The fair child grew up to be a still fairer woman. From childhood to womanhood her pathway was blooming with flowers, and overarched by a sunny sky. Scarcely one day of her life had been clouded when the sun rose on her happy bridal morning.

How had those years dealt with her slave sister, the little playmate of her childhood? She, also, was very beautiful; but the flowers and sunshine of love were not for her. She drank the cup of sin, and shame, and misery, whereof her persecuted race are compelled to drink.

In view of these things, why are ye silent, ye free men and women of the north? Why do your tongues falter in maintenance of the right? Would that I had more ability! But my heart is so full, and my pen is so weak! There are noble men and women who plead for us, striving to help those who cannot help themselves. God bless them! God give them strength and courage to go on! God bless those, everywhere, who are laboring to advance the cause of humanity!

X

A Perilous Passage
in the Slave Girl's Life

After my lover[3] went away, Dr. Flint contrived a new plan. He seemed to have an idea that my fear of my mistress was his greatest obstacle. In the blandest tones, he told me that he was going to build

---

[3] A free black carpenter had courted Jacobs and wanted to buy her freedom, but Norcom forbade their marriage.

a small house for me, in a secluded place, four miles away from the town. I shuddered; but I was constrained to listen, while he talked of his intention to give me a home of my own, and to make a lady of me. Hitherto, I had escaped my dreaded fate by being in the midst of people. My grandmother had already had high words with my master about me. She had told him pretty plainly what she thought of his character, and there was considerable gossip in the neighborhood about our affairs, to which the open-mouthed jealousy of Mrs. Flint contributed not a little. When my master said he was going to build a house for me, and that he could do it with little trouble and expense, I was in hopes something would happen to frustrate his scheme; but I soon heard that the house was actually begun. I vowed before my Maker that I would never enter it. I had rather toil on the plantation from dawn till dark; I had rather live and die in jail, than drag on, from day to day, through such a living death. I was determined that the master, whom I so hated and loathed, who had blighted the prospects of my youth, and made my life a desert, should not, after my long struggle with him, succeed at last in trampling his victim under his feet. I would do anything, everything, for the sake of defeating him. What *could* I do? I thought and thought, till I became desperate, and made a plunge into the abyss.

And now, reader, I come to a period in my unhappy life which I would gladly forget if I could. The remembrance fills me with sorrow and shame. It pains me to tell you of it; but I have promised to tell you the truth, and I will do it honestly, let it cost me what it may. I will not try to screen myself behind the plea of compulsion from a master; for it was not so. Neither can I plead ignorance or thoughtlessness. For years, my master had done his utmost to pollute my mind with foul images, and to destroy the pure principles inculcated by my grandmother and the good mistress of my childhood. The influences of slavery had had the same effect on me that they had on other young girls; they had made me prematurely knowing, concerning the evil ways of the world. I knew what I did, and I did it with deliberate calculation.

But, O, ye happy women whose purity has been sheltered from childhood, who have been free to choose the objects of your affection, whose homes are protected by law, do not judge the poor desolate slave girl too severely! If slavery had been abolished, I, also, could have married the man of my choice; I could have had a home shielded by the laws; and I should have been spared the painful task of confessing what I am now about to relate; but all my prospects had been blighted by slavery. I wanted to keep myself pure; and, under the most adverse circumstances, I tried hard to preserve my self-respect; but I was struggling alone in the powerful grasp of the demon Slavery; and the monster proved too strong for me. I felt as if I was forsaken by God and man; as if all my efforts must be frustrated; and I became reckless in my despair.

I have told you that Dr. Flint's persecutions and his wife's jealousy had given rise to some gossip in the neighborhood. Among others, it chanced that a white unmarried gentleman had obtained some knowledge of the circumstances in which I was placed. He knew my grandmother, and often spoke to me in the street. He became interested for me, and asked questions about my master, which I answered in part. He expressed a great deal of sympathy, and a wish to aid me. He constantly sought opportunities to see me, and wrote to me frequently. I was a poor slave girl, only fifteen years old.

So much attention from a superior person was, of course, flattering; for human nature is the same in all. I also felt grateful for his sympathy, and encouraged by his kind words. It seemed to me a great thing to have such a friend. By degrees, a more tender feeling crept into my heart. He was an educated and eloquent gentleman; too eloquent, alas, for the poor slave girl who trusted in him. Of course I saw whither all this was tending. I knew the impassable gulf between us; but to be an object of interest to a man who is not married, and who is not her master, is agreeable to the pride and feelings of a slave, if her miserable situation has left her any pride or sentiment. It seems less degrading to give one's self, than to submit to compulsion. There is something akin to freedom in having a lover who has no control over you, except that which he gains by kindness and attachment. A master may treat you as rudely as he pleases, and you dare not speak; moreover, the wrong does not seem so great with an unmarried man, as with one who has a wife to be made unhappy. There may be sophistry in all this; but the condition of a slave confuses all principles of morality, and, in fact, renders the practice of them impossible.

When I found that my master had actually begun to build the lonely cottage, other feelings mixed with those I have described. Revenge, and calculations of interest, were added to flattered vanity and sincere gratitude for kindness. I knew nothing would enrage Dr. Flint so much as to know that I favored another; and it was something to triumph over my tyrant even in that small way. I thought he would revenge himself by selling me, and I was sure my friend, Mr. Sands, would buy me. He was a man of more generosity and feeling than my master, and I thought my freedom could be easily obtained from him. The crisis of my fate now came so near that I was desperate. I shuddered to think of being the mother of children that should be owned by my old tyrant. I knew that as soon as a new fancy took him, his victims were sold far off to get rid of them; especially if they had children. I had seen several women sold, with his babies at the breast. He never allowed his offspring by slaves to remain long in sight of himself and his wife. Of a man who was not my master I could ask to have my children well supported; and in this case, I felt confident I should obtain the boon. I also felt quite sure that they would be made free. With all these thoughts revolving in my mind, and seeing no other way of escaping the doom I so much dreaded, I made a headlong plunge. Pity me, and pardon me, O virtuous reader! You never knew what it is to be a slave; to be entirely unprotected by law or custom; to have the laws reduce you to the condition of a chattel, entirely subject to the will of another. You never exhausted your ingenuity in avoiding the snares and eluding the power of a hated tyrant; you never shuddered at the sound of his footsteps, and trembled within hearing of his voice. I know I did wrong. No one can feel it more sensibly than I do. The painful and humiliating memory will haunt me to my dying day. Still, in looking back, calmly, on the events of my life, I feel that the slave woman ought not to be judged by the same standards as others.

The months passed on. I had many unhappy hours. I secretly mourned over the sorrow I was bringing on my grandmother, who had so tried to shield me from harm. I knew that I was the greatest comfort of her old age, and that it was a source of pride to her that I had not degraded myself, like most of the slaves. I wanted to confess to her that I was no longer worthy of her love; but I could not utter the dreaded words.

As for Dr. Flint, I had a feeling of satisfaction and triumph in the thought of telling *him*. From time to time he told me of his intended arrangements, and I was silent. At last, he came and told me the cottage was completed, and ordered me to go to it. I told him I would never enter it. He said, "I have heard enough of such talk as that. You shall go, if you are carried by force; and you shall remain there."

I replied, "I will never go there. In a few months I shall be a mother."

He stood and looked at me in dumb amazement, and left the house without a word. I thought I should be happy in my triumph over him. But now that the truth was out, and my relatives would hear of it, I felt wretched. Humble as were their circumstances, they had pride in my good character. Now, how could I look them in the face? My self-respect was gone! I had resolved that I would be virtuous, though I was a slave. I had said, "Let the storm beat! I will brave it till I die." And now, how humiliated I felt!

I went to my grandmother. My lips moved to make confession, but the words stuck in my throat. I sat down in the shade of a tree at her door and began to sew. I think she saw something unusual was the matter with me. The mother of slaves is very watchful. She knows there is no security for her children. After they have entered their teens she lives in daily expectation of trouble. This leads to many questions. If the girl is of a sensitive nature, timidity keeps her from answering truthfully, and this well-meant course has a tendency to drive her from maternal counsels. Presently, in came my mistress, like a mad woman, and accused me concerning her husband. My grandmother, whose suspicions had been previously awakened, believed what she said. She exclaimed, "O Linda! has it come to this? I had rather see you dead than to see you as you now are. You are a disgrace to your dead mother." She tore from my fingers my mother's wedding ring and her silver thimble. "Go away!" she exclaimed, "and never come to my house, again." Her reproaches fell so hot and heavy, that they left me no chance to answer. Bitter tears, such as the eyes never shed but once, were my only answer. I rose from my seat, but fell back again, sobbing. She did not speak to me; but the tears were running down her furrowed cheeks, and they scorched me like fire. She had always been so kind to me! *So* kind! How I longed to throw myself at her feet, and tell her all the truth! But she had ordered me to go, and never to come there again. After a few minutes, I mustered strength, and started to obey her. With what feelings did I now close that little gate, which I used to open with such an eager hand in my childhood! It closed upon me with a sound I never heard before.

Where could I go? I was afraid to return to my master's. I walked on recklessly, not caring where I went, or what would become of me. When I had gone four or five miles, fatigue compelled me to stop. I sat down on the stump of an old tree. The stars were shining through the boughs above me. How they mocked me, with their bright, calm light! The hours passed by, and as I sat there alone a chilliness and deadly sickness came over me. I sank on the ground. My mind was full of horrid thoughts. I prayed to die; but the prayer was not answered. At last, with great effort I roused myself, and walked some distance further, to the house of a woman who had been a friend of my mother. When I told her why I was there, she spoke soothingly to me; but I could not be comforted. I thought I could bear my shame if I could only be reconciled to my grandmother. I longed to open my heart to her. I thought if she could know the real state of the case, and all I had been bearing for years, she would perhaps judge me less harshly. My friend advised me to send for her. I did so; but days of agonizing suspense passed before she came. Had she utterly forsaken me? No. She came at last. I knelt before her, and told her the things that had poisoned my life; how long I had been persecuted; that I saw no way of escape; and in an hour of extremity I had become desperate. She listened in silence. I told her I would bear anything and do anything, if in time I had hopes of obtaining her forgiveness. I begged of her to pity me, for my dead mother's sake. And she did pity me. She did not say, "I forgive you"; but she looked at me lovingly, with her eyes full of tears. She laid her old hand gently on my head, and murmured, "Poor child! Poor child!"

XII

FEAR OF INSURRECTION

Not far from this time Nat Turner's insurrection broke out; and the news threw our town into great commotion.[4] Strange that they should be alarmed, when their slaves were so "contented and happy"! But so it was.

It was always the custom to have a muster every year. On that occasion every white man shouldered his musket. The citizens and

---

[4]Nat Turner's slave insurrection, the bloodiest in American history, raged for two days in August 1831, in southern Virginia, around forty miles from Edenton; Turner remained at large for nine weeks.

the so-called country gentlemen wore military uniforms. The poor whites took their places in the ranks in everyday dress, some without shoes, some without hats. This grand occasion had already passed; and when the slaves were told there was to be another muster, they were surprised and rejoiced. Poor creatures! They thought it was going to be a holiday. I was informed of the true state of affairs, and imparted it to the few I could trust. Most gladly would I have proclaimed it to every slave; but I dared not. All could not be relied on. Mighty is the power of the torturing lash.

By sunrise, people were pouring in from every quarter within twenty miles of the town. I knew the houses were to be searched; and I expected it would be done by country bullies and the poor whites. I knew nothing annoyed them so much as to see colored people living in comfort and respectability; so I made arrangements for them with especial care. I arranged everything in my grandmother's house as neatly as possible. I put white quilts on the beds, and decorated some of the rooms with flowers. When all was arranged, I sat down at the window to watch. Far as my eye could reach, it rested on a motley crowd of soldiers. Drums and fifes were discoursing martial music. The men were divided into companies of sixteen, each headed by a captain. Orders were given, and the wild scouts rushed in every direction, wherever a colored face was to be found.

It was a grand opportunity for the low whites, who had no negroes of their own to scourge. They exulted in such a chance to exercise a little brief authority, and show their subserviency to the slaveholders; not reflecting that the power which trampled on the colored people also kept themselves in poverty, ignorance, and moral degradation. Those who never witnessed such scenes can hardly believe what I know was inflicted at this time on innocent men, women, and children, against whom there was not the slightest ground for suspicion. Colored people and slaves who lived in remote parts of the town suffered in an especial manner. In some cases the searchers scattered powder and shot among their clothes, and then sent other parties to find them, and bring them forward as proof that they were plotting insurrection. Everywhere men, women, and children were whipped till the blood stood in puddles at their feet. Some received five hundred lashes; others were tied hands and feet, and tortured with a bucking paddle, which blisters the skin terribly. The dwellings of the colored people, unless they happened to be protected by some influential white person, who was nigh at hand, were robbed of clothing and everything else the marauders thought worth carrying away. All day long these unfeeling wretches went round, like a troop of demons, terrifying and tormenting the helpless. At night, they formed themselves into patrol bands, and went wherever they chose among the colored people, acting out their brutal will. Many women hid themselves in woods and swamps, to keep out of their way. If any of the husbands or fathers told of these outrages, they were tied up to the public whipping post, and cruelly scourged for telling lies about white men. The consternation was universal. No two people that had the slightest tinge of color in their faces dared to be seen talking together.

I entertained no positive fears about our household, because we were in the midst of white families who would protect us. We were ready to receive the soldiers whenever they came. It was not long before we heard the tramp of feet and the sound of voices. The door was rudely pushed open; and in they tumbled, like a pack of hungry wolves. They snatched at everything within their reach. Every box, trunk, closet, and corner underwent a thorough examination. A box in one of the drawers containing some silver change was eagerly pounced upon. When I stepped forward to take it from them, one of the soldiers turned and said angrily, "What d'ye foller us fur? D'ye s'pose white folks is come to steal?"

I replied, "You have come to search; but you have searched that box, and I will take it, if you please."

At that moment I saw a white gentleman who was friendly to us; and I called to him, and asked him to have the goodness to come in and stay till the search was over. He readily complied. His entrance into the house brought in the captain of the company, whose business it was to guard the outside of the house, and see that none of the inmates left it. This officer was Mr. Litch, the wealthy slave-holder whom I mentioned, in the account of neighboring planters, as being notorious for his cruelty. He felt above soiling his hands with the search. He merely gave orders; and, if a bit of writing was discovered, it was carried to him by his ignorant followers, who were unable to read.

My grandmother had a large trunk of bedding and tablecloths. When that was opened, there was a great shout of surprise; and one exclaimed, "Where'd the damned niggers git all dis sheet an' table clarf?"

My grandmother, emboldened by the presence of our white protector, said, "You may be sure we didn't pilfer 'em from *your* houses."

"Look here, mammy," said a grim-looking fellow without any coat, "you seem to feel mighty gran' cause you got all them 'ere fixens. White folks oughter have 'em all."

His remarks were interrupted by a chorus of voices shouting, "We's got 'em! We's got 'em! Dis 'ere yaller gal's got letters!"

There was a general rush for the supposed letter, which, upon examination, proved to be some verses written to me by a friend. In packing away my things, I had overlooked them. When their captain informed them of their contents, they seemed much disappointed. He inquired of me who wrote them. I told him it was one of my friends. "Can you read them?" he asked. When I told him I could, he swore, and raved, and tore the paper into bits. "Bring me all your letters!" said he, in a commanding tone. I told him I had none. "Don't be afraid," he continued, in an insinuating way. "Bring them all to me. Nobody shall do you any harm." Seeing I did not move to obey him, his pleasant tone changed to oaths and threats. "Who writes to you? half free niggers?" inquired he. I replied, "O, no; most of my letters are from white people. Some request me to burn them after they are read, and some I destroy without reading."

An exclamation of surprise from some of the company put a stop to our conversation. Some silver spoons which ornamented an old-fashioned buffet had just been discovered. My grandmother was in the habit of preserving fruit for many ladies in the town, and of preparing suppers for parties; consequently she had many jars of preserves. The closet that contained these was next invaded, and the contents tasted. One of them, who was helping himself freely, tapped his neighbor on the shoulder, and said, "Wal done! Don't wonder de niggers want to kill all de white folks, when dey live on 'sarves" [meaning preserves]. I stretched out my hand to take the jar, saying, "You were not sent here to search for sweetmeats."

"And what *were* we sent for?" said the captain, bristling up to me. I evaded the question.

The search of the house was completed, and nothing found to condemn us. They next proceeded to the garden, and knocked about every bush and vine, with no better success. The captain called his men together, and, after a short consultation, the order to march was given. As they passed out of the gate, the captain turned back, and pronounced a malediction on the house. He said it ought to be burned to the ground, and each of its inmates receive thirty-nine lashes. We came out of this affair very fortunately; not losing anything except some wearing apparel.

Towards evening the turbulence increased. The soldiers, stimulated by drink, committed still greater cruelties. Shrieks and shouts continually rent the air. Not daring to go to the door, I peeped under the window curtain. I saw a mob dragging along a number of colored people, each white man, with his musket upraised, threatening instant death if they did not stop their shrieks. Among the prisoners was a respectable old colored minister. They had found a few parcels of shot in his house, which his wife had for years used to balance her scales. For this they were going to shoot him on Court House Green. What a spectacle was that for a civilized country! A rabble, staggering under intoxication, assuming to be the administrators of justice!

The better class of the community exerted their influence to save the innocent, persecuted people; and in several instances they succeeded, by keeping them shut up in jail till the excitement abated. At last the white citizens found that their own property was not safe from the lawless rabble they had summoned to protect them. They rallied the drunken swarm, drove them back into the country, and set a guard over the town.

The next day, the town patrols were commissioned to search colored people that lived out of the city; and the most shocking outrages were committed with perfect impunity. Every day for a fortnight, if I looked out, I saw horsemen with some poor panting negro tied to their saddles, and compelled by the lash to keep up with their speed, till they arrived at the jail yard. Those who had been whipped too unmercifully to walk were washed with brine, tossed into a cart, and carried to jail. One black man, who had not fortitude to endure scourging, promised to give information about the conspiracy. But it turned out that he knew nothing at all. He had not even heard the name of Nat Turner. The poor fellow had, however, made up a story, which augmented his own sufferings and those of the colored people.

The day patrol continued for some weeks, and at sundown a night guard was substituted. Nothing at all was proved against the colored people, bond or free. The wrath of the slaveholders was somewhat appeased by the capture of Nat Turner. The imprisoned were released. The slaves were sent to their masters, and the free were permitted to return to their ravaged homes. Visiting was strictly forbidden on the plantations. The slaves begged the privilege of again meeting at their little church in the woods, with their burying ground around it. It was built by the colored people, and they had no higher happiness than to meet there and sing hymns together, and pour out their hearts in spontaneous prayer. Their request was denied, and the church was demolished. They were permitted to attend the white churches, a certain portion of the galleries being appropriated to their use. There, when everybody else had partaken of the communion, and the benediction had been pronounced, the minister said, "Come down, now, my colored friends." They obeyed the summons, and partook of the bread and wine, in commemoration of the meek and lowly Jesus, who said, "God is your Father, and all ye are brethren."[5]

XIII

THE CHURCH AND SLAVERY

After the alarm caused by Nat Turner's insurrection had subsided, the slaveholders came to the conclusion that it would be well to give the slaves enough of religious instruction to keep them from murdering their masters. The Episcopal clergyman offered to hold a separate service on Sundays for their benefit. His colored members were very few, and also very respectable—a fact which I presume had some weight with him. The difficulty was to decide on a suitable place for them to worship. The Methodist and Baptist churches admitted them in the afternoon; but their carpets and cushions were not so costly as those at the Episcopal church. It was at last decided that they should meet at the house of a free colored man, who was a member.

I was invited to attend, because I could read. Sunday evening came, and, trusting to the cover of night, I ventured out. I rarely ventured out by daylight, for I always went with fear, expecting at every turn to encounter Dr. Flint, who was sure to turn me back, or order me to his office to inquire where I got my bonnet, or some other article of dress. When the Rev. Mr. Pike came, there were some twenty

[5]Matthew 23:8 (slightly misquoted).

persons present. The reverend gentleman knelt in prayer, then seated himself, and requested all present, who could read, to open their books, while he gave out the portions he wished them to repeat or respond to.

His text was, "Servants, be obedient to them that are your masters according to the flesh, with fear and trembling, in singleness of your heart, as unto Christ."[6]

Pious Mr. Pike brushed up his hair till it stood upright, and, in deep, solemn tones, began: "Hearken, ye servants! Give strict heed unto my words. You are rebellious sinners. Your hearts are filled with all manner of evil. 'Tis the devil who tempts you. God is angry with you, and will surely punish you, if you don't forsake your wicked ways. You that live in town are eye-servants behind your master's back. Instead of serving your masters faithfully, which is pleasing in the sight of your heavenly Master, you are idle, and shirk your work. God sees you. You tell lies. God hears you. Instead of being engaged in worshipping him, you are hidden away somewhere, feasting on your master's substance; tossing coffee-grounds with some wicked fortuneteller, or cutting cards with another old hag. Your masters may not find you out, but God sees you, and will punish you. O, the depravity of your hearts! When your master's work is done, are you quietly together, thinking of the goodness of God to such sinful creatures? No; you are quarreling, and tying up little bags of roots to bury under the door-steps to poison each other with.[7] God sees you. You men steal away to every grog shop to sell your master's corn, that you may buy rum to drink. God sees you. You sneak into the back streets, or among the bushes, to pitch coppers. Although your masters may not find you out, God sees you; and he will punish you. You must forsake your sinful ways, and be faithful servants. Obey your old mistress. If you disobey your earthly master, you offend your heavenly Master. You must obey God's commandments. When you go from here, don't stop at the corners of the streets to talk, but go directly home, and let your master and mistress see that you have come."

The benediction was pronounced. We went home, highly amused at brother Pike's gospel teaching, and we determined to hear him again. I went the next Sabbath evening, and heard pretty much a

[6]Ephesians 6:5
[7]Pike preached against practicing African folk magic.

repetition of the last discourse. At the close of the meeting, Mr. Pike informed us that he found it very inconvenient to meet at the friend's house, and he should be glad to see us, every Sunday evening, at his own kitchen.

I went home with the feeling that I had heard the Reverend Mr. Pike for the last time. Some of his members repaired to his house, and found that the kitchen sported two tallow candles; the first time, I am sure, since its present occupant owned it, for the servants never had anything but pine knots. It was so long before the reverend gentleman descended from his comfortable parlor that the slaves left, and went to enjoy a Methodist shout. They never seem so happy as when shouting and singing at religious meetings. Many of them are sincere, and nearer to the gate of heaven than sanctimonious Mr. Pike, and other longfaced Christians, who see wounded Samaritans, and pass by on the other side.[8]

The slaves generally compose their own songs and hymns; and they do not trouble their heads much about the measure. They often sing the following verses:

> Old Satan is one busy ole man;
>   He rolls dem blocks all in my way;
> But Jesus is my bosom friend;
>   He rolls dem blocks away.

> If I had died when I was young,
>   Den how my stam'ring tongue would have sung;
> But I am ole, and now I stand
>   A narrow chance for to tread dat heavenly land.

I well remember one occasion when I attended a Methodist class meeting. I went with a burdened spirit, and happened to sit next a poor, bereaved mother, whose heart was still heavier than mine. The class leader was the town constable—a man who bought and sold slaves, who whipped his brethren and sisters of the church at the public whipping post, in jail or out of jail. He was ready to perform that Christian office anywhere for fifty cents. This white-faced, black-hearted brother came near us, and said to the stricken woman, "Sister, can't you tell us how the Lord deals with your soul? Do you

[8]Luke 10:33–37.

love him as you did formerly?"

She rose to her feet, and said, in piteous tones, "My Lord and Master, help me! My load is more than I can bear. God has hid himself from me, and I am left in darkness and misery." Then, striking her breast, she continued, "I can't tell you what is in here! They've got all my children. Last week they took the last one. God only knows where they've sold her. They let me have her sixteen years, and then— O! O! Pray for her brothers and sisters! I've got nothing to live for now. God make my time short!"

She sat down, quivering in every limb. I saw that constable class leader become crimson in the face with suppressed laughter, while he held up his handkerchief, that those who were weeping for the poor woman's calamity might not see his merriment. Then, with assumed gravity, he said to the bereaved mother, "Sister, pray to the Lord that every dispensation of his divine will may be sanctified to the good of your poor needy soul!"

The congregation struck up a hymn, and sung as though they were as free as the birds that warbled round us,—

> Ole Satan thought he had a mighty aim;
> He missed my soul, and caught my sins.
> Cry Amen, cry Amen, cry Amen to God!
>
> He took my sins upon his back;
> Went muttering and grumbling down to hell.
> Cry Amen, cry Amen, cry Amen to God!
>
> Ole Satan's church is here below.
> Up to God's free church I hope to go.
> Cry Amen, cry Amen, cry Amen to God!

Precious are such moments to the poor slaves. If you were to hear them at such times, you might think they were happy. But can that hour of singing and shouting sustain them through the dreary week, toiling without wages, under constant dread of the lash?

The Episcopal clergyman, who, ever since my earliest recollection, had been a sort of god among the slaveholders, concluded, as his family was large, that he must go where money was more abundant. A very different clergyman took his place. The change was very agreeable to the colored people, who said, "God has sent us a good man this time." They loved him, and their children followed him for a smile or a kind word. Even the slaveholders felt his influence. He brought to the rectory five slaves. His wife taught them to read and write, and to be useful to her and themselves. As soon as he was settled, he turned his attention to the needy slaves around him. He urged upon his parishioners the duty of having a meeting expressly for them every Sunday, with a sermon adapted to their comprehension. After much argument and importunity, it was finally agreed that they might occupy the gallery of the church on Sunday evenings. Many colored people, hitherto unaccustomed to attend church, now gladly went to hear the gospel preached. The sermons were simple, and they understood them. Moreover, it was the first time they had ever been addressed as human beings. It was not long before his white parishioners began to be dissatisfied. He was accused of preaching better sermons to the negroes than he did to them. He honestly confessed that he bestowed more pains upon those sermons than upon any others; for the slaves were reared in such ignorance that it was a difficult task to adapt himself to their comprehension. Dissensions arose in the parish. Some wanted he should preach to them in the evening, and to the slaves in the afternoon. In the midst of these disputings his wife died, after a very short illness. Her slaves gathered round her dying bed in great sorrow. She said, "I have tried to do you good and promote your happiness; and if I have failed, it has not been for want of interest in your welfare. Do not weep for me; but prepare for the new duties that lie before you. I leave you all free. May we meet in a better world." Her liberated slaves were sent away, with funds to establish them comfortably. The colored people will long bless the memory of that truly Christian woman. Soon after her death her husband preached his farewell sermon, and many tears were shed at his departure.

Several years after, he passed through our town and preached to his former congregation. In his afternoon sermon he addressed the colored people. "My friends," said he, "it affords me great happiness to have an opportunity of speaking to you again. For two years I have been striving to do something for the colored people of my own parish; but nothing is yet accomplished. I have not even preached a sermon to them. Try to live according to the word of God, my friends. Your skin is darker than mine; but God judges men by their hearts, not by the color of their skins." This was strange doctrine from a southern pulpit. It was very offensive to slaveholders. They said he and his wife had made fools of their slaves, and that he preached like a fool to the negroes.

I knew an old black man, whose piety and childlike trust in God were beautiful to witness. At fifty-three years old he joined the Baptist church. He had a most earnest desire to learn to read. He thought he should know how to serve God better if he could only read the Bible. He came to me, and begged me to teach him. He said he could not pay me, for he had no money; but he would bring me nice fruit when the season for it came. I asked him if he didn't know it was contrary to law; and that slaves were whipped and imprisoned for teaching each other to read. This brought the tears into his eyes. "Don't be troubled, Uncle Fred," said I. "I have no thoughts of refusing to teach you. I only told you of the law, that you might know the danger, and be on your guard." He thought he could plan to come three times a week without its being suspected. I selected a quiet nook, where no intruder was likely to penetrate, and there I taught him his A, B, C. Considering his age, his progress was astonishing. As soon as he could spell in two syllables he wanted to spell out words in the Bible. The happy smile that illuminated his face put joy into my heart. After spelling out a few words, he paused, and said, "Honey, it 'pears when I can read dis good book I shall be nearer to God. White man is got all de sense. He can larn easy. It ain't easy for old black man like me. I only wants to read dis book, dat I may know how to live; den I hab no fear 'bout dying."

I tried to encourage him by speaking of the rapid progress he had made. "Hab patience, child," he replied. "I larns slow."

I had no need of patience. His gratitude, and the happiness I imparted, were more than a recompense for all my trouble.

At the end of six months he had read through the New Testament, and could find any text in it. One day, when he had recited unusually well, I said, "Uncle Fred, how do you manage to get your lessons so well?"

"Lord bress you, chile," he replied. "You nebber gibs me a lesson dat I don't pray to God to help me to understan' what I spells and what I reads. And he *does* help me, chile. Bress his holy name!"

There are thousands, who, like good Uncle Fred, are thirsting for the water of life;[9] but the law forbids it, and the churches withhold it. They send the Bible to heathen abroad, and neglect the heathen

[9]"And whosoever will, let him take the water of life freely" (Revelation 22:17).

at home. I am glad that missionaries go out to the dark corners of the earth; but I ask them not to overlook the dark corners at home. Talk to American slaveholders as you talk to savages in Africa. Tell *them* it is wrong to traffic in men. Tell them it is sinful to sell their own children, and atrocious to violate their own daughters. Tell them that all men are brethren, and that man has no right to shut out the light of knowledge from his brother. Tell them they are answerable to God for sealing up the Fountain of Life from souls that are thirsting for it.[10]

There are men who would gladly undertake such missionary work as this; but, alas! their number is small. They are hated by the south, and would be driven from its soil, or dragged to prison to die, as others have been before them. The field is ripe for the harvest, and awaits the reapers.[11] Perhaps the great grandchildren of Uncle Fred may have freely imparted to them the divine treasures, which he sought by stealth, at the risk of the prison and the scourge.

Are doctors of divinity blind, or are they hypocrites? I suppose some are the one, and some the other; but I think if they felt the interest in the poor and the lowly that they ought to feel, they would not be so *easily* blinded. A clergyman who goes to the south, for the first time, has usually some feeling, however vague, that slavery is wrong. The slaveholder suspects this, and plays his game accordingly. He makes himself as agreeable as possible; talks on theology, and other kindred topics. The reverend gentleman is asked to invoke a blessing on a table loaded with luxuries. After dinner he walks round the premises, and sees the beautiful groves and flowering vines, and the comfortable huts of favored household slaves. The southerner invites him to talk with these slaves. He asks them if they want to be free, and they say, "O, no, massa." This is sufficient to satisfy him. He comes home to publish a "South-Side View of Slavery," and to complain of the exaggerations of abolitionists. He assures people that he has been to the south, and seen slavery for himself; that it is a beautiful "patriarchal institution"; that the slaves don't want their freedom; that they have hallelujah meetings, and other religious privileges.[12]

[10]See Psalms 36:9.
[11]See Revelation 14:15.
[12]After a short tour of the South, Nehemiah Adams, a Boston clergyman, defended slavery in his *A South-Side View of Slavery; or, Three Months in the South in 1854* (1854).

What does *he* know of the half-starved wretches toiling from dawn till dark on the plantations? of mothers shrieking for their children, torn from their arms by slave traders? of young girls dragged down into moral filth? of pools of blood around the whipping post? of hounds trained to tear human flesh? of men screwed into cotton gins to die? The slaveholder showed him none of these things, and the slaves dared not tell of them if he had asked them.

There is a great difference between Christianity and religion at the south. If a man goes to the communion table, and pays money into the treasury of the church, no matter if it be the price of blood, he is called religious. If a pastor has offspring by a woman not his wife, the church dismiss him, if she is a white woman; but if she is colored, it does not hinder his continuing to be their good shepherd.

When I was told that Dr. Flint had joined the Episcopal church, I was much surprised. I supposed that religion had a purifying effect on the character of men; but the worst persecutions I endured from him were after he was a communicant. The conversation of the doctor, the day after he had been confirmed, certainly gave *me* no indication that he had "renounced the devil and all his works." In answer to some of his unusual talk, I reminded him that he had just joined the church. "Yes, Linda," said he. "It was proper for me to do so. I am getting in years, and my position in society requires it, and it puts an end to all the damned slang.[13] You would do well to join the church, too, Linda."

"There are sinners enough in it already," rejoined I. "If I could be allowed to live like a Christian, I should be glad."

"You can do what I require; and if you are faithful to me, you will be as virtuous as my wife," he replied.

I answered that the Bible didn't say so.

His voice became hoarse with rage. "How dare you preach to me about your infernal Bible!" he exclaimed. "What right have you, who are my negro, to talk to me about what you would like, and what you wouldn't like? I am your master, and you shall obey me."

No wonder the slaves sing,—

> Ole Satan's church is here below;
> Up to God's free church I hope to go.

---

[13]Impertinent gossip (?).

Elizabeth Cady Stanton

1815–1902

ELIZABETH CADY grew up in a strict Presbyterian household in upstate New York, the daughter of a distinguished lawyer and judge. She first became aware of the legal oppression of women through hearing about her father's cases. When her only brother died, she tried to make up for his loss by learning Greek and becoming an expert horseback rider; but her father only responded, "Ah, you should have been a boy!" She married Henry Stanton, a gifted abolitionist speaker, in 1840, and had seven children. She wrote in old age that they "lived together without more than the usual matrimonial friction for nearly half a century." Accompanying him to the World Antislavery Convention in London, she was radicalized by the organizers' refusal to seat women delegates and by meeting Lucretia Mott, the first woman she had known who did not hesitate to challenge male wisdom and authority.

In 1848, she and Mott organized the first Women's Rights Convention in Seneca Falls, for which Stanton wrote a Declaration of Sentiments, modeled on the Declaration of Independence. In 1851, she met Susan B. Anthony, with whom she worked closely for almost fifty years; her speeches, in fact, might be considered joint productions. Anthony collected data, while Stanton articulated arguments; Anthony circulated petitions and organized conventions, while Stanton delivered speeches. When Stanton was totally immersed in domestic obligations, Anthony exhorted her and gave her practical help with children and housework.

During the summer and autumn of 1859, feminists organized by Anthony canvassed New York State, circulating petitions to the legislature for a constitutional amendment to allow women to vote and for laws to give married women control over their property and equal custody over their children. Anthony urged Stanton to address the legislature, and Stanton agreed if Anthony, with her practical knowledge of the situation, would come over "and start me on the right train of thought." The result was the great speech of 1860, which succeeded in persuading the legislators to enact laws securing married women's rights to their property and their children. Two years later, they repealed parts of these laws—taking advantage of the fact that women still had no votes. After the Civil War, Stanton and Anthony continued to work tirelessly for women's suffrage, touring the country, giving speeches, editing the feminist newspaper *The Revolution,* and organizing the National Woman Suffrage Association, of which Stanton was president.

BIBLIOGRAPHY
Banner, Lois. *Elizabeth Cady Stanton: A Radical for Woman's Rights.* Boston: Little, Brown, 1980.
Stanton, Elizabeth Cady, Susan B. Anthony, and Matilda Joslyn Gage. *History of Woman Suffrage.* Vol. 1. New York: Fowler and Wells, 1881. Reprint New York: Arno and The New York Times, 1969.
Stanton, Theodore, and Harriot Stanton Blatch, eds. *Elizabeth Cady Stanton, As Revealed in Her Letters, Diary, and Reminiscences.* 2 vols. New York: Harper and Brothers, 1922. Reprint New York: Arno and The New York Times, 1969.

Letters to Susan B. Anthony

Seneca Falls, March 1, 1853

Dear Friend,—I do not know whether the world is quite willing or ready to discuss the question of marriage. I feel in my innermost soul that the thoughts I sent the convention are true. It is in vain to look for the elevation of woman so long as she is degraded in marriage. I hold that it is a sin, an outrage on our holiest feelings, to pretend that anything but deep, fervent love and sympathy constitute marriage. The right idea of marriage is at the foundation of all reforms. How strange it is that man will apply all the improvements in the arts and sciences to everything about him, animate or inanimate, but himself. If we properly understood the science of life, it would be far easier to give to the world harmonious, beautiful, noble, virtuous children, than it is to bring grown-up discord into harmony with the great divine soul of all. I ask for no laws on marriage. I say with Father Chipman, remove law and a false public sentiment, and woman will no more live as wife with a cruel, bestial drunkard than a servant, in this free country, will stay with a pettish, unjust mistress. If lawmakers insist upon exercising their prerogative in some way on this question, let them forbid any woman to marry until she is twenty-one; let them fine a woman $50 for every child she conceives by a drunkard. Women have no right to saddle the state with idiots who must be supported by the public. You know that the statistics of our idiot asylums show that nearly all are the offspring of drunkards. Women must be made to feel that the transmitting of immortal life is a solemn, responsible act, and should never be allowed except when the parents are in the highest condition of mind and body. Man in his lust has regulated long enough this whole question of sexual intercourse. Now let the mother of mankind, whose prerogative it is to set bounds to his indulgence, rouse up and give this whole matter a thorough, fearless examination. I am glad that Catholic priest said of my letter what he did. It will call attention to the subject; and if by martyrdom I can advance my race one step, I am ready for it. I feel, as never before, that this whole question of woman's rights turns on the pivot of the marriage relation, and, mark my word, sooner or later it will be the topic for discussion. I would not hurry it on, nor would I avoid it. Good night.

Seneca Falls, December 1, 1853

Dear Susan,—Can you get any acute lawyer—perhaps Judge Hay is the man—sufficiently interested in our movement to look up just eight laws concerning us—the very worst in all the code? I can generalize and philosophize easily enough of myself; but the details of the particular laws I need, I have not time to look up. You see, while I am about the house, surrounded by my children, washing dishes, baking, sewing, etc., I can think up many points, but I cannot search books, for my hands as well as my brains would be necessary for that work. If I can, I shall go to Rochester as soon as I have finished my Address and submit it—and the Appeal too for that matter—to Channing's criticism. But prepare yourself to be disappointed in its merits, for I seldom have one hour undisturbed in which to sit down and write. Men who can, when they wish to write a document, shut themselves up for days with their thoughts and their books, know little of what difficulties a woman must surmount to get off a tolerable production.

Peterboro, September 10, 1855

Dear Susan,—I wish that I were as free as you and I would stump the state in a twinkling. But I am not, and what is more, I passed through a terrible scourging when last at my father's. I cannot tell you how deep the iron entered my soul. I never felt more keenly the degradation of my sex. To think that all in me of which my father would have felt a proper pride had I been a man, is deeply mortifying to him because I am a woman. That thought has stung me to a fierce decision—to speak as soon as I can do myself credit. But the pressure on me just now is too great. Henry sides with my friends, who oppose me in all that is dearest to my heart. They are not willing that I should write even on the woman question. But I will both write and speak. I wish you to consider this letter strictly confidential. Sometimes, Susan, I struggle in deep waters. I have rewritten my "Indian," and given it into the hands of Oliver Johnson, who has promised to see it safely in the *Tribune.* I have sent him another article on the "Widow's Teaspoons," and I have mailed you one of mine which appeared in the Buffalo *Democracy.* I have sent six articles to the *Tribune,* and three have already appeared. I have promised to write for the *Una.*[1] I read and write a good deal, as you see. But there are grievous interruptions. However, a good time is coming and my future is always bright and beautiful. Good night.

As ever your friend, sincere and steadfast.

Seneca Falls, July 20, 1857

Dear Susan,—I was glad to hear of Lucy Stone. I think a vast deal of her and Antoinette Brown. I regret so much that you and Lucy should have had even the slightest interruption to your friendship.[1] I was much interested in the extract from her letter; although I agree with her that man, too, suffers in a false marriage relation, yet what can his suffering be compared with what every woman experiences

---

[1] A woman's rights newspaper edited by Paulina Wright Davis.

[1] Lucy Stone was a feminist and abolitionist particularly known for her insistence on women's independence in marriage. Antoinette Brown, her sister-in-law, was the first formally educated woman minister. Anthony resented Stone's (temporary) abandonment of public affairs for motherhood.

whether happy or unhappy? I do not know that the laws and religion of our country even now are behind the public sentiment which makes woman the mere tool of man. He has made the laws and proclaimed the religion; so we have his exact idea of the niche he thinks God intended woman to fill. A man in marrying gives up no right; but a woman, every right, even the most sacred of all—the right to her own person. There will be no response among women to our demands until we have first aroused in them a sense of personal dignity and independence; and so long as our present false marriage relation continues, which in most cases is nothing more nor less than legalized prostitution, woman can have no self-respect, and of course man will have none for her; for the world estimates us according to the value we put upon ourselves. Personal freedom is the first right to be proclaimed, and that does not and cannot now belong to the relation of wife, to the mistress of the isolated home, to the financial dependent.

Seneca Falls, July 4, 1858

Dear Susan,—I went to Junius[1] and read my address on suffrage, which was pronounced very fine. I feel that two or three such meetings would put me on my feet. But, oh, Susan, my hopes of leisure were soon blasted. The cook's brother was taken sick with a fever a few days after you left, and she was obliged to go home. So I have done my work aided by a little girl ever since. But I went to Junius in spite of it all. I see that Mr. Higginson[2] belongs to the Jeremy Bentham school, that law makes right. I am a disciple of the new philosophy that man's wants make his rights. I consider my right to property, to suffrage, etc., as natural and inalienable as my right to life and to liberty. Man is above all law. The province of law is simply to protect me in what is mine.

Seneca Falls, July 15, 1859

Dear Susan,—Well, here is the tract.[1] I think it is about right now that the best part is all cut out! I should have sent it long ago, but as I

[1]Possibly a misprint for "Julius," a family nickname for Stanton's cousin and close friend Elizabeth Smith Miller.

[2]The Reverend Thomas Wentworth Higginson, a worker for abolition and woman suffrage.

[1]The Appeal to the Women of the Empire State to sign a petition asking the legislature to legalize married women's property rights and woman suffrage.

have had to change servants, I had little time to give to writing. Mary went into the factory, as she was tired revolving round the cook stove—I couldn't blame her—and Susan got sick and went home. So imagine me with strange servants, my boys home on their vacation, and excuse my seeming neglect of all your epistles. But when you come, I will try and find time to grind out what you say must be done. In the past, we have issued all kinds of bulls under all kinds of circumstances, and I think we can still do more in that line, even if you must make the puddings and carry the baby[2] while I ply the pen.

Seneca Falls, December 23, 1859

Dear Susan,—Where are you? Since a week ago last Monday, I have looked for you every day. I had the washing put off, we cooked a turkey, I made a pie in the morning, sent my first-born to the depot and put clean aprons on the children, but lo! you did not come. Nor did you soften the rough angles of our disappointment by one solitary line of excuse. And it would do me such great good to see some reformers just now. The death of my father, the worse than death of my dear Cousin Gerrit, the martyrdom of that grand and glorious John Brown[1]—all this conspires to make me regret more than ever my dwarfed womanhood. In times like these, everyone should do the work of a full-grown man. When I pass the gate of the celestial city and good Peter asks me where I would sit, I shall say, "Anywhere, so that I am neither a negro nor a woman. Confer on me, good angel, the glory of white manhood so that henceforth, sitting or standing, rising up or lying down, I may enjoy the most unlimited freedom." Good night.

[2]Her seventh and last child, born in March.

[1]Gerrit Smith, Stanton's beloved cousin and neighbor, had introduced her to liberal ideas, notably abolitionism; he supported Brown's attempt to inspire slave rebellions through the raid on Harper's Ferry (October) and became temporarily insane as a result of Brown's execution (December 2).

Speech to the New York State Legislature, February 18, 1860

Gentlemen of the Judiciary:—There are certain natural rights as inalienable to civilization as are the rights of air and motion to the savage in the wilderness. The natural rights of the civilized man and woman are government, property, the harmonious development of all their powers, and the gratification of their desires. There are a few people we now and then meet who, like Jeremy Bentham,[1] scout the idea of natural rights in civilization, and pronounce them mere metaphors, declaring that there are no rights aside from those the law confers. If the law made man too, that might do, for then he could be made to order to fit the particular niche he was designed to fill. But inasmuch as God made man in His own image, with capacities and powers as boundless as the universe, whose exigencies no mere human law can meet, it is evident that the man must ever stand first; the law but the creature of his wants; the law giver but the mouthpiece of humanity. If, then, the nature of a being decides its rights, every individual comes into this world with rights that are not transferable. He does not bring them like a pack on his back, that may be stolen from him, but they are a component part of himself, the laws which ensure his growth and development. The individual may be put in the stocks, body and soul, he may be dwarfed, crippled, killed, but his rights no man can get; they live and die with him.

Though the atmosphere is forty miles deep all round the globe, no man can do more than fill his own lungs. No man can see, hear, or smell but just so far; and though hundreds are deprived of these senses, his are not the more acute. Though rights have been abundantly supplied by the good Father, no man can appropriate to himself those that belong to another. A citizen can have but one vote, fill but one office, though thousands are not permitted to do either. These axioms prove that woman's poverty does not add to man's wealth, and if, in the plenitude of his power, he should secure to her the exercise of all her God-given rights, her wealth could not bring

---

[1] Jeremy Bentham, a British political-legal philosopher, argued that the laws should promote the happiness of the community, but criticized the concept of natural rights.

poverty to him. There is a kind of nervous unrest always manifested by those in power, whenever new claims are started by those out of their own immediate class. The philosophy of this is very plain. They imagine that if the rights of this new class be granted, they must, of necessity, sacrifice something of what they already possess. They can not divest themselves of the idea that rights are very much like lands, stocks, bonds, and mortgages, and that if every new claimant be satisfied, the supply of human rights must in time run low. You might as well carp at the birth of every child, lest there should not be enough air left to inflate your lungs; at the success of every scholar, for fear that your draughts at the fountain of knowledge could not be so long and deep; at the glory of every hero, lest there be no glory left for you. . . .

If the object of government is to protect the weak against the strong, how unwise to place the power wholly in the hands of the strong. Yet that is the history of all governments, even the model republic of these United States. You who have read the history of nations, from Moses down to our last election, where have you ever seen one class looking after the interests of another? Any of you can readily see the defects in other governments, and pronounce sentence against those who have sacrificed the masses to themselves; but when we come to our own case, we are blinded by custom and self-interest. Some of you who have no capital can see the injustice which the laborer suffers; some of you who have no slaves, can see the cruelty of his oppression; but who of you appreciate the galling humiliation, the refinements of degradation, to which women (the mothers, wives, sisters, and daughters of freemen) are subject, in this the last half of the nineteenth century? How many of you have ever read even the laws concerning them that now disgrace your statute-books? In cruelty and tyranny, they are not surpassed by any slaveholding code in the Southern States; in fact they are worse, by just so far as woman, from her social position, refinement, and education, is on a more equal ground with the oppressor.

Allow me just here to call the attention of that party now so much interested in the slave of the Carolinas,[2] to the similarity in his condition and that of the mothers, wives, and daughters of the Empire State. The negro has no name. He is Cuffy Douglas or Cuffy Brooks,

---

[2] The Republican party was generally opposed to slavery, although it did not officially advocate abolition.

just whose Cuffy he may chance to be. The woman has no name. She is Mrs. Richard Roe or Mrs. John Doe, just whose Mrs. she may chance to be. Cuffy has no right to his earnings; he can not buy or sell, or lay up anything that he can call his own. Mrs. Roe has no right to her earnings; she can neither buy nor sell, make contracts, nor lay up anything that she can call her own. Cuffy has no right to his children; they can be sold from him at any time. Mrs. Roe has no right to her children; they may be bound out to cancel a father's debts of honor. The unborn child, even by the last will of the father, may be placed under the guardianship of a stranger and a foreigner. Cuffy has no legal existence; he is subject to restraint and moderate chastisement. Mrs. Roe has no legal existence; she has not the best right to her own person. The husband has the power to restrain, and administer moderate chastisement.

Blackstone declares that the husband and wife are one, and learned commentators have decided that that one is the husband.[3] In all civil codes, you will find them classified as one. Certain rights and immunities, such and such privileges are to be secured to white male citizens. What have women and negroes to do with rights? What know they of government, war, or glory?

The prejudice against color, of which we hear so much, is no stronger than that against sex. It is produced by the same cause, and manifested very much in the same way. The negro's skin and the woman's sex are both *prima facie* evidence that they were intended to be in subjection to the white Saxon man. The few social privileges which the man gives the woman, he makes up to the negro in civil rights. The woman may sit at the same table and eat with the white man; the free negro may hold property and vote. The woman may sit in the same pew with the white man in church; the free negro may enter the pulpit and preach. Now, with the black man's right to suffrage, the right unquestioned, even by Paul, to minister at the altar,[4] it is evident that the prejudice against sex is more deeply rooted and more unreasonably maintained than that against color. As citizens of a republic, which should we most highly prize, social privileges or civil rights? The latter, most certainly.

---

[3] In his *Commentaries on the Laws of England* (1765–1769), William Blackstone enunciated the common-law principle that, when a woman married, her identity was submerged in that of her husband.

[4] Paul decreed that women must not speak in church (I Corinthians 14:34–36), but said nothing about blacks.

To those who do not feel the injustice and degradation of the condition, there is something inexpressibly comical in man's "citizen woman." It reminds me of those monsters I used to see in the old world, head and shoulders woman, and the rest of the body sometimes fish and sometimes beast. I used to think, What a strange conceit! but now I see how perfectly it represents man's idea! Look over all his laws concerning us, and you will see just enough of woman to tell of her existence; all the rest is submerged, or made to crawl upon the earth. Just imagine an inhabitant of another planet entertaining himself some pleasant evening in searching over our great national compact, our Declaration of Independence, our Constitutions, or some of our statute-books; what would he think of those "women and negroes" that must be so fenced in, so guarded against? Why, he would certainly suppose we were monsters, like those fabulous giants or Brobdignagians of olden times, so dangerous to civilized man, from our size, ferocity, and power. Then let him take up our poets, from Pope down to Dana;[5] let him listen to our Fourth of July toasts, and some of the sentimental adulations of social life, and no logic could convince him that this creature of the law, and this angel of the family altar, could be one and the same being. Man is in such a labyrinth of contradictions with his marital and property rights; he is so befogged on the whole question of maidens, wives, and mothers, that from pure benevolence we should relieve him from this troublesome branch of legislation. We should vote, and make laws for ourselves. Do not be alarmed, dear ladies! You need spend no time reading Grotius, Coke, Puffendorf, Blackstone, Bentham, Kent, and Story[6] to find out what you need. We may safely trust the shrewd selfishness of the white man, and consent to live under the same broad code where he has so comfortably ensconced himself. Any legislation that will do for man, we may abide by most cheerfully. . . .

But, say you, we would not have woman exposed to the grossness and vulgarity of public life, or encounter what she must at the polls. When you talk, gentlemen, of sheltering woman from the rough winds and revolting scenes of real life, you must be either talking

[5]Alexander Pope, the greatest English poet of the eighteenth century, and Richard Henry Dana, Sr., a nineteenth-century American poet and essayist. Her point is that poets have traditionally overidealized women.

[6]Distinguished legal philosophers, who flourished from the seventeenth to nineteenth centuries in the Netherlands, England, Germany, and America.

for effect, or wholly ignorant of what the facts of life are. The man, whatever he is, is known to the woman. She is the companion, not only of the accomplished statesman, the orator, and the scholar; but the vile, vulgar, brutal man has his mother, his wife, his sister, his daughter. Yes, delicate, refined, educated women are in daily life with the drunkard, the gambler, the licentious man, the rogue, and the villain; and if man shows out what he is anywhere, it is at his own hearthstone. There are over forty thousand drunkards in this State. All of these are bound by the ties of family to some woman. Allow but a mother and a wife to each, and you have over eighty thousand women. All these have seen their fathers, brothers, husbands, sons, in the lowest and most debased stages of obscenity and degradation. In your own circle of friends, do you not know refined women whose whole lives are darkened and saddened by gross and brutal associations? Now, gentlemen, do you talk to woman of a rude jest or jostle at the polls, where noble, virtuous men stand ready to protect her person and her rights, when, alone in the darkness and solitude and gloom of night, she has trembled on her own threshold, awaiting the return of a husband from his midnight revels?—when, stepping from her chamber, she has beheld her royal monarch, her lord and master—her legal representative—the protector of her property, her home, her children, and her person, down on his hands and knees slowly crawling up the stairs? Behold him in her chamber—in her bed! The fairy tale of "Beauty and the Beast" is far too often realized in life. Gentlemen, such scenes as woman has witnessed at her own fireside, where no eye save Omnipotence could pity, no strong arm could help, can never be realized at the polls, never equaled elsewhere, this side the bottomless pit. No, woman has not hitherto lived in the clouds, surrounded by an atmosphere of purity and peace—but she has been the companion of man in health, in sickness, and in death, in his highest and in his lowest moments. She has worshipped him as a saint and an orator, and pitied him as madman or a fool. In Paradise, man and woman were placed together, and so they must ever be. They must sink or rise together. If man is low and wretched and vile, woman can not escape the contagion, and any atmosphere that is unfit for woman to breathe is not fit for man. Verily, the sins of the fathers shall be visited upon the children to the third and fourth generation. You, by your unwise legislation, have crippled and dwarfed womanhood, by closing to her all honorable and lucrative means of employment, have driven her into the garrets and dens of our cities, where she now revenges herself on your innocent sons, sapping the very foundations of national virtue and strength. Alas! for the young men just coming on the stage of action, who soon shall fill your vacant places—our future Senators, our Presidents, the expounders of our constitutional law! Terrible are the penalties we are now suffering for the ages of injustice done to woman.

Again, it is said that the majority of women do not ask for any change in the laws; that it is time enough to give them the elective franchise when they, as a class, demand it.

Wise statesmen legislate for the best interests of the nation; the State, for the highest good of its citizens; the Christian, for the conversion of the world. Where would have been our railroads, our telegraphs, our ocean steamers, our canals and harbors, our arts and sciences, if government had withheld the means from the far-seeing minority? This State established our present system of common schools, fully believing that educated men and women would make better citizens than ignorant ones. In making this provision for the education of its children, had they waited for a majority of the urchins of this State to petition for schools, how many, think you, would have asked to be transplanted from the street to the schoolhouse? Does the State wait for the criminal to ask for his prison-house? the insane, the idiot, the deaf and dumb for his asylum? Does the Christian, in his love to all mankind, wait for the majority of the benighted heathen to ask him for the gospel? No; unasked and unwelcomed, he crosses the trackless ocean, rolls off the mountain of superstition that oppresses the human mind, proclaims the immortality of the soul, the dignity of manhood, the right of all to be free and happy.

No, gentlemen, if there is but one woman in this State who feels the injustice of her position, she should not be denied her inalienable rights, because the common household drudge and the silly butterfly of fashion are ignorant of all laws, both human and Divine. Because they know nothing of governments, or rights, and therefore ask nothing, shall my petitions be unheard? I stand before you the rightful representative of woman, claiming a share in the halo of glory that has gathered round her in the ages, and by the wisdom of her past words and works, her peerless heroism and self-sacrifice, I challenge your admiration; and moreover claiming, as I do, a share in all her outrages and sufferings, in the cruel injustice, contempt, and ridicule now heaped upon her, in her deep degradation, hopeless wretchedness, by all that is helpless in her present condition, that is false in law and public sentiment, I urge your generous consideration; for as my heart swells with pride to behold woman in the highest walks of literature and art, it grows big enough to take in those who are bleeding in the dust.

Now do not think, gentlemen, we wish you to do a great many troublesome things for us. We do not ask our legislators to spend a whole session in fixing up a code of laws to satisfy a class of most unreasonable women. We ask no more than the poor devils in the Scripture asked, "Let us alone."[7] In mercy, let us take care of ourselves, our property, our children, and our homes. True, we are not so strong, so wise, so crafty as you are, but if any kind friend leaves us a little money, or we can by great industry earn fifty cents a day, we would rather buy bread and clothes for our children than cigars and champagne for our legal protectors. There has been a great deal written and said about protection. We, as a class, are tired of one kind of protection, that which leaves us everything to do, to dare, and to suffer, and strips us of all means for its accomplishment. We would not tax man to take care of us. No, the Great Father has endowed all his creatures with the necessary powers for self-support, self-defense, and protection. We do not ask man to represent us; it is hard enough in times like these for man to carry backbone enough to represent himself. So long as the mass of men spend most of their time on the fence, not knowing which way to jump, they are surely in no condition to tell us where we had better stand. In pity for man, we would no longer hang like a millstone round his neck. Undo what man did for us in the dark ages, and strike out all special legislation for us; strike the words "white male" from all our constitutions, and then, with fair sailing, let us sink or swim, live or die, survive or perish together.

At Athens, an ancient apologue tells us, on the completion of the temple of Minerva, a statue of the goddess was wanted to occupy the crowning point of the edifice. Two of the greatest artists produced what each deemed his masterpiece. One of these figures was the size of life, admirably designed, exquisitely finished, softly rounded, and beautifully refined. The other was of Amazonian stature, and so boldly chiselled that it looked more like masonry than sculpture. The eyes of all were attracted by the first, and turned away in contempt from the second. That, therefore, was adopted,

[7]Mark 1:24.

and the other rejected, almost with resentment, as though an insult had been offered to a discerning public. The favored statue was accordingly borne in triumph to the place for which it was designed, in the presence of applauding thousands, but as it receded from their upturned eyes, all, all at once agaze upon it, the thunders of applause unaccountably died away—a general misgiving ran through every bosom—the mob themselves stood like statues, as silent and as petrified, for as it slowly went up, and up, the soft expression of those chiseled features, the delicate curves and outlines of the limbs and figure, became gradually fainter and fainter, and when at last it reached the place for which it was intended, it was a shapeless ball, enveloped in mist. Of course, the idol of the hour was now clamored down as rationally as it had been cried up, and its dishonored rival, with no good will and no good looks on the part of the chagrined populace, was reared in its stead. As it ascended, the sharp angles faded away, the rough points became smooth, the features full of expression, the whole figure radiant with majesty and beauty. The rude hewn mass, that before had scarcely appeared to bear even the human form, assumed at once the divinity which it represented, being so perfectly proportioned to the dimensions of the building, and to the elevation on which it stood, that it seemed as though Pallas herself had alighted upon the pinnacle of the temple in person, to receive the homage of her worshipers.

The woman of the nineteenth century is the shapeless ball in the lofty position which she was designed fully and nobly to fill. The place is not too high, too large, too sacred for woman, but the type that you have chosen is far too small for it. The woman we declare unto you is the rude, misshapen, unpolished object of the successful artist. From your standpoint, you are absorbed with the defects alone. The true artist sees the harmony between the object and its destination. Man, the sculptor, has carved out his ideal, and applauding thousands welcome his success. He has made a woman that from his low standpoint looks fair and beautiful, a being without rights, or hopes, or fears but in him—neither noble, virtuous, nor independent. Where do we see, in Church or State, in schoolhouse or at the fireside, the much talked-of moral power of woman? Like those Athenians, we have bowed down and worshiped in woman, beauty, grace, the exquisite proportions, the soft and beautifully rounded outline, her delicacy, refinement, and silent helplessness— all well when she is viewed simply as an object of sight, never to rise one foot above the dust from which she sprung. But if she is to be raised up to adorn a temple, or represent a divinity—if she is to fill the niche of wife and counsellor to true and noble men, if she is to be the mother, the educator of a race of heroes or martyrs, of a Napoleon, or a Jesus—then must the type of womanhood be on a larger scale than that yet carved by man.

In vain would the rejected artist have reasoned with the Athenians as to the superiority of his production; nothing short of the experiment they made could have satisfied them. And what of your experiment, what of your wives, your homes? Alas! for the folly and vacancy that meet you there! But for your clubhouses and newspapers, what would social life be to you? Where are your beautiful women? your frail ones, taught to lean lovingly and confidingly on man? Where are the crowds of educated dependents—where the long line of pensioners on man's bounty? Where all the young girls, taught to believe that marriage is the only legitimate object of a woman's pursuit—they who stand listlessly on life's shores, waiting, year after year, like the sick man at the pool of Bethesda,[8] for someone to come and put them in? These are they who by their ignorance and folly curse almost every fireside with some human specimen of deformity or imbecility. These are they who fill the gloomy abodes of poverty and vice in our vast metropolis. These are they who patrol the streets of our cities, to give our sons their first lessons in infamy. These are they who fill our asylums, and make night hideous with their cries and groans.

The women who are called masculine, who are brave, courageous, self-reliant and independent, are they who in the face of adverse winds have kept one steady course upward and onward in the paths of virtue and peace—they who have taken their gauge of womanhood from their own native strength and dignity—they who have learned for themselves the will of God concerning them. This is our type of womanhood. Will you help us raise it up, that you too may see its beautiful proportions—that you may behold the outline of the goddess who is yet to adorn your temple of Freedom? We are building a model republic; our edifice will one day need a crowning glory. Let the artists be wisely chosen. Let them begin their work. Here is a temple to Liberty, to human rights, on whose portals behold the glorious declaration, "All men are created equal." The sun has never yet shone upon any of man's creations that can compare with this.

[8]John 5:5–7.

The artist who can mold a statue worthy to crown magnificence like this, must be godlike in his conceptions, grand in his comprehensions, sublimely beautiful in his power of execution. The woman—the crowning glory of the model republic among the nations of the earth—what must she not be? (Loud applause.)

Elizabeth Stuart Phelps

(1815–1852)

ELIZABETH STUART, the fifth of nine children, was the daughter of an invalid mother and a prominent professor at Andover Theological Seminary. Her first published pieces, written as a teenager, appeared in the religious magazine edited by the director of her boarding school. After years of publishing nondescript anonymous pieces in periodicals and children's books, she won international recognition with her novel *The Sunny Side; or, The Country Minister's Wife* (1851), written with her characteristic realism. *The Angel Over the Right Shoulder* appeared in 1852.

She had married Austin Phelps, a young minister, in 1842, and had borne three children. He got a parish in Boston, where she spent six happy years, delighting in the varied life, society, and cultural resources of a great city. But when he decided to accept a faculty position at Andover, which entailed crushing economy as well as a restrictive environment, she felt it her duty to conceal her despair. Despite her struggles with depression, she always exerted herself to look at "the sunny side." Like Mrs. James in *The Angel Over the Right Shoulder,* Phelps was torn between duty to her family and duty to use her talent. She did not give up self-fulfillment as her heroine did, for she reserved two hours per day for her writing; but she paid for her choice. According to her daughter, who adopted the same name and became a more famous writer, it was the struggle between thwarted creativity and relentless domestic obligation that killed her at the age of thirty-seven.

BIBLIOGRAPHY

Fetterley, Judith, ed. *Provisions: A Reader from Nineteenth-Century American Women.* Bloomington: Indiana University Press, 1985.

Phelps, Elizabeth Stuart. *The Angel Over the Right Shoulder; or, The Beginning of the New Year.* Andover: W. F. Draper, 1853.

Ward, Elizabeth Stuart Phelps. *Chapters from a Life.* Boston: Houghton Mifflin, 1896.

The Angel Over the Right Shoulder

"There! a woman's work is never done," said Mrs. James; "I thought, for once, I was through; but just look at that lamp, now! It will not burn, and I must go and spend half an hour over it."

"Don't you wish you had never been married?" said Mr. James, with a good-natured laugh.

"Yes"—rose to her lips, but was checked by a glance at the group upon the floor, where her husband was stretched out, and two little urchins with sparkling eyes and glowing cheeks were climbing and tumbling over him as if they found in this play the very essence of fun.

She did say, "I should like the good, without the evil, if I could have it."

"You have no evils to endure," replied her husband.

"That is just all you gentlemen know about it. What would you think if you could not get an uninterrupted half hour to yourself, from morning till night? I believe you would give up trying to do anything."

"There is no need of that; all you want is *system*. If you arranged your work systematically, you would find that you could command your time."

"Well," was the reply, "all I wish is that you could just follow me around for one day, and see what I have to do. If you could reduce it all to system, I think you would show yourself a genius."

When the lamp was trimmed, the conversation was resumed. Mr. James had employed the "half hour" in meditating on this subject.

"Wife," said he, as she came in, "I have a plan to propose to you, and I wish you to promise me beforehand that you will accede to it. It is to be an experiment, I acknowledge, but I wish it to have a fair trial. Now to please me, will you promise?"

Mrs. James hesitated. She felt almost sure that his plan would be quite impracticable, for what does a man know of a woman's work? Yet she promised.

"Now I wish you," said he, "to set apart two hours every day for your own private use. Make a point of going to your room and locking yourself in; and also make up your mind to let the work which is not done, go undone, if it must. Spend this time on just those things which will be most profitable to yourself. I shall bind you to your promise for one month—then, if it has proved a total failure, we will devise something else."

"When shall I begin?"

"Tomorrow."

The morrow came. Mrs. James had chosen the two hours before dinner as being, on the whole, the most convenient and the least liable to interruption. They dined at one o'clock. She wished to finish her morning work, get dressed for the day, and enter her room at eleven.

Hearty as were her efforts to accomplish this, the hour of eleven found her with her work but half done; yet, true to her promise, she left all, retired to her room and locked the door.

With some interest and hope, she immediately marked out a course of reading and study for these two precious hours; then, arranging her table, her books, pen and paper, she commenced a schedule of her work with much enthusiasm. Scarcely had she dipped her pen in ink, when she heard the tramping of little feet along the hall, and then a pounding at her door.

"Mamma! mamma! I cannot find my mittens, and Hannah is going to slide without me."

"Go to Amy, my dear; mamma is busy."

"So Amy busy too; she say she can't leave baby."

The child began to cry, still standing close to the fastened door. Mrs. James knew the easiest, and indeed the only way of settling the trouble, was to go herself and hunt up the missing mittens. Then a parley must be held with Frank, to induce him to wait for his sister, and the child's tears must be dried, and little hearts must be all set right before the children went out to play; and so favorable an opportunity must not be suffered to slip, without impressing on young minds the importance of having a "place for everything and everything in its place." This took time; and when Mrs. James returned to her study, her watch told her that *half* her portion had gone. Quietly resuming her work, she was endeavoring to mend her broken train of thought, when heavier steps were heard in the hall, and the fastened door was once more besieged. Now, Mr. James must be admitted.

"Mary," said he, "cannot you come and sew a string on for me? I do believe there is not a bosom in my drawer in order, and I am in a great hurry. I ought to have been downtown an hour ago."

The schedule was thrown aside, the work-basket taken, and Mrs. James followed him. She soon sewed on the tape, but then a button needed fastening, and, at last, a rip in his glove was to be mended. As Mrs. James stitched away on the glove, a smile lurked in the corners of her mouth, which her husband observed.

"What are you laughing at?" asked he.

"To think how famously your plan works."

"I declare!" said he, "is this your study hour? I am sorry, but what can a man do? He cannot go downtown without a shirt-bosom!"

"Certainly not," said his wife, quietly.

When her liege lord was fairly equipped and off, Mrs. James returned to her room. A half an hour yet remained to her, and of this she determined to make the most. But scarcely had she resumed her pen, when there was another disturbance in the entry. Amy had returned from walking out with the baby, and she entered the nursery with him, that she might get him to sleep. Now it happened that the only room in the house which Mrs. James could have to herself with a fire was the one adjoining the nursery. She had become so accustomed to the ordinary noise of the children that it did not disturb her; but the very extraordinary noise which Master Charley sometimes felt called upon to make, when he was fairly on his back in the cradle, did disturb the unity of her thoughts. The words which she was reading rose and fell with the screams and lulls of the child, and she felt obliged to close her book, until the storm was over. When quiet was restored in the cradle, the children came in from sliding, crying with cold fingers—and just as she was going to them, the dinner-bell rang.

"How did your new plan work this morning?" inquired Mr. James.

"Famously," was the reply, "I read about seventy pages of German, and as many more in French."

"I am sure *I* did not hinder you long."

"No—yours was only one of a dozen interruptions."

"Oh, well! you must not get discouraged. Nothing succeeds well the first time. Persist in your arrangement, and by and by the family will learn that if they want anything of you, they must wait until after dinner."

"But what can a man do?" replied his wife; "He cannot go downtown without a shirt-bosom."

"I was in a bad case," replied Mr. James, "it may not happen again. I am anxious to have you try the month out faithfully, and then we will see what has come of it."

The second day of trial was a stormy one. As the morning was dark, Bridget overslept, and consequently breakfast was too late by an hour. This lost hour Mrs. James could not recover. When the clock struck eleven, she seemed but to have commenced her morning's work, so much remained to be done. With mind disturbed and spirits depressed, she left her household matters "in the suds," as they were, and punctually retired to her study. She soon found, however, that she could not fix her attention upon any intellectual pursuit. Neglected duties haunted her, like ghosts around the guilty conscience. Perceiving that she was doing nothing with her books, and not wishing to lose the morning wholly, she commenced writing a letter. Bridget interrupted her before she had proceeded far on the first page.

"What, ma'am, shall we have for dinner? No marketing ha'n't come."

"Have some steaks, then."

"We ha'n't got none, ma'am."

"I will send out for some, directly."

Now there was no one to send but Amy, and Mrs. James knew it. With a sigh, she put down her letter and went into the nursery.

"Amy, Mr. James has forgotten our marketing. I should like to have you run over to the provision store and order some beef-steaks. I will stay with the baby."

Amy was not much pleased to be sent out on this errand. She remarked that "she must change her dress first."

"Be as quick as possible," said Mrs. James, "for I am particularly engaged at this hour."

Amy neither obeyed, nor disobeyed, but managed to take her own time, without any very deliberate intention to do so. Mrs. James, hoping to get along with a sentence or two, took her German book into the nursery. But this arrangement was not to Master Charley's mind. A fig did he care for German, but "the kitties," he must have, whether or no—and kitties he would find in that particular book— so he turned its leaves over in great haste. Half of the time on the second day of trial had gone when Amy returned and Mrs. James, with a sigh, left her nursery. Before one o'clock, she was twice called into the kitchen to superintend some important dinner arrangement, and thus it turned out that she did not finish one page of her letter.

On the third morning the sun shone, and Mrs. James rose early, made every provision which she deemed necessary for dinner, and for the comfort of her family; and then, elated by her success, in good spirits, and with good courage, she entered her study precisely at eleven o'clock, and locked her door. Her books were opened, and the challenge given to a hard German lesson. Scarcely had she made the first onset, when the doorbell was heard to ring, and soon Bridget, coming nearer and nearer—then tapping at the door.

"Somebodies wants to see you in the parlor, ma'am."

"Tell them I am engaged, Bridget."

"I told 'em you were to home, ma'am, and they sent up their names, but I ha'n't got 'em, jist."

There was no help for it—Mrs. James must go down to receive her callers. She had to smile when she felt little like it—to be sociable when her thoughts were busy with her task. Her friends made a long call—they had nothing else to do with their time, and when they went, others came. In very unsatisfactory chit-chat, her morning slipped away.

On the next day, Mr. James invited company to tea, and her morning was devoted to preparing for it; she did not enter her study. On the day following, a sick headache confined her to bed, and on Saturday, the care of the baby devolved upon her, as Amy had extra work to do. Thus passed the first week.

True to her promise, Mrs. James patiently persevered for a month in her efforts to secure for herself this little fragment of her broken time, but with what success, the first week's history can tell. With its close, closed the month of December.

On the last day of the old year, she was so much occupied in her preparations for the morrow's festival that the last hour of the day was approaching before she made her good night's call in the nursery. She first went to the crib and looked at the baby. There he lay in his innocence and beauty, fast asleep. She softly stroked his golden hair, she kissed gently his rosy cheek, she pressed the little dimpled hand in hers, and then carefully drawing the coverlet over it, tucked it in, and stealing yet another kiss, she left him to his peaceful dreams, and sat down on her daughter's bed. She also slept sweetly, with her dolly hugged to her bosom. At this her mother smiled, but soon grave thoughts entered her mind, and these deepened into sad ones. She thought of her disappointment and the failure of her plans. To her, not only the past month, but the whole past year seemed to have been one of fruitless effort—all broken and disjointed—even her hours of religious duty had been encroached upon and disturbed. She had accomplished nothing that she could see, but to keep her house and family in order, and even this, to her saddened mind, seemed to have been but indifferently done. She was conscious of yearnings for a more earnest life than this. Unsatisfied longings for something which she had not attained often clouded what, otherwise, would have been a bright day to her; and yet the causes of these feelings seemed to lie in a dim and misty region, which her eye could not penetrate.

What then did she need? To see some *results* from her life's work? To know that a golden cord bound her life-threads together into *unity* of purpose—notwithstanding they seemed, so often, single and broken?

She was quite sure that she felt no desire to shrink from duty, however humble, but she sighed for some comforting assurance of what *was duty.* Her employments, conflicting as they did with her tastes, seemed to her frivolous and useless. It seemed to her that there was some better way of living, which she, from deficiency in energy of character, or of principle, had failed to discover. As she leaned over her child, her tears fell fast upon its young brow.

Most earnestly did she wish that she could shield that child from the disappointments and mistakes and self-reproach from which the mother was then suffering; that the little one might take up life where she could give it to her—all mended by her own experience. It would have been a comfort to have felt that, in fighting the battle, she had fought for both; yet she knew that so it could not be—that for ourselves must we all learn what are those things which "make for our peace."

The tears were in her eyes as she gave the good-night to her sleeping daughter; then, with soft steps, she entered an adjoining room, and there fairly kissed out the old year on another chubby cheek, which nestled among the pillows. At length she sought her own rest.

Soon she found herself in a singular place. She was traversing a vast plain. No trees were visible, save those which skirted the distant horizon, and on their broad tops rested wreaths of golden clouds. Before her was a female, who was journeying towards that region of light. Little children were about her, now in her arms, now running by her side, and as they traveled, she occupied herself in caring for them. She taught them how to place their little feet; she gave them timely warnings of the pitfalls; she gently lifted them over the stumbling-blocks. When they were weary, she soothed them by singing of the brighter land, which she kept ever in view, and towards which she seemed hastening with her little flock. But what was most remarkable was that, all unknown to her, she was constantly watched by two angels, who reposed on two golden clouds which floated above her. Before each was a golden book and a pen of gold. One angel, with mild and loving eyes, peered constantly over her right shoulder; another kept as strict watch over her left. Not a deed, not a word, not a look, escaped their notice. When a good deed, word, look, went from her, the angel over the right shoulder, with a glad smile, wrote it down in his book; when an evil, however trivial, the angel over the left shoulder recorded it in his book—then, with sorrowful eyes, followed the pilgrim until he observed penitence for the wrong, upon which he dropped a tear on the record, and blotted it out, and both angels rejoiced.

To the looker-on, it seemed that the traveler did nothing which was worthy of such careful record.

Sometimes, she did but bathe the weary feet of her little children, but the angel over the *right shoulder*—wrote it down. Sometimes, she did but patiently wait to lure back a little truant who had turned his face away from the distant light, but the angel over the *right shoulder*—wrote it down. Sometimes, she did but soothe an angry feeling or raise a drooping eyelid, or kiss away a little grief; but the angel over the right shoulder—*wrote it down.*

Sometimes, her eye was fixed so intently on that golden horizon, and she became so eager to make progress thither, that the little ones, missing her care, did languish or stray. Then it was that the angel over the *left shoulder* lifted his golden pen, and made the entry, and followed her with sorrowful eyes until he could blot it out. Sometimes, she seemed to advance rapidly, but in her haste the little ones had fallen back, and it was the sorrowing angel who recorded her progress. Sometimes, so intent was she to gird up her loins and have her lamp trimmed and burning,[1] that the little children wandered away quite into forbidden paths, and it was the angel over the *left shoulder* who recorded her diligence.

Now the observer, as she looked, felt that this was a faithful and true record, and was to be kept to that journey's end. The strong clasps of gold on those golden books also impressed her with the conviction that, when they were closed, it would only be for a future opening.

Her sympathies were warmly enlisted for the gentle traveler, and with a beating heart she quickened her steps that she might overtake her. She wished to tell her of the angels keeping watch above her—to entreat her to be faithful and patient to the end—for her life's work was all written down—every item of it—and the *results* would be known when those golden books should be unclasped. She wished to beg of her to think no duty trivial which must be done, for over her right shoulder and over her left were recording angels, who would surely take note of all!

Eager to warn the traveler of what she had seen, she touched her. The traveller turned, and she recognized or seemed to recognize *herself*. Startled and alarmed, she awoke in tears. The gray light of morning struggled through the half-open shutter, the door was ajar, and merry faces were peeping in.

"Wish you a happy new year, mamma,"—"Wish you a *Happy New Year*,"—"a happy noo ear."

She returned the merry greeting most heartily. It seemed to her as if she had entered upon a new existence. She had found her way through the thicket in which she had been entangled, and a light was now about her path. The *Angel Over the Right Shoulder* whom she had seen in her dream, would bind up in his golden book her life's work, if it were but well done. He required of her no great deeds, but faithfulness and patience to the end of the race which was set before her. Now she could see plainly enough that, though it was

---

[1]Allusion to Christ's parable of the wise and foolish virgins (Matthew 25:1–13).

right and important for her to cultivate her own mind and heart, it was equally right and equally important to meet and perform faithfully all those little household cares and duties on which the comfort and virtue of her family depended; for into these things the angels carefully looked—and these duties and cares acquired a dignity from the strokes of that golden pen—they could not be neglected without danger.

Sad thoughts and sadder misgivings—undefined yearnings and ungratified longings seemed to have taken their flight with the Old Year, and it was with fresh resolution and cheerful hope, and a happy heart, she welcomed the *Glad* New Year. The *Angel Over the Right Shoulder* would go with her, and if she were found faithful, would strengthen and comfort her to its close.

Frances Ellen Watkins Harper

(1825–1911)

FRANCES ELLEN WATKINS was born to free parents in Baltimore and lost her mother before she was three. She attended her clergyman uncle's school for free black children and continued her education by reading on her own when, just before she was thirteen, she took a job as housekeeper in a book dealer's family. She was publishing poetry and prose in Baltimore newspapers while still in her teens. Preferring to live in free territory, she moved North and taught school. She was moved by the increasingly severe pro-slavery laws of the 1850s to devote her life to working for abolition. From 1854 to 1860 she lectured full-time for various Anti-Slavery Societies. She was a spellbinding orator. Her poems can be best appreciated as compositions meant to be declaimed from the platform. Her *Poems on Miscellaneous Subjects* were published in 1854 and often reprinted.

In 1860 she married Fenton Harper and settled on a farm in Ohio; they had one daughter. After her husband's death in 1866, she returned to public life, lecturing to blacks and whites on their responsibilities after emancipation. She continued to publish poetry, as well as the novel *Iola Leroy* (1892). She spoke and wrote for blacks' and women's rights throughout her long life, which extended from the Underground Railroad to the antilynching movement and the campaign for women's suffrage.

BIBLIOGRAPHY

Watkins (Harper), Frances Ellen. *Poems on Miscellaneous Subjects.* Philadelphia: Merrihew and Thompson, 1857.

The Slave Mother

Heard you that shriek? It rose
    So wildly on the air,
It seemed as if a burdened heart
    Was breaking in despair.

Saw you those hands so sadly clasped—
    The bowed and feeble head—
The shuddering of that fragile form—
    That look of grief and dread?

Saw you the sad, imploring eye?
    Its every glance was paid,
As if a storm of agony
    Were sweeping through the brain.

She is a mother, pale with fear,
    Her boy clings to her side,
And in her kirtle vainly tries
    His trembling form to hide.

He is not hers, although she bore
    For him a mother's pains;
He is not hers, although her blood
    Is coursing through his veins!

He is not hers, for cruel hands
    May rudely tear apart
The only wreath of household love
    That binds her breaking heart.

His love has been a joyous light
    That o'er her pathway smiled,
A fountain gushing ever new,
    Amid life's desert wild.

His lightest word has been a tone
  Of music round her heart,
Their lives a streamlet blent in one—
  Oh, Father! must they part?

They tear him from her circling arms,
  Her last and fond embrace.
Oh! never more may her sad eyes
  Gaze on his mournful face.

No marvel, then, these bitter shrieks
  Disturb the listening air:
She is a mother, and her heart
  Is breaking in despair.

The Slave Auction

The sale began—young girls were there,
  Defenceless in their wretchedness,
Whose stifled sobs of deep despair
  Revealed their anguish and distress.

And mothers stood with streaming eyes,
  And saw their dearest children sold;
Unheeded rose their bitter cries,
  While tyrants bartered them for gold.

And woman, with her love and truth—
  For these in sable forms may dwell—
Gazed on the husband of her youth,
  With anguish none may paint or tell.

And men, whose sole crime was their hue,
  The impress of their Maker's hand,

And frail and shrinking children, too,
  Were gathered in that mournful band.

Ye who have laid your love to rest,
  And wept above their lifeless clay,
Know not the anguish of that breast,
  Whose loved are rudely torn away.

Ye may not know how desolate
  Are bosoms rudely forced to part,
And how a dull and heavy weight
  Will press the life-drops from the heart.

The Dismissal of Tyng[1]

"We have but three words to say, 'served him right.'"
                    Church Journal (Episcopal)

Served him right! How could he dare
  To touch the idol of our day?
What if its shrine be red with blood?
  Why, let him turn his eyes away.

Who dares dispute our right to bind
  With galling chains the weak and poor?
To starve and crush the deathless mind,
  Or hunt the slave from door to door?

[1]The Reverend Tyng is unidentified, but the important point of Harper's satire is that so-called Christian churches, even in the North, supported slavery and condemned abolitionists.

Who dares dispute our right to sell
  The mother from her weeping child?
To hush with ruthless stripes and blows
  Her shrieks and sobs of anguish wild?

'Tis right to plead for heathen lands,
  To send the Bible to their shores,
And then to make, for power and pelf,
  A race of heathens at our doors.

What holy horror filled our hearts—
  It shook our church from dome to nave—
Our cheeks grew pale with pious dread,
  To hear him breathe the name of slave.

Upon our Zion, fair and strong,
  His words fell like a fearful blight;
We turned him from our saintly fold;
  And this we did to "serve him right."

The Colored People in America

Having been placed by a dominant race in circumstances over which
we have had no control, we have been the butt of ridicule and the
mark of oppression. Identified with a people over whom weary ages
of degradation have passed, whatever concerns them, as a race, concerns me. I have noticed among our people a disposition to censure
and upbraid each other, a disposition which has its foundation
rather, perhaps, in a want of common sympathy and consideration,
than mutual hatred, or other unholy passions. Born to an inheritance
of misery, nurtured in degradation, and cradled in oppression, with
the scorn of the white man upon their souls, his fetters upon their
limbs, his scourge upon their flesh, what can be expected from their

offspring, but a mournful reaction of that cursed system which spreads its baneful influence over body and soul; which dwarfs the intellect, stunts its development, debases the spirit, and degrades the soul? Place any nation in the same condition which has been our hapless lot, fetter their limbs and degrade their souls, debase their sons and corrupt their daughters, and when the restless yearnings for liberty shall burn through heart and brain—when, tortured by wrong and goaded by oppression, the hearts that would madden with misery, or break in despair, resolve to break their thrall, and escape from bondage, then let the bay of the bloodhound and the scent of the human tiger be upon their track;—let them feel that, from the ceaseless murmur of the Atlantic to the sullen roar of the Pacific, from the thunders of the rainbow-crowned Niagara to the swollen waters of the Mexican gulf, they have no shelter for their bleeding feet, or resting-place for their defenceless heads;—let them, when nominally free, feel that they have only exchanged the iron yoke of oppression for the galling fetters of a vitiated public opinion;—let prejudice assign them the lowest places and the humblest positions, and make them "hewers of wood and drawers of water;"[1]—let their income be so small that they must from necessity bequeath to their children an inheritance of poverty and a limited education,—and tell me, reviler of our race! censurer of our people! if there is a nation in whose veins runs the purest Caucasian blood, upon whom the same causes would not produce the same effects; whose social condition, intellectual and moral character, would present a more favorable aspect than ours? But there is hope; yes, blessed be God! for our down-trodden and despised race. Public and private schools accommodate our children; and in my own southern home, I see women whose lot is unremitted labor saving a pittance from their scanty wages to defray the expense of learning to read. We have papers edited by colored editors, which we may consider it an honor to possess and a credit to sustain. We have a church that is extending itself from east to west, from north to south, through poverty and reproach, persecution and pain. We have our faults, our want of union and concentration of purpose; but are there not extenuating circumstances around our darkest faults—palliating excuses for our most egregious errors? and shall we not hope that the mental and moral aspect which we present is but the first step of a

---

[1] Joshua 9:21–27. This text was often used to rationalize enslavement of a people.

mighty advancement, the faintest coruscations of the day that will dawn with unclouded splendor upon our down-trodden and benighted race, and that ere long we may present to the admiring gaze of those who wish us well, a people to whom knowledge has given power, and righteousness exaltation?

Louisa May Alcott

1832–1888

LOUISA MAY ALCOTT was the second of the four daughters of
Amos Bronson Alcott, the Transcendentalist philosopher and friend
of Ralph Waldo Emerson and Henry David Thoreau. She was closer,
however, to her mother, Abba, the original of Marmee, beloved
center of the March family in *Little Women* (1868). After his progressive school in Boston failed (1840), the idealistic but impractical
Bronson was never steadily employed; so the family subsisted pre-
cariously on handouts from his friends and whatever his wife and
daughters could earn. They were not financially comfortable until
Louisa established her success with *Little Women*. She had been publishing anonymously in magazines from 1852, as well as teaching,
sewing, and doing domestic work. When the Civil War broke out,
she was eager (like her autobiographical heroine Jo March) to take
an active part; she volunteered as a nurse in 1862 and was assigned
to the Union Hotel Hospital in Washington, a poorly run institution
that had been inadequately converted from a hotel. After six weeks,
she contracted typhoid fever and was invalided home.

She developed her letters to her family into *Hospital Sketches,*
which were published in the *Commonwealth Magazine* and then in
book form (1863). She was also turning out Gothic thrillers, published anonymously, to support her family. She was now able to
write full time, except when she had to return home to deal with
some family crisis. *Little Women,* a critical and financial success,
established her reputation; and she followed it up with sequels and
other juvenile fiction. *Work* (1873), a novel for adults, relates many
of her own efforts to support herself. Although she devoted herself
and her earnings to her family, Alcott worked for women's rights:
she wrote for the *Woman's Journal,* edited by Lucy Stone and Henry

Blackwell; led a counterdemonstration by local women at a celebration of the nation's centennial on July 4, 1876; and was the first woman to register to vote in Concord in 1879.

Hospital Sketches established Alcott as a serious writer. She wrote in her journal that they "never made much money, but showed me 'my style,' and taking the hint, I went where glory awaited me"—that is, to *Little Women*.

BIBLIOGRAPHY
Alcott, Louisa May. *Hospital Sketches*. Edited by Bessie Z. Jones. Cambridge: Harvard University Press, 1960.

Saxton, Martha. *Louisa May: A Modern Biography*. New York: Avon Books, 1978.

Stern, Madeleine. *Louisa May Alcott*. Norman, Okla.: University of Oklahoma Press, 1971.

from Hospital Sketches

III

A DAY

"They've come! they've come! hurry up, ladies—you're wanted."

"Who have come? the rebels?"

This sudden summons in the gray dawn was somewhat startling to a three days' nurse like myself, and, as the thundering knock came at our door, I sprang up in my bed, prepared

> To gird my woman's form,
> And on the ramparts die,

if necessary, but my room-mate took it more coolly, and, as she began a rapid toilet, answered my bewildered question,—

"Bless you, no child; it's the wounded from Fredericksburg;[1] forty ambulances are at the door, and we shall have our hands full in fifteen minutes."

"What shall we have to do?"

"Wash, dress, feed, warm and nurse them for the next three months, I dare say. Eighty beds are ready, and we were getting impatient for the men to come. Now you will begin to see hospital life in earnest, for you won't probably find time to sit down all day, and may think yourself fortunate if you get to bed by midnight. Come to me in the ball-room when you are ready; the worst cases are always carried there, and I shall need your help."

So saying, the energetic little woman twirled her hair into a button at the back of her head, in a "cleared for action" sort of style, and vanished, wrestling her way into a feminine kind of pea-jacket as she went.

I am free to confess that I had a realizing sense of the fact that my hospital bed was not a bed of roses just then, or the prospect before me one of unmingled rapture. My three days' experiences had begun with a death, and, owing to the defalcation of another nurse, a somewhat abrupt plunge into the superintendence of a ward containing forty beds, where I spent my shining hours washing faces, serving rations, giving medicine, and sitting in a very hard chair, with pneumonia on one side, diptheria on the other, five typhoids on the opposite, and a dozen dilapidated patriots, hopping, lying, and lounging about, all staring more or less at the new "nuss," who suffered untold agonies, but concealed them under as matronly an aspect as a spinster could assume, and blundered through her trying labors with a Spartan firmness, which I hope they appreciated, but am afraid they didn't. Having a taste for "ghastliness," I had rather longed for the wounded to arrive, for rheumatism wasn't heroic, neither was liver complaint, or measles; even fever had lost its charms since "bathing burning brows" had been used up in romances, real and ideal; but when I peeped into the dusky street lined with what I at first had innocently called market carts, now unloading their sad freight at our door, I recalled sundry reminiscences I had heard from

---

[1]On December 13, 1862, the Union Army, under Major General Ambrose Burnside, had been routed at Fredericksburg, Virginia, by a smaller Confederate force; Union losses were 1,284 killed and 9,600 wounded. Alcott had arrived at the hospital on December 14.

nurses of longer standing, my ardor experienced a sudden chill, and I indulged in a most unpatriotic wish that I was safe at home again, with a quiet day before me, and no necessity for being hustled up, as if I were a hen and had only to hop off my roost, give my plumage a peck, and be ready for action. A second bang at the door sent this recreant desire to the right about, as a little woolly head popped in, and Joey (a six years' old contraband[2]), announced—

"Miss Blank is jes' wild fer ye, and says fly round right away. They's comin' in, I tell yer, heaps on 'em—one was took out dead, and I see him,—ky! warn't he a goner!"

With which cheerful intelligence the imp scuttled away, singing like a blackbird, and I followed, feeling that Richard was *not* himself again,[3] and wouldn't be for a long time to come.

The first thing I met was a regiment of the vilest odors that ever assaulted the human nose, and took it by storm. Cologne, with its seven and seventy evil savors, was a posy-bed to it; and the worst of this affliction was, everyone had assured me that it was a chronic weakness of all hospitals, and I must bear it. I did, armed with lavender water, with which I so besprinkled myself and premises, that, like my friend, Sairey, I was soon known among my patients as "the nurse with the bottle."[4] Having been run over by three excited surgeons, bumped against by migratory coal-hods, water-pails, and small boys; nearly scalded by an avalanche of newly-filled tea-pots, and hopelessly entangled in a knot of colored sisters coming to wash, I progressed by slow stages upstairs and down, till the main hall was reached, and I paused to take breath and a survey. There they were! "our brave boys," as the papers justly called them, for cowards could hardly have been so riddled with shot and shell, so torn and shattered, nor have borne suffering for which we have no name, with an uncomplaining fortitude, which made one glad to cherish each as a brother. In they came, some on stretchers, some in men's arms, some feebly staggering along propped on rude crutches, and one lay stark and still with covered face, as a comrade gave his name to be recorded before they carried him away to the dead house. All was hurry and confusion; the hall was full of these wrecks of

[2]Former slave who had escaped to the Union side.

[3]"Conscience avaunt, Richard's himself again" (Colley Cibber's alteration of William Shakespeare's *Richard III,* V, iii). (Alcott's note.)

[4]Sairey Gamp is a drunken nurse in Charles Dickens's *Martin Chuzzlewit* (1843–1844).

humanity, for the most exhausted could not reach a bed till duly ticketed and registered; the walls were lined with rows of such as could sit, the floor covered with the more disabled, the steps and doorways filled with helpers and lookers on; the sound of many feet and voices made that usually quiet hour as noisy as noon; and, in the midst of it all, the matron's motherly face brought more comfort to many a poor soul than the cordial draughts she administered, or the cheery words that welcomed all, making of the hospital a home.

The sight of several stretchers, each with its legless, armless, or desperately wounded occupant, entering my ward, admonished me that I was there to work, not to wonder or weep; so I corked up my feelings, and returned to the path of duty, which was rather "a hard road to travel" just then. The house had been a hotel before hospitals were needed, and many of the doors still bore their old names; some not so inappropriate as might be imagined, for my ward was in truth a *ball-room,* if gun-shot wounds could christen it. Forty beds were prepared, many already tenanted by tired men who fell down anywhere, and drowsed till the smell of food roused them. Round the great stove was gathered the dreariest group I ever saw—ragged, gaunt and pale, mud to the knees, with bloody bandages untouched since put on days before; many bundled up in blankets, coats being lost or useless; and all wearing that disheartened look which proclaimed defeat, more plainly than any telegram of the Burnside blunder. I pitied them so much, I dared not speak to them, though, remembering all they had been through since the rout at Fredericksburg, I yearned to serve the dreariest of them all. Presently, Miss Blank tore me from my refuge behind piles of one-sleeved shirts, odd socks, bandages and lint; put basin, sponge, towels, and a block of brown soap into my hands with these appalling directions:

"Come, my dear, begin to wash as fast as you can. Tell them to take off socks, coats and shirts, scrub them well, put on clean shirts, and the attendants will finish them off, and lay them in bed."

If she had requested me to shave them all, or dance a horn-pipe on the stove funnel, I should have been less staggered; but to scrub some dozen lords of creation at a moment's notice, was really— really—. However, there was no time for nonsense, and, having resolved when I came to do everything I was bid, I drowned my scruples in my washbowl, clutched my soap manfully, and, assuming a businesslike air, made a dab at the first dirty specimen I saw, bent on performing my task *vi et armis* if necessary. I chanced to light on a withered old Irishman, wounded in the head, which caused that portion of his frame to be tastefully laid out like a garden, the bandages being the walks, his hair the shrubbery. He was so overpowered by the honor of having a lady wash him, as he expressed it, that he did nothing but roll up his eyes, and bless me, in an irresistible style which was too much for my sense of the ludicrous; so we laughed together, and when I knelt down to take off his shoes, he "flopped" also and wouldn't hear of my touching "them dirty craters. May your bed above be aisy darlin', for the day's work ye are doon!—Woosh! there ye are, and bedad, it's hard tellin' which is the dirtiest, the fut or the shoe." It was; and if he hadn't been to the fore, I should have gone on pulling, under the impression that the "fut" was a boot, for trousers, socks, shoes and legs were a mass of mud. This comical tableau produced a general grin, at which propitious beginning I took heart and scrubbed away like any tidy parent on a Saturday night. Some of them took the performance like sleepy children, leaning their tired heads against me as I worked, others looked grimly scandalized, and several of the roughest colored like bashful girls. One wore a soiled little bag about his neck, and, as I moved it, to bathe his wounded breast, I said,

"Your talisman didn't save you, did it?"

"Well, I reckon it did, marm, for that shot would a gone a couple of inches deeper but for my old mammy's camphor bag," answered the cheerful philosopher.

Another, with a gun-shot wound through the cheek, asked for a looking-glass, and when I brought one, regarded his swollen face with a dolorous expression, as he muttered—

"I vow to gosh, that's too bad! I warn't a bad looking chap before, and now I'm done for; won't there be a thunderin' scar? and what on earth will Josephine Skinner say?"

He looked up at me with his one eye so appealingly that I controlled my risibles, and assured him that if Josephine was a girl of sense, she would admire the honorable scar, as a lasting proof that he had faced the enemy, for all women thought a wound the best decoration a brave soldier could wear. I hope Miss Skinner verified the good opinion I so rashly expressed of her, but I shall never know.

The next scrubbee was a nice looking lad, with a curly brown mane, and a budding trace of gingerbread over the lip, which he called his beard, and defended stoutly, when the barber jocosely suggested its immolation. He lay on a bed, with one leg gone, and the right arm so shattered that it must evidently follow; yet the little Sergeant was as merry as if his afflictions were not worth lamenting over, and when a drop of two of salt water mingled with my suds at the sight of this strong young body, so marred and maimed, the boy looked up with a brave smile, though there was a little quiver of the lips, as he said,

"Now don't you fret yourself about me, miss; I'm first rate here, for it's nuts to lie still on this bed, after knocking about in those confounded ambulances, that shake what there is left of a fellow to jelly. I never was in one of these places before, and think this cleaning up a jolly thing for us, though I'm afraid it isn't for you ladies."

"Is this your first battle, Sergeant?"

"No, miss; I've been in six scrimmages, and never got a scratch till this last one; but it's done the business pretty thoroughly for me, I should say. Lord! what a scramble there'll be for arms and legs, when we old boys come out of our graves, on the Judgment Day: wonder if we shall get our own again? If we do, my leg will have to tramp from Fredericksburg, my arm from here, I suppose, and meet my body, wherever it may be."

The fancy seemed to tickle him mightily, for he laughed blithely, and so did I; which, no doubt, caused the new nurse to be regarded as a light-minded sinner by the Chaplain, who roamed vaguely about, informing the men that they were all worms, corrupt of heart, with perishable bodies, and souls only to be saved by a diligent perusal of certain tracts, and other equally cheering bits of spiritual consolation, when spirituous ditto would have been preferred.

"I say, Mrs.!" called a voice behind me; and, turning, I saw a rough Michigander, with an arm blown off at the shoulder, and two or three bullets still in him—as he afterwards mentioned, as carelessly as if gentlemen were in the habit of carrying such trifles about with them. I went to him, and, while administering a dose of soap and water, he whispered, irefully:

"That red-headed devil, over yonder, is a reb, damn him! You'll agree to that, I'll bet? He's got shet of a foot, or he'd a cut like the rest of the lot. Don't you wash him, nor feed him, but jest let him holler till he's tired. It's a blasted shame to fetch them fellers in here, along side of us; and so I'll tell the chap that bosses this concern; cuss me if I don't."

I regret to say that I did not deliver a moral sermon upon the duty of forgiving our enemies, and the sin of profanity, then and there;

but, being a red-hot Abolitionist, stared fixedly at the tall rebel, who was a copperhead, in every sense of the word, and privately resolved to put soap in his eyes, rub his nose the wrong way, and excoriate his cuticle generally, if I had the washing of him.

My amiable intentions, however, were frustrated; for, when I approached, with as Christian an expression as my principles would allow, and asked the question—"Shall I try to make you more comfortable, sir?" all I got for my pains was a gruff—

"No; I'll do it myself."

"Here's your Southern chivalry, with a witness," thought I, dumping the basin down before him, thereby quenching a strong desire to give him a summary baptism, in return for his ungraciousness; for my angry passions rose, at this rebuff, in a way that would have scandalized good Dr. Watts.[5] He was a disappointment in all respects (the rebel, not the blessed Doctor), for he was neither fiendish, romantic, pathetic, or anything interesting; but a long, fat man, with a head like a burning bush, and a perfectly expressionless face: so I could hate him without the slightest drawback, and ignored his existence from that day forth. One redeeming trait he certainly did possess, as the floor speedily testified; for his ablutions were so vigorously performed that his bed soon stood like an isolated island, in a sea of soap-suds, and he resembled a dripping merman, suffering from the loss of a fin. If cleanliness is a near neighbor to godliness, then was the big rebel the godliest man in my ward that day.

Having done up our human wash, and laid it out to dry, the second syllable of our version of the word war-fare was enacted with much success. Great trays of bread, meat, soup and coffee appeared; and both nurses and attendants turned waiters, serving bountiful rations to all who could eat. I can call my pinafore to testify to my good will in the work, for in ten minutes it was reduced to a perambulating bill of fare, presenting samples of all the refreshments going or gone. It was a lively scene; the long room lined with rows of beds, each filled by an occupant, whom water, shears, and clean raiment had transformed from a dismal ragamuffin into a recumbent hero, with a cropped head. To and fro rushed matrons, maids, and convalescent "boys,"[6] skirmishing with knives and forks; retreating with empty plates; marching and counter-marching, with unvaried

---

[5] The Reverend Isaac Watts, author of widely known moralizing hymns.
[6] Convalescent soldiers were used as ward aides.

success, while the clash of busy spoons made most inspiring music
for the charge of our Light Brigade:

> Beds to the front of them,
> Beds to the right of them,
> Beds to the left of them,
>   Nobody blundered.
> Beamed at by hungry souls,
> Screamed at with brimming bowls,
> Steamed at by army rolls,
>   Buttered and sundered.
> With coffee not cannon plied,
> Each must be satisfied,
> Whether they lived or died;
>   All the men wondered.[7]

Very welcome seemed the generous meal, after a week of suffering, exposure, and short commons; soon the brown faces began to
smile, as food, warmth, and rest did their pleasant work; and the
grateful "Thankee's" were followed by more graphic accounts of the
battle and retreat than any paid reporter could have given us. Curious contrasts of the tragic and comic met one everywhere; and some
touching as well as ludicrous episodes might have been recorded that
day. A six-foot New Hampshire man, with a leg broken and perfo-
rated by a piece of shell so large that, had I not seen the wound, I
should have regarded the story as a Munchausenism,[8] beckoned me
to come and help him, as he could not sit up, and both his bed and
beard were getting plentifully anointed with soup. As I fed my big
nestling with corresponding mouthfuls, I asked him how he felt during the battle.

"Well, 'twas my fust, you see, so I ain't ashamed to say I was a
trifle flustered in the beginnin', there was such an all-fired racket; for
ef there's anything I do spleen agin, it's noise. But when my mate,
Eph Sylvester, caved, with a bullet through his head, I got mad, and
pitched in, licketty cut. Our part of the fight didn't last long; so a

[7]Travesty of Alfred Tennyson's "The Charge of the Light Brigade" (1854). Alcott's realistic portrayal of the soldiers' suffering contrasts with Tennyson's glorifi-
cation of suffering caused by blundering officers during the Crimean War.

[8]Baron Munchausen's *Travels* (published by Rudolph Erich Raspe, 1785), are
filled with wildly exaggerated stories.

lot of us larked round Fredericksburg, and give some of them houses a pretty consid'able of a rummage, till we was ordered out of the mess. Some of our fellows cut like time; but I warn't a-goin' to run for nobody; and, fust thing I knew, shell bust, right in front of us, and I keeled over, feelin' as if I was blowed higher'n a kite. I sung out, and the boys come back for me, double quick; but the way they chucked me over them fences was a caution, I tell you. Next day I was most as black as that darkey yonder, lickin' plates on the sly. This is bully coffee, ain't it? Give us another pull at it, and I'll be obleeged to you."

I did; and, as the last gulp subsided, he said, with a rub of his old handkerchief over eyes as well as mouth:

"Look a here; I've got a pair of earbobs and a handkercher pin I'm a goin' to give you, if you'll have them; for you're the very moral o' Lizy Sylvester, poor Eph's wife: that's why I signalled you to come over here. They ain't much, I guess, but they'll do to memorize the rebs by."

Burrowing under his pillow, he produced a little bundle of what he called "truck," and gallantly presented me with a pair of earrings, each representing a cluster of corpulent grapes, and the pin a basket of astonishing fruit, the whole large and coppery enough for a small warming-pan. Feeling delicate about depriving him of such valuable relics, I accepted the earrings alone, and was obliged to depart, somewhat abruptly, when my friend stuck the warming-pan in the bosom of his night-gown, viewing it with much complacency, and, perhaps, some tender memory, in that rough heart of his, for the comrade he had lost.

Observing that the man next him had left his meal untouched, I offered the same service I had performed for his neighbor, but he shook his head.

"Thank you, ma'am; I don't think I'll ever eat again, for I'm shot in the stomach. But I'd like a drink of water, if you ain't too busy."

I rushed away, but the water-pails were gone to be refilled, and it was some time before they reappeared. I did not forget my patient patient, meanwhile, and, with the first mugful, hurried back to him. He seemed asleep; but something in the tired white face caused me to listen at his lips for a breath. None came. I touched his forehead; it was cold: and then I knew that, while he waited, a better nurse than I had given him a cooler draught, and healed him with a touch. I laid the sheet over the quiet sleeper, whom no noise could now disturb; and half an hour later, the bed was empty. It seemed a poor requital for all he had sacrificed and suffered,—that hospital bed, lonely even in a crowd; for there was no familiar face for him to look his last upon; no friendly voice to say, Good bye; no hand to lead him gently down into the Valley of the Shadow; and he vanished, like a drop in that red sea upon whose shores so many women stand lamenting. For a moment I felt bitterly indignant at this seeming carelessness of the value of life, the sanctity of death; then consoled myself with the thought that, when the great muster roll was called, these nameless men might be promoted above many whose tall monuments record the barren honors they have won.

All having eaten, drank, and rested, the surgeons began their rounds; and I took my first lesson in the art of dressing wounds. It wasn't a festive scene, by any means; for Dr. P., whose Aid I constituted myself, fell to work with a vigor which soon convinced me that I was a weaker vessel, though nothing would have induced me to confess it then. He had served in the Crimea, and seemed to regard a dilapidated body very much as I should have regarded a damaged garment; and, turning up his cuffs, whipped out a very unpleasant looking housewife, cutting, sawing, patching and piecing, with the enthusiasm of an accomplished surgical seamstress; explaining the process, in scientific terms, to the patient, meantime; which, of course, was immensely cheering and comfortable. There was an uncanny sort of fascination in watching him, as he peered and probed into the mechanism of those wonderful bodies, whose mysteries he understood so well. The more intricate the wound, the better he liked it. A poor private, with both legs off, and shot through the lungs, possessed more attractions for him than a dozen generals, slightly scratched in some "masterly retreat"; and had any one appeared in small pieces, requesting to be put together again, he would have considered it a special dispensation.

The amputations were reserved till the morrow, and the merciful magic of ether was not thought necessary that day, so the poor souls had to bear their pains as best they might. It is all very well to talk of the patience of woman; and far be it from me to pluck that feather from her cap, for, heaven knows, she isn't allowed to wear many; but the patient endurance of these men, under trials of the flesh, was truly wonderful; their fortitude seemed contagious, and scarcely a cry escaped them, though I often longed to groan for them when pride kept their white lips shut, while great drops stood upon their foreheads, and the bed shook with the irrepressible tremor of their tortured bodies. One or two Irishmen anathematized the doctors with the frankness of their nation, and ordered the Virgin to stand by them, as if she had been the wedded Biddy to whom they could administer the poker, if she didn't; but, as a general thing, the work went on in silence, broken only by some quiet request for roller, instruments, or plaster, a sigh from the patient, or a sympathizing murmur from the nurse.

It was long past noon before these repairs were even partially made; and, having got the bodies of my boys into something like order, the next task was to minister to their minds, by writing letters to the anxious souls at home; answering questions, reading papers, taking possession of money and valuables; for the eighth commandment[9] was reduced to a very fragmentary condition, both by the blacks and whites who ornamented our hospital with their presence. Pocket books, purses, miniatures, and watches were sealed up, labelled, and handed over to the matron, till such times as the owners thereof were ready to depart homeward or campward again. The letters dictated to me, and revised by me, that afternoon, would have made an excellent chapter for some future history of the war; for, like that which Thackeray's "Ensign Spooney"[10] wrote his mother just before Waterloo, they were "full of affection, pluck, and bad spelling;" nearly all giving lively accounts of the battle, and ending with a somewhat sudden plunge from patriotism to provender, desiring "Marm," "Mary Ann," or "Aunt Peters," to send along some pies, pickles, sweet stuff, and apples, "to yourn in haste," Joe, Sam, or Ned, as the case might be.

My little Sergeant insisted on trying to scribble something with his left hand, and patiently accomplished some half dozen lines of hieroglyphics, which he gave me to fold and direct, with a boyish blush that rendered a glimpse of "My Dearest Jane" unnecessary, to assure me that the heroic lad had been more successful in the service of Commander-in-Chief Cupid than that of Gen. Mars; and a charming little romance blossomed instanter in Nurse Periwinkle's[11] romantic fancy, though no further confidences were made that day, for Ser-

---

[9]"Thou shalt not steal" (Exodus 20:15).
[10]A very young officer in William Thackeray's *Vanity Fair* (1847–1848).
[11]Alcott called herself Tribulation Periwinkle in these sketches.

geant fell asleep, and, judging from his tranquil face, visited his absent sweetheart in the pleasant land of dreams.

At five o'clock a great bell rang, and the attendants flew, not to arms, but to their trays, to bring up supper, when a second uproar announced that it was ready. The newcomers woke at the sound; and I presently discovered that it took a very bad wound to incapacitate the defenders of the faith for the consumption of their rations; the amount that some of them sequestered was amazing; but when I suggested the probability of a famine hereafter to the matron, that motherly lady cried out: "Bless their hearts, why shouldn't they eat? It's their only amusement; so fill every one, and, if there's not enough ready tonight, I'll lend my share to the Lord by giving it to the boys." And, whipping up her coffee-pot and plate of toast, she gladdened the eyes and stomachs of two or three dissatisfied heroes by serving them with a liberal hand; and I haven't the slightest doubt that, having cast her bread upon the waters, it came back buttered, as another large-hearted old lady was wont to say.

Then came the doctor's evening visit; the administration of medicines; washing feverish faces; smoothing tumbled beds; wetting wounds; singing lullabies; and preparations for the night. By eleven, the last labor of love was done; the last "good night" spoken; and, if any needed a reward for that day's work, they surely received it, in the silent eloquence of those long lines of faces, showing pale and peaceful in the shaded rooms, as we quitted them, followed by grateful glances that lighted us to bed, where rest, the sweetest, made our pillows soft, while Night and Nature took our places, filling that great house of pain with the healing miracles of Sleep and his diviner brother, Death.